THE SECRET OF ANATOMY

MARK MORRIS was born in 1963 and now lives in the village of Boston Spa, near Leeds, with his wife, Nel. In 1988 he became a full-time writer on the Enterprise Allowance Scheme and a year later saw the release of his first novel, *Toady*. He has since published two more novels, *Stitch* and *The Immaculate*; his work has received considerable critical and popular acclaim. Mark also writes short fiction, articles and reviews for a variety of horror anthologies and magazines.

MARK MORRIS

THE SECRET OF ANATOMY

HarperCollins*Publishers*

HarperCollins*Publishers*
77–85 Fulham Palace Road,
Hammersmith, London W6 8JB

This paperback edition 1995

1 3 5 7 9 8 6 4 2

First published in Great Britain by
Judy Piatkus Publishers (Ltd) 1994

Copyright © Mark Morris 1994

Interior illustrations are reproduced from
Gray's Anatomy copyright © Longman Group Limited 1980

The Author asserts the moral right to
be identified as the author of this work

ISBN 0 00 649043 3

Set in Sabon

Printed in Great Britain by
HarperCollinsManufacturing Glasgow

This one's
for Pete and Nicky Crowther,
with love.

Acknowledgements

There's a whole bunch of people involved this time round. I'd especially like to thank:

Peter Robinson of McAlpine Helicopters and the staff at the West Yorkshire police helicopter base for advice on helicopters;

Arek and Jean Hersh for advice on Judaism, and for providing Nel and me with a Spanish retreat when we most needed it;

Julie Akhurst for reading the damn thing in first draft, and for taking the time to write copious notes full of insight, criticism and encouragement (good luck in Australia, Julie);

Nick Royle, prize Chiseller, for advice on London locations and for a million and one other favours;

Pete and Nicky Crowther for setting the ball rolling in the first place;

Kate Callaghan for her incisive and detailed editing;

Nel for . . . well, everything really.

Other people who helped in a variety of ways during the writing of this book include:

Clive Barker, Ramsey and Jenny Campbell, Peter Coleborn, Lucinda Culpin, Steve and Marilyn Gallagher, Ian Glasper and the 'Mushroom' crew, Colin Greenland, David Howe, Dave Hughes, Steve Jones, Graham and Sue Joyce, Joel Lane, Steve and Mel Laws, Kev Mullins, Kim Newman, Imogen Parker, Judy Piatkus, Jim and Sandra Pitts, Seamus Ryan, Mike Marshall Smith, Chris Westwood, Conrad Williams.

I'd like to point out that I've taken great liberties with

many of the locations in this book, for which I claim artistic licence. Any factual errors are because I didn't ask enough (or the right) questions and not because I was given erroneous information.

Finally, I'd like to say a huge, albeit belated, thank you to Leeds United for winning the 1992 league championship.

1

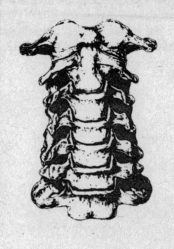

Feeling Bad

1

The beach was as grey as his mood the day that David Fox looked out to sea and wondered how and when all the bad stuff would end.

It was December, and cold. An aggressive wind gnashed at his slight frame, snapping his trouser cuffs, trying to tear his coat from his back. David screwed up his eyes, unimpressed by its bared teeth. He had lived with his own storms for two months now; storms which reduced this sea-squall to insignificance. Having paused for a moment, he strode on, his clothes and his blond hair flapping like flags.

He looked down as he walked, watched the pressure of his feet squeeze the moisture from the sand with each step. The retreating sea had left debris behind – straggles of seaweed, lumps of sodden paper with their colour bled away, cans so rusted it was impossible to tell what they had once contained.

A tiny crab, almost translucent, burrowed frantically into the sand as his foot descended, an inch from its scuttling legs. David wished *his* problems could have so simple a solution. But there was no running away from the turmoil of his own thoughts. They rode everywhere with him, hostile passengers, their jabbering voices filling his head. Even now he could hear their poisonous words; they made him feel victimised, desperate. So desperate, in fact, that instead of going to work that morning, he had driven sixty miles to the seaside town of Starmouth, intending . . . what?

'Suicide.' He spoke the word and was surprised by it. It tasted strange, like a fruit whose plump colourful flesh concealed a flavour that was bad and bitter.

Suicide? Had he really come here with such a notion? He looked out to sea again, and suddenly recalled a conversation he'd had not so very long ago with his friend, Ralph Joyce.

Ralph was an avuncular man, big and bespectacled, with a laugh that could rattle china. When they were seven years old, Ralph had bowled over a bully who was using his fists to persuade David to relinquish a whole week's dinner money. In this way a friendship had been born, and it was one that had endured despite that great leveller – distance. Even during Ralph's two-year sojourn in California back in the seventies, the two had kept in touch.

Now Ralph lived in Bristol with his American wife, Diane. A medical man, he had finally achieved his ambition of opening his own practice in 1985. Diane described him as 'that great contradiction in terms, a sensitive gynaecologist'. The conversation which now sprang to David's mind had taken place the last time he, Ellen and the girls had spent a weekend with the Joyces in Bristol.

It was one of those two-thirty in the morning conversations. Ellen and Diane had gone to bed over two hours before, sleepy with too much food and wine, bored with obscure schoolboy reminiscences. David and Ralph were sitting in front of a log fire that would have graced Henry VIII's banqueting hall, Ralph's Old English sheepdog, Boss, snoring on the rug between them. Ralph was holding up his brandy glass, squinting at its contents as though looking for foreign bodies. It was their third nightcap, and it would not be their last.

'If you were to kill yourself,' Ralph said after a few minutes of companionable silence, 'how would you go about it?'

David sipped his brandy and blinked at his host. Though he was not really drunk, he felt relaxed enough to melt.

'Is that a serious question?' he asked.

Ralph shrugged with his face, jutting out his bottom lip. 'Well . . . semi,' he said.

David looked into the fire, its movements so subtle they almost defied the eye.

'I don't know,' he said after a moment. 'It wouldn't be anything painful.'

'Painful?'

'You know . . . like hanging. Slashing my wrists. Crashing my car into a wall. I wouldn't fancy any of that.'

'What about jumping off a tall building?'

'Urgh . . . no.'

'Why not? It'd be quick. And you'd make an impact.'

David grimaced at the joke. 'What if you changed your mind on the way down? Besides, I don't like heights.' He was silent for a moment, then he said, 'No, I think I'd just take a load of pills washed down with a bottle of whisky. I'd tuck myself up in bed and drift away.'

'It's not always that easy, you know.'

'What do you mean?'

'Sometimes people who do that die by choking on their own vomit. Or they start to have convulsions and die in terrible pain. Or they're found too soon, and saved, and then spend the rest of their lives brain-damaged.'

David sighed. 'Well, what would you suggest?'

'I think I'd have the booze and pills and everything, but instead of tucking myself up in bed, I think I'd drown myself.'

Though he felt as if the fire was slowly roasting the left side of him, David shuddered. 'Drown yourself? You wouldn't!'

'Why not?'

5

'Well, it's the thought of it. Inhaling all that water. You'd be panicking and kicking. It'd be horrible.'

'Not if you were completely out of your head. Not if you were exhausted. I'd swim out to sea as far as I could, and then I'd just let myself sink. Apparently drowning is quite a pleasant death. The denial of oxygen is supposed to bring on a feeling of euphoria.'

David shook his head and then wished he hadn't; it made him realise he was drunker than he'd thought. 'All the same,' he said, 'what about afterwards? You'd be all white and bloated. All the fish and things would have eaten your eyes.'

'Where did you get that from?'

'Well . . . that's what they do, isn't it?'

'I don't know,' admitted Ralph. He shrugged. 'Maybe. I suppose it all depends on how long you're out there for.' He raised his arms, slopping brandy on to his hand. 'But so what? You'll be dead. Past caring.'

'Nevertheless,' said David, 'I wouldn't fancy it.'

Another short silence descended. The fire popped and hissed like roasting meat; the clock on the mantelpiece ticked sonorously. Boss groaned in his sleep, right hind foot jerking, claws scraping the rug.

'He's dreaming of the prairies,' said Ralph.

'How do you know all this?' asked David.

'All what?'

'All this stuff about drowning? How do you know it's so pleasant?'

Ralph looked as though he was about to get pompous, then he smiled widely. 'Well,' he said, 'it's a well-known fact, isn't it? Besides, it stands to reason.'

'Does it?'

'Of course.'

'I don't see how. No one's ever talked to someone who's drowned themselves before, have they?'

Ralph's eyes twinkled like a Christmas card Santa's as

6

he reached for the brandy bottle. 'True,' he conceded, then held up the bottle. 'Fancy another?'

It was not long after this that David had begun to feel unsettled. It was a feeling that seemed to have crept up on him unawares, insinuated itself into his consciousness until finally it was dictating his every move, his every decision. At the time it had seemed a gradual process, but viewed with hindsight it became clear that it had all happened very, very quickly. One day he had been content with his life, sliding happily through the groove he'd carved for himself, and the next, for no reason at all, it had all seemed so pointless and stifling; he had wanted to scramble his way out of the groove, to destroy everything he'd lived and worked for and start again.

Mid-life crisis. That was what they called it. Before now David had regarded the concept as a myth, or at least a nebulous thing, vague and without substance. If he was going to suffer one at all – and he doubted it – it would be little more than a glitch, a bumpy patch which he would ride over and then forget.

How wrong he was. If someone had told him six months ago that he would be standing on a grey beach in a grey town a week before his fortieth birthday, pondering on suicide as a viable proposition, he would have laughed hard and long in their faces.

While he'd been thinking, his feet had carried him some four hundred yards further along the beach. Before him crouched the pier, hunchbacked and creaking on its stilts as though ready to pounce. David walked underneath it, water dripping around him. Beyond it, the beach dwindled to rock pools and caves, and beyond that, trying to puncture the scowling sky, was the fairground, silent now for winter.

Suicide. Could he *really*, if it came down to it, stride out into the sea, among waves that looked like shifting slabs of concrete? Could he simply drift out there, waiting for water to fill the places where his life had been? He shook his head, part frustration, part despair, part amusement, part anger at himself. He had no intention of doing away with himself, nor ever really had. So what *had* possessed him to drive all this way out here today? He had made nothing more than an empty statement, a dramatic gesture known only to himself. His emotions, so unpredictable, so volatile, just lately, boiled into rage inside him. He hated this, this turmoil, this confusion. It was like a pain so bad he wanted to gnaw it away.

He turned and began to stalk back along the beach, towards the steps that led up to the promenade where he'd parked his car. There was little evidence of Christmas here on the seafront; a few coloured lights twinkling from the direction of the hotels further along the promenade, but that was all. He wondered whether Ellen knew that he'd not turned up for work that morning, and felt a sudden rush of shame. He had put her through hell the last couple of months, her and the girls. Numerous times he'd wanted to apologise for his behaviour, to make it up to them, but the monster that had taken residence inside him had not allowed him to do so.

It was only when you were in the throes of such an experience that you realised just how appropriate all the old clichés were. Like the familiar refrain of the murderer: 'It was like someone else was killing the girl, like I was just watching what was going on through someone else's eyes.' Or 'It was like I was possessed,' or 'I wasn't myself,' or 'I couldn't help what I was doing.' To David, such excuses had always seemed a convenient way of passing the buck, of shifting the responsibility for foul deeds on to an agent as mystical as it was unpunishable.

But now he found he identified with such self-justifications, and to do so was frightening. It really *did* feel as though there was someone or something inside him, some malign presence, manipulating his emotions and deeds, putting words into his mouth. It felt almost like a kind of possession, but more subtle than that. The influence came not from outside but from some deeper, darker part of him, a part which had reared its head only briefly, and at his behest, in the past, but which had now risen despite him and was claiming ascendancy.

From the corner of his eye, David glimpsed a flash of light somewhere out at sea, and he turned instinctively to look. He might have thought it was the sun glinting on the waves if it wasn't for the fact that clouds dark as smoke were amassing on the horizon, climbing towards him like a slow tidal wave. A boat then, perhaps? But there were no boats, unless one had just slipped out of sight, beyond the horizon. He stood for a moment, blinking away the after-effect of the light, a green sun which flared behind his eyelids, and wondered where it could have come from, for there was no evidence of it now. After a moment he shrugged irritably and moved on. He had taken no more than a step when his right foot clunked against something.

He looked down, and was surprised to see a bottle lying at his feet, which he could have sworn hadn't been there a moment ago. The bottle could have been half-submerged in sand, however. It was mushy here; it sucked at the soles of his shoes, hungry but toothless. He stooped and plucked the bottle from the soft mouth of the beach, remembering holidays where he, Ellen and the girls had spent hours exploring coastal rock pools, picking up old bottles like this one, oddly shaped stones and shells, the empty carapaces of crabs. This bottle was small with squared-off sides, and looked as though it had been in the sea for a long time. The movement of sand and salt over its surface had scratched it almost opaque.

It was odd, but the bottle felt warm as flesh in David's hand, and somehow soothing. It gave him a ripple of pleasure, almost of security, which was not unlike the feelings associated with lying in a warm cosy bed at night and listening to rain battering the window. Without quite knowing why, he held the bottle up to the sky's dubious light. He saw immediately that there was something inside it, something tubular, possibly a scroll of paper. Despite himself, he felt a flicker of excitement. Could he really have found a message in a bottle?

Less than five minutes later he was sitting in a café on the promenade, shuddering the cold out of him. As a middle-aged woman with a plastic Snoopy apron took his order for coffee and apple pie, the sky split and he had to raise his voice above the rain. When the woman had gone, David draped his coat over the back of his chair and slipped his hand into the right hip pocket. The texture of the bottle against his fingers was comforting, as if the glass was projecting its own nature on to his mind – scouring his thoughts smooth, erasing the sharp edges.

David had always liked rain, the more torrential the better. As a boy he had driven his mother to distraction, coming home as he often did with his hair dripping and his face shining wet.

'David, look at you! Why didn't you put your hood up?' she would wail.

To which he would reply, 'I didn't want to. I like getting wet.'

'But you'll catch your death,' she would say.

'No, I won't,' he would reassure her, 'it's only water.'

He wanted to tell her that she was more likely to catch her death smoking all those cigarettes than he was by getting his head wet. But he never did. His mother had been a skittish, fragile person. He had always been afraid that criticism, however slight, would be liable to snap her in two.

The rain beat harder against the window, turning the road to grey-blue metal. Clouds the colour of smoke boiled overhead, giving the day a flat, grainy twilit feel. The sea frothed and roared and lunged at the shore. A plastic bag fled along the promenade in panic, pursued by a Kentucky Fried Chicken box and a magazine that was spreading its wings and trying to fly.

The woman came back, appearing from a door behind a counter trimmed with red tinsel. She was carrying a tray which she set on the table before him. A large shaggy Alsatian prowled into the room at her heels and made straight for the bedraggled Christmas tree in the corner, black snout twitching.

'Don't you dare, King,' the woman snapped. 'If you want to go out you can go on the yard. Come here.'

The dog gave her a bland look but complied. The woman scribbled out David's bill and tucked it very obviously between the coffee pot and a jug of milk. David thanked her, but she was already striding across the room, shooing back the Alsatian, which was gazing at her dolefully from the doorway.

The apple pie was too sweet, the pastry damp, but David relished it. That was another thing – a couple of months ago, he had been a health-conscious man of the nineties, but now he just didn't give a shit. It was almost as though by stuffing himself full of junk he was raising two fingers to the world, or as though he was punishing not himself but the beast inside him. He was drinking heavily too, and the more he drank the more furious he became. Subconsciously he would be thinking, 'See how you like *this*! And *this*!' as each new shot of alcohol hit his system.

After his plate was emptied, he found his fingers straying once more to the booty in his pocket. Whilst caressing the rough-smooth glass he glanced surreptitiously at the half-open door behind the counter, as if his actions were somehow shameful. Although eager to examine the bottle, he was reluctant to do so in public, though exactly why he couldn't say. Finally, his heart pumping, he pocketed the knife from his plate, left some money – including a hefty tip to compensate for the pilfered cutlery – on the table, and walked out of the café.

The wind took hold of him immediately and bullied him all the way to his car. Normally David liked to turn his face to the rain but on this occasion he was forced to bow his head, and reached his destination half-blind and with his scalp stinging. Nevertheless as he slid into the driver's seat he felt invigorated. With hands that felt gloved in ice he switched on the engine so that the heater could warm him through. Then he turned on the interior light and took the bottle from his pocket.

In this light it resembled crystal. Or rather, something crystalline – more ancient and unusual than crystal itself. Here in the car he felt safe, able to examine his treasure without the threat from prying eyes.

He drew the stolen knife from his pocket and began to scrape at the stuff around the bottle's neck that sealed it. At first he had thought it was some natural cement formed by the accumulation of flotsam in the water, but on closer inspection he decided that it was more likely to have been caked around the bottle cap by whoever had tossed the vessel into the sea. It took David some five minutes of busy work with the knife before the sealant finally gave up its grip. By this time his right wrist was aching and his flesh felt prickly inside his layers of clothing. He switched off the heater and glanced at the world through the windscreen. Rain still drummed on the roof and writhed on the glass, fracturing the scene into obscure splinters of light and shadow.

As he unscrewed the cap of the bottle, another odd thought occurred to him, simply slipped into his mind as if it had been placed there, like an envelope into a slot. He felt that once he read the note that would be it, there would be no turning back. By the simple act of viewing whatever was on that paper he would be committing himself. But to what?

The cap came off grittily, and so fumble-fingered was he that David dropped it between the driver's and passenger's seats. He swore, then upended the bottle into his palm. The tightly rolled tube of paper slipped easily into his hand as though it had been waiting to do so.

He unrolled the paper, which was nothing more than a page from a cheap notepad. It was yellow and brittle, but not so far gone that it crumbled at his touch. Carefully, little by little, he revealed its message.

His first thought was that the author was unused to writing with a fountain pen given the smudged lettering and the fact that the nib had torn the paper in at least three places; his second thought, that this was the handwriting of a child. He scanned the note quickly, but by the end realised that he had digested only a fraction of its meaning. He took a deep breath and started again.

PLEASE HELP!
MY NAME IS JOHN MARSHALL. I LIVE AT
58 CRANLEIGH PARADE, LONDON, N15. I
AM ELEVEN YEARS OLD. TODAY'S DATE IS
22ND JUNE, 1953. I LIVE WITH MY MUM
AND DAD, CELIA AND MALCOLM. MY
MUM IS NICE BUT MY DAD IS TRYING TO
KILL US. THIS IS NOT A JOKE. IF WE DO
NOT GET HELP SOON WE WILL BE DEAD.
PLEASE CALL THE POLICE OR TRY TO HELP
IN ANY WAY YOU CAN.
THANK YOU.
JOHN MARSHALL

2

'I'm at my wits' end, Diane. I dread to think what might have happened to him.'

'Hey, calm down. Nothing's happened. I'm sure of it.'

'But what if he's ... you know ... done something stupid?'

'Killed himself, you mean?' said Diane, ever the pragmatist. 'No, not David. Look, just relax, Ellen, okay? He'll be home soon. He probably just decided to take the day off, that's all.'

The conversation had been circling in such a manner for the last ten minutes or so. It seemed to Ellen to match the feeling of doom that was circling her too, like a shark. The nightmare had started just before midday when a colleague of David rang to enquire why he had not shown up for work that morning. Normally Ellen would have shrugged off the anomaly, but David had been so weird these last couple of months – cold, distant, erratic, given to fits of rage at the most innocuous of provocations – that the news had immediately set alarm bells ringing in her head. As the day progressed, and phone calls to family and friends drew a yawning blank, the alarm bells had increased in volume and tempo. Something had happened to David, she was sure of it. She called the police and told them everything she could think of, pausing intermittently to control her cracking voice, then she called Diane back.

Even without the grounding of history behind them, Diane and Ellen had become almost as close as their husbands were to each other over the past seven years.

However, they had not always liked one another; their friendship had been preceded by conflict and barely concealed hostility. Initially Ellen thought of Diane as a gum-cracking, loud-mouthed California bimbo, whereas Diane for her part regarded Ellen as a repressed, tight-assed, double-talking Brit. They had warmed to each other gradually, even reluctantly, over the months following their original high-voltage encounter, which had taken place in a Japanese restaurant called, of all things, Big Fish.

Both women agreed the real turning point had come after a night spent bowling, and eating Lebanese food. It was a Friday. Ralph and Diane had travelled up from Bristol that afternoon to spend a weekend with the Foxes in Leeds. Neither woman had been looking forward to the encounter very much, but they knew their husbands were and so kept their reservations to themselves. As it turned out, the bowling, suggested by David, had been a great success. Usually conversation between the two women started out politely, albeit distantly, and ended up with them spitting bullets at each other. With the bowling, however, there had been interaction without much need for conversation, so by the time they entered the restaurant around ten everyone was feeling relatively relaxed and pleasantly drunk. Halfway through the main course, David made a comment about his food which made both women shriek with laughter. They looked at each other, surprised by their simultaneity, which set them off again.

'See,' Ralph piped up, 'I told you you'd love each other, given time.'

It wasn't love, not then, but it was a start. After floundering for months on the rocks, the women had finally found some common ground which was firm beneath their feet. In the months ahead they were to stride across that ground together with ever-increasing confidence.

'Tell me what you really think, Diane,' Ellen said now. 'If there's one person I can rely on for straight answers, it's you.'

'Okay, you wanna hear it?'

'You know I do.'

'Okay, here goes.' Deep breath. 'I think he's having an affair.'

Ellen opened her mouth but her throat had been stunned into silence. Suddenly her skin felt cold and tight. Now that Diane had said the words it sounded like the obvious solution, and she couldn't believe that the suspicion hadn't been in her mind all along. But the fact was, the possibility had never, at any time, occurred to her. Why not? Had she simply disallowed it entry? The concept of David with another woman, naked in bed with another woman, kissing another woman as passionately as he kissed her (*used* to kiss her), was absolutely unthinkable.

David would never do that to her. Never.

Would he?

'Ellen?' Diane's voice was all concern. 'Honey, are you okay?'

Ellen was trying to speak but no words were coming out. Finally she managed to make some kind of sound.

'What was that?' said Diane.

With a supreme effort, Ellen said, 'You don't *really* think that, do you?' Her voice was a plea, as if she believed that Diane's dismissal of her own suggestion would make its possibility a nonsense.

Neutrally Diane said, 'Don't you?'

Ellen ran her fingers up her cheek and through her hair. Her hand was trembling with a ferocity that frightened her.

'I don't know,' she said, and could say no more. Her thoughts were whirling vertiginously, too chaotic to contrive words that would form a measured response.

'Well, of course,' Diana said, 'I may be wrong. I haven't been there with you the last two months. I only know what's been going on through what you've told me. But from what you *have* said, that's the way it looks to me.'

'What should I do?' Ellen whispered.

'Confront him with it, I guess. That's what *I'd* do.'

'But he's been getting so mad.'

'Mad?'

'Angry. Furious. At everything. Sometimes I think he's going to hit me. Or one of the girls.'

Diane sighed. 'Honey, you're the one should be getting mad. You're the one with a *right* to be mad. Just face him with it, see what he says. Threaten to leave him if he doesn't tell you.'

'I don't want to leave him,' Ellen said, and now she heard the tears behind her voice, running to catch up. 'I just want things to be back the way they were.'

Diane sighed again, deeper this time. There was a pause in which Ellen could almost hear her friend thinking. Finally she said, 'Listen, what if I ask Ralph to come up there, take David out to lunch, talk to him? Would that help?'

'I don't know.'

'Well . . . do you want me to ask him or not?'

'I . . . yes. Yes, please. Thanks, Diane.'

'No problem. Listen, if you want anything, anything at all, just ring me, okay? Any time of the day or night. I'll be here.'

'Thanks, Diane.'

'Hey, I mean it. Three o'clock in the morning, you want me, you ring me. Okay?'

'Yes, I will.' Ellen's guts were churning so violently she thought she might faint. She leaned back against the wall to take some of the weight off her feet. It didn't help much.

'How bad is this hurting the girls?'

'Bad, I think. They try not to show it, but they go round looking scared all the time. Scared of David. You can see it in their eyes, in the way they hold themselves. It's breaking my heart.'

'That *is* bad,' confirmed Diane sadly. 'You want to send them here for the weekend? Kim would be pleased to see them, and we all know Olly will.'

Kim and Olly were Diane's children from her first marriage. Sixteen-year-old Oliver had a crush on the Foxes' oldest daughter, Rachel, who was fourteen. Jane and Kimberley were both ten. Ellen recalled once remarking scornfully to David, 'Kimberley? What sort of a name's *that*?'

'I don't know,' she said.

'Well . . . have a think about it. No pressure. But you know they're always welcome here.'

'Yes. Thanks. Again.'

'Hey, no need. You'd do the same for me.'

'Yes.' Ellen closed her eyes as a sudden wave of misery washed over her. 'Oh God,' she said, 'I don't know what's worse. The thought of David killing himself or the thought of him having an affair.'

'Yeah,' said Diane sympathetically. 'It's a bummer both ways. But look, maybe we're both wrong. Maybe things are just getting on top of him and he went off to be by himself for a while.'

'Maybe,' said Ellen, but she sounded unconvinced.

Two things happened simultaneously then which made her turn round. Jane stepped out of the lounge door into the hall, en route from the kitchen – where she'd been making a jam sandwich for herself – to her bedroom; and there was the sudden roar of a car engine in the drive, followed by a sweep of white light across the stained glass of the front door.

As abruptly as they had made their presence known, engine and lights were extinguished. There was a beat of silence then where mother and daughter looked at each other, both fearful for different reasons.

The moment was broken by Diane's voice on the telephone saying, 'Ellen? Are you still there?'

'Er . . .' Ellen brought the receiver up to her ear. Her hands felt clumsy. 'Yes, but . . . listen, I think David's home.'

'Okay. Speak to you later.'

'Okay,' said Ellen and fumbled the receiver back into its cradle.

Jane was looking at the sandwich in her hand, one corner of which was oozing jam, with a stricken expression. Ellen felt her heart tearing. Had things got so bad that the prospect of being caught snacking between meals by her father elicited such fear in the girl?

'Up to your room quickly,' said Ellen. 'I want to talk to Dad.'

Jane scampered up the wide staircase, gratitude on her face. She was still in her school uniform, one sock up, one down. Ellen felt her heart tear a little more at the sight. Just recently she had found poignancy in the simplest of things, had become increasingly conscious of form and texture, depth and plane. She had experienced this heightening of awareness only once before, and that had been after her father had died very suddenly of a heart attack at the age of fifty-six. Then, as now, she had felt like an open wound, her emotions raw and horribly vulnerable. She remembered how the tiniest, the most banal, of details had elicited tears. Finding two of his golf tees in the fruit bowl; taking back his library books, one of which was half-read and his place marked with a brown envelope; coming across two tickets to a dinner dance which was to have taken place the Saturday after his death; seeing his battered road atlas on the back seat of his car and remembering him saying, 'I must get another one of these. They've built a lot of new roads since this was published.'

She braced herself as she heard the car door slam, saw David's shape loom at the front door. At least he's alive, she thought, but the surge of relief she had felt on hearing the car was gone now, replaced by her fear of where he'd been, what he'd done. Would she be able to smell it on him? Perfume; sex; guilt? Would she be able to read it in his face, hear it in his voice, taste it in his mouth when (if) he kissed her?

He came in, scowling as if he resented having to come back here day after day. Ellen remembered Diane's words – *Honey, you're the one should be getting mad. You're the one with a* right *to be mad* – but she couldn't just turn her anger on and off like a tap. Instead she forced a smile which fluttered at her lips, and said, 'Hi.' She didn't know what to do with her hands; they hovered uncertainly at her sides.

David looked at her, still scowling, and muttered, 'Hi,' back. One tiny syllable, and yet Ellen felt a plug being pulled in the pit of her stomach. There was no feeling in the greeting, no warmth, nothing. If she had kept her mouth shut, she felt sure David would simply have walked past her without a word.

'So,' she said as he closed the door behind him, 'where have you been?'

He turned back and there was a blankness on his face that was frightening. In a voice just as expressionless he said, 'What are you talking about?'

'Tony called. He said you didn't show up for work today.'

David's eyes briefly met hers – a rare occurrence these days – before skittering away. He shrugged and said, 'Oh.'

His indifference roused the first spark of anger in her. She welcomed it. She took a step towards him.

'So where *have* you been?' she said, her voice firmer this time.

'Nowhere.'

'*Nowhere?* Come on, David, I've been worried sick about you.'

His brow furrowed, though not in anger, and just for an instant Ellen thought she had got through to him. She was no fool, but she was so desperate for things to be back to normal that she had a momentary vision of reconciliation – David gathering her into his arms, showering her with kisses, apologies.

Then, as though she had made her desire too obvious, as though he could read it in her face, he withdrew. His furrowed brow smoothed out, his expression became blank, unencouraging, like a visor sliding down.

'There was no need,' he mumbled, half-turning away, peeling off his wet overcoat.

'But where have you *been?*' she demanded. Her anger was prickling now, but she was fearful too. Her voice wavered as it increased in volume.

He swung back on her, half-removed overcoat swirling like a cape. Spittle flew from his mouth as he snapped, 'Nowhere. I told you. Nowhere. What does it fucking matter?'

He hardly ever used that word when the girls were within earshot, and his use of it now was like a blow to her, more evidence that he just didn't care any more.

'Don't use that language with me!' It was more plea than threat.

'What, English?'

'You know what I mean.'

'Well get off my f . . . bloody back then. Stop hounding me.'

'I'm not hounding you, David. I just want to know where you've been.'

He snapped. It was sudden and terrifying, as always. He lunged towards her, making her flinch. '*Why?*' he yelled. '*Why do you need to know? What's the matter with you? You're bloody obsessed!*'

His voice echoed in the wide high-ceilinged hall. Ellen imagined the girls cowering upstairs, terrified. Jane would probably be crying now, giving vent to the kind of misery that was inconsolable. She looked at her husband, his face red, his reason and his patience gone, superseded by a primitive sickening rage.

How can this be happening? she thought. What has gone so wrong between us?

In a small tight voice, a tone that she hoped would soak up his anger, she said, 'I'm not obsessed, David. There's nothing wrong with me. You didn't turn up for work today and nobody knew where you were. It's only natural for me to be worried.' She hesitated, then said, 'I love you, David.'

His snort of exasperation was like another blow, a harder one. She was cowed by her husband's fury, though something inside her, some part of her, wanted to beat its fists against his chest, scream at him, make him see how . . . how *unfair* he was being, how close he was to tearing the family apart.

'Where were you?' she persisted.

'*For God's sake!*' He swiped at his head, clawed at his scalp, as if it was *she* that was driving him mad, as if she was the unreasonable one.

'Where were you?' She heard her voice fading, and hated the fact. If he didn't answer this time, she felt she would not be able to ask again.

He shuddered, sighed, looked up at the ceiling. When he replied it was quietly, silkily, through gritted teeth. 'If you must know, I went for a drive. I wanted to be on my own for a while. To think.'

'A drive? Where?'

'Just around. To the coast.'

'The coast? Why the coast?'

He gave her a strange look that made her feel uncomfortable. 'I . . . wanted to be somewhere different. And near to the sea. I . . . wanted . . .' He shook his head. 'It doesn't matter.'

Ellen didn't want to move, or even to breathe too loudly for fear of breaking this moment. She felt as though David had not been this close to opening up to her, letting her in, for weeks.

'Please tell me,' she said quietly. She wanted to add how much she needed him, how much she thought he needed her, how much she loved him and wanted him back the way he was . . . but she made the words stay silent in her head. It would be the wrong move just now to lay bare her heart. Too much too soon.

He looked troubled, and turned away from her again. 'I don't want to talk about it,' he growled, and she knew that she was losing him once more.

The knowledge made her desperate. 'Please,' she said, moving forward, touching his shoulder. The muscles bunching, tensing, under his jacket felt like a hand pushing her away. 'David,' she said, 'we need to talk.'

'Not now.' He began to walk away from her.

'When?'

'I don't know. Don't hassle me.' Trailing his overcoat he began to walk up the stairs.

She took a few steps after him, and closed her hand over the square post that supported the banister. She gripped it so hard it dug into her palm, leaving a white divot that would later feel tender without her remembering why. 'David,' she said, but he turned the corner and was suddenly out of her sight.

'I've got work to do.'

'David, please . . .'

He didn't reply. His footsteps grew fainter as they spiralled to the top of the house. She heard the door of his study open, then close with the finality of a full stop at the end of a sentence. Immediately it had done so, her body sagged; she felt drained, exhausted. Her unspoken

23

thoughts, what she wanted to articulate to her husband, and couldn't, what they *needed* to say to each other, felt like sharp, heavy lumps of metal, sticking in her stomach and her chest and her gullet. There was a pressure building and building inside her head, inside the house. If it wasn't released soon, she felt sure it would rip all their lives apart, like a gas explosion. What was *wrong* with him? What had happened to change him so drastically? Ellen felt poised, in limbo. Desolate. Confused. Angry. Something had to happen soon. It *had* to. She couldn't go on like this.

She walked across the silent hall and into the sitting room, too empty even to cry.

3

Danny was five and he could only write little words. That fact didn't matter, however, when Teddy was around. It felt a bit like a dream when Teddy spoke to him or when Teddy made him do things, as if there was a part of Danny that wasn't quite there. His Aunt Mathilde had a funny word for it. *Fyoog* she called it, or at least that's what it sounded like. His Aunt Mathilde had lots of funny words. *Animis* was one, and *orricle* and *flux*. She spoke all these words to Danny as if she expected him to understand them and he just nodded and tried to look as though he did so as not to disappoint her.

His hand stopped writing and Danny was fully awake again. Teddy had finished. He looked at the words Teddy had made him write in purple crayon on the back of his Teenage Mutant Ninja Turtles comic, but he didn't know what any of the words meant. He looked around his bedroom, which was cosy in the subdued light from his Glo-Bug. There was a poster for *Jurassic Park* on the wall which the nice girl in W.H. Smith's had let him have, and there was his clown, Patootie, sitting at the end of his bed, and some of his toys were on the floor and not in the toy chest where they were supposed to be, and his soldiers were all standing in groups on the shelves and windowsills in readiness for tomorrow's battle.

Danny liked his room and he liked his Aunt Mathilde. After his mummy and daddy went to the angels he had come to live with her, and she was nice because she nearly always gave him everything he wanted. She even let him have monsters, which his mummy and daddy never had because they said they would give him nightmares. But they didn't give him nightmares. Instead Danny's monsters protected him from the baddie monsters outside. He heard the baddie monsters sometimes, screaming and howling in the distant dark, but although he sometimes felt a little scared, he never really felt in danger. He knew that his wallpaper dinosaurs would protect him, and his dragon money box, and the funny talking robot that Bernard had given him on his fifth birthday. Bernard told him the robot came from a telly programme which Danny had never heard of called 'Doctor Who', and that the robot's name was a Dalek. He said that he would get Danny some videos of proper Daleks but he hadn't yet. The Dalek said things like 'Exterminate, exterminate,' and 'What are your orders?' in a funny voice that sounded like Aunt Mathilde when she was angry.

Danny was getting very excited about Christmas, which was only a week and a bit away. The thought of Santa landing on the roof of the house, climbing down the chimney and leaving loads of presents wrapped up under the Christmas tree was the most exciting thing in the world. Danny couldn't understand why his Aunt Mathilde didn't feel just as excited as he did. He had the feeling that she wouldn't even have had a Christmas tree and all the decorations if Danny hadn't said he wanted them. A week and a bit . . . In Danny's world that seemed such a long time; he feared it would never come. He imagined Santa and his helpers in the toy factory in Greenland getting all the presents ready for the children, putting things in boxes, wrapping them in brightly coloured paper, and the thought made him feel sick with excitement.

It was very windy outside, the kind of windy that Aunt Mathilde always said was 'wailing like a banshee'. Even so, when the wind dropped a little, Danny heard voices from downstairs, so soft and low that he couldn't make out any of the words. Teddy had given Danny a message to give to his aunt, not just the one he had written down but another one as well. Danny knew he would have no trouble remembering the message. Teddy would remember it for him. He always did.

Danny got out of bed, his feet searching for his Turtle slippers. He kicked his plastic Roman soldier's sword halfway across the room before he found them, by which time he was feeling a bit cold. He went downstairs, clutching his comic, the cool darkness pressing against him and making him feel a little scared. His fear faded, however, as he descended each step, and the voices of his aunt and her friends grew louder and louder, louder than the wind outside. Now he could distinguish one voice from another, and he could even hear separate words, though he didn't really listen to what was being said because it was grown-up talk and he wasn't really interested in it. Grown-ups talked about boring things which were hard to understand. He reached for the door handle which was level with his nose, pulled it down and pushed the door open.

The voices stopped as if by opening the door Danny had switched them off. There wasn't proper light in the room, which wasn't unusual. Aunt Mathilde didn't like strong light; she said it hurt her eyes. In the daytime she kept the curtains half-closed and when she went out she wore dark glasses, even when it was dull and rainy. Sometimes people looked at his Aunt Mathilde and said things about her and laughed at her. She didn't seem to see them but Danny did, and it made him feel nervous and scared and confused. He was not too young to have noticed that his aunt was a bit different from most people, and he thought vaguely that it was because she was different that people laughed at her. She wore long flowy dresses like fairies might wear, and brightly coloured waistcoats with sparkly bits on that she let Danny dress up in sometimes. She also wore lots of

27

beads and bangles that meant Danny could hear her coming even when she was miles away, and sometimes she wore a thing round her head that made her look like a pirate. Also she was fat all over like a barrel; Danny liked to tickle her smooth white chins and make her giggle. She had very long hair and purple lips and fat warm hands with black fingernails. Danny had no idea how old she was; he guessed about a hundred.

Danny blinked as he stood in the doorway, trying to adjust his eyes to the flickering candlelight. The people in the room were like shadows outlined in a wavy orange glow. The settee and the chairs were full of them, and someone – Bernard, it looked like – was sitting cross-legged on the hearth, so close to the fire that it must have been burning his back.

Heads turned to look at him, and just for an instant Danny was scared. Just for an instant he thought that these weren't people at all but something else, monsters dressed as people perhaps. Their eyes looked all shiny and wet in the candlelight, and Danny heard a faint squeaking sound which he thought was somebody's unoiled head rotating until he realised it was the castors of the old red armchair, which sometimes squeaked when you moved about on it. A bulky shape moved away from the rest, and in the gloom seemed to slide towards him like oil. Then the shape said, 'Hello, Danny,' and he recognised Aunt Mathilde.

'Hello,' said Danny and, his fear fading quickly now, moved into the room. As he got used to the candlelight he recognised the faces that were smiling at him with glistening teeth, greeting him in soft friendly voices. It *was* Bernard who was sitting by the fire, and as well as him Danny recognised Tammy and Mr Worthington and the little man with the funny voice and the purple neck, and one or two others who never spoke much but always smiled at him as if he were an old friend.

'What can we do for you, little man?' Mr Worthington asked. Danny liked it when Mr Worthington called him little man. It made him feel important.

Danny held the comic out for his aunt. 'Teddy drew some words for you and he told me something as well.'

Danny sensed the thrill of excitement ripple round the room, and although he didn't fully understand it, it pleased him nevertheless.

Aunt Mathilde took the comic from him with a chubby hand. In her high fluttery voice that reminded him a bit of a bird, she asked, 'What did Teddy tell you, Danny?'

It was not often that Danny had such a large audience. Usually when Teddy told him things there was only his Aunt Mathilde to pass the message on to. Now, though, everyone was looking at him, and, it seemed, hanging on his every word. He couldn't remember quite what Teddy had told him but he hoped that once he opened his mouth and began speaking, the words would just come, as they always did. He opened his mouth – and sure enough the words flowed out.

'We have to get the bottle back. Mr Worthington has to go and fetch it.'

Mr Worthington seemed to flush beneath his white moustache, though it was difficult to tell in the dim light. He looked pleased, as if it was an honour to be chosen.

'If I may just ask,' he said in a quiet voice, 'what exactly is "the bottle" and where do I find it?'

Danny said nothing. There were no more words. He looked at his aunt, who silently handed the Teenage Mutant Ninja Turtles comic to Mr Worthington.

Mr Worthington took the comic and held it up to the light of a candle flame. He was silent for a few moments, his brow furrowed, as he deciphered the words scrawled in purple crayon. Everyone in the room seemed to be holding their breath; the windows rattled beneath a sudden onslaught of wind. Wood collapsed in the fire with a soft crumbling sound. 'It's a name and address,' Mr Worthington said. 'It must belong to the bottle's owner.' Everyone listened as he read it aloud.

4

There was a commotion on the street, as there so often was these days. Violet marked her place in the Mary Wesley novel she was reading and got out of bed to investigate.

She was seventy-six years old, and remarkably agile. So agile, in fact, that there were times when she felt compelled to pretend she wasn't. It was a strange but not uncommon attitude, this idea that old people should *act* old, that they should be forgetful and out of touch, that they should shuffle along with the aid of a stick and be martyrs to arthritis and rheumatism. What was surprising and sad, Violet found, was that the attitude was not confined to the younger generations; it prevailed even amongst her peers. Every Thursday she attended the Senior Citizens' coffee morning at the Headingley Community Centre, close to the cricket ground. Hilda Moffat, seventy-three years old and confined to a wheelchair, would invariably regale her with the words, 'Good morning, Violet. Still as fit as ever, I see!' Violet would laugh and wave, though she would detect more than a hint of envy, even disapproval, in Hilda's voice. And Hilda was not the only one who showed resentment; in fact, there were times when Violet was made to feel unbearably guilty for being fit. That was when she would pretend to be afflicted with some ailment or other, to keep the peace. The only problem with this was that sometimes she would forget what she had claimed to be suffering from the week before, whereupon Hilda or one of the others would observe loudly and pointedly, 'That lumbago of yours seems to have cleared up *very* quickly, Violet.'

Violet pottered over to the window and eased back the edge of a curtain to peer out. My, but it was windy tonight. Her neighbours' bushes across the road were thrashing about as if trying to tear themselves from the earth, and hedges were rippling like sheets on a washing line. Violet could see television aerials waving back and forth, clattering against chimney stacks. Her own television reception had been poor that evening, the picture crackling and stuttering, threatening to break up. Some of the slates on the roofs of the houses opposite looked none too secure; there was one slate in particular she could see, resting in the open guttering that rimmed the roof of number 11, just waiting to fall. It was not the wind, however, that had drawn Violet to the window. It was the sound of raised voices that were audible even above the wind.

Just students, she realised, half a dozen or so of them, probably on their way back from the pub. They were shouting drunkenly to one another, laughing like hyenas. Three of them were eating pizza from flat square boxes. As Violet watched, one of the students, his long hair flailing in the wind and lashing his face, launched his pizza box into the air like a frisbee. Violet winced as the wind caught the box and sent it crashing into the side of the new black Golf GTi that belonged to Stephen and Beverley, the nice young couple that lived next door. The students laughed and walked on. Violet watched them let themselves into number 21, one of the more ramshackle, through terraces further up the street. She let the curtain drop back and then, tutting, returned to her bed and her book.

Things had changed so much since she had first moved into this house with her husband, William, who had died in 1984. That had been in 1939, over fifty years ago now.

They had been married in January, had moved into this place in the spring, and then – irony of ironies – had been separated by the war for the best part of the next six years. It was then, of course, that she had begun to have her doubts about what she and the others were supposedly working towards. When so much misery was involved, when thousands of young lives could be simply snuffed out like so many candles, how could the end possibly justify the means? However it was not until 1944 that she had finally plucked up the courage and got out. The decision was a dangerous one to take; even now, though she had not been active for half a dozen years, she was constantly wary of a hand on her shoulder, a stranger at the door. Of course, such a campaign by those who still believed in the cause would be time-consuming and inadvisable. Still, you never knew. Instructions from on high were unpredictable at the best of times, and once received could not be ignored.

There were lots of students living in this area now, and lots of Asian families. Not that Violet minded either (though the students could be a bit noisy sometimes, especially late at night); it was simply different to how it used to be, that was all. What *was* unpleasant, though, was the amount of crime in the neighbourhood, which seemed to be escalating all the time. Hilda Moffat was always banging on about being able to remember a time when you could go out and leave your windows open and your door unlocked, even at night, and though Violet found the woman's bitterness tiresome, she had to admit that she could remember such a time too. Nowadays, though, you had to keep everything constantly secure, and even then you couldn't guarantee that you wouldn't come back from the shops to find your front door hanging off its hinges. Only last spring she had seen four lads pull up in a car in the middle of the day and kick down the front door of one of the student houses opposite. She had called the police, but the lads had been in and out in two minutes, laden down with videos and TVs and hi-fi equipment. She had even managed to write down the car registration number, but it turned out the car had been stolen earlier that day.

It was a vicious circle really; the more crime there was, the more overcrowded the prisons became, and therefore the more lenient were the sentences for such 'trivial' offences as house-breaking and stealing cars. Joe, her son, who lived the other side of Headingley, only a few minutes' drive away when the traffic on Otley Road was light, was for ever exhorting her to move out of the area, to find a nice bungalow in Yeadon or Calverley or one of the other villages a bit further out. But Violet was adamant; until the day came when she was too infirm to climb the narrow twisting staircase in her little back-to-back, she would be staying put.

She couldn't concentrate on her book now but was not particularly tired. She decided to go downstairs, make herself a cup of Horlicks and fetch the book which Joe and Dorothy had bought her for her birthday, *The Gardener's Encyclopaedia Of Plants And Flowers*. She could browse through that, look at the lovely photographs, without having to concentrate too intensely. That was the only real drawback about this house – she wished she had more garden, or at least she wished she had had more in the past. Violet loved gardening, though it was a nuisance here with all the cats leaving their little deposits. She got out of bed again and put on her slippers. She was reaching for her dressing gown when the telephone began to ring downstairs.

Who could this be, so late at night? She looked at the alarm clock on her bedside table. It was almost half-past eleven. Joe sometimes rang her late on, but always before eleven o'clock. She felt a twinge of apprehension, and hoped that everything was all right, that there was nothing wrong with Dorothy or the children, or Joe himself come to that. As she descended the stairs she told herself that it would be a wrong number or something equally silly. Nevertheless she felt a little tense as she lifted the receiver and said, 'Hello?'

'Violet? Is that really you?'

She was taken aback at the unexpected greeting. 'Er . . . yes, it is. But . . . well . . . I'm afraid I don't know who you are.'

'You mean you don't recognise my voice?' the caller said, gently teasing. 'I'm deeply hurt.'

Violet thought about it. The voice *did* sound familiar, though she couldn't think why. Then all at once a name and a face rose from the murk of her memories.

'Max?' she ventured.

'You *do* remember! So Violet, tell me, how have you been?'

'Fine,' said Violet, recalling the little Jewish tailor with the bald head and the mutton-chop whiskers. Entering Max's poky shop in East London had always been like stepping into a scene from a Dickens novel. She had said as much to Max once and he had chuckled as if delighted by the idea. Certainly with his pince-nez and his flowery waistcoats he himself seemed to cultivate the image of a Dickens character. Violet had always liked Max, had always found him unfailingly cheerful and sensitive, but his calling on her now, after all these years, could be nothing other than ominous.

'And how are you?' she asked automatically when what she really wanted to know was: Why are you calling me?

'Things could be better,' said Max sadly. 'My poor wife, Jean, is not so well and I'm afraid that business is slow. This recession, I'm afraid, is affecting us all. Also my eyesight is not as good as it used to be. To be truthful, Violet, I'm thinking of selling up, moving out of the East End altogether. You know, things just aren't the same as

35

they used to be. *People* aren't the same. There is no sense of community any more.'

It disturbed Violet a little to find that Max was voicing an opinion that was so similar to her own thoughts of a few minutes before. It only added to the sense of unease, of disorientation that she was already feeling. Unable to stand it any longer, she asked, 'What's happening, Max?'

'Happening?' he repeated, puzzled.

'I mean . . . why are you ringing me? Now? After all these years? Something's happening, isn't it?'

Max chuckled. 'You were always very astute, Violet. You know, this is what I like about you. Your intelligence and your warmth.'

'Max,' said Violet firmly.

He sighed, and suddenly his voice was serious. 'It's nothing much,' he said. 'At least we hope not. We need you to do something for us, that's all.'

Her heart sank. 'I'm an old lady, Max. I'm seventy-six. Why does it have to be me?'

'Because you're close,' he said, his voice gentle and apologetic, 'because you're discreet and because you're intelligent.' When she didn't reply he repeated, 'It's nothing much. Truthfully. It may be of no importance whatsoever.'

'All right,' she said in a heavy voice, 'what is it?'

'It concerns a bottle . . .' Max began.

5

Rachel came awake with a start, sensing a presence beside her bed. Cool darkness flooded into her hot eyes and made them sting. She was lying on her back, the duvet askew, one foot exposed and frozen, her fists clenched. She felt horribly vulnerable, her confusion a weight that pinned her to the mattress. In the dream that seemed to have accompanied her out of sleep, something had been pursuing her, though exactly what she was unsure.

A rustle of movement beside her made her body jerk in a spasm of shock. Her eyes blinked frantically into the darkness above her face. She could see nothing, and yet she had the impression that something was looming over her. Her arms came up instinctively. Though she had no desire to make contact with the intruder, her greater fear was that it might touch her face.

'Rachel.' The voice was plaintive and, just for an instant, terrifyingly unrecognisable. 'Rachel, wake up.'

Each syllable was a blade of sound, cutting away the membrane of half-sleep that still clung to her. Her confused thoughts settled; her body relaxed back into itself.

Her lips and tongue felt like drying slabs of meat which had congealed together. She opened her mouth, unpeeling one from the other, and murmured, 'Jane,' the word emerging stale and sticky. She saw her sister move closer, black on black, smelled her clean blonde hair before feeling tendrils of it tickle her face. She wafted them away ill-temperedly and groaned, 'Whaddya want?'

'Can I sleep with you?' Jane pleaded.

'No, go away. The bed's not big enough for two.'

'Please.' Jane's voice was little more than a whimper. 'I don't like it on my own.'

Rachel groaned again and propped herself up on her elbow. Her eyes were adjusting to the dark now. Her sister was a brownish blur with a paler blur for a face, her bedroom a fuzzy approximation of itself.

'You're not on your own, Jane. I'm here, and Mum and Dad are just up the corridor.'

'It's not the same,' said Jane. 'When I'm in bed it feels like I'm the only person in the world. *Can* I sleep in your bed? *Please?*'

Rachel scowled. Jane had been doing this a lot just lately, and Rachel invariably ended up pushed against the wall with no covers and her sister's elbows digging her in the ribs every two minutes. It didn't matter that she was a head taller than her little sister. Somehow Jane had a knack of monopolising bed space.

This time she decided to put her foot down. 'No, Jane. Go back to your own bed. I'd quite like to get a decent night's sleep for once.'

She braced herself for a further volley of exhortations, but surprisingly they didn't come. She wondered why – and then Jane started to sob.

'Hey, hey,' Rachel said softly, sitting up, 'what's the matter, Ratbag?'

Through her tears, Jane said, 'I duh–don't like it when Daddy shouts.'

'Hey, come here.' Rachel reached out her arms and hugged her sister. 'Has Dad been shouting at you?'

'N–no. He's been shouting at Mummy again.'

'You mean earlier this evening?'

Rachel felt Jane nodding against her chest.

'Yeah, I heard it too.' She paused, then said reluctantly, 'Okay, you can get into my bed, but only on the condition that you keep to your own side and don't take all the covers. Okay?'

'Okay,' said Jane.

'Come on then.' Rachel flipped back the duvet and Jane crawled in beside her. 'Do you want a cuddle?' Jane nodded again.

Rachel wrapped her arms around her sister. 'You feel like a big warm teddy bear in these pyjamas,' she said.

Jane didn't reply and for a few minutes the girls were silent. Rachel began to drift off to sleep, despite the fact that Jane's hair was tickling her chin.

Then Jane said, 'Rachel?', jerking Rachel from her doze.

'Hmm?'

'Why does Daddy keep shouting at Mummy all the time?'

Rachel stared over her sister's head at her darkened room. The crouching figure in the corner was an armchair with her clothes dumped on top of it. 'I don't know,' she said. 'He's probably just going through a bit of a bad time at the moment, that's all.'

'Why?'

'I don't know. Maybe he's got some problems at work or something.'

'But it's nearly Christmas. He should be happy.'

Rachel smiled. Had *she* really viewed life in such simple terms only four years ago? She thought maybe she had.

'Yeah,' she said, 'you're right. He should be happy.'

'So why isn't he?'

'I don't really know, Jane. Why don't you ask him?'

'He'd just shout at me too.'

'He might not.'

'He would. He shouted at me yesterday for leaving my skipping rope on the drive.'

Rachel didn't reply. She couldn't really think of anything to say. Dad's behaviour was upsetting and baffling her as much as it was Jane. And Mum was being really secretive about it too, trying to pretend that nothing was wrong. It had been going on for a while now, but it had been getting worse just lately. Last week she and Mum had been alone in the kitchen, washing up after the evening meal (Dad usually did it, but he'd gone stomping off upstairs, having eaten his food in a grumpy silence), and after a few false starts she had finally plucked up the courage to ask, 'Mum, is Dad okay?'

Mum had looked startled, and a bit guilty. 'Yes,' she had said, 'why do you ask?'

'I've just noticed that ... well ... he's not really been himself lately. I just wondered if something was the matter.'

'Oh no,' Mum had said in a voice so casual that Rachel knew she was lying, 'everything's fine. He's just a bit tired, that's all.'

'Oh,' Rachel had said, and had left it at that. Usually she felt able to talk to Mum about personal stuff, but on this occasion it was as though an invisible barrier had sprung up between them, denying her entry.

'Rachel?' Jane said again.

'Yeah?'

'Mummy and Daddy aren't going to get divorced, are they?'

The question surprised Rachel and frightened her, as if she half-believed that Jane's mere voicing of the possibility might make it come true.

'Of course not,' she snapped. 'What makes you say that?'

'Michaela Trewson in our class's mummy and daddy got divorced. She says they used to argue all the time. She lives with her mummy now and only sees her daddy on Sundays.'

'Well, that's not going to happen to *our* parents,' Rachel said fiercely, 'so you can put that idea out of your head. You have to argue *a lot*, much more than Mum and Dad have been arguing, to get divorced. You have to have stopped loving each other, and Mum and Dad haven't stopped doing that.'

'Haven't they?'

'No, they haven't. And they never will. Everything'll be all right, you'll see.'

'Will it?'

'Yes.'

'Okay,' Jane said, evidently reassured, and snuggled down deeper in the bed, arching her back a little, taking up just a bit more room. 'I'm going to go to sleep now.'

'Yeah, me too,' said Rachel, though distractedly; she was thinking about what Jane had said. *Would* her parents split up? The idea was unthinkable. But how bad *were* things between them? And what did it really take to end a relationship like theirs, a relationship which formed the solid rock on which she had built her own life?

Suddenly she was frightened, more frightened than she had ever been before. There were times when she felt so grown up, and times, like now, when she felt like a child lost in the darkness. *Please don't split up*, she prayed silently into the darkness, *please don't split up*. She closed her eyes to aid her prayer and hugged her sister tighter.

6

David was at work the next day when the telephone rang.

'Hello.'

'Greetings.'

'Oh. Ralph. How are you?'

If he detected a lack of enthusiasm in his best friend's tone, Ralph Joyce didn't let on. 'Hale and hearty,' he proclaimed in a voice which proved it. 'How about yourself?'

'Oh . . . not too bad. Busy. You know.'

'How are things in the film world? All cameras rolling?'

David made complementary noises to accompany his friend's chuckles. He had trained as a journalist and now worked for a company called Imperial Vision, editing a magazine which was rather grandly entitled: *Creative Eye: The Cinema and Video Quarterly.*

'Much the same,' he said. 'What can I do for you?'

Even this question, innocuous though it seemed, was indicative of the way David's attitude to life had changed these past few months. There was a time not long ago when Ralph would not have needed a reason to ring, and David would not have asked for one.

'I'm here as an Angel of Mercy, come to shed some light on your miserable existence,' said Ralph.

'What?'

'How about lunch tomorrow?'

David mentally recoiled from the suggestion. 'Tomorrow? I . . . I don't know. Are you in Leeds?'

'Well, Bradford actually. Gynaecologists' convention.

Gruesome bunch of people, gynaecologists. Can't stand the buggers. Actually, you'd be doing me a favour. It would get me out of having to socialise if I said I was meeting an old friend for lunch. What do you say? My shout.'

David hesitated. His instinct was to say no, he was too busy, appointments to keep, blah, blah, blah. But he'd never been able to lie to Ralph; in fact, he found it easier deceiving Ellen. Besides, a liquid lunch with his old friend, as this would inevitably turn out to be, might help take his mind off things.

'Fat chance,' he thought, and then realised he'd spoken out loud.

'What was that?' said Ralph.

'Er . . . nothing, just . . . er . . . it doesn't matter.' To avoid having to explain he blurted, 'Where shall we meet?'

'How about that place where they do those excellent chicken fajitas and serve Mexican beer?'

'The Filling Station?'

'That's the feller! Let's meet there at . . . twelve-thirty?'

'Better make it one,' said David, and immediately felt dismayed at the pointlessness of his suggestion. There was no *reason* why he'd said one, except a desire to put the encounter off as long as possible.

'One it is then,' said Ralph. 'Be there or be somewhere else.'

David chuckled dutifully at the familiar phrase, though in truth even this made him feel miserable. It was yet another example of how distanced he felt from his old life, how hard he found it to identify with the man he had been just a few months before. He muttered a farewell and put the phone down quickly. For a few moments he simply sat and stared at his desk, depressed by the exchange, his stomach hollow, a pulse beating hard in his throat.

Why couldn't he tell someone what was wrong? Why couldn't he talk to Ralph? Why couldn't he talk to *Ellen*,

43

for God's sake? He had always been so open in the past, so what was the difference now? He supposed it was because the problem this time was that *everything* was the problem. He felt trapped, suffocated by the web of his life. All at once, everywhere he looked there was something he wanted to break away from. He knew that if he verbalised this, confessed it to Ellen or to Ralph, they would try their hardest to be sympathetic, understanding. But underneath they would be terribly hurt, Ellen particularly, and their overwhelming urge would be to stifle him even more, to further tighten the bonds that he felt were restraining him.

He expelled a sigh that released none of his tension. It was only 11:45, but David decided it was time for lunch. As he swung his overcoat over his shoulder, the weight of the bottle in his pocket bumped against his hip. He told Becky, his secretary, that he would be back for his one-thirty meeting, and left.

The streets of Leeds were submarine-grey with the rain that had fallen. Now, though, a sun which seemed to give off no heat at all was struggling manfully to establish itself. David screwed up his eyes against the unexpected glare from a puddle as he walked up towards the Headrow. His hand crept into his overcoat pocket and closed around the bottle.

Immediately it soothed him. Its texture, its shape, its coolness seemed to diffuse through his skin and into his mind, unravelling the hard painful knot of his thoughts. The sensation was a strange one. Though David had heard of the supposed healing power of crystals, he had always regarded the notion with more than a little scepticism. Yet the bottle was performing a not dissimilar function, acting as a kind of focus for his thoughts, an outlet for his insecurities. Last night, whilst brooding, he had sat and stared at the bottle for hours, his eye drawn by the intricate play of light on its scoured surface. Crazy though it seemed, after a while he had felt almost as though the bottle was trying

44

to tell him something. Or rather . . . no, the sensation was more ambiguous and less mystical than that. It was as though the bottle, by his concentrating on it, was acting as a key to his innermost thoughts – thoughts buried so deeply that he was certain of neither their content nor their relevance. David had had the feeling that he was on the verge of remembering something important, revelatory even, or of discovering some piece of information about himself, something so intrinsic that he would wonder how he could ever have overlooked it.

He pressed a cool hand to his forehead, which felt hot, headachy. It all sounded so vague and weird, but then nothing seemed to make sense any more. Maybe his strange ideas had come from the half-bottle of whisky that he'd drunk alone in his study, which had resulted in him slumping asleep over his desk, his head resting on his arms. He'd woken at dawn feeling stiff and cold. Unable to bear the thought of crawling into bed beside Ellen and waking her up, he'd showered and then put back on the clothes he'd been wearing all night. He had crept downstairs, where he'd drunk two cups of black coffee and stared glumly as the sky changed from a deep salmon-pink to a dull dishcloth-white. As soon as he heard sounds of stirring from upstairs, he had grabbed his briefcase, hurried into the hall, opened the front door, shouted, 'Right, I'm off!', and exited, trapping Ellen's awkward questions, which he felt sure she would have sent to pursue him, inside the house.

He had reached the Headrow and crossed the busy road almost without knowing it. Now he was striding across the grey-flagged plaza before the art gallery. A Henry Moore sculpture of a reclining woman – voluptuous, faceless – lolled on a metal base beside the wide steps up to the main doors.

The library, which was David's destination, was a building of grimy ashlar which seemed to crouch shyly in the shade of the expansive art gallery. It had always seemed to David as if the library was reluctant to be discovered, and he liked it for that very reason. On the section of plaza in front of the library a group of people were studiously watching a game of chess being played on a giant chess board. The players were an enormous dread-locked black man, stripped to the waist despite the coldness of the day, and a tiny hunched pensioner wearing a cloth cap and fingerless gloves, whose stubbled jaw worked with the slow deliberation of a cow chewing cud.

David bypassed them, and hurried up the steps into the library. The reference library, on the third floor, was a long rectangular room – or rather, two rooms, separated by an arch. Dominating the centre of the main room was a row of tables, flanked on all sides by elaborate arches within which bookshelves were housed. At this time of day the room was almost empty: a few students pored resentfully over essays, a middle-aged man in half-moon spectacles consulted a leather-bound book whose cover was so worn it was impossible to make out the title, and a large woman with prematurely grey hair, wearing a voluminous red and black lumberjack shirt, scowled as she consulted an array of road atlases, her lips moving as if she were mouthing curses or incantations.

David located the telephone directories, found the appropriate one for London, and took a seat beside a girl who was hunched over a book on the Spanish Civil War, her face hidden behind a curtain of ginger corkscrew curls. His hand stole surreptitiously into his pocket and sought the silky grittiness of the bottle's surface once more. He touched it with his fingertips as if for luck, then withdrew his hand and opened the directory roughly in the middle. He found himself looking at the name Nibbins, which he thought sounded like some kind of corn snack. He flipped backwards quickly until he came to the start of the M's. He had read John Marshall's note so many times that he

46

had no need to refer to it. He knew the message, together with the name and address he was looking for, verbatim.

There were a great many Marshalls, almost six pages' worth. The M. Marshalls, which took up three-quarters of a column, began on the third page. David's finger travelled down the list, his eyes flickering over address after address. Even if the note was not a joke, it was surely too much to hope that Malcolm Marshall was still living in the house he had occupied forty years ago – in which case David's little investigation would be over before it had even begun. What David would do if Marshall *was* still living at 58 Cranleigh Parade he had no idea; probably nothing. The note had simply piqued his curiosity a little, that's all. No, that was a lie. It had piqued his curiosity a lot. Nevertheless, if the bottle itself had not made him feel so . . . so odd, following up the information on the note would probably have become one of those little tasks he was always meaning to do but would never actually get around to.

Suddenly his finger stopped. There it was, even after all these years: Marshall M., 58 Cranleigh Parade. David felt strange in a way he couldn't explain. Seeing Marshall's existence confirmed in print was a little spooky. David licked his lips, read the name and address again just to be sure, then murmured, 'Excuse me,' to the cascade of ginger curls beside him. The curtain of hair rippled then swished aside; a very lovely face with pale skin, freckles and green eyes raised its eyebrows enquiringly.

'Sorry to bother you but could I borrow your pen a minute?' David asked.

'Sure,' said the girl and held out her black biro for him to take.

David thanked her and scribbled down Malcolm Marshall's telephone number on the back of his hand. He returned the pen, then pushed his chair back, stood up and thoughtfully returned the telephone directory to its place on the shelf. He cleared his throat and decided that the library was dry and stuffy and that he needed a drink. Though insipid, the sunlight as he stepped outside seemed harsh after the gloom of the library. He screwed up his eyes to reduce its glare.

Between the library and the art gallery was a wine bar called Stumps, which David took two steps towards, then stopped. No, some of the trendies from work went in there; he'd look for somewhere else. He hurried across the plaza, breath puffing out in a steamy cloud, hand clenched around the bottle in his pocket as though it were a fetish. From the corner of his eye he saw a hand stretching out towards the sleeve of his overcoat, and he flinched away, thinking it belonged to one of the down-and-outs who congregated around the art gallery steps.

'Excuse me.' The voice belonged to a woman. David glanced around, still walking, and saw an old lady, well-dressed in a yellow mac, tweedy skirt, thick tights and brown suede fur-lined boots with a zip up the front. He halted and smiled vaguely, thinking she probably wanted directions to somewhere.

The old lady looked like everyone's idea of a rosy-cheeked grandma. Her complexion was healthily pink, her eyes a pale clear blue. Her tightly curled hair was so white it seemed to glow, as if it had somehow managed to trap and enhance the meagre sunlight.

'I wonder if I could talk to you for a minute?' she said.

Immediately David was wary. If she'd wanted directions she would surely have begun by saying, 'I wonder if you can tell me where . . .' or something along those lines. But the way she had phrased her sentence sounded like the start of a conversation in which she would do most of the talking. He decided that she was either conducting a survey, collecting for charity or selling religion. However he maintained his smile and said, 'What about?'

The woman looked a little embarrassed. 'It's a bit

difficult to explain. I don't really know what it's about myself, to be honest. I've . . . been asked to have a word with you.'

'Have a word?' said David guardedly. 'By who?'

'Um . . . well, I can't really tell you that, I'm afraid. You wouldn't know him anyway.'

David looked about, as if expecting to see whoever had asked this woman to contact him standing nearby, watching the exchange. He saw no one. No one, that was, except for office workers on their lunch breaks, mothers pushing prams, shoppers laden down with plastic bags full of Christmas gifts. David had hardly given Christmas a thought this year. In his present state of mind he'd simply wanted to blot it out, forget about it. He blew out a plume of air and stuffed his hands into the pockets of his overcoat. He remembered that Ellen had given him this overcoat as a Christmas present last year. She always referred to it as his 'Bogart'.

'Look,' he said reasonably, stepping away from the old woman, 'I think you've got the wrong person here.'

'No, I haven't,' said the old lady almost apologetically. 'You're David Fox. I've been watching you.'

She might have been a harmless-looking old lady but on hearing this David felt the first stirrings of alarm.

'Watching me?' he said in surprise, his voice rising enough to make heads turn. 'What do you mean?'

'Oh dear,' said the woman. 'I'm afraid I'm not handling this terribly well.'

She seemed genuinely distressed, and David, despite his trepidation, felt a little sorry for her. 'Look,' he said gently, 'did someone put you up to this? Did Ellen ask you to keep an eye on me?'

The old woman shook her head. 'No, no, it's nothing like that. It's just . . . oh dear, it's silly really. It's just . . . well . . . I want to buy the bottle you found.'

David felt the jitterings of a pulse in his throat. 'The

49

bottle? How did you know about that?'

The woman's hand fluttered in the air, dismissively, nervously. 'How I know isn't really important. The thing is, I've been asked to buy it from you.'

'Why?'

'I honestly don't know. Those were just the instructions I got. I didn't ask questions.'

David put a hand to his head. 'Well . . . who gave you these instructions?'

'I'm not sure I'm allowed to tell you,' said the woman apologetically.

With a sudden flash of inspiration David asked, 'Was it Malcolm Marshall?'

The woman looked shocked; it was evident she recognised the name.

'It was, wasn't it?' David said. 'It *was* him!'

The woman shook her head slowly. 'No,' she said. 'No, it wasn't Malcolm Marshall.'

'Who then?'

The woman regarded him thoughtfully, lips pursed as if she were weighing up the pros and cons of revealing the information. Finally she said, 'It was a man called Max Fleischer.'

'Max Fleischer?' David looked puzzled. 'I've never heard of him.'

'There's no reason why you should have.'

'But . . . who is he? I mean . . . how does he know about the bottle? Why does he want it?'

The old lady looked weary. 'I honestly don't know.'

'But you must know who he is! You're not telling me a stranger walked up to you, introduced himself as Max Fleischer, and told you to try and buy an old bottle off me?'

'No, I'm not telling you that.'

'What then?' said David.

The old lady sighed. She looked nervous and upset and

uncomfortable. David felt more sorry for her than ever, but he had to know who and what was behind her strange offer.

'Max is an old friend of mine,' she said at last. 'He lives in London, in the East End. He's a tailor. Last night he rang me up and told me to approach you and to offer to buy the bottle you'd found. He said it was important, but I honestly don't know any more than that.'

David stared at the old woman and found it hard to believe she was telling anything but the truth. Nevertheless he shook his head. 'I still don't understand. I still think it sounds weird.'

'Yes,' agreed the woman, 'it does sound weird, but there you are.'

She spoke with such resignation that David, despite himself, couldn't help smiling.

'Am I allowed to ask you what *your* name is?'

The woman grimaced. 'I'd rather you didn't.' Then she immediately conceded, 'Violet.'

'Violet what?'

'Just Violet. I don't want to get any more involved than I am already.'

'Involved in what?'

'I've told you, I don't know.'

David sighed. 'Of course you don't,' he said.

For a few seconds neither of them spoke. They had reached, it seemed, a kind of natural deadlock. Then, tentatively, Violet asked, 'So . . . are you prepared to sell me the bottle?'

'I don't know,' said David. 'It depends what you're offering.'

'Five hundred pounds,' Violet said quickly, slipping her hand into her pocket as if she intended to pull out the money there and then.

'Five hundred pounds? You're joking!'

What David meant, of course, was that he was

surprised to have been offered so much, but misunderstanding him, evidently flustered, Violet blurted, 'A thousand then.'

This time David was so surprised he couldn't even repeat the figure. He simply gaped at the old woman.

Violet's breath was coming quickly, wreathing her chin in little white puffs of steam. She looked terribly nervous, as if she wanted this to be over and done with as quickly as possible.

David was thinking hard. He had no idea who this Max Fleischer was or how he could possibly know about the discovery of the bottle, but his guess was that Fleischer was working for, or somehow involved with, Malcolm Marshall. No one else would offer to pay such a ridiculous amount of money for an old bottle – or rather, he thought, for the damning evidence contained within John Marshall's message.

Quietly, testing the water, he said, 'He killed them, didn't he?'

Violet looked alarmed. 'What? Who killed who?'

'Malcolm Marshall. He killed his son, John, and his wife, Celia. Almost forty years ago. He did, didn't he?'

The old lady was shaking. She looked as though she wanted to flee, and was about to do so at any moment. 'I don't know,' she said. 'I don't know what you're talking about.'

David nodded almost compassionately. 'I'm sorry, but yes, you do. You know who Malcolm Marshall is. I could tell by your face when I mentioned his name.'

Violet was extremely agitated now but she shook her head adamantly. 'No, I don't,' she said. 'I've never heard of him.'

David stared at her. Her nervousness was making him feel calm. 'Ten thousand pounds,' he said evenly.

Violet blinked, and was momentarily shocked into stillness. 'I beg your pardon?' she said after a moment.

'Ten thousand pounds for the bottle.'

She looked at him a moment longer, then began to nod slowly, gratefully. 'All right.'

David's calm crumbled. He stumbled back a step as if she'd pushed him. 'You're joking!' he exclaimed again.

Violet shook her head, evidently pleased that he had come up with a figure, eager to get this over and done with. 'No, if that's what you want.'

'You mean you'd be prepared to pay me –' he lowered his voice '– ten thousand quid? Just like that? Would this Fleischer guy agree to that?'

Violet nodded. 'I've been told to pay whatever you ask for.' Then she immediately put a hand to her mouth. 'Oh dear. I don't think I should have told you that.'

'Whatever I ask for? *Whatever* I ask for?'

'Within reason, of course,' Violet amended, though her tone was not convincing.

David's heart was beating fast. He placed a palm on his forehead and it came away gleaming with sweat. 'Whatever I ask for,' he murmured to the sky. 'I don't believe this. *I do not believe it.*'

'Are we agreed then?' said Violet tentatively.

'What?'

'Ten thousand pounds. Is that what we're agreed on?'

David stared at the woman. Part of him insisted that this was all a big joke – finding the bottle, the note, the offer of money – that it was all a hugely elaborate set-up. But he knew in his heart that it was not. It was deadly serious. And he knew also that there was no way he could take the money, hand over the bottle and simply walk away.

And so he shook his head slowly and said, 'No.'

'Pardon?' said Violet, taken aback.

'I'm sorry, no. I've changed my mind.'

'What do you mean?'

'The bottle's not for sale.'

53

'But . . . but I was going to give you ten thousand pounds.'

'I know,' said David, 'which is precisely why the deal's off. I want to know why you'd quite happily hand over such a huge amount of money for an old bottle containing a message that's nearly forty years old. Even if what the note says is true, it's surely not worth that, is it? Not after all this time?'

'I don't know anything about a message,' said Violet despairingly. 'I was just asked to buy the bottle.'

'So you'd just take the bottle without the note?'

Violet looked confused. 'I don't know.'

David shook his head. Even if this guy, Max Fleischer, was operating under Malcolm Marshall's instructions, there was still something very wrong about this whole scenario. Forgetting for the moment the question of how they even knew that he had the bottle, David couldn't understand why they would then send an ill-informed old woman, who obviously didn't even want to be here, after him. It was either very bad planning or something so sinister that he didn't even want to begin to think about it.

'Look,' said David, 'you tell Mr Fleischer that I'll speak to him personally. If he explains exactly what's going on, then maybe I'll think about selling the bottle to him.'

Violet looked as though she was contemplating whether or not to argue further. Then her shoulders slumped and she said, 'Oh well, I tried.' She pulled a face and continued, 'Max told me that if you wouldn't sell the bottle I was to tell you that others would be coming after it, and that they might not be as . . . well, as polite as I am.'

David's stomach squirmed. 'Is that a threat?' he asked.

The old woman looked almost comically alarmed. 'Oh dear, I don't think so. At least, not by me. No, I think Max meant it as . . . as a warning.'

'A warning? Against whom?'

'I don't know,' said Violet so quickly that David knew it was a lie. 'I'm just repeating what Max told me.' She looked around as though she'd just decided to do a spot of shopping and was not sure which shop to go in first. 'Well, I must be going,' she said inappropriately. 'I'll tell Max what you said. Yes, I . . . goodbye.'

Without waiting for a reply, which David did not give anyway, she turned and walked quickly away. David watched her, unmoving, until the crowd had swallowed her up, and then he hurried in the opposite direction.

7

Although David had looked around, half-expecting to see some dark and sinister figure observing the exchange between himself and Violet, he had not noticed a tall white-haired man in a grey pin-striped suit sitting on a bench thirty yards away eating a cheese and salad baguette. If David *had* noticed the man he would simply have dismissed him as just another city gent taking a lunch break – idling for an hour or so, watching the world drift by, picking crumbs from his white moustache, throwing titbits for fat pigeons to bicker over. If David had glanced at the man at just the right moment, however, their eyes might have met, and he might have noticed a covert but intense expression on the man's face, and he might have become suspicious. If Violet Turner had noticed the man, she might well have turned a deathly shade of pale and run as fast as her legs could carry her in the opposite direction.

Michael Piers Worthington had not seen Violet for many years but he had recognised her instantly. He cursed the fact that she had got to David before him. He didn't know why the item he had been sent to retrieve was so significant, but if the oracle said it was, then there was no questioning the matter. He had been given carte blanche to use whatever method he deemed necessary to recover the bottle. Subtlety of course was preferable, but if that was to prove unproductive then he was not averse to using stronger tactics.

What did please him about the exchange between Violet and Fox was that the old woman seemed extremely

agitated, which would suggest that she was having difficulty persuading Fox to hand the bottle over. However,
the fact that she was here at all was disturbing; it raised
the question of how those recidivist bastards had come by
their information so quickly. Worthington's hatred of
Violet and her ilk burned in his belly like bile. Like the so-
called hunt saboteurs who were continually showing up at
his Sunday meets and spoiling the day for everyone, they
were an ignorant and disruptive rabble.

'You're joking!' he heard Fox say even from this
distance. Glancing up, he saw the blond-haired man take
a stumbling step back before recovering his composure.
Worthington gave a slight smile. He had been here right at
the beginning, had been just about to make his own move
in fact when the old woman had stepped in literally
seconds before him, and he was as certain as he could be
that the bottle had not yet changed hands. Of course, the
bottle *could* have changed hands at some earlier meeting,
and what he was witnessing now might simply be the
preamble to payment, a last-minute attempt by the old
woman to get David to accept a lower price. However,
Worthington didn't think so. From the surprised and
suspicious look on Fox's face when the old woman had
first clutched his sleeve, he was fairly certain that this was
the first time Violet Turner and David Fox had met.

All of which meant that things were not turning out
quite as badly as had first appeared. Once Fox had given
the old woman the brush-off, which Worthington in
his arrogance believed was about to happen any second
now, he would step in and make his offer. Worthington
knew he could be *far* more persuasive than the old
woman. He had, after all, been practising the art of
persuasion for over forty years. As Managing Director of
IMI Pharmaceuticals, Worthington enjoyed a certain
reputation. He did nothing to quell the whispers that he
was a dangerous man to know and an even more

dangerous one to cross; indeed, he revelled in his image, which if truth be known was not entirely unjustified. Not that David Fox would know who he was, but that didn't matter. Once Worthington had brought the full force of his personality to bear on the man, he felt sure that the bottle would be as good as in his pocket. And if not . . . well . . . there was more than one way to skin a cat.

His reverie was interrupted by a smell so sharp and revolting it brought instantaneous tears to his eyes. The smell was like a distillation of everything bad – diarrhoea, rotting cheese, chronically unwashed armpits. As a shadow fell over him, bringing the stench closer, he propelled himself in a swift and undignified sideways shuffle to the other end of the bench. However the action failed to halt the progress of either shadow or smell, both of which loomed closer, like death. Worthington jumped up and turned to face his tormentor, rearing back like a nervous horse as he did so.

The swaying, grinning creature before him could barely, in Worthington's opinion, be described as a man. He was filthy, unshaven, drunk and dressed in rags. Worthington hated tramps; they offended his sensibilities. He resented paying his not inconsiderable taxes merely to keep such no-hopers in a constant state of inebriation. As far as he was concerned, there was absolutely no excuse in this day and age for such degenerate behaviour. In a low, steely-calm voice he muttered, 'Please go away.'

The man simply stood there, tottering, as though he hadn't heard. After a few moments he slurred, 'I'll tell you what, mate, you seem like a really nice bloke.'

'I'm not, I assure you,' Worthington murmured. 'And if you don't leave now I'll prove it by tearing your fucking liver out with my bare hands.'

The man blinked as if surprised by the dichotomy of calm voice and vicious words. 'Hey now,' he said compan-ionably, 'there's no need for any of that. You're all right, you are, you're a good lad.'

'Fuck. Off.' Worthington's voice was so cold it would have frozen fire.

The tramp, however, blundered obliviously on.

'Nah, nah, just listen a minute. I won't keep you for a minute. You're all right, you are. I just wanted a favour, that's all. You'd help out a mate, wouldn't you?'

'If I had time, I'd take pleasure in feeding you to the pigeons piece by piece. Now get out of my way, you stinking scrap of shit.'

The tramp, still swaying drunkenly, did not look particularly put out by either the threat or the insult. 'Now then, I know a nice lad like you would help out a good mate at Christmas – Happy Christmas, by the way. Now then, I just need twenty pence for a cup of tea.' He spread his hands and shrugged, demonstrating what a reasonable man he was and how meagre his request.

Worthington took a quick look around to ensure that no one was watching, then he turned back to the tramp and gave him his special smile. He allowed the smile to linger for three seconds to ensure that the image penetrated the man's alcohol-sodden brain. He even unfurled his yellow tongue and allowed it to drool briefly over the glistening white pyramids of his teeth. 'I'll give you one more chance,' he said reasonably. 'If you leave now I'll allow you to keep your face.'

The tramp's expression was comical to behold, so comical in fact that Worthington could not help but chuckle. First of all he flushed an interesting puce colour, which drained almost immediately from his face to leave his skin, even his lips, bloodless as old dough. His eyes stretched wide as though pinned back, his mouth twisted like that of a stroke victim straining for speech. He began to make a strange noise, as though imitating a geiger counter encountering traces of radioactivity. Finally he managed to sigh out a single word:

'Glory.'

Worthington, restored to normality, smirked beneath his white moustache. 'Very appropriate,' he said. 'Now, if you'll excuse me.' He sidestepped the tramp, wrinkling his nose fastidiously as he did so, and fixed his eyes back on the spot where Turner and Fox had been debating.

Fury rose in him when he realised they had gone.

Frantically he swung this way and that, hoping to catch a glimpse of one or both of them weaving through the lunch-time crowds. His search was in vain, however. During the two or three minutes that the tramp had distracted him, they had evidently concluded their business and made themselves scarce. Livid, he strode briskly after the tramp, who was now loping unsteadily across the plaza. When he was just a couple of yards away he glanced quickly around, pulled a small stiletto dagger from the inside pocket of his pin-striped suit and stabbed it quickly in and out of the tramp's back as he passed behind him.

Worthington had moved perhaps ten yards further when the tramp's legs buckled and he fell. At first no one seemed to notice, or care. It was only when blood started to fan out from the tramp's body on to the grey flagstones, causing someone to scream, that a crowd began to form around the old man.

Worthington glanced back once but did not linger to see whether the tramp lived or died. He hoped it would be the latter, because he was still holding the stiletto in his hand, the blade pointing upwards into his sleeve, and he didn't want to have stained the cuff of his shirt with blood for nothing.

Dealing with the tramp made him feel a little more cheerful, though losing track of the bottle still worried him. As he walked back to his car he decided that the wisest thing to do would be to pay Violet a little visit. The reasoning behind this was simple: if Violet *did* have the bottle it was vital to retrieve it as quickly as possible, before she had time to pass it on. If, however, David Fox still had the bottle, which seemed more probable, then the matter was perhaps not *quite* so urgent. Worthington was gambling on the fact that Fox had no inkling of the bottle's importance and was holding on to it simply because Violet Turner's clumsy approach had aroused his curiosity. Assuming that Violet had not managed to procure the bottle, her next move would presumably be to report back and inform the rest of her rabble about what had occurred. Worthington hoped she would wait to get home before doing this and not use a public phone box, otherwise the scum could be putting contingency plans into action whilst he was twiddling his thumbs. The worst scenario, of course, was that Violet had the bottle and was now on her way to a post office to get rid of it. This possibility made Worthington's heart beat a little faster, though he didn't think even the rabble would be so stupid as to resort to posting the bottle. After all, letters and parcels could be intercepted. No, if they had any sense they would hold on to the damn thing.

He reached his car and pressed the button on the pad of his keys which switched off the alarm and unlocked the doors. He had decided to use Gillian's Renault today; his mustard-yellow Rolls was far too ostentatious for this kind of business. Seated inside, he drew the stiletto carefully from his sleeve, took a pristine white handkerchief from his left trouser pocket and wrapped the knife up in it. When he examined the cuff of his suit he found a spot of blood the size of a penny on the silk lining and more blood speckled the sleeve of his white shirt.

'Dear me,' he murmured. He opened the glove compartment and took out his car phone. Hoping the surrounding buildings would not choke the line, he dialled Mathilde Cowper's number. He shuddered when the phone was picked up, half-expecting Danny, speaking in

61

the voice of the oracle, to say, 'You've failed, haven't you, Mr Worthington.'

However it was Mathilde who answered the phone. 'Hello?' she said, suspicious as ever.

'Mathilde, it's Michael.'

'Michael! Have you got it?'

'Almost,' he said vaguely. 'I just need a little information.'

'What is it you want to know?'

'You were friends with Violet Turner, weren't you?'

'Violet? Yes, I was. Why?'

Bracing himself, Worthington asked, 'I don't suppose you happen to remember her address?'

8

Ten minutes after his conversation with Violet, David was sitting at a table in The White Horse, nursing a pint of bitter and picking unenthusiastically at his ploughman's lunch. He kept replaying the exchange with the old woman over and over in his mind, trying to make sense of her extraordinary offer. His original theory that Malcolm Marshall was somehow at the bottom of all this still seemed the most feasible, but what he couldn't work out was how Marshall knew he had the bottle in the first place. He could only assume that Marshall must somehow have *known* that the bottle was going to be washed up on Starmouth beach yesterday, which itself seemed an impossibility. But if somehow he *had* known, and had sent someone to retrieve it, then whoever had been sent must have seen David pick the bottle up and then followed him all the way home. But if the note was genuine, then that meant that the bottle had been in the sea for nearly forty years. And if it wasn't genuine, if the note and the bottle had simply been made to *look* old and the bottle had been planted at the water's edge, then why the hell would anyone be prepared to pay ten thousand quid for it?

Though the mystery intrigued him, his frustration over its apparent inconsistencies gnawed at his belly like indigestion. Was he overlooking something obvious? If so, he couldn't think what. He chewed grimly on a piece of orange cheddar which tasted of the clingfilm it had been wrapped in, and looked around. Despite the mediocre food, The White Horse was one of David's favourite pubs.

It was situated on the outskirts of the city centre, by the side of the River Aire. This was an area of considerable expansion and refurbishment at present, new flats, office blocks and trendy restaurants continuing to spring up despite the recession. The White Horse, however, seemed determined to resist the implied pressure to upgrade itself accordingly. It stood in the midst of all this pristine modernist splendour like a scruffy snot-nosed child at a society wedding.

Like its primarily Bohemian clientele, it was a pub that cared little for surface glamour. It was shedding curls of green paint from its doors and windowsills, rising damp crawled like fungus up its side wall, and its roof was so humped and uneven it resembled a dinosaur's back.

The interior was much the same. The decor was minimal – no carpets, scratched and battered tables, seats worn to a shine through years of use. However, the atmosphere was relaxed and the beer exceptional.

At this time of day the pub was quiet, tranquil almost. One or two regulars murmured at the bar, interspersing their conversation with gulps of Old Peculiar; a couple of lads in dusty overalls played pool in a raised alcove. The pub cat, Jess, slunk between table legs like a feline femme fatale. A bearded man wearing a cream fedora tried to tempt her with a sliver of prawn cocktail crisp. She sniffed it and then disdainfully turned her back and sauntered away.

David finished his first pint quickly and ordered another, with a whisky chaser. He spent the next hour staring into the middle distance, drinking steadily as he tried to piece together a workable solution to the bottle's riddle in his mind. His inability to do so exasperated him, added to which the alcohol he had consumed made him melancholy. Finally, after four pints and three whiskies, he pushed aside his plate of limp salad, plastic cheese and congealed pickle, and stood up.

His head spun, as if his brain was set on a turntable inside his skull. His bladder was a swollen balloon. David walked carefully to the toilet, negotiating a wide arc around a small plastic Christmas tree on a table against the wall. The tree had been sprayed with some white fluffy substance which was supposed to resemble snow, but which looked instead like a dusty accumulation of cobwebs. All at once David felt an urge, which he managed to repress, to sweep the tree from the table. It was normally about this time that he and Ellen took a day off work to spend Christmas shopping together. They would buzz around like little kids, excited and happy, spending far more money than they had intended. They would eat lunch in a pub or a teashop, shop until late and then dine in one of Leeds' numerous restaurants before going home.

David normally loved the week before Christmas; for him, it was always a time of great anticipation. He would invariably be so pleased with the presents he had bought for Ellen and the girls that he could barely wait to see their faces when they opened them. As he stepped through the door into the toilet, he felt choked and sick and frustrated in the knowledge that there would be none of that this year. Because of the way he was feeling, because of his stupid hormones or something, the thought of trying to cope with all that joy, all that happiness, was unbearable.

He locked himself into a cubicle, the walls of which were decorated with lengthy and misspelled sexual fantasies. The stench was pretty nauseating; David held his breath whilst he urinated. As he was zipping himself back up, he heard the toilet door opening, its hinges wheezing like an asthmatic. Slow footsteps approached, echoing slightly. David jumped as someone rapped on the door of his cubicle, five hard-knuckled knocks.

Irritably he muttered, 'Hang on. I won't be a minute.'

'Mr David?' The voice surprised him, not only because

it had used his name but because it was shy and timid, the voice of a child.

'Who's that?' said David warily.

'It's John, Mr David. I need your help. Please say that you'll come.'

'John?' said David, 'John who?' And then all at once he remembered the note in the bottle and a chill passed through him.

'John?' he repeated uncertainly. He was confused, his thoughts muggy with drunkenness. Suddenly he didn't feel very well; he wanted to sit down.

'Yes, Mr David. Please say you'll help. Please.' There was desperation in the boy's voice.

David said nothing. As if John's voice was implementing it, the pounding in his head was becoming ever more vigorous, his stomach flipping over and over like a snowball gaining momentum as it rolls downhill.

'*Please!*' the boy implored as if David's silence was a refusal. 'Please say you'll help, Mr David. Please, please, *please!*'

He began to pound on the door with his fists. David could see the wood shaking. He looked down suddenly at the gap between the bottom of the cubicle door and the floor, and saw a pair of black leather shoes, grey school socks.

'Stop!' David cried. He put a trembling hand on the door and immediately the boy on the other side stopped pounding. 'Stop,' he said again, his voice trailing into a whisper. 'I . . . I don't know who you are.'

'Yes, you do, Mr David,' the boy said matter-of-factly. 'You found my bottle. You read my note.'

David's rapidly escalating nausea was making him sweat. He could almost feel himself going white, the blood draining from his face. His vision was blurring, and trying to focus was making him feel even worse. He closed his eyes, leaned into the corner between door and wall to support his weakening legs, and muttered, 'No. That can't have been you.'

'Yes, it was, Mr David. You read my note. Now I need you to help me.'

David was now feeling so sick he didn't know where to put himself. He felt his legs giving way, his body sinking, his sweaty forehead squeaking as it slid down the wall. 'Just go away,' he whispered. 'Go away.'

'I can't,' said the boy. 'Not until you promise to help me.'

'Oh God,' David moaned. He crossed his arms over his stomach, bowed his head, as if that would reduce the nausea that was flooding through him. 'Oh God, this isn't happening. It isn't real.'

'Just say it, Mr David. Just say it and I'll go.'

David was no longer sure whether the boy's voice was inside his head or outside the cubicle door. Now, with his eyes squeezed shut and nausea filling his thoughts and his belly, he was not even sure whether his sight of the boy's feet through the gap in the bottom of the door had been real or imagined. What he did know was that he wanted to be alone to concentrate on not feeling any worse than he already was. And so he whispered, 'All right, I'll help you. Just go now, please.'

'Promise?' said the boy. 'Cross your heart and hope to die?'

'Yes,' David sighed.

'All right,' said the boy, apparently satisfied. 'Thank you, Mr David. Thank you . . .'

The boy's voice faded on that last word, seemed to sigh away as though carried by a summer breeze. David crouched there in the dank smelly silence of the toilet cubicle for another minute or so and then cautiously opened his eyes.

The black shoes and grey socks, if they had ever been there at all, were gone.

It was ten minutes later when David opened the toilet door and stepped out into the soothing normality of the pub. It felt as though a long time had passed since he had entered the toilet; certainly the pub seemed busier now. Cutlery scraped across plates, pool balls clicked, the fruit machine burbled and flashed. David felt a little better now that he had vomited a good deal of the liquid from his belly into the stained toilet bowl, and had then staggered out of the cubicle to one of three sinks on the opposite wall where he had washed his face and rinsed out his mouth with cold water that smelled of chlorine. His reflection in the cracked and speckled mirror above the sink had been ghastly. Though the skin around his eyes was dark, the rest of his face – including his lips – was white and clammy-looking.

He needed some fresh air. His head was thick, his stomach raw and hollow. He felt slightly distanced from his surroundings, as if what he was seeing was merely an assimilation of reality. Outside the pub, David slipped his hand into the pocket of his Bogart and touched the bottle. It was almost certainly wishful thinking that made the bottle appear to act as a focusing dial, clarifying his thoughts. However, it could not be denied that the idea to ring Malcolm Marshall sprang into his mind the instant his fingers made contact with the bottle's silky-rough surface. He took his hand from his pocket, looked at the telephone number written in biro on the back, then sighed and began to trudge the short distance into the city centre.

As he walked he made a deal with himself: if there was a phone booth available at the railway station he would call Marshall, if not he would scrub the number from his hand and forget about the whole thing. However, when he arrived to find that every booth was occupied, he instantly changed his mind. His need to know what was going on, and something else too (a sense of . . . duty? Inevitability?), was too strong.

Three minutes later, even as he was dialling Marshall's number and wondering just what he was going to say, it occurred to David that this was the first time in two months or more that anything had managed to spark his interest. The phone rang five times (David counted each double-burr, promising himself that when they numbered ten he would replace the receiver, collect his fifty-pence piece from the slot and walk away) before it was picked up. There was a pause which seemed longer to David than it actually was, and then a gruff, tired voice said, 'Hello?'

David swallowed. 'Mr Marshall?'

'Yes.'

'Mr Marshall, I . . .' David began, and then realised he didn't know what to say. He experienced a flare of panic which took him back momentarily to the time when he was ten at junior school and had been playing Joseph in the Christmas Nativity play. Things had been going fine until the moment Adam Horton, who was playing the innkeeper, flung out his arm dramatically and proclaimed, 'There is no room at the inn!' David had opened his mouth to respond, only to find that the words he had learned so carefully, and had practised and practised with his mother at home, were no longer in his head. Back then his mind had frozen solid for an eternally drawn-out ten seconds before his line, 'But we must have shelter,' had popped out of his mouth as if it had bypassed his brain entirely.

This time, however, David had no rehearsed lines to regurgitate. He took a deep breath in the hope that it would get his locked thoughts turning again, and hardly aware of what he was saying, he blurted out, 'Mr Marshall, are you there?'

'Yes,' said Marshall in a voice that sounded brittle.

'Sorry about that, I thought we'd been cut off,' David said. 'Mr Marshall, my name is . . . er . . . Adam Horton. I'm an old friend of John's.'

Did that really sound as unconvincing as David thought it did? Apparently so, for there was a heavy and prolonged silence at the other end of the line. The silence seemed to rush from the earpiece, to clog David's head. He wanted to put the phone down and walk away, but instead found himself saying, 'Mr Marshall, are you still there?'

His own voice sounded hollow and distant in his ears, and Marshall's voice was more than tired this time. It sounded cold and dead, eerie in its lifelessness. 'John's not here,' he said.

David suppressed an urge to shudder. 'Oh,' he said, 'right. Well, I . . . er . . . just wondered whether you could give me his number – his phone number, that is. I thought, you know, that I'd give him a call. Surprise him.'

'When did you know John?' Marshall asked tonelessly.

Perhaps to make up for the old man's unresponsiveness, David felt a need to be overly chatty and cheerful. 'Oh, it must be . . . forty years ago now. We were at school together. Great mates we were, but I left when I was . . . ten. Or thereabouts.'

Another silence. David had the sudden absurd idea that if he didn't fracture it with sound, Marshall would somehow use the silence to ensnare him.

'Mr Marshall, is something wrong?' he said briskly.

'John's dead.' The words, though not unexpected, were so blunt they seemed shocking.

'Dead?' David murmured. 'But . . . how? When?'

'A long time ago. I don't want to talk about it.'

'But . . . how did he die, Mr Marshall?'

A pulse began ticking uncomfortably in David's throat. He swallowed, as if in the belief that the pulse could be dislodged like a troublesome hunk of bread. He felt sure that he couldn't say anything this time, not until Marshall did. He was contemplating again whether to simply put down the phone and forget about the whole thing when Marshall said quietly, 'Why don't you stop messing about?'

The pulse was now so strong that David felt certain it would strangle his speech. He cleared his throat twice but eventually managed to say, 'What do you mean?'

Another silence, though shorter this time, more a pause than anything. Marshall's voice was slow and measured, and dry as old leaves being crushed against the earpiece. 'Why don't you ask me outright what you want to know?'

'I . . .' floundered David, and then repeated helplessly, 'What do you mean?'

'Why don't you ask me whether or not I killed my son?'

David could think of nothing coherent to say. He felt defenceless, as if Marshall had ducked beneath his opening jabs and caught him a good one on the chin. 'Well I . . . I . . . I don't know,' he stammered at last, voice dwindling.

Marshall's tone was almost sympathetic as he delivered the knockout blow.

'I think you're out of your depth, Mr Fox.'

David slammed the phone down, his hand spasming away from it as if it had turned into a scorpion. He could not have been more shocked had Marshall materialised behind him and tapped him on the shoulder. He shot out of the phone booth and began to hurry across the ticket area, his overcoat flying behind him. His entire body was cold and greasy with sweat; his mind was spinning. He found no comfort in the straggling queues of people at the ticket booths, the general hubbub. Indeed, he felt hemmed in, restricted; he felt a need to get outside where he could move more freely.

The fact that Marshall had used his name seemed to confirm David's theory that he was behind the approach by the old woman, but still it had been a shock. It made him feel that there was nowhere to hide, that he was being observed wherever he went. Thinking of the quiet, almost casual, threat implied in Marshall's voice encouraged a rash of goosebumps across David's shoulder blades and down his arms, caused the hair to bristle on the back of his neck. Why didn't he just give the bottle back to them? It meant nothing to him, despite the note, despite the strange occurrence in the pub toilet and his vow to help what might or might not have been the ghost of John Marshall.

But David knew that he couldn't give the bottle back, just as he knew that his assertion that the bottle meant nothing to him was untrue. Curiosity had hold of him now ... or rather, something more than curiosity – an obsessive need to find out just what was going on. Yesterday on Starmouth beach he had stared out to sea and thought (albeit only semi-seriously) about suicide. Was it too dramatic to say that the bottle, or more specifically the mystery connected to it, was his lifeline, something to which he was now clinging eagerly in the hope that it would prevent him from going under? To admit such a thing was frightening, for it suggested that his situation was even more desperate than he wished to believe. He wondered what his attitude to the bottle would have been had he found it six, or even three, months ago. But his mind was in such turmoil, his thoughts and emotions so arbitrary and untrustworthy, that the only reply he could come up with was: I don't know.

As he strode across town, wiping sweat from his brow despite the cold day, his eyes darting to examine the face of each passer-by, David wondered what he should do next. As far as he could see, there were two alternatives: either give the bottle back and try to forget about the whole thing, or keep hold of it and try to find out what was going on. He realised that he had already decided that the second alternative was the only one he could follow, in which case he had to decide on the best way to go about it. He could either play the passive role by sitting tight and waiting for them to come to him, or he could play the detective, acting on information he already had and following up any leads which might sprout from this information.

The idea of sitting tight did not appeal to David for a number of reasons. First of all, it would put him instantly on the defensive rather than the offensive; secondly he felt driven, impatient for answers; and thirdly he did not want his family involved or even asking questions, and he wanted to avoid – if it wasn't already too late – Marshall and whoever was working for him finding out where he lived.

So that left only one possible course of action, which was to go on the attack. And the only starting point David could think of was to travel to London and keep tabs on Marshall, and whilst there to try and discover the real story behind John Marshall's apparent death.

Passing beneath rows of grinning plastic Santas clinging to lamp posts, he told himself over and over that it was crazy to even consider travelling to London on what amounted to little more than a whim. Each time, however, the intractable answer came back: I know, but I'm going to do it anyway.

The only other question to consider, therefore, was, when should he go? And again the answer came back immediately: Why not now?

Why not indeed? After all, today was Thursday 17th December (exactly a week away from David's fortieth birthday), and on Thursdays, Fridays and alternate weekends, Ellen worked at the Rose Lodge Residential Home as a care assistant. This meant that until the girls came home from school the house would be empty, which gave David ample opportunity to return there, throw some things into a bag, scribble a note to Ellen and leave.

He was in no fit state to drive but he had no choice; he needed the car. He felt nervous as a truant as he crossed the company car park behind the Imperial Vision building, unlocked his car and got in. It was almost 1:45 p.m. They would all be wondering why he hadn't shown up at the editorial meeting. Until yesterday he'd managed not to let his personal problems affect his work. Vaguely he wondered what the reaction would be to this latest development, but in truth he didn't much care. The magazine, even his job, seemed trivial. Let Tony Cabanas take over as editor; he'd been wanting to for long enough.

It was not until he was safely inside the car and had started the engine that David glanced up at the building itself. God, the place was hideous! Among an intricately patterned framework of steel, hundreds of windows gazed forlornly back at him. Behind some of them, like grubs in glass tanks, David glimpsed movement: his colleagues, his co-workers, his fellow human beings. Disturbingly they seemed to twitch and flounder as though suffocating, fighting for air. David felt utterly divorced from them.

No one seemed to be looking his way. No one rushed out to challenge him as he drove off. David's journey home was dream-like, his movements mechanical. He felt enclosed within a protective bubble, felt as though the traffic around him was a cheap backdrop, not really there. All at once he was sitting in a motionless car on the road outside his house. He turned and looked at it as though he'd never seen it before.

A memory, sharp as lemon, filled his mind: the first day he and Ellen had seen this place. She had been five months pregnant with Jane, and had looked at least seven months; Jane had been a big baby, despite being almost two weeks premature. Rachel had been three at the time and a bit whiny. David remembered she had been right in the middle of her 'daddy' phase, clinging to him as much as possible, constantly trying to play him off against Ellen in that surprisingly manipulative way that children have.

He and Ellen had loved the place immediately. Up until

a couple of months ago he'd still loved it. Now, though, its familiarity depressed him. It was a big house, so big that many of its neighbours had been converted into flats, or even hotels. It was stone-built, late Victorian, with long windows that let in plenty of light, and a gargoyle called Horace over the door.

They'd bought it relatively cheaply and had done it up little by little. Now it was worth a small fortune. Ellen's dad had lent them a lot of money over the years. He'd died before they got a chance to pay him back, before he could buy that villa in Spain he'd always wanted.

David had always been sentimental, though as he let himself into the house a flood of emotion came over him that teetered dangerously towards the maudlin. He hadn't felt like this since the last day in his and Ellen's previous house, which had been the first one they'd bought together. That had been a little back-to-back just outside Huddersfield. Even now he could remember hoovering the attic bedroom which had been cleared of everything but the carpet they were leaving behind, and thinking: As soon as I finish this, I'll go out, lock the door behind me and probably never return. Half an hour later, after handing the keys over to the young couple who were buying the house off them, Ellen had actually wept a few tears in the car and David had felt like doing so too.

But there was no need to feel that way about this house, was there? he told himself almost angrily. For God's sake, it wasn't as though he was never coming back. His emotions were a mess at the moment, that was all it was, the negative ones far too close to the surface, bobbing up indiscriminately like pieces of driftwood.

He went upstairs and packed a suitcase as quickly and economically as possible. He found it hard restricting himself to essentials – now that the crunch had come, there was so much he wanted to take with him – but at last he was ready to go. He had no idea how long he would be gone for, and tried to block out the thought of how miserable Christmas would be for Ellen and the girls if he didn't return in time for it. The future was a grey fog, an unknown territory. All he could do was blunder blindly into it and hope for the best.

Suitcase beside him, he sat at the desk in his study and spent the next half-hour trying to compose a note to Ellen. How much should he tell her? How much *could* he tell? How could he possibly expect her to understand when he understood so little himself? He tried a number of different tacks, but at last decided that simple and short was best. The note which he sealed in an envelope and left propped against a vase of marigolds on the kitchen table read:

> My Dearest Ellen
> I have to go away for a while. I'm sorry. I love you.
> David

He then spent the next ten minutes just wandering around the house, touching things, feasting with his eyes. All the while he told himself there was no need for him to be doing this, that he would be back soon enough, yet all the same he couldn't deny that he felt a desperate urge, almost a kind of hunger, to commit as much of this as he could to memory. There was a lot of film and TV stuff around which he had collected over the years and which until recently had given him an incredible amount of happiness. There were framed movie posters and rare postcards, a vast video collection, a veritable library of books and magazines, as well as film props and models and other assorted merchandise. In truth, there was a whole life here, and it was not just his life but it was the life of the family, of all four of them. Everywhere he looked, David was beset with memories so poignant that they hurt. There were paintings and bowls and rugs which he and Ellen had bought together over the sixteen years or so since they had first started going out. There were masks from their honeymoon in Venice; a tapestry from their trip to Peru in 1985; a mother and child carved in wood from Kenya. And there were the girls' things too; David found he couldn't bear to actually go into their rooms and look at all the toys and games and clothes that had made birthdays and Christmases so special in the past. He lingered at the mantelpiece in the lounge, where the photograph of all four of them together in Wales last year brought a plum-sized lump to his throat. How could he find anything but joy in all this? How could he leave it all behind? What was *wrong* with him, for God's sake?

Breathing hard, he picked up his suitcase and carried it into the hall, his self-loathing so acute that it was making his already tender stomach throb with pain as though from an ulcer. As he left the house, locking it firmly behind him, and got into his car he had the disturbing impression that he was fading and shrinking, dwindling to nothing. He twisted the ignition key savagely, slammed the car into gear and roared away, leaving slewed brown marks in the gravel. He resisted the urge to look back, but his angry defiance felt hollow and pointless. The more distance he put between himself and what he was leaving behind, the more insubstantial he seemed to become.

9

When Violet walked away from David Fox she was feeling churned up with guilt and failure, but Max made her feel much better. As soon as he picked up the phone, apologies began to spill from her, but he soothed them away with his kindness and understanding and reassurance. He told her that she had done her best and that he was grateful, and he even apologised for imposing this burden upon her. It was unfair of him, he said, and he hoped that Violet would accept his personal and most sincere apologies.

'Thank you, Max,' Violet said, touched by his sincerity and relieved by his good grace. 'So what do I do now?'

'Nothing,' said Max. 'Go home and forget about the whole thing. Enjoy Christmas with your family.'

'But what about the bottle?'

'Let *us* worry about the bottle. Contingency plans are already being set in motion.'

Violet felt momentarily alarmed. 'You won't harm Mr Fox, will you?'

Max's tone was one of genuine hurt. 'Of course not. You should know us better than that, Violet.'

'I do,' said Violet, shamefaced. 'I'm sorry. Again.'

She could almost hear the smile in Max's voice. 'No, that's all right. You do well to ask. You liked Mr Fox, did you?'

Violet considered the question. 'He was suspicious of me, but . . . yes, I got the feeling that he was a nice young man.'

'And your instincts are usually right,' said Max. 'You

were always an excellent judge of character, Violet.'

'And you were always an old flatterer, Max Fleischer. Still are from the sounds of it.'

'True, true, but I only flatter those who deserve it. Tell me again,' he said, changing tack abruptly but making it sound like a natural progression of the conversation, 'what Mr Fox said about Malcolm.'

Violet told him, and imagined the little man listening intently, his pince-nez perched on the end of his nose, his head nodding unconsciously now and again.

When she had finished he murmured, 'And he obtained this information from a message that he found inside the bottle?'

'Well, he didn't actually say that.'

'No, but it seems a fair assumption – and the motives of the Flux would be far more explicable as a consequence, wouldn't you agree?'

Violet couldn't help but shudder a little and glance around at the street outside the transparent phone box. The street was thronged with people, the road choked with traffic, but no one seemed the slightest bit interested in her. It was the first time she had heard the group referred to by name in years, and she felt a little thrill of dread. It was only partly true that the group had ears everywhere. Referring to them by name was hardly likely to bring the wrath of God down on her, but still . . .

'I suppose so,' she said. 'Don't think I'm being funny, Max, but to be honest I'd rather not talk about it.'

'Of course not,' said Max. 'I'm sorry, Violet, truly.'

'It's all right. It's just me. I'm not as . . . strong as I used to be.'

'I don't think any of us are,' said Max, his voice wistful and sympathetic.

Violet pressed her free hand against her ear as a truck roared by outside, and said into the noise, 'Are you sure there's nothing else that you want me to do?'

'Just one thing,' replied Max.

Violet felt immediately resentful; just when she thought she was off the hook it seemed she was about to find herself snagged again. 'What's that?' she said sharply.

'Don't be a stranger,' said Max. 'Call me sometimes. Even if it's only to moan about the state of the world, or even the price of bread.'

Immediately Violet felt ashamed. 'I promise,' she said. 'I'm sorry I couldn't get your bottle for you.'

'We'll get it,' said Max airily. 'Goodbye, Violet. Happy Christmas.'

Violet was about to echo the sentiment and then remembered Max's faith.

'Happy . . . Chanukah,' she said. 'Is that right?'

Max seemed genuinely delighted. 'Yes,' he said. 'Bless you, Violet.'

Violet hadn't realised just how much Max's request had been preying upon her until she was free of it. Stepping from the phone box felt almost like liberation. Light-hearted, she fluttered around the shops, enjoying the Christmas bustle, buying little presents for Joe and Liz's children to go with the ones she had already bought – a confectionary box each, a Chalet School book for Kirsty from Waterstone's, a Subbuteo team for Andrew from Lewis's toy department where a crying child was being dragged towards Santa's Grotto.

Violet remembered the Christmases of her youth, where a bowl of oranges on the table had been a rare treat and a bar of chocolate an even rarer one. Nowadays Christmas was a commercial marathon, and that was a shame, for Violet felt it obscured the true meaning of the festival, which was not so much a religious one in her eyes but simply a time of peace and goodwill. She didn't begrudge the children their mountain of gifts (indeed, when it came to spoiling them she was the worst culprit), but she did hate the appearance of Christmas lights as early as

October, especially when it was unlikely they would be taken down until February. Nevertheless she felt good today, so good in fact that she walked around with a smile on her face that she was barely aware of. She caught the bus home and bought herself a strawberry gateau from the baker's on the corner to celebrate feeling good.

Laden down with presents and food, she walked back to her little back-to-back with its blue-painted front door and postage-stamp garden (which was currently strewn with cat pepper in an attempt to discourage the little darlings from using her flowerbeds as a toilet). She fumbled her key from her purse and managed to unlock and open the door without dropping anything.

Her good mood persisted for only two seconds longer, when it was snuffed out like a bug on a window. This was because the first thing she saw when she entered the house was Michael Piers Worthington sitting on the settee in her lounge, sipping tea from one of her best china cups.

She barely managed to avoid dropping everything in shock. Like the rest of her body, her arms felt suddenly weak and trembly. However she was able to lower her purchases on to her old leather armchair before swaying and clutching at the wall for support. Her hand bumped the print of a painting of Richmond Castle and knocked it slightly awry. The idea of fainting, like a band of blackness that was as fleeting and intense as light flashing on a knife blade, passed across her mind before she willed it away. When Worthington spoke, his voice seemed simultaneously as thick as treacle and as dry and echoey as the clunk of footsteps on the bare wooden floorboards of an empty house.

'Hello, Violet. I won't ask if you remember me, for I can see that you do.'

The voice that Violet managed to dredge from deep inside her was old and rusty and barely recognisable.

'What do you want?'

Worthington smiled and put his cup and saucer down carefully before replying, 'I think you know.'

'I don't,' said Violet.

Worthington smiled quickly without showing his teeth. 'Don't be obtuse, Violet. You're a little too old and a little too tired for these sorts of games.'

Violet's dizziness had passed, but her heart was still pumping hard and a sweat that turned instantly chilly was oozing from her skin.

'You're no spring chicken yourself,' she said, and was pleased by the spark of anger in her voice.

Worthington leaned forward a little. 'But I'm hardly decrepit,' he murmured. 'And my abilities have not decreased one iota. I'm still dangerous. Deadly, in fact . . . very deadly.'

'Is that supposed to frighten me?'

'Not particularly. But I can see that it does.'

Violet pushed herself away from the wall, welcoming the anger that was rising in her now. It was a shaky and fearful sort of anger, but it was anger just the same.

'How did you get into my house?' she demanded.

Worthington proffered her another smile – quick and patronising. 'Please,' he said as if she had insulted his intelligence, 'let's not get embroiled in trivialities.'

Violet took two further steps into the room and pointed at the door behind her. 'Will you please get out of my house?'

'Of course,' said Worthington to her surprise, and then added, 'but not just yet. First I want to know where the bottle is.'

'What bottle?'

Worthington drew his breath in with a hiss, and Violet stepped back involuntarily. 'Come now, Violet,' he said, his voice steady, 'don't try my patience. Just tell me where it is.'

Violet was not aware she had been retreating until she

backed into the dining table in the alcove beneath the window.

'I haven't got it,' she retorted, trying – and failing – to prevent her voice from rising shrilly. 'I haven't got it and that's the truth.'

Worthington's icy gaze bored into her, then a mirthless smile crossed his face. 'I believe you,' he said magnanimously.

Violet made an attempt to compose herself which was almost credible. 'Good. Would you go now please, then?'

Worthington shook his head, tutting in a way that made Violet think crazily of Skippy the bush kangaroo.

'Oh no, no, no, not until you tell me everything that you know.'

'I don't know very much,' Violet said warily, watching Worthington closely, all too aware of his unpredictable moods. However he simply stared at her, coolly and appraisingly, and then raised his eyebrows as an indication that she should continue.

'I was . . . I was asked to try and buy the bottle from a man whom I had never met before. I tried, but he wouldn't sell it to me . . . And that's all.'

She spread her hands, palms upwards, as though to prove her honesty. Worthington sighed.

'No,' he said, 'that's not all. Please tell me the rest.'

'What rest?'

Worthington got up and strolled over to the mantelpiece. He selected a miniature Chinese vase from the ornaments displayed there and threw it almost casually across the room. It shattered against the opposite wall.

'That,' he said conversationally, 'could so easily be your skull. Now tell me everything. Who asked you to buy the bottle? What reason did they give for doing so? What did they tell you about David Fox? I want to know it all.'

Violet felt a hot and grinding pain in her belly. The pain was part anger, part fear, part frustration, but most of all it was resentment and a sense of injustice, directed against both Max and Worthington, who were symbols of the opposing factions in this dispute. Violet wanted no part in this, she just wanted to live out her life, quietly and calmly, with her past firmly behind her where it belonged. She had been dragged into this business against her will and now she was being victimised, indeed terrorised, for what amounted to only a very minor role in something she did not, and had no wish to, understand.

She felt like telling Worthington all this but knew it would be pointless. She told him, therefore, everything that he wanted to know in the hope that after she had done so he would leave and that would be an end to it.

However he didn't leave. He simply stood where he was, looking at her thoughtfully, apparently mulling over all that she had told him.

Eventually he murmured, 'Max Fleischer. I might have guessed that Yid bastard would be behind this. Rather a pity that Adolf Hitler was got at before the plan could come to fruition, don't you think?'

Violet said nothing, and after a moment Worthington smiled as though at a private joke.

'Where did the Jew get his information from?' he asked her.

'I don't know,' said Violet, and added quickly, 'and that's the truth. He just rang me up last night out of the blue. I hadn't heard from him in years. I didn't ask any questions. I didn't want to get any more involved than I had to.'

Worthington snorted. 'It's a bit late for that.' He pushed himself away from the mantelpiece; Violet tensed. As though sensing her unease, and wishing to reassure her, Worthington beamed. Then he murmured, 'And now the question to be asked is, what shall we do with you?'

Violet's stomach clenched at his words. She should have known she wouldn't be permitted to simply put this whole unpleasant affair behind her. Nevertheless she said as reasonably as she could, 'Why do you have to do anything? I've told you everything I know. Why can't you just go away and leave me alone? You and everybody else?'

Worthington tilted his head, pursed his lips in mock sympathy. 'I wish I could,' he said, 'truly I do. Especially with Christmas so close and all. But the thing is . . . I'm afraid I can't. If I just walked out of here, then I wouldn't be doing my job properly, would I? As our American friends would say, I wouldn't be covering all the bases. You'd be a loose end, you see, Violet. And much as I like and admire you personally, I'm afraid loose ends have to be tied up.'

Violet wanted to say something scathing, wanted to tell him to stop behaving like a third-rate gangster, but she didn't have the courage. All she could manage was to ask a question whose answer she dreaded. 'What are you going to do?'

Worthington grinned, showing his teeth this time, but it was not a nice grin. It was the kind of grin a shark might give its prey, a grin of ravenous anticipation.

'Well,' he said, 'the way I see it I have two options. Either I can take you with me or I can kill you. Now . . . which shall I choose?'

Violet's heart felt as if it was beating against the base of her throat, clamouring to get out. The saliva was congealing in her mouth, turning her voice thick and clumsy.

'Why can't you just go away and leave me alone?' she pleaded again. 'I never wanted anything to do with this in the first place.'

Worthington frowned and put a finger to his lips. 'Shh, I'm thinking.'

Violet considered making a break for the front door but even at this stage she was reluctant to provoke

Worthington, reluctant to prompt events. She still clung to the possibility that the man might simply leave, that he was saying all these things merely to frighten her, and she didn't want to jeopardise that possibility. She still didn't *quite* believe that he was serious, even a moment later when he raised his head slowly to look at her and said, 'I've decided to kill you.'

The second following his statement, which had been delivered quietly and calmly, seemed suspended, held in stasis by Violet's sudden inability to breathe. It was broken only when she finally managed to draw a loud hissing breath and to whisper the only word she was capable of:

'Why?'

Worthington shrugged. 'Because taking you with me would be too much of an effort. Let's face it, old woman, you're neither use nor ornament. Besides,' he said, grin widening as he spoke, 'I like killing people, and I rarely get the opportunity these days.'

What happened next Violet had seen only once before, and that a long time ago. Even back then, when such wonders were commonplace, she had found the sight sickening and horrifying. This time she thought she might die from sheer terror even before Worthington had completed his transformation, which would spoil *his* fun certainly, but wouldn't do her a great deal of good either. She tried to ignore what was happening in front of her and to concentrate on rediscovering the pivot of her own animis. However it was difficult, like looking for a favourite party dress in an attic room heaped with old clothes. She knew if she had time she could rediscover it. But time was a commodity which, for her, was in very short supply.

She forced herself to close her eyes, to concentrate, forced her mind to wrench itself away from what Worthington was doing. Within the Flux, Worthington was known as

Glutton, or, more grandly, the Man of Mouths. He had once boasted to Violet that he had three hundred and ninety-nine of them and that they were capable of consuming *anything*. As an initial demonstration of his skills, he had transformed before an audience of six Flux members, including Violet, and consumed an entire double-decker bus in less than fifteen seconds.

Violet had never liked Worthington. He had a personality which these days would probably be termed sociopathic. Within the Flux his extraneous pursuits were known about but largely ignored, an attitude which Violet had felt reprehensible and which was just one of the reasons why she had left. As well as killing people for pleasure, Worthington was a sexual deviant, his tastes ranging – so she had heard – from children to corpses, both male and female. Once, at a party, he had sidled up to her, the worse for drink, and had hissed, 'Just imagine, Violet, almost four hundred tongues! What woman wouldn't kill for that? See me upstairs in ten minutes.' Without waiting for a reply he had swayed away, cocktail in hand. Violet had left immediately and had not felt safe until she was back home with William.

Try as she might, Violet tried to block the memory of Worthington's transformation from her thoughts but it was no use. She could hear it happening again right in front of her, a wet sharp sound, like the smacking of many lips, that seemed to go on for ever. She remembered how his body had ballooned as though with red wounds, to become something that was no longer recognisable as human. He had appeared to expand, to unravel; it had been almost like seeing him explode, though in a way that was horribly slow and horribly controlled.

She heard a crunching, juddering sound and knew that it was the noise of her furniture being forced back against the walls as Worthington's body swelled. His transformation must be almost complete now. She could stand it no longer; she opened her eyes.

The sight was so horrible that she could not even scream. She saw mouths of all shapes and sizes, slobbering, chomping, writhing. She saw thousands of shiny bared teeth, tongues straining hungrily. Some of the tongues were yellowish-white in colour, and reminded her of maggots wriggling in a mountain of meat.

Violet noticed that the mouths closest to her were puckering their lips, as if kissing the air. Was it possible that they were pinpointing her position by taste alone? Were they tasting her aura? The air around her?

She knew she didn't have much time. For the moment Worthington was stationary, acclimatising himself to his transformation. However, he would not stay that way for long. Within seconds he would start quivering and rippling his way towards her, his myriad mouths opening and closing as though talking without sound.

She became aware of a rustling movement behind her and glanced over her shoulder. A column of Worthington's slug-like flesh had oozed over the settee, and was now wavering from side to side by the front door like a gigantic blind worm, or a snake mesmerised by the music from a charmer's pipe. With terrifying speed, the column suddenly elongated, striking out like an eel at the light with its frilly shade dangling from the ceiling in the centre of the room. Violet saw a large jagged-toothed mouth open at the top of the column and close around the light, shade and all. There was a brief crunching sound and the column descended, leaving behind a shred of flex which dangled from the ceiling like a nerve ending.

Either Worthington was building up his strength, flexing his muscles as it were, or he was toying with her. Though she knew its protection would be minimal, she sidled around the dining table that had been pressing into her back and reached for one of the spindly wooden chairs tucked beneath it in the hope of using it as either a shield

88

or a weapon.

It was only as she did this that she realised her hand was becoming transparent. So it *was* working! Somehow, blundering about in her own thoughts, she had unknowingly tapped into her animis, the energy at the core of her being that powered her ability. She had rediscovered the skill she had not used in years: she had made herself invisible. She closed her eyes in order to concentrate, just as Glutton began rolling towards her like an awesomely fat cartoon drunk. There was hardly any distance to cover, no more than eight feet. Within seconds he would snap her up like a dog devouring a biscuit.

The instant she closed her eyes, however, Violet felt the strange sensation that preceded full invisibility flood through her. She had always thought of it as being like turning into running water, a living waterfall. She felt light and strong and supple as an athlete, felt her clothes slide away from her and crumple to the ground. She was aware of physical sensation such as cold and heat and pain, texture and substance, only peripherally, like a cool breeze passing across partially numbed flesh.

Less than a second after closing her eyes, she opened them again. Even now, invisible and insubstantial, she thought in terms of the body despite being bodiless. Glutton was still rolling towards her, moving at strolling pace, which, despite his claims, was perhaps his limit these days. Behind Violet was her large front window, flanked on either side by smaller windows. From the windowsill was a four-foot drop on to a narrow paved border, or even on to her tiny lawn if she could propel herself outwards far enough.

In her present state she was most akin to air, which meant that she could not pass through solid objects. However she *could* impose herself physically on the real world if she concentrated hard enough. She reached out what she imagined to be her hand and tried to grasp the

89

dining chair that she had been hoping to use as a weapon before her animis had taken effect. At first it was like trying to clutch a hologram, but after a moment's intense concentration, a moment in which Glutton rolled another two or three feet closer, the chair became real and solid in her grip. Strong as a weightlifter now, she swept it up and hurled it through the big front window.

The window exploded outwards, vomiting glass. The chair bounced across the lawn and skidded into the flowerbeds where it came to rest, upside-down, one of its legs broken and hanging on threads of wood. In that instant, as though sensing his prey was about to escape, Glutton seemed to gather himself and launch his bulk across the room towards her. He made a terrifying sound as he did so, as though each mouth was screaming its own individual war-cry. Though she had no voice herself, Violet added her own internal scream to the cacophony. A split-second later she leaped at the jagged star-shaped hole in the glass.

Glutton ploughed into the dining table and chairs, shattering them like matchwood. His mouths, chomping hungrily, devoured the lot in seconds. Even flying splinters were snatched from the air with tongues like whips and swallowed.

Violet, meanwhile, was landing on her lawn and rolling on broken glass as if it were no more substantial than cotton wool. She knew she was safe now, for the time being at least, but she was scared nonetheless, scared of Worthington's fury, of his madness and his hatred. If neighbours were standing open-mouthed on the street, or even peering from behind lace curtains to see what was going on, she had no inkling. Fluid as the fittest stuntman, she allowed her momentum to help her rise to her feet, and then she was up and running, or rather gliding, flowing, her only thought being to put as much distance as possible between herself and the monster behind her.

10

As soon as she heard Ellen speak her name, Diane knew that something was wrong.

'What's happened?' she snapped.

Ellen sounded so distraught it sent a chill through her. 'It's David. He's gone!'

'Gone? What do you mean, gone?'

'I came back from work today and there were his things all . . .' The rest of the sentence broke down into a rushed tearful babble.

'Hey, hey, take it easy, you'll hyperventilate. Calm down and take a few deep breaths. Then start again. Slowly.'

The sounds at the other end of the line suggested that Ellen was trying to do so. When she resumed a minute or so later she sounded a little better – still wretched, but more coherent, on top of her emotions.

She told Diane how she had come home from work to be informed by Jane that there was a letter from Daddy. At first she had misunderstood. 'A letter *from* Daddy? Surely you mean a letter *for* Daddy?' As soon as she saw the envelope propped up on the kitchen table she had feared the worst, had felt something convulse in her stomach. It had been evident the girls too were not unaware of the implications. Rachel was mooching around, trying to look nonchalant and succeeding only in looking terribly worried, whereas Jane was being all skittish and silly, playing the little innocent girl, a role she was rapidly growing out of and which she only reverted to nowadays as a form of defence.

It had been a bad day all round for Ellen. She had arrived at work only to find that Mrs Montgomery, her favourite resident, had died earlier in the week after the latest of a series of chest infections. Because of the upset of this and her ongoing worries about David, she had not been concentrating properly on the way home and had driven her Metro into the back of a Land Rover, not hard but enough to cause a bit of damage and shake her up. The letter from David had been the final straw. 'It's not fair,' she said to Diane, voice trembling, threatening to break up again. 'What have I done to deserve this?'

'Not a thing,' said Diane firmly. She heard Ralph – he was not a quiet man – coming up behind her and turned to face him.

He had his eyebrows raised. 'What's going on?'

'Your friend has left his wife.' She knew the accusatory tone of her voice was unfair but she couldn't help it.

'David? No, you're kidding.' Kidding was a word Ralph had picked up in America and which he still used now and again. Diane found his use of Americanisms amusing, for Ralph was the most English of Englishmen. However she was not smiling now.

'Would I joke about something like this?'

He frowned. 'I didn't mean it literally. How's Ellen?'

Diane smothered the mouthpiece with her hand. 'Not good. I'll tell you everything in a little while, okay?'

'Of course.' Ralph lumbered forward and kissed his wife on the forehead. 'I'll pour you a gin.'

'Thanks, I need one.' When Ralph had gone she uncovered the mouthpiece and said, 'Sorry about that. It was just Ralph being nosey.'

'Do you think he might know where David has gone?'

'I doubt it. Why should he?'

'Well, I thought . . . with them being friends . . .'

'No. Ralph would have told me, I know he would. Something as serious as this, he wouldn't keep it to

92

himself.'

Ellen sighed. After a moment, tentatively, she said, 'All the same . . . could you ask him? I mean, if he has any idea at all . . .'

'Sure,' said Diane, 'I'll ask him.' She hesitated only a moment before plunging in. 'Did David give any reason why he left?'

'No,' said Ellen. 'His note was very short. It just said that he had to go away for a while and that he loved me.'

'What a creep,' Diane couldn't prevent herself from saying. She looked up as Ralph reappeared with a full glass and handed it to her. He indicated rather unnecessarily that he would be in the lounge. She nodded.

As if she had no wish to hear the answer, Ellen said, 'Do you still think he might be . . . you know . . .?'

'Having an affair?'

'Yes.'

'Who can say? I mean, it's a possibility but then I haven't seen David for a while. I don't really know what's been happening, what's been going on in his head.'

'No.' Ellen sighed. There was a pause and then abruptly she wailed, 'Oh, why did he go away? What's so wrong that he couldn't talk to me?'

'Hey, hey, take it easy,' said Diane. 'Don't torture yourself. None of us has any answers. I guess we just have to sit back and see what happens.'

'That's easy for you to say.'

Diane was a little taken aback by the venom in her friend's voice. 'Yeah,' she murmured, 'I guess it is.'

'Oh God, Diane, I didn't mean to take it out on you.'

'Hey, no, that's okay. You yell and throw things if you want to. It'll probably do you good.'

There was a half-hearted chuckle at the other end of the line.

'So . . . what you gonna do now?' asked Diane.

'I don't know. What can I do? Tell the police, I suppose,

though I don't suppose they'll do anything. I mean, no crime has been committed.'

'Maybe it has,' said Diane.

'What do you mean?'

'Well . . . hey, I'm not accusing David or anything, but that could be another reason for his going away.'

'You think David's a criminal?'

'Well . . . not so much a criminal exactly, but . . . you know . . . I'm just exploring possibilities, throwing up theories.'

'What do you think he might have done?'

'I'm not saying he's done anything.'

'But you think he might have?' Ellen's tone was not exactly one of anger, but it seemed as though it could become so at any moment.

Diane took a deep breath and said firmly, 'Ellen, I don't know, okay? I *don't know*. I didn't mean to insinuate anything. I was just . . . I don't know . . . just shooting off my mouth as usual.'

Ellen sighed. 'I'm sorry.'

'There's no need to apologise.'

'Yes, there is. I'm just taking my anger and frustration out on everyone around me when the only person who really deserves it is David.'

'Yeah, well, that's the way it goes. Will you tell the police tonight?'

'I suppose so, though I don't really feel up to it. I just want to go off somewhere quiet and close my eyes and forget about everything.'

'Where are the girls?'

'In the lounge. Rachel's trying to do her homework and Janey's got her drawing book and pens spread all over the floor. They're both very upset, I think, but they're putting on a brave face for me.'

Diane felt a lump in her throat and cleared it. She glanced at her watch and saw it was not yet seven o'clock.

She did a brief calculation and then said, 'Why don't Ralph and I come up?'

'Up? You mean here?'

'No, to Glasgow. Of course there.'

'Tonight?'

'Yeah.'

'Oh no, you couldn't. It's much too far.'

'Nah, it's only a couple of hours. We'd be there in no time.'

'Oh no, thanks, Diane, but I'd feel terrible thinking of you setting off from Bristol tonight. You couldn't be here before midnight.'

'The way Ralph drives, we'd be there by ten.'

'No, but still, it's too far. What about the children? And Boss?'

'We'll leave them with the Morgans. They love kids *and* dogs, and the kids love staying there; they get spoiled rotten.'

'I don't know,' said Ellen doubtfully, but Diane could tell from her voice that the idea appealed.

'Look, the bottom line is this. If you want us to come, we'll come. It's no problem. Ralph was coming up tomorrow as it is. If you don't want us there, if you'd rather be on your own –'

'Oh no, it's not that,' said Ellen quickly.

'So you want us to come, right?'

'I feel terrible.'

'We're coming,' said Diane. 'See you in a few hours.'

There was silence on the other end of the line. No, not quite silence. Diane could hear sounds so tiny that they were barely even squeaks or whimpers. She thought that Ellen might be weeping and trying to hide it. 'You okay?' she asked, and immediately thought: Dumb question.

A few more seconds of silence, then Ellen managed, 'Yes.'

'Okay. See you soon. Put the kettle on.'

'I will. Bye.'

'Bye, honey.'

Diane put the phone down, looked at the wall, expelled a heartfelt sigh, closed her eyes briefly. She picked up her drink and swallowed most of it in two gulps, then walked across the hall into the lounge.

Ralph looked up from his *Guardian*, eyebrows raised. 'So what's been happening?' he said.

Diane smiled sweetly and finished her drink. 'Put your shoes on, honey. We're going to Leeds.'

11

Blinded by her tears, it took Ellen three attempts to get the telephone receiver back into its cradle. When she had finally done it, she stumbled over to the stairs and sat down, aiming to remain there until she had managed to bring her emotions back under control. She didn't want the girls to see her crying, though she was certain that they had at least guessed by now that something was badly wrong. She felt like the little boy in the story with his finger jammed in the dyke. The dyke was the unstable barrier containing the full force of her emotions. If she weakened, the torrent would sweep in and carry her away.

Ironically, it was Diane's selfless generosity that had almost caused the barrier to crumble. Now it was up to Ellen to effect a few hasty repairs before the girls discovered the damage and started to demand answers. She would tell them, of course she would, but now was not the time, not whilst her emotions were so fragile. When she felt stronger, strong enough to bear some of their shock and despair, she would tell them. She tried to ignore the little voice that asked her whether she would *ever* feel strong enough.

She wiped her eyes with a handkerchief that she had tucked up her sleeve, and blew her nose. The girls' suspicions would be confirmed when Ralph and Diane arrived anyway; she would *have* to tell them then. She still couldn't believe what an abrupt nosedive her life had taken. Up until recently, she had always counted herself a very fortunate person. She had had a wonderful life with few traumas. Her childhood, in the Yorkshire village of Beckford, had been a happy and loving, even magical one. When she brought it to mind, it was always in an idealistic way, which she knew couldn't be wholly accurate and yet which part of her felt certain was. She recalled hot summer days spent playing in the local woods with her friends, Susan and Claudia, running through meadows of buttercups whose vibrancy dazzled her eyes. She recalled the smells of the trees and the grass, green and alive, and of the flowers, their fragrance so glorious it was like the smell of joy itself. She remembered Christmases where everything was perfect, and where she was so full of happiness and excitement that she could almost feel her body buzzing with it. She remembered the whole family eating fish and chips out of newspaper on Saturday lunchtimes, and then her father and her elder brother, Ben, going off to watch Leeds United play football whilst she went shopping with her mother in the village, or helped her to bake a cake in the warm kitchen at home, feeling very important measuring out ingredients and sifting the flour through a sieve.

There was so much more she remembered – hide and seek, and roast beef on a Sunday, and trips to the seaside, and their German Shepherd, Pippa, who was so big and gentle and whose coat was soft and warm. And her father serenading her mother around the house until she giggled and told him not to be silly. And liquorice twists from Taylor's all-purpose store. And 'Yellow Submarine' by the Beatles. And her favourite teacher, Mrs Speed, who had big round glasses and frizzy hair and always told brilliant ghost stories on the last day of term.

Her blissful childhood and relatively trouble-free adolescence had then been followed by three years at Hull University studying History. Despite being away from home for the first time, she had settled in quickly to University life. She had made some good friends, joined a few clubs, kept up with her studies, and had done all the crazy, exciting things that students were supposed to do. Looking back on that time now, she saw it as a kind of social whirlwind interspersed with intense, sometimes frenetic, periods of study. Her energy had been sky-high then. She had thought nothing of staying at a night club until two or three in the morning and then getting up five hours later for a nine o'clock lecture.

After graduating in 1974 with a very creditable 2:1, Ellen had then spent two wild years in London with a Uni friend of hers, Joanna Gregson. She had shared so much with Jo, had experienced so much *life*, that she now found it sad and a little frightening to think that the two of them had drifted so far apart. It was not that a rift had ever developed between them, it was simply that pledges of undying friendship made the best part of two decades ago now seemed somehow immature and impractical, even unimportant. Lives change, people change, priorities change. Even so, Ellen occasionally toyed with the idea of dropping Jo a line, just to enquire how she was and what she was doing, perhaps even to suggest that the two of them get together for old times' sake. But she never carried the idea through. There were lots of reasons why. Mainly it was because she was afraid that seeing Jo again would be the same as losing her for ever. She saw as inevitable the prospect that she and Jo would no longer have anything in common except the past, that they would have nothing to talk about beyond what was dead and buried. And then they would realise that they had become two very different people, and they would go their separate ways, both mourning the loss of that which could never be recaptured.

Not that Ellen had any regrets. Far from it. She had left London at the right time, moving back up North at the age of twenty-three to take up a post as junior archivist for the Harrogate and District Council. She had been lucky to get the job, and to this day believed that she *had* got it only because the interviewer, a quietly spoken man called Tom Ramage, had secretly fancied the pants off her. She moved into a flat in the city centre, made another batch of new friends, and saw her parents, with whom she had always maintained a good relationship, once or twice a week.

And then, at a New Year's Eve party in 1976, she had met David. Within a month they were an item, within three months they were madly in love, and nine months after their first meeting, in September 1977, year of the Queen's Silver Jubilee and the Sex Pistols, they were married.

They had always planned to have children, though perhaps not as soon as they did. However, they were both still delighted when, only a few months after their wedding, Ellen discovered she was pregnant. Rachel was born on 9th October 1978, two months after they moved into their first house just outside Huddersfield, having spent the first ten months of their marriage in rented accommodation. They spent four very happy years in that house, and then in August 1982, when Rachel was almost four and their new daughter, Jane, two months old, they moved to the house where they had lived ever since.

And things had just continued to get better. Ellen had loved the new house immediately, despite all the work that had needed to be done to it, and now, over a decade later, she still loved it. She loved its nooks and crannies, its high-ceilinged rooms and wide staircase, its long garden out the back, and Horace the gargoyle above the front door, who Jane still maintained had once winked at her when she had said hello to him. She loved her daughters, who had grown up into exactly the kind of people she had wanted them to. And she loved David, who had continued to be not only her husband and her lover but also her best friend. Indeed, up until two months ago, when the cracks had suddenly and shockingly started to appear and widen in their relationship, she had found him as warm and funny and kind and gentle and attractive as ever.

Of course, her life had not been *all* sweetness and light. Her father's death in 1984 had shaken her to the core. However, though it hadn't seemed so at the time, that had been a natural trauma, the kind of thing that everyone had to face sooner or later. David's recent behaviour, though upsetting and bewildering, might have seemed in months and years to come like a natural trauma too, a rough patch which they would eventually ride over together, if it wasn't for the fact that he had now taken the problem beyond what Ellen saw as its acceptable boundaries by running out on the three of them.

Ellen sniffed, composed herself, tucked her handkerchief back into her sleeve and stood up. She hoped the girls hadn't been listening to her on the phone. She had tried to keep it down, but if they had been listening at the door they would have heard most of her side of the conversation with Diane. Her stomach was jumping with nerves as she braced herself to stroll into the lounge. She would know soon enough; she would know as soon as she saw their faces.

She began to walk forward, but had taken only one step when the doorbell rang. It was so unexpected it made her jump. Her immediate thought, before she had time to realise how ludicrous it was, was: Ralph and Diane have arrived. Then she thought: *It's David! He's come back!* Her heart and stomach lurched as she plunged for the door, forgetting that David had his own key. She pulled the front door open and discovered to her disappointment that it was not her husband who stood there.

The man was taller than her husband, older, smarter, more distinguished. He had white hair and a white moustache. When Ellen opened the door he was already smiling, as if he had fixed the expression beforehand.

'Oh, hello,' she said, unable to keep the disappointment out of her voice.

The man's smile widened, his lips stretching over his teeth. 'Mrs Fox?' he enquired.

He's a policeman, she thought suddenly, a policeman come to tell me something awful about David! 'Y–Yes,' she all but whispered.

'Mrs Fox, I wonder, is your husband in?'

It took a moment for her to realise that if he had been the harbinger of bad news he would not have asked her this question. Her shoulders sagged in partial relief. 'No,' she said. 'No, I'm afraid he isn't.'

Was that anger that flashed across the man's face? The expression was so fleeting that Ellen could not be sure. 'Ah,' the man said. 'I don't suppose you have any idea when he might be back?'

I wish I knew, Ellen almost replied. 'No,' she said, 'I'm afraid I don't.'

'Is it likely to be some time this evening? I could wait.'

Ellen felt an urge to tell the man to fuck off. His enquiries were like knives twisting in her belly. That, of course, would have been unfair. He was not to know how much he was hurting her with his questions.

'No,' she said, 'he's gone away for a while. I'm not sure when he'll be back.'

The man pursed his lips beneath his moustache, scrutinised her as if trying to decide whether or not she was telling the truth. At last he said, 'Does he have an address where I could contact him at all?'

'No,' said Ellen.

The man looked sceptical.

'Look, Mr . . .'

'Johnson.'

'. . . Mr Johnson. You've come at a very . . . difficult time. I don't know where David is and I don't know when he'll be back.'

Ellen was going to explain further but couldn't. However she decided that she had been plain enough without actually having to spell out the situation.

'Ah,' Johnson said, 'I see,' and at least had the good manners not to look embarrassed. 'In that case, Mrs Fox, I won't trouble you any further. Goodnight.' He turned abruptly and began to walk away.

Ellen, realising belatedly that this strange visit might just possibly have something to do with David's disappearance, called, 'Excuse me.'

The man turned back, his face half in shadow. 'Yes?'

'I wonder . . . that is, could you tell me what it was you wanted to see David about?'

The man blinked slowly, like a reptile. Even in the semi-darkness Ellen saw the action quite clearly.

'It was nothing much,' he said. 'A business matter, that's all. It can wait. Goodnight, Mrs Fox . . . and Merry Christmas.'

'Yes,' Ellen said. She hesitated before replying, 'Merry Christmas,' by which time the man was out of earshot. It hurt her to say the words; each syllable was like a stone that almost choked her. She closed the front door, snapping off the cold as though it were a solid thing. She suddenly felt exhausted, felt imbued with a depression so absolute that her whole body seemed weighed down, as if with sandbags. There had been something about that man that she hadn't liked, something . . . something repellent.

She shivered.

12

The meat in the bacon burger tasted like leather doused in salt. After two bites, David dumped it back into its polystyrene box and closed the lid. He took a gulp of tea, swilling the tepid bitter liquid around in his mouth to rid himself of the taste. He'd not eaten a take-away burger for about ten years, not since Ralph had told him that fifty per cent of the meat was comprised of offal, eyeballs, testicles, skin and hair. After tasting this one, he thought it would probably be another ten years before he tried one again. Propping his elbows on the table, he held his cup in both hands like a religious offering and looked around.

He was in a motorway service station. He'd forgotten which; after a while they all blurred into one. Humanity – grimy, tired, bad-tempered from travelling – passed back and forth in front of his eyes like zombies in a George Romero film. David had been on the road for almost two hours. Back home, unbeknownst to him, the girls had arrived home from school and had found his letter on the kitchen table. He had a pain in the centre of his forehead from scowling concentratedly through the drizzle on the windscreen. He'd wanted to do the journey without stopping, but had found his mind starting to meander down the spiral staircase towards sleep, had found himself snapping it back with increasing regularity. Even then he might have carried on if he hadn't seen a car upside-down on the opposite carriageway, another crumpled like an accordion. There was a confusion of swirling lights from ambulances and police cars, people wandering around dazed on the hard shoulder. It had all seemed too much like an omen.

He finished the tea and immediately poured what was left from the metal teapot into his cup. Part of his exhaustion was from trying to suppress his thoughts and emotions. At the moment he was clinging rather desperately to a sort of equilibrium. He was trying to outrun what he'd left behind – longing, regret, guilt – whilst rushing headlong towards uncertainty, possibly even danger. However it was best not to think of all that until he had to. If he didn't keep his mind in check, it might overwhelm him, drag him down. Closing his eyes he put his finger on the point of pain in the centre of his forehead and rubbed gently. His other hand crept into his pocket and touched the bottle. The pain began to ease.

He froze when he felt the presence of someone standing by his left shoulder. Despite the bustle of the service station, the clatter of crockery, the drone of conversation, David suddenly felt very alone. He opened his eyes, and saw oatmeal-coloured walls, plastic seats, formica table-tops, a television screen relaying a constant flow of travel information. People drank tea, chewed pastry, shovelled chips, but they seemed not quite there: pretend-people; phantoms. David twisted his head so violently that muscles crunched in his neck.

A boy stood silently by his table, no more than two feet from his left shoulder, staring at him.

David's hands began to tremble; moisture drained from his mouth. The boy had dark tousled hair, a blue anorak, jeans. His face was chubby, his lips pushed forward in a sullen pout. He was perhaps six or seven years old.

For an age man and boy stared at each other, the boy stock-still, the man swallowing, twitching. At last, in a hoarse whisper, David said, 'John?'

The boy didn't respond.

'I'm coming, John,' David said. 'I'm coming to help

you.'

The boy's gaze shifted from David's face and alighted on the polystyrene box that David had pushed across the formica surface. Pointing he said, 'Don't you want your burger, Mister?'

'I . . . what?' David looked at the box as if he had never seen it before. Then he shook his head. 'No. I don't.'

'Can I have it then?' said the boy.

Before David could reply a woman's voice snapped him from his daze. 'Lee, what the hell do you think you're doing?'

The boy jumped back guiltily. 'Nothing, Mummy, honest.'

'How many times have I told you not to talk to strangers?' She glared at David, and despite himself David felt guilty.

'I wasn't doing anything,' Lee protested. He flinched as his mother shot out a hand and grabbed his arm.

'Just come and sit down and behave. I'll give you such a smack in a minute.'

'I wasn't doing anything,' the boy wailed again. 'It's not fair.'

The woman spun her son round so that he stumbled and almost fell and then dragged him, blubbering, away.

For a few moments David couldn't stop trembling. He felt profoundly shaken by the encounter. Though it hadn't really been funny, he began to giggle, and within moments was shaking uncontrollably, tears trickling down his face, hand clamped over his mouth to stifle his laughter. It was a hard, dry, somehow desperate mirth. It hurt his stomach and his throat, and he wanted it to stop. It took a long time before it did, but at last his stomach began to settle, his heart to slow into its proper rhythm. He stood up, feeling drained and depressed. It was time to go.

13

If she didn't know better, Mathilde would have put Danny's agitation down to pre-Christmas excitement. Maybe it was partly that, because although he was apt to be irritable after a fugue, he was not generally quite so unpleasant as he had been today. He'd woken up crying, and from that point on things had deteriorated. During breakfast he'd thrown his cereal spoon at Merlin the cat, and then had launched into the most tumultuous tantrum when Mathilde had scolded him for doing so. He had been argumentative and aggressive about *everything* – getting dressed, getting washed, brushing his teeth, combing his hair. Even her suggestion that they go down to the shops and buy some sweets – something he normally loved to do – had met with a sullen refusal.

'Why don't you watch some of your cartoons then?' she had said.

'Don't want to,' he had snapped.

'How about helping me make some mince pies for Christmas Day?'

'Don't want to, don't want to, don't want to!'

Now Mathilde's patience was exhausted, as was she. Normally she was very possessive of Danny, not because she loved him particularly, but because it was an honour to be chosen as the oracle's guardian. Today, however, she would have been grateful to have had him taken off her hands by Tametia or even Bernard. She was sitting now on the settee in her lounge, sipping camomile tea to calm her nerves and waiting for her five o'clock appointment to show up.

The settee, and indeed the rest of her furniture, was just like her – old, plump, misshapen and comfortable. Mathilde Cowper was sixty-one years old and had been a professional herbalist (and sometime clairvoyant) since the mid-sixties. Although she liked occasional company, she had never felt any urge to marry, partly because she regarded herself as strictly asexual, and partly because she had no wish to share her secrets. The darkest of those secrets concerned something that had happened in America almost a quarter of a century ago.

She had been in her thirties, one of the oldest, when she first started travelling with the group that were later to become known as The Family. She was not proud of what she had precipitated in Los Angeles, but neither was she ashamed. What had happened over those two crazy summer weeks in 1969 had been not only inevitable, but vital to the furtherance of the pattern.

She turned her thoughts back to the present before the memories became too specific, and to the sound of Danny crashing about upstairs. Every so often there was a thump which made the ceiling shake, but Mathilde merely flinched and tried to ignore it. At least he had finally found something to preoccupy him; he was having a war with his soldiers lined up against a giant Dalek. Because of his mood it was a particularly savage war. She could hear him shouting, 'Exterminate, exterminate,' in imitation of the Dalek's grating tones.

Her five o' clock appointment (the first of that day because, owing to Danny, she had had to cancel the others) was not a great success. The middle-aged woman who came to see her was evidently nervous, as if she regarded Mathilde as some sort of sorceress, and seemed to feel a constant need to make excuses for being there at all.

'I only decided to try you because my friend suggested

it,' she said, not for the first time. 'You treated her for her neuralgia last year – Margaret Farrel.'

'Oh yes, I remember Margaret,' Mathilde said, though her recollection was only a vague one. 'How is she?'

'Oh, she's fine. Those capsules you gave her have helped tremendously. What was it you put in them?'

Mathilde couldn't help feeling that the woman had asked her the question to be reassured that the ingredients didn't include wing of bat, toe of newt, that sort of thing.

'Hops, camomile, lemon balm, skullcap and Jamaica dogweed,' she said, raising her voice above Danny's din.

It now sounded as though he was hitting the floor with a sledgehammer. She hoped he wasn't destroying the Dalek that Bernard had bought for him. Bernard was a sweet and sensitive soul, easily upset. If he found out Danny had smashed up the present which he'd chosen so carefully, he'd be devastated.

The woman glanced at the ceiling nervously, as if expecting it to collapse in on them.

'My grandson,' Mathilde explained. 'He's playing upstairs.'

Things rapidly went from bad to worse. The woman was reluctant to discuss her ailments, proclaiming herself 'a bit run down, that's all'. It was obvious that she wanted to get away, but Mathilde felt duty-bound to get to the heart of the woman's problem and discuss it with her, if only for the hour that the woman had booked. It turned out that the woman, whose name was Dorothy Mullins, was suffering from headaches, constipation, tiredness and occasional nausea – in fact, a general lassitude which was not uncommon, and which Mathilde explained was more than likely the result of the cumulative build-up of toxins over many years. She launched into her usual spiel – there was no miracle cure, if the woman was going to change she had to really want to, and even then it was going to take a good while before she really started feeling the benefits. She had just started delving into the specifics of the woman's diet – already knowing by this time that at the end of the session the woman would smile sweetly, thank her very much, and never come back again – when everything went quiet upstairs.

Immediately the knot of tension that had been present all day began to tighten between Mathilde's breasts. The house suddenly seemed not just quiet but silent, as if somehow the very air had stopped moving. Mathilde's voice faltered, then wound down. Mrs Mullins, who had been looking uncomfortable as Mathilde explained to her about the need to flush out the encrusted mucus which would undoubtedly be lining her bowel walls, looked at first puzzled and then concerned.

'Mrs . . . Cowper,' she ventured, 'are you all right?'

Mathilde looked at her, perhaps a little wide-eyed, for the woman seemed slightly startled. 'Yes,' she said uncertainly, and then even more uncertainly, 'The noise has stopped.'

Mrs Mullins smiled a little. 'The war must be over,' she said.

'Yes,' said Mathilde, but the woman's words did little to reassure her. She became aware of the clock ticking on the mantelpiece, the growl of a car going past outside, and realised that the house was not really as silent as she had thought.

She stood up, her beads and bangles jangling, and said, 'I must just . . . go and see if he's all right.'

'All right,' said Mrs Mullins like an echo, though the look on her face suggested that she thought Mathilde's concern a little unnecessary.

Mathilde turned towards the door. The curtains were pulled across the window, the sky almost full dark outside, but pain prickled at the backs of her eyeballs nevertheless. She was wondering whether to cross to the sideboard, where her black spectacles were propped on their folded arms, the round lenses like beetles, and whether Mrs Mullins would think her strange for doing so, when she heard the sound of a door opening upstairs and then soft footsteps on the landing.

She felt suddenly nervous, felt an urge to propel Mrs Mullins out of the house before Danny showed himself. But it was too late now. Mathilde could hear the boy walking slowly downstairs.

'Excuse me a moment,' she said, and crossed the room swiftly, her purple diaphanous skirt flowing behind her, sandals squeaking, bangles chattering on her wrists. She opened the door just enough to allow her to slip through. The staircase was to her left. She turned and looked up it.

Danny was about halfway down, descending slowly. His body was stiff and straight, almost military in its bearing, his pace measured. His arms were held rigidly out in front of him, and in his hands he held his teddy bear, its limbs splayed, its blue eyes glassy as death. As if Mathilde's appearance was his cue, he began to speak in a brittle squeaky voice that was not his own, repeating the same phrase over and over, and at each syllable he gave his teddy bear a little shake so that its head nodded back and forth in a ghastly imitation of life. At first his voice was too quiet for her to hear the words, but it gradually increased in volume until by the time he reached the bottom he was practically shrieking.

'Mr Fox is coming,' Teddy told her through its thin slash of a mouth, its head nodding back and forth. 'Mr Fox is coming, Mr Fox is coming, Mr Fox is coming, Mr Fox is coming . . .'

2

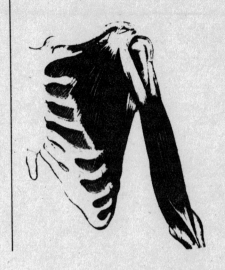

Missing Persons

14

David was quickly coming to the conclusion that in London the term 'rush-hour' was a redundant phrase. 'Rush-day' would be more appropriate, of which there were seven in a week, each lasting for twenty-four hours. He had hit the outskirts at around six-thirty, and had managed to crawl no more than eight miles in the forty minutes since. He was tired, nauseous from smoke fumes, and he needed a pee badly. Every five minutes he had to wave away gangs of kids armed with buckets and cloths, who loomed from the darkness, wanting to clean his windscreen and charge him exorbitantly for the privilege.

As he came to a halt again, vehicles ahead of him as far as the eye could see, David opened his glove compartment and took out his London A-Z. Switching on the light, he found Cranleigh Parade and tried to work out his own position in relation to it. He was surprised to find that he was closer than he'd thought. On a sudden impulse he decided to drive past, look at the place – no more than that – and then find a B & B.

Straddling the road a couple of hundred yards ahead was a viaduct, its brickwork black as tar. Fumes swirled like fog beneath its arch; it was a miracle, thought David, that the drivers stuck under there didn't suffocate. He found the viaduct on the map. If he took a left just before it, down Conduit Road, he should be able to work his way round to Cranleigh Parade via more residential, and hopefully quieter, streets. Conduit Road was only a hundred and fifty yards away, but it still took David almost five minutes to reach it. When he did, he swooped down it like a prisoner in a chain-gang attempting a getaway.

He drove for a while through a no-man's-land of suburbia: lines of tall, tightly packed houses set back from the road, some guarded by rows of sickly saplings; cars parked nose to tail on both sides of every street. There were hardly any people about, and very few lights shining in the houses. Rival football teams jostled for graffiti-space on the walls. He noticed a lamp post that had become a gallows, supporting a doll with no legs hanging from a wire noose.

He was making good progress until what looked like a through-road in his A-Z ended in a line of bollards and an ominous metal barrier with a no-entry sign in the middle of it. He doubled back, watched by an old guy who was standing motionless in a garden with a broom in his hand. It was eerie, this place, unnaturally quiet and very dark. Even the street lights seemed mugged by smog.

Trying to follow a map and drive at the same time was not easy, especially when the streets were as mazy as this. David was looking at the street names with growing desperation, unable to find them on his map, when suddenly he turned left at a junction and found himself on Cranleigh Parade.

It was a long road, and surprisingly wide. The houses were an unsettling mix of the well cared for and the neglected. David crawled along, on the look-out for numbers on gates or front doors. At last he saw one, 146, and a little further along, 134. His foot jerked on the accelerator, putting on a spurt of speed. The ache in his bladder was expanding into his stomach, making him feel sick. Ahead of him, something with flashing eyes loped across the road and into the black shadow-land between two cars. David touched the brake gently as he came parallel with the space into which the creature had vanished. He couldn't be certain, but he thought it had been a fox.

Whatever it was, it seemed to have gone now. He puffed out a long breath and rubbed the palm of his right hand vigorously across his forehead. He felt tired and hungry and more than a little depressed. He wished he could be happy again, wished someone could just take his mind apart like a car engine, fix what was wrong and then put it back together. He wanted all this business with the bottle not to be important to him, or at the very least he wanted to know why it *was* so important. The bottom line was, he wanted his old self and his old life back, wanted to be able to go home to Ellen and the girls and rediscover the contentment and love that had been so mysteriously denied him these past few weeks.

He touched the accelerator and edged forward, his restless eyes searching out numbers on walls and garden gates. Here was 72; he counted down under his breath: 'Seventy, sixty-eight, sixty-six, sixty-four, sixty-two, sixty.'

And then there was no more breath. The car cruised to a halt before an unspectacular house. Wooden gate and door painted royal blue, small, neatly trimmed lawn, net curtains, hanging basket, rose bushes thorny and scrawny in preparation for winter.

'Number 58 Cranleigh Parade,' David whispered. He sucked in a breath which felt hard in his lungs, sharp-edged, like pieces of broken porcelain.

Number 58 Cranleigh Parade.

My mum is nice but my dad is trying to kill us.

'*I think you're out of your depth, Mr Fox,*' a voice whispered in David's ear. His hands tightened on the steering wheel until it creaked.

'Fuck you,' he hissed. 'Fuck you.'

The street was silent. There was a light on in number 58. David put out his hand to the gear stick. As he did so he heard the thump of something landing on the back of the car and in his rear-view mirror he glimpsed a snarling long-snouted face and yellow eyes . . .

He cried out, jerking his feet from the pedals, making the car lurch forward and stall. He twisted in his seat, restricted by the seatbelt. The fox, if indeed it had been there, had gone now, perhaps frightened away by the sudden movement of the car.

David forced himself to calm down, and eventually even to smile. It couldn't have been a fox, it must have been a dog. Foxes didn't attack cars, they didn't leap up snarling and glaring. Foxes were timid creatures in human company, quick and cunning and silent. David took a quick look round but he saw no sign of the animal now. Maybe it was hiding under the car. If so, tough. It would move soon enough when he started the engine.

Nothing came out from under the car when the engine roared to life. David eased forward slowly, hoping not to feel a bulky obstruction beneath a wheel, the sickening crunch of bones. But the car moved forward freely. David touched the accelerator, changed into second gear. The shock had made his head swim. He looked once more at 58 Cranleigh Parade, but nothing had changed. As he drove away, he couldn't help glancing into his rear-view mirror, but all he saw were the lozenge-shaped blocks of street lamps, like yellow eyes observing his departure.

15

The girls were now in bed, though Diane doubted they were sleeping. When she and Ralph had arrived at the Foxes' house at 10:20, the girls had both still been up, keeping Ellen company.

Rather than leaping to greet them as she usually did, her face wreathed in smiles, Jane had seemed almost resentful to see them, as if she knew that their arrival meant that things had become very serious. Rachel had been calm and quiet, but it was a carefully orchestrated calmness, both touching and heart-rending to see.

As for Ellen, she had obviously been trying to hold herself together for the girls' sake, though Diane could see the strain on her fine-boned face, the look in her eyes of shocked bewilderment. When Ellen hugged her, Diane felt the tension in her body, felt her friend's hands digging into her shoulders, clutching her as if she never wanted to let go. When Ralph enclosed Ellen in a bear-hug, his size making her look like a little girl, Diane thought: My God, it's like David died!

It was now twenty minutes after their arrival. They were sitting in the lounge in front of the fire, Diane cradling a whisky she didn't particularly want. Jane had been reluctant to leave her mum to go to bed, had looked at the Joyces almost as if they were strangers that Ellen needed protecting from, but Rachel had taken charge, showing a maturity beyond her years.

'Come on,' she had said. 'It's past bedtime and we've got school in the morning. Mum wants to talk to Uncle

Ralph and Aunty Diane.'

Jane had taken her sister's hand, albeit reluctantly. She'd kissed everyone goodnight, stopping in front of Diane and saying, 'Will you still be here in the morning?'

Diane glanced at Ellen. 'I think so,' she said. 'Is that all right?'

Jane appeared to consider the question carefully, then nodded. 'Yes, I like it when you and Uncle Ralph come to visit us. It's just . . .' She trailed off, wrinkling her nose.

'What, honey?' said Diane gently.

'It's just funny when Daddy's not here, that's all. Do you know how long you'll be staying for?'

Diane smiled sadly. 'No, honey,' she said. 'How long do you think we should stay?'

Jane looked quickly at Ellen, but her mother offered her no support. Uncertainly she said, 'Until Daddy gets home.'

Diane's eyes were sore. She felt tired but was bracing herself for a long night. Ralph was looking at David's note, frowning as if trying to deduce some hidden meaning in the simple message, whilst Ellen watched him nervously. Glancing around the room, Diane noticed a framed photograph on the mantelpiece which showed David, Ellen, Jane and Rachel, their arms flung around each other's shoulders, their hair flying in a strong wind, their mouths wide with laughter. She had taken that photo herself the summer before last, on top of a hill in Wales. It had been a wonderful holiday, so many good memories: the seafood restaurant in Laugharne; the windswept beaches; watching the sun go down as they ate barbecued food in the garden of their holiday cottage. She felt an urge to stand in front of the photograph, shield it from Ellen's gaze. Ellen looked fragile as the finest crystal. Diane felt on tenterhooks, thought that the slightest wrong move on her part would shatter her friend into a million pieces.

Ralph shook his head wearily and passed the note back

to Ellen.

'Well,' said Ellen, 'what do you think?'

It was rare that Ralph was lost for words, but now Diane could see that he was floundering. Finally he said, 'I honestly don't know. He doesn't tell us much, does he? He says that he loves you.'

Ellen's body seemed to sag, her face falling, as if she was disappointed with his response.

'Did you call the police?' asked Diane.

Ellen looked guilty. 'I . . . no. I didn't think they'd be interested.'

'I think you should call them, let them know what's going on.' Diane caught Ralph's eye, the tiny shake of his head, and she fell silent.

'Would you like us to call them?' he asked gently.

Ellen shrugged, was silent for a long while. At last she said, 'I don't know. . . . Not tonight.'

Ralph enfolded her right hand in his two big paws and patted it awkwardly, affectionately. 'All right,' he said, 'we'll leave it till the morning. I don't suppose it'll make any difference.'

'How much do the girls know?' said Diane. 'Did you show them the letter?'

Ellen shook her head. 'I told them that David had had to go away for a while and I wasn't sure when he'd be back.'

'Did they believe you?'

'I don't know . . . No. They both know something's very wrong. It's been patently obvious these last couple of months. I think Rachel probably guesses the truth. I don't know about Janey. I know she's very confused, very scared.'

'Do you think you *will* tell them?' asked Ralph.

Ellen hesitated, then she said, 'I think they have a right to know, don't you?'

Diane nodded. 'I think they do. After all, it's not as if

any of this is your fault.'

Ellen looked at her. 'Isn't it?'

'Of course not! And don't go thinking it is. Jesus, Ellen, it's David who's to blame here, pure and simple.'

'But I keep thinking, maybe I drove him to it. I keep going over and over in my mind what it is I did wrong.'

Diane was angry and frustrated. She had never seen her friend so uncertain. 'You didn't do anything wrong,' she flared. 'It's that creep who's in the wrong, not you.'

'Okay, that's enough,' said Ralph. When Diane glared at him he said, 'None of this is helping matters.'

Diane pursed her lips and controlled herself with an effort. She knew what Ralph had said was true but keeping calm had never been her strong point.

'What do you think we should do next?' Ralph asked Ellen.

Ellen shook her head. 'I don't know. I just feel . . . at a loss. I can't think straight.'

'We gotta find David,' Diane said as if it was obvious. 'We gotta make him talk to us.'

'But how?' said Ellen. 'He could be anywhere.'

'If I may make a suggestion,' said Ralph and they both looked at him. 'I think tomorrow morning, after we've told the police, I should go to his work and speak to his colleagues, see if they can give us any information. They might even let me look through his desk. There might be a clue to his whereabouts there.'

'Yeah, good idea,' said Diane. 'And I could maybe make some phone calls, speak to everyone we can think of that David might know.' She crossed to Ellen and put an arm round her shoulders. 'We'll find him, honey. You'll see.'

16

After leaving Cranleigh Parade, David had driven aimlessly for twenty minutes until he eventually saw a cardboard sign sellotaped to the inside of a window promising BED AND BREAKFAST. The house was tall and thin, imposingly Victorian, its stonework blackened by grime. In the front garden, emaciated trees raised their limbs to the night sky as if worshipping the shrouded moon. When David got close enough to ring the bell, he saw the tracks and pockmarks of ivy which had been forcibly ripped from the stonework, a few withered strands still clinging in defiance.

The woman who answered his summons had grey hair so brittle-looking it seemed you could snap it from her head like twigs. She wore a plastic apron advertising Bourneville Chocolate, and spoke in a slow drawl that David guessed might be either Scottish or Irish before deciding it was probably Canadian. The floor of the house was littered with children's toys, the owner of which clung to his mother's skirt and gaped at David as if he had two heads and purple skin. The boy, perhaps four years old, had black tousled hair and over-bright eyes. He reminded David of Damien from the original *Omen* film.

At least his room was clean and warm with a lock on the inside of the door. He had his own sink and a colour television at the end of the bed. He didn't know how long he was planning to stay, and told the woman so. She looked wary, and seemed set to probe him with questions, until David gave her three days' cash in advance. Now he was lying on his bed, his body almost humming with stillness and fatigue. His suitcase stood in the middle of the floor, waiting to be unpacked.

Through the wall came the muffled sound of a television. The programme was obviously a situation comedy, and a fairly raucous one at that. David thought that the intermittent explosions of canned laughter were the most depressing sounds he had ever heard.

He couldn't think of anything he wanted to do right now, except sleep. His mind was crowded with queries, anxieties, but the instant he closed his eyes they receded, or perhaps it was he that receded from them. As he began to slip deeper into the soft treacle-warmth of his own fatigue, his mind seemed to become empty and buoyant as a balloon. Darkness enfolded him like a sea of balm, soothing, caressing, erasing his troubles. The darkness had a voice, the voice of a mother reassuring a child. It whispered to him, weaving a cocoon of gentleness around him. He opened himself up to the darkness and its voice, wanting it to fill him, yearning to become a part of it.

The darkness obliged, rushing into him, soaking into his pores like water into a sponge. David was drowning, his senses filling with velvet blackness. It was the most exquisite sensation he had ever experienced. The voice of the darkness seemed to come from within him now, its constant *hushhh* like waves kissing the shore on a calm, clear day. Almost imperceptibly, over a span of time that seemed to David to encompass hours, the voice changed, its wordless whisper breaking into a pattern, into two syllables repeated over and over.

At first the word, though mesmeric in its effect, was meaningless to David. He was barely aware of adding his own voice to the voice of the darkness, joining it in its devotions. Gradually the word began to insinuate itself into his consciousness, and he realised that it was a word familiar to him; indeed, a word so familiar that he felt himself inextricably linked with it. His own voice began to rise above the voice of the darkness until at last he felt he was shouting out the word, as if demanding that its meaning be revealed to him.

'Da–vid, Da–vid, Da–vid,' he chanted.

It was with a shock of realisation that he recognised his own name.

He rose up through the darkness like a torpedo through murky water, and broke the surface gasping and floundering. He opened his eyes with an effort, but for a few seconds saw nothing; darkness seemed to cling to his vision like clots of matter. When his eyes did finally focus, he could make little sense of the sight before him. His mind felt swaddled; disorientation mugged his thoughts. Even now he was unsure whether he was awake or asleep, or perhaps stranded in some way station in between.

A figure was sitting cross-legged at the end of his bed. David couldn't see its face because it was obscured by a mask of golden light. The origin of the light was David's bottle, which, impossible though it seemed, was glowing like a lantern. Equally impossible was the fact that the bottle was hovering in mid-air, a few inches above the figure's cupped hands. Apart from the bottle's light the room was in darkness.

'Who are you?' David heard himself asking. The words seemed to slur, and to echo in his ears.

David was not sure whether the figure actually spoke to him or whether he simply heard its words in his mind. Though its voice was deep, rich, melodious, paradoxically it still seemed the voice of a child.

'I think you know,' the figure said, and then added teasingly, 'Do you know, Mr David?'

David felt a shiver pass through him. He pinched his leg. It hurt. But even now he was not sure whether he was awake. 'John?' he ventured.

The figure chuckled. Its laughter was light and silvery,

its unseen features swarmed with light. 'John,' it repeated as though tasting the word. 'As good a name as any.'

David felt confused, though not frightened. Indeed, he felt calm, relaxed, oddly reassured by the presence of this intruder. 'What do you want?' he asked.

He was unsure whether the figure's reply was an answer to his question or not. 'The bottle is yours now. It belongs to you. Look after it, David. Use it wisely.'

The figure spread its hands and, as though released from some invisible forcefield, the bottle began to float across the length of the bed towards David, the light pulsing within it dazzling him, flooding his vision.

The figure became little more than a shadow behind the wall of light. All at once David became anxious that if he lost sight of the figure completely it would fade away, that somehow only his acknowledging its existence kept it there.

'What do you mean?' he said. 'How do I use it?'

'It's part of you, David. Cherish it as you would yourself.' The figure's voice sounded blurred now, as though distorted by wind or water. Its outline was beginning to break up, to bleed into the darkness around it.

'Don't go,' David called. 'I don't know what you mean.'

'Match your energy with that of the bottle, David. But don't waste it. Use it only when there is no other way. Its energy . . . limited . . .'

The voice collapsed into a slow, dragging groan, then faded into nothing at all. The figure itself seemed to unravel, to be picked apart by the darkness that sucked it back into itself. For a few seconds after the figure had gone, the bottle continued to glow, then that too waned like a torch with a failing battery. Abruptly the bottle dropped from the air, into a hand that David wasn't even aware he had been holding outstretched in readiness.

No evidence now remained that anything out of the

ordinary had happened, and despite what he'd heard and seen, David suddenly found himself wondering just what had. His thoughts seemed to be drifting above him, difficult to grasp; his mind still felt, as it had felt throughout his exchange with the figure, as though it was hovering on the edge of sleep. Perhaps his effort to put his thoughts in order expended more energy than he realised, for all at once fatigue was sapping the strength from his limbs, turning his mind into a dark treacly soup from which nothing of worth could be salvaged.

As though pushed by invisible hands, he felt himself sinking backwards. He clutched the bottle to his chest as tightly as his ebbing strength would allow, determined that no one would take it from him. The instant his head touched the pillow he felt his eyelids sliding down like shutters. His inability to stop them was oddly liberating. His remaining thoughts, half-formed and isolated now, winked out like extinguished lights.

For a period that seemed deliciously timeless, David was granted the most profound sleep that he had had in months. His first conscious thought was one of dismay at being dragged back from near-oblivion by a vague inkling that something both distant and obscure was demanding his attention, nibbling at the outer edge of his consciousness.

As he rose up through the murky layers of his own sluggish mind, the inkling progressed into a vibration and from there into a definite sound. But what kind of sound? It was certainly not a voice. Images began to flutter in his mind's eye – old doors, unoiled swings, chalk scribbling on a blackboard – as though his brain was involuntarily flipping through a visual index file, trying to find a match for the auditory stimulus that was coaxing him awake.

At last his fuzzy thoughts sharpened sufficiently for him to recognise the sound as somewhere between squeaking and scratching. What could that mean? Mice? He struggled to open his eyes, but the muscles needed to do so felt too weak to unmesh his knotted eyelashes. He sat up, groaning, sleep still draped around him like a thick swathe of material. He rubbed at his eyelids until at last he was able to prise them apart, and only then did he wonder, with a mild flare of panic, where the bottle had gone.

He saw it almost immediately, beside him on the bed, half-hidden by bedclothes. The meagre light reflected in its scoured surface looked bluish, giving the impression that the bottle was made of metal rather than glass. The light being reflected was that of the moon, which was spying on David through the window that he now turned his face towards. Through eyes that were gritty slits he saw that the moon was wearing a moustache of cloud. What shocked him enough to widen his eyes further, however, was the sight of the black jagged cracks etching their way across its milky surface.

Almost immediately he realised that they weren't cracks at all, but merely the outermost twigs of a leafless tree branch. In this light, the tree and its neighbours looked charred; though motionless, they appeared to be squirming in pain. A patch of shadow at the bottom left-hand corner of the uncurtained window suddenly unfurled itself and turned to regard him with a flash of yellow eyes.

He jumped so violently that pain splayed out across his head, as though his brain had jerked against the ceiling of his skull. The shadow, sleek and still unfurling, slid along the ledge outside the window. It raised a paw on which David could see silky pads, the tiny white hooks of claws. In a curiously human gesture, it tapped its paw against the window, claws clicking and squeaking against the glass.

It was a cat, that was all, probably cold and hungry, wanting to be let in. It opened its mouth and mewed, exposing needle-teeth and a delicate pink tongue. Its fur was a beautiful silver-grey, thick and lustrous. It prowled back and forth along the window ledge, looking at David, an appeal in its yellow eyes.

'Hello,' David said, a yawn in his voice. 'Who do you belong to then?'

The cat mewed loudly as if trying to explain, and pawed once more at the window.

'Do you live here, is that it?' David said. 'Do you want to come in?' He reached out for the catch and the bar that would open the window, the cat watching him with what he fancied was an expression of eager anticipation.

The cat backed along the window ledge to enable David to shove the window open, then slid through the gap like oil and into the room. 'You're a friendly one, aren't you?' David said, washed by a cool breeze that roused him a little more. The cat, ignoring him, dropped noiselessly from windowsill to floor, then padded across the few feet of floor space and sprang up on to his bed.

It made straight for the bottle, which it leaped upon as though it were prey. David thought that the cat must have mistaken a flash of moonlight on the bottle's surface for movement. The cool air was refreshing, so he left the window open and strolled across the room, bending down over his bed and reaching out to pick the cat up. 'Come on,' he said, 'let's put you out in the hall. Shit!' He managed to snatch his hand away just in time as the cat whirled and spat at him and slashed out with unsheathed claws.

'You little bastard,' David muttered. 'Out you go now.' He half-turned, intending to open his door and then shoo the cat into the hall.

As he did so he noticed something strange out of the corner of his eye. He turned back to look at the cat, which was writhing among the bedclothes as though luxuriating in the crumpled warmth. Was it David's imagination or did the cat appear to be changing shape and colour, to be swelling, bloating, as though about to explode? He shook his head, blinked, and took a step closer to the bed.

Impossible though it seemed, it was true. The cat was growing before David's eyes. Already it was twice its previous size and its fur had changed colour from silver-grey to a streaky mustard yellow. I'm dreaming, he thought, but he knew he was not. Something frightening and inexplicable was happening here. Fear rising in him, he was about to tear open the door and flee, then remembered the words of the dark figure: look after the bottle, cherish it. *It's part of you*; wasn't that what the figure had said?

He lunged for the bed, his hand stretching for the bottle. Instantly the cat roared and slashed out at him again with a paw that was now the size of his hand. David retracted his hand just in time, feeling the wind of its claws across his knuckles. His mind boggling, he realised that the cat was now no longer a cat at all, but a small, and rapidly growing, tiger.

There was no way he could retrieve the bottle. Better just to cut and run. But the words of the dark figure had had a profound effect on him, had seemed to confirm, or pull into sharp focus, the half-formed thoughts that had been lurking deep in his mind ever since he had picked the bottle up just forty or so hours before. He felt certain that the bottle was not merely important, but absolutely *crucial* to whatever future awaited him. The bottle itself, its mystery, and the presence and words of the wraith connected with it had wormed their way into his psyche, riddled him, given him a vocation when he most needed one.

He couldn't simply let all of that go now. He glanced around quickly, saw his suitcase still sitting on the floor, waiting to be unpacked. He took two quick steps towards it, scooped it up and then swung it towards the still-growing cat. He opened his hand on the upward swing, and the suitcase flew through the air and struck the tiger. The animal yowled and scrabbled for purchase on the bed, its talons shredding the coverlet and slicing deep into the mattress beneath it.

David took his chance and dived once more for the bottle. His hand closed around it just as the animal growled and batted the suitcase away. David rolled off the bed, the tiger springing after him. He hit the floor with a thump and immediately rolled into a ball, squeezing his eyes tightly shut, aware that nausea or adrenalin or something was rushing through him, making the hand that was holding the bottle tingle like an electric shock.

He braced himself as much as he was able for the weight of the tiger's body landing on him, for the sensation of its teeth and claws ripping his flesh apart. Time seemed to slow down, as if some malicious god was relishing the prospect of his imminent demise. The moon's light turned the darkness behind his eyelids a shimmering ice-blue. He couldn't judge the tiger's position by the sounds it was making because the rush of his own body was deafening him, a torrent of blood and pulses.

He waited and waited, expecting unbelievable pain at any moment, but nothing happened. Finally he opened his eye, performing the tiny movement excruciatingly slowly as if afraid that even this might goad the poised animal to attack. Instantly his vision was flooded by white-blue light far too piercing to be the light of the moon. For long seconds the light filled him, blinded him, so that he saw nothing but its coruscating ice-patterns. Then, little by little, either the light faded somewhat or his eyes became accustomed to its glare, and he was able to discern its source. It was the bottle, clenched in his right fist. It was not glowing with a soft yellowish light as it had done when the figure had been present, but blazing with a light that was hard and blue-white and brilliant as a glacier.

David opened his other eye, and then, after a moment, cautiously raised his head. The bottle's light had formed a nimbus around him, a glassy shining igloo. Beyond this barrier the tiger prowled, back and forth, back and forth, never taking its eyes off him. It was growling, evidently both frustrated and uncertain. Still moving slowly, David sat up, legs crossed in front of him, and held up the bottle.

It was beautiful, bathing the room in its icy radiance. David could see the bones of his hand, red as embers, through the skin of the hand that held the bottle aloft. He felt as though his hand should be burning, but it wasn't. Despite the situation, he felt only the most profound sense of peace he had ever experienced. He had the impression that he was feeding the light just as the light was feeding him. There was a tugging sensation deep in the centre of his being, which, though not unpleasant, was nevertheless persistent.

He could have sat there for hours, entranced, if it hadn't been for the tiger. It was full-grown now and still prowling agitatedly. Its eyes were flat blue-white discs, reflecting the light. It curled back its lips in a snarl, revealing teeth thicker and longer than David's fingers.

All at once it backed away, swishing its tail, and then with a roar launched itself at the barrier of light. David felt a surge within him, and immediately beams of ice-blue light, pure and piercing, were lancing from the bottle like the points of a star. They struck the tiger in several different places, unerring as harpoons. The tiger screamed like a human being and twisted in mid-air as its fur began to smoulder and char, revealing dark flesh that immediately blistered like burning plastic.

The creature hit the floor with a shuddering thump and began to thrash about in an attempt to evade the spears of light. Its eyes were blazing red as though aflame, and as David watched it began to transform once again, though this time seemingly involuntarily as though its molecules had gone haywire. It shrank from tiger back to cat, and then transmuted to snake to lizard to some formless confusion of bone and muscle before finding its way back to cat once more. Though the creature was certainly no normal animal, its suffering nevertheless distressed David, but he was not sure how to stop the power surging through him, was not even sure whether it was the bottle that was using him or he that was using the bottle.

Finally, with a screech that seemed as full of rage as it was of pain, the cat, its smoking fur writhing as though infested, turned and leaped for the open window. It hit the sill gracelessly, still trailing beams of light like glowing silver threads, scrabbled up on to it, and from there launched itself towards the branches of a tree, whereupon it became lost amid a black tangle of limbs and darkness.

Instantly the light from the bottle began to fade, and as it did so David began to feel tired again, and then more than tired; fatigue washed over him like a faint, making him feel giddy and sick and light-headed. He placed the bottle on the bed, then dragged himself over to the window and closed it. Only then did he realise that someone was banging on his door and calling his name. He wondered how long that had been going on.

'Just a minute,' he called wearily and climbed shakily to his feet, using the windowsill as support. He took a few deep breaths, then walked unsteadily to the door and opened it a crack. Mrs Macau, the landlady, stood there, in a dressing gown made of stitched-together hexagons of padded pink silk.

'Mr Fox,' she said through gritted teeth, 'could you please explain yourself.'

It was a demand rather than a question. David blinked at her, barely able to keep his eyes open, and in what he hoped was an innocent and accommodating voice, said, 'Sorry?'

'I hope you are, Mr Fox, I really do, because I simply cannot tolerate this sort of behaviour in my house.'

David restrained himself from telling her to piss off, which he felt entitled to do after everything that he'd

133

experienced tonight. Instead he forced a smile and said, 'I'm sorry, have I done something to offend you?'

'Not only me, Mr Fox, but all my other guests too. You've woken up the whole house with your racket.'

'Ah,' said David, wishing she would go away and let him get some sleep, 'yes, I'm sorry about that. I was . . . er . . . having a nightmare. I must have been sleepwalking, blundering about, banging into things. I do that sometimes.' When she pursed her lips and deepened her frown, he added hastily, 'But not often. Only very occasionally. It won't happen again.'

She yanked the two sides of her dressing gown tighter together as if his eyes had been straying to her non-existent cleavage. 'It had better not, Mr Fox. I won't have my sleep disrupted, or that of my guests.'

She made it sound as if they were all her personal friends with him the only outsider. David forced a smile and said, 'Sorry again, Mrs Macau. Goodnight.'

'What's left of it,' she muttered and stomped away.

David closed the door, sighing with both dismay and relief. He dragged off most of his clothes and then slumped on to his bed, grabbing the bottle and hugging it to him, curling his body foetally around it. The bottle was chipped and scoured, dull and unimpressive now, like something worthless spat out by the sea. Oddly the shredded sheets smelled vaguely of a perfume David didn't recognise; an exposed spring jutting from the slit mattress poked him in the ribs and he shifted position slightly, wondering sleepily how he was going to explain that to Mrs Macau. As his eyes slid closed and sleep began to fold its black wings over him, his last conscious action was to wonder how he could even think of sleeping after all that had happened tonight.

17

Jean had put on a brave front, as she always did, but she couldn't disguise from Max the pain and fear she felt. When the doctors had taken her breast, it seemed as if they had taken most of her lifeforce with it, as if the spark that ignited her body had seeped like blood from the wound they had made.

This, for Jean, had been hard to take, almost as hard as the loss of her breast. She had always been a very active woman, burning with energy and enthusiasm, rushing here and there in a way which made Max feel giddy sometimes, made him feel as if he was the calm eye at the centre of a hurricane. Now, though, just getting out of bed made Jean feel tired, sitting upright exhausted her, and walking up and down stairs or preparing a meal was quite simply an impossible feat.

Seeing her nowadays, particularly when he caught her unawares, sipping water or reading a magazine, filled Max with a poignant, almost overwhelming at times, blend of emotions. Love, of course, was what he felt most keenly, but there was also pride and a kind of wistful melancholy. Jean had never been a big woman – she had always been too energetic to put on even an ounce of extra weight – but now her sinewy toughness had deteriorated into scrawny frailty. For the first time she looked truly old, looked as if the entire weight of her sixty-four years was bearing down on her shoulders. It made Max realise that not only Jean but he too was winding down, that they were getting towards the end of their lives. And sometimes, despite his faith, the thought of their parting made him feel desolate.

It was quiet in the room, and smelled faintly of burning candle wax and Jean's medication. An hour ago there had been ten minutes of shouting and singing and scuffling as the pub-goers were turned out for the night, but now only the muffled growl of an occasional car engine disturbed the peace.

Candlelight pulled the shadows of the room into long brown toffee-shapes, limned Jean's features in a golden glow which, from certain angles, recaptured the strong smooth beauty of her youth with such conviction that Max had to look twice to convince himself she had not somehow slipped backwards in time. There had been moments during her illness when she had seemed almost . . . ethereal. It was as if she had been hovering in the doorway between life and death, and as if some of the light from the other side had slipped through, briefly illuminating the drabness, enfolding her in an aura that was almost saintly. These moments, though fleeting, had been so awesome that Max had felt the breath lurch and then stop in his throat, tears spring unbidden to his eyes, moisture drain from his mouth.

He and Jean had always favoured candlelight. The first time they had made love, in Lodz over forty years ago, had been by candlelight. He had even proposed by candlelight. And if Max had his choice he would like to die by candle-light as well, slipping into the soft silent flicker of the flame, peacefully, unhurriedly, painlessly.

He stopped reading for a moment and looked up at his wife. Her eyes were closed, and he could tell by the way she breathed that she was asleep. She slept so often and so deeply these days. It was as if sleep was the norm for her now, as if she felt most at home swimming beneath the silent waters, entering the waking world only for brief gulps of air before plunging beneath the surface again.

He put down the book he had been reading to her, Graham Greene's *Brighton Rock*. He had been surprised by her choice but she had insisted on something 'tough and lively'. They had always read to each other, ever since Max could remember. He did all the reading now, though. Speaking for more than a few minutes at a time tired her out.

It was late, after twelve. Max sighed out as much of the day's worry as he could and pushed his pince-nez up on to his forehead with a broad stubby hand. His fingers were fat and blunt, the tips calloused by his work, but there were some who said he had the touch of an angel with needle and thread. He stood up, feeling fat and old and tired. When the chair creaked he thought for a moment it was the sound of his own body.

Tiptoeing so as not to disturb Jean, he made his way along the little hall to the bathroom. Not that he was likely to disturb her anyway. She probably wouldn't have stirred even if he had dropped an anvil on to a metal tray right beside the bed. He turned on the bathroom light and peered at the face that stared back at him from the mirror. Once he had been handsome but that face looked shapeless to him now, baggy and wrinkled, all dewlaps and grey whiskers, with the features just sort of dunked carelessly into the middle of it all.

He bared his teeth at himself. They looked yellowish-grey in the apricot light. He reached for the toothpaste and murmured, 'Stop feeling sorry for yourself, Max Fleischer. At least they are all your own.'

The water was running when he thought he heard the jingle of the doorbell downstairs in the shop, so he was not sure if it had been his imagination or some other sound far away in the night. He turned off the tap and cocked his head to the left, his mouth full of minty foam, water running down his wrist and dripping off his elbow on to the floor.

There was no mistaking it the second time with the house so silent. Max felt a wriggle of unease in his belly and glanced at his watch on the shelf by his head, though he knew perfectly well that it was after twelve and far too late for callers.

Who, then, could this be? A would-be intruder would not ring the doorbell, and it was positioned in such a manner that it was impossible to press against accidentally.

He put down his toothbrush, rinsed his mouth out quickly and dried his hands and his face. In his shirt-sleeves, braces flapping against his thighs and buttocks, he crept downstairs.

The key chattered in the lock that marked the boundary between shop and flat, causing Max to grit the teeth he had been cleaning just moments before. A nasty suspicion was forming in his mind which he hoped would not be realised. He pushed the door into the shop slowly open.

Despite the shutters, geometrical shapes of brownish light from the street lamps outside lay here and there, having seeped through whatever crevices they could find. Max's big old Singer sewing machine crouched like a dog on a nearby bench; his tailor's dummy – armless, headless and whose lower body was a single wooden spindle ending in three splayed castors – stood in the corner, wearing the half-finished jacket of a double-breasted suit. Max was relieved to see that the shop door was closed and the windows intact. Perhaps the ringing of the bell had been nothing more than a prank by some malicious passer-by. He stepped carefully down the three small steps until he was standing on the shop floor. He looked round slowly, scrutinising each shadow, each patch of gloom, but it was clear that the shop was empty.

He shook his head, and was about to go upstairs again, when he was startled by half a dozen rapid knocks on the front door. Because of the roller-blind which he pulled down at night, he was unable to see through the wire-mesh grille which protected the upper pane of glass in the door. The knocking caused him to utter a small cry of shock and to step backwards, as if he had been pushed lightly in the chest. Recovering, he edged towards the door, wanting to clear his throat but not daring to make a sound.

He stood beside the door, listening, for ten long seconds before he could stand it no longer. Finally he cleared the phlegm from his throat and tentatively asked, 'Who's there?'

He knew if it was them they would not need to knock. There were those within the Flux who could ooze beneath his door, or slip through his keyhole, or even walk through solid objects as if they didn't exist. But many of them, he knew, saw their assignments not merely as steps towards achieving an objective, but as excuses for satisfying their own warped desires. Too many of them liked to tease and terrify; too many of them gained pleasure from the act of inflicting pain and causing death.

With hindsight, Max couldn't believe he had stayed with the organisation for so long, especially after the horrors of the concentration camps where his own people, indeed some members of his own family, had suffered horribly for the cause. Of course, he had been young then, idealistic, easily manipulated. Now he worked to thwart the Flux's plans, to try to prevent what they saw as inevitable. It was a dangerous occupation, but he was not alone in his endeavours. Though he knew it would not be in the Flux's interests to launch a campaign of violence against him and his colleagues, it was nevertheless always a possibility. A kind of uneasy stalemate existed at the moment, but it was one that relied on the whims of the oracle. This fact worried Max greatly. The oracle was unpredictable at the best of times, like an unstable dictator with nuclear capabilities at his fingertips. All it would take would be a fit of pique, or even an order misinterpreted, and the results could be cataclysmic, echoing and echoing until there was nothing left. The Flux saw itself as infallible, unshakeable, but all Max saw were the ever-widening cracks in its foundations.

Such thoughts had been circling in his mind for years, black and troublesome as flies, and they buzzed briefly again now as he stood by the door in his quiet dark shop, wondering if the day he had been dreading for so long had finally come. If it had, all implications for the time being would be forgotten; the matter would become one of basic priorities. He would simply fight until there was nothing left. He would defend Jean until his lungs were devoid of breath.

'Who's there?' he said again, his voice a little stronger now. 'Answer me.'

No reply except the hissing of the night, which was in truth the sound of Max's own body, his animis readying itself for battle.

All at once, Max felt a surge of anger, and welcomed it. If it *was* them, how dare they try to intimidate him. He was not one of their sacrifices; he ought to be shown a little more respect. This again, he knew, was his animis at work, eradicating the fear in his system, saturating each cell. He felt the tips of his fingers tingling, and knew he was as ready as he ever would be. He thrust the key into the lock of the door and twisted it, then tugged the door defiantly open.

It was like opening the door of a freezer store. The night air swept in like a solid thing, chilling him instantly. Max gave a quick shiver, then his animis adapted to the change in temperature, boosting the cells in his body. Max saw a sheen of water droplets hanging in the air in front of him, opening like a curtain as he stepped forward – or at least, he thought he did. When the animis kicked in, so much was imagery, interpretation. That was what came of being part visionary, he supposed.

His breath seemed to ripple in front of him like a heat wave. The streets were shiny with winter, the sky like black ice. Despite the cold wind, there was a spiky brittle stillness in the air that was like expectation. Max looked left and right, squinted into the shadows clotted beneath hedges and between cars as if by so doing he could penetrate the darkness there. He stepped forward again, his carpet slippers making a harsh sound, like sandpaper, on the gritty pavement. All at once, instinctively, he stretched out a hand as if to clear cobwebs from in front of his face. His body gave a jolt of shock when another hand closed around his own.

The sensation was only momentary, but so tangible that Max snatched his hand back the instant he felt it released, became aware of his animis scorching through his veins, turning his blood to fire. He waded forward but there was nothing solid in front of him.

'What are you?' he muttered. 'Show yourself.'

Sensing movement behind him, he whirled. The door to his shop shifted perhaps half an inch, as if someone had entered, brushing against it as they did so.

'Hey!' shouted Max, and ran back inside. The door to the stairs and the flat above was ajar, as he had left it. He felt panicky now, but for Jean, not for himself. His feet boomed on the floorboards as he ran towards the door. He reached it and pulled it all the way open, then stopped.

There was a sound behind him, a tight rhythmic squeaking, like unoiled hinges. He turned again, feeling a little helpless, feeling as if he was being given the run-around. At first he saw nothing, then he noticed his tailor's dummy turning slowly on its spindle, as if someone was standing behind it, spinning it. Almost as soon as he noticed the dummy it stopped spinning, creaking as it came to rest.

Max stared hard at the air itself, trying to detect some

sign of the invisible creature moving through it. He had no doubt now that a member of the Flux was here in the shop with him. Suddenly the door to his shop swung shut with a bang. His head snapped round. His animis was flooding his system now, he was brimming with it. His fingers itched terribly.

Despite himself, despite his fear for Jean, he felt wonderful. This, too, was the animis's doing. It was like a drug. It made him feel young again, his body vibrant with power. Later, he knew, he would be drained, would need to sleep for twelve, sixteen, perhaps twenty hours. But for now he felt lethal as a tiger, ready to pounce, felt the old familiar lusts pounding through his body, screaming for release. He was both invigorated and shamed by them. Experience had enabled him to control his power over the years, but it was still a struggle, like willing himself to stay awake when he was dead tired. He had the will, though, to hold himself back, to tell himself that whatever happened he would not be the aggressor.

Moments after the door had closed, the dummy began creaking again. This time, though, it did not spin. What happened was that the unfinished jacket it was wearing began rising into the air. Max watched as the jacket was pulled from the dummy and then flapped for a moment in the air like washing on a line. Then all at once the right sleeve of the jacket began rising into the air from the shoulder as if something solid was being pushed into it. When the sleeve was full and fat, the jacket gave a little shrug and then the left arm began to fill up too. Seconds later, the sleeves came down and invisible hands tugged the two sides of the jacket together.

It was only now, with the invisible body partly clothed, that it began to form. It started as a greasy white shimmering in the air, like globules of oil coming together, knitting into a definite shape. First the head and the thin legs, globules becoming fibres which lashed for a moment, blind and fat as worms, before twining and blending together. When the basic shape had been formed, the stuff of its creation continued to slither and shift, refining itself. Texture was added, skin, hair, features, fingernails. A glossy bubble formed and then tore across the front of the head and became a mouth. Something twitched within the mouth and was suddenly a tongue. Lips and teeth came into being, wrinkles, sags, the intricate shells of the ears. Nostrils, eyes, eyebrows, a forehead pared to fineness by the forming bone structure. The body was still partly unfinished when Max recognised it and stepped forward.

'Violet,' he said like an apology as the figure swayed and then crumpled to the floor. He crouched down by the gasping figure and turned it gently over. Violet was still clutching the jacket about her thin frame, perhaps partly through modesty, but mostly because she desperately needed the heat. Her eyelids fluttered and blue eyes focused for a moment on Max.

'Found you,' she whispered. 'Couldn't remember . . . couldn't speak . . .' The effort proved too much and she slipped into unconsciousness.

'Shh,' Max said. 'Shh. Sleep now.'

Maybe it was his unreleased animis which gave him the strength, but when he picked Violet up she seemed as light as a feather.

18

It didn't take David long to find it. All he did was work forward from the date on John Marshall's note, 22nd June 1953.

Walthamstow Library was far smaller, and more modern, than its counterpart in Leeds, but it was well enough equipped to suit David's purpose. He arrived at 9:45, and had to wait almost twenty minutes before a microfiche reader became free. He spent the time flipping through the morning papers and taking nothing in, constantly touching his overcoat pocket to ensure that the bottle was still there.

All morning he had been puzzling over last night's events, wanting to convince himself that the whole thing had been nothing more than an overly vivid dream. It was difficult, especially when confronted by the evidence of the torn mattress and the shredded sheet, but if it hadn't been a dream, if it had all really happened just as he remembered it, then that meant that in the space of a few hours his whole perception of what was real, of how things worked, had been turned upside-down and inside-out. David had always retained an open mind about the supernatural, or thought he had, but now that he actually found himself faced seriously with the prospect of such things as ghosts and magic bottles and shape-shifting creatures, he found his mind shying away like a nervous horse, wanting to construct barriers of denial and logic around itself. Perhaps he himself had damaged his bedding during his nightmare, perhaps what he had told Mrs Macau had indeed been true. That that particular exchange had taken place he had no doubt whatsoever. Although she had not referred to their conversation directly this morning, the black looks she had given him as he devoured a cholesterol-packed breakfast had made her disapproval of his behaviour all too apparent.

After breakfast he went back to his room and lay on his bed for a while and tried to decide how he really felt about what had apparently happened. Was he denying it simply because it seemed expedient to do so? Was he afraid that if he allowed this through, then it would be too much like admitting that he was beginning to lose his mind? It was frightening to think that the supernatural might be more than a construct of fanciful minds, but didn't part of him find the prospect exciting too, invigorating even? Certainly for the first time in weeks he had woken up with something else on his mind other than his own emotional problems. Thinking this reminded him that Ellen and the girls would be waking up this morning – if indeed they had been able to sleep at all last night – not knowing where he was or what he was doing. Immediately he felt guilty and ashamed, told himself he ought to call them, let them know he was all right. However the fact that he couldn't bring himself to do so just yet, that the prospect of Ellen's hurt and anger drew a shudder from him, made him feel even worse.

By nine-thirty he was coasting past Malcolm Marshall's house again, but it was as unimpressive as before. Indeed, in the daylight, Cranleigh Parade seemed shabbier than he remembered it.

As a girl with hennaed dreadlocks and long black fingernails switched off her microfiche reader, gathered up her belongings and pushed back her chair, David stood up. He was sliding into the still-warm seat almost as soon as she'd vacated it, which earned him a look of impatience. He smiled at her, and she responded by wrinkling a nose in which glinted a stud inset with a turquoise stone before stomping off. The cubicle smelled of earth and incense; it was a nice smell, vaguely erotic.

The *TW Gazette*, as the librarian had called it, was a broadsheet, though its tone was that of a polite tabloid. Considering the editions he was scanning were forty years old, David suspected it might have been considered rather trashy in its day. Primarily a paper centring on affairs in North London, its outlook was nevertheless broad enough to encompass national issues and even European politics. The world at this time was still in a state of flux after the war. It was an age of hope and reconstruction, but also uncertainty. The new Queen was barely a year on the throne and patriotism was high.

The story David was looking for was not front page news. He found it on page 5 of the 5th October edition. Filling barely a column, the story was unsensationally headlined: WIFE AND SON GO MISSING. The head and shoulders photograph of Malcolm Marshall beneath the headline was only marginally bigger than a postage stamp.

David peered at the photograph, but it told him little about the man he was investigating. Evidently much reduced, Marshall's eyes, nose and mouth were simply triangles of shadow. David did not think he would recognise Marshall from this photograph, even if he walked past him on the street. The only impression he was able to gain was that Marshall seemed to be (or had once been) a bull-necked man with a bony face and short-cropped hair. David read the article. Its tone was dry.

> Mr Malcolm Marshall, of Cranleigh Parade, North London, today appealed to the general public to look out for his wife, Celia, and son, John, who have been missing from the family home since Saturday. Mr

Marshall, a furniture maker, last saw them on Saturday morning before leaving the house to attend a local football match.

At first, Mr Marshall thought the two of them had gone shopping, but became worried later in the evening when they failed to return home. After contacting various relatives, to no avail, he decided to call the police.

Mrs Celia Marshall is thirty-four years old and is described as slim and blonde-haired. She was wearing a red dress and a white cardigan when Mr Marshall last saw her, but also missing from the house is a blue knee-length overcoat and a headscarf. John Marshall is eleven years old. He is a thin, dark-haired boy with a pale complexion. He may be wearing a navy-blue blazer and shorts.

Mr Marshall commented today: 'I'm worried half to death. I just want to know where Celia and John are. They've gone without any spare clothes or even, it seems, any money. If you're reading this, Celia, please get in touch immediately.'

David cleared his throat. It was dry and hot in the library. He shrugged off his Bogart, feeling the bottle bump against his hip. He glanced round, then surreptitiously took the bottle from his overcoat pocket and placed it on the floor between his feet. Making a note of the date and page number of the article on the ring-binder pad in front of him, he continued his search.

It only took him a couple of minutes to find the next article. On page 2 of the 8th October edition of the *Gazette*, was a longer headline:

MOTHER AND SON STILL MISSING
CAN YOU HELP?

David felt uncomfortable staring at the faces of Celia and John Marshall. He couldn't help feeling they were staring back out of the page at him. Celia Marshall was an attractive woman, if a little thin-lipped. But it was the photograph of John Marshall which claimed most of David's attention.

He felt sweat trickling between his shoulder blades, around which his flesh seemed to flinch. All at once it seemed as though the sounds of activity in the library behind him were receding. He was ensconced with the past, communing with the photograph of a long-dead boy. Yesterday's exchange with Malcolm Marshall rose in his mind.

'I think you're out of your depth, Mr Fox.'

Even through the dubious medium of a forty-year-old newspaper photograph, John Marshall looked a sickly, frightened boy. His eyes were large and dark, his features soft, delicate, almost feminine. Instinctively David reached out and touched the screen, his fingertips brushing John Marshall's pale cheek. He felt an emotion welling in him that he could not identify. Regret, was it? Not quite, but it seemed the closest approximation.

He continued with his search. The next headline, on Monday 12th October, made him draw his breath in sharply.

FATHER QUESTIONED
OVER FAMILY'S DISAPPEARANCE

Mr Malcolm Marshall, whose wife and son went missing over a week ago, was today being questioned by police about their disappearance.

According to Mr Marshall, his wife, Celia, and son, John, left the house in Cranleigh Parade, on Saturday October 3rd whilst he was attending a local football match and have not been heard from since.

Last night Mr Marshall was seen leaving the house accompanied by two police officers. He was bundled into a police car and driven away. Although it is not certain at this time whether he has been arrested, a police spokesman later confirmed that Mr Marshall was helping them with their enquiries.

David skim-read the rest of the article but it told him nothing new. He wound the handle on the microfiche reader as fast as he could, looking for the next development.

On the next day's edition of the newspaper, Tuesday 13th October, the story became front page news for the first time. POLICE IN GRISLY SEARCH the headline screamed, below which was a sub-heading: IS THIS A HUNT FOR MURDER VICTIMS?

Most of the space on this page was taken up by two photographs. The main photograph depicted what appeared to be a group of policemen doing a spot of gardening in front of a nondescript background. Most of the policemen were carrying shovels and wearing overcoats. In the foreground a senior officer in a peaked cap was bent almost double, black-gloved hand stretched out as though to pick something interesting up off the ground.

David peered hard at the senior officer, whose face was the only one in the photograph that was not blurred. He had bushy eyebrows and a moustache that seemed to be imitating them. Below the photograph the caption read: Inspector Kerslake directs the police search at 58 Cranleigh Parade.

The other photograph was of Malcolm Marshall. It was the same one that had accompanied the original article, but four times larger. David couldn't prevent a shudder rippling down his back as he studied the man's face.

As the reduced photograph had intimated, Marshall was a bull-necked man whose bone structure made his face appear angular with shadow. The sight of him did not inspire confidence in David. The man's broad forehead and prominent brow reduced his eyes to tiny glints of light in pools of darkness. He had high sharp cheekbones and hollow cheeks, which accentuated his most attractive feature – a mouth and jawline that any Hollywood star would have killed for. All in all, David thought that Marshall looked like a boxer. He couldn't help but imagine that sharp-featured bullet-head sprouting from huge domed shoulders and a well-developed torso.

Even remembering that Marshall would be a pensioner by now did little to ease David's mind. The fact that he was very possibly a murderer seemed to render his age irrelevant.

David pressed the palm of his left hand against his forehead in an attempt to cool it, but without success. He began to read the text of the article, but Marshall's shadowed eyes kept distracting him. Eventually David tore a sheet of paper from his ring-binder pad and placed it over Marshall's face.

In fact, there was little in the article that couldn't be gleaned from the accompanying photographs. Presumably as a result of last night's questioning, the police had decided to dig up Marshall's garden. It was only press speculation, albeit reasonable to assume, that the object of their search was the bodies of Celia and John Marshall.

The TW Gazette took up the story the following day

with the front page headline: 'I HAVE NOTHING TO HIDE', accompanied by a new photograph of Malcolm Marshall. In this one he was wearing an overcoat and hat, which made him look like a tough private eye. Again the text of the story was evident from the headline: the police had found nothing, they had let Marshall go and he was now proclaiming his innocence. There was a terse statement from Inspector Kerslake, 'This particular line of enquiry is now closed and we are pursuing others,' and a fresh appeal from Malcolm Marshall, 'Please, if anyone knows where Celia and John are, ask them to get in touch with either me or the police. I'm at my wits' end.'

Over the next week there were several short reports of the police search extending to include areas of wasteland, canals, abandoned buildings. POLICE FEARS FOR MISSING MOTHER AND SON was a side-heading on page 1 of the Saturday 24th October edition of the *Gazette*, where readers were reminded that Celia and John Marshall had been missing for exactly three weeks, and where Inspector Kerslake publicly admitted for the first time, 'Exhaustive police enquiries have revealed nothing. We now have very genuine fears for the safety of Mrs Marshall and her son, John. It's a very real possibility that they may have been kidnapped or worse.'

David made his notes and then wound the machine on. But although he searched for another hour, and covered a whole year's worth of editions of the *TW Gazette*, he found no further reference to the story.

He sat back, groaning a little at the pain it caused him when he eased his back from the position it had been locked into. He felt sweat beneath his armpits, a sheen of it across his forehead. His feet were numb from clutching the bottle between them; when he moved them slightly, pins and needles started dancing.

Because the story had petered out, he could only assume that there had been no further developments. Celia and

John Marshall had never been found, and no charges were ever brought against anybody. Yesterday on the phone, Malcolm Marshall had told David that John was dead, but had he said that because he knew it for a fact or simply because he had become resigned to the likelihood of it? The police must have had *something* pretty strong on Marshall to treat him the way they had during the enquiry. But what? Circumstantial evidence that had never been proven? Perhaps Marshall had said something to make them suspicious, contradicted himself in some way? David picked up the bottle, having already decided on his next course of action. He would find Inspector Kerslake, presuming of course that the man was still alive, and he would do his utmost to get him to talk about Malcolm Marshall.

19

Whilst David was poring over old newspapers in Walthamstow Library, Ralph was conducting an investigation of his own. He waited for over half an hour in the Reception area of the Imperial Vision building before being allowed in to see David's assistant, Tony Cabanas. The Imperial Vision building was ghastly, a soulless edifice of steel tubing and vast windows. The Reception area was ghastly too. Dominated by mirrors and smoked glass, it had a ceiling which seemed to be made of irregularly shaped steel toilet rolls, and furniture which was upholstered in creamy-brown plastic, and which it proved impossible to sit on without sliding forward.

Ralph leafed uninterestedly through a 1989 edition of *Country Living*, which was the only magazine on the glass-topped table before him, until Tony Cabanas became free. David had once described Cabanas as Leeds' answer to Gordon Gekko, so when Ralph entered David's office to find a man with slicked-back hair and red braces unfurling like a snake to greet him, he didn't know whether to laugh or recoil.

He found the ensuing conversation with Cabanas slightly unreal. It was almost as if the man's identification with Gekko, Michael Douglas's character in the film *Wall Street*, had become so deeply rooted in his personality that he could not speak without it sounding as if he was delivering glib double-barbed phrases from a film script. Ralph soon found he was having to fight to eradicate the sensation that he and the assistant editor were swapping lines from a movie.

After some preamble, and a handshake that felt to Ralph as if he was clutching a live eel, they got down to the nitty-gritty.

'How has David seemed to you these last few weeks?' Ralph asked.

Cabanas appeared to give the question some thought, appeared to be debating with himself over what his answer should be. He glanced quickly at Ralph as if assessing him, linked his hands together and placed them before him on the desk-top. Finally he said, 'We–ell . . . far be it from me to cast aspersions, but it was obvious to everyone that David was having problems of one sort or another.'

'Was it?' said Ralph.

'Oh yes. You could tell that much from his work. To be perfectly honest, it's not been up to the standard we expect here.'

'We? You mean, the company?'

'Of course. Who else? I'm only repeating what I've heard, you understand.'

'And who did you hear this from? One of David's superiors?'

'Not directly.'

'Who then?' pressed Ralph.

Cabanas smiled indulgently. 'I can't really remember. It was just an office rumour. These little whispers filter down all the time.'

Ralph sighed inwardly. Cabanas was as elusive as an oil slick, and as distasteful. 'Did David ever give you any indication that he might do something like this?'

'Leave us in the lurch, you mean?' Cabanas smirked to give the impression he was joking. 'To be honest, David *has* been rather unreliable recently – taking extra-long lunch breaks, skipping meetings, coming in late. I've been doing my best to cover for him but it's not been easy.'

'Have you spoken to him about it? About how he's been feeling?'

'Not really. David's not a big communicator.'

'You surprise me,' said Ralph. 'I've known David for years and I've always found him to be a very approachable chap.'

'Oh please, don't get me wrong,' Cabanas said. 'David and I get on like a house on fire. I just didn't feel as though it was my place to pry, that's all.'

'Even though it was badly affecting his work?'

Cabanas shrugged. 'I guess we all go through bad patches at one time or another. Naturally I was very concerned about David, but I just thought he'd get over it.'

Ralph sighed and picked up a letter-opener which, judging by the pile of sliced-open envelopes by Cabanas's right hand, the assistant editor had been using not long ago. He toyed with it, turning it over in his hands three or four times, before realising it was in the shape of a naked woman of cartoon proportions, her long legs the blade, tapering to a point.

Cabanas watched him, a little warily Ralph thought. Perhaps he thought Ralph was planning to steal the implement, or even stab him with it.

'Didn't David say anything at all to you?' Ralph asked. 'Didn't he even give the merest hint of where he might be going?'

'Sorry.' Cabanas smiled and spread his hands. 'As far as I, and everyone else, was aware, David *promised* he would be at the one-thirty editorial meeting.'

There was little else left to say. Ralph put the letter-opener back down on the desk.

'Oh well,' he said, 'thanks for your help.'

'My pleasure. I hope you find David. We all want him back as quickly as possible.'

'I'm sure you do,' said Ralph drily. He stood up, and

155

then added, as if it were an afterthought, 'You don't mind if I have a quick poke around in his desk, do you? There might be something in there that'll tell us where he's gone.'

Cabanas paused – but only for a second. 'Be my guest,' he said, waving at the drawers.

Ralph circled the desk as Cabanas pushed his seat back to allow him access. Up close, he could smell Cabanas's aftershave, which stung his sinuses a little, like freezing cold air. Ralph was aware of Cabanas's stillness; he was like a reptile, poised. Generally Ralph was unfazed by authority or pretension or insincerity, but Cabanas made him feel uncomfortable, and that fact annoyed him. He looked through David's desk briskly, almost aggressively, but found nothing.

'No luck?' said Cabanas in a voice that made Ralph want to knock his teeth out.

'No,' said Ralph heavily. He banged the last drawer shut and walked back round the desk. 'Thanks again for your help.'

Cabanas stood up smoothly. 'Not at all. Any time.' Before Ralph could turn away, he thrust out his hand. The handshake was more vigorous than before, over-familiar. 'It was good to meet you. And don't worry about David, I'm sure he'll turn up.'

In the outer office, Ralph chatted briefly with David's secretary, Becky, a friendly, dark-haired girl. She was obviously concerned about David, but couldn't enlighten him either. All she was able to add to what he already knew was that David had left for an early lunch immediately after speaking to Ralph on the phone yesterday and had promised to be back for his one-thirty meeting. Finding this out made Ralph feel guilty. Had David taken off because he had guessed Ralph's arranging to meet him for lunch the following day had been more than a casual invitation? Maybe he had even checked up to find out whether there *was* a gynaecologists' convention in

Bradford – which of course, there wasn't.

Ralph killed time in Leeds city centre for a couple of hours, and then wandered along to The Filling Station, where he and David had arranged to meet, and stood at the bar until 1:30, watching the arrivals. It was surely too much to hope that David would actually arrive at the rendezvous, and of course he didn't. Frustrated, Ralph drove back to the house, hoping the girls had had better luck with their phone calls.

The first thing he heard when he entered the house was the sound of laughter, which surprised him and gave him hope. It only took him a few moments, however, to realise that the laughter was not the natural, uninhibited sound it was supposed to be, but was instead a little forced and hollow. He closed the door quietly and took off his coat, listening all the while to the sounds coming from the kitchen. Diane was talking loudly and rapidly, telling a funny story about a friend of a friend of hers who had started going out with Lord somebody-or-other's son.

'But when she said bathroom, she really meant toilet, and of course the room she was shown into didn't have a toilet in it. There was just a shower and a sink, but she was really desperate for a pee and she was too embarrassed to go back out and explain what she'd really meant, so what she did was . . .'

Ralph had heard the story a number of times before, had even related it himself on a couple of occasions, but it depressed him to hear it now. Diane sounded like a stand-up comedian desperate for laughs, and Ellen like a punter determined to have a good time no matter what.

He clumped through the house towards the kitchen, purposely making a noise so that he wouldn't make the girls jump or catch them unawares. Semicircles of Christmas cards, suspended on red ribbon, festooned the walls in the lounge, though Ralph noticed that that morning's delivery was scattered unopened on the settee, seven or eight envelopes of varying sizes and colours. It would normally be about this time that David and Ellen would be fetching the tree from old Mr Murray's place over in Wharfedale. Ralph knew that decorating the tree and the house was a family tradition with the Foxes, and usually took place the weekend that the girls broke up from school.

That morning, during a breakfast eaten largely in strained and exhausted silence, Ralph had noticed Jane's eyes flickering from one adult to the next while she worked her way stolidly through her bowl of Frosties. He had known she was building up to something, and sure enough, in a small and tentative voice, she had finally ventured, 'Mummy?'

'Hmm?'

'Are we going to have a tree this year?'

Ellen had winced and closed her eyes briefly, as if she'd unexpectedly swallowed something sharp. In a voice which was composed, but which was also so steely that it broached no further argument, she had replied, 'I don't know. I haven't really thought about it.'

Despite her mother's warning tone, it had been evident that Jane had had to struggle hard with herself not to express her dissatisfaction with this state of affairs. In the end, though, partly due to a warning scowl from her elder sister, she had dumped her spoon in her bowl, splashing milk on to the table, and had stomped out, proclaiming bad-temperedly that she was going to brush her teeth.

Because he and Diane had shot up here on the spur of the moment last night, and because their time since had been pretty full – comforting Ellen, concocting plans to find David, trying to stay positive – it had taken this short exchange between Jane and her mother to make Ralph realise what an awkward situation he and Diane had actually got themselves into. Christmas was only a week away, and although it sounded selfish, he didn't see why they should have to disregard the festivities this year just because it appeared that Ellen was going to. That wouldn't be fair on Olly and Kim – *especially* on Kim, who like Jane was just at that age where Christmas was the most exciting thing in the world. The problem was, though, if they *were* going to have a normal family Christmas, then they couldn't really afford to stick around here very much longer. They themselves still had the tree to buy, as well as most of the food and about half the presents.

Ralph had been mulling the problem over all morning – on the drive into Leeds, and then later, while he'd been strolling round town and standing at the bar in The Filling Station. He was an easy-going sort of bloke, but he had to admit this problem was getting to him a bit. He felt a nervous sort of urgency, he felt indecisive, and he felt resentful towards David for running off and mucking everyone about. Why did the silly bugger have to leave just before Christmas? Couldn't he at least have waited another couple of weeks? Ralph knew he was being selfish but he couldn't help it. Even the possible solutions he had been coming up with just seemed to throw out more problems.

The obvious solution seemed to be to ask Ellen and the girls to spend Christmas with them in Bristol, but he doubted whether Ellen would agree to that. She'd surely want to stay at home in case David came back, and even if they could persuade her, he doubted that she'd be in the mood to don paper hats, pig out in front of the telly and play drunken party games. What if he and Diane just took the girls with them then? But he'd feel awful leaving Ellen to spend a miserable Christmas on her own, and he doubted whether Rachel, at least, would want to leave her mum at such a time. Just Jane on her own then? But would she want to be away from her family at Christmas? He doubted it.

Bracing himself, stomach knotted with tension, he stepped into the kitchen.

Ellen and Diane were making mince pies – or rather, Diane was making them, pressing circles of pastry into their moulds in the bun tin, her sleeves rolled up, her hands ghostly with flour, a large jar of opened mincemeat standing by her elbow.

Ellen was sitting at the breakfast table, her hand curled protectively around a mug from which drifted tendrils of steam. She had one leg tucked beneath her, her hair pulled back into an untidy ponytail. She looked pale and tired. The wan smile on her face slipped when she looked up as Ralph entered, as if it had been something so fragile that her sudden movement had destroyed it.

'Any chance of a cup of tea?' Ralph said, nodding at Ellen's mug.

'In the pot,' said Diane. As Ralph poured it she said, a little tetchily, 'Where've you been? You've been gone a hell of a long time.'

'Did you find out anything?' said Ellen. She sounded almost afraid to hear his answer.

Ralph shook his head, hating himself for disappointing her. 'Not a thing. You?'

'We phoned everyone we could think of, however obscure,' said Diane, and pulled a disgusted face. 'Zilch.'

'Now everyone knows that David's run out on me,' said Ellen miserably, 'and we're no nearer to finding him.'

Ralph sat down beside her, placing a big hand on her shoulder and squeezing it briefly. 'At least people are aware now,' he said. 'If David *does* turn up, they'll know to ring you.'

It was evident from Ellen's expression that she regarded this as small consolation.

'Where have you been anyway?' said Diane. 'We were starting to think that you'd run out on us too.'

Ralph showed by his expression that he didn't think this

was a very tactful thing to say. However Ellen didn't appear to respond to her friend's comment.

'In a pub,' said Ralph. Before either of them could say anything, he explained why.

He finished his lukewarm tea in four gulps and washed his cup at the sink. 'Did the police come?' he asked.

'Yeah, they came,' said Diane, rolling her eyes, 'for what good it'll do.'

'What did they say?'

'They weren't interested,' said Ellen. 'I told you they wouldn't be.'

'Did you tell them everything?'

'Of course we did,' said Diane, 'but you could see what they thought. As if they know anything about anything.'

'So they actually said they weren't interested?'

'No, they said they'd keep an eye open,' said Diane. 'Which, roughly translated, means, "Go and waste somebody else's time, lady."'

'At least they know,' said Ralph.

'Big deal. The only way they'll get interested is if David tries to rob a bank or if they have to fish him out of a river somewhere.'

Ralph clenched his teeth and gave his wife an anguished look.

'It's okay,' said Ellen unexpectedly. 'We've talked about the possibility of David committing suicide. Neither of us thinks it's very likely.'

'Oh,' said Ralph. 'Right.'

'Do you?' said Ellen.

'What? Think David would commit suicide?' He looked from Ellen to Diane, and then back to Ellen again. Finally he shook his head. 'No. I can't say the thought hasn't crossed my mind, but . . . no. I can't see it somehow.'

Ellen looked momentarily relieved, then said, 'So . . . what can we do now?'

Ralph looked at Diane and then shrugged. 'I don't

know,' he admitted.

'I know what I'm going to do,' said Diane. 'I'm going to finish these.' She rolled the remainder of her pastry into a ball, smoothed it out with a rolling pin and used the pastry cutter to make corrugated circles. Ellen watched her glumly. Ralph made a fresh pot of tea.

A little later, they were all sitting in the lounge, Ralph leafing through the *Yorkshire Evening Post* which had just come through the door. The smell of mince pies was permeating the room and making Ralph realise how hungry he was. The pile of Christmas cards, still unopened, had been moved from the settee to the blanket box which served as a coffee table in order to give them all room to sit down.

Abruptly Ellen stood up and made for the door.

'Where're you going?' asked Diane.

'I won't be a minute. I'm just going to fetch something.'

Ralph and Diane looked at each other as they heard the front door open, the same unspoken question occupying them both: Should we go after her?

Before either of them could decide, Ellen was back, carrying a large road atlas. She sat down and began to look through it.

'What are you doing?' said Diane.

There was a pause as Ellen turned to a particular page, and then she said, 'The day before yesterday, when David didn't go to work at all, he said he'd driven to the coast. I was just trying to work out whereabouts he might have meant. I thought maybe he might have gone there again.'

Ralph put down his newspaper and leaned forward, the springs of the settee creaking beneath his weight. 'That's as good a theory as any,' he said. 'Let's have a look.'

They pored over the book, working out the possibilities. However, even allowing for the fact that David had had to drive there and back in a day, it soon became apparent that there were a great many alternatives to choose from.

'We ought to make a list,' said Ellen, 'check these out.'

Gently Ralph said, 'To be honest, Ellen, I don't know if it's really worth it. Look at all these places: Scarborough, Blackpool, Filey, Skegness, Starmouth, Southport . . . and these are just the holiday towns. Let's face it, David could have gone anywhere. It'd be like looking for a needle in a haystack.'

'We could get lists of all the hotels and ring them up one after the other,' said Ellen stubbornly.

'You're joking. Every other building is a hotel or a boarding house in these places.'

There was a pause of perhaps two seconds, and then suddenly Ellen hurled the atlas across the room. It struck one of the speakers of the stereo, making it rock, and fell to the floor, pages splayed like the wings of an injured bird.

She jumped up, her body ramrod-straight, her arms stiff by her sides, fists clenched. 'Well, you bloody think of something then!' she shouted. 'At least I'm trying to do something constructive instead of sitting on my arse reading the paper!'

Bursting into tears, she stormed out of the room and up the stairs.

Ralph sat stunned for a moment, then looked bewilderedly at his wife. 'Did I deserve that?'

Diane gave him a sympathetic look. 'She's just upset, honey. I'm sure she didn't mean it. She's just hitting out. I'll go and talk to her.'

She followed Ellen out of the room, though at a more sedate pace. Ralph expelled a huge sigh and walked across to pick up the atlas. By the side of the stereo, where the atlas had fallen, was a pair of French windows, the long central panes of which were surmounted by smaller panes of stained glass. Ralph straightened, smoothing the atlas's bent cover, and glanced out of the windows.

'Hey!' he exclaimed.

The view from the windows was of the back edge of the garage, to the right of which was a large chunk of the back lawn with a hedge at the far end which separated the Foxes' garden from the one behind. As Ralph had looked up, he had seen a figure duck back into the hedge. Though he had glimpsed the figure for only a moment, Ralph was sure he had been dressed in tight-fitting black clothes, had been wearing gloves and a baseball cap which partially obscured his face, and had had something bulky slung around his neck which might have been binoculars.

Ralph could see a small gap in the hedge where the man had pushed himself through. It might have been his imagination, or just the effects of the wind, but he was sure he could also see the leaves and twigs there vibrating back and forth, echoing the man's passage. Tossing the atlas on to a chair, Ralph looked quickly around, grabbed the fire poker, and tried the handle of the French windows. They were locked, and although it wasted precious seconds, he couldn't help rattling them back and forth in frustration.

Knowing it was very likely that the man was halfway to Halifax by now, Ralph hurried across the lounge, into the hallway, out of the front door and round the side of the house. A crisp cold wind stiffened his cheeks. The sky was in the intermediary stage between late afternoon and early twilight, pearly and flat. Conversely, because of the onset of darkness, the lines and shadows of the garden seemed well defined, each individual leaf and blade of grass etched with a thin outline of charcoal shadow. Hefting the poker, Ralph marched across the lawn, his feet crunching as if the ground was brittle with frost, his breath hanging wraith-like on the air.

The gap in the hedge was hardly man-sized but was certainly noticeable. Ralph wondered how long the man had been here, watching the house. As he drew closer, he saw that twigs had been broken, leaves bent and crushed, the ground flattened. There were one or two footprints in the dirt which told Ralph that the man had been wearing trainers.

With an effort, he pushed himself through the gap that the man had made and peered left and right. There was no sign of the intruder now, and although there were a number of places where he could be hiding – behind a fence or a tree, in a shed, perhaps even crouched low behind a bush – Ralph thought it more than likely that he had scarpered. Sighing, he pulled himself back through the hedge, snagging his sweater on a twig and swearing as a long thread unravelled from it. Now that his adrenalin was settling a little, he was uncomfortably aware of the concrete-heavy beat of his heart.

His heartbeat bumped up another notch when he heard footsteps on the gravel drive around the side of the house. Had the intruder doubled back somehow? Was he now taking the opportunity to have a quick shufti at the front of the house? Ralph hurried across the lawn, panting slightly, the poker gripped tight by his side. He came around the side of the house, began to raise the poker like a conductor raising his baton . . .

And saw Jane, reaching out for the front door, her school satchel flung over her shoulder, a paper hat from a Christmas cracker on her head.

Jane froze and looked at him with open mouth and wide eyes. At last she blinked slowly, her mouth closing and then opening again like that of a goldfish. A puzzled frown wriggled across her forehead. And finally, in a tone that was somewhere between wonder and irritation, she enquired, 'What *are* you doing, Uncle Ralph?'

20

Elliott Lloyd was some kind of financial wizard. He worked for some South American bank or other, investing people's money. He had explained it all to Tametia once but she hadn't been particularly interested. She had been a panther at the time. She was nearly always a panther with Elliott.

It gave Tametia great satisfaction to tell him that she wouldn't be available this afternoon. There had been a time, back in Edinburgh, when she would have done anything, no matter how repugnant, to any man, no matter how unclean, if it meant money in her pocket at the end of it. Those had been desperate days. Too often she had performed only to have her face laughed or spat into, or even slapped, when it came time for her to demand payment. She often entertained the notion of returning to her old haunts, using the special abilities of the Flux to track the men down, looking deep into their eyes and kissing them oh so tenderly as she ripped them apart.

Maybe one day she would actually do it. God knew, there were times when she felt her past pressing in on her with such force that she thought she might be crushed between the jaws of her memories. Someday she would have to face that past and eradicate it, otherwise she would never be free of it. She realised Elliott was still bleating plaintively into her ear, offering her ten per cent above her usual fee. She smiled; she loved the sound of powerful men pleading.

'I'm sorry, darling,' she purred into the mouthpiece. 'It's

not a question of money. You'll just have to dampen your ardour for today. It'll make it all the better the next time.'

'But I *need* you, Tam,' he said. She imagined him sitting at his snooker table-sized desk in his vast wood-panelled office, wearing his Armani suit and silk tie, his blond Vidal Sassoon-cut fringe drooping aesthetically across one eye, his tanned and impossibly beautiful face fixed in a petulant pout.

'I know you do, sweetie,' she said, and couldn't help adding, 'far more than I need you.'

There was a stunned silence which delighted her. Elliott simply could not conceive of the possibility of rejection.

'You . . . you bitch!' he finally managed, his voice a pathetic and astonished squeak of protest.

'I can be if that's what you want,' said Tametia. 'Literally, in fact.'

Elliott did not join her in her amusement. Like a spoiled schoolboy he said, 'Oh come on, Tam, it's not fair. We had a date for this afternoon.'

'A date?' said Tametia. 'An appointment, you mean.'

'I like to think of them as dates,' said Elliott sulkily. 'You mean more to me than just . . . you know.'

'Fucking an animal,' said Tametia coldly, and felt a savage satisfaction in the knowledge that Elliott would now be shrivelling inside his expensive suit, turning crimson beneath his tan.

'I was going to say . . . the physical side of our relationship.'

'Relationship?' said Tametia. 'Since when has what we do become a relationship?'

Elliott was a squirming thing, a fish on a hook. But what made him so loathsome was that he was a fish who was desperate to be caught.

'There's no need to be so hostile, Tam,' he said. 'You know how much you mean to me, how much I like you.'

'Yeah,' she said with heavy emphasis.

He gave a small despairing sigh that made her want to throw up. 'When *can* I see you then?' he asked in a small voice.

'I don't know. Give me a call some time next week.'

'Next week? What's wrong with tomorrow?'

'Tomorrow's Sunday, Elliott.'

'So?'

'Sunday's my day of rest. Besides, shouldn't you be spending the day with your wife and child? They hardly see you. You spend ninety per cent of your time working, and the other ten is spent out with the boys or fucking with me.'

'I wish you wouldn't use that phrase,' said Elliott, his voice all petulance again.

'What phrase? Fucking?'

'Yes.'

'What would you call it then?'

'Making love.'

Tametia laughed hard and long into the mouthpiece. 'You're a sick man, Elliott. Priceless but sick. You know that?'

Elliott stayed silent.

'Oh dear,' said Tametia. 'Have I offended you?'

'I don't have to take this, you know,' Elliott said tightly. 'I could go elsewhere.'

'Really? You know someone else who can provide the same service as me?'

Again Elliott said nothing.

Tametia sighed, tiring of the game, and said, 'Call me next week, Elliott. Tuesday or Wednesday. I might be able to see you then.'

'Tuesday or Wednesday!' He sounded devastated. 'And what do I do in the meantime?'

'Tie a knot in it,' said Tametia. 'Or buy a hamster.'

'You're the sick one,' he said in disgust.

'Goodbye, Elliott. Give my love to your wife.'

She put down the phone before he had a chance to reply, then went back into the bathroom to bathe her wounds, which were still hurting.

Despite the pain and what it might mean, she felt a little more cheerful than she had done ten minutes ago. Next time she saw Elliott he would be an emotional mess, she knew, all helpless lust and hurt ego, but she could handle that. What she couldn't handle was David Fox and his fucking bottle.

She had received the call from Mathilde on Thursday evening, and it had seemed a simple enough assignment at the time. Mathilde told her that Fox had evaded Worthington and was now in London with the bottle. As Worthington had been ordered to stay in Leeds, where Bernard would soon be joining him, and given alternative instructions, it was now up to Tametia to get the bottle. Exactly how she retrieved the object was up to her, though the minimum amount of incident would be preferred at this stage.

Though the task did not sound a particularly difficult one, Tametia's instructions, as usual, filled her with both nervousness and excitement. Nervousness because beneath the fine clothes and expensive perfume and delicate features, beneath the shell of arrogance and aloofness which she had constructed around her, there still existed that frightened and abused little girl from the slums of Edinburgh whose only ambition was to be accepted and praised and, ultimately she supposed, loved.

And excitement because if she did this right, if she managed to accomplish what the venerable Mr Worthington had apparently failed to achieve, then she would get that acceptance and that praise, she would be embraced by the Flux, would feel (for a while at least, until the uncertainties began to gnaw at her confidence once again, as they always did) like an integral cog in a vast and powerful machine.

She flinched as she dabbed TCP into one of the wounds on her back. The pain flared up, sharp and hot, like someone holding a match to her skin. Tametia moaned, the muscles bunching in her neck and shoulders. The pain was a symbol of her failure, and it made her feel helpless and scared and angry. She *would* get the bottle. She had no idea how she would get it, but ultimately she was determined not to fail. Unless she received instructions to the contrary, she was obliged to pursue this matter until either it reached a successful conclusion or she died in the attempt.

Of course, like every other Flux member, Tametia knew that whatever happened was meant to happen, that events that seemed to work against the Flux were just as much part of the pattern as those that worked for it. Even the Schism, the ex-members of the Flux who now strove to thwart its plans, were ultimately working towards the Flux's final objective, and they were fools if they thought otherwise. The pattern, which had begun to weave its intricate tapestry even before the first of the nails was driven through Jesus Christ's wrist on the cross, was complex beyond comprehension, but so intrinsically true, so breathtakingly whole, that her doubts were fleeting, her faith well-nigh unbreakable.

However, despite her belief in the immutability of the pattern, this did not mean that Tametia did not believe that the pattern could be shaped, moulded, that within the apparent confines of predestination there was room for free will and individuality. Tametia saw no conflict in this viewpoint at all. If she shaped her own destiny, fought against the odds, then it was the pattern's will that she do so. Or rather, not so much the pattern's will but whatever lay behind it. To call it God was to diminish it somehow. Indeed, to try to articulate its state, or even understand it, was a pointless exercise, for it was everything, it was infinity. There were no words possible to describe its size, its power, its glory, just as there were no minds that could understand its motives.

She dragged her thoughts back to her present predicament. Examining her back in the mirror, she could not help but release a moan of distress. Two of the purple-black patches of skin were big as dinner plates, the third a little smaller, saucer-sized. She could have sworn they had not been *quite* so big when she had examined them earlier.

She dropped the wad of TCP-soaked cotton wool into the hollow pink porcelain pig which she used as a waste bin and then probed hesitantly at one of the blemishes with a slender, beautifully manicured forefinger. The flesh was still weeping a little, and felt disconcertingly soft beneath the thin membrane of skin, like bruised and mushy banana.

The thought of what might be happening inside her body filled Tametia with dread. She was terrified of dying, but it was not death itself which frightened her as much as the prospect of the pain that would inevitably precede it, and most of all the prospect of losing her looks, of turning into a hag.

She had seen it happen to her mother when she was eleven years old. The spinal cancer had taken hold quickly. From the first symptoms to her mother's delirious morphine-drenched death had taken a little over three months. Before the cancer her mother had looked much as Tametia did now: small and delicately boned, with an ethereal beauty that was exemplified in her porcelain-white skin and lustrous raven-black hair. On her deathbed, her mother, forty-four years old, had been unrecognisable, a dry haggard thing, less than five stones in weight and twisted with pain, her skin a sickening mustard-yellow due to the ravaging effects of the disease in her liver.

Since then, Tametia had been terrified of going the same way. Though her animis protected her to some extent –

containing certain recuperative qualities, boosting her resistance to infection, slowing her body's natural ageing processes – it was no elixir of life. If something really virulent took hold when her animis was dormant, then not only would it not be able to cope, but it would actually become poisoned and would eventually wither and die, thus depriving her of the ability that made her unique. For this reason she viewed her animis not with any sense of reassurance but as just another faculty that could be taken from her.

The prospect that the damage done to her the night before last was not only permanent but spreading through her body like a virus terrified her. The light from that bottle, or whatever it really was, had cut into her animis like a laser through jelly, filling her with fire, sending her system haywire. Although her animis had been fully active, it had proved frighteningly ineffective in countering the threat. Tametia had been aware of it thrashing and squirming like a wounded octopus. She had not dared try to change since, except back to her normal shape, and that had been hard enough, involving lots of mess and pain inside, and nausea which made her vomit not only her stomach contents but also a lot of blood.

She flexed her back again cautiously and winced at the pain. The bruised areas felt like hollows filled with sharp objects which ground against one another when she moved. Her back was so tender she couldn't even wear a bra. Carefully she pulled on a cerise Naf-Naf sweatshirt, a pair of tight white leggings, white ankle socks and pumps patterned in a colourful floral design. She probed gently at the skin beneath her cheekbones as though checking for slackness, then painstakingly cleansed her face and applied her make-up.

She grimaced at the result. She had always had pale skin, but today she looked so wan that the make-up gave her the appearance of a painted doll. She walked along the hallway and into the spacious lounge of her Bloomsbury flat, dismayed by the grinding pain in her back at each step.

She crossed the lounge gingerly and entered the kitchen through a louvred sliding door on the far side of the room. Her kitchen was large, like every other room in her flat. It had been designed by Roland Collier, an architect and client. Because it was fashioned in yellow and green stained pine, Tametia called it her Canary Kitchen. Roland's designs were a little manic, like the man himself. At first glance the rooms he created looked cluttered, haphazard, even somewhat surreal, full of strange curves and angles like something from *Alice in Wonderland*. The Canary Kitchen was no exception. It was crammed with drawers and shelves and cupboards which initially looked higgledy piggledy, but once you'd got used to it had a clever and complex symmetry. Tametia was just in the process of soaking some of her home-made muesli in freshly squeezed apple juice from organically-grown apples when the phone rang.

She jumped at the noise and then cried out; the sudden movement made her back feel as though someone was scraping rusty nails down it. If this is Elliott again, she thought furiously, he'll get more than he fucking bargained for next time I'm a panther. She entered the lounge as quickly as her back would allow her and picked up the phone.

'What?' she snapped.

'Tametia, this is Mathilde.'

Her spirits plummeted. 'Mathilde,' she repeated woodenly.

'How are you feeling, dear?' Mathilde's voice was all motherly concern, but behind it Tametia heard the insinuation: *Because we want that bottle now.*

'I don't know,' said Tametia. 'My back still hurts, and you should see the marks. They're horrible, Mathilde.'

Even as she said the words she realised how they sounded – like a whiny excuse, an admission of defeat. Before Mathilde could comment therefore, she added, 'But I won't give up. I'll get that bottle for you.'

'I don't doubt it,' said Mathilde sweetly. 'In fact, that's why I'm ringing. I've got information that will help you.'

'From Danny?' said Tametia.

'From the oracle.' Though there was no inflection in Mathilde's words, they sounded nevertheless like a mild rebuke.

'That's what I meant,' said Tametia. She had never liked the term 'oracle'. It had been coined a long time ago and sounded a bit naff to her, a bit Dennis Wheatley mumbo-jumbo. It didn't help that it was also the name of a TV information service. 'What did he say?' she asked.

Mathilde told her – about the man named Burgess and how she would find him. And before long, despite the pain and her fear of what it might mean, Tametia was sighing with relief.

21

The child, whom David simply thought of as Damien, pointed at the TV and burbled incoherently. He turned and fixed his over-bright eyes on David as if seeking approval. David forced a smile and nodded, feeling uncomfortable. The cartoon only added to his belief that just lately the world had shifted disconcertingly out of phase, shunting him into a reality that was subtly different to the one he was used to. The creatures in the cartoon looked like brightly coloured condoms wearing armour. They spoke in squeaky American accents and argued a lot. Like the situation comedy that had assailed him through the wall of his room a couple of nights before, the programme – its sickening primary colours, its crude artwork – made him obscurely depressed.

Yesterday, after completing his investigations in Walthamstow Library, David had spent hours walking round the area, asking the proprietors in every shop and pub he passed whether they had ever heard of an Inspector Kerslake, now retired. He had never realised before just how appropriate the phrase 'banging your head against a brick wall' was. By the time he returned to the B & B, around ten-thirty, he had a headache that felt akin to his brain being squeezed between the corrugated jaws of a very large vice.

He'd been frustrated, miserable, exhausted and hungry. He sat in his room watching 'Whose Line Is It Anyway?' and eating a takeaway Chinese which had turned cold and glutinous in its tin-foil tray during the ten-minute walk home. He was especially fed up because not only had his enquiries come to a dead end, but he had encountered discouragement and even, in one or two cases, barely restrained hostility. It had reached the stage where he almost dreaded having to say the word 'Inspector', because the instant he did so he would see shutters come down behind eyes, lips clamp tight, and nostrils flare as if he had suddenly become nothing more than a bad smell in a small room.

And what was even worse was the fact that he was going to have to go through it all again today if he wanted to continue pursuing this particular line of enquiry. He did wonder whether speaking to Kerslake would actually achieve anything in the long run, or whether he was simply pussyfooting around the periphery in order to put off the inevitable encounter with Malcolm Marshall. This thought depressed him somewhat, but he tried to deal with it by telling himself firmly that forewarned was forearmed.

He sat now in the big kitchen-cum-dining room, shovelling down his fried breakfast as quickly as he could in order to escape before Damien started climbing on him. The toddler had a habit of doing this. Yesterday David had entered the kitchen to find the boy hanging like a chimpanzee from the neck of an old man. The man looked about to expire, or at least buckle under the toddler's weight, but had never once complained. Damien's mother had been bustling constantly in and out, but appeared not to notice that her son was strangling one of her elderly guests.

It was crazy but David was already missing Ellen and the girls so much it hurt. He'd spent the last two months ignoring them, resenting them, but now that they weren't around he felt like a big chunk of himself had been torn away. He ought to ring them, he told himself for the umpteenth time, and once again felt like a shit for not yet feeling ready to take a walk through that particular minefield. Perhaps it was only an excuse, but at the moment his life felt like a series of wounds that had to be cleaned and stitched up not only one at a time but also in the correct order.

Ten minutes later he was standing on the street outside the house, the smell of exhaust fumes filling his nostrils. It was a drizzly, cold day. He pulled his Bogart around him, feeling the reassuring weight of the bottle in his right-hand pocket counterbalanced by the London A-Z in his left. David liked his Bogart. It made him feel crumpled and ordinary but at the same time kind of stylish, like Bob Peck in *Edge of Darkness*. He liked its deep pockets, the way it flapped around him when he was striding, the way he could casually flip up the collar when it was cold or raining and it would stay where he had put it and wouldn't hang like limp bat wings and make him look stupid.

Today, though, he was wishing he had some other coat to wear. Today he didn't *want* to look like Bob Peck. He didn't want to look remotely like a policeman, didn't want to feel as though there were daggers, even imaginary ones, pointing at his back wherever he went.

Because the pubs didn't open until eleven, David spent the first two hours of that day wandering in and out of local shops, asking questions. He received a slightly better reaction than yesterday, but only because he had learned a little from that experience and had now come up with what he thought was a feasible excuse for his search. Whenever anyone threatened to become obtuse or hostile, David told them that Kerslake used to be a friend of his father's and that he was planning a surprise party for the old man's eightieth birthday, trying to track down as many of his old friends as he could. This seemed to go down quite well with most people, especially the older shop owners who were appreciative of such things. One or two of them even admitted to remembering Kerslake from his days on the manor, though none of them had any idea of his present whereabouts.

By 11:20, David was feeling weary. His feet were aching and he was damp and cold from the rain which had been falling lightly all morning. He decided it was time to hit the pubs. On his perambulations he had noted down in his A-Z the whereabouts of any he passed. He consulted the book now and saw that the nearest was a couple of streets away. Memorising the route, he slipped the A-Z back into the pocket of his Bogart and hurried in that direction, collar turned up, head hunched against the rain.

The pub, The George IV, was a large seedy-looking establishment positioned just off the intersection of two main roads. Fish and chip wrappers from the shop next door dozed in its shadow or scuttled drunkenly along the pavement outside. A large white graffito on its side wall read JESUS EATS CHILDREN. When he was a few feet from the main door of the pub a black fuzz of litter on its top step unfurled and streaked away from him. It was a cat.

He went inside. The room he walked into was so gloomy that he could barely make out the bar until his eyes had adjusted. The threadbare flock wallpaper had acquired a sludgy brown film, which David guessed from the smell was the accumulation of by-products from cooking fat, cigarette smoke and sweat. The place was warm, but unpleasantly so, the air hazy and thick, almost sticky in texture. David took off his Bogart and carefully draped it over one arm. He felt the weight of the bottle, swaying slightly in its pouch of material. He wanted to reach into the pocket and close a hand around it, whether for reassurance or simply to steady it he was not sure. However he felt reluctant to do so here, as if the bottle would be perceived as something valuable, like a wallet fat with money.

He made his way to the bar, feeling as though his rubber-soled shoes were clinging leech-like to the carpet with each step, tearing off wads of fluff and fibres as he pulled away. The pub's customers seemed little more than bulky brown shadows. When he looked closely he saw slow turtle-like faces regarding him. A bar stool loomed like a brown-capped mushroom. He put his hand out and felt its stickiness. Somewhere in the haze at the other end of the bar, glasses chinked, a cash register pinged, a buzz of words was exchanged. Then the barman was sliding towards him, plump and slug-like.

'Yes, mate?' he said in a North London accent. He had greased wavy hair, a mottled bug-eyed face. Fuzzy blue tattoos bruised his hairy arms. He wore a white t-shirt with a Southern Comfort logo on it, stained yellow beneath the armpits.

'Er . . . a bottle of Beck's, please,' said David.

'Bottle o' Beck's,' repeated the barman as if correcting David's pronunciation. He turned to a fridge behind him, which opened with a sucking sound. 'Want a glass with this?' he asked, holding up the bottle like a cudgel.

'Er . . . no thanks,' said David.

The barman nodded and picked up a bottle opener that was sitting on a ledge by the cash register. He removed the metal cap with a flick of the wrist and placed the bottle on the bar in front of David. David handed him a five-pound note. As the barman turned again to the cash register, David heard a loud gulping noise by his left elbow. He turned to see a scrawny old man in a tartan cap perched on a bar stool four feet away. The man was tilting a pint glass up to his mouth and drinking noisily.

The old man gasped and thumped his glass down rather too heavily, as if the weight of it had been getting too much for him. Beer slopped up the inside of the glass and out, splashing the cuff of the man's blue serge suit. He caught David's eye and winked, simultaneously cupping his grizzled chin to catch the beer which was dribbling down it. David smiled quickly, then turned back to the barman who was holding out his change.

The barman dropped coins into David's cupped palm, his fingertips, cold and damp as clay, brushing David's hand. Before the man could turn away, David leaned forward and, his voice unconsciously quietening a little, said, 'Excuse me.'

The barman looked surprised. His upper lip glistened with sweat. 'Yeah?'

'I wonder if you can help me. I'm looking for a bloke called Kerslake. He used to be an Inspector in the police force around here.'

The barman immediately looked wary, raising his head a little, eyes narrowing. It was a response that David was used to. 'Oh yeah?' he said. 'You one of them, are you?'

'What?' said David.

'Copper.'

'Oh.' He smiled nervously. 'No, it's just that . . . well, this Kerslake bloke used to be a friend of my dad's.' He told his lie, at which he was now becoming adept.

The barman said, 'Your dad was one then, was he?'

'A policeman? No. He was just . . . a neighbour of Kerslake's. They used to go out drinking together, playing golf, that sort of thing.'

The barman shrugged dismissively and started to turn away. 'Can't help you, pal. I've never heard of the bloke,' he said.

David watched him walk down to the other end of the bar, feeling belittled, dismissed. He closed his hand around the bottle of Beck's, his thumb creating a channel through the frost of condensation. He took a sip of the beer and got nothing more than a mouthful of bubbles.

'What was your pa's name?' asked the old man.

David glanced at him. The old man had swivelled on his stool and was now facing him, leaning forward a little, thin legs together, bony knees jutting at a thirty-degree angle. He resembled a rather dishevelled leprechaun perched on top of a toadstool. He had spoken, however, not in an Irish accent but in a thick Glaswegian one.

Now that the man was facing him, David observed two things about him which he had not noticed before. One was the startlingly incongruous presence of a large gold loop in the old man's left ear, and the other was a maroon birthmark which started just above the man's jawline and covered the left side of his throat, and which, in the dim light of the pub, looked disconcertingly like a splash of blood.

'Burton,' said David, pulling the name from nowhere. 'James Burton.'

The old man smiled crookedly and nodded. David couldn't help thinking that somehow the old man knew he was lying, but was smiling in admiration of the quickness of his response to an unexpected question.

'Burton, eh?' the old man said. 'Ah canna say ah knew anyone o' that name. He was a copper too, ye say?'

'No,' said David, shaking his head. 'He was just a friend of Inspector Kerslake's. A neighbour.'

'Ah well, ah wouldna know him then. Kerslake didna live around these parts, just worked here. He had a nice hoose up Borehamwood way, if ah remember right.'

'Did you know Inspector Kerslake well then?' David asked. He waited patiently while the old man picked up his glass and gulped down the last of his beer.

When he had done, the old man released a gasp of contentment and placed his empty glass with loving care on the bar. 'Great drop o' beer, that is,' he said meaningfully.

David suppressed a sigh. 'Can I get you another?'

The old man's wizened face lit up with surprise and delight. 'Ah well noo, that's verra decent of you, young feller. I'll hae a wee drop o' the same in there, if you don't mind.'

David bought the old man a drink and watched as he sucked noisily at the cloudy liquid. When the old man's mouth was free again, David prompted, 'You were going to tell me about Inspector Kerslake.'

'Name's Willie,' said the old man, extending a hand. 'Willie McQueen.'

David took the hand and shook it. Despite McQueen's diminutive stature, his hand was larger and chunkier than David's, the skin rough and calloused. David was surprised at the strength of his handshake.

'David,' he said, and was about to use his proper surname when he remembered to say, 'Burton.'

'Pleased to meet you, David.' McQueen winked again, the skin around his eyes crumpling like old brown paper. 'You're not from around these parts, are you?'

'No,' said David, 'I'm from Leeds. You don't sound as though you're from around these parts either.'

McQueen chuckled. 'True enough. Ah'm what you might call a dispossessed Scotsman. From good auld Glasgee, God bless her and all who sail in her.'

'You must have been here a while,' said David. When McQueen frowned enquiringly, he added, 'To know Kerslake, I mean.'

'Oh aye. Back after the war, you know, this was where the work was. Or so we all thought anyway.'

'Do you know if Kerslake still lives in . . . where was it? Borehamwood?' David asked.

McQueen pursed his lips. 'Och no. He retired from the force and moved out nearer ti the coast.'

'I don't suppose you have any idea which coast he moved to?'

'Aye, well, it wasna really the coast. It was just *nearer* ti the coast. Somewhere outside Ipswich. No far from Felixstowe.'

'Do you know where exactly?' David asked. Though only half-full, the pub now felt very warm. He took a swig of his beer. The cold liquid felt good on his tongue and throat but he winced at the spark of pain it ignited in his temples.

'Ah canna remember exactly,' McQueen said slowly, screwing up his eyes as if gazing into the dim and distant past. 'It was just a wee village. Began with an S.'

'S,' said David. He didn't know enough about the area to even hazard a guess.

The Scotsman gazed up into the murky air as if the answer was there somewhere, waiting to be plucked out. Perhaps it was, for suddenly his face cleared. 'Sholten,' he said, then rather spoiled it by adding, 'Something like that anyway.'

'Sholten,' David repeated. He had never heard of the place.

'Aye. Something like that.'

David took another swig of Beck's, but found that he didn't really want the beer after all, that he was now too eager to check out what the old man had told him. He shrugged himself into his Bogart, grimacing at its clamminess.

McQueen lowered his glass and wiped a hand across his mouth. Sounding genuinely disappointed, he said, 'You're not going already, are you?'

'Sorry, but I'm not actually feeling too well,' David lied. 'I think I've got a touch of the flu coming on. I'm going to go home to bed.'

McQueen nodded shrewdly. 'Oh aye, best thing. You don't want ti be poorly for Christmas, do you?'

As he said this, he gestured vaguely around him. David looked up and was surprised to see cheap foil lanterns drooping from the ceiling, loops of coloured crepe paper stuck to the wall behind the bar with drawing pins. He hadn't even noticed the Christmas decorations before, and now that he looked properly he realised they were all around him. Grinning Santas made of thin moulded plastic beamed inappropriately from the toilet doors. A large fringed streamer made of gold foil was redly emblazoned with the words HAPPY CHRISTMAS.

In David's eyes, instead of cheering the place up, the decorations only served to make it more depressing than it was already. The streamers and lanterns were old and grubby and a bit battered. It made Christmas seem like an obligation to be cheerful rather than a genuine celebration.

He mustered a smile. 'No,' he said, 'I don't.' He hesitated only a second before holding out his hand. 'Nice to have met you, Mr McQueen.'

'Oh aye,' said McQueen, shaking David's hand with warmth and vigour. 'Likewise.'

'And thanks for the information about Kerslake.'

'Nae problem. Ah hope you find the owd bastard. Give him my regards if you do.'

'I will,' said David. He began to walk away. 'Cheerio.'

'Aye, be seeing you.' When David was by the door he heard a shout. 'Thanks for the drink, pal.'

David raised a hand without looking back and stepped outside. Instantly he was forced to screw up his eyes; although it was a dull day, the sky was bright as an interrogation lamp after the dimness of the pub. Despite wondering earlier whether he was skirting the real issue, McQueen's information had imbued him with a sense of urgency. Consulting his A-Z, he saw that Walthamstow Library was at least two or three miles away. He decided to walk back to his car and drive there.

Sliding into the driver's seat ten minutes later, David reached immediately for his road atlas but found no reference to a place called Sholten in the index. Indeed, there seemed to be no village beginning with the letters S-H anywhere near Ipswich. Patiently he consulted all the S's, and eventually discovered that there was in fact a village called Solden about five miles from the town. Armed with this information, David drove to Walthamstow Library, hoping it had a big enough reference section to provide him with an Ipswich and district telephone directory.

It did, and furthermore it had only one Kerslake in it. The initial was D., and the address was 22 Blackett Road, Solden. 'Bingo', whispered David, and wrote down the address and phone number, feeling very pleased with himself. He drove back to the B & B, telling himself that his good work had earned him the right to a couple of hours' rest.

He lay in a hot bath for almost an hour, lulled by the steady drip of water from the faulty hot tap. Because it was Saturday afternoon, most of the tenants seemed to be out and so he was not disturbed, though he could hear the drone of a football commentary from somewhere. When he reluctantly dragged himself out of the bath he felt enervated by warmth, but immediately began to shiver as the cold air found the water on his skin. He draped his towel around his shoulders and dried himself slowly.

As he dressed he thought once again about ringing Ellen, and this time found to his surprise that his mind didn't recoil from the idea. Maybe the success of his investigations had made him confident that any problem, if approached correctly, could be overcome. He dressed slowly as he pondered the idea, then all at once decided, as though it was a snap decision, to go for it. He felt nervously excited as he descended the stairs, like a schoolboy about to ring a girl in his class to ask for a date.

He stacked his change on the shelf by the telephone in the hall, and dialled the number. As he listened to the phone ringing, he stared at the print of an oil painting on the wall which depicted an orange and blue swan enfolding its wings around a naked man. Sweat, which was the result of his hot bath and his trepidation, prickled on his forehead and he palmed it away. From the direction of the dining kitchen he heard Elmer Fudd say, 'You smart alec wabbit.'

Usually around this time on a Saturday, Ellen would be out in the garden until it got too dark to see, wearing her canvas gloves and wielding secateurs. Jane would probably be sitting cross-legged in front of the TV, watching 'Jim'll Fix It' or 'Brookside'. Rachel would be helping with the dinner, or she might be up in her room, listening to CD's or stretched out on her bed reading a book, something by Anne McCaffrey or Melanie Rawn. David smiled wistfully at the image – and then his face fell as he realised what day it was.

It was the Saturday before Christmas. If he had been at home and everything had been normal, they would be fetching the boxes down from the attic now, unpacking the decorations from their tissue paper nests in readiness to dress the tree that he and Ellen would have bought that afternoon.

The pips went. He put the money in, his stomach clenching, telling himself how ridiculous it was that he should feel nervous. When the pips had subsided, a voice he didn't immediately recognise said, 'Hello?'

'Oh,' said David, 'I think I've got the wrong –'

'David!'

His name was blurted at him like an insult, and suddenly he recognised the voice, the Californian accent.

'Diane,' he said.

'David, where the hell *are* you?' She sounded like a mother scolding a child who is late home.

'What are you doing there?' said David.

'We're having a party, what do you think? Where are you, David? What the *fuck* is going on?'

David winced. Diane had a temper that could terrify Rottweilers. 'Is Ellen there?' he asked.

'Why?' snapped Diane.

'Because I want to speak to her, of course.'

'Oh right, *now* you want to speak to her. Why couldn't you speak to her before you decided to run away?'

David knuckled more sweat from his forehead. '*Is* she there?' he asked in a calm voice.

There was a short pause, then Diane said reluctantly, 'Yeah, she's here.'

'Well, could you get her for me please?'

There was a clunk as the receiver was put down. David expected to hear Diane bawling Ellen's name but he didn't. She probably didn't want to broadcast to the girls that he was on the phone. He was just debating whether he had time to put the receiver down, take out his handkerchief and swab his neck and face when a breathless, emotion-filled voice said, 'David.'

'Hello, Ellen,' David said.

'David, where are you?' The question was a plea from the heart.

Feeling like a shit, wondering whether this had been such a good idea after all, David said, 'I'm sorry. I can't tell you that.'

'Why not? Why did you just leave, David?'

'I had to, Ellen, that's all.'

'But *why*?'

'I . . . can't explain. It's too complicated.'

'Well, are you in . . . trouble or something?'

'Trouble?' said David. 'No, not really. It's just . . . things were getting on top of me. I had to get away for a while, be on my own.'

There was a pause. David decided that this had definitely not been one of his better ideas. Ellen was hurting enough already, and he, by his evasiveness, was simply twisting the knife, making her hurt all the more.

Her pain was evident in her voice now. 'Why couldn't you talk to me about it? We used to talk about everything.'

'I don't know,' said David. Silently he cursed himself:

don't leave it like that, you shit. Explain to her how you feel.

'Was it . . . problems at work? Or with the police? Or is there . . . someone else involved?'

David didn't understand what she meant at first by 'someone else'. Then it dawned on him and he was horrified. It had never occurred to him that she might be thinking this way.

'God no,' he said. 'It's nothing like that, honestly. There's no one else involved at all, and it's not your fault. It's just me, Ellen. I was feeling . . . I don't know . . . trapped. Stifled. Desperate. I can't really explain it. I just . . . needed to get away. I thought I was going mad.'

'But why, David? Nothing's changed, has it? You were always happy before, weren't you?'

David felt frustrated, almost angry, both at his inability to explain and at Ellen's inability to understand.

'That's just it,' he said. 'Nothing *has* changed, not for a long time. I've hit a brick wall in my life.'

'But I thought you were *happy*.' Ellen's voice was chalky with desperation.

'I was. . . . It's just . . . oh, I don't know. Recently I've started to feel hemmed in. I can't explain why. I don't really *know* why. Maybe it's my hormones or something.'

The silence was keenly painful, felt by both of them. When Ellen next spoke, it sounded like the vocal equivalent of treading barefoot over broken glass.

'So,' she said, 'where does that leave us now?'

'I don't know,' said David, and wanted to scream at himself.

'Well . . . are you coming back?'

'I don't know. Probably. Eventually.'

'When?'

'I don't know. Ellen, I'm sorry, but . . . I just can't put a time limit on this thing. I have to sort my own head out first.'

'Couldn't you do that at home? Couldn't I help you? Couldn't *we* help you? All of us?'

'I don't know,' said David like a stuck record. 'I don't think that would be a very good idea.'

'Well, why not?'

'I just don't. There are too many ... distractions at home. Too much pressure.'

'But David, we need you! We love you!'

'I know. And I love you. Honestly I do. It's just ... I have to sort myself out. I have to know where I'm going in life.'

'And meanwhile we have to just sit and wait for your decision?'

'I'm sorry, Ellen. I'm really sorry.'

'The girls are missing you like mad, you know. Jane doesn't understand why you've gone away.'

'I know. I'm sorry.'

'Do you want to talk to her, explain to her just what's going on?'

'No.'

'But you expect me to, don't you? You leave me with all the shitty stuff to do.'

'I didn't plan for it to be like this.'

'Oh well, that's all right then, isn't it?'

'Please, Ellen, don't be like this.'

'Like what? Upset? What do you expect me to be like? Do you expect me to just carry on as normal?'

'No, of course not.'

'What then? Jane was asking yesterday whether we were going to have a Christmas tree this year. What shall I tell her, hey?'

'I don't know.'

All the anger drained from Ellen's voice and suddenly the desperation was back again. 'Please come back, David. Please come back for Christmas.'

David didn't know whether he had ever felt as awful as

he did at that moment. 'I don't know if I can, Ellen. I can't promise anything.'

'*Please*. I'm begging you, David. For the girls' sake.'

David felt choked, could barely get out his words. 'I've got to go . . . I've got to . . .'

He slammed down the phone, stood shaking and sweating, panting as if he'd just run a race. From the kitchen Bugs Bunny said, as though addressing him, 'Ner . . . what's up, doc?'

22

The pub was called The Blue Posts and was on Rupert Street, just off Shaftesbury Avenue. It was still early evening, but already the place was busy and getting busier. Nevertheless Tametia noticed him immediately upon entering, a small scruffy unremarkable man sitting on his own in the corner. It was Paxton, one of the telepaths, who had found him during a scan of the area. He had reported back to Mathilde, who had used her contacts to gather more information about the man before passing what was relevant on to Tametia.

Tametia watched the man for a while like the predator she was. He was perhaps twenty-six or twenty-seven years old, podgy with bad skin and small darting eyes. He wore a grubby camouflage jacket over a thick greying Arran sweater. The skin of his throat was red raw and fuzzy with stubble (bum-fluff they used to call it at school), as if he had nothing to shave with but a blunt knife.

The more she watched him, the easier Tametia felt this would be. Even from right across the room, she could see the way his hand shook as he lifted the pint glass to his lips, the way his head swooped towards the alcohol. He gulped the beer as if it was the first he'd had for months, then glanced around almost guiltily, his small eyes flickering like trapped insects.

Tametia was dressed to kill tonight, in a black sleeveless figure-hugging dress, the skirt ending less than an inch below her underwear. Her dark hair tumbled about her pale smooth shoulders; it had taken her over an hour to achieve the effect of windswept abandon. She still thought her complexion was ghastly, the skin almost translucent around her eyes where pale blue veins looked like bruises beneath the surface, but she had done what she could with make-up and hoped that the lighting in the pub would do the rest. She concealed her pain very well, even when people – men mostly – pressed against her back or placed their hands directly on her wounds, not always unintentionally. To anyone else, the straightness of her back would seem simply a sign of her elegance. Tametia waited for just the right moment, which was when her prey's glass was almost empty, and then she glided across.

She was aware of the many admiring glances she drew as she crossed the floor but she ignored them all studiously. Her prey was lifting his glass again. As he took what was destined to be his last swallow of beer ever, she slid into the seat beside him.

The instant she did so, bracing herself against the pain in her back, Burgess jumped as if someone had dropped an ice cube down his collar. He didn't only look at Tametia, he gawped at her. Tametia assessed him quickly and coolly, taking in every aspect of his appearance. She noticed the sweat on his cheeks, the flecks of yellow wax in his ears, the dirt beneath his fingernails, the sickle-shaped scar on his upper lip.

'Hello, Dean,' she purred at him, and then, without waiting for a reply, 'You know who I am, don't you?'

Burgess dropped his almost-empty glass into his lap. It tipped over and splashed beer over the thigh of his jeans. His eyelids fluttered briefly as if he was about to faint, and then slowly he nodded.

Tametia's lips, full and purple with lipstick, curled into a smile. She leaned close enough for him to feel her warm sweet breath on his acned cheek.

'*Who* am I?' she murmured. 'I want to hear you tell me.'

Burgess's lips moved but no sound came out. Despite

the throbbing pain in her back, Tametia was enjoying this. Burgess reminded her of some of the men to whom she had once sold her body. Seeing what an inadequate wreck he was, how much control she had over him, was like an indication of how much progress she had made since those dark submissive days in Edinburgh. Knowing it would scare him witless, she tapped gingerly into her animis, shifted her molecules just a little, though it hurt like hell to do so, just enough to give him a glimpse of cold yellow snake-eyes. Quietly, almost whispering, she repeated, 'I want you to tell me, Dean. I want you to tell me who I am.'

He struggled desperately to speak. His breath smelled of old meat, bad digestion. Finally he made a kind of strangled sound.

'What did you say?' she demanded, hissing. 'You'll have to repeat it. I didn't hear you.'

Burgess made a supreme effort. 'The Alien.' The word was somewhere between a whisper and a sob.

Tametia smiled and caressed the knot of his hands which were now pressed hard into his lap. His flesh was cold and clammy as tripe. He was trembling so much that she felt sure people would begin to notice before too long. 'That's quite correct, Dean,' she said soothingly. 'I *am* the Alien. Take a gold star and go to the top of the class.'

Burgess squeezed his eyes shut and then opened them again. His breathing was quick and shallow. He made Tametia think of the birds she had encountered when she'd been a cat, so transfixed by terror that they had been unable to fly.

'Tell me, Dean,' she said conversationally, 'do you know why I'm here?'

Burgess twitched his head. Tametia took the movement to be a nod.

'Well, in that case,' she said, 'perhaps you'd care to enlighten me. I want us to be perfectly sure that we understand each other.'

Burgess opened his mouth and tried to speak again, but all that emerged was a hitching and gurgling of breath.

'Don't be afraid,' she said, and suddenly remembered the catchline for a film called *The Fly*, which, because of her own ability, she'd found interesting and amusing. *Don't be afraid*, the posters had said, *Be very, very afraid*. Or something like that. She grinned and said, 'I'm not going to hurt you. I'm here to help. You should know that.'

Burgess's head turned very slowly, as if he was suffering from chronic neck ache. He still looked terrified, but there was a little hope in his piggy eyes now, a plea for reassurance. His slack wet lips moved again and he mumbled, 'You've come to tell me what to do.'

'That's right!' Tametia exclaimed delightedly as if he was a child grasping a complicated notion. 'That's very, very good, Dean. And *will* you do whatever I tell you?'

'Yes,' he whispered.

'Even if it's something terrible? Even if it's the most terrible thing in the world?'

He nodded again, eagerly now, wanting to please her.

'Why?' she asked.

Burgess looked momentarily alarmed, as if it was a trick question, and then he said, 'Because the boy in the lights told me to.'

Tametia felt an urge to laugh; she stifled it. 'And do you know who the boy in the lights is?' she asked him.

He looked at her blankly, and then alarm crept across his face again. His bottom lip began to tremble. He shook his head.

'But you know who sent him, don't you?' she coaxed gently.

He looked for a moment as though he didn't – and then an expression of awe appeared on his podgy features. 'Oh,' he whispered, like a deaf boy hearing music for the first time. Despite his fear he started to smile. 'Yes,' he breathed like a lover.

'Who was it, Dean? Who sent him?'

Burgess gazed at her, mouth open and smiling. He said nothing.

'Who, Dean? You have to tell me.'

He was still smiling. He swallowed, took a deep breath. '*Him*,' he said.

This was all going wonderfully, just as Mathilde had said it would. 'That's right, Dean, it *was* him. And you know you have to obey him, don't you?'

Burgess nodded.

'And you know what will happen if you *don't* obey him, don't you?'

He shuddered. 'Yes,' he said.

'Good,' said Tametia, her voice soft, reassuring, mesmeric. 'We knew we could rely on you, Dean. We knew that you were our man.' She held out her hand, and Burgess, after a moment, took it like a hesitant child.

'Are you ready?' asked Tametia.

He nodded.

'Then let's go,' she said.

23

After the phone call, David felt dreadful. It had been a bad idea, a really terrible idea; no wonder he had shied away from it on previous occasions, he should have realised what would happen. Rather than patching things up a little between himself and Ellen, he had succeeded only in tearing the wound wide open again, making it gape and bleed and susceptible to infection.

He went upstairs and lay on his bed, feeling sickened, furious with himself. How could he have been so stupid, so insensitive? His thoughts buzzed like faulty circuits in his cluttered head until he could stand it no longer.

He sat up abruptly, swung his legs from the bed and reached for his Bogart. Fuck his investigation, fuck the bottle, fuck everything. Tonight he was going to go out and get absolutely rat-arsed, he was going to drink until he collapsed in a pile of his own puke.

It was dark and cold and still drizzling, but he stomped to the nearest tube station, Seven Sisters, his coat flapping about him, the bottle bumping against his thigh like a revolver. He sat on the hot smelly tube, glaring into space until he reached King's Cross, where he changed to the Piccadilly Line and caught a train to Covent Garden.

There he found a large pub, loud and well lit, the door wreathed with strings of brightly coloured light bulbs around each of which was a halo of twitching glowing fibres that were rain. He marched in like a gunfighter, elbowing people out of the way and ignoring their protests. It was hot and crowded in the pub. Steam rose from his wet hair and from the shoulders of his Bogart.

The heat made his head feel as though it was melting from the inside. From the juke box in the corner, Annie Lennox roared that she needed a man. The guy standing next to David at the bar looked like a male model. He was wearing an immaculately tailored suit and flashing impossibly white teeth as he talked money with the beautiful girl beside him. His hand was clasped around a bottle of pale lager in which bobbed a chunk of lime.

'Sol, please,' said David when his turn came, reading the name of the lager through the condensation on the bottle.

He stood against a wall, drinking his beer and watching people. He used to feel self-conscious in a pub on his own, but now he didn't care what anyone thought. In less than an hour he drank four bottles of Sol but he didn't feel the slightest bit drunk. All that happened was that his self-loathing lost its edge and became a dull ache inside him, leaving him tired and melancholy.

When he left the pub the drizzle had turned to a hard freezing rain which bounced up off the gleaming pavements and made a noise like escaping gas. He stood watching the rain for a minute in the sheltering recess of the pub doorway, then he pulled up the collar of his overcoat and ventured out. The rain drummed on the thick canvassy material of his Bogart; his feet spanked the wet pavement.

David walked quickly but he didn't run. Though his face was streaming with water after less than a minute, he relished the rain's relentless muscular power. Reflections of lights trailed in puddles, twitching as they drowned. The red neon sign of a Chinese restaurant called Hoo Sun seemed to drip like blood. The smell from the restaurant doorway tweaked David's hunger into life, made him decide he'd rather eat than drink. He licked the rain from his lips as he pondered what he fancied. How about some pasta, something rich and tomatoey?

The Italian restaurant, called Casa Romana, was on James Street near the tube station. Painted on the large front window was a fat Italian cartoon chef carrying a column of toppling pizzas. The waiters inside looked so typically Italian that David wondered whether they were consciously parodying themselves. On the wall behind the bar was a framed photograph of the Sampdoria football team. One of the waiters made a joke about the rain which David didn't quite catch, but which he smiled at anyway.

After transferring his wallet and the bottle to the capacious pockets of his grey chinos, David peeled off his coat and hung it up. He was handed a towel which smelled of lavender to dry his hair, and then shown to a table. The place was about half-full and, though open-plan, was set at two different levels. Though the lighting was subdued, the candles which flickered on each table were mainly for effect. David followed the narrow-hipped waiter who'd made the joke about the rain as he weaved between tables like a fish slipping between rocks. David's table was at the back of the room, on the higher level, which suited him. He had to ascend three carpeted steps to get there. As soon as he sat down, the waiter opened a menu into his hand.

David wondered whether the Pavarotti, which was playing discreetly in the background, was for the tourists or whether it was all the Italians listened to. He ordered garlic bread, spaghetti bolognese and a bottle of red house wine. When he blew his nose, hoping he wasn't catching a chill, the young couple on the next table giggled. David glared at them only to realise that they were too enamoured with each other to have been laughing at him.

The garlic bread was strong enough to clear anyone's sinuses. The bolognese was as rich as he'd hoped it would be and shimmering with grease. When he dabbed his lips on his napkin, he left two orange crescents on the white material. People came and went but the restaurant remained about half-full. The bottle in David's pocket pressed coldly against his thigh.

He was thinking about dessert when he saw the man outside in the rain. At first he thought nothing of him; people had been passing the big front window all evening, blurred by the rain on the glass as if they themselves were made of it, smears of featureless colour. One or two had stopped to glance at the restaurant's menu before hurrying on. All had been hunched and wreathed against the elements, squeezing themselves compact to prevent the cold and the wet getting in.

This man, however, was different. David's attention was caught and then held because of the way he approached the restaurant – purposefully, upright, as if oblivious to the weather. David could not see the man clearly, especially since he approached the restaurant on a line with the painting of the fat chef, so that his and the chef's forms seemed to merge together into a wavering blur. However he could see enough to discern that the man was wearing a greeny-brown jacket so saturated by rain that it looked like mud.

A number of people turned to look when the man marched right up to the window, cupped his hands around his eyes and peered in. Now David could see that the rain had made the man's skin look shiny as plastic. Instinctively he hunched forward in his seat and brought a loosely clenched fist up to conceal the lower half of his face, though he had no reason to believe that the man might be looking for him. Indeed, it was impossible to tell exactly what the man *was* looking at, for his eyes were dark clots in his face.

The waiters, and many of the customers too, seemed to treat the man's behaviour as a joke. The barman said something in Italian, making the rest of the waiters laugh. One, whose chinless face seemed too narrow for its thick dark moustache, strode to the door of the restaurant, calling something over his shoulder which revived the laughter before the previous outburst had died. The instant he opened the door, however, admitting the scuttling sound of the rain, the man detached himself from the window and walked quickly away.

The waiter came back in, shrugged, and said something else in Italian. The waiter who was serving David tapped his head and muttered something; David caught the word '*matto*' which he thought meant 'insane'. People settled down again, turning their attention back to their meals. A couple in their fifties, the man moving slowly as though his pendulous stomach was a burden he was trying not to dislodge, stood up to leave.

David viewed their slow progress to the door, where they paused to drag on heavy coats, only peripherally. When they tugged the door open, grimacing at the rain, he was nodding his thanks to the waiter who had come to clear the debris of his main course away. Seconds later there was an almighty bang like an explosion, which stung David's ears and which echoed and re-echoed both in the high-ceilinged room and in his head. David saw everyone jolt upright in their seats even as he was doing so himself. Heads turned to the door, a ripple of movement like a Mexican wave. The fat man who had been on the verge of leaving was now backpedalling, strangely graceful as he floundered into the edge of a table and knocked it over. It had all happened so quickly that David didn't know what the man was doing or what the bang had been. Even when the man collapsed and the table collapsed on top of him, he didn't realise.

The truth began to dawn when someone started screaming, though even then the woolly sense of unreality persisted. David noticed that the picture of the Sampdoria football team had been obscured by a splash of what looked like blood. And then, as if his senses were filtering the information through only fragmentarily, he noticed that there were more splashes of blood, a lot of them – on the floor, on the side of the bar, on a white tablecloth, and on a waiter's face and then on his hands as he tried to swipe the stuff away as if it were a spider's web.

David saw the fat customer's feet pedalling slowly, and then, before stopping, shuddering and thumping the floor as if he was having a fit. David noticed some small details very clearly – the fat customer's very shiny shoes, a woman's mouth hanging open as if showing a dentist her fillings, a man's hand still curled around a glass of red wine on his table as if protecting it from harm.

The scruffy man who had been looking through the window then walked into the restaurant carrying a gun. There was no anger on his face or urgency in his movements. He just strolled casually in, as if about to order a takeaway. The man was wearing a soaking wet camouflage jacket and it seemed to David as if he was carrying his gun in a very professional manner, diagonally across his chest, left hand almost at shoulder height, supporting the barrel.

Still no one moved or made a sound, apart from the fat man's wife, who had been the one who'd screamed and who was now having hysterics. She was holding her clenched fists up to her face, pushing her knuckles hard into her cheekbones. Her screams were raw and primal, eyes stretched wider than seemed possible.

Calmly the gunman raised his weapon and shot the woman. There was a thick copious spray of maroon and then she was flailing backwards as if someone had shoved her very hard in the chest. The large front window with the painting of the cartoon chef on it exploded with the impact of the woman's body. She did a grotesque back-flip into the street and then pieces of glass, some as large as guillotine blades, were falling on to and around her body.

Because the second retort of the shotgun was still ringing in David's ears, the shattering glass and the ensuing panic sounded like a film with a defective sound-track. People were rising from their seats or diving beneath tables, or just sitting there staring, their faces wide with shock. One or two people dived through the broken window into the street; David saw one man roll over and over in the rain before hitting his head on the wheel of a car that was parked by the roadside and curling up in pain like an endangered hedgehog. What was perhaps most reprehensible, and yet at the same time oddly understandable, was that people were grabbing complete strangers and using them as shields. One man actually pushed a teenage girl towards the gunman, evidently in the hope that she would act as a distraction while he made a break for it. The man's ploy worked very well indeed; as the girl staggered towards him, the gunman swivelled and shot her calmly in the throat.

While all this was going on, David just sat at his table, staring at the carnage, so stunned that it was only after the girl had been killed that he realised the sweet menu was still propped casually open in his hands. He dropped it now, his fingers springing apart as if the laminated card had suddenly become very hot. The echo of the latest shotgun blast was still repeating in his ears, though with decreasing volume; he very clearly heard the slap of the menu as it hit the glass-topped table.

David's emotions had been so stunned by the enormity, the *impossibility*, of what was happening, that he felt like a spectator, emotionally and physically divorced from the proceedings, on the surface, at least. All that changed, however, when the gunman rotated slowly, like a human radar, and looked at him. David stared straight into the gunman's calm, even serene, face, and at that moment he knew, without a shadow of a doubt, that he was the man's target. It occurred to him, in a dreamy kind of way, that maybe this was what everyone in a similar situation thought, that staring into the eyes of such a man was like gazing at your own death.

It must have been no more than a minute since the gunman had entered the restaurant, yet it seemed like an age. In that short time the whole world had changed irrevocably. In the instant that David's and the gunman's eyes met, everything else seemed to fade: the screaming and shouting and crashing of furniture became nothing more than background noise, the milling people simply extras in a disaster movie.

The gunman hefted his weapon and began to walk calmly towards David. It was only now that David realised how hopelessly he had dealt with this situation, and more than anything he felt annoyed with himself. Somewhere deep inside him was a fear so intense that it was turning his innards to water. On the surface, however, he could feel only anger with himself; he had often wondered how he would deal with a situation like this and now he knew. By doing nothing, by just sitting there like a dork. He might as well have the words CANNON FODDER tattooed across his forehead.

The gunman was raising his gun now and pointing it at David. Behind the gunman, in a kind of background blur, David saw overturned tables and broken crockery, was vaguely aware of lumpy dark things strewn about that might have been anything from discarded handbags to spilled food to bits of people. The young girl who had been shot in the throat was lying on her back in her orange dress amid the debris. All that could be seen of the middle-aged couple were their legs, the man's protruding from beneath the edge of the table that had collapsed on to him, the woman's resting crookedly on the jagged lip of the broken window. Some people were still leaving the restaurant, whereas others, evidently trampled in the crush, were lying on the floor groaning or shuffling about on hands and knees. David was vaguely aware of dark figures running back and forth in the rain outside, or huddled in heaps. He could hear crying, shouting, sounds of anger and shock and disbelief, and underlying it all, like static, the clattering hiss of the rain.

These images, profuse and subliminal, were part of the terrible chaos that was the gunman. What was happening here was so wrong, so intrinsically opposed to everything that made life seem good and meaningful, that David felt poised on the edge of the most awful darkness. The gunman was still raising his gun; he seemed to be doing so in slow motion. His face, pallid, plump and flecked with acne, was blank as a mask.

As the muzzle of the gun rose to meet his face, David's mind began to pick up speed, his thoughts to race, and he found himself wondering whether he was actually going to experience that old cliché of his life flashing before his eyes. But it was regret that filled him – regret that he would never again see Ellen and the girls, regret that he had caused them so much sorrow, regret that he had left nothing behind, no legacy, no achievements to speak of, regret that he would never now solve the mystery of the bottle.

The bottle! After what it had done to the tiger, wasn't there a chance that . . .?

Frantically he groped for it, turning the lining of his pocket inside-out as he yanked it out.

He held it aloft, and immediately felt the familiar tugging deep in the core of him. Almost instantaneously the bottle blazed into light, consuming David's hand in a ball of white-blue fire. David felt confidence, strength, power flowing through him. He felt as though he had the energy of a star at his fingertips, waiting to be unleashed.

He looked at the gunman and saw that he was standing transfixed, the light reflecting on the gun barrel and the man's wet shiny skin and the broken glass, turning the raindrops to crystal, the glass-topped table in front of him to a sheet of ice. He saw also that the man's fat white finger was still resting on the trigger of his gun, and he knew that the minutest pressure would propel a bullet across the short distance to his head, where it would shatter his skull into coin-sized fragments and tear apart the soft grey meat of his brain.

The light filled the gunman's eyes like lenses made of ice. For long, long seconds David and the gunman remained poised in their respective positions, as though engaged in some mental battle which required the utmost concentration. Was it only David's imagination or was the bottle's light not quite so fierce as it had been the first time he had used it? Certainly on that occasion he had used the bottle's power instinctively, his emotions meshing with the raw energy it was providing, the full force of which had been turned against the tiger. Now, though, he sensed that the light required a greater mental contribution from him to make it work, felt as though the force of his emotions had to be more sharply focused to compensate for the very slight reduction in the bottle's own energy output. He closed his eyes to aid his concentration, tried not to think of the gunman's finger on the trigger, of the bullet waiting to be discharged. Could it be that the bottle's energy was like a battery pack for his own will? He tried not to think of that just now, tried to concentrate on the matter in hand. Mentally he felt as though he were pushing, straining to hold on.

Then all at once whatever was opposing him seemed to give way, to crumble, and he felt a surge of energy inside him so strong it made him cry out and open his eyes. The gunman's face looked fat and white and blank as a snowman's now. He was still pointing the gun at David, but his grip was slackening, and almost at once David saw the gun barrel droop like a wilting erection. The gunman's lips began to move as if he was murmuring a mantra to himself. David saw beams of ice-blue light lance from within the heart of the bottle's radiance and sketch crazy patterns on the gunman's face. The gunman's eyes were not just reflecting the light now, they seemed to be absorbing it, like pads of blotting paper absorbing ink. David felt triumphant, in full control, but only for a moment. His triumph turned to shock when the gunman flipped the gun around, closed his lips around the barrel and pulled the trigger.

With the gunman's death, the light began rapidly to fade. David, feeling shell-shocked and almost exhausted enough to drop, stumbled past the gunman's body and across the debris-strewn floor of the restaurant. He grabbed his Bogart from the coat-rack as he passed and dragged it on as he began to walk away, his feet spattering the drowned streets, pushing between people stunned with grief and confusion and terror. No one tried to stop him, to take his arm and ask what had happened in there. No one even looked at him; he moved through the crowds and away as if he were invisible. And though he was conscious, it was on a primary level only. His mind worked like a machine, efficiently and unfeelingly, doing just enough to get him home, but denying him emotions or autonomous thought. It was comforting in a way to be so detached, to have his opinions and his feelings taken away from him. It was like sleeping without dreams and yet being conscious at the same time.

Back in his room at the B & B, an hour or so later, the full horror of what he had experienced began to punch through his defences. He sank on to his bed, curled foetally around the bottle, and braced himself as well as he was able for what he felt sure would be a long and terrible night.

24

Teddy was holding his hand and letting him watch a film in his head. It was a scary film, but it was also exciting. Danny felt as if he were floating above a big room where people were eating food. Most of Danny's attention was focused on a man sitting on his own near the back of the room, eating a plate of spaghetti and meat. Danny could smell the food and it made him hungry. He could hear people talking, the clunk and clatter of pots and pans and knives and forks. Like in a real film, Danny kept jumping from this place to another one, cutting between two scenes that he felt would very soon join together and become one. The first place was cosy and warm, but this second place was dark and frightening. It was like one of those films where you see something through a monster's eyes. You crash and jolt through the undergrowth and you hear its heavy breath, and then you come into a clearing and you see who you're going to kill and you speed up as you rush towards them. And the people who you're going to kill, usually a couple kissing, hear you and turn slowly, and when they see you they start to scream. They try to run but they're much too slow, and you, the monster, catch up with them and their screaming mouth fills the screen and then everything goes red . . .

This was a bit like that, but Danny wasn't in a monster's head, not really. The head he was inside belonged to a man. Danny knew, or somehow sensed, that the man wasn't normal however. Perhaps it was Teddy who told him, though Danny couldn't remember Teddy actually saying anything. The thing was, Danny knew that this man had odd ideas about how things worked, and that these ideas had been somehow mucked about with, made to grow into something that was terrifying and dangerous. Being in the man's head was like being at the bottom of a horrible pit. Danny heard sounds – crashing, screaming, awful sounds – echoing all around him in the darkness, and he kept thinking he could see things out of the corners of his eyes that made him want to scream himself.

So Danny kept jumping between the two places. One minute he was in the warm cosy room watching the blond-haired man eating his spaghetti, and the next he was inside the other man's head, looking out through the man's eyes, moving through rainy streets he didn't recognise and hearing the man's soft breathing and seeing his breath coming out in little white clouds.

And soon, just as Danny knew they would, the two scenes came together like two bits of a jigsaw that look completely different until you try them and find they're a perfect fit. Through the scary man's eyes, Danny saw a big lit-up window with a picture of a fat man carrying pizzas painted on it, and he knew that this was the place where the blond-haired man was eating his spaghetti.

Still inside the scary man's head, Danny went up to the window and looked through it. The glass was smeary with rain, but Danny could see the blond-haired man sitting at a table on a little balcony near the back. As if he knew he was being watched, the blond-haired man lifted a hand up in front of his face in an attempt to hide himself from view. Danny became aware that people were laughing at him – or rather, at the scary man – and the dark insect-thoughts in his head became even more crawly, like ants whose nest is disturbed.

It was at this moment that Danny knew something really bad was going to happen. All of a sudden he wanted to be away from here, wanted to fly away from this place and be back at home in his nice warm bed. But Teddy wouldn't let him. He could only watch helplessly as the man walked away from the restaurant and down a dark alley nearby where rain was battering on the lids of metal dustbins and dripping from a light over a door that looked as if it was never used. The man walked up to the fourth dustbin along, trampling on black bin bags that made Danny think of dead seals. One of the bags burst open and stuff came out like guts – shredded paper, chicken bones, rotting vegetables, slimy cans. The man opened the bin and looked inside. He reached in and pulled something out that was long and thin and wrapped in newspaper. Danny saw the man's stubby hands pulling the newspaper away, saw the gleam of metal underneath. Danny felt very scared and, despite himself, also a bit excited when he realised it was a real live gun.

The man picked up the gun and then went back down the alley and on to the street, walking like a robot. Danny travelled with the man as he walked back towards the restaurant, the rain still beating down. He was only a few feet from the restaurant door when it opened and a man in a big coat came out, his fat body filling the doorway like a barrier.

Without even thinking about it the man raised his gun and shot the fat man. The fat man threw up his arms and blew backwards as if he were pretending the wind was too strong for him. Danny wanted to squirm and scream and run away, but he was held fast and struck dumb, forced to watch the terrible things happening in front of him. He'd seen the Terminator shoot people, and policemen on telly, and cowboys, but this was different. This wasn't all slick and exciting and glamorous, it was ugly and empty and horrible.

The restaurant was hot and bright after the rain. The smell of meat and oil made Danny feel sick. Danny saw faces surrounding him, staring at him, faces with open mouths and big eyes. A woman was screaming. The man with the gun turned calmly round and shot her. She blew backwards like the fat man and hit the large front window, which smashed. Her body fell out into the street, and the rain and the cold blew in. People started to scream and scramble over each other like starving dogs who'd been thrown a piece of meat. Danny wanted to shout at the man to stop, or at the very least to close his own eyes, but he couldn't.

There was blood everywhere and soon there were overturned tables and broken crockery and spilled food and handbags and lots of other things as well. A girl in an orange dress sort of fell towards the man as if she was going to try and wrestle the gun away from him. He turned and shot her too. The noise was tremendous. Her head was almost ripped from her shoulders as her throat exploded. Danny cowered in the stinking pit of the man's mind, listening to the man's twisted thoughts slithering and scuttling around him in the darkness.

Now the scary man turned slowly and looked at the blond-haired man. The blond-haired man just sat there with a stunned expression on his face. The scary man began to walk towards the blond-haired man, raising the gun. Danny's senses were packed with smells and sights and sounds, all of them terrible.

The scary man pointed his gun straight at the blond-haired man's face and began to pull the trigger. Danny wanted to shout at the blond-haired man to move out of the way. He couldn't understand why the man was just sitting there. And then Danny saw a brilliant blue-white light travelling up the blond-haired man's body, surrounding him like a block of ice. The light grew brighter and brighter, and suddenly it was filling the scary man's head, rushing into his mind through his eyes.

All the scuttling things in the pit were killed instantly, like spiders set on fire. The scary man's mind became clean and empty and pure. Danny felt himself lifted up by the light, carried away as if on a cloud. Distantly he heard another bang and then he felt himself spinning, rushing through the blue-white brightness, as his final link with the scary man was snapped like an elastic band. His whole vision, all his senses, filled with a terrific whiteness that was like light and noise, both at the same time.

And then at last the brightness and the noise faded away. When it was gone completely he opened eyes that felt as if they had been glued closed and found himself sitting on his bed, his back against the wall, holding Teddy by the hand. His lips felt glued closed too. He stuck his tongue against the back of them, forcing them apart. His eyes were sore, like when he was in the swimming baths for too long and he opened them underwater. His arms and legs tingled like pins and needles.

Teddy's rage was sudden and powerful. It rushed through Danny like a black thunderbolt, filling him with such pain that he couldn't even scream. He felt himself being lifted up, but not like before, not like when the white light had done it. This time he felt as if hooks were plunging into his body, wrenching him into the air. He kicked with his legs, thrashed about, but it made no difference. He saw the bed below him and knew he was rising up to the ceiling of his room. He was in agony, such agony that he felt himself starting to faint. He opened his mouth but still no sound came out. And then he felt himself clutched as if in some enormous invisible claw, pulled back and hurled forward.

The wall rushing towards him was the last thing that Danny ever saw. The impact of the little boy's body with the wall was of such ferocity that he was instantly killed. The body slid to the floor, leaving a sizeable smear of itself behind. But despite the fact that it had no life left in it, the body was then picked up and thrown at the wall again and again and again, until parts of it were strewn around the room, until it was no longer recognisable as a human being. The force that Danny had called Teddy played with the boy's body as a cat might play with a shrew, played with it until there was almost nothing left to play with. And then, its anger exhausted, it moved on, searching for another host, another tender mind to infiltrate. It already knew where it would find one.

25

Sunday morning was bright but bitterly cold. David welcomed the brittle silver dawn like a long-lost friend. There had been moments during the night when he felt that time had stopped, as though the events that had taken place earlier that evening had been so terrible that they had shocked the great motors of the universe into immobility.

He had been sick twice during the early hours, and each time his nostrils had filled with the stink of blood and garlic and meat as if he had carried some of the horror back with him, as if it had infected him in some way. Though he felt enervated by his ordeal, he had not slept. He had remained curled up like a foetus on his bed, the bottle clutched to his midriff, afraid to close his eyes because every time he did so he saw the fat man flailing backwards, the woman erupting with blood and performing her terrible back-flip through the window, the young girl in the orange dress stumbling forwards and then being blown back by the force of the blast as her throat and jaw exploded.

The dawn, thankfully, dissipated these images a little. At least, it encouraged David to get up from his bed and peel off his Bogart which, he now discovered, was still damp from last night's rain. He went over to the window and watched a pale sun striving to haul itself above the spiky grey horizon of the city. The sun extended talons which tore the darkness softly apart like old denim, revealing the pallid skin of daylight beneath.

The light acted as a gentle probe, coaxing at David's mind, thawing the shock from around it. Sluggishly at first, his thoughts reawakened; he began to ask himself questions about last night, tried to find reasons, to make some sense out of the senselessness of it all.

Had he really been the gunman's target or had the gunman marched unhesitantly towards him and pointed the gun at his face because he had simply sat there, offering himself as a target, whilst all around him people had been diving for cover? David didn't know, and he guessed there was no way of finding out, not immediately anyway. An idea that he suspected had been in his head for a long time, frozen and dormant within the glacier of his shock, now wriggled free of the ice and surfaced with its arms waving. Did the gunman have something to do with Marshall, with David's investigation? Was Marshall really prepared to stop at nothing to get the bottle back, and if so, then what should David's next move be? The obvious thing to do would be to dump the bottle into the nearest dustbin, go home and forget about the whole thing. And yet even after all this, David knew he couldn't do that.

He pushed the heels of his hands into his aching sockets and spread his fingers over the front of his skull as if to prevent it splitting with the weight of his thoughts. He still didn't know what to think about all the really weird stuff that had been happening. The instinctive part of him believed fervently that he had seen exactly what he thought he had, whereas the logical part insisted it was all dreams and delusions, the mental aberrations of an over-wrought mind. Could hallucinations really be so vivid, seem so real? And if the bottle's power hadn't deflected the gunman away from David last night, then what had? The easiest thing, he decided, was to keep his mind as empty as possible, just to plod on with the day-to-day stuff and try not to think about anything else. The only thing that was certain in all of this was that he couldn't stop now, he had to go on. Though he was terrified and confused, he was also more curious than ever.

Later, having had another long soak in the bath, and having skipped breakfast which he couldn't face, he walked to his car. The streets were drying out quickly. In the dips and hollows between paving slabs, the water was hardening to ice. The cold gnawed at the tips of David's ears, made the shaving cut on his chin throb coldly. The instant he got into the car and shut the door the windows steamed up.

The engine gave a hypothermic splutter when he turned the ignition key but refused to awaken until he'd pulled out the choke. He checked his watch; it was 9:25. David estimated it would take him between an hour and ninety minutes to reach Solden. He wanted to catch Kerslake in the best of moods, to time it so that he'd neither be so early that he'd get the man out of bed, nor so late that he'd interrupt his Sunday lunch. He turned on the heater to clear the windows and pulled away from the kerb. Realising that it was almost time for the news, he turned on the radio.

The shooting was the lead story. Despite having braced himself for it, David felt his stomach turning over, largely because he found it hard to equate the newsreader's calm voice and clinical phraseology with the terrible chaos of last night.

'At least three people were shot dead in a restaurant in Central London last night by a gunman who then turned his gun on himself,' the newsreader said. 'The gunman, who has not yet been identified, walked into the Casa Romana restaurant on James Street at around 10 p.m. and apparently began firing at random. The dead have not yet been named, but are thought to include a teenage girl.'

The newsreader paused and David tensed, expecting him to add, 'Police are anxious to trace a blond-haired man who was seen walking away from the scene in a trance-like state . . .' But he didn't. Instead he said, 'Prime Minister, John Major, has said that Britain will make no concessions to –'

David turned the radio off.

He drove in silence for a while and then put some music on, Nigel Kennedy playing Vivaldi's 'Four Seasons'. Considering the day and the hour, the roads were surprisingly busy, particularly with lorries thundering towards Felixstowe. The East Anglian countryside was pretty but uninspiring, or perhaps it was simply that David was in no mood to appreciate it. The flat landscape provided no protection from the sun, which had scaled a grey hillside of cloud and was now glowering down at him, throwing sheets of cold white light across his windscreen and making his sleep-starved eyes hurt. He was so busy fumbling in the glove compartment for his sunglasses that he almost missed the turn-off for Solden.

He veered into the left-hand lane without indicating or checking his mirror. He raised a hand in shaken and embarrassed apology as the car behind him blared its horn. As he pulled off, slowing down, the car accelerated past him, a black Mini whose young bespectacled driver mouthed what was quite definitely not an endearment. David grimaced, and again acknowledged his mistake with a raised hand. He felt very tired and depressed.

Flat endless fields spread themselves on either side of him, divided by hedges from which sprouted the occasional gesticulating tree. He climbed a gentle incline, at the top of which was a junction whose left fork was signposted: Solden 1. Just before he entered Solden itself, a small field of sheep furnished him with a memory of Jane, aged four, pointing out of the car window during a family day out to the seaside and shouting, 'Look, Daddy, cloud-dogs!' He was smiling painfully as he drove into the village, where a metal sign greeted him with the words:

Solden Welcomes Careful Drivers.

The village was pretty, picturesque, prompting such phrases as 'olde-worlde' and 'rustic charm' to pop immediately into the mind. Normally David found such places restful, imbued with a sense of gentle history. The surroundings would make him imagine fondly that the people who lived here enjoyed long, happy, uncomplicated lives. Today, though, he felt almost contemptuous of the rambling architecture, much of which was smothered with Virginia creeper, the immaculate gardens, the village green complete with duck pond, the tiny post office which was really just someone's front room, the tea-shop (or rather tea-shoppe) called Quaintways.

He couldn't help thinking that the whole place was a sham, that the people who lived here were simply burying their heads in the sand. Didn't they realise what an awful place the world really was? How could the inhabitants of places such as Solden live with themselves when elsewhere people were being shot dead for no reason?

It was an unfair and illogical viewpoint, he knew, but he couldn't help it. After last night, everything seemed soured and pointless and hypocritical and uncaring. However much he tried to convince himself that this wasn't the case, the feeling refused to go away. He pulled up at a newsagent's and asked the way to Blackett Road. Less than two minutes later he was parked outside Kerslake's house.

It was only when he had switched off the engine and unfastened his seatbelt that he found himself wondering whether this was the right Kerslake, after all. He'd tracked the man down only by making a number of assumptions. At no stage had he bothered to check his facts. What if this wasn't the right Kerslake? Well then, he thought, I'll make my apologies and leave and then I'll . . . I'll go back. But to do what? To fart around some more? To think up some other pointless task which would put off what he should *really* be doing, which was confronting Marshall?

He told himself angrily that what he was doing was gathering information, arming himself, acting on the words of that very wise old saying which went: Know Thine Enemy. And besides, this *was* the right Kerslake, he knew it was. He got out of the car and slammed the door as if shutting the argument inside.

Kerslake's house was a large stone cottage, the right side of which was festooned with the inevitable Virginia creeper. Behind waist-high double gates, one of which bore an ominous 'Beware Of The Dog' sign, a long gravel drive led to a newish-looking garage which was tucked between the house and a screen of conifers that separated the Kerslakes from their neighbours on the left. Looking and listening for signs of a dog, David unlatched the gate and entered, his feet crunching on the gravel drive. To his right, beyond a line of shrubs, was the front garden, comprising a large expanse of lawn, flowerbeds which were sparse and dark at this time of year, and another line of conifers on the far side, planted so closely together that they formed an impenetrable barrier.

David walked to the front door, studiously avoiding looking into the window that he passed. He raised his hand to the doorbell but paused before pressing it. It suddenly occurred to him that he didn't know what to say, how to approach this. He had meant to work it out beforehand, but with all that had happened the intention had completely slipped his mind.

He stood in the cold, thinking furiously. He would have gone back to the car if he hadn't had to pass that window again. Why didn't he just tell Kerslake the truth? Not the whole truth, of course – he'd be dumb to mention all the weird stuff that had been happening – but he could tell Kerslake about finding the bottle and the note, could even show him the note to prove that he wasn't a crank.

He put his hand into the pocket of his Bogart, still

clammy from last night's rain, and touched the bottle. Its texture and coolness against his skin reassured him, as always. He unscrewed the cap of the bottle and prised out the note, which took a little time as it was not so tightly rolled as before. He put the note into his right-hand pocket and the bottle into his left. He still felt oddly reluctant to show the bottle to anybody.

Now he rang the bell and waited nervously, licking his dry lips, clearing his throat. At first he heard nothing, then the distant barking of a dog reached his ears. The barking grew louder, was accompanied by the sound of paws galloping across a carpet. 'Shit,' David said and jumped back when something thudded against the other side of the door. Was it his imagination or had he seen the wood shiver?

David liked dogs, but this sounded like a bloody big one. He realised that his hand was creeping instinctively towards the bulge of the bottle in a way that reminded him of a gunslinger reaching towards his weapon. He imagined himself retreating down Kerslake's drive, pursued by a slavering Rottweiler which he was deterring with bolts of light from his weathered old bottle that was really a laser gun. The image coaxed a small smile out of him.

The attack on the door continued unabated for perhaps fifteen seconds, then a voice which belonged to an elderly woman shouted, 'Barney! Get down! Barney!' The dog continued to bark but ceased its attack on the door. David heard a man saying mildly, 'Give over, Barney, you daft bugger. Put him in the kitchen, Mabel.'

There were further sounds of scuffling, then the sound of Barney being led away, still barking intermittently. David heard a door closing somewhere at the back of the house. The instant it had done so, the front door opened.

'Sorry about that,' said the old man who stood there. 'He wouldn't hurt you but some people are a bit wary.'

David blinked and responded automatically, 'What sort is he?'

'Black labrador. Daft as brushes, really, the lot of them.'

David nodded and chuckled, though his response was more a screen to hide his surprise than anything else. Although the photograph of Kerslake in the *Walthamstow Gazette* had been taken almost forty years ago, David had been expecting someone broad-shouldered, square-jawed, still imposing despite his years. This man, however, was very thin, haggard even, wearing a brown cardigan that seemed too heavy for his narrow stooped shoulders. Black and grey checked carpet slippers, frayed at the points where the man's big toes pushed against the lining, jutted from the bottoms of baggy green corduroy trousers.

'I'm sorry to trouble you on a Sunday,' David said, 'but . . . are you Mr Kerslake?'

The man was clean-shaven with stone-grey hair receding from a broad bony forehead, and he wore large square spectacles with thick black rims. 'That's right,' he said.

'Is that . . . I mean, are you the same Mr Kerslake who used to be an Inspector in the Metropolitan police force back in the fifties?'

The man frowned. Though he made no perceptible move, he seemed suddenly wary. 'Do you mind telling me who *you* are?' he said, avoiding the question.

'Yes,' said David, 'sorry. My name's David Fox. I'm . . . um . . . I'm just following up some information.'

Kerslake took off his spectacles, giving David the immediate impression that he was doing so in case of trouble, and slipped them into the breast pocket of his shirt. Immediately thick wiry eyebrows which had been concealed behind the spectacle rims sprang up like tiny grey springs uncoiling in slow motion.

'Information? What do you mean?' he said, his voice noticeably frostier now.

David tried to keep his own voice light and friendly. 'It's quite a long story,' he said, 'and it actually started on Starmouth beach of all places.' He told Kerslake about finding the bottle with the note inside, and then he reached into his pocket with numb fingers and pulled the note out. He offered it to Kerslake, who took it automatically. 'I think this will probably explain things better than I could.'

Kerslake peered hard at David for a moment, then he began to unroll the note, his thin hands trembling, either with age or cold or uncertainty.

'Careful,' David said, 'it's quite old,' but Kerslake made no sign that he had heard. He held the note up close to his face, squinting as though he couldn't quite decipher the childish script.

David watched him closely, feeling unaccountably nervous, like a child showing his father a poor school report. The note in Kerslake's hand began to shake, the dry paper crackling like fire heard from a distance. All of a sudden Kerslake made a distressed sound, a sort of stifled moan, and let the note slip from his grasp.

David instinctively shot out a hand and caught the note in mid-air. The paper felt like autumn leaves in his grip but it did not crumble. Kerslake's face had drained of colour; his bloodless lips were quivering as if from intense cold. Now the old man did not only look haggard, he looked frail enough to snap.

'Mr Kerslake, what's the matter?' David asked, alarmed. The old man looked so unsteady on his feet that it seemed the slightest breeze would push him over. David reached out a hand to steady him, but rather than accepting it, Kerslake recoiled, lost his footing and stumbled into the frame of his own front door.

For a horrible moment, David thought Kerslake was going to collapse. If he did, David fully expected to hear the sound of bones snapping like parched twigs. Kerslake, however, did not collapse. He clutched the doorframe and managed to steady himself. His bloodless lips toiled for a moment and then he croaked, 'Who *are* you?'

David was startled by the question. 'I've already told you,' he said gently. 'My name's David Fox.'

'You know what I mean.' The venom in Kerslake's voice was unmistakable. 'Who *are* you?'

David just stared at Kerslake, unsure what was expected of him. At last, guardedly, he said, 'Everything I've told you is the truth, Mr Kerslake. I am who I say I am. Who else would you expect me to be?'

Kerslake seemed not even to hear him. His eyes were wild now; frothy spittle had collected at the corners of his mouth.

'Why don't you leave me alone?' he said. 'I've done nothing to harm you, have I?'

'No,' David agreed.

'Then why have you come here?'

'I've told you,' said David. 'I found the note. It intrigued me, that's all.' He paused. He wasn't going to go through the whole story again, especially when it was pretty obvious that Kerslake was not really listening to him. Instead he asked, 'Why are you so scared, Mr Kerslake?'

Kerslake seemed to respond to the direct question. He licked his lips, blinked rapidly, and now when he looked at David he seemed actually to be focusing on him again.

'Let me give you some advice,' he said, his voice still roughened but a little calmer now. 'Go back home, throw the note away, forget about it.'

'Why?' David asked.

'Never mind why, just do it.'

Now David was getting scared again, and his fear was making him angry. 'Why should I? I can't unless you give me a reason, can I?'

'That's up to you,' Kerslake said, 'but you'd be wise to take my advice.'

'But why won't you tell me *why* you've given me this

advice? There's nobody listening.'

'I'm not prepared to discuss it any further. It was all over a long time ago for me.'

Kerslake was beginning to retreat into his house. Any moment now he would slam the door in David's face.

Desperately David said, '*What* was all over a long time ago? What happened, Mr Kerslake? Were you threatened? Did Marshall threaten you?'

Kerslake grinned a humourless grin. It made his face look like a skull. 'You don't know the half of it,' he said.

'No, I don't,' said David, 'because you won't tell me.'

'Goodbye, Mr Fox,' Kerslake said, and started to swing the door closed.

'If Marshall threatened you, maybe we can do something about it,' David called desperately into the narrowing gap.

The door continued to close on him. Instinctively, David stuck his foot between door and jamb.

Kerslake looked down and then up at him. He was furious, his forehead crinkling, his pale sunken cheeks flushing red.

'Get your bloody foot out of my door.'

'Not until you tell me what's going on.'

'Get your foot out of my door or I'll set my dog on you.'

'You said it was as daft as a brush.'

'I'll call the police then. I've told you I don't want to talk to you.'

'I only want to know about this one case,' David said. 'What possible harm could it do? Like you said yourself, it was all over a long time ago.'

'Go away,' Kerslake said. His voice was getting high and scratchy now, both with rage and fear, and he was trembling badly. David felt wretched, no better than a thug taking advantage of an old man's frailty. However, he had to give it one more try.

'*Please*, Mr Kerslake,' he said.

But Kerslake just muttered doggedly, 'Go away.' David left his foot where it was for two seconds more, and then reluctantly removed it. The door was slammed in his face.

'Fucking hell,' he snarled, and had to restrain himself from kicking at the wood in exasperation. He took a step back and looked up at the house, half-expecting to see Mrs Kerslake peering down at him from one of the higher windows. But there was no sign of anyone. 'What the bloody hell did Marshall do to you?' he said, loud enough for Kerslake to have heard had he been standing on the other side of the door.

The question, emerging as vapour, curled away unanswered. David sighed, and then, with a quick look round, took the bottle from his pocket, rolled up the note and pushed it inside. He put the bottle back into his pocket, hesitated a moment, then walked slowly down the drive and out to his car.

Unsettling thoughts and turbulent emotions filled his mind all the way to London.

26

Whenever anyone walked past Ellen's door, they did so on tiptoe, terrified of waking her. No one was particularly eager for a repeat of last night's performance. David's phone call had been the battering ram which had finally demolished the already weakened floodgates. Of course, it had been Diane and Ralph who had had to bear the brunt of the ensuing deluge of Ellen's emotions.

She had spent the evening weeping and ranting, and had finally been led up to bed, exhausted, at 2:30 a.m. by Diane. The Joyces had barely been able to keep up with her wildly fluctuating outbursts. One minute she had been vicious in her condemnation of David, calling him every name under the sun, and the next she had been blaming herself for not providing him with the support and sympathy that he had evidently been crying out for. By the time Diane came downstairs, having watched her friend slip into a deep but perhaps not altogether restful sleep, she too was feeling more tired than she could ever remember being.

Ralph made them both cocoa, and they sat at opposite ends of the settee, facing each other, warming their hands on the mugs. For a long time they simply sat there, sipping their drinks, too tired to move or talk or even to think. Ralph looked at his wife's face, slackened by fatigue, at the dark blotches around her eyes, and he wondered if he looked just as bad. He certainly felt it, felt as though he had diverted every ounce of energy he had into comforting Ellen, and that she had sapped that energy from him, using it like fuel to feed the furnace of her emotions.

Eventually, after a silence that stretched into minutes, he said, 'You okay?'

Diane looked at him, eyes hooded as if her eyelids were made of lead, and gave a tiny nod. 'Uh-huh.'

Ralph sighed. 'What a night.'

'Mm.'

'Poor Ellen.'

'Yeah.'

Diane blew a thin sigh from between her lips and her eyelids drooped closed.

'Come on,' said Ralph with no urgency whatsoever, 'we can't sleep here. Let's go to bed.'

'Mm. Intwominutes.' Diane's voice was a sleepy burr, the words running together.

Ralph couldn't be bothered to argue. He closed his own eyes. 'Okay,' he murmured. 'Two minutes.'

Four hours later he woke up, freezing cold, with a stiff neck, an aching back and a full bladder.

He shivered and groaned and eased himself gingerly into a sitting position. Propping his spectacles on his forehead he massaged his face with his hands. His moving about woke Diane, who wrapped her arms around herself and asked, 'What time is it?'

'Half-six,' said Ralph.

'Jesus.' Diane pushed her hair away from her face. 'I feel like death warmed over.'

'This time I'm definitely going to bed,' said Ralph, pushing himself to his feet. Diane extended a hand and he helped her up. They switched off the lights in the lounge and pulled out the plugs of the lamps and the TV before creeping upstairs. They could see through the open curtains in their bedroom that it was still dark outside, though the quality of the darkness suggested that dawn was perhaps not too far away. A light rain was falling, silver and soft, the first of the downpour that had blanketed the South some hours previously. After they had both visited the bathroom, Ralph pulled the curtains closed, then he and Diane tugged off their clothes, which they left in crumpled heaps beside the bed, before slipping between sheets which seemed cold enough to have been refrigerated.

They cuddled up, seeking heat in one another's naked bodies. Though cool to start with, the bed was comfortable, and Ralph's body still felt drained of all its energy, weighed down with fatigue. However, despite this, he found that he couldn't sleep. He closed his eyes and lay quietly for a time, but the thoughts in his head refused to drift, to become nonsensical and break apart. Eventually he opened his eyes and realised it was a little lighter than before. He couldn't help thinking that the breaking dawn was hinting that he should be up and about, despite last night. Diane was breathing heavily beside him, her lips slightly parted. Her hair smelled faintly of some nice but unidentifiable perfume. Ralph watched her face for a while. His hand, resting on her hip, felt like part of her. He moved it and felt her skin slide like silk beneath his touch. When he spoke her name softly, she opened her eyes at once.

'Hi,' she murmured.

'Sorry. Did I wake you?'

'Course you did. Asshole.' But there was no anger in her voice.

'Sorry,' said Ralph.

'That's okay. What time is it now?'

'I don't know. Half an hour after we came to bed. Or maybe an hour.'

'Is that all?' She rolled wearily on to her back. 'Shit, what a night.'

'I couldn't sleep,' said Ralph.

'So you woke me up to tell me?'

'Something like that.'

'Thanks.'

'Sorry.' He was silent for perhaps ten seconds. 'To be honest, I've got things on my mind.'

'Who hasn't?' she said, but she rolled over to face him again. 'Do you want to talk about it?'

'Do you mind?'

She stretched languidly, then made a V on the pillow with her arm and propped her head on her hand. 'Go ahead,' she said. 'You talk, I'll listen.'

Ralph shuffled down in the bed and kissed her right breast.

'If that's the kind of talking you've got in mind, then forget it. I'm too tired,' she said, not unkindly.

Ralph emerged from beneath the covers and kissed her on the lips. 'No,' he said, 'it's not that. I was just thinking . . .'

'What?'

'Well, how long do you see us staying here? We should really be getting home, you know.'

Diane reached out and stroked her husband's hair as if it were a cat. 'I know it,' she said, 'but Ellen needs us right now. We can't just walk out on her.'

'Our children need us too,' said Ralph. 'It's Christmas in five days. We can't let them down.'

'I know that, Ralph, but . . . well, it's a tough situation.'

'What does that mean?'

'It means . . . oh, I don't know . . . that we should give it another day or two before making a decision.'

'But there are things to do, Diane. You know what Christmas is like. We can't leave everything until the last minute.'

'What Ellen's going through is more important. The kids will understand.'

'I don't want them to have to understand. I think we should talk to Ellen, make *her* understand. We can always come back in a week or so.'

'A week's a long time, Ralph. I'd feel bad leaving her on her own.'

'Well, let's suggest that she and the girls come back with us then. But I want a proper Christmas, for Kim's sake more than anything. I don't see why we should have to suffer too.'

'That's a really shitty attitude, you know, really selfish.'

'Well, I'm sorry, but that's the way I feel. Sometimes you have to be selfish, otherwise people just walk all over you.'

There was a short, simmering silence, and then Diane said, 'Okay, but you tell her.'

'I will. I'll ask her if she wants to come back and celebrate Christmas with us, and if she doesn't, well then, that's her choice.'

Diane turned her back on him, yanking the bedclothes over her shoulder. 'Is that all you wanted to talk about?'

'Well, yes, really.'

'Okay then. Goodnight.'

'Night,' said Ralph. He lay on his back and listened to his wife's quick breathing become slower, deeper, more relaxed. It took a long time, and it wasn't until he was sure she was asleep that he felt able to close his own eyes. However sleep still eluded him, and so eventually he got out of bed, got dressed and went downstairs.

By the time Jane padded downstairs in her Snoopy nightshirt, clutching the cuddly owl called Oliver that she had previously been growing out of, Ralph had made himself a bacon sandwich which he felt he deserved, and was currently drinking his third cup of coffee whilst working out a list of things that might help in finding David. He was writing the list to assuage the guilt that he assured himself he shouldn't really be feeling.

Jane walked into the kitchen on the balls of her feet, blinking sleepily. 'Hello, Uncle Ralph,' she said, and plonked herself down on the chair beside him.

'Hello, sweetie,' said Ralph. He gave the girl a brief hug

and kissed the top of her blonde tousled head. 'Did you sleep okay?'

'I had nasty dreams.'

'Oh dear. What about?'

'I can't remember. People were shouting and hurting each other. They weren't very nice.'

'Well, that won't do, will it?' said Ralph. 'Would it make you feel better if I made you some breakfast?'

'Can I have a bacon sandwich like you?'

'Course you can. How many slices?'

'What of? Bread or bacon?'

'Both.'

She considered the question carefully and then, with absolute certainty, said, 'Three.'

'Three it is,' said Ralph, smiling. He got up and walked over to the grill. As he peeled away three slices of bacon, he said, 'Aren't your feet cold?'

Jane's toes were curled over. Now she flexed them. 'A bit,' she admitted.

'Haven't you got any slippers?'

'Upstairs.' She shuffled over to Ralph's seat and looked at the pad he had been writing on. 'What's this?' she asked.

Ralph considered lying or changing the subject, but then decided that there wasn't much point. 'It's a list of things I've thought of that might help us to find Daddy,' he said.

'Oh.' She was silent for a few moments. Ralph glanced at her and saw that she was deep in thought about something. Eventually, guardedly, she asked, 'Uncle Ralph?'

'Yes?'

'Why did Daddy go away?'

Ralph placed the bacon on the sheet of tin foil on the grill and turned it on. 'Didn't Aunty Diane explain all that last night?'

'Well, ye–es, but . . .' She screwed up her nose.

'What did Aunty Diane tell you?' he asked her.

Jane had been so distressed by her mother's behaviour last night that it had seemed kinder to explain to the girls exactly what was going on. Rachel, of course, had guessed by this time that her father had run out on them, though having it confirmed had still hit her hard. However, after the initial tears, after Jane had been taken up to bed by Ralph and was being read a story by him until Rachel came up to keep her company, Diane had filled Rachel in on all the details that they knew. After this, Rachel's reaction had been one of puzzlement, and even guarded optimism.

'So Dad did say he was going to come back?' she said, trying not to sound too eager.

'Well . . . he intimated it. But he didn't say when,' Diane replied cautiously.

'I'm sure he'll come back,' Rachel said. 'He just has to sort himself out, that's all.'

'That's what we're all hoping, honey.'

'Next time he rings, can I speak to him?'

'What for?'

'I just want to talk to him, tell him that . . . that I understand, and that we love him and we want him to come back.'

Diane felt her throat getting tight. It had been, and would continue to be, an emotional evening.

She made a couple of attempts to speak and eventually managed to say, 'Well, we don't know if he is going to ring again, but if he does, then sure, you can speak to him. You'd better ask your mum, but I don't think she'll mind. I'll talk to her for you.'

After this, Rachel had gone to bed not quite cheerfully but certainly feeling much better than anyone else. As Diane told Ralph later, in one of the quiet snatched moments when Ellen seemed to be coping enough to be left on her own, Rachel was at the age where she was too old to be frightened and upset simply because everyone else was, and too young to understand how complicated and uncertain the situation really was.

These thoughts scuttled through Ralph's head in a second or less as he waited for Jane's reply. He already knew the answer to his question – Diane had told him what she'd told the girls – but he wanted to hear it from Jane's point of view.

'She said Daddy had gone away to . . . to think about things. She said he had a lot to think about and that he needed some time on his own.'

'That's right, honey,' said Ralph.

'But why can't he stay here to think about things, Uncle Ralph? I could've helped him. I'm good at thinking.'

'I'm sure you are, sweetie, but the things Daddy has to think about are very complicated.'

'What are they?'

'I can't really say. They're so complicated even I can't explain them very well.'

Jane thought about that one for a few seconds and then said, 'Why couldn't Mummy help him, then?'

Despite himself Ralph was feeling a little trapped, a little on edge. 'I don't know,' he admitted, and turned to the grill pan to turn the spitting, shrinking bacon over with the tip of his finger.

'Is it going to take him a long time to think about things, Uncle Ralph?'

Ralph licked a smear of hot bacon fat from his finger and said, 'It might take him a little while, sweetie. We're not really sure.'

'But he will be back for Christmas, won't he?' Jane's voice had risen in alarm.

'We're hoping so,' said Ralph, but he must have betrayed himself with his face or his voice because she burst abruptly into tears.

'Hey, hey,' Ralph said softly, crossing to her, enfolding her thin body in his bulky embrace.

Jane buried her face in the hollow above his stomach. Her voice muffled by his sweater and her own tears, she wailed, 'I want Daddy to come back. I want Daddy to come back for Christmas.'

Ralph had not hated his best friend until that moment, but he hated him now, the emotion keen and ubiquitous as pain. His voice barely audible above the spitting meat on the grill, he said, 'Shh, don't cry, sweetie. Everything will be all right. Don't worry.'

'It won't be. It won't be all right.'

'It will. I promise. Your Aunty Diane and I have come here to make things better.'

'How?' sobbed Jane.

How indeed? thought Ralph. 'By helping to look for your daddy and bring him back,' he said.

Jane raised her head and looked at him. Her eyes were red, her cheeks shiny with tears. 'Will you bring him back for Christmas?'

'We'll try,' Ralph promised, and gave her an extra-tight squeeze. 'We'll try our very hardest.' Jane clung to him so tightly that Ralph had to say, when it seemed she never wanted to let him go, 'And now I'd better see to this bacon otherwise you'll be having a charcoal sandwich.'

27

Because that bitch, Violet Turner, had eluded him, Worthington had made Mary Pritchard suffer before devouring her. He'd taken small dainty bites, nibbled her away piece by piece. It was amazing, given her age, that she had managed to stay alive so long.

Worthington kept telling himself that the reason Violet had escaped was that he had been too complacent, but really he knew it was more than that. Despite his animis's restorative powers, and despite his public claims to the contrary, he was beginning to feel his age. A complete transformation now took a great deal of energy. There had been a time when he'd been able to transform and strike in about three seconds. Now, though, it took him a minute or so after transforming before he was able to move at anything faster than a snail's pace.

With Violet, he'd been banking on the fact that her fear and age, and her inactivity these past few years would have caused her animis to seize up like an engine in a disused car. It seemed at first that that was what might have happened, but then her animis had kicked in, good as new, and she'd managed to get away.

It was easier to change back. You just let go, like a weightlifter dropping a weight. The reversion was not exactly instantaneous, but it was very quick.

Nursing his rage, he had set fire to the house and then got out quickly. Despite the broken window, the din that that must have caused, no one challenged him, though a minute or so later, driving along, a police car had raced by him, its lights flashing, and had turned into the road that he'd just driven out of. Worthington, exhausted and angry, had then taken a wrong turning and got stuck in a long string of cars escaping from Leeds city centre. It had been light when he left Violet's house, though somewhat hazy, but by the time he finally cruised into a parking space opposite Fox's house and extinguished his lights, it was dark as midnight.

He watched Fox's house for a little while as he composed himself, then he got out of his car, walked across the road and up the drive and knocked on the front door. The woman who answered his knock was highly desirable, and distressed but trying not to show it, which made her more desirable still. He gave her a false name, and told her, when she asked him, that he wanted to see David about a business matter. She told him that she didn't know where David was and that she didn't know when he'd be back. Though he was angry, Worthington believed her.

Reluctantly, he had got back into his car and driven away. He stopped at the first phone box he came to and called Mathilde. He hated having to confess his failure to that fat hippy drop-out, even though he knew she would not admonish him for his lack of success, that she had no authority to do so.

He was not altogether surprised to discover that Mathilde already knew about his failure. The boy had slipped into another fugue state and informed her that Fox was on his way to London. To his annoyance, Worthington's suggestion that he follow Fox, continue his pursuit of the man into the capital, was knocked back. Contingency plans were already in operation, Mathilde informed him smugly. Worthington couldn't help feeling he'd been snubbed until she gave him new instructions and he decided he liked these a whole lot better than the old ones.

The only drawback was that they'd sent Bernard to assist him. Bernard was like a little kid who had never grown up. Some, generally the more spineless of the Flux's members in Worthington's opinion, saw this as a positive and appealing quality in Bernard, an intense sensitivity, an empathic awareness of his environment. Worthington, however, regarded the guy as a pathetic wimp, no more, no less. Added to which, he was as thick as a brick shithouse, which made him a liability. What the hell he thought he was doing dressing up like a burglar in a 'Carry On' film and skulking around in the bushes in the Foxes' garden and almost getting caught, Worthington had no idea. He'd got so annoyed about that he'd slapped Bernard across the face and knocked him down. Bernard had crawled into a corner, whimpering like a kicked dog and had sat there for the rest of the evening, watching him with those big brown cow-eyes of his, bony knees drawn up, hand pressed over the slap-mark as if trying it for size.

Since then the two of them had communicated only when they had to. Bernard had spent most of his time reading in his room, or mooching around looking bored, or watching TV and bemoaning the fact that the late Mrs Pritchard did not have a video recorder on which he could play his 'Doctor Who' videos, a batch of which had taken up most of the space in his rucksack.

Three days Worthington had been cooped up here now waiting for the go-ahead. Two of them he'd had to endure with Bernard, who had arrived on Friday morning. The old woman had not had many phone calls – just two or three – since Worthington had been here, and only one person had come to the door who hadn't been readily identifiable as a milkman or a meter reader, and that had been an elderly man in a hat and a brown coat who had stood around for ages, peering up at the house as though inspecting the guttering, before leaving. Nevertheless, if things dragged on much longer, chances were that somebody, a neighbour or a friend or a relative, would start to get worried or suspicious. All it might take for the police to turn up on the doorstep was for a doting son or daughter to try ringing a mother who was generally in the house all day. For this reason, Worthington was very, very uptight. If he didn't get the word soon, he was going to have to take the initiative and damn the consequences. After all, whatever happened it was all part of the pattern. That much was unquestionable.

It was now Sunday morning. Worthington was in his normal place in the attic room, watching the Foxes' house across the road through a pair of binoculars, when the phone began to ring for the fourth time that weekend.

Immediately his head snapped up, like a deer sensing danger on the air. His tongue flickered out to moisten his lips as he heard the phone ring once, twice, three times. Then the phone cut off and there was a pause of perhaps ten seconds before it started ringing again. It was the signal he'd been waiting for. Worthington dropped the binoculars and ran for the attic stairs, his footsteps echoing in the dusty carpetless room.

He entered the hallway to find Bernard reaching out for the phone. 'Don't touch that!' he barked. Bernard shrank back, pulling clenched fists up under his chin as if afraid Worthington might chop off his hands as a punishment. Worthington shot Bernard a contemptuous look before snatching up the phone.

'Worthington,' he snapped, and then he listened for a few moments, his frown deepening. 'That's all we need,' he said finally.

He listened some more and then he said, 'So what are we supposed to do in the meantime? Sit here and twiddle our thumbs?'

He listened to the jabbering, confused, emotional voice on the other end, and then he said, 'For God's sake, pull yourself together. The kid wasn't important. It's what happens now that we've got to think about.' He smiled savagely at the reaction he had provoked, and then said, 'No. To be honest, I couldn't care less. Listen, I'm going to go ahead with the plan. It's getting too dangerous to wait any longer.'

Worthington was aware that Bernard was watching him, trying to be as covert as possible when standing only six feet away. He felt a renewed stab of contempt for the boy (hardly that at twenty-five, but Worthington couldn't think of him as a man), whose hands were intertwining ceaselessly. Bernard looked a mess, his dark hair long and tousled, his limbs thin and white, his Cyberman t-shirt stained with baked bean juice. As Worthington caught his eye, Bernard's gaze skittered away, his unshaven cheek twitching. Worthington was going to enjoy telling him about the boy. He knew how fond Bernard was of children.

'Well, what would *you* suggest?' he said sarcastically into the mouthpiece. He listened to the answer. 'Exactly. Which is why I'm going ahead.'

He put the phone down without saying goodbye, and turned to Bernard. 'The boy's dead. The oracle killed him yesterday morning. There's been no contact since so we might as well go ahead with the plan.'

He knew his bluntness would have an effect. Bernard looked almost comically upset. His bottom lip, rubbery and wet, drooped over his chinless jaw.

'Dead?' he said, his voice small and broken and a bit whiny. 'Oh no, not Danny.'

'Yes, Danny. For God's sake, you should know by now that the oracle never keeps them around for too long.'

'But . . . but he was only a little boy. I thought he'd be okay for a while. I was going to buy him some Dalek videos.'

Worthington reached Bernard in three strides and, without preamble, grabbed him round the neck with his right hand and shoved savagely. Bernard's eyes squeezed shut and his tongue popped out of his mouth as he stumbled backwards, his arms pinwheeling wildly for balance. His head struck the wall with a sound like a billiard ball hitting concrete, and from his throat came a noise a character in a comic might make: 'Gnn.'

'Don't be so pathetic!' Worthington snarled at him. 'The kid is dead. He's not important and he never was. He was dead the minute the oracle chose him. Cannon fodder, that's all.'

Bernard was curled up in a ball, groaning, both hands pressed to the back of his head. Worthington watched him contemptuously for a moment, then said, 'Get up. I don't want to waste any more time. I'll see you in the sitting room in two minutes.'

When Bernard staggered into the sitting room ninety seconds later, Worthington was sitting on Mary Pritchard's settee, looking relaxed and immaculate and distinguished as always. Bernard had one hand still pressed to the back of his head. He took it away now and showed it to Worthington. 'Look,' he said, 'blood.'

Worthington looked but was not impressed. 'So? We all have to bleed a little now and again.'

'You could have knocked me out or worse, then we wouldn't have been able to do this.'

'Oh, stop whining, you little shit. Come and sit down and we'll get started.'

Bernard pouted, looked momentarily as though he might have something more to say on the subject. Then he wiped his bloody fingers on his Cyberman t-shirt and complied with Worthington's request.

He sat at the other end of the settee from Worthington, leaving a big enough gap for a fat man to have squeezed between them. Worthington made a sound of exasperation, half-sigh, half-snarl. 'Closer. I want to see as well. Without me to guide you, you might as well have your eyes closed.'

Bernard swallowed and edged closer, though not so close that he and Worthington were actually touching.

'Do you have a mirror?' Worthington asked.

'Oh.' Bernard looked flustered. 'No. I'll . . . go and get one.'

'No need.' With a flourish, Worthington produced a small hand mirror from the inside breast pocket of his beautifully tailored grey jacket and handed it to Bernard.

'Thanks,' said Bernard, flushing at his own lack of foresight. He pushed his dark curly hair nervously out of his eyes, but the instant he released it, it just flopped back again.

He hunched over, getting comfortable, then took the mirror in both hands, his elbows resting on his knees to keep it steady, and gazed into it. A silence seemed to settle about the room, a motionlessness. Even the light rain falling outside seemed to make no sound.

The seconds ticked on, stretched into minutes, and Worthington began to get impatient. 'How long do we have to wait?' he muttered finally. 'I don't want to spend all morning looking at your ugly face.'

Bernard sighed and lowered the mirror, his concentration broken. 'I almost had it then,' he said almost petulantly. 'You'll have to keep quiet or I'll never get an image.'

'Trust you to have an ability that takes for ever to show itself,' Worthington complained.

'It works better when I'm not nervous,' Bernard said quietly.

He braced himself, uncertain how Worthington was going to react. It was the man's unpredictability that made him so terrifying. It was an unpredictability, however, that only embraced the more negative aspects of the personality. Worthington never did anything unexpectedly nice. He could either not react at all or he could fly into a violent rage at the slightest provocation.

This time Worthington just sighed and said, 'Oh, for God's sake, just get on with it.'

Bernard did his best to compose himself, taking air deeply into his lungs through his mouth and letting it out slowly, trying to open a channel into his animis. Unlike most members of the Flux, Bernard could not just turn his ability on and off whenever he felt like it. He had to get himself into a certain state of mind, had to feel relaxed. His system just seemed to seize up when he felt even the slightest bit stressed.

Having Worthington sitting beside him, gawping over his shoulder, and sensing the man's disdain and impatience, was not therefore an ideal situation for Bernard. He held up the mirror and stared hard into it, trying to pretend he was alone, trying not to smell Worthington's expensive aftershave. It was hard and it took a long time, but at last, little by little, he felt that he was slipping deeper inside himself, drawing his animis out. It was a sublime feeling, like his idea of how an orgasm should be. By now he was sweating; time had become meaningless. He clenched his teeth between parted lips and gasped, as if in ecstasy or pain.

'It's coming,' Worthington hissed, and in that moment he sounded like a doctor urging a mother who was giving birth. Worthington's voice was a minor distraction at this stage but nothing more. Bernard had control of the situation now. It would take a great deal more than a few whispers to sever the connection. His reflection in the mirror was blurring, becoming insubstantial as the face of a ghost. His eyes, dark blots, were the last to go, but eventually even they were swallowed up by the swirling grey stuff that had crept in from the edge of the mirror and which resembled not so much smoke or mist but colourless lava.

Excruciatingly slowly, a picture began to form in the

glass. Like a polaroid exposed to the light, it started as a series of indiscernible shadows, of flecks and dots, vague blobs of colour. Worthington leaned forward, narrowing his eyes as if that would make the picture clearer. It took two or three minutes for the shapes to form into something recognisable.

'It's a room,' he breathed. He could make out a carpeted floor, walls with pictures on, a table against the wall, various hazy objects jumbled on it. As if reacting to his voice, the picture suddenly became sharper, and Worthington saw that it wasn't a room, not really.

'No,' he said, 'it's a hallway.' The objects on the table were a telephone, an answering machine perched on a block of telephone books, a jar of pens and a pad, a cactus in a pot and a pile of unopened letters.

There were doors leading off from the hallway, and the edge of a wide staircase to the left. Looking into the mirror was like watching the film of someone exploring a house with a hand-held camera. The image in the mirror shifted as if the someone were veering left, towards the staircase. Then it was moving past the staircase, still panning left. A doorway loomed up, the door half-open.

Bernard, Worthington knew, was exploring the Foxes' house, assessing the lie of the land. Worthington watched as Bernard entered the doorway, and he saw in the mirror a sitting room where a big bespectacled man was sitting in an armchair reading the *Sunday Observer*. Bernard approached the man and leaned over him. His face loomed up large in the mirror. The man did not react, merely carried on reading his newspaper. His image receded as Bernard moved away.

There was a closed door leading off from the lounge. As Bernard approached it, it grew bigger, filling the mirror, and then it seemed to just melt away and the image that replaced it was that of a kitchen. Greasy breakfast plates were stacked by the sink, there was a half-empty pint of milk and a jar of coffee on the wooden table in the middle of the room. There were no people in the kitchen, however. Bernard moved back into the lounge, where the bespectacled man was now picking his nose, unaware that he was being watched.

Bernard went upstairs. The steps glided by in the mirror like an escalator. There were lots of doors here, made of pine which had been stripped and waxed. The carpet was oatmeal-coloured and the wallpaper was a tasteful and not too busy William Morris design.

The first room Bernard entered through its closed door was a bathroom. The room was wood-panelled to hip level, except around the bath where it was tiled in blue and white checks. Steam speckled the glass of framed pictures on the walls: lots of images of fish and some movie posters – *The Maltese Falcon*, *Brief Encounter*, and here was Humphrey Bogart and Ingrid Bergman in *Casablanca*, the poster so dog-eared in its frame that it might have been an original.

The steam was rising from the bath, in which a very attractive blonde-haired woman was reclining. Her eyes were closed, her hair was fanning out in the water, soapy bubbles frosted her large breasts which were breaking the surface. Worthington craned forward and murmured appreciatively, 'Very nice indeed. It's not often that one sees a natural blonde.' Bernard made no reply. Worthington glanced at him. Bernard's eyelids were flickering over a dull trance-like stare; saliva dribbled from the corner of his mouth, creating a slick wet trail to his weak sloping chin.

To Worthington's regret, Bernard's vision veered away from the naked woman in the bath, out of the bathroom and further along the landing. To the left was another doorway, the door ajar. Inside a woman was sitting up in a double bed, her back propped by a mass of pillows, sipping a cup of tea or coffee. Worthington recognised this woman; it was David Fox's wife. She looked a mess, tired and drawn with red puffy eyes. She was talking to a teenage girl, who was sitting cross-legged on the edge of the bed like a Buddha, leaning forward. The girl, wearing a baggy denim shirt and black leggings, was very pretty.

Worthington made an appreciative sound in his throat and a little smile of anticipation played about his lips. Even though her shirt was very baggy, he could see the points of her budding breasts pushing against the material. She looked so fresh and unsullied, so . . . ripe. Worthington was going to enjoy this assignment very much. Three such pretty captives as these promised endless hours of fun.

Bernard's gaze wavered away from the girl comforting her mother, back to the door of the room and out on to the landing. The next two rooms were empty – a small toilet and a study. The last on this landing, before the stairs corkscrewed higher, was full of toys and dolls, posters on the walls, a shelf of books with brightly coloured spines. This room belonged to a child, younger than the teenager who had been sitting on her mother's bed. However the camp bed, set at right angles to the more permanent wooden bed, suggested that not only the little girl was sleeping here at the moment. Worthington, who was a cruel man but not a stupid one, quickly deduced that David Fox's family had taken his departure rather hard. Fox's wife was upset because she thought her husband had run out on her. His daughters were both sleeping in the little girl's room either to keep one another company during this difficult time or because the teenage girl's room had been given over to the friends who had no doubt come running the instant the crisis broke.

The little girl whose room this was was sitting on the floor, one leg tucked beneath her, the other sticking straight out, toes pointing at the ceiling. She was engrossed in whatever she was drawing and colouring in on a large pad, her head bowed, blonde hair hanging like a curtain over her face. Different coloured felt tip pens were strewn around her on the carpet. The picture in the mirror tilted over the girl's shoulder, and Worthington saw that she was carefully colouring a lion's tongue pink, the pen making a squeaky scratching noise. The little girl's own tongue was stuck out as if in imitation of the lion.

'*Four* pretty captives,' Worthington murmured, feeling himself going all tingly inside. He gazed at the little girl's bare leg. Her flesh was so smooth and pink and plump, so delectable.

Bernard's gaze panned up, sweeping almost carelessly around the room. As it flashed across a poster on the wall, Worthington grabbed Bernard's arm and squeezed it. 'Stop!' he commanded.

Whether it was the authority in his voice or the pressure of his hand was uncertain, but his order certainly got through to Bernard. The image in the mirror juddered to a halt, came to rest on a wardrobe door.

'Go back,' Worthington hissed. 'Go back slowly.'

Bernard complied, the image in the mirror back-tracking, like a film running in reverse. When it came to the poster again, Worthington said, 'Stop.'

The image in the mirror stopped.

Worthington looked at the poster. It depicted four young men, their teeth impossibly white, their complexions faultless. Their haircuts were neat and trendy, as were their clothes, and they were all sickeningly good-looking. They were famous enough for even Worthington, who loathed pop music, to recognise the latest teeny-bop sensation. At the bottom of the poster, in big bouncy banana-yellow letters was their collective name: SMILE.

'There,' Worthington said through lips that had curled in a savage grin. 'That's the one.'

Bernard's eyes opened wide and his lips peeled back

245

over a hiss and a spray of spittle. It was an expression of such manic intensity that even Worthington almost shuddered.

28

Jane heard a noise behind her. She twisted round, supporting her weight with her left hand. It had been a funny noise, like the crackle a sweet wrapper makes when you scrunch it up. The noise had made her jump a bit, because despite turning to look she knew that it couldn't really have come from behind her. Behind her there was only the wall.

Nevertheless, she *had* turned, and now she wrinkled her nose and frowned, her heart beating a bit faster than usual. What had she expected to see? She wasn't sure. An insect perhaps, so big it clicked and crackled when it moved. Or, more likely as she thought about it, a poster peeling itself from the wall because its sellotape was so old it had lost its stickiness.

But she could see nothing. All her posters were in place and there was no giant insect. Unless . . . She scrambled to her feet, her left leg bristling with pins and needles. Unless the insect had dropped off the wall and behind her bookcase, and was now creeping up on her unseen.

In her hand, like a pitiful weapon, she held a green felt tip pen. Her drawing book was still open on the floor, the jungle scene she'd been doing half-coloured in. She'd enjoyed doing the lion and the monkey but she'd been getting a bit bored with doing the trees, and especially of colouring in all the leaves. She had been wondering whether to give it up for now and go and talk to Rachel and Mummy, even though Rachel had told her she wanted to talk to Mummy alone for a while, but now she knew she couldn't do anything until she'd found out what that noise was.

She took a step towards the bookcase and then stopped. For a few seconds she wavered with indecision. She didn't really want to look for the thing on her own. What if it was just waiting for her to get close enough so that it could scuttle up her leg or, even worse, leap at her face? She decided to go downstairs and get Uncle Ralph. She wished Daddy were here; if he had been, she'd have asked him. She remembered once when Daddy had caught a daddy-long-legs that had been ticking and buzzing around her light. She'd been having hysterics, but he'd just snatched it out of the air like a magician and tossed it out of the window.

Dropping her pen, she backed out of the room, then turned and jogged down the landing. Even now she hunched her shoulders together, half-afraid that the thing might take a giant flying leap at her back. She slowed momentarily by her mother's door, from behind which she heard the soft murmur of voices. The sound was soothing but it also made her feel a bit lonely, a bit left out. From behind the bathroom door, where Aunty Diane was having a bath, she heard the lap of water.

Uncle Ralph looked up from his newspaper, smiling as always, when she entered the room. 'Hello, sweetie,' he said. 'What's happening?'

'Uncle Ralph,' she said, 'will you come upstairs? I think there's a big spider in my room.'

He closed his newspaper, folded it and put it on the arm of the chair. Pulling a face, he said, 'Urgh, we can't have that, can we? Whereabouts is it?'

'On my wall. But then it dropped behind the bookcase.'

He stood up, placed a reassuring hand on her shoulder. 'How big is it?' he asked.

'I don't know,' she said. 'I haven't seen it. I only heard it.'

He was escorting her out of the room, but now he faltered momentarily. 'Heard it? How do you know it was a spider?' he said.

Perhaps a little unkindly she thought, Daddy wouldn't have asked questions, he'd have just gone up there and dealt with it. 'I heard it walking,' she said, and as she said it she felt suddenly convinced that that was what she *had* heard, 'I heard its legs moving.'

Uncle Ralph raised his eyebrows, but he said, 'Okay. Well, let's go and see, shall we?' He strode upstairs, Jane behind him.

In her room he looked enormous as a giant. Despite his size he was not a clumsy man, but Jane imagined him clumping across the floor, oblivious to what lay beneath his feet, stamping on felt tip pens which would split and burst like stick insects, ingraining the carpet with rainbow blood. To prevent this happening, she slipped past him and gathered up her pens and drawing book, keeping a watchful eye out for the big spider she now felt certain was in here somewhere. Arms laden, she took two quick steps and then leaped on to her bed. For the split-second that she was in the air she was terrified that the creature was going to emerge from beneath the bed and pounce, attaching itself to her flailing leg.

It didn't. The creaking bed-springs seemed to echo her gasps of relief. Uncle Ralph looked around the room, up at the walls even though she had already told him that it had fallen behind the bookcase. 'Whereabouts did you hear it?' he said.

She pointed to his feet. 'That's where I was sitting, and then I heard it on the wall and then I think it dropped behind the bookcase.'

He cleared his throat and moved over to the bookcase. He loomed over it, put his head to the wall and closed one eye, trying to peer behind the bookcase without touching it. 'I can't see anything,' he said. 'I'm going to have to pull it away from the wall. Shout if you see anything moving.'

Jane nodded dumbly, her eyes wide and fearful. Uncle Ralph braced himself, then took hold of the top of the bookcase with both hands. He lifted it away from the wall and set it down, his cheeks turning red with the effort. Jane gasped, and Uncle Ralph said quickly, 'What can you see?'

Jane thought it had been the spider, but it was only a shadow. 'Nothing,' she admitted.

Uncle Ralph rolled his eyes, but good-humouredly. 'You'll have me as jumpy as you soon,' he said.

Carefully he got down on his hands and knees and stuck his head into the gap behind the bookcase. Jane tensed, half-expecting him to suddenly scream and emerge into the light, the spider clamped to his face like that thing in *Alien*, pictures of which Jason Darlington had brought to school. He didn't scream though, he just shuffled around for a bit, and eventually in a slightly muffled voice he said, 'I can't see anything.'

Jane felt herself relax a fraction, but then he said, 'Hang on a minute, there *is* something.'

His head emerged, his face flushed, hair a bit tousled. He shifted position slightly so that he could reach into the gap with his arm. He pawed around for a few seconds, eyes narrowed as if he was seeing with his fingers.

'What is it?' Jane asked in a hushed voice.

'Aha,' he said and pulled his arm out. He held out what he had found between his thumb and index finger. 'A 2p coin,' he said, and flipped it towards her. Jane flinched back instinctively and the coin landed beside her on the bed. It was coated in a layer of sticky dust.

Uncle Ralph clambered to his feet as she picked up the coin and rubbed a thumb across it. 'Well,' he said, 'if there was a spider, it's not there now.' Jane examined the pad of her thumb, to which the dust had adhered in a blue-grey crescent. Uncle Ralph began, 'What exactly was it that –'

and there he stopped.

There was something in the wardrobe.

Jane and Uncle Ralph looked at each other. It was evident to each of them that the other had heard it. From the wardrobe had come a kind of shuffling scrape and then a bump as if something was moving around, trying to get comfortable. Whatever had made the sound, it was a damn sight bigger than a spider.

Jane hugged her colouring book to her chest as though it were a shield. Her hand, white-knuckled, was still gripping her felt tip pens, a multi-coloured bouquet of stalks without flowers. 'What was that, Uncle Ralph?' she whispered.

He tried to look calm and casual, but Jane could see he was only pretending. 'I don't know,' he murmured. 'Let's have a look, shall we?'

He looked around as though all at once he'd forgotten where the wardrobe was, then when he lifted Jane's hockey stick from the corner where it had been propped, she realised he'd been looking for a weapon and that made her more scared than ever.

He walked back to the wardrobe and put his hand on the door. Before pulling it open, he glanced back at Jane and raised his eyebrows as though there was really nothing to worry about. She was so scared she could barely breathe, never mind smile. She couldn't even begin to guess what terrible thing might be in the wardrobe. As Uncle Ralph hefted the hockey stick in his hand and began to pull the door open, Jane's eyes flickered almost unconsciously to his left, where she suddenly noticed something very strange indeed.

Her eyes had returned there, she realised now, because she'd noticed it before but had been so taken up with the spider that it hadn't really registered. The strange thing was this: her poster of SMILE now no longer depicted the members of the band. Above the banana-yellow letters was now simply a shimmery blue background, like a distorted mirror.

She opened her mouth to speak, to cry out, to do something, but she was too late. Uncle Ralph had now pulled the wardrobe door open. She saw Donny first, his dark hair and eyebrows, his tanned complexion, his big heart-melting grin. Almost before Uncle Ralph could even show his surprise, Donny stepped out of the wardrobe and punched Uncle Ralph right in the face, smashing his glasses.

Uncle Ralph dropped the hockey stick and started to stagger backwards, slivers of broken glass falling out of his eyes like shattered light. Before he could fall against anything and make a noise, Donny grabbed him by the front of his sweater and yanked him forwards as if to kiss him. Donny didn't kiss him though; he head-butted him in the face. Uncle Ralph was twice as big as Donny, but Donny seemed ten times as strong. Making a sort of snorting noise, like a pig asleep, Uncle Ralph slid to the floor.

Jane was unable to make any kind of sound until she saw the mask of blood that Uncle Ralph's face had become. Red bubbles were oozing slowly from his mashed nose; his eyes were closed but all around them slick-red shards of glass were sticking out of his skin like strange stubble. The twisted frames of his spectacles still clung to his face like a weird insect, or the skeleton of one. Donny moved smoothly towards her, still grinning. There was not a mark on his face.

She felt the piercing scream rising up through her and opened her mouth to let it out. Before she could do so a hand, tight as a clamp and smelling of nothing, slid round her face from behind and blocked its release. There had been something under her bed, after all; it had been Marc, Smile's drummer. He yanked her head back against his chest so she was looking up at him. He was smiling too.

He had long bleached hair and was wearing eye-liner.

Lee and Kris, the other two members of Smile, came out of the wardrobe behind Donny. Coat hangers jangled as they did so, but still it must have been a terrible crush in there.

The scream was still there inside Jane, wanting to come out. Worse, it seemed to be building up and up, and if she didn't release it soon, she felt she might burst. She began to wriggle, but Marc's hand just tightened over her mouth and his other arm came round her body and held her still. He was so strong he seemed as if he was made of steel rather than flesh and blood. The arm across her chest, holding her arms to her sides, was solid as a safety bar on a funfair ride.

Donny, Lee and Kris filed from the room, grins still fixed to their faces. Marc lifted Jane up as if she was hollow and followed them, carrying her. She closed her eyes as he stepped over Uncle Ralph, who was leaking blood into her carpet and whose breathing sounded like shifting sludge. Tears squeezed out from behind her eyes and blurred her vision. She blinked them away in time to see Donny and Kris stop by her mother's bedroom door, Lee walk on a little further and then stop by the bathroom door.

Never for one instant did Jane think that this was the real Smile. She'd seen the real Smile interviewed by Phillip Schofield on 'Going Live', and they were dead nice and friendly and into conservation and Children In Need and things like that. She did not find it hard to accept that this Smile, the Smile who had punched Uncle Ralph's face in and who now held her captive, were not human. She'd seen the evidence with her own eyes, was still seeing it. This Smile had climbed out of her poster. They had fixed grins like wax dummies, and eyes that were flat and glossy, like magazine paper.

She didn't know how or why her poster had come alive,

and neither did she know why these monsters who looked like her favourite pop group were being so horrible. They didn't speak or even look at each other, they didn't communicate at all. Yet Donny, Kris and Lee all stepped forward at exactly the same time, raising their arms, and threw themselves at the doors they were standing in front of.

The bathroom door flew open as if hit by a car, the bolt on the inside useless as plasticine. The door to Mummy's bedroom, attacked by both Donny *and* Kris, tore right off its hinges and flew inwards as if a bomb had gone off beside it. The noise was tremendous, but over very quickly. The three Smile monsters strode into the respective rooms. When the doors had burst open, Jane had heard all three women scream. Now she heard Mummy's panicked shriek, 'Who are you?', and Aunty Diane's rather more abrasive, 'What the hell's going on here? Get out of here, you –' before her voice abruptly cut off.

Jane squirmed as much as she could, panic-stricken by the thought of what terrible things might be happening in those rooms, of Mummy and Rachel and Aunty Diane being hurt. She tried to bite the hand clamped over her mouth but it was no use. She could hear struggles and half-smothered cries, but that was all.

Marc, who had been standing motionless outside her bedroom at the end of the corridor, now began to walk forward again as if in response to some unspoken command. As he neared Mummy's room, from which Jane could hear only silence now, she could feel her panic growing inside her, thumping with a red juicy rhythm in her head. Her heart was pounding frantically, her chest heaving. She could hardly breathe; her nostrils seemed unable to draw in the amount of air she felt she needed. She wanted desperately to open her mouth, to gulp at the air, but Marc's hand was still clamped over the bottom half of her face. She felt sure she was going to suffocate or faint; black stars were pricking her vision. She did her very best to blink them away as Marc came level with Mummy's bedroom.

He walked straight past but she caught a one-second glimpse of what was happening in there. Donny had his hand on the back of Mummy's neck and was pushing her face into the pillow, and Kris was doing the same to Rachel. Rachel was limp, but Mummy was still struggling feebly. Donny and Kris were not finding it a strain to hold Mummy and Rachel down. They were doing it effortlessly, and as usual their expressions were fixed, their grins unchanged.

Jane was still trying to cope with the awful freezing shock of seeing her mother and sister being casually suffocated when Marc walked past the bathroom door and she saw what was happening in there too. Lee was sitting on the edge of the bath, holding Aunty Diane's head under the water with one hand, whereas his other hand was encircling both her ankles and holding her feet clear of the water. Jane realised this must be to prevent Aunty Diane getting her feet entangled in the plug chain and pulling the plug out. Aunty Diane was splashing and convulsing, but not much; her arms were waving ineffectually as if she couldn't control them any more. Lee, of course, was sitting motionless, grinning vacantly at Humphrey Bogart who was speckled with condensation. Tendrils of steam curled about the room and drifted out of the door, performing slow and ghostly acrobatics.

Marc started to carry Jane downstairs. She saw the hallway below her, jolting closer, the banister rails lurching by on her left. But then the hallway began to recede, to disappear down a long dark tunnel, and all the sounds she could hear lost their sharpness, became fuzzy and distorted and meaningless. Fizzy black shapes seethed across her vision. She felt herself spiralling down and down. She felt horribly sick; her heart was crashing inside her like waves in a thunderstorm. She struggled desperately to stay afloat but then the silent shriek of her panic torpedoed up through the dark water and swallowed her whole.

3

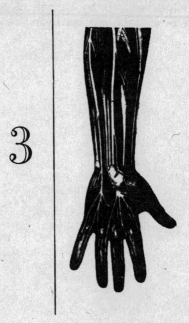

Legion Street

29

Mabel Kerslake's concern for her husband was tempered by her frustration at his secretiveness. He had always been the same, keeping things to himself, refusing to show his true feelings, but rather than getting used to it over the years, his emotional impotence infuriated her more now than ever before. The reason for this, she supposed, was that she had once believed that as the years passed he would mellow, open up to her, learn to trust her. The fact that he hadn't felt almost like a betrayal. Though she loved him deeply, she didn't feel she knew him very well.

Even when their six-year-old son, Thomas, had died of hepatitis some forty years before, Derek had failed to display any outward signs of grief. Colleagues of his had been weeping at the funeral, but Derek had stood almost to attention at the graveside, staring defiantly into space, maintaining his stiff upper lip.

And then there had been that strange period after he had retired from the force, completely out of the blue, at the age of forty-three. They'd suffered financially because of that, but Derek had been so well respected that a few strings had been pulled and they had managed to come out of it better than they deserved. It had been an astonishing decision for Derek to make, but the only reason he would give her for having made it was that he had had enough of policing, he wanted to get out. Mabel had known there was more to it than that, but Derek had adamantly refused to discuss the matter. On one occasion he had even got so angry with her constant questioning that he had punched a dent in the kitchen wall, which wasn't like him at all. That had been a very strange and unsettling year; though Derek had frequently insisted that nothing was wrong, he had been constantly on edge – unable to sleep, picking at his food, glancing out of the window whenever he thought she wasn't looking.

All sorts of things had gone through her mind at the time: Derek was having a nervous breakdown; he'd been involved in something shady and quietly removed himself to avoid a public scandal; one of the cases he was working on had upset him badly; some criminal or other had made threats against him.

One by one she had considered these possibilities, and one by one had rejected them. Though emotionally stunted, Derek was a rock; he was simply not the sort of man who would have a breakdown of any kind. There was no question of him having been involved in anything the slightest bit suspect either; he was whiter than white, his morals impeccable. And as for having been driven out by a case he was working on, or by a criminal making threats against him, well, that was downright ludicrous. Derek had been involved in all sorts of grisly things in his time, and had met all sorts of awful people, and he had never taken any of it to heart before. He'd been involved, for instance, in the tracking down of Lawson Gallagher, that dreadful man who gassed his lodgers and ate parts of them and kept what was left underneath the floorboards. 'All part and parcel of the job,' he would say matter-of-factly when she remarked how terrible it must be for him, dealing with such things on a day-to-day basis.

Besides, as far as she could recall, his final case had been nothing out of the ordinary: a missing persons case in North London, a mother and son who were never found. If she remembered rightly, the husband had been suspected of murdering them, but nothing had ever been proven and no charges ever brought against him.

Though she had felt guilty about doing so, Mabel had gone behind Derek's back and spoken to some of his colleagues about his behaviour and his decision. But nothing they told her had shed any light on the matter; they had genuinely been as perplexed as she was.

All in all, it had been a disquieting and bewildering episode from the past which she had no wish to re-experience. The only problem was, when Derek had come back into the house that morning, having spoken on the doorstep to whoever had rung the bell and set Barney off, the look on his face had brought all those dreadful old memories flooding back.

'Who was that?' she called from the kitchen when she heard the front door slam. She guessed it must have been someone annoying, perhaps a zealot peddling religion, because Derek was not normally a man who slammed doors.

She heard his footsteps coming down the hallway, but they stopped short of the kitchen, turning instead into the sitting room. 'Derek, who *was* that?' she called again. No reply. She tutted and addressed Barney, who was prancing restlessly by her left leg, urging her with his eyes to drop a morsel of food his way.

'Your dad gets deafer by the day. He'll soon be as deaf as a doorpost, won't he?' she said.

Barney whined and salivated to demonstrate how hungry he was.

'Yes, he will,' she answered herself. 'Let's go and ask him if he wants some tea, shall we?'

She came out of the kitchen and bustled along the hallway, Barney skipping at her heels like the puppy he hadn't been for a long time. The sitting room door was ajar, which was another of Derek's annoying little habits. Mabel was for ever telling him to close doors and keep the heat in.

Today, however, she wasn't in the mood for arguments,

not on the Sunday before Christmas, with a warm fire blazing, a roast in the oven and Gregory Peck on the telly this afternoon. As she reached out a hand to push the door all the way open, she was saying, 'I've made some tea, dear. Oh, and I saw that squirrel in the back garden again this morning. I'm getting a bit worried about him. If he doesn't hibernate soon, he might – Derek, whatever's the matter?'

Derek was curled up in his favourite armchair, looking as pale as the cotton wool snowman that little Emily from two doors down had made for Mabel at school. He was clutching his midriff as if he had the most dreadful stomach ache, and just for an instant, Mabel, who at sixty-six was sixteen years younger than her husband, thought that this was it, the moment she had been dreading all her married life.

Then, at the sight of her, Derek seemed to recover a little. His hands, long and white, the skin almost translucent, grabbed the arms of his chair and he pushed himself a little more upright in his seat. He cleared his throat and said unconvincingly, 'Nothing's the matter. I'm fine.'

'You don't *look* fine,' said Mabel firmly. 'You look ill. You're terribly pale.'

'I'm *fine*,' Derek repeated irritably. 'It's just the cold, that's all. It's bitter out there. I'll be all right when I've warmed up.'

Mabel was not convinced. 'You look as if you've seen a ghost,' she said. 'The cold doesn't do that to you. If anything it brings the blood to the surface, puts a bit of colour into your cheeks.'

Derek scowled. 'Oh, for God's sake, stop fussing, woman. I've told you, I'm perfectly all right.'

'You haven't got any pains in your chest?'

'Of course not.'

She sighed and decided to try a different tack. 'Who was

that at the door?'

It was odd the way Derek looked away from her, somehow furtive. 'Nobody,' he muttered.

'Oh, I suppose it was just the wind knocking, was it?'

He scowled again, his eyebrows bristling. 'It was just a salesman,' he said.

'What was he selling?'

'Does it matter?'

'Probably not. I'm just curious, that's all.'

'Oh . . . I don't know. Brushes or something.'

'On a Sunday?'

'Well . . . perhaps he wanted to make a bit of extra for Christmas.' Then another thought occurred to him and he clutched at it eagerly. 'Anyway, Sunday's the day when you're most likely to catch people in, isn't it?'

For an ex-policeman who should have been used to questioning techniques, Derek didn't lie very well. However, by the same token he didn't crack either. If Derek wanted to keep something to himself, then he would do so, and no amount of pestering would wheedle it from him, however unconvincing his story.

Barney wandered over, wagging his tail, and began to sniff at Derek's knee. Mabel watched her husband fussing over the dog, playing gently with Barney's soft ears, stroking his sleek black head. Despite the fire and the roast, their old artificial but much-loved Christmas tree twinkling away in the corner, the prospect of Gregory Peck on the telly, the day had been spoiled for her now. She was anxious without really knowing why; she knew Derek had been upset in some way, but she couldn't think by whom or what it might have been about. She wished she'd answered the door; then at least the threat, if there was one, would not have been so faceless. *Could* it have simply been a salesman that had upset him? Someone young and bolshy and aggressive, someone who'd intimidated him, made him feel old? She couldn't really believe that, and yet she wanted to, she wanted to believe it was that simple. She watched him stroking Barney for a bit longer, his hands still trembling on the dog's fur, his eyes avoiding contact with hers. Finally she said, 'Well, if you're sure you're all right, I'll make us that cup of tea, then I'll get on with the dinner.'

He looked up at her now and managed to muster a smile. 'I'm fine, love,' he assured her.

'All right then,' she said, and left the room.

Ten minutes later she was checking the meat in the oven when the sound of the doorbell drilled through the house for the second time that morning. Hastily she closed the oven door and peeled off her oven gloves as she crossed the linoleum. 'I'll get it,' she called, and almost ran down the hallway before Derek could respond. When she reached the front door she was breathless, her heart going nineteen to the dozen. She opened the door and shivered as a sheet of freezing cold air billowed over her.

The man on the doorstep was small and old and scruffy. When he saw her, his face, brown and wrinkled like old leather, creased into a yellow-toothed grin. He was wearing a blue serge suit and a tartan cap. A large gold loop pierced his left earlobe, dangling above a maroon birthmark which covered part of his jaw and the left side of his throat.

'Mrs Kerslake?' he said in a thick Glaswegian accent.

'Yes,' said Mabel Kerslake wearily, drawing herself in a little. However much she tried not to judge by appearances, she couldn't help thinking that this man looked like one of the drunks who staggered round Ipswich town centre on a Saturday afternoon, breathing fumes on people whom they asked for money.

'Ah wonder if ah can speak ti yer husband?'

'Well . . . I don't know. What about?' she said.

The little man chuckled vapour and glanced to his right as if he'd seen movement there. 'It's just a wee bit of unfinished business.'

'Unfinished business? From when?'

'Oh . . . a long time ago.'

Behind her, muffled by the closed door of the sitting room, Mabel could hear Barney barking again. All at once the barking increased in volume and she heard Derek say, 'Stay there, good lad.' She turned to see him closing the sitting room door, shutting Barney inside. He looked up, his expression unreadable, and began to shuffle towards her. 'Who's at the door?' he asked, his tone of voice making it sound as if he was frightened of the answer.

Before Mabel could say anything, the little man had slipped past her, into the house.

'Long time no see, Derek,' he said.

The effect on Derek was horrifying. His whole face seemed to gape – his mouth, his eyes – and he staggered backwards as if he'd been pushed. He raised his hands in a warding-off gesture, twisting his head aside like a baby refusing a mouthful of food. He was moaning something as he fell, his legs giving way like rotten splints. On his back, he drew in his limbs like an insect and tried to shuffle away.

'Derek!' Mabel screamed and flew to her husband. She lowered herself down beside him too quickly, pain flaring in both her knees. She reached for him and he flinched, then, realising who it was, groped for her and pulled her close. His grip on her arm was so tight it hurt more than her throbbing knees. She cradled his head and twisted to look at the little man.

'Who are you?' she demanded, her voice shrill. 'What do you want?'

The little man looked at her with an expression of guilty apology. He spread his hands as if that would prove he was harmless.

'Ah'm sorry,' he said, and sounded as if he meant it. 'Ah didnae want this. Ah just want ti talk.'

'*Who are you?*' she repeated, screaming the question at him. In the sitting room Barney was going mad, throwing himself against the door.

'Ma name's Willie McQueen. I knew yer husband a long time ago. I knew him when he left the force.'

Mabel was terrified, but she was also furious, more furious than she could ever remember being. It was only Derek's behaviour that was terrifying, and that was because she honestly believed he might die of fear, right here and now.

'Do you know *why* he left the force?' she spat at the little man.

'Oh aye,' he said.

'*Then tell me!*' she screamed. 'Tell me what's going on?'

'It's a long story,' said Willie firmly. 'I don't know if we've got time for it.'

Mabel glanced down at her husband. His eyes were squeezed tight and he was muttering words that she could not make out. Though he was not a Christian she thought he might be praying, exhorting a God he had never believed in to deliver him from this evil. She kissed his cold ancient face and looked up at Willie McQueen.

'Tell me,' she hissed.

30

The first thing that David did when he arrived back in London was to find the nearest pub and start drinking. Although after leaving Kerslake he needed a drink and felt he deserved one, he had the good sense to wait until he passed Newbury Park tube station before turning off the A12 and parking the car.

The pub he walked into was called The Regent. Cigarette smoke was so thick inside that it blurred and greyed outlines like fog. The ceiling was low, and inlaid with plastic beams that were trying their hardest to look like old wood. Four pot-bellied men were playing a raucous game of darts in the corner. A Sunday league football team, their hair still wet from the shower, their sports bags resting between their feet like obedient pets, were having an after-match drink and arguing about the game. In the time it took for David to cross the carpet to the bar, he gathered that the team had lost 5–2 and that the ref had been a wanker.

He ordered a pint of bitter with a whisky chaser and started to drink. The barman, red and plump and pink-eyed as though stuffed with blood, was friendly but not chatty. That suited David fine. He was happy to sit at the bar and drink and let the jabbering conversation of the footballers and the dart-players' gurgling laughter wash over him. His thoughts were a tangled knot again, and he wanted the opportunity just to sit on his own and pick them apart, or, failing that, to soak them with alcohol until they drowned.

The smoke made his eyes sting, his chest grow tight. In one corner of the room, perched on a shelf, John Craven was talking to an old man from inside a television screen. David stared at the programme for a bit, but didn't really take in what was being said. It was a conservation programme, or something to do with country matters at any rate. John Craven was tramping round a lot of fields and woods wearing wellies and a thick jacket. His hair was much greyer than the last time David had seen him, but apart from that he didn't look much different. David had drunk three pints and was just downing his third whisky when the programme finished and the lunch-time news came on.

Just as it had been on the radio that morning, last night's shooting at the Casa Romana was the lead story. David felt a horrible rumbling chill in the pit of his stomach as coverage began. He didn't know what was worse, seeing people falling silent and twisting their heads towards the TV as some in the pub did, or seeing people ignoring the TV completely, carrying on talking and joking and laughing as though nothing had changed.

'The victims of last night's shooting at the Casa Romana restaurant in Central London have been named by police,' the newsreader began, his neutral tone and immaculate appearance seeming somehow inappropriate, even tasteless, to David. 'The middle-aged couple have been named as Mr Kenneth Drinkwater, a fifty-four-year-old art gallery owner, and his fifty-two-year-old wife, Lillian, who was a secretary at an East London primary school. The other victim was seventeen-year-old Amanda Murray, who was with her boyfriend, Vincent Latimer. The couple were at the restaurant celebrating Mr Latimer's eighteenth birthday when the gunman, who police named earlier as twenty-seven-year-old Dean Burgess, burst in at around 9:30 last night. This report from Larry Jensen.'

The picture changed to that of a thin pale-faced young

man with spiky brown hair. He was wearing a shirt and tie beneath an expensive-looking overcoat, and holding a microphone. It was evidently very cold; his eyes were watery, his nose was bright red and every time he spoke his breath emerged as a plume of vapour. Across the road could be seen the Casa Romana, its large front window like a gaping black mouth lined with jagged teeth of broken glass. The reporter, his face and voice grave, began to recount last night's events, telling David what he already knew. Behind him, police tape, closing off the area around the restaurant to the public, rippled and snapped in the wind like bunting left over from a carnival. David thought he could see a large dark stain on the pavement outside the restaurant, but he wasn't sure.

As the report wore on, David began to feel more and more as though memories he'd managed partly to suppress were blossoming like poisonous fungi in his mind. First there were the witnesses to the shooting, who looked as shell-shocked as he felt and who thankfully made no mention of a blond-haired man with a strange glowing bottle. Then there was a profile of the gunman, Dean Burgess, who was apparently all the normal things that psychotics are supposed to be. Over an array of mostly blurred photographs of Burgess at various stages of his short life, a verbal portrait was painted of an unemployed loner who had an obsessive interest in all things military and a large collection of pornographic material in his filthy one-room flat in Dagenham. He had lived with his widowed mother until the age of twenty-five, and had a previous conviction for indecent exposure. The tone of this profile infuriated and appalled David; it seemed somehow smug, reassuring, as though the media had moved in on this situation and diminished it with their slick neat theories, imposing order on a chaos they couldn't possibly comprehend.

After profiling Burgess, there was a profile of the

seventeen-year-old girl, Amanda Murray. Her smiling face filled the screen, and was then replaced by the haggard tear-stained face of her grandmother, who, in a broken voice, described her as a lovely girl who'd do anything for anybody, who liked to go dancing, who wanted to be a hairdresser. At this point, David slid from his stool and loped towards the toilet, his stomach cramping, the horror of his memories surging up through him like bile. The toilet door banged shut behind him, and he found himself in a small square room like a cell.

Three urinals, like giant shells, were attached to the wall. There were two sinks, a hand dryer, a condom machine and a single cubicle. David plunged at the cubicle and shoved the door open. The instant he saw the toilet he swooped towards it and vomited.

It was the third time he had vomited in twelve hours, and his stomach and throat felt scoured. He half-expected to see blood in the toilet bowl, but there was only the liquid he had drunk. The watery vomit stank of whisky. David wiped round the seat with toilet paper, his hand shaking. He dropped the paper into the bowl and pulled the chain, then lowered the seat cover and sank down, his head in his hands.

He felt awful, truly awful. He'd felt bad enough before, but after witnessing last night's shooting and coming close to being one of the victims, he couldn't shake off the feeling that beneath the surface of order and respectability the world was a rotten, evil place where nothing made sense. He remembered reading an article about how the witnesses to the massacre in Hungerford, where a man called Michael Ryan had gone berserk with a shotgun, were coping two or three years on. Many of them were still undergoing counselling, suffering from nightmares or nervous disorders. It was a while since he had read the article, but he thought he remembered reading that someone had even committed suicide, unable to cope with their terrible memories. David wondered whether he should seek help, at least the help of his family and friends if not professional advice, but how could he simply go home and admit that he needed it after all he had been through here, after coming so far? But then again, how far had he come, really? What, in all honesty, had he achieved? Things were happening to him of which he had no comprehension. He had come to London with a purpose, an objective, and though the mystery of the bottle intrigued him more and more, he also felt as though his life was now more out of control than ever.

He took a deep breath and sat up. His stomach and throat were sore, his head ached. He reached into his pocket and took out the bottle. Would things get less complicated if he smashed this, or left it here and walked away and never came back? He looked at the bottle for a while, and then he pressed it to his forehead, rolling it slowly back and forth across his sweaty skin. The bottle was cool, its texture soothing. He closed his eyes.

When he opened them again he felt calmer. The confusion was still there, and the guilt and shock and misery and anger and all the other stuff that filled his head nowadays, but David felt as though he could just about function again despite it. His headache had eased too. He expelled a long breath, then stood up and put the bottle in his pocket. Beyond the cubicle door he heard the toilet door squeal open, then bang shut.

It was only a small room, but the footsteps that he heard approaching the cubicle seemed to take a long time to do so. His throat seemed to pinch itself shut, his forehead to prickle, as he remembered a similar occasion in Leeds just a few days ago, days that now felt more like weeks. The footsteps stopped outside the cubicle. There was a pause and then the rap of knuckles on the wooden door. David didn't dare turn and look down at the gap beneath the door for fear of seeing a pair of shiny black shoes, grey school socks.

He tried to breathe without making a sound, tried to stand absolutely still. A man's voice with a heavy London accent said, 'You gonna be long in there, mate? I'm dying for a crap.'

David almost giggled, but managed to smother it by clearing his throat. 'No,' he said, 'won't be a minute.' He flushed the toilet again, unlocked the cubicle door and pulled it open.

'Cheers, mate,' said one of the footballers and slipped past him, into the cubicle.

David rinsed out his mouth and splashed some water on his face, then he left the toilet and the pub. Outside the air felt sharp and clean, and so cold that his first breath caused pain to flash through his head. Although he was over the limit he felt sober enough to drive back to the boarding house, and did so. The first thing that greeted him as he walked through the door was his landlady standing there with her arms folded.

She looked as if she'd adopted the stance earlier and had been waiting for him to come back ever since. Her lips were pursed, which emphasised the wrinkles around her mouth, and her grey brittle hair was pulled back in an untidy ponytail.

'Oh,' said David, 'hi,' and wondered whether he should mention the state of the bedding and the mattress before she did.

She, however, didn't mention the bedding at all. Instead she said, as though in disapproval, 'Mr Fox, there have been two phone calls for you this afternoon.'

'Phone calls?' said David, and only just managed to stop himself exclaiming, 'But nobody knows I'm here!' Instead he asked, 'Who from?'

'The caller didn't leave his name. It was a man, the same man both times.'

'Well . . . did he leave a number? Or a message?'

'He said he'd call back again later.'

'Oh. Right. Well . . . thanks. Thanks very much.' He smiled and started to trudge upstairs.

'There is one other thing, Mr Fox?'

David turned back. 'Yes.'

'Your rent. Are you intending to stay very much longer?'

David wrote a cheque for four more days. It would be Christmas Day on Friday. He couldn't bring himself to write a cheque to cover that too; the prospect of it was too depressing. He went upstairs, turned the TV on and flopped on to his bed. He lay back, staring at a live football match without really taking it in.

Who could have phoned him? A man, Mrs Macau had said. Had Ralph managed to track him down? David realised the prospect of that did not alarm him as much as he had thought it would. If Ralph *had* found him, had he told Ellen or did he plan to speak to David secretly first, find out what was going on? If that was the case, then he would tell Ralph everything, David decided.

But what if it wasn't Ralph? Who else could it be? The police? But they wouldn't phone, would they? They would come round and see him personally. Another possibility suddenly occurred to him, one that made him sit bolt upright and stare at his door like someone alone in a house who has heard strange noises outside. Could it have been Malcolm Marshall? All at once that seemed the most likely possibility of all. But Marshall lived close enough to come and see him personally too, didn't he? David did not find that thought particularly comforting.

He got up and locked his door, then lay back down on the bed. He felt restless now. He both wanted the phone to ring and he didn't. He stared at the football match, trying to focus his mind on the game. After a few minutes he did something he would have thought himself incapable of under the circumstances. He fell asleep.

'For you! For you! For you!' The cry, like a siren with a human voice, was accompanied by pounding. David was torn from the soft skin of sleep feeling raw and vulnerable and disorientated. His arm shot out and then pain lanced up it; his clenched fist had smashed against the wall. The pain roused him but he was still confused. He looked around, blinking, with no idea of where he was.

He half-fell off the bed, staggered to the door and pulled it open. Damien was gazing up at him with his dark glittering eyes. 'For you! For you!' he shrieked in David's face.

'What the hell do you want?' David growled.

'For you,' Damien repeated, lowering the decibel level only slightly.

'What is?' David snapped.

'Telephone!' Damien shrilled. 'Telephone! Telephone! Telephone!'

The significance of that took a moment to seep into David's brain, but when it did he suddenly felt wide-awake. His eyes opened as wide as the devil-child's and he muttered, 'Oh God, right.'

He plunged past the boy and clattered down the stairs. The telephone receiver was waiting for him, off the hook and lying on its back on the hall table. David snatched it up. 'Hello?' he said.

'Am I speaking to David Fox?'

'Yes. Who is this?'

'Never mind that. Just listen.'

'What do you mean? I –'

'Just listen, Mr Fox, or you will never see your wife and daughters again. That I can promise you.'

It was a line David had heard a million times on TV cop shows, but hearing it for real was not the slightest bit funny. He felt himself go cold all over.

'What do you want?' he said softly.

'The bottle, Mr Fox, that's all. The bottle in exchange

274

for your friends and family. I'm going to give you an address, Mr Fox. I want you to be there at nine o'clock tonight and I want you to bring the bottle with you. I want you to hand it over and then tomorrow morning your family and your friends will be released. It's as simple as that, Mr Fox. Do you understand what I've told you?'

David couldn't believe that this was happening. He said, 'You've kidnapped my family?'

The man sighed. 'Yes. And your two friends, Ralph and Diane Joyce.'

'How . . . I mean . . . how do I know you're telling the truth?'

'Oh dear, how tedious,' said the man. Then David heard him say, 'Bring Fox's wife over here.'

David listened hard but heard nothing. Then all at once, shockingly, he heard Ellen say, 'David? Is that you?'

'Ellen!' David cried. There was no response. 'Ellen!' he shouted.

'Don't draw attention to yourself, Mr Fox,' the man said. His voice was calm and cultured and mocking. 'If you do as I say, nobody will be hurt. Now, here's the address. Can you remember this?'

'Yes,' said David. He could think of nothing else to say. He wanted to scream and shout, but he was terrified that if he did so the man would hurt Ellen and the girls. He listened as the man told him the address, repeated it over and over to himself though he knew he would not forget it.

'Nine o'clock tonight,' the man repeated. 'You hand over the bottle and your family and friends will be released tomorrow morning.'

'Why not tonight?' said David, his voice wavering up and down the scale. 'Why can't you bring them with you?'

'Use your head, you fucking moron,' the man said wearily. 'It's to stop you informing the police, of course.'

'But . . . but how do I know you'll let them go? How do

275

I know?' David was trying to prevent himself from sobbing out the words, trying to keep his voice steady.

'You'll have to trust me, won't you?' the man said smugly, and put the phone down.

31

Jane watched the man with the white hair and moustache put his mobile phone back into his pocket, and wished she could wake up in bed and find that it had all been a dream. She knew she wouldn't, even though so much of what had been happening felt as if it was too weird to be real. After being carried downstairs by Marc and passing out, she remembered nothing before waking up here, in this horrible, scary place. Because of the white-haired man, she was too scared even to move or make a sound. She just lay where she was, looking up at his cruel face, unable to stop trembling.

At least Mummy and Rachel and Aunty Diane and Uncle Ralph were sort of all right, although they were tied up just like she was, and each of them had thick brown tape wrapped round and round their heads, covering their mouths. When she'd first woken up to find the tape over her mouth, Jane had panicked, thinking she couldn't breathe. Then she found that if she calmed herself down a bit, which was not easy, and didn't move around so much, she was able to breathe through her nose. The worst thing about the tape was that it pulled all your hairs really hard even if you just moved your head a little bit. It also made the bottom half of your face really hot, as if the skin wanted to sweat but couldn't.

Jane could tell by everyone's eyes that they were very scared, but that they were trying to pretend they weren't for her sake. Except for looking scared, though, everyone looked okay, apart from Uncle Ralph, who looked awful.

His nose was one huge purple-black bruise, all crusted with dried blood, and the flesh around his eyes was swollen and black too and covered with little cuts, reducing the eyes themselves, one of which was bright red as if full of blood, to slits.

When she had woken up, there had been just the five of them in what she had thought at first was a dungeon. They had all been half-lying, half-leaning in a row against a stone wall that was damp and smelly and dirty and very, very cold. Jane had been lying at the end of the row, next to Mummy. Then there was Rachel, then Aunty Diane, then Uncle Ralph, whose breathing sounded like someone stirring a bowl of gravel with a stick. All of them were dirty, and Mummy's and Rachel's eyes were all red as if they'd been crying. Mummy was just wearing a dressing gown and her nightdress; her feet were bare and covered in dirt and one of them was bleeding. Aunty Diane, who had been naked the last time Jane had seen her, was now wearing a baggy black t-shirt that had faded to a greeny grey and a pair of jeans, with a hole in the knee, that looked too big for her. Her feet had been bare and dirty too (although now, of course, they were bleeding a lot worse than Mummy's after what that horrible man had done to her), and her hair was wet-looking and hung down in matted rat's-tails.

Looking around, Jane had quickly realised that they were not in a dungeon but in a cellar. It was a very damp and dirty cellar, full of cobwebs and rusty old tools and bits of wood and broken flower pots and other rubbish. There was an old cracked sink against the right-hand wall, above which were taps that were covered with some sort of yellowy-grey gunge. Above these was a window, perhaps just large enough for a small child to squeeze through. The window contained reinforced glass and was covered in grime and swathed in cobwebs, but it still admitted enough light for them to see by. The only door to the cellar was up a narrow flight of stone steps on the far wall.

Before the man with the white hair had come down into the cellar, Jane had heard people moving about in the house above. She'd heard their feet clumping on floorboards, the buzz of their voices from which, by some acoustic quirk, the odd word had emerged crystal-clear. There was nothing special or even sinister about the words she heard, though they enabled her to guess that there were at least three people in the house, one of which was a woman. She heard the woman say two words, 'before' and 'everything', and she heard someone else say 'consciously' and the other person say 'whenever' and 'certain'.

And then the door had opened, throwing light on to the stairs, and the white-haired man had come down and he had been horrible. He had stood looking at them for a while, all neat and smug in his pin-striped suit, and then he had smiled, though not in a friendly way, and had said, 'Good afternoon. I trust you're all comfortable?'

Nobody had said anything, of course, though Aunty Diane had tried to, making muffled 'Mmmm-mmmm' noises behind her gag. The man had walked forward and squatted down, tilting his head towards her.

'I'm sorry,' he had said. 'I'm afraid I didn't quite catch that.'

So quickly that Jane had jerked her head back, startled, bumping it on the wall, Aunty Diane had then sort of spun round on her bottom and lashed out with her bound legs. Her feet, though bare, would have made contact with the man's head, probably sending him sprawling, if they had been allowed to. Like a striking cobra, so fast that Jane saw the movement as nothing more than a blur, his arm shot up and his hand snapped round her left foot, stopping the momentum of the swing in mid-air.

The man seemed completely unruffled by Aunty Diane's

attempt to kick him.

'I'm afraid that wasn't very nice,' he said pleasantly.

Then he turned his head and sank his teeth into the bottom of Aunty Diane's left foot until blood was running down it and dripping on to the floor, and Aunty Diane was writhing and squealing, and everyone else was squealing and trying to kick out at him too.

Jane squeezed her eyes tight shut and would have blocked her ears too if she'd been able to do so. Just as the muffled squealing reached fever pitch, and she thought her head was going to pop with the sheer awfulness of the sound, the squealing faded into puppy-like whimpering, and she opened her eyes.

The white-haired man was standing up again, blood smeared all round his mouth and coating his moustache. He reached gingerly into his pocket with bloody fingers and plucked out a wad of something small and white, which became a fluttering bird when he flicked his wrist, or at least Jane thought it had before realising it was a handkerchief. The man walked over to the cracked sink and twisted one of the taps. It squeaked and spluttered, then coughed up some rusty spurts of water. After a few seconds, the water began running more freely. The man put his handkerchief under the water until it was soaked, then wrung it out and used it to wipe the blood from his face and hands.

Aunty Diane, meanwhile, had her head bowed and her face creased up with pain. Tears were running out of her eyes and dripping off the end of her nose. Her feet were red with blood, which welled up from a crescent of teeth-marks on the sole of the left one. Her toes on that foot were curled inwards and the foot itself was taut and bent like a banana.

The white-haired man, his face clean, scrunched up his now bloody handkerchief and threw it at Aunty Diane. She turned her head away, but it still hit her on the cheek and flopped on to her stomach.

'You're welcome to use this,' he said, 'but don't think I'm washing your feet for you.' He seemed to find this funny and chuckled to himself. 'Well,' he said, 'that was fun. Now, where were we?' He appeared to consider the question for a moment, and then his face brightened. Looking at Mummy he said, 'Oh yes. I was just about to molest your youngest daughter. You haven't any objections, have you?'

Mummy's eyes opened wide and she began to moan behind her gag.

'Thought not,' said the man brightly and walked slowly towards Jane.

Jane felt something inside her shrinking away, trying to hide. She began to whimper like Aunty Diane was now doing, and drew up her knees, her feet dragging across the gritty floor. Beside her, Mummy looked as if she was having a fit. Her eyes were wide and full of outrage and terror. She was rocking back and forth, thrashing like a worm on a fish-hook.

The horrible man crouched in front of Jane and bared his teeth in the horriblest grin she had ever seen. Though he had wiped the blood from his face, his teeth were still pink with it, and up this close Jane could see tiny beads of glittering redness still clinging to the white wirv strands of his moustache. His eyes were horrible too, flat and silver like metal, like the eyes of a robot. He reached out a hand towards her and she twisted away, wishing she could push herself right inside the rotten damp plaster of the wall, out of his reach.

His hand, warm and dry and smelling of soap, touched her cheek. He stroked it gently and crooned, 'Beautiful girl.' Almost idly he glanced to his right where Mummy was trying to shuffle into a position where she could put herself bodily between the man and Jane. 'Oh, for God's sake,' he murmured, then he stood and picked Jane up and carried her to the other side of the room.

Jane began to cry but that didn't seem to perturb the man one bit. He put her down, got down on all fours in front of her and ran his tongue up her bare leg, from her ankle to her knee. Across the other side of the room, Mummy was thrashing from side to side, Uncle Ralph too, and Rachel had tears pouring down her face. Instinctively Jane was trying to keep her knees as tightly together as she could. She wasn't sure exactly what was going to happen, but she knew it was going to be awful.

And then light tumbled down the steps again and the white-haired man twisted his head towards it. As footsteps clacked on the stone steps, Jane saw a terrifying expression cross the man's face, a look of absolute fury and frustration and hatred. He looked like an animal, or worse than an animal. He looked like madness. He looked Jane directly in the eyes and in that instant she thought she was going to die. Then he hissed, 'Later,' and scrambled to his feet.

He was brushing the dirt from the knees and elbows of his suit when an old fat woman and a young gangly nervous-looking man entered the cellar. The fat woman looked at him through spectacles so dark you could not see her eyes, her bangles and beads jangling. 'What are you doing?' she asked suspiciously.

'What does it look like?' the white-haired man spat back at her. 'Checking the hostages.'

The woman made a clucking noise with her tongue. 'Hostages. You make everything sound so dramatic. This isn't Beirut, you know.'

'What would you suggest calling them, then?' the man asked, contempt in his voice.

'Why do we have to call them anything?' said the fat woman.

'What about prisoners?' the young man suggested timidly, flashing an almost shameful glance at Jane, who was breathing quickly and heavily, trying to blink tears out of her eyes.

'Shut up, *Bernard*,' said the horrible man.

Bernard visibly flinched.

The fat woman stepped towards the horrible man. Even though Jane couldn't see her eyes, she could tell that she was furious.

'No names!' she snapped at him. 'That was stupid and irresponsible. You know the rules.'

The horrible man gestured dismissively at the four older captives. 'What does it matter if they hear our names?' he said. 'We can make them forget easily enough. Besides, they won't get out of here alive in any case.'

'That's enough!' barked the fat woman. She was quivering with rage now. She took another step forward as if she was planning to strike the horrible man. He stood his ground, and though he was stone-faced, Jane could see that he was daring her to try it, perhaps even hoping that she would.

She didn't. Instead she said again, more quietly, 'That's enough.' Though she was facing the horrible man, Jane knew she wanted them all to hear her when she said, 'These people are distressed enough as it is. Now, nobody is going to get hurt here. Are they?'

Her voice hardened on those last two words. The horrible man just stared at her for a long, long moment, still as a mannequin, his face like stone. Then he smiled, gave a snort of laughter, and in a voice so calm it made Jane shiver, he said, 'I think you ought to remember something, *fat lady*. I think you ought to remember that your authority is not what it was. Your charge is dead, or had you forgotten? Had it slipped your mind that your precious little Danny was no more?' Suddenly his arm snapped out as if to punch the old woman. Bernard gave a startled shriek. But instead of punching her, the horrible man opened his fist and patted her non-too-gently on the cheek, making the flesh wobble like jelly. 'In which case,' he continued, 'I think it would be very wise on your part to show me a little more respect. Don't you?'

The fat woman stood her ground, but refused to get annoyed, even though, by patting her cheek, the horrible man had tried to make her look small and stupid. She let him have his say and then she replied, in just as silky a voice as his, 'You know as well as I do that it's not just my authority you're opposing. If something happens here because of your . . . lack of control, and you jeopardise this assignment, then it won't just be me you'll be answering to.'

The horrible man sneered. 'And *you* know just as well,' he said, 'that if something happens here, then it will be because it was *meant* to happen. The pattern, fat lady. Always remember the pattern.'

'That's exactly what I *am* doing,' the fat woman said curtly. Then, as if she couldn't keep the argument up any longer, she sighed, shook her head and reached out to touch the horrible man's arm. 'Please,' she said, her voice softer as if prepared to make friends again, 'let's play this one by the book. We can't afford any mishaps. It's a very delicate time, but with Danny dead, things are in a state of . . .'

'Flux?' suggested the horrible man, smiling as if he'd made a joke.

'Flux,' said the woman, smiling too. 'So let's just carry things through as we were instructed, shall we?'

The horrible man spread his hands. 'Of course. It never crossed my mind to do otherwise.'

The fat woman looked at him, but because of her dark glasses, it was hard to tell what she was thinking. Eventually she said, 'Good,' then she looked around as if it was the first time she had been in here. She pointed at Jane. 'Why is the little girl over here? And why is that woman's foot bleeding so badly?'

Worthington glanced at Jane, and then at Aunty Diane, as if he had only just noticed them. 'The girl was being disruptive,' he said, 'agitating the adults, so I decided to move her. While I was doing so the woman tried to attack me. She was so frenzied that only violence would subdue her. I used the minimum force necessary.'

On occasion, Jane had heard Mummy and Daddy using the phrase, 'If looks could kill . . .', and now, looking at Mummy and Aunty Diane and Uncle Ralph, she suddenly knew exactly what that phrase meant. They were glaring at the white-haired man as if they wanted to kill him. Jane wondered whether they really would kill him if they got the chance. She thought maybe they would.

Maybe she would too. She thought she would be prepared to do anything to get away from here, though she didn't like to think that she might have to. She was so glad that the fat woman and the young man had come down when they did, but she was still shivering with fear, so scared that she thought her breath might freeze into a solid block in her throat and suffocate her.

'I suggest that we keep these people together and that they be watched at all times. If all goes to plan, they won't be here for too long,' the fat woman said.

The horrible man smiled. 'Whatever you think is best.' The fat woman glanced at him sharply to see if he was teasing her, but if he was there was no way of telling.

'Would one of you move the girl back over beside her mother, and then bathe this woman's foot?' the fat lady said.

There was a pause while nobody moved, and then Bernard scuttled forward. 'I–I'll do it,' he said.

Jane went rigid when the young man bent towards her, but he twitched a reassuring smile at her and picked her up gently and carefully. Jane heard his heart beating very fast through his thin chest as he carried her back over to Mummy and set her down. Oddly it reminded her of the time she'd held a baby chicken in her hands when her class had gone on a trip to the urban farm in Leeds. It had been smaller than a tennis ball and so fragile that it seemed a sneeze would kill it. She had been able to feel its tiny heart pulsing so fast, as if about to beat its way out of its chest. The experience had frightened her a little, for it made her realise that life for this little thing was so frail and uncertain. All it would take for that life to end was for her to squeeze her fists together; she doubted she would even need to exert much pressure.

After laying Jane carefully beside Mummy, Bernard scampered away, up the cellar steps, presumably to fetch some water to carry out the second part of the fat lady's instructions. Jane was a little sorry to see him go. Though the fat lady was not cruel like the white-haired man, she was not friendly either; Bernard seemed to be the only one who might be nice given half a chance. Through the open cellar door, Jane heard the sound of water spattering into a bucket or a plastic bowl. It made her think of being at home and having to wash up after dinner, a chore she hated. She thought that if God allowed them to get out of this, she would gladly wash up for ever.

While Bernard was upstairs, the white-haired man took his mobile phone out of his pocket and began to jab out a number. Upstairs, Bernard turned the tap off, and now Jane could hear the high-pitched brr-brr sound of the phone at the other end of the line. It rang about four times and then was replaced by a Munchkin voice so tiny that Jane could not make out the words.

'I'd like to speak to David Fox, please,' the horrible man said. 'I believe he's one of your guests.'

Daddy! The horrible man was going to speak to Daddy! Beside her, Jane felt Mummy sort of jerk, saw her head snap up, eyes go wide with surprise. What did this mean? Surely this man couldn't be a friend of Daddy's? But if he wasn't, how did he know where Daddy was? When she'd spoken to Uncle Ralph (had it only been this morning?), even he hadn't known where Daddy was.

The horrible man waited for a bit and then the Munchkin voice came back. 'I see,' he said, 'thank you . . . No, I'll call later.' As he stuffed the phone back into his pocket he said to the fat lady, 'Not in.'

The fat lady looked a bit anxious. 'Where is he then? And where's McQueen? Why hasn't he called in?'

'Relax,' said the horrible man, 'everything's fine.'

'But what if –'

'Shh.' The horrible man put a finger to his lips. 'Don't even think it.'

The fat lady looked anxious, looked as if she wanted to say more, but eventually just nodded.

'Have faith,' the horrible man said. 'No one can hide from us. You ought to know that.'

She still looked unsure, her mouth set in a pert line, but then she seemed to relax a little. 'I know,' she said. 'You're right, of course. I'm just . . . so impatient. I can't stand the thought of any more delays.'

The horrible man smiled. He looked relaxed and confident, looked also to be enjoying the fat lady's anxiety. 'Faith,' he reminded her. 'The pattern is already set. We can influence it, but we can't change its course.'

Bernard reappeared, carrying a red plastic washing-up bowl, sloshing with steaming water. The fat lady glanced at him, then said to the horrible man, 'You'll ring again soon?'

'Every half-hour,' the horrible man promised her.

Jane was relieved to see the fat lady and the horrible man go upstairs. They left with the fat lady repeating her orders to Bernard: to bathe Aunty Diane's feet and then to sit and guard the captives.

The three adults and Rachel watched Bernard warily as he approached with his bowl of steaming water. He looked nervous, his body a mass of tics and twitches. He set the bowl down by Aunty Diane's bleeding feet and then straightened, his head jerking up to look at the five captives, glancing quickly from one to the next, unwilling to maintain eye contact for too long. In a shy stuttering mumble, he said to Aunty Diane, 'I . . . uh . . . I'm going to bathe your feet now, okay? It might s–sting a bit, 'cos I put some TCP in the water to stop the cut going septic.'

He glanced up at Aunty Diane from beneath his fringe of untidy black hair. She was controlling the pain better now. She looked at him as steadily as she could and nodded.

'Okay,' said Bernard, giving her a quick nervous smile before his glance skidded away. 'You . . . er . . . you won't t–try anything, will you? Only it'll b–bring him back.'

Aunty Diane shook her head very deliberately from side to side.

'Right,' said Bernard. 'Well, h–here goes then. I'll try to be as gentle as I can.'

He squatted down and pulled out the sponge he had been soaking in the bowl of warm water and squeezed it. Water ran over his hand and drooled back into the bowl with a sound like someone going to the toilet. He shuffled forward, gave a quick reassuring grin to nobody in particular, then examined Aunty Diane's foot.

'That's nasty,' he said, and glanced up quickly at Aunty Diane. 'He did this to you.'

It was more a statement than a question, but Aunty Diane nodded anyway. Bernard looked down at her foot again, his head moving quickly, twitchily, like a bird's. Almost to himself he murmured, 'I don't like him. I'm not on *his* side, not really. We just believe in the same thing, that's all.'

He touched Aunty Diane's foot with the sponge. She flinched, her eyes creasing up. Bernard jumped, snatching his hand away, spattering his Cyberman t-shirt with water. 'Sorry, sorry,' he moaned. He sounded genuinely distressed.

Aunty Diane calmed down. She said, 'Mmmm-mmmm,' through the brown tape over her mouth. Bernard glanced at her. She raised her feet a little, indicating that he should carry on.

'A–Are you sure?' he said.

She nodded.

'Okay.' With infinite care he washed her feet with the sponge. Soon her feet were as clean as they must have been in the bath earlier. The water in the bowl, by contrast, was cloudy and rust-coloured. The horrible man's teeth-marks stood out like a crescent of red melon seeds on her white skin.

'Th–that should be okay for a bit,' Bernard said. 'I haven't got any p–plasters or anything.' He screwed up his face in apology, then stood up and carried the bowl over to the cracked sink. He emptied the dirty water down the plughole, then rinsed the bowl out.

'Mmmm-mmmm,' Aunty Diane said.

Bernard turned to look at her.

Aunty Diane was gesturing with her head towards Uncle Ralph, the brown tape pulling at her hair.

Bernard frowned, puzzled. 'I'm sorry, I d–don't . . .' and then it dawned on him what she was trying to say. 'Oh, right. You want me to c–clean up your husband's face, yeah?'

Aunty Diane nodded.

Bernard looked uncertain. His gaze scuttered to the cellar steps. 'Well, I–I don't know. Er . . . he might not like it. He told me to s–stay down here and . . . uh . . . keep an eye on things. He didn't say I could clean up everybody.'

'Mmmm,' Aunty Diane said, and nodded towards the cracked sink. Again Bernard looked momentarily confused, and then a smile flickered across his face.

'Right,' he said. 'I could . . . uh . . . use this sink here, yeah, and he w–wouldn't . . . er . . . know.'

'Mmm,' Aunty Diane said with a brief nod.

Bernard chuckled. It was a child-like sound. 'Yeah,' he said. He held the bowl under the tap and turned it on. As water filled it he said apologetically, 'It's ... uh ... just cold water, I'm afraid, but it'll have to do.' He turned the tap off and carried the bowl over to Uncle Ralph. Uncle Ralph sat still, closed his eyes and tried not to wince as Bernard carefully washed the dried blood from his face.

When he had done, Uncle Ralph looked better, though not much. Bernard emptied the bowl again, then sat down, his back against the opposite wall. There was silence for a time. The five of them looked at Bernard, Bernard looked at his feet or down at the floor, anywhere but at them. At last Bernard began to speak haltingly, still looking down as though addressing his shoelaces.

'I'm ... er ... sorry that you're tied up. But ... you know ... that's ... er ... how it has to be for now. Er ... what Mr W–' He paused, blinked, knowing he'd almost caught himself out, then shook his head. He continued, speaking more slowly, as though mentally examining each word before allowing it to leave his mouth. 'What *he* said earlier ... about ... you know ... killing you and that ... well, it's not true. We ... that is, me and ... well ... *her* ... we won't let him do it. He's a nutter, you know. He's not like the rest of us. And ... anyway, that's all. I ... er ... just wanted you to know that ... er ... everything's going to be okay.'

He looked up, reddened, flashed a quick half-hearted smile, then looked down at the floor again. His hands intertwined, long fingers flexing and unflexing. He shivered, gave a short nervous laugh. 'C–cold in here,' he said.

More time passed. After a while, because Bernard's hair was hanging down from his bowed head, hiding his face, Jane thought he had gone to sleep. Then abruptly he stirred, half-raised himself from the floor and took something from his back pocket. It was a very tatty paperback, folded in half. He flipped through it, looking for his place, which he eventually found, marked with a bus ticket. He started to read, but almost immediately realised that Jane was looking at him. He looked up, his eyes meeting hers for a brief second before sliding away. He smiled shyly and held up the book so that she could see the cover.

The artwork comprised of a number of images: a scowling black-haired man, a young couple, the man dressed in a kilt, and a bulky bear-like creature with a gaping fanged mouth and small green eyes. In large black letters on the cover were the words : DOCTOR WHO. And then in smaller blue letters underneath: AND THE ABOMINABLE SNOWMEN.

'It's . . . er . . . well, you can see. It's Doctor Who. I'm . . . er . . . a big fan. Have been since I was a kid.' Bernard gave Jane one of his quick shy smiles and said, 'Do you know Doctor Who?'

She nodded.

Bernard visibly brightened. A spark seemed to jump into his eyes. Suddenly, enlivened by the subject, much of his shyness seemed to vanish.

'Do you like it?' he said.

In truth, Jane wasn't bothered. She could take it or leave it. However, she nodded to please him.

'Yeah, it's great, isn't it?' said Bernard, looking fondly at the cover of his book. 'I'll read this to you if you like. I'm on page 47, but I don't mind starting again. I've read this book dozens of times already. I've had it for years. Do you want me to? Er . . . read it, I mean.'

Anything would be better than waiting in silence for whatever was going to happen. Jane nodded, wincing as the tape that was round the lower half of her face tugged at the hairs on the back of her neck.

'Great,' said Bernard, genuinely pleased. Jane thought he looked really nice when he grinned like he was doing now. 'How about you other folks?' he asked, his voice the strongest it had been since he had entered the cellar with the fat lady, his stammer almost gone. 'Do you mind if I read out loud?'

Mummy, Rachel, Aunty Diane and Uncle Ralph all shook their heads.

'Great,' said Bernard again, but before he could start, the cellar door opened and footsteps descended.

Immediately, his expression changed from delight to cringing disappointment. Like a threatened hedgehog, he curled himself into a ball. The horrible man swaggered into the cellar, the fat lady waddling behind him. The horrible man shot Bernard a contemptuous look and said, 'This cellar suits you, Bernard. You blend in well with these miserable surroundings.'

Bernard said nothing, just huddled even more tightly into himself. The horrible man rolled his eyes and snorted air out through his nose as if to show that Bernard wasn't worth bothering about. He looked at the five captives in his sneery gloating way, then without another word, took his mobile phone from his pocket and tapped out a number.

Much the same thing happened as before. The horrible man asked to speak to Daddy and was told that Daddy wasn't in. He said he would call later and put the phone back into his pocket. The fat lady said anxiously that she didn't like it, that she was afraid something might have gone wrong. The horrible man told her to relax, that nothing had gone wrong, that everything was under control. However, he was scowling as he said it, and Jane thought that maybe even he wasn't as sure as he had been.

They left the cellar, but not before the fat lady had told Bernard that it would be getting dark soon, and that he would find candles and matches in the drawer of the old dressing table which was standing in the corner by the sink, all scratched and chipped and covered in cobwebs.

When they had gone, Bernard took out the book which he had tucked guiltily into the waistband of his jeans as if it was a dirty magazine. He glanced at the cellar steps, perhaps to make sure the horrible man was not still lurking there, trying to catch him out. Then he flashed a smile at them, said, 'Here goes,' opened his book and began to read.

To Jane's surprise he read quite well, slowly and clearly; she had thought he would rush and stammer. When she closed her eyes, he reminded her a bit of Daddy, who until recently had read to her quite often. Bernard's voice was different to Daddy's, but he got you involved in the story and did slightly different voices for each character, just like Daddy did. At school, when they had to read out loud, some of her classmates (especially the boys) went too fast, missing out words, stumbling over others, trying to get their page over with as soon as possible. Jane hated that, because all you heard was their embarrassment at having to read, you didn't hear the story at all. If it was a good book, she would take it home and re-read everything that had been read aloud in class that day. When she read aloud, the teacher, Mrs Levison, always said, 'Well done, Jane, that was very good.'

Time felt different here. When you couldn't do anything, when you were scared and wondering what was going to happen, time moved very slowly indeed. It sounded silly, but as well as being scared and uncomfortable, Jane was also very bored. For this reason, and because Bernard read so well, she became completely embroiled in the story he was telling, saw it all happening very clearly in her head. She saw the monastery, the snowbound mountains of Tibet, the characters as clear as day, and the huge Yeti ambling down the mountainside, roaring and snarling and flexing their claws.

She didn't know how long he was reading for before she fell asleep, but it seemed like a long time. It seemed longer than half an hour, which was how long the horrible man said he was going to wait between phone calls to Daddy. She fell asleep not because the story was boring, but because it relaxed her, made her forget how scared she was, and the exhaustion that came with being scared all the time dragged her down into blackness. Bernard's words started to echo, to overlap, so that soon it sounded like a dozen Bernards were reading to her, and each was a few words behind the one before. The words, plaiting together, formed a cocoon of sound, like a lullaby, through which nothing could penetrate. Feeling safe and snug in her cradle of words, Jane allowed herself to dream.

The dream, however, was like a betrayal of the fact that she had allowed herself to sleep, for the place in which she found herself was not a nice place. She appeared to be in the courtyard of a castle, or perhaps a monastery like the one in the story Bernard had been reading to her. It was dank and cold and dark as the onset of night, and there were grey stone walls looming up on all sides of her, so high that they made Jane feel dizzy to look at them, so high that she could see only a smoky mass of shadow where the ceiling ought to be. There were arches leading out from the courtyard in all directions, perhaps a dozen in all, through which Jane could see suggestions of other courtyards like this one, with other arches like bullet shapes cut out of black paper stuck on to the grey walls. If each of these arches led to a dozen other arches, and then each of those led to a dozen more, how many would that be? How many different routes would she have to choose from? She tried to do the sum in her head, but the numbers defeated her. It was hundreds, she knew that, maybe even thousands. But one place, one building, couldn't have thousands of rooms, could it? It would have to be bigger than . . . than Buckingham Palace. Maybe as big as a whole town, or bigger still.

She shivered and looked around, wondering where she

should go. As if her ears had been stuffed with fog before, she suddenly became aware of two sounds. One was the slow steady drip . . . drip . . . of water all around her, as if the monastery was made of grey ice that was melting, and the other was the low faraway tolling of what Jane imagined to be a great bell.

The sound of the bell seemed to vibrate through her feet, into her stomach and throat, as if encouraging her to tremble. She didn't know why, but she couldn't help thinking that the sound was like a warning that something dark and dangerous was on its way, heading straight for her, something that would do terrible things to her if she didn't run as fast as she could.

And so she ran, suddenly full of terror she couldn't express or understand, a terror that was more feeling than thought. The grey stone walls, crawling with a foggy darkness that looked as if it was trying to gather itself into a solid shape, seemed to sway and rock above and around her like the view of the world on a fairground ride that spins and swoops. The arches seemed to jostle for her attentions – pick me, pick me, they seemed to cry – and once chosen they sucked her in like giant mouths. The monastery was like a vast living thing that kept folding back on itself, or that she seemed to make grow bigger and bigger the further she progressed. She ran, her breath tearing at her lungs, through mouth after mouth after mouth. And all the time the bell tolled and tolled, growing neither louder nor softer, as if it was somehow inside her, like her own crashing heart.

And then, just when she thought she could run no more, when her legs felt brittle and hollow and her breath moved inside her like nails, she found she had to run faster, and faster still, because suddenly she *knew* that there was something behind her, something terrible in pursuit. She could sense it rather than see it, a grunting slavering thing in the shapeless dark. It was all the bad things she had ever known coming for her, all her fears rolled into one. It was the darkness itself and it was spiders and Daddy shouting and going away and the horrible man with the white hair and Smile coming out of her poster and hurting Mummy and Rachel and Uncle Ralph and Aunty Diane. It was a thing made of pain and fear, a thing whose fingers were knives, whose teeth were splinters, whose eyes were scorpions, whose breath was fire. If it saw you, you died; if it touched you, it owned your soul for ever and ever. And it was coming, it was coming, it was right behind her. It came like a tidal wave, devouring everything before it.

There was no escape, but she ran anyway, and without realising when the change had happened, she suddenly found that she was no longer in the monastery but in a forest, fleeing between trees that snagged at her clothes and hair like long crooked fingers. The ground was uneven and a bit squishy as if it had been raining. The trees were creaking, the undergrowth rustling, sounds that were like the voice of the forest, muttering in terror because it also knew that the bad thing was coming to consume it. Jane was sobbing now, and her legs felt like they were made of iron, and they wouldn't work, and she kept slipping and stumbling forward on to her knees. She could hear the thing behind her now, making its terrible sound that was like a hundred different sounds, like screaming and whistling and howling and grunting and moaning and whimpering, and she could feel its breath at her back, cold as the Arctic and rotten as a mountain of dead fish.

If it sees me, she thought, I'll die. And if it touches me, it will own my soul for ever and ever.

It was just behind her, just through the trees, towering above her, swooping down, the trees crashing in its wake, its footprints leaving a trail of ash.

She scrambled to her feet, then slipped and fell down again, knocking the breath from her body.

If it sees me, I'll die. If it touches me –

'Jane.'

She looked up. At first she thought it was a tree that had spoken, or the thing at her back, sending out voices to kiss and coax and tease. Then she noticed the figure standing in the shadows of a tree ten feet away, its body black as the branches that seemed to pierce it, black as the clumps of leaves into which its head merged. The figure stuck out its arm, and Jane saw that it was brandishing a fistful of felt tip pens. Oddly, although it was dark, she could see the colours of the pens clearly, as if they were imbued with their own special and subtle light; she saw orange and yellow, red and pink and two shades of green, brown and purple, light blue and dark blue (*royal* blue, Mummy called it).

'Take them, Jane,' the figure said. 'Quickly.'

Jane reached out her hand, and suddenly she was no longer ten feet from the figure but standing right in front of it. She took the felt tip pens.

'Choose a colour,' the figure said.

'Purple,' Jane replied without hesitation; this was her favourite.

'Now colour out the trees behind you. Colour in the gaps. Quickly.'

She turned and began to do as the figure had instructed. She didn't know how it worked, but she seemed to know what to do. She took the lid off the purple pen and coloured in the gaps between the trees until her wrist ached and there were no gaps left and the pen was squeaking and running out.

'Now,' the figure said, 'choose another colour.'

'Orange,' said Jane.

'Use that for the sky,' the figure said.

Jane coloured in the sky, leaving no gaps for the bad thing to get through. When she had finished she was panting and her hand felt like it was dropping off.

'Well done, Jane,' said the figure, and suddenly, though the forest was dark, Jane could see who the figure was.

'Daddy!' she cried.

'Shh,' said Daddy, but he was smiling. 'Don't tell him that I'm here.'

'Who?' said Jane.

'You know. He's been trying to ring me up.'

Jane looked around, suddenly wary. It was quiet again now, the trees still. 'Is he here?' she whispered.

'He'd come if he knew I was,' Daddy said. He held out his hand and said, 'Come on, Janey, let's go home.'

Though Jane took his hand, which was warm and comforting and familiar, she said, 'I can't.'

'Why not?'

'What about Mummy and Rachel and Aunty Diane and Uncle Ralph? Can't we help them?'

Daddy frowned thoughtfully. Jane felt safe and confident now in the knowledge that he would know what to do.

'I don't know if *I* can help them,' he said, 'but maybe I can help you to help them.'

'How?' asked Jane. 'What do I have to do?'

'You trust me, don't you, Jane?' Daddy said.

Jane wrinkled her nose. It seemed a funny sort of question for Daddy to ask. 'Yes, Daddy,' she said.

'Enough to take me back to where Mummy is?'

Jane didn't know how she was going to do that, but if Daddy knew a way, then that was fine with her.

'Yes, Daddy,' she said again.

'Are you absolutely certain, Jane? You have to trust me completely to let me come back with you.'

The serious look on Daddy's face made Jane feel a little uneasy, but also proud because she felt as though he was asking her something very important, something that only she could answer.

'Course I am, Daddy,' she said. 'Can we go now?'

Daddy smiled again. 'Yes,' he said, 'we can. Come on.'

They began walking through the forest, Daddy's hand enclosing hers so warm that it seemed to make her glow, to make her sleepy, like being wrapped in a cosy duvet on a cold winter's morning. She felt as though his hand was melting its warmth over her, seeping into her skin and through her veins, numbing her senses. At first she thought it was this, the warmth enfolding her thoughts and making them slow and woozy, that was causing her to hallucinate. Certainly she was seeing things at the edge of her vision that, when she turned sleepily to look, were no longer there.

But what was she actually seeing? Or rather, what did she *think* she was seeing? She scowled, concentrated hard, trying to make sense of the half-glimpsed images.

She *thought* . . . she thought she saw trees moving. Not actually tearing themselves from the ground and shambling towards her, but subtly altering their shapes, twisting their branches to new positions as if made of rubber. Or maybe it wasn't the branches of the trees that were moving, but something *in* the branches. Also, she thought she saw dark figures scuttling from trunk to trunk, like shadows playing hide and seek.

The wind had picked up again, rattling leaves so dry they sounded like crisp wrappers, so it was hard to tell, but she *thought* she could hear things too. Padding footsteps, the kind of rustling sounds only a human being, or an animal equally as large, could make.

Several times she shook her head and blinked her eyes in an attempt to clear her senses. It was no good. Even when she squeezed her eyes tight shut and counted slowly to ten, which she did more than once, the instant she opened them again she saw dark shapes flit across the edge of her vision. On one occasion she spun to look, hoping to nail at least one of the shapes with her gaze. All she saw were trees sprouting from undergrowth that shivered in the wind.

She told herself that she had no need to be scared now that Daddy was with her. Daddy knew how to deal with every situation. He was going to come to where Mummy and the others were and set them all free. There was no longer any need to flinch at shadows. With Daddy beside her she could be happy and fearless. She was about to voice her anxieties, hoping that by doing so Daddy would smile and tell her, in his gentle way, that she had nothing to worry about, when a dark troll-like figure stepped from behind a tree directly in front of them.

Jane let out a yelp of panic and jerked back so violently that she almost pulled her hand from Daddy's grasp. In response, Daddy's hand spasmed tightly around her own; Jane knew he was only reacting to her panic, gripping her hand hard to stop her from falling over, but just for a second it seemed as though he was trying to crush the bones in her hand. Her cry of shock changed, therefore, to a moan of pain; for a long giddy moment she thought she was going to faint. She moved her mouth; her lips and tongue felt large and rubbery. Nevertheless she managed to mutter, 'Daddy, you're hurting me.'

'Sorry, petal,' said Daddy, looking down at her, 'I thought you were going to fall. There's nothing to be frightened of. It's only a child.'

His words reassured Jane a little, who blinked the smog of threatened unconsciousness away, and focused on the figure which had stepped from behind the tree. Jane could see that the figure was not the least bit troll-like, after all, but was that of a young girl, maybe four or five years old. In the meagre light, her naked body looked grey. She was holding something in her arms, a bundle, that Jane had taken at first to be a grotesque pot belly. When she looked closer, she saw that it was a Cabbage Patch Doll. The girl was looking at them coyly, sucking her thumb.

'Hello,' said Jane uncertainly. 'Who are you?'

Before the girl could answer, something large and dark dropped from a tree to their right and landed with a thump on the ground, making Jane jump. She thought it was a full sack until it straightened and she realised it was a boy.

Like the little girl, the boy too was naked. However, he was older than the girl, older than Jane even, perhaps twelve or thirteen, and Jane felt herself blushing as her eyes flickered instinctively and fascinatedly to his willie.

The boy seemed unaware of the effect he was having on her, unembarrassed by his nakedness. He strolled forward, a scowl on his face that was directed not so much at Jane but at Daddy. He had blond hair and looked a bit like Jason Donovan. In any other circumstances, Jane would have considered him very nice-looking. She was getting to the stage where she was seeing boys as more than just irritating and clumsy and stupid; there were one or two in her class that she really liked, and she went all hot and embarrassed when those particular ones smiled at or spoke to her. She and her friends, Meryl and Stephanie, had recently taken to drawing up a Boy Chart in the backs of their rough books at school. There they would give boys marks out of ten in whatever categories they could think of: 'Looks' was subdivided into 'Smile', 'Eyes', 'Hair' and 'Body – How Athletic?', whereas other categories included 'Trendiness' and 'Music Taste' (liking Smile, at least before today, had always been a big plus).

The boy walked up to the little girl and put his hand on her shoulder, like an older brother protecting his sister from bullies. There was a rustling of undergrowth to Jane's left and another figure appeared, another girl this time, perhaps Rachel's age. She had long hair that fell about her shoulders, and boobs that were bigger than Rachel's but not as big as Mummy's, and hairs on her fanny that Rachel had told her were called pubes and that Mummy had said started to grow on all girls when they were about twelve years old.

The girl had taken only two steps towards them when there was more movement, this time to Jane's right, and two more children appeared, a boy and a girl, perhaps her age or a bit younger, holding hands.

Then another boy fell from a tree, landing on the balls of his feet and springing immediately upright like an animal. Then, in quick succession, two more children fell from trees, a young boy and a teenage girl, and landed within a second of each other, the boy rolling over in the undergrowth before rising to his feet.

And suddenly figures were appearing from behind trees and dropping from the concealing darkness of branches like strange fruit in such numbers that Jane could not keep account of them all. They made a heavy pattering and rustling sound as they appeared, like jungle rain. They came from all around – in front, behind, to the left and the right – and soon had formed a thickening circle of naked human flesh around Jane and Daddy.

Jane was tense, alarmed even, but not really scared, not with Daddy beside her. Daddy was a grown-up, after all, and these were just children, and though many of the children looked angry, they made no move to attack. They didn't even come all that close to Jane and Daddy; the nearest child to Jane was at least ten feet away. Jane tried to tell herself that there was nothing to be scared of, nothing to worry about, but if the children didn't mean them harm, then why had they surrounded them, blocking off all hope of escape?

After what seemed like a very long time, but was probably no more than a minute or two, something happened. The children were standing seven or eight deep now and were packed quite tight; Jane estimated that there must be a few hundred of them. After taking up their positions they had been standing motionless, like an army, but now, directly in front of Jane and Daddy, there was a ripple of movement. For an instant Jane saw the children as a single creature, and the movement as a sign that it was about to speak. As it turned out, this was true in a way, for all at once the two children directly in front of Jane, a boy of seven or eight with dark curly hair and a blonde-haired girl a little older, moved apart like the lips on a mouth, allowing an older girl, older than any of the other children, to step into the circle.

The girl was perhaps sixteen, and had boobs that seemed to point upwards in different directions like the eyes of an iguana. Her hair was brown but with blonde streaks in it that flashed like gold in the semi-light, and she had a lot of hair around her fanny, so much in fact that you couldn't even see the fanny itself. She wasn't really pretty but she wasn't ugly either. She looked strong and determined, as if she had never been afraid in her life. Despite herself, Jane found herself admiring the girl. She was so striking that Jane didn't realise at first that she wasn't alone. It was a subtle movement of the girl's body that made Jane look down to where a small boy was clinging to the girl's hand. Despite his big eyes, the boy seemed withdrawn, lost in his own thoughts. He had a teddy bear jammed beneath his armpit and was greedily sucking the thumb of his free hand.

Jane was almost surprised when the girl spoke. The children had been so silent up to now that she had been wondering whether they could.

'I'm Yvonne,' the girl said, 'and this is Danny.' She nodded at Daddy. 'Thanks to him, we're all trapped here. For ever. This is our eternity.'

The girl's voice was calm and quiet, but there was a bitterness there, and she said 'eternity' in such a way that the very word seemed to bring alive its meaning. Jane shivered and looked up at Daddy.

'What does she mean?' she whispered.

Yvonne answered before Daddy could. 'We're here to

303

warn you, Jane. We don't always get the chance. Don't go with him. Don't trust him. He's not who you think he is. He'll use you just as he used us. And when he's done he'll spit you out like a piece of gristle and you'll end up here, with us. This is a trap, Jane, that he sets again and again and again. He's a hunter, but he needs people like you, like us, to survive. He's like a vampire who needs to be invited to cross a threshold, but once he's over he'll suck you dry. Do you understand what I'm telling you, Jane? Without a willing host he's nothing, he's powerless. If you tell him to go, he'll have to go, he'll have to look elsewhere. We know we can't save everyone, we know he'll get someone eventually, but we'll save who we can because it's all we can do. He's responsible for everything that's bad in the world, Jane, and he's getting stronger all the time, he's gradually eating away at the good, overwhelming it. Soon he'll be so strong that he won't need people like us. He'll be able to do whatever he wants.'

Yvonne stopped talking and looked at Jane, a plea in her eyes, willing her to understand. But Jane didn't understand. The girl's words just confused her.

'I don't know what you mean,' she said. 'This is my Daddy. He's going to help me.'

'No,' said Yvonne firmly. 'It's not your Daddy, and he helps no one but himself. He's trying to trick you, Jane. He's just exploiting the situation you're in. Do you want me to tell you what he does? Do you want me to tell you my story, which is the same as everyone else's story here? He came to me when I was miserable and angry and thought that no one understood me. He wormed his way in when I was at my most vulnerable, and because I was weak and needed a friend I welcomed him. That's how he works, Jane, through persuasion. He's weak at first, but once he's taken a hold he never lets go. He gets stronger, far stronger than you. He takes you over, controls your thoughts, makes you do things that you didn't want to do, that you didn't know you were capable of doing. Do you know what he made me do, Jane? He made me kill my parents with a hammer when they were asleep. I couldn't do a thing about it. He used me like a machine, he *possessed* me. You read about it in the paper sometimes, people being possessed by demons, doing terrible things, things you wouldn't think a human being was capable of. It was like being trapped in a tiny corner of myself, screaming to be let out, while he went ahead and used my body and my mind. Afterwards, he made me find some people who looked after me, hid me away. They called themselves the Flux and they did what he told them through me. They thought he was God. Or *a* god. They called me their oracle. It was like being on drugs the whole time, but just before the end I felt myself becoming more lucid, and I realised he was weakening, just a little. That was when he made me kill myself. He made me throw myself off a motorway bridge in front of a lorry. Then he moved on, probably to a little kid like Danny. They're weaker, more pliable, you see, more open to persuasion. But they have disadvantages too. They're less physically strong. And it's harder to hide little kids. They don't run away like teenagers, they only get abducted, so people never stop looking for them, and that can be dangerous.'

She had been speaking with a quiet intensity, almost as though she was trying to hypnotise Jane into believing her, so that when she stopped the silence seemed to rush into the spaces where her voice had been, making Jane feel dizzy.

Jane didn't know what to think. Could this girl, Yvonne, really be telling her the truth? She sounded convincing and earnest, but Jane didn't want to believe her. When Jane had seen Daddy (could someone really look and sound so much like Daddy but not *be* Daddy?) she had thought all their problems were over, had thought they were going to be a family again, and now this girl was taking all that away from her. Even if the girl was trying to help, even if she was trying to save her as she claimed, Jane couldn't help hating her a little bit.

She turned and looked up at Daddy. 'Is it true what she says?' she asked miserably.

Daddy looked a little sad, which immediately made Jane feel ashamed that she had asked the question. 'What do you think?' he said quietly.

Jane looked from Yvonne to Daddy, then back to Yvonne again. She didn't know what to think. All she knew was that she hated Yvonne for having planted this seed of doubt in her mind.

To save her having to reply, Daddy squeezed her hand and said, 'It's all right, petal, don't get upset. I know how confusing this all is.'

'You *are* my Daddy, you *are*,' Jane wailed as though trying to convince herself.

'Of course I am. You know I am.'

'Then why did she tell me you weren't? Why did she say that?'

'Because I'm not the one who's trying to trick you, Jane. She is,' Daddy said.

Jane felt relief wash over her, felt as though this was just the reassurance she had been waiting for. 'How?' she asked.

'By trying to make you let go of my hand. While you're with me you're safe, but if you let go . . .' He left the sentence unfinished.

'But why would she do that?'

'Because she's lonely, Jane. They're all lonely, even together. You mustn't really blame them, but they want to break us up so that they can keep you here. They know that without me you'd never find your way out.'

'That's not true, Jane,' said Yvonne. 'He's just tying you in knots, making you confused. Look around you. There are hundreds of us. How can we be lonely? How can keeping you here, one more person, make us less lonely?'

'Because Jane is alive and you're not.' It was the first time Daddy had addressed Yvonne directly. He spoke firmly, like he sometimes spoke to Jane when she complained about going to bed at half-past nine. In a gentler voice he said, 'This is a dead place, Jane. Though you may not realise it, we both shine here like fires in the darkness. They –' he indicated the silent ranks of naked children '– want to warm themselves on your fire until it goes out, which it will if you stay here, believe me. They just want to remind themselves what it feels like to live again. But we have to keep the fire burning, for Rachel's sake and Mummy's.' He cocked his head as if listening for something, and then said, 'There isn't much time, Jane. I'm going to let you decide, but you have to do it quickly. Do you believe me and take me back to Mummy and Rachel, or do you believe them and stay here and lose everything?'

'Do you take him back and become lost like us or do you let go and find your own freedom?' countered Yvonne.

A sudden gust of wind snatched Jane's hair and set it flailing about her face. She saw the trees ripple as if they were no more than a backcloth. Carried on the wind, still faint but growing louder, came a crackling sound, like and yet unlike radio static.

She had to make a decision. Now. But really, when she thought about it, there was no decision to be made. She gripped Daddy's hand tighter and shouted, 'Come on, Daddy, come on.'

She ran at Yvonne, intending to barge her way through. The wind was screaming now and buffeting her, no longer a wind but a hurricane. Something was happening to Yvonne and to all of the children. They were blurring, running together, breaking up, as if made of sand that the hurricane was tearing apart.

Head down, eyes screwed almost shut, Jane ran. She knew that Daddy was still with her only by the fact that she could feel nothing but warmth where her left hand should be. She ran instinctively, dodging trees that were shredding anyway and would probably have spun apart like smoke if she had collided with them. Flashbulbs began to burst in her vision, intense light that seemed to suck her thoughts from her head. She felt herself becoming weightless as if she were leaving her body behind. She was soaring, soaring into a light brighter than the sun . . .

She woke up.

Physical sensations, hard and real, flooded into her. Her arm hurt, her back hurt, her head throbbed because it had been resting against the cold stone wall. She blinked eyes which were gummy and gritty, swallowed spit that tasted like someone else's bad breath. At first everything was vague, fuzzy, made of shades of light and dark.

One of those shades of light was brighter than the rest and moving, flickering, dancing. She stared at it, felt it soothing her, and eventually her eyes focused like a camera and she realised it was a candle flame. Now everything else came into focus, and she saw that the room was different, that the light had changed and made everything softer, more shadowy. At first, even after seeing the candle, she couldn't work out why, but then all at once it hit her: it was night-time. Jane couldn't believe that just this morning she had been sitting on her bedroom floor, drawing and colouring. That seemed like days ago now.

The first person she saw was the horrible man. He was talking into his mobile phone, grinning that nasty grin of his. Jane heard him say, 'Don't draw attention to yourself, Mr Fox. If you do as I say, nobody will be hurt.' She didn't hear the rest of what he said because those two words, 'Mr Fox', seemed to boom in her mind like an echo. Daddy! He was talking to Daddy! She felt a crushing disappointment. Had it all been just a dream then? It had seemed like so much more.

Now she began to see other things. Mummy was on the other side of the room rather than beside her (perhaps it had been her moving, or her warmth being taken away, that had woken Jane up) and Bernard was winding more of the brown tape around her head. He looked a bit sorry about what he was doing, but he was probably just following the horrible man's orders, so Jane could forgive him a little. The fat lady was in the cellar too, listening to what the horrible man was saying. Jane twisted her head, gritting her teeth against the pain of the tape pulling her hair, and saw that Rachel, Aunty Diane and Uncle Ralph were still in the same places they'd been in when she'd fallen asleep. Aunty Diane caught her eye and winked. Jane tried to wink back, but she hadn't quite mastered the art; she couldn't close one eye without the other closing too. Aunty Diane nodded secretly towards the horrible man, and Jane tried to focus on what he was saying. It was hard though; she still couldn't believe that Daddy was on the other end of that phone.

And then it became easier to hear what he was saying because the man used the F-word which shocked Jane. She had never heard an adult use it before, only kids in the playground. The man called Daddy a 'fucking moron', and then said, 'It's to stop you informing the police, of course.'

There was a pause then, during which the horrible man's smile widened, and then he said, 'You'll have to trust me, won't you?' before breaking the connection.

'Well?' said the fat lady impatiently as the horrible man tucked the phone back into his pocket.

'He'll be there. I told you everything was fine, didn't I?' He brushed past the fat lady and made for the cellar steps. 'Come on,' he ordered. 'There's a great deal to do.'

The fat lady waddled after him. 'Put this one back with the others,' she told Bernard, indicating Mummy, 'and watch them. If all goes to plan, it's nearly over.'

Bernard nodded and the fat lady huffed her way up the cellar steps. Jane's head was reeling. She hadn't heard the whole of the conversation between Daddy and the horrible man, but enough to guess that Daddy had to go somewhere and do something if he wanted her and Mummy and everyone else back. She hoped that the horrible man wasn't going to kill Daddy. She felt panic rising within her; she needed help more than ever.

Silently, with her mind, she said, 'Oh Daddy, where are you?'

She was surprised when a voice came back, speaking to her inside her head, a voice which although it said, 'Here I am,' didn't sound like Daddy's voice at all.

32

The address David had been given was on the Hob Lane Estate, which was situated in an amorphous no-man's-land somewhere between Wanstead and Walthamstow. Terrified of getting lost and being late for his rendezvous, David had set off ridiculously early and, inevitably perhaps, *had* got lost, stopping only when the increasingly narrow, run-down and ill-lit streets he was attempting to negotiate came to an abrupt halt at a chain-link fence.

He should have checked his route more carefully, of course, but he was so wound up that the thought of stopping and doing something as methodical as looking at a map was anathema to him. He stopped the car but left the engine idling, and snatched up his A-Z from the passenger seat, cursing its pages for not turning quickly enough, cursing God for not only allowing his wife and children to be kidnapped but for getting him lost as well. 'What have I done to you, you vindictive bastard?' he muttered, looking around for a street sign. He couldn't see one. Of course. Thank you, God.

Beyond the chain-link fence was a steep bank that dropped six or eight feet to a basin of solid blackness. It could have been scrubland or playing fields, a quarry or a disused railway track; in this light, or rather lack of it, it was impossible to tell. Across the nothingness, miles away it seemed, David could see lights twinkling, so indistinct that they could have been anything from lanterns to houses. He looked for an unpopulated area on his map and eventually, by process of elimination, found what seemed to be a correlation between the map and his actual position. The scrubland was labelled as a playing field and was at the end of a street called Mullet's Rise. If this was where he was, there was no wonder he had got lost; the street system looked to have been fashioned on the maze at Longleat, which he and Rachel had once spent over an hour wandering through without getting anywhere. Trying to control his urge to slam the car into gear and simply tear back the way he had come and hope for the best, he found a stub of pencil in the glove compartment and shaded in what appeared to be the quickest route back.

With the A-Z bent open and held against the steering wheel with the thumb of his right hand, David reached the Hob Lane Estate within twenty minutes. It was still only 8:15, three-quarters of an hour before the rendezvous time, but David wouldn't feel reassured until he was actually at the address that the caller had given him. That particular information was branded on his mind: Flat 5, Coronation House, Legion Street. David eased the car through the estate in third and sometimes second gear, his eyes flickering between the A-Z and the actual streets represented by its gridded lines, and hoped he was driving quickly enough not to be picked up as a kerb crawler – not that there was any evidence of the Great British Constabulary around here.

The estate itself looked like Beirut on a bad day. Many of the houses were boarded up, their roofs stripped by thieves, their brickwork defaced by graffiti or scorched by fire. A gutted car sat in a patch of black stubble in a school playing field. Rubbish fluttered and flapped like the scabs peeled from diseased buildings. Street lamps, more often than not, were smashed or festooned with all manner of ornamentation: tyres, bicycle frames, items of clothing. To cause so much destruction must have required a great amount of energy, yet the people David saw hanging around the streets, most of them teenagers in dark clothing and baseball caps, appeared listless to the point of inertia.

He could see four blocks of flats, one of which must be Coronation House, looming above the houses like colossi. They were positioned in a way that reminded him of the four corner towers of a castle. All they lacked were the linking walls from which boiling tar could be tipped on to the heads of unwary passers-by. Spotting the flats was far easier than reaching them, however. If they resembled a castle, then the intricate pattern of streets and squares and cul-de-sacs that jigsawed around them was the barrier of thorns that he had to hack his way through.

It was 8:35 when he finally did, pulling into a parking area beside a Sierra with a bent aerial and furry seats. The flats towered above him, grey and dreary and somehow pitiless. When he switched off the engine, silence rushed into the car and his head, so profound it was like a scream that hurt his ears.

He swallowed, took some deep breaths, got out of the car. The cold hit him immediately, wheedled its way into his bones, making him shudder and drag his Bogart tightly around him. He felt the bottle bump against his hip, and thought how unimportant the phone call had made it and its mystery to him, how nothing else mattered now except getting his family back, or at least ensuring their safe release. He could hardly believe it was Christmas Day on Friday, had only remembered now because he could see, looking up, coloured spots of light in more than one window of the block of flats he was closest to, and through the window of a flat on the fifth floor the jagged outline of a Christmas tree. He dared not believe that he might be with his family at Christmas; he dared not even wish it. He began to walk towards the nearest block of flats, his footsteps clacking like horses' hooves on cobble-stones, a freezing wind bringing a sudden flurry of sleet from nowhere, which stung his face and speckled the shoulders of his Bogart.

A concrete canopy, perched on squared-off columns, jutted from the base of the block of flats like a petulant bottom lip. Attached to the canopy was a large plastic sign, black letters on a white background, some of which were missing. The sign announced the building as COR NAT ON HOUSE, yet although his search was over, David felt little relief. Hesitating only a little, he passed beneath the canopy and headed for the double doors in front of him. The doors were made of wood, inset with panes of smashed security glass, the splinters held in place by their mangled wire frameworks. As he passed the concrete columns he glanced left and right; they were so wide he could almost believe they had been designed as ambush aids for muggers. There was a sign above the doors which read: IN THE INTERESTS OF SECURITY PLEASE KEEP THESE DOORS LOCKED AT ALL TIMES. Nevertheless the left-hand one was propped open with a piece of wood. David wondered, with more than a little trepidation, whether this was for his benefit.

He pushed the door all the way open. It was ill-fitting, perhaps kicked out of shape by past intruders, and slid and squeaked grittily across the tiled floor beyond. David stepped inside the building, which was no warmer than outdoors and no more welcoming. He found himself in an entrance hall which smelled stale as mildew, and whose greying walls were noticeboards for all manner of graffitists. There were two light fittings in the ceiling but only one unshaded bulb burned. The other fitting was a sooty socket which extended black greasy tendrils across the ceiling.

Directly in front of David, its doors again spectacularly defaced by graffiti, was a lift. To his left and right, irregularly lit corridors led to ground-floor flats. Clearly the architects of Coronation House and its neighbours had been much taken with the notion of symmetry. Everywhere David looked, the lines and angles were regular, undemanding to the eye, unenticing to the imagination. More plastic signs were bolted to the walls, the one at head height to David's right informing him that Flats 1–6 could be located down the right-hand corridor.

It was perhaps inevitable, and very possibly intentional, thought David, that this corridor was in darkness. The meagre yellowish light from the bare bulb in the entrance hall ventured a little way, far enough at least to illuminate a pale blue door with a number 1 screwed to it, but beyond that were merely shadows and uncertainty.

Heart chopping, David edged into the corridor. His shadow ballooned before him, head elongating across the thinly carpeted floor, creasing to climb walls veined with graffiti. The corridor was just wide enough for David to have reached out and touched both sides with his fingertips if he had wished. As the dankly odoured darkness slipped its arms around him and drew him in, David opened his eyes wide, willing them to adjust.

They did so, enough at least for him to be able to tell that the corridor ahead of him was deserted. David slipped his hand around the bottle and crept forward, feeling absurdly like a cop moving into position for a drug bust, hand curled protectively around his gun. Though the bottle was a comfort, his senses felt heightened by apprehension, felt like wire stretched to its limit. He could hear the sound of carpet fibres being crushed beneath his feet. He could *feel* the darkness; it had a grimy greasy texture, left a taste in his mouth like coal. He passed another door and mouthed, 'Two,' to himself. Then he was falling.

It was like a funhouse trick, as if a section of the floor was on castors. David didn't realise what had happened until his foot swooped backwards, his knee buckled and the carpet was rising to meet him. One hand was still in his pocket, curled around the bottle, so he was unable even to break his fall. He landed heavily on his left side, taking most of the impact on his shoulder and hip. The bottle felt like a mallet slamming into his pelvis.

He lay there, bathed in pain for a few moments, gasping to refill his lungs with air. Then he struggled groggily to his knees, gritting his teeth against the flaring pain in his side. Fortunately the bottle had not broken, though the hand that had been holding it felt as though it was. David pulled it gingerly from his pocket, half-expecting it to be pulsing red like a hand slammed in a door in a cartoon. He flexed and unflexed it experimentally. It hurt, but not enough to be broken; in fact, even now the burning pain was subsiding a little. He looked around and saw something black on the carpet behind him, about the size of a shoe. When it didn't move he nudged it gingerly with his foot. It rattled, a familiar sound that made him think, oddly, of Jane. With his good hand he picked the object up and immediately realised why the sound had reminded him of his daughter. What he held was a roller skate.

Had it been planted deliberately? If so, it was a pretty childish trick. He tossed the skate to one side, where it clattered and came to rest, and then clambered painfully to his feet. He rotated his shoulder slowly, and then his hip, like a geriatric attempting aerobics. Both joints flared with pain but he didn't think anything was seriously amiss. He moved on, taking great care this time where he put his feet.

He passed another door which he assumed must be flat 3, and then, a dozen or so paces later, flat 4. Here he paused, peering into the darkness ahead. Although he could make out the general shape of the corridor, it was too dark for him to see as far as the door to flat 5. He came to a halt, his face creasing up with the effort of listening, but heard only silence. Maybe the bottom flats were long-abandoned – too damp, too rat-infested, too vandalised – but unless the walls were unbelievably thick, he should have been able to hear something from the floors above – TVs, music, babies crying, people yelling at one another. The fact that he heard nothing couldn't help making him feel, paranoically perhaps, that the entire population of Coronation House were in cahoots against him.

Partly to establish a sense of perspective, partly to ensure that nothing was creeping up behind him, David turned and looked back the way he had come. He was shocked by how far away the light was; it hovered in the darkness, like a faintly luminous postage stamp held at arm's length. He thrust his injured hand into his pocket and closed it once more, briefly, around the bottle, then he turned again and began to walk forward, counting his footsteps under his breath, trying to ignore the throbbing in his bruised joints. All at once the wall to his right, which looked to David like an expanse of steel wool viewed through dark glasses, seemed to pour forth a column of blackness that rose and swayed and reached for him.

David cursed his imagination even as he stepped backwards out of its clutches. It was not a living thing at all, but a doorway, blacker than the darkness around it, given life only by his own perception of its outline curling and shifting. All the same, it required just as much caution as if it had been a breathing creature. If he had guessed right, and he was sure he had, then this was the doorway to flat 5.

He stood and stared at it for a moment, and listened hard, trying to discern some clue to what lay beyond the opening. He saw and heard nothing. The blackness, which only the impurity of his own vision seemed to cause to drift and shimmer, might as well have been a void. He saw no door this time; either it had been opened inwards as far as it would go or it had been removed. He opened his mouth and breathed deep and slow, like an athlete trying to relax himself before an event. Then, once again, he slipped his aching hand into his pocket and squeezed the bottle.

It was warm, or perhaps his hand was cold, though he couldn't believe that, not the way it was throbbing. He remembered being cold when he had come into the building, but at some stage he had started sweating; he felt a trickle of perspiration scurrying down his forehead, towards his eye. He swiped at it with his free hand, smearing it across his skin like a bug. He wiped the hand on the leg of his trousers, then extended it towards the doorway. The blackness lapped at his hand before swallowing it.

The room felt colder than the corridor, as though, by some convolution of geography, the doorway led back to the outside world. A chill travelled up David's arm and made him shudder. He pulled his hand back slowly and curled it into a fist. What was waiting for him in there? Would it be better just to walk in or to call out first? He decided on the latter, but it was only when he opened his mouth to do so that he realised how dry his mouth had become. His first attempt to conjure a voice from it resulted in a wordless croak. He swallowed, cleared his throat and licked his lips, trying to generate some saliva, and finally he called, 'Hello. Is there anybody there?'

He had meant to make the request sound casual, but instead his voice came out rough and wavery, and made him think of a medium conducting a seance. Whether he expected a reply or not, he still jumped out of his skin when it came, even though the voice was calm and cultured, the voice of a politician or a public school headmaster.

'Do come in, Mr Fox,' said the unseen man at the end of the voice, for all the world as if inviting David into an oak-panelled office for a friendly chat. Recovering from his shock, David peered hard in the direction from which the voice had come, but the room's darkness continued to defy his eye.

'Who are you?' he asked, mentally cursing the wavering uncertainty in his own voice.

'All in good time.' The words seemed to ooze from the darkness. 'Come along, Mr Fox. Don't be afraid.'

'Why aren't there any lights?' David said. It occurred to him that with his family and friends being held hostage he was perhaps not asking the most pertinent questions here. But he couldn't help it; he felt vulnerable as a sheep in a roomful of butchers.

'Who knows?' said the voice. 'Perhaps someone forgot to pay the electricity bill.'

'Are you the man who phoned me?' David suddenly became aware that his left hand was hurting again and realised that he was squeezing the bottle so hard it was liable to shatter in his grip. He tried to force himself to relax a little.

'Yes,' the man said, and then abruptly his voice hardened. 'Now come in.'

David felt as though he should be furious, should be storming in here, hands outstretched, searching for this man's throat. He felt guilty that he wasn't, even though he knew that anger would do nothing more than cloud his vision, make him reckless. It certainly wouldn't help Ellen and the girls and the Joyces. The only thing that would was if he remained calm and demurely accepted the man's conditions.

Moving tentatively, wary of traps, he edged forward into the blackness. He raised his right hand protectively as the shadowy suggestion of shape and form he had experienced in the corridor degenerated into a darkness more profound than he had ever known, and the clammy chill of the place settled on his skin. David peered ahead until his eyes ached but could not even see the hand that he had raised in front of his face. He moved forward perhaps half

319

a dozen slow shuffling steps before coming to a halt. His lips were trembling, his fear compounded by the cold, as he said, 'Okay, I'm here. What happens now?'

'Walk forward,' said the voice. It was somewhere in front of him, but exactly how close he was not sure. 'Take four steps and then stop.'

David did so, testing the firmness of the ground with the tips of his toes at each step before putting his full weight on his leading foot. He didn't want to find himself suddenly plunging forward into empty space, into a hole in the floor, or even down a flight of stairs. The floor was uncarpeted, and, guessed David, made of concrete, judging by the way it deadened his footfalls. After four steps he stopped again. His left hand was still in his pocket, trying to derive what comfort he could from the bottle, his right still wavering in front of his face as if to protect it from attack. All the things they could do to him kept flickering through his mind: a bullet through the brain, a knife across the throat, acid in the eyes.

'Okay,' he said. 'Now what?'

There was no reply.

He gripped the bottle tighter, as though in the hope it might absorb his sudden surge of panic. 'Where are you?' he called.

Somehow, silently, while David had been moving forward, the man had been moving too, had managed to get behind David without him even knowing about it. 'Watch,' the man said, so close that David fancied he could feel the warmth of the man's breath on his ear. He twisted his head but the man said sharply, 'Don't turn round. Don't even move. Just watch.'

It was hard but David complied. He faced forwards again, remained absolutely still and peered into the darkness. Though the bottle was a comfort, it didn't prevent him feeling afraid. He saw shapes begin to swirl in front of him, but they were not quite forming, they were breaking apart just as he was on the verge of recognising what they were. He saw colours – purples, browns, deep blues – and even though he knew that really it was just his mind trying to make something out of the nothingness, he felt rigid with apprehension. He closed his eyes briefly but there was no escape there; swirling shapes were forming from the darkness behind his eyelids. When the orange pinpoint of light appeared somewhere in front of him, David thought that this was simply a product of his mind too.

Even when the light spread, became more defined, he still believed that he was imagining it. His mind was creating something he craved, something for his deprived senses to focus upon, something to warm the chill from his bones. 'Stand still,' the man behind him ordered, and it was only now that David realised he had actually taken a step towards the light. He stood still, blinking, trying to clear his mind. 'Look at the light,' the man said. 'Don't take your eyes off it.'

So it was not in his mind at all; it *was* real. David was not sure whether to feel frightened or reassured by the fact. The light was the colour of a candle inside a Halloween pumpkin, but its texture was odd. It seemed somehow contained, controlled; it seemed to spread slowly, like liquid or corrosion.

A shape was becoming defined by the light, but for now its nature defeated him. He saw something spinning slowly, a whirlpool made of solids that glowed like phosphorescence. Without question it was mesmerising, even beautiful. David was only vaguely aware that he was gripping the bottle as if his life depended on it.

'Do you see?' the man behind him murmured. 'Do you see what you're dealing with?'

'Yes,' David said, though he was not sure that he did.

'We need the bottle, Mr Fox,' the man said. 'We need the bottle more than you do.'

The man's words nudged David part-way from the reverie which his contemplation of the light had become. He half-turned his head, then remembered and turned back again before the man could say anything. 'Why?' he dared to ask, his curiosity, for the moment at least, overriding his fear. 'What's it for?'

'It's for us,' the man said. 'That's all you need to know. You just hand it over, walk away and tomorrow you can resume your life.'

'But . . . Ellen. And Jane and –'

'Shh, Mr Fox. No more questions. Just be grateful that we're being so gentle with you, particularly after the way you treated poor Tametia.'

'Tametia?'

'The cat. Her condition, unfortunately, is still deteriorating.'

'Yes,' David breathed, 'the cat. Oh!'

The exclamation was David's response to his sudden recognition of the form the light had taken. It was that of a man, his skin smooth, his head bald and featureless, as if his body was encased in luminous tight-fitting rubber. He was curled up in the foetal position, and the most astonishing thing of all was that he was spinning slowly in mid-air as if cradled within the revolving framework of a giant sphere. Now that he was whole, he lent a dim illumination to the rest of the room. Despite what the man had told him about not turning his head, David could not resist looking round.

The room was bare of furniture and carpets, and the walls, though a few scraps of floral wallpaper still clung to them like flaking skin, were grey and blotched with damp. There was a heavily boarded window behind the revolving figure, a closed door that led presumably to the rest of the flat. The floor, as David had guessed, was concrete, untidy with bits of rubble, broken glass and cigarette butts. Somewhat reassured to find himself in a real place, albeit a hovel, and wondering vaguely where else he might have been expecting to find himself, he drew the bottle from his pocket.

'Ah,' the man behind him murmured, 'the object in question. Very good. You may turn round. Slowly.'

David did as instructed, showing his back to the glowing spinning figure. The owner of the voice, standing a few feet behind him, looked more or less as David had imagined he would. Though the man's face betrayed his age as around sixty, his body seemed to belong to a much younger man. He had a physique that suggested power; he was tall, upright, with broad shoulders and narrow hips. He was soberly but immaculately dressed, in grey pin-striped suit, white shirt and grey silk tie. He had dove-white hair with a moustache to match, and given a bushy beard could have played Father Christmas if it hadn't been for his eyes, which were devoid of warmth.

David saw now that apart from himself and the man there were two other men in the room. They were big and burly and silent, standing one on either side of the door through which David had entered, like nightclub bouncers. They made David feel very uneasy.

'If I give you this,' he said, 'what happens then?'

The man smiled – or at least his mouth did; his eyes remained cold. 'You walk out of here, you get into your car and you go home. Tomorrow you will be joined by your wife and daughters and your two friends. What happens from then on, Mr Fox, is your own affair. Our only stipulation, naturally, is that you keep quiet about everything that has happened to you these past few days.'

'And if I don't?' said David.

'Oh dear, what a tedious question. Well now, first of all, nobody would believe you anyway, and I can guarantee that you would find no evidence whatsoever to support your wild stories. And secondly ... oh, I suppose one of your daughters will meet with a fatal accident. Or perhaps your wife. Something along those lines.'

The man smiled again and smoothed his moustache. David nodded and held up the bottle. It felt warm as a kitten in his hand, felt like a living thing, like flesh.

'Okay then,' he said, feeling as though he was relinquishing part of himself, 'take it.'

The man reached out his hand and David placed the bottle into it. Instantly the man closed his fingers around it and took three steps back from David. 'Thank you, Mr Fox,' he said, the tone of his voice suddenly changing, becoming sharper, colder. He crooked a finger at the two men by the door, then pointed at David. 'Kill him,' he said, 'slowly and painfully.'

David's stomach dropped into his boots. He backed away as the two thugs ambled towards him. 'W–what do you mean? You can't do this,' he stammered.

The white-haired man smiled. 'I can do whatever I like, Mr Fox.'

'But we had a deal,' David wailed. He was still backing away even though he knew there was no escape, holding up his arms in a warding-off gesture even though he knew physical resistance would prove futile.

The man snorted disdainfully, pulling a face as if David had committed a social faux pas. 'So what?'

'But my family –'

'Your family are dead, you stupid moron. I fucked your little girl, made her swallow my come, before I slit her throat.'

David felt as though he had been doused in icy water. His whole body seemed to clench, to freeze, with the shock of what he had just heard. For a moment he couldn't react – couldn't speak or move, couldn't even breathe. Then a rush of heat melted the shock, transforming it into such rage that he felt his heart would burst with it, and he roared like an animal, the echo of the sound booming around him in the empty room, and launched himself at the white-haired man.

The thugs reached David first, slamming into him, smashing the breath from his body, grabbing his arms and twisting white agony into his muscles, bearing him struggling to the floor. David's rage intensified along with his pain, was indistinguishable from it. He could only see sizzling redness in front of his eyes. He writhed and kicked and spat and swore, but even his fury, his desire to tear the white-haired man apart with his bare hands, did not lend him the strength to overcome his assailants. The frustration was worse than the pain in his arms, which felt as though they were being crushed by tanks. The inability to do anything, to exact the revenge he felt entitled to, was like being forced to turn all his rage and violence against himself.

And then suddenly one of the thugs screamed, and David felt the pressure on his left arm lessen, felt as though his arm was floating upwards on a bed of pins and needles. He blinked through the red haze that was gauzing his vision, and became aware of fire dancing atop a black hulk, a teardrop of white-yellow flame splashing the blotchy walls with its erratic light, agitating the shadows. Had he done this? he wondered, but if so, what exactly *had* he done? He stared, uncomprehending, for perhaps five long seconds, and then all at once, like a camera pulling a picture into focus, everything became clear; he suddenly realised what he was looking at.

One of the white-haired man's henchmen was staggering about the room with his hair on fire.

David had less than a second to wonder what was going on, because almost immediately the second thug cried out too and then he was jumping up, staggering about, beating at the flames in *his* hair. If it hadn't been so grotesque, if the men's screams hadn't been so piercing, if the smell of crisping hair and then blistering flesh had not been so pungent, so stomach-turning, it would almost have been funny.

For a few seconds, David lay on the floor, bewildered by what he was seeing, aching arms outspread like a horizontal crucifixion. One of the men was spinning in small circles in the middle of the room now, ducking and weaving like a boxer, as though believing he could dislodge the flames or somehow evade them like a swarm of wasps. The other man was sinking to his knees, semi-conscious, the flames dying but only after having left the flesh of his head bubbling and charred. David had the impression there were other people in the room, an extra two or three shadowy figures. This was confirmed when he heard the white-haired man snarl, 'What the hell do you think you're up to, McQueen?'

The name rang a bell, but David had no time to think about it just now. He was free, and there was the white-haired man, the man who claimed to have killed his family and raped his youngest daughter, standing just a few feet away, his attention distracted, the bottle still clutched in his right hand. Gritting his teeth against the busy tingling pain in his arms, David pushed himself into a sitting position and then scrambled to his feet. As he lunged, arms outstretched, the white-haired man half-turned towards him and thrust his right arm towards David, either instinctively using the bottle as a shield or intending to smash it into David's face.

David's instincts, however, were quicker, perhaps because he was younger, perhaps because his sense of self-preservation was so strong, or simply because he was fuelled by rage. As the white-haired man jabbed the bottle towards his face, David half-twisted, shot out a hand and grabbed the neck that was jutting from the man's wrist. For a few moments, David and the man grappled like relay-racers squabbling over the baton. All David's rage was directed at the white-haired man, all his hate and energy; he screamed it into the man's face. He felt waves of it surging through him, threatening to engulf him, convulsing him like sickness.

The bottle, like a lamp plugged into a power source, suddenly erupted with light.

Even before David could screw up his eyes against the glare, the light had engulfed the white-haired man from head to toe. Though David felt no pain, the man evidently did; he threw back his head and screamed. Within the inferno he resembled a negative. His skin and teeth and hair were blue-black, his pupils and tongue and suit of a white so piercing it was like staring at the sun through a telescope.

The bottle's white-blue fire embraced the man, and then, even as David watched, began to slice him apart with flames like piercing silver daggers. The heat and radiance were tremendous, but neither David nor the man could let go of the bottle; it fused them together like Siamese twins. Not that David wanted to let go. Though the bottle was feeding on his rage, it was also swelling it, amplifying it; David felt gorged with the yearning to see this man suffer for what he claimed to have done. The man was shimmering now like a mirage, his body blurring, the light opening bloodless cuts in him. No, they were not cuts. They were more like . . . more like mouths. Mouths that snapped and snarled like a pack of wild dogs devouring their prey, and then screamed when they filled with light.

Despite his wish to see this man dead, the sight repulsed David and he closed his eyes. Instantly he felt as though he was slipping down into the redness inside his own body, felt as though his mind was breaking apart and gushing through his own hot veins, his senses filling with the juicy roar of his own blood, the muffled pumping rhythm of his heart. Suddenly and alarmingly, his centre of balance tilted. He opened his eyes and immediately whiteness poured into them, of such intensity that he thought his retinas had shrivelled like cellophane. He staggered and dropped to one knee, his hand slipping from the bottle at last. All at once he felt exhausted, as though the energy of his rage had been sucked from him, as though his body was a machine that a moment ago had been roaring and churning with life but which had now run dry of fuel.

He slumped to the ground, rested his cheek against the cold gritty concrete, closed his eyes once again, and slept. How long he lay there he was not sure. Perhaps only for a few seconds, because he became aware, almost immediately it seemed, of something tugging at his right arm, of a voice urging, 'Come on, son. Come on, wake up.'

David groaned, rolled on to his back, opened his eyes. He saw a face looming over him, the features rudimentary as though scratched in with charcoal, bleached of texture by the light that made the room bright as a freezer store. Nevertheless he recognised the face almost immediately.

'McQueen,' he mumbled groggily. 'I met you in the pub.'

'Aye, that's right, son,' the Scotsman said. 'Now come on. Ah havena the strength ti carry you.'

Aided by McQueen, David sat up and looked around. The two thugs were lying unconscious on the floor, wisps of smoke curling from their charred scalps. The white-haired man was unrecognisable as a human being now: still entwined within a vortex of light, he had become an amorphous thing, a shifting column of snapping writhing mouths. What was most abhorrent about the creature, if creature it could be called, was the fact that it appeared to be devouring itself.

David turned away, sickened. 'Come on, son,' McQueen said. 'Just pick up the bottle and let's git oot o' here.'

He nodded towards the cocoon of light, which even now was dwindling, taking the self-devourer with it. David turned and saw the bottle, only flickering intermittently now like a stuttering firefly, lying a little apart from the self-devourer's death-throes. Tentatively he reached out and picked it up, his hand mere inches from the bubbling soup that the self-devourer had become. He dropped the bottle into his pocket and then, aided by McQueen, hauled himself to his feet.

Together the two of them stumbled towards the door. David glanced back once, saw the self-devourer dwindling like a spent firework, saw that the spinning man had also gone. Out in the corridor he slumped against McQueen, his legs buckling beneath him once again. The little Scotsman struggled to keep him upright.

'Come on, son,' McQueen urged. 'Not far ti go now.'

But David felt suddenly overcome by grief and shock and reaction. He slumped to the ground, McQueen letting him down gently, and said, 'Leave me.'

McQueen frowned and took his arm again, attempting to drag him to his feet. 'Don't be daft, son. You can't stay here.'

'Why not?' David said. 'I've got nowhere to go. He . . . that thing in there . . . killed my family.'

The Scotsman crouched down beside David and placed a reassuring hand on the back of his neck. Gently he said, 'Did he tell you that?'

David gave the slightest of nods.

'Well, he's lying then,' said McQueen. 'Take it from me, David, your family are okay, still very much alive at any rate.'

David looked up. There was hope in his eyes, hope that seemed almost afraid to show itself for fear of being dashed.

'Really?' he said, both wonderment and caution in his voice.

'Aye, really. You don't want ti listen ti Worthington. He's just an evil bastard. He likes upsetting people.'

David felt joy gathering inside him, a radiant all-encompassing joy that was pushing his lips wide in a grin.

'I don't believe it,' he said. 'I don't believe it!' Then the grin faltered. 'How do you know?'

McQueen patted David's back. 'Trust me. Ah know. Worthington was lying. Ah'll explain everything once we're out o' this place, once we're far away from here.'

David scrambled to his feet, Willie's news having filled him with fresh impetus.

'Okay,' he said, and the two men began to make their way down the corridor. 'Who are you, really?' David asked him. 'How did you know I was here?'

'We've been keeping tabs on you for a while,' McQueen said. 'Ah knew about Worthington's phone call. How ah knew and who ah am will have ti wait till later.'

'Why not now?'

'It's too dangerous. Look, ah promise ah'm a friend and ah promise all your questions will be answered eventually. But noo isn't the time. You'll just have ti trust me.'

'Do you know where my family are?' David asked as they entered the foyer and made for the main doors.

'Not exactly, but ah can find oot. Noo, no more talking. Okay?'

David looked set to argue, then reluctantly nodded. 'Okay,' he conceded.

Willie pushed open the doors and the two men walked out of the building. The cold outside hit David like a battering ram. Still weakened by his ordeal, he reeled and would have fallen had McQueen not been supporting him. 'Over here,' McQueen shouted, and staggering like a couple of drunks, the two of them made their way towards a car that was idling further down Legion Street. Though the car was partially obscured by swirling sleet which seemed to swarm like moths in the headlight beams, David could see more than one dark figure inside it. He skidded to a halt, making McQueen stop too.

'Hang on,' he said. 'I don't know about this. Who's in that car?'

330

'Just friends. It's okay, son, honestly. D'you really think ah'd try anything, having seen whit that bottle can do?'

'I've got my own car,' said David.

'Aye, but there's no one sittin' in it who can help you, is there? No one who knows whit's goin' on?'

David looked at McQueen. The Scotsman was right, of course. 'Okay,' he said finally, 'I'll come with you. But you know what'll happen if you try anything.'

'Oh aye,' said McQueen. 'You've got the bottle, just like on the milk advert. Noo come on, ah'm freezing ma bollocks off standing here.'

The two of them splatted through the thin mush of sleet to the car. When they were still a few feet away, David saw the figure in the passenger seat reach round and open the back door for them. David got into the car first, noting as he did so that it was a brand new BMW. The car was warm inside and smelled of new leather. He slid along the seat to a position behind the driver, allowing McQueen room to get in too. The Scotsman did so, slamming the door, shivering the cold out of him. His tartan cap and the shoulders of his jacket were flecked with sleet which was already melting. The man who had opened the back door of the car for them was still twisted round in the front passenger seat, staring at David. David stared back. Somehow he had a feeling that they had met before, but he couldn't for the life of him remember where or when. Finally the man extended a large meaty hand for David to shake.

'I'm the reason you came here, Mr Fox,' he said. 'I'm Malcolm Marshall.'

4

The Schism

33

Jane's body felt like a house that had been invaded by something very bad and very strong, and though it was her own house, the place that she filled perfectly, she had been forced into its tiniest cupboard, crammed into a smothering darkness where she couldn't move. The bad thing, meanwhile, was making her body its own, using it, hurting it, filling it with its evil. Jane felt all the pain of this, the sense of violation, but she was powerless to stop it.

Sometimes the thing used her voice; Jane was aware of her mouth opening and words coming out, but they were not her own words. Sometimes she was left in the darkness of the tiny cupboard inside herself, and sometimes, when the thing let her or perhaps felt that it didn't matter, she sort of knew what was going on. She didn't actually *see* what the thing was using her body for and what it saw out of her eyes, it was more like she dreamed it, or as though the thing had used her eyes and then had planted what it had seen into her thoughts, her memories. Jane was scared, more scared than she had been of the white-haired man. Being tied up in the cellar had been bad enough, but being trapped inside herself, unable to move or speak or even to think properly, was far, far worse.

She knew now she should have listened to the girl in the wood, Yvonne. She should never have trusted the thing that had pretended to be Daddy, should never have brought it back with her. She didn't really know where that place that it had come from had been. Although she had been asleep, it had been a place beyond dreams, beyond thoughts. She realised now that the thing that had been chasing her through the monastery and then the woods, and the thing that had claimed to be Daddy, were one and the same. It had tricked her, and now, she supposed, it would do whatever it was going to do to her and then spit her back into the place where the other children were, where she would remain for ever and ever.

She wanted to cry. She wanted to scream and kick and struggle, to shout for Mummy and Daddy to help her. But she couldn't. She was lost in the darkness, trapped in there. She was filled with the horrible fear, with the terror, that she would never get out, never see Mummy and Daddy ever again.

34

When David awoke, nudged gently by McQueen, he felt
he'd been sleeping for hours. He opened his eyes, fully
expecting daylight to pierce them, but all he saw were
trees on either side of the road, paper-white in the lurching
headlights, scribbling their uppermost branches on to a
night sky dominated by grey cloud which choked the
moon. Immediately he wondered how he had managed to
sleep through the hammering that the uneven road was
giving to the car's suspension. He must have appeared
bewildered for McQueen said encouragingly, 'We're
nearly there, son.'

David looked around, trying to spot something that
even vaguely suggested a destination. All he could see
were trees and more trees, behind which was a blackness
that he assumed became hedges or fields in the daylight.
Though the question of his whereabouts was uppermost in
his mind, he automatically found himself asking, 'What
time is it?'

McQueen looked at the watch on his scrawny wrist,
angling it towards the light. 'It's almost two-thirty, son.'

'In the morning?'

McQueen gave him a look.

'Sorry,' said David. 'Stupid question.' He struggled
upright, groaning as the anaesthetic of sleep began to fade
from his shoulder and hip and the pain in them
reawakened. His head felt thick and dull, his mouth
gummy. 'Whereabouts are we?' he asked now. 'I don't
recognise this place.'

From the front seat, Marshall said quickly, 'It's best if you don't know.'

Although he had felt trustful enough to sleep in the company of these men, the merest hint of equivocation still made David uneasy. Suspiciously he said, 'But you told me earlier that when we arrived you'd answer all my questions.'

'We haven't arrived yet,' Marshall said, 'not quite.' He twisted in his seat to look at David, the darkness reducing his features to a series of black inverted triangles. 'Please be patient, Mr Fox. And if you remember, we had an agreement: absolute silence.'

David sighed in exasperation, but gave a resigned nod and settled back in his seat. He rotated his aching joints, wincing as something clicked in his neck. He tried closing his eyes again, but that, combined with the jolting of the car, made it feel as though heaviness was trapped inside his skull, so he opened them again. He looked out at the countryside, the liquid darkness of which made him impatient for it to change, and then at the back of Malcolm Marshall's head.

Marshall must have been seventy or so now but he still looked like a boxer. He didn't actually have a neck as such; his head sprouted direct from his broad shoulders. Everything about him suggested compacted strength, from his partly shaven head, the stubble grey as rock, to his knuckly features and chunky hands. Even the hairs growing out of his nose made David think of iron filings. He resembled, thought David, a barrel-chested troll, or a stubbier version of Desperate Dan.

When Marshall had first turned round, thrust out his hand and introduced himself, David had panicked despite the bottle. He could admit to himself now that he had spent most of his time in London contriving activities to avoid confronting Marshall, as a result of which Marshall had become more than just a man in David's mind – he had become a symbol, a kind of bogeyman, the pivot around which, and perhaps because of which, all the other events were revolving. Finally coming face to face with him had not only shocked David but had also given him a terrible sense of inevitability. He had flinched from the proffered hand, had scrabbled at the door handle but found the door to be locked with no apparent means of opening it from the inside. 'Let me out,' he had shouted. 'Open this door or I'll use the bottle. I mean it.'

Calmly Marshall had withdrawn his hand and then held both of them up, showing David his palms. 'Hey, calm down, son,' McQueen had said. 'We're no your enemies, we're your friends – Mr Marshall included, whatever you might think.'

David had rounded on McQueen, had seen flecks of spit arc from his mouth as he snapped, 'You tricked me, you bastard. I suppose you're going to tell me you didn't know that he's the reason I came to London? The note in the bottle's about him. He killed his wife and child!'

McQueen and Marshall exchanged a glance. The man in the driving seat, who was concentrating on driving and whom David had not yet even noticed, said nothing – did not even turn round.

'Aye,' said McQueen. 'We guessed as much About the note, I mean.'

'He threatened me,' David said.

'No,' said Marshall, speaking for the first time since he had introduced himself, 'that's not true. I simply warned you, Mr Fox, and with good reason. If you remember, my exact words were, "I think you're out of your depth."'

Marshall may have looked tough, but his voice was weary, even brittle. It did not seem much of an Achilles heel, but it gave David a smidgen of confidence nonetheless, enough at least to inject some aggression into his voice.

'You killed your wife and son,' he said.

Marshall looked at him steadily, his expression unchanging. Then, slowly, he began to shake his head. 'No,' he said in a quiet voice, 'I didn't.'

David grimaced contemptuously. 'Then who did?'

Marshall glanced at McQueen again, and the Scotsman gave a slight nod, perhaps of approval or temperance.

'It was my son, John, who killed Celia, my wife,' Marshall said in a voice so flat that David knew he was trying to suppress his emotions, 'and then I killed what John had become.'

'Which was?' said David.

'Noo's not the time ti discuss this,' interjected McQueen. 'You'll get all your questions answered, son, believe me, but not here.'

'Why not? What's wrong with here?'

McQueen glanced out of the window as though his eye had been drawn by something, and seemed relieved to see only dark streets lashed by sleet. 'It's no safe,' he said. 'There's a chance this conversation's being monitored.'

'Monitored?' said David, thinking of spy films, electronic bugs. 'By whom?'

McQueen raised his eyebrows, but seemed resigned to answering at least some of David's questions. 'By the people who're holding your family and friends hostage.'

'What do you know about them?' said David. 'And more to the point, who are you people?'

McQueen looked pained. 'Please, David, it's all verra complicated. Like ah say, ah promise ah'll answer all your questions when we get where we're going.'

'Where's that?' David asked, undeterred.

'You don't really think ah can tell you that just noo, do you?' Willie said. 'Ah mean, come on, be reasonable.'

'Are we going to rescue Ellen and the girls?'

'Aye, eventually, hopefully. Let's get ourselves safe first, eh?'

David sat back, frustrated. Glancing out of the window,

he saw a bouncer the size of a sumo wrestler standing outside a pub plastered with a huge pink banner announcing XMAS KARIOKI TONITE.

'How do I know you're not bullshitting me?' he said, calmer now but still very much on his guard. 'How do I know you're not just after the bottle too?'

'Ah guess you don't,' Willie said. 'You just have ti trust us. But do you really think we'd try and take the bottle off you after seeing what it can do?'

'No,' conceded David cautiously, 'I suppose not, but I wish you'd tell me something. I'm burning with curiosity here. Can't you tell me anything at all?'

McQueen sighed and turned to the driver, whom David now really noticed for the first time. He was in his thirties, a handsome Pakistani with a closely trimmed beard. He wore tinted spectacles and a suit that made him look like a foreign diplomat.

'What do you reckon, Ishvak?' McQueen said.

Without turning his head, his voice soft and measured, Ishvak replied, 'I think it will be all right. There's nothing specific coming through at the moment as far as I can tell. I don't think they expected this.'

McQueen nodded and turned back to a baffled David. 'All right, son, we can talk for a short while. What do you want ti know?'

David was frowning at the back of Ishvak's head. 'What did you mean just then,' he said, '"there's nothing coming through"?'

Ishvak looked at David in the rear-view mirror, his eyes dark and implacable behind the tinted lenses of his spectacles. 'Just that, Mr Fox,' he said softly.

'But . . . I mean . . . coming through *where*?'

For a few seconds there was just the purr of the engine, the sigh of the heater, the wet sweep of the windscreen wipers. David was about to speak again when Ishvak asked unexpectedly, 'Do you believe in the powers of the mind, Mr Fox?'

David raised his eyebrows in surprise, and thought immediately of how the bottle seemed able to convert his own thoughts and emotions into a kind of raw energy that he could use like a weapon. Was this what Ishvak was alluding to? 'What kind of powers?' he asked cautiously.

Ishvak was still watching him in the mirror as though assessing his reactions, glancing at the road only intermittently. 'What would you say, Mr Fox, if I told you I was telepathic? If I told you I could hear thoughts just as clearly as you could hear . . . well, this radio?'

David was aware that all three men were staring at him. 'W–well, I don't know,' he stammered. 'Are you serious?'

'What do you think, Mr Fox?' Ishvak said quietly, his expression never changing.

'I think you are,' said David. He looked at McQueen and saw an expression of sympathy on the face of the little Scotsman. 'Look . . . what's going on here? I mean, who *are* you people?'

Before Willie could reply, Marshall rumbled, 'I don't think it's wise to discuss this now. We should wait until we're at the safe house.'

'Oh come on!' David exclaimed. 'You can't leave me dangling in the air like this. I'll go mental if you don't tell me *something*.'

Willie glanced at Ishvak, who said, 'Still quiet. But make it quick.'

'Okay,' said Willie, 'ah'll make a deal wi' you, son. Ah'll explain as much as ah can in two minutes, then we'll have ti have absolute silence for the rest o' the journey. Agreed?'

'How long will the journey be?' David asked. 'Are you allowed to tell me that?'

'A few hours,' Willie said.

'A few *hours*! Where the hell are we going?'

'You're wasting your own time here, Mr Fox,' Marshall said.

David glared at him, then sighed. 'Okay, okay, agreed,' he said. 'Go on.'

'Right,' said Willie, 'well, the people who have got your family are a society that call theirselves the Flux.'

'The Flux?' David felt compelled to interrupt. 'I've never heard of them.'

'They're a secret society.'

'Like the Masons?'

Willie smiled as though at a private joke. 'Aye, something like that. Anyway, ti cut a long story short, the Flux want your bottle, which as you know is why they kidnapped your family, ti use as a bargaining lever. They sent Worthington along ti get it, who's an evil bastard and plays by his own rules, but luckily for you we were there too.'

'So who are you lot then? And how did you know I'd arranged to meet Worthington?'

'Ah was coming ti that. Oor own group is opposed ti the Flux.'

'Why?'

'Och, the whys and wherefores o' that will have ti wait till later. It's a long and complicated story. Let's just say for noo, we don't agree wi' what the Flux is doing, we think they're . . . what's the word ah'm looking for?'

'Misguided,' supplied Ishvak.

'Aye, misguided, that's it. You see, we were all Flux members at one time, and as far as the Flux is concerned, ah still am. Ah found oot what Worthington was planning, got a couple of the boys together and we came along ti . . . er . . .'

'Intercept,' said Ishvak.

'Aye, that's it, intercept,' said Willie.

'So you're like . . . a double agent then?' David said, struggling to take all this in.

Willie seemed delighted with the label. 'Aye, a double agent. That's what ah am!'

343

David shook his head. 'This is ah .-. well, pretty unbelievable.'

'Aye,' said Willie sympathetically, 'it is.'

'So . . . why *are* the Flux after the bottle, and what is the bottle exactly? I mean, I've seen what it can do, but what do they want it for? And how did they know I had it in the first place?' David pressed a hand to his forehead as though afraid it would split with the sheer volume of questions queuing up to be answered.

Willie glanced at Ishvak, who gave a slight nod which David assumed meant it was still okay to go on. 'Ti be honest, son, we don't really know what the bottle's for just yet, and neither do the Flux as far as ah know. The reason they're after it is because . . . ah well, this is a wee bit complicated. Let's just say they have a guiding force, which they call the oracle, which tells them to . . . er . . . do things. It was the oracle that told them ti get the bottle and where ti find it.'

'Oracle?' said David, pulling a face. 'I don't understand what you mean. What is this oracle?'

'I'm afraid that information will have to wait, Mr Fox,' said Ishvak a touch imperiously. 'It's rather too complex to go into here.'

David frowned, but let the matter pass for the time being. 'Don't *you* know what the bottle's for?' he asked, looking at Marshall.

'Why should I know?' Marshall said with a scowl.

'Well, it was your son who wrote the note, wasn't it? And that's another thing. Why, if he was in the danger he claimed to be in, would he write a note and put it in a bottle instead of doing something more direct, like phoning the police? I mean, it doesn't make sense.'

Marshall looked at David as if he was stupid. 'Don't you understand yet, Mr Fox? My son didn't write that note.'

'Then who did?' said David, confused.

344

'We believe the note in the bottle was just a means to an end, Mr Fox,' Ishvak said. 'It was calculated to lead you to us.'

'Me specifically?' said David.

Willie frowned. 'How do you mean, son?'

'I mean, did the bottle want *me* to find you or just whoever picked it up off the beach?'

'Ah,' said Willie, 'now there's a question.'

'And one to which, unfortunately, we have no answer as yet,' added Ishvak.

David looked thoughtful. 'If it *was* for me,' he murmured, half to himself, 'then how do I fit into all this?'

'I think we should shut up now,' Marshall said. 'You must have heard enough, Mr Fox, to satisfy your curiosity for the time being.'

'There's still one question you haven't answered,' said David.

Marshall scowled. 'Well, I don't –'

'Just this one and then I promise I'll be quiet.'

Willie glanced at Ishvak, who nodded, 'Go on then,' said the Scotsman.

'Who *did* write the note and put the bottle into the sea for me to find?'

'Och,' exclaimed Willie as though David had come up with the question to end all questions, 'ah'm afraid, son –'

'Don't tell me,' said David, 'it's too complicated to go into here.'

Willie smiled and spread his hands apologetically. 'Sorry, son. We're no just being difficult for the sake of it, you know.'

'I believe you,' said David. He slumped back in his seat. 'Do we have to keep completely silent?'

'Aye, just ti be on the safe side.'

'Are the Flux telepathic too?'

'Some of them,' said Ishvak.

'Then can't they just read our thoughts if they want to?'

345

'I've created a psychic barrier,' said Ishvak, 'albeit a temporary, hastily constructed affair.'

'A *what*?'

'Think of it as the mental equivalent of a scrambler that distorts radio waves. If the Flux try to read our minds, all they will pick up will be directionless static.'

Despite himself, David laughed. 'This is unbelievable. It's like the bloody Twilight Zone.'

'Please,' said Marshall with a pained expression, 'could we be quiet? Even if the Flux don't pick up on our thought patterns, they'll pick up our voices if we don't shut up.'

'Malcolm's right,' said Willie. 'It's time we had a bit o' hush.'

'Can't we even play I-Spy?' said David.

Marshall glared at him.

'Sorry.'

David settled back, trying to make himself as comfortable as possible, and wondered how he was going to prevent himself going mad with curiosity over the next few hours. *Few* hours? What did that mean? Two? Four? Six? How far could you get in two hours? Up to Birmingham? And how about six? As far as Newcastle, maybe even into Scotland? Or maybe they were heading south, down to Cornwall or Portsmouth or Southampton. Or into East Anglia. Or maybe even Wales or . . face it, Fox, he told himself, you could be going *anywhere* in the British Isles. So here you are with three weird guys telling weird stories, one of whom you previously suspected (still suspect?) of murdering his wife and son. Is this a healthy position to be in? And yet, he thought, looking around, he felt more secure here than he had done in a long while. Despite everything, despite the surliness of Malcolm Marshall, the implacability of Ishvak, the grizzled seediness of Willie McQueen, he couldn't help feeling that these men were, for the most part, telling him the truth, however bloody crazy that truth seemed to be. Certainly

346

the barely contained panic of less than an hour before, and even the trauma of last night's shooting, now seemed a little distant (albeit temporarily perhaps), swamped by his curiosity. But why should this be? Was it because for the first time since he had picked up the bottle some of his responsibility had been taken from him? Or was it simply because, based on what McQueen had said, he now felt a little more optimistic about the fate of his family and friends?

Although he would not have believed it possible, he felt his eyelids drooping closed. As his adrenalin ebbed, he realised how bone-weary he was. It was warm in the car, and for the time being inactivity had been forced upon him; others were taking the initiative. His eyes flickered open and then closed again; lulled by the engine, he felt he could sleep for days. He slipped his hand into his pocket and gripped the bottle, wondering whether he dared give himself up to sleep. The bottle was warm and comforting. It seemed to relax him, to drain the tension from his muscles as though urging him to sleep. Even now David didn't believe his buzzing, wary mind would let him rest, but the instant he closed his eyes he felt himself spiralling down into welcoming darkness. He remembered nothing more until McQueen coaxed him awake almost five hours later.

He was staring out of the window again when he felt the car slowing down. He looked to the front and saw a gap in the trees ahead on the left-hand side of the road, marked by gateposts that lacked a gate. Ishvak turned the wheel smoothly and the car bumped through the gap and began to jolt up a track even muddier than the road had been. David didn't realise how tense the driver had been until he saw his shoulders slump, the furrows in his brow smooth out.

In the front seat, Marshall noticed it too. 'It's safe now?' he said.

'Absolutely,' Ishvak replied. 'The barriers are up, and they are exceptionally strong ones. Mr Hollis has excelled himself this time. He must be exhausted.'

David looked from one man to the other. 'I take it we can talk now?' he said.

'Aye, son,' replied Willie.

'So who's Mr Hollis?'

'Another member of our group,' said Ishvak. 'He's a telepath like me. You'll meet him in a few minutes – if he's not dead to the world, that is.'

'And he's created psychic barriers around this place, like the one you created around the car?'

'Oh, far more sophisticated. This place has always been protected to some extent, which is why we use it as a safe house, but Mr Hollis has strengthened existing defences quite considerably – I read the influence of his mind pattern everywhere; it's like a signature to me. The barrier I created around the car was flimsy, the work of a few minutes, whereas the ones around the safe house are the result of hours of concentration built upon years of consolidation.'

'Which is why we can talk noo,' said Willie. 'There's one or two in the Flux can tune themselves ti any conversation anywhere they like, but the barriers here keep oor sound in and them oot.'

'You mean they've got, like, supersonic hearing, like Superman?' said David.

Marshall frowned. 'This isn't the joke that you seem to think it is, Mr Fox.'

Before David could reply, Ishvak pointed ahead with his left hand and said, 'Here we are.'

David looked where Ishvak was pointing and saw what he at first thought was the flicker of a fire up ahead. However he quickly realised it wasn't a fire at all, but the lights from the windows of a house, glimpsed between tree branches. The drive, or rather track, up to the house, wound in and out of the trees like a slalom course. Finally, however, the trees thinned out and the track widened into a yard. Now the house could be seen as clearly as the cloud-choked moon and its own illumination would allow. It appeared to be a large stone farmhouse, with outbuildings clustered around it. Brownish light which the orange curtains couldn't contain gave limited definition to the yard, highlighting objects which would otherwise have melted shapelessly into the night. Here was an old water pump, there the twisted frame of a child's tricycle. Part of the yard was cobbled, and each smooth stone wore a skull-cap of dim light. As the yard opened up before them and the house came fully into view, David asked, 'So are you allowed to tell me now where we are?'

McQueen smiled. 'This is the safe hoose which is furthest away from London in this country. We're in Cumbria as a matter of fact, no far from Carlisle.'

'Carlisle!' echoed David, and wondered why he was surprised. After all, they had been travelling for hours. Ishvak swung the car round in front of the house and brought it to a standstill. David watched him switch off the car's heater, then the lights and then the engine, feeling a little tense, wondering, now that they were here, what he had let himself in for.

'You know, Mr Marshall, you were right,' he said.

Marshall turned. 'About what?'

'I *am* out of my depth.'

Marshall chuckled and Willie joined in. Ishvak gave a rather smug smile.

'Let's go inside,' Willie said. 'You can meet the others and then we'll have a nice long chat over a cup o' tea.'

'How many of you are there here?' David asked.

'Oh, a fair few.'

Ishvak pressed a button on his key ring and the car's central locking system disengaged. McQueen opened his car door, muttered 'Jesus, it's cold,' and clambered out.

Marshall climbed out of his side a little awkwardly, making David realise that he wasn't as physically powerful as he appeared: the years had taken their toll. He opened his own door and stepped on to muddy slippery cobbles. McQueen was right; it *was* cold.

They walked up to the farmhouse and McQueen knocked on the door. Despite the barriers that Ishvak had described, the woman's voice asking, 'Who's there?' was cautious.

'It's me, Willie,' said McQueen.

There was the sound of a key turning in a lock and the door opened.

'Did Patrick not know we were coming?' said McQueen a little mischievously to the girl who stood there.

She was perhaps eighteen, blonde and fresh-faced, and wearing a chunky patterned cardigan over a Friends Of The Earth t-shirt and a pair of snug-fitting jeans.

'Willie!' she exclaimed, and flung her arms around him. 'Oh, it's so good to see you all. Come in, come in.'

She stood aside and they all filed in, David at the rear. He smiled at the blonde girl and was surprised when she took his hand and said, 'Hello, David.'

He was murmuring his reply when McQueen said, 'You still havenae answered ma question.'

'What question was that?' said the girl.

He gave a mock sigh and rolled his eyes. 'Does no one ever listen ti me? I was asking why Patrick didnae know we were coming. I thought mebbe he was losing his touch.'

'Patrick is exhausted,' the girl said. 'He's been strengthening the barriers all afternoon. Ishvak must have sensed them.'

'I did,' said Ishvak, stepping through an arch in the right-hand wall towards a large open fire on the other side of the room. 'He's done very well.'

The girl closed the door, shutting out the cold. 'Patrick

says we're impregnable here now.'

Ishvak, holding out his hands to the flames, shook his head. 'Nowhere's impregnable, and we shouldn't become complacent enough to think otherwise. Their resources are still greater than ours.'

'Oh, you're such a pessimist,' said the girl, wrinkling her nose.

'Not at all. I'm a realist.'

Whilst this exchange was going on, David was looking around, taking in his surroundings. The room they had walked into was a large kitchen-cum-dining room, most of the floor space occupied by a rough-hewn wooden table which was strewn with used tea and coffee mugs, and surrounded by an assortment of chairs. The huge pot sink and the cupboards to the left of the door looked as if they had been there since the house was built, as did the enormous black cooking range which dominated the left-hand wall. The more modern items – fridge freezer, washing machine, plastic Kenwood kettle – appeared incongruous by comparison and somehow impermanent. The room beyond the arch which Ishvak had stepped through was a lounge set at a slightly lower level. It was carpeted in burgundy and dominated by a blazing log fire. Two settees and various armchairs, all of which were threadbare and none of which seemed to match each other, were arranged around the fire in a vague semicircle. It was evident the place was not a family home; though comfortable, there were no knick-knacks on the mantelpiece, no pictures on the walls, no books, no plants, no photographs. The only luxury items, in fact, were a portable TV sitting in one corner facing the wall as though in disgrace, and, oddly, a small artificial Christmas tree decorated with red tinsel on a battered side table, above which, tacked to the wall, was a loop of red ribbon supporting a dozen or so Christmas cards.

The blonde girl noticed David looking at the tree and

said a little ruefully, 'I did that to cheer the place up a bit. After all, it *is* nearly Christmas.'

David smiled. 'It looks really nice,' he said. 'Gives the place a bit of . . . er . . . sparkle.'

She responded to his smile with one of her own. 'You must be parched. Do you want a drink? Tea? Coffee? Beer?'

'Tea would be great.'

'You wouldnae have a wee drop o' Scotch?' said McQueen, who had now joined Ishvak by the fire.

The girl smiled again. 'What do you think, Willie? We knew you were coming.'

'Och, you're a wee angel.' McQueen winked at David who was hovering between the kitchen and lounge, feeling, despite the blonde girl's friendliness, wary and out of place.

All three men were now basking in front of the fire, its yellow glow illuminating their faces. 'Please, Mr Fox,' Ishvak said, 'join us.' He patted the seat on the settee beside him.

David nodded and walked over, sitting where Ishvak had indicated. Within seconds he felt hot enough to remove his Bogart. He started to do so, but when he felt the weight of the bottle in his pocket he had second thoughts. He shrugged his coat back on, and was soon sweating so profusely that he had to swab his forehead with his sleeve.

The girl went into the kitchen, reappearing moments later with a tumbler of Scotch and a promise that the tea wouldn't be long. 'You're like a den of thieves, you lot, all huddled together like that,' she said as she handed Willie his glass.

Willie swallowed half the whisky in one go, then gave a blissful sigh. 'Come and sit wi' us, Tippi,' he said. 'Where is everyone, by the way? I thought we'd get more of a welcome than this.'

'Oh, I'm not good enough for you, am I?' said the blonde girl, perching on the arm of McQueen's chair.

'Och, you're a sight for sore eyes, girl. Ah just thought, wi' things as they were, there'd be a wee bit more ... urgency.'

'It is three o' clock in the morning, you know.'

'Aye, but even so.'

'Besides, nobody knew what was really happening.' The girl looked suddenly serious. 'We didn't know whether you'd bring David back or even yourselves.' She suddenly put her arm around the little Scotsman and kissed the top of his grizzled head. 'It is good to see you, you old sod. It's good to see all of you.'

She looked happy and embarrassed. David was surprised to see her eyes shining with what looked like tears that she managed to blink back before they could fall.

McQueen slipped an arm around the girl's waist and squeezed, then he looked at David. 'Och, we havenae even introduced you two, have we?' he said. 'David, this is Tippi.'

'Hi again,' said Tippi.

'Hello,' said David.

'Go on, ask me the question that everyone else asks?'

David looked at her, feeling foolish, and still incredibly hot in his overcoat. 'What's that?'

Like a child reciting lines, Tippi said, 'That's an unusual name. Where does it come from?' And then, reverting to her normal voice, 'As if there's a shop somewhere that sells stupid names.'

Automatically David said, 'I don't think it's a stupid name.'

Tippi gave him a look. 'You're just saying that.'

'No, honestly, I think it's a nice name. And I bet I can guess where it came from.'

Tippi's face broke into a grin. 'Okay then, go on.'

'Your parents were Tippi Hedren fans, right?'

'More or less. My mum was a Tippi Hedren fan. She met her once, about a million years ago in Gibraltar, and she always said that if she ever had a daughter she'd call her Tippi. So here I am.'

David smiled and nodded, but wasn't sure what else to say. Tippi excused herself and went to fetch the tea. As she clattered about in the kitchen, Marshall said mildly, without taking his eyes from the flames, 'If you don't take off your coat, Mr Fox, you'll melt. None of us are going to try to steal that bottle of yours, you know.'

David swallowed and looked at Marshall's glowing profile. His face blushing red, he stammered, 'I know. I was just . . . it was just that . . .' He left the sentence unfinished, and instead began to wriggle his way out of his Bogart. He winced as pain flared in his left shoulder.

'Are you hurt, David?' asked Tippi, reappearing from the kitchen with a tray of steaming mugs. She looked and sounded genuinely concerned.

'No, not really,' said David, his Bogart now crumpled behind him. 'I've just got a few bruises, that's all. It's my shoulder and hip mainly . . . and my hand. Nothing to worry about.'

He opened and closed his hand as if to demonstrate its flexibility. Tippi put down the tray and sat beside him on the settee, Ishvak shuffling along to give her room.

'Let me see,' she said.

'No, really, it's all right. It's not serious or anything.'

'Relax, Mr Fox,' said Ishvak. 'Tippi's a healer. She'll take your pain away for you.'

David felt uncomfortable, but offered no further resistance as Tippi placed one hand on his shoulder and the other on his elbow and began to squeeze gently. He hoped she wasn't going to ask him to strip to the waist; that would give him a sense of vulnerability he could do without. Her fingers were strong, and he hissed in pain as they probed at the left side of his body, pinpointing the tender spots with surprising accuracy. She even trailed her fingers across his ribs before murmuring, 'Ah,' and closing a palm over his aching hip bone.

'You took quite a bashing, didn't you, David?' she said. 'What happened?'

He pulled a rueful face. 'I stepped on a roller skate, among other things.'

She smiled, though not unkindly, and said, 'Just relax, this'll only take a minute. Don't be alarmed if it feels a bit weird.'

She clamped her right hand over his shoulder, her left over his hip, then she drew a deep breath and closed her eyes. David looked at the three men, each of whom were watching what was happening with what he could only describe as expressions of professional interest. In all honesty he felt a bit silly. He didn't really expect anything dramatic to happen, and so when he felt a fluttering in his shoulder he thought at first it was his imagination.

'Here it comes,' Tippi murmured, 'here it comes.'

The fluttering intensified, became a tickling, wriggling sensation. David's eyes opened wide. What the hell was happening? It felt as though his nerves or his muscles were jumping about under his skin, as though blood was racing upwards through his veins towards his shoulder. It was not actually an unpleasant feeling, but it was an uncommon one and therefore alarming.

He looked at Tippi, whose face had turned pale. She had a sheen of sweat on her forehead, and a prominent tracery of blue veins beneath each of her closed eyelids. She frowned a little, pursed her lips, as though concentrating hard, then slowly lifted her hand from his shoulder. David felt a tugging sensation, and looked to see what was happening.

He was astonished to see something swirling up out of his shoulder into her open palm. It was dark grey like

355

smoke, but more sinewy, as though made of thick rubbery coils. Perhaps the oddest thing of all was that, although he could see it, it appeared to be not quite there. He blinked several times, almost as if he believed it was a blemish on his eyeball. But the thing continued to coil out of his shoulder and wrap itself around Tippi's hand, like the grey ghost of some tentacled undersea creature.

The entire process took perhaps fifteen seconds. When Tippi broke her connection with him, she was panting slightly, her face shiny with sweat, as if she had been running for several minutes. Her face was now pasty white, her lips and the skin around her eyes dark as bruises. She lifted her hand slowly away from his shoulder and held it in the air as if the hazy grey mass coiled around it was dangerous, like a snake.

Then, with a whiplash movement, she shook the thing free. It flew from her hand like a thick loose glove made of swirling shadow, straight into the fire. Immediately the fire flared, became twice its previous size; for a few seconds its flames burned a bright luminous green. David stared, eyes wide, until the fire shrank back to its normal size and colour. He had seen some amazing things these past few days, yet despite the frequency of the miracles he had witnessed, each seemed no less astounding.

'How did you do that?' he asked.

Tippi was pushing the hair back from her face, wiping the sweat from her forehead. Already the colour was returning to her cheeks. Instead of answering David's question she asked, 'How's your arm?'

Gingerly David rotated his shoulder in its socket and was not entirely surprised to find that the pain had gone completely. He examined his hip; there was no tender spot. 'Better,' he said. 'Completely better. What did you do?'

'I extracted your pain,' said Tippi.

'That grey stuff you threw on the fire . . . that was my

pain?'

She nodded.

'But how did you do it? I mean, pain's not a . . . not a solid thing, is it?'

'It's a gift,' said Tippi. 'It's my gift. We've all got one.'

David looked at her, and then at the others. They were all looking back at him, like psychiatrists assessing the reactions of an interesting patient. David pointed first at Ishvak, then at Tippi. 'You're a telepath, you're a healer, you've told me about someone who can hear conversations over great distances. I mean, who *are* you people, really?'

Marshall grunted, though whether in amusement or disgust David was unsure, and lofted one of the logs, which were stacked in a basket beside the fire, on to the flames.

'I think it's time to fetch the others,' Ishvak said.

'I'll go,' said Tippi, standing up. She still had damp strands of hair clinging to her forehead, but her normal colour had returned.

'How many of you are there in the house?' David asked, as he heard Tippi clumping up a flight of uncarpeted stairs.

'About a dozen,' said Ishvak. 'It's not wise to congregate in very large groups unless it's absolutely necessary.'

'Why not? Because of the Flux?'

Ishvak looked at McQueen, who said, 'Aye, that's right, son. But wait till the others get here and then we'll tell you everything from the beginning.'

David heard movement upstairs now, muffled voices. 'How many of you are there altogether?'

McQueen shook his head at David's persistence, but he was smiling. 'Here in the UK or worldwide?' he said.

David blinked. 'You mean . . . you've got members all over the world?'

'Oh, aye,' said McQueen.

'Every year we get together and have a big party,' muttered Ishvak.

Such was the bitterness in the bearded man's voice that David didn't realise at first that he was joking. Ishvak was gazing into the fire, lips set in a terse line, reflections of flames slithering across the lenses of his spectacles, hiding his eyes. Addressing McQueen, David asked, 'This group of yours, does it have a name?'

'Aye, well, sort of,' said McQueen. 'Because we split away from the Flux, we've become known over the years as the Schism.'

'The Schism?' repeated David as though testing the word. 'So how come, if you, and presumably the Flux, have got members worldwide, I've never heard of you before?'

Ishvak leaned back, smoothing imaginary creases from his suit with exquisitely manicured hands. 'It's best if you allow us to start from the beginning, Mr Fox,' he said. 'If you ask arbitrary questions, then you're just going to get a jumble of answers that will confuse you.'

Patronising bastard, thought David, and then remembered that Ishvak could read minds. He squashed the thought as though it were a mental bug, glancing quickly at Ishvak to see whether he had picked up the insult. If he had, there was no indication of the fact.

'All right,' said David, 'but can't you at least answer my original question?'

'Which was?' said Ishvak with a sigh.

'How many of you are there?'

'Depends,' grunted Marshall.

'On what?'

'Whether you're talking about just our group,' said Ishvak, 'or . . .' he hesitated before finishing, a little lamely, 'all people with abilities.'

'Okay,' said David, 'how many of *you* are there, *your* group, in this country?'

Ishvak raised his eyebrows and pushed out his bottom lip. 'Two hundred?' he ventured, looking at McQueen.

'Aye,' confirmed McQueen, 'aboot that.'

'And what about all together?' said David.

Again Ishvak looked at the Scotsman. 'Seven, eight hundred?' he said.

McQueen nodded.

'And what about worldwide?' said David.

This time Ishvak shook his head. 'Thousands. I couldn't begin to put a figure on it.'

Thousands. Thousands of people in the world with extraordinary, perhaps even superhuman, abilities. It was a mind-boggling concept, though perhaps the most amazing thing of all was not simply that these people existed, but that they had managed, if McQueen and co. were telling him the truth, to gather together to form what amounted to a huge global society. It was impossible to comprehend, in this day and age, that such a group could exist and yet remain secret. How had they done it? David was aching to know, but now he heard footsteps on the stairs again, descending this time.

The door into the sitting room opened and a little man entered wearing a flowery waistcoat over a white shirt with sleeves rolled up to the elbows. With his bald head, mutton-chop whiskers and pince-nez, he looked like one of Santa's elves. Behind him came Tippi, and behind her David caught a glimpse of the old woman who had approached him in Leeds, offering to buy the bottle, just a few days ago. He was unable to comment on the fact, however, for the little man was waddling across, both hands outstretched in greeting, a smile lighting up his face.

David automatically stood up, turned and offered his hand, and the old man enfolded it in both of his and began pumping it up and down. 'David!' he exclaimed as though greeting a friend he had not seen in a long time, 'How lovely to meet you at last!'

'Er . . . thanks. Nice to meet you too,' David replied, bewildered.

'You must tell me everything that's been happening to you. We've all been on tenterhooks here, not knowing how things were going to turn out.' He released David's hand and raised both of his as though stopping David from launching into an immediate account of that evening's events. 'But all in good time. First of all, I expect you're wondering who we all are and why you've been brought here. Allow me to introduce myself. My name is Max Fleischer.'

The name rang a very large bell in David's mind. 'It was you who told this lady –' he indicated Violet '– to try to buy the bottle from me.'

Fleischer seemed delighted by David's ability to remember. 'Quite right, quite right, and although your refusal to sell saved us a great deal of money it also caused us much anxiety.' He patted David's arm. 'But all's well. Here you are now, all in one piece and with the bottle intact, I take it?'

David might have found Fleischer's joviality irritating had the little man not been so instantly likeable. It was, however, in a curt voice that he said, 'All's *not* well. Apparently this other group, the Flux, are holding my wife and children and two of my friends hostage. The ransom they wanted was the bottle, but when I went to meet them tonight to hand it over, they took the bottle and tried to kill me.' He quickly told Max the rest of the story, aware as he did so of how sketchy and inadequate his words were in describing what in truth had been an incredible event.

Instantly Max became a model of concern and understanding. Placing a hand on David's shoulder, he said, 'My dear boy, please accept my apologies. It was very insensitive of me not to consider the plight of your loved ones.'

'That's okay,' David said.

'On the contrary. Naturally we'll do all we can to help you. But you must understand that the situation we're involved in here is a very delicate and dangerous one, and requires the utmost caution. Though it may seem unnecessarily time-consuming to you, our first task is to make sure you know exactly who we are and what you'll be dealing with in the days ahead. You do understand?'

'Yes,' said David, then gave a short, mirthless laugh. 'Well, to be honest, no, not really. I'm a bit confused by all this.'

'I don't blame you,' said Max, patting David again on the shoulder in what seemed a gesture of genuine affection. 'We'll try to make it as clear as possible though, I promise you.' He excused himself and moved aside, and was greeted, rather respectfully, David noticed, by the men who had brought David here. As the old woman, Violet, moved forward, David overheard McQueen ask Fleischer how Jean was, and Fleischer's voice seemed to lose some of its zest. 'Not so well,' he replied. 'All this excitement is not good for her. Tippi is helping a great deal, of course, but I fear that Jean has more pain in her than the poor girl can handle.' David did not hear what was said next, for his attention was diverted by the old lady who was moving hesitantly forward to greet him.

'We meet again,' said David, taking the old woman's proffered hand.

'Hello, dear,' said the old lady. 'Rather a lot seems to have happened since Thursday, doesn't it?'

David smiled at the understatement and nodded. 'You can say that again.'

'It reminds me of that old Chinese curse . . . how does it go now? May you live in interesting times.'

'I wish my life wasn't quite so interesting at the moment,' David said. 'I wish I'd left that bottle where I found it.'

'Don't blame yourself, dear. It was probably fate.

Unavoidable.'

'Maybe,' said David. A brief pause followed, which he prevented from becoming prolonged by asking the first question he could think of: 'Is Violet your real name?'

'Oh, yes,' she said. 'I'm impressed that you remembered.'

'I'm hardly likely to forget someone who offers me ten thousand pounds for an old bottle, am I?'

The old lady laughed. 'No, I suppose not,' and then added, self-deprecatingly, 'I wasn't very good at it, was I?'

'Well, to be honest, no,' said David. 'But maybe that was Max's fault, getting you to do his dirty work.'

'I like you,' said Violet, 'you're a very tactful young man.'

'Am I allowed to ask you what your surname is now?'

'It's Turner. I didn't tell you before because I didn't want to get any more involved than was necessary.' She sighed a little wistfully. 'It doesn't much matter now, of course.'

Oddly, despite the situation and all that had led up to it, David couldn't help feeling that he was in the midst of a social gathering here. It was like being a guest at a cocktail party without cocktails, with people milling around, engaging in chit-chat. He was peripherally aware that five or six more people had entered the room behind Violet, and were now renewing acquaintances with the three men who had brought him here, or just hovering, perhaps waiting their turn to speak to him. Though he felt more inclined to be trustful of these people than before, he still stood close to the settee, keeping his Bogart, and therefore the bottle, within reaching distance.

'Let me introduce you to a few more people,' Violet said. 'This is Richard Hodge and his wife, Melanie; this is Imogen Butterworth; and over there talking to Willie is Patrick Hollis – he's the one with the leather coat on – and Jack Livermore.'

If they were close enough, David said hello to people as

they were introduced. Everyone looked as though they had got out of bed especially to meet him, except for Imogen Butterworth, a willowy, graceful, somewhat reserved woman in her fifties, who was fully dressed, demurely made-up and had not a hair out of place. She looked and spoke, thought David, like the kind of woman you would imagine teaching elocution lessons in a finishing school for young ladies. Nevertheless, though he only exchanged a few words with her, he was sure he detected a warmth behind her restraint, a gentle humour in her hazel eyes.

The Hodges were in their early thirties, both attractive and fit-looking, the sort of people who looked as if they played a lot of sports and went for long country walks at the weekend. Richard Hodge was wearing a t-shirt and baggy tracksuit bottoms and white socks. Melanie wore a blue towelling dressing gown over a long nightshirt with a picture of Yogi Bear and Booboo on it. They had the rumpled appearance of people who had been asleep for a while, but despite this they were cheerful and seemed genuinely pleased to meet him. Richard Hodge's handshake was firm and dry and warm, and immediately made David remember something his father had once told him: that a man with a firm handshake was someone you could rely on – a piece of advice which David had always regarded rather dubiously.

Though Violet had pointed them out, it was actually Willie who introduced David to Hollis and Livermore. Hollis was wiry and grizzled, his fuzzy sideburns appearing to make up for his thinning hair. With his mottled complexion and shrewd eyes he looked more like a rogue and a drinker, and therefore a perfect companion for Willie. He was wearing a short black leather coat which had seen better days over his otherwise naked upper torso, and a pair of faded jeans which threatened to burst open under the weight of a hairy pot belly. Willie's advice to David on introducing his friend was, 'Don't believe a single word he says, and whatever you do, don't let the bugger sell you a car.'

Both men laughed at this, and David laughed too, though he was not sure whether Hollis actually was a car salesman or whether Willie had been making a joke. 'Nice to meet you, mate,' Hollis said in an odd accent which seemed to fall somewhere between Merseyside and New Zealand, and shook David's hand, his grip bony and surprisingly strong. David found it hard to believe that astounding mental feats could be ascribed to this shabby, rather dissolute-looking man.

'It's a disguise,' Hollis said.

'What?' replied David, taken aback.

'This scruffy exterior. If you don't draw attention to yourself, you're harder to find.'

David took a step back as if the extra few inches would make a difference. 'You read my mind!' he exclaimed.

'Sorry, mate,' said Hollis cheerfully. 'Bad habit of mine. It often saves time, especially with the birds. Know what I mean?'

He cackled and Willie joined in. The two men reminded David of the crows from *Dumbo*. He tried to kill the image before Hollis picked up on it, but it was impossible just to block your thoughts, or even to control them.

'What's it like reading minds?' he asked. 'Do you know what everyone's thinking *all* the time?'

'Bloody hell, you're joking,' said Hollis. 'I only read 'em when I want to. It's like with a book, you only know what's inside if you pick it up and open it. Christ, if I knew what everybody was thinking all the time I'd go stark staring bloody mad.'

'Let me introduce you ti Jack,' said Willie, indicating the man standing patiently on Hollis's left. He looked like a retired army colonel, tall and broad and straight-backed, with a beaky nose and bristling eyebrows. He was wearing an old-fashioned maroon dressing gown, with tie-ups resembling curtain tassels, over a pair of pale blue pyjamas and brown and white checked slippers. Like the Hodges, he had the rumpled, slightly bloated look of someone who had just got out of bed, yet he had evidently taken a few moments to rub some Brylcreem on to his sparse grey hair and comb it ruthlessly back over his scalp in an effort to make himself look presentable.

'Pleased to meet you, young man,' he said, his voice clipped and plummy, his handshake short and sharp as if he was trying to tug David's arm off at the wrist.

'You too,' said David, and then couldn't think of much else to say.

He was saved from having to make smalltalk by Tippi, who surprised him by appearing at his side and slipping an arm through his. David was touched by the companionable gesture, not least because she reminded him a little of Rachel, who would sometimes come up behind him when he was washing up or cooking, put her arms around his waist and rest her head between his shoulder blades.

'I see you've met everyone,' she said. 'Are you ready to do some serious listening?'

'Definitely,' said David.

'Okay. Ishvak wants us all to sit round the table in the kitchen, and Max is happy to go along with that. I think Ishvak feels more comfortable sitting on hard chairs around a big table – makes him feel he's in a board meeting.'

There was a general movement towards the kitchen. 'What does Ishvak do?' David asked.

'He owns a shipping company or something.' She lowered her voice. 'He's seriously loaded. We're talking mega-bucks. In fact, it was him who was putting up most of the money to buy the bottle from you.'

David wondered whether being able to read minds was a big advantage in the business world, but he tried not to wonder about it too much. Having two mind-readers, or telepaths, or whatever they called themselves, in the room made him feel distinctly uncomfortable. He picked up his Bogart from the settee and allowed Tippi to lead him into the kitchen. Already Ishvak was settling himself at the head of the table, hands meshed together on the table-top, speaking earnestly to Max, who was sitting down beside him.

'I'll make some coffee,' Richard Hodge announced as everyone sat down. 'Who wants some?'

Everyone did, except for Imogen Butterworth, who wanted Darjeeling tea, Willie, who requested another Scotch, and Hollis, who asked Max to reach behind him and chuck him one of the cans of Special Brew out of the fridge.

Ishvak unmeshed his hands and rapped hard on the table so that everyone stopped talking and looked at him. 'Right,' he said, 'I don't think we need say much in the way of preamble. You've all met Mr Fox, and basically all we're here to do is exchange a large amount of information as quickly and concisely as possible. Now, if no one has any objections, I'm going to act as spokesman this evening –'

'Morning,' Hollis muttered before ripping the ring pull from his can.

Ishvak frowned irritably. 'I beg your pardon?'

'It's morning. Three twenty-two a.m. to be precise.' He grinned and raised his can. 'Cheers.'

Willie chuckled. Ishvak gave him a withering look. 'Quite so,' he said tersely, 'which of course makes it even more imperative that we don't waste time. I'm sure we could all do with some sleep.'

Most people concurred, but David wasn't one of them. Despite the time he felt surprisingly fresh and alert. This was partly due to the deep sleep he'd had in the car, but mostly it was because it seemed he was finally on the verge of finding out exactly what was going on.

He was going to have to wait just a little longer yet, however, because the next thing Ishvak said was, 'But before I start, I think it would be a good idea if Mr Fox filled us in on what's been happening to him these past few days.'

David looked up in surprise. 'Me? But I thought you knew everything about me.'

'Not everything,' said Ishvak. 'Perhaps you'd be good enough to take us through your movements these last few days, starting with the day you found the bottle?'

David looked around the table, a little daunted by the request. There was so much that *had* happened, and a great deal of it bewildering, that the prospect of recounting it all seemed a mammoth task. He looked down at the scuffed stained wood of the table-top, wondering where to start. At last, however, he said, 'Okay, I'll try. I guess it all started because I've been feeling . . . well . . . pretty depressed lately.' He smiled self-consciously and glanced round the table once more. No one was laughing at him or pulling a face or giving him a pitying look. Encouraged by the response, he went on.

It took him almost three-quarters of an hour to tell his story, at the end of which his throat felt raw. However, he found the experience rewarding, cathartic even. Finally being able to recount the incredible events of the past few days to an attentive audience made him feel almost light-headed with relief.

'Thank you, Mr Fox,' Ishvak said softly when he had finished. 'Most enlightening.'

It was hard to tell whether Ishvak was being genuine or not; his expression remained deadpan, his voice without inflection. 'And now,' Ishvak said, 'here is our story. You already know that as a group we each possess one particular ability that makes us something . . . other than ordinary human beings. Sometimes, as in the case of Mr

Hollis and myself, our abilities are duplicated. You know that Mr Hollis and myself are both telepaths and that Tippi is able to extract pain. To add to that, Mrs Butterworth can become a perfect facsimile of whomsoever she chooses, Mrs Turner has the power of invisibility, Mr Livermore is able to plant whatever disease or illness he wishes into a person's body simply by touching them, Mr Hodge has the ability to send selected people to sleep in an area around him for a little while –'

'Like a party political broadcast,' interjected Hollis, eliciting a ripple of laughter.

Ishvak raised his disapproving voice above the laughter: 'Mrs Hodge can breathe life into inanimate objects, and Mr Marshall is pyrokinetic; he can create fires just by thinking about them.'

He drew breath, and was about to continue when David snapped his fingers and exclaimed, 'Of course, the two thugs in Coronation House. Worthington's henchmen. It was you that set them on fire, wasn't it?'

He directed the question at Marshall, who inclined his head only slightly as though reluctant to admit responsibility.

Ishvak said a little tersely, 'If I may continue, Mr Fox?'

David wafted a hand as though offering him the table. 'Sorry. By all means.'

Ishvak waited a couple more seconds, either to emphasise his disapproval or to ensure absolute silence, and then said, 'Mr Fleischer has the ability to manipulate memories and dreams, and Mr McQueen here can conjure up people's fears in their minds and use them against them.' He paused and looked at David almost smugly, like a scientist who has just unveiled a series of startling new discoveries.

David, feeling that a comment was called for, said, 'This is all just amazing. You sound like a bunch of super-heroes – the X-Men or something.'

Ishvak raised his eyebrows condescendingly, but a couple of other people chuckled. 'We're not superheroes, David,' Max said, 'not by a long way. We're human beings like yourself, with all the usual faults and foibles. It's just that, physically, we have . . . how can I put it? . . . a little bit extra. Each of us has a skill which sets us not above but . . . apart from our fellow men, and which, used independently of our compatriots, is generally of limited use. It is only together, our abilities complementing each other, that we are strong.' He turned to Ishvak sitting beside him and said with a beaming smile, 'But I'm being terribly rude, interrupting our friend here. Perhaps you'd like to take up the story, my boy?'

Ishvak gave Max a tight smile of acknowledgement and nodded. 'Moving away from our group for a moment, I'd like to tell you about the people who are holding your family and friends hostage,' he said.

Across the table from David, Hollis belched quietly. David wondered if that constituted his opinion of his fellow telepath or of the Flux.

'As you know, they call themselves the Flux,' Ishvak continued, undeterred. 'Across the world, people like us are either members of the Flux or members of the Schism. However it wasn't always like this. Up until this century only the Flux existed. Indeed, many of the people in this room – Mr Fleischer, Mr Hollis, Mrs Turner, Mr McQueen, Mrs Butterworth, Mr Marshall and Mr Livermore – were once members, but left when they began to question the methods that the Flux was employing in an attempt to achieve its goal.'

'And what is its goal?' asked David.

Ishvak frowned. 'If you'll bear with me, Mr Fox, I'll come to that eventually.' As David apologised, he continued, 'The Flux is an organisation which spans the world. It has thousands of members in every country you can name. It's a very old organisation, almost certainly the oldest in the world. Its origins predate Christ.'

'You're joking!' David blurted.

Ishvak scowled, exasperated at having been interrupted again. 'You think so?'

David looked round the table, perhaps in the hope that someone would back him up. 'It's just . . . I mean . . . how can it predate Christ? That's impossible! How can it have been going on all this time without anybody ever hearing of it?'

'Oh, people hear of it,' Willie said. 'People find oot about it all the time.'

'So how come it's never been exposed, or you either for that matter?'

'People are made to forget,' said Richard Hollis. 'It's as simple as that.'

'What do you mean,' said David, '"made to forget?"'

Max chuckled. 'It's not what you think, David, believe me. Our friend Richard meant nothing sinister by his statement. It's merely that, with our combined abilities, it has never been difficult to cover our tracks. If someone discovers something about us, we are able to call on members who can literally extract that information from them, erase that part of their life, without them knowing anything about it. No doors are closed to us, David. We have influence everywhere . . . or at least, the Flux has such an influence. Our own group, pitiful though it may be in comparison, exists merely to thwart their plans.'

'But why?' asked David. 'What are they after?' A thought occurred to him and his eyes widened. 'World domination, is that it? Christ, it is, isn't it? They want to take over the world.'

Max shook his head. 'No, David, think about it. That isn't it at all. If that was the case, they could have done it very easily, many thousands of years ago. No, the Flux don't work towards their *own* ends. They have a guiding hand.'

'A guiding hand? You mean . . . there's someone who gives them orders?'

Before replying, Max turned to Ishvak and said, 'Oh dear, I'm doing it again, aren't I? Would you like to . . .'

Wearily Ishvak shook his head, apparently resigned to having his lecture blossom into a discussion. 'No,' he said, 'you go ahead.'

'Thank you,' said Max. 'How kind.' He turned back to David, then frowned. 'Oh dear, I've quite forgotten where we were.'

'I think you were about to tell David about the oracle, Max,' Tippi said gently.

'The oracle. Oh yes.' His face took on a sombre expression. 'For as long as I can remember, the guiding hand I was talking about has always been referred to as the oracle. The oracle, we believed, was the voice of . . .' Instead of speaking he made an expansive gesture with his hands as if imitating a flower erupting into bloom, and looked meaningfully upwards.

'God?' said David, unable to keep the incredulity from his voice.

Max looked a little surprised, almost as if he had not actually considered the prospect before. 'God, yes . . . or more than God perhaps. We thought the oracle was . . . *everything*. All creation. Perhaps God's creator and its own.' He frowned hard as if unable to express what he was really trying to say. 'It's difficult, thinking back, to recall exactly what we did believe. The oracle was the voice of the pattern. It perpetuated the pattern by using the Flux and its abilities as . . . as instruments.'

He looked to Violet as if for assistance, but David said, 'Hang on a minute. What's "the pattern"? I don't quite understand.'

Violet said, 'The pattern is everything that happens. Every leaf that falls, every bird that sings, every . . .' She groped for another image '. . . every time anyone is born or dies, they are perpetuating the pattern, contributing to it.'

David was trying to grasp what these people were attempting to explain to him, but it seemed so abstract it was in danger of slipping through his fingers like sand. 'So you're saying that the world and everything that happens in it, from the tiniest, most insignificant thing to the biggest catastrophe, is part of some huge pattern, like fate has already been mapped out beforehand?' He looked hopefully at Violet, but she shook her head.

'Not mapped out. The pattern can be changed, channelled, by the will of the oracle. But at the same time everything that happens is *meant* to happen. Even if we thwart the Flux's plans, then that, so the oracle would have the Flux believe, is part of the pattern too.'

'So . . . you can never win, can you? I mean, whatever you do, you're all just part of the machinery?'

'That's what the Flux believe,' said Melanie Hodge.

'But you don't?'

'We don't, no,' said Max. 'We believe that the idea of the pattern is merely a convenient conceit used by what lies behind the oracle to keep its followers from losing faith.'

'Okay,' said David, 'so, according to the Flux, everything that happens is like a great big pattern, right, and the oracle is like the thing that keeps this pattern going along the right lines and the Flux is like the tools it uses; it tells them to do certain things, yes, so that the pattern is maintained?'

'A little simplistic,' said Max, 'but yes, that's basically it.'

'Okay,' said David. 'Two questions, or at least two that spring immediately to mind. First, if the pattern is supposed to continue to keep the world going, why are you trying to stop it? And second, what does this oracle look like? What form does it take? Is it just like a booming voice that you hear in your head or what?'

'We left the Flux,' said Max, 'or at least I did and Jack did and Violet did, around the time of the Second World War. Though you'll never read it in any of the history books, though you'll never find even the merest hint of a suggestion of it anywhere, the Flux, directed by the oracle, actually set the wheels of that war in motion. Out of the oracle's instructions came suffering and death on a massive scale, worldwide conflict, and the horrors of the concentration camps where thousands, *millions*, of my people were forced to endure the most appalling atrocities. At the centre of all this pain and horror and misery was one man, one small, seemingly insignificant man.'

'Adolf Hitler,' said David.

Max nodded gravely. 'Quite so. Adolf Hitler. And it soon became clear to us, having left the Flux, having shaken ourselves from its trance, as it were, that the oracle, or whatever lies behind it, almost . . . came through in that man.'

'Came through?' said David.

'This is what we believe the pattern is for, what the Flux are being manipulated towards. We believe now that what lies behind the oracle is evil, not just something that *is* evil, but evil itself, the essence of all the cruelty and horror that happens in this world. The oracle preaches death and destruction and misery. Kill this person, explode that bomb, start that fire. Through the Flux it often sets in motion events that build and build and eventually result in catastrophe, like dropping a small pebble into a lake and generating ripples which spread and spread. We believe that the evil feeds on the energy of all this misery and pain. Everything bad that happens in the world enables its power to grow.'

'And you think that when it gets strong enough, it will actually break through physically into this world?' said David.

'Yes, as it has tried to do before.'

'To do what?'

'Who knows?' said Max. 'Destroy it and move on, perhaps? Maybe that is its only ambition, to destroy and thus perpetuate itself.'

'So what stopped it breaking through before?' said David. 'What stopped it during the war, for instance?'

'We think it was too eager,' said Max. 'It spread itself too thinly, tried to do too much in too short a time. Certain of us . . .' He cocked his head to one side and rotated his hands, searching for the phrase '. . . woke up to ourselves, you might say, realised that what was happening could not possibly be the product of a benevolent force.'

Jack Livermore spoke up for the first time. 'We began to disobey its orders, to undermine the Flux's work. Eventually a small group of us made it behind enemy lines and assassinated Hitler.'

This, more than anything that had gone before, made David's stomach lurch purely because it seemed such an outrageous statement to make.

'*You* killed Hitler?' he exclaimed. 'I thought Hitler committed suicide?'

'We made it look like suicide. We changed the memories of the people that were there at the time, and we used our abilities to get away, leaving no trace whatsoever. We were very lucky. The Flux, or rather the thing that was controlling them, was so desperate to come through it had started making mistakes.'

'You killed Hitler,' said David wonderingly, still unable to get his head round the concept. 'Were you the one who pulled the trigger?'

'No,' said Livermore brusquely. 'I was there, that was all. I saw the deed done.'

David pressed a palm to his forehead. 'This is unbelievable,' he said, and laughed, perhaps just a little

374

hysterically. 'Totally and utterly crazy.'

Tippi put an arm around him. 'I know,' she said, 'but it's also true. You do believe us, don't you?'

Hollis was coming to the end of his second can of Special Brew. 'He believes us,' he said. 'He's not happy with the idea, but he's seen too much not to believe.'

'Are you reading my mind again?' said David irritably.

'Sorry, mate, just monitoring your progress, making sure you don't blow a fuse. Have one of these.' He held up his can. 'It'll make you feel better.'

'Thanks,' said David. 'I will.'

Tippi fetched it for him. There were only two left in the fridge, so she tossed the other to Hollis. He caught it one-handed, like a baseball catcher.

'Okay,' said David after breaking open the can and gulping down enough beer to give him a transitory buzz, 'so Hitler was killed, and then what? Nazism broke up, we won the war . . .'

'And the evil, which had been weakening the membrane which separated it from this world, suddenly found that the focus of its power had been destroyed,' said Ishvak.

David nodded slowly. 'And I suppose the oracle just told the Flux that its defeat was part of the pattern too?'

'Of course,' said Max, 'as was the rift in the Flux itself.'

'But you don't believe that?' said David.

'No. We believe it is an indication that the evil is not omnipotent as the Flux believe. We think it *can* be defeated. At least . . . this is what drives us on.'

David thought about what he had been told for a moment, taking another long swig of beer in the process. Then he said, 'So . . . how come the Flux don't realise that what they're doing is evil? I mean, surely if this oracle was really the voice of God, it would be telling them to use their powers to do good, not evil.'

Before Max could reply, Hollis said, 'Half the buggers in the Flux are evil bastards nowadays anyway.

Something's happened these last fifty years or so; things have changed. Either the force behind the oracle is getting stronger and affecting them, or it's somehow putting out feelers, attracting more and more nutters, siphoning out all the good 'uns.'

'But in our day,' Max added, 'we did these things because we believed it was a regrettable means to a glorious end. We believed, I suppose, that we were exorcising the evil by allowing it release, and that this would eventually pave the way for . . .' Again he floundered, seemingly lost for words.

'The coming of great good,' said Violet, but even she didn't sound sure.

'The coming of *ultimate* good,' amended Max. 'We felt we were cleansing the world.'

'Like squeezing the pus from a wound to clean it,' said Hollis, a phrase which made Melanie Hodge screw up her face and say, 'Thank you for that one, Patrick.'

Hollis grinned. David said dubiously, 'To be honest, that sounds like a bit of a flimsy excuse to me. I mean, surely that's the kind of thing that the Nazis themselves believed, that the Jews were unclean or whatever and that they needed to be destroyed, together with anyone else who opposed Nazism, to make way for their glorious master race?'

'Exactly right,' said Max, 'but we were manipulated by the oracle, we were made to believe absolutely in its integrity. We were fanatics in a way, I suppose. We had tunnel vision.' He shook his head as if trying to clear a cloud of confusion from his mind. 'Looking back to how I was, I see a different person with a completely different state of mind. We all do. We didn't realise it at the time, but we were completely in thrall to the oracle.'

'You were brainwashed, you mean?'

'Exactly! We were brainwashed, but in an incredibly subtle and sophisticated way. It was like . . . like . . .'

'Like the Moonies,' suggested David. 'That's all the Flux is really, isn't it? It's a crackpot religion, but an incredibly powerful and dangerous one, manipulating the workings of the world into ... into one big ceremony that will eventually result in the coming of their God.'

'You've got it spot on,' said Richard Hodge. 'Only they've been conned, haven't they? It's not God who's coming at all, is it, but –'

'The Devil,' said Hollis in a dark, dramatic voice.

'The Devil?' repeated David, shuddering despite himself. 'You don't think it's *really* him, do you?'

'It's evil,' said Max simply. 'It's only human beings who have given it a name and a personality. If you want to call it the Devil, then it's the Devil.'

David's heart was hammering hard. He gulped down so much beer this time that he almost choked. The escalation of events since Thursday was incredible. From finding an old bottle on a beach he'd progressed to discussing the coming of Satan with a bunch of superhumans. And perhaps what was most crazy of all was that he found he believed every word that was being said here. He placed the cold can against his forehead for a moment in the hope that it would aid him in organising his thoughts. There was so much he still wanted to ask, so many grey areas. After a moment he said, 'So, getting back to my earlier question – what does this "oracle" look like? Is it a person or a presence or what?'

As soon as he asked the question, he thought of the spinning, glowing figure that had materialised in the empty flat in Coronation House. Could that have been the oracle?

Hollis, however, surprised him by saying, somewhat bitterly, 'It's a kid.'

'A kid? You mean a child?'

'Yes. Or rather, it's not one kid but a load of kids. The oracle speaks through 'em. It chews 'em up and spits 'em out like . . . like jelly babies.'

The disgust on his face was evident, but David said, 'I don't quite understand what you mean.'

'I mean, the oracle chooses a kid, right – any kid from the age of, say, three or four to sixteen – and it . . . I dunno . . . takes them over, possesses them. It uses them for a bit, speaks through them, gives orders, stuff like that, and then eventually it just . . . kills them and moves on.'

'It kills the children?' said David, appalled.

Hollis nodded curtly. 'Yep.'

'But . . . but why? How?'

'Why, I don't know. I guess it can only use them for a certain time. It burns them up or something maybe, or maybe they start to get wise to it and fight back. As for how, well, there's loads of different ways. Some kids commit suicide – maybe that's the only way they can escape. Others have fits and stuff or just drop dead of so-called natural causes. Some are even found ripped apart as though they've spent the afternoon in a cage full of lions. I even know of one occasion where a kid just burst into flames. There's a word for it . . .'

'Spontaneous combustion,' said Melanie Hodge.

'All right, two words then,' Hollis muttered darkly.

Before David could express the horror that he was feeling, Willie said, 'The latest kid, Danny, just got torn apart. He was only five. A nice little kid.'

David shook his head slowly. 'That's really horrible. So, is there just one child for the whole world which the oracle speaks through, or is there one for . . . for every faction of the Flux?'

'For every country, aye,' said Willie.

'But what about the parents of these children?' asked David, half-dreading the answer even before he had finished asking the question.

Hollis shrugged. 'Quite often they're orphans, or kids living rough on the streets. They get the call and seek out the nearest Flux member to 'em. Sometimes, though, the kids have got parents, and when that happens either the parents have a terrible accident, courtesy of the Flux of course, or the kids are just made to kill their own parents and then disappear, and with the Flux's abilities it's easy to make a disappeared kid stay disappeared.'

David shook his head again, sickened. The thought of a child being forced to kill its own parents was somehow worse than the thought of deliberately setting into motion a war in which millions of people would die. 'And you were party to this?' he said accusingly, looking round the table at the ex-members of the Flux.

Max and Violet nodded shamefacedly, but Marshall met his gaze with a defiant one of his own and barked, 'Don't you judge us. You weren't there. You don't know what it was like.'

David was a little surprised at the vehemence of his reaction. Marshall looked fearsome as a roused bulldog, his eyes flashing, his cheeks glowing red. David realised he had overstepped the mark a little and he mumbled an apology. 'You're right,' he added, 'I wasn't there. I can't imagine what it must have been like. I can't imagine my head being messed about like that.'

Imogen Butterworth placed an elegant long-fingered hand over Marshall's clenched red fist on the table-top. 'Why don't you tell him the whole story, Malcolm?' she urged gently.

Marshall was breathing hard, staring at the table-top now, his mouth set in a terse line, his jawbone clenching and unclenching. He appeared at first not to have heard her, but then he gave a single brusque nod and his head snapped up.

Looking directly at David, speaking in a growl, he said, 'My son, John, the one who supposedly wrote the note in that bottle of yours, was one of the oracle's *children*.' He virtually spat out the words like a piece of rotten fruit.

'Maybe the oracle thought it was a joke using my boy like that, or maybe it decided to make an example of me, show the rest of the Flux who was boss, or maybe test my loyalty, I don't know. Anyway, I made it clear I wasn't happy about the situation, as a result of which the oracle killed my wife, Celia, used John's body to . . . to strangle her to death. When I found out what had happened I went berserk. I used my ability on John, burned him up. I wasn't killing him, not really. He was dead the minute the oracle chose him. I was just . . . cleansing him, putting him out of his misery.

'Anyway, because the oracle was then between hosts and because I just didn't care what the hell happened any more, the Flux were a bit slow to sort things out, and before they could I was arrested and the story appeared in the papers. We always tried to keep Flux members from being implicated in crimes, you see, not that there was any *real* danger of the Flux being exposed, of course, because it had the resources to cope with stuff like that easily, even after the event, but it was just to keep things nice and neat and efficient, to keep so-called little people, like policemen and newspaper reporters, from poking around. I didn't say anything to the police at the time about the Flux, of course, because I knew they wouldn't believe me, and even if they'd been prepared to investigate my claims they wouldn't have found any evidence to support them, but I did a lot of thinking while I was in custody and I left the Flux soon after. I only wish I'd come to my senses in time to save my family, but I didn't, of course . . . I didn't.'

Abruptly his voice turned brittle and then tailed away. His head drooped like a wind-up toy which had come to the end of its spring. Imogen Butterworth put her arm around him and whispered something in his ear. There was a pained silence around the table, broken after a few seconds by Willie, who said quietly, 'Ah helped ti clear up afterwards, dealt wi' Kerslake, but ah didnae make a verra good job of it. Ah was so disgusted wi' the way Malcolm had been treated that ah tried ti leave cracks where ah could in the hope that one day the whole fucking castle would collapse around the Flux's ears. No real chance o' that, o' course, but it made me feel better. Pardon ma language, by the way.'

David nodded vaguely, feeling bad about his accusatory outburst of a few minutes before. Awkwardly he said, 'I'm sorry, Mr Marshall, about what I said earlier. I didn't realise.'

Marshall made a slight gesture of acknowledgement with his hand, but didn't look up. David wondered why the evil that lay behind the oracle had put its grand plan in potential jeopardy by using Marshall's son. If it had acted purely out of malice, then surely that was a weakness? Or was the evil so arrogant that it believed it could just go ahead and do whatever it liked, could be as sloppy and inconsistent as it wished, and then simply get the Flux to paper over the cracks later?

His head was spinning with ideas and counter-ideas, thoughts and theories and suppositions. This whole concept of the Flux and the oracle and the pattern seemed like a recurring puzzle, each answer erupting into yet more questions. Turning to look at Max, David asked, 'So why don't you just expose the Flux? Match your abilities with theirs?'

Max smiled wanly. 'It sounds easy, doesn't it? But the Flux outnumber us by four to one, and our abilities, though undoubtedly impressive, are limited in certain areas. Besides, who would believe us? There is no evidence at all to implicate the Flux in anything anywhere. We would sound like crackpots. And even if, miracle of miracles, the Flux were exposed, how would the world defend itself against them? With weapons? With sheer weight of numbers? I don't think so.'

'So what *is* the answer?' David said, frustrated. 'Or isn't there one?'

'All we can really do,' said Richard Hodge, 'is keep tabs on what's going on, and when something big does happen, try to stop it. In the meantime, we just hamper the Flux's progress however we can.'

'It doesn't sound a very positive strategy,' said David.

'Well, what would you suggest?' said Melanie Hodge.

David's mind was reeling so much that he was in no state to suggest anything. 'I don't know,' he admitted. He gulped down the last of his beer, then asked, 'How come the oracle doesn't just tell the Flux to get rid of you? I mean, if you lot are hampering its plans so much, why doesn't it just send out an order to hunt you all down and get you out of the way?'

'I'd like to see it bloody try,' said Hollis. 'We'd give it a run for its money.'

There was a general rumble of support for Hollis's defiant statement, though Max merely smiled, placed his palms together and upright as though in preparation for prayer and waited for the rumble to die down.

When it did he said, 'Some of our number *have* died at the Flux's hands in the past – indeed, Violet here barely escaped death just a few days ago. However, in general, I believe that the oracle wants to avoid direct confrontation. Although the Flux outnumber us greatly, we're still too large a group for them to obliterate in one go. If they did force us to go to war with them, then we would have to, and who knows, we might, by some miracle, even win. But neither our group, nor, I suspect, the Flux is prepared to risk such an eventuality whilst there are still other alternatives. The results of such a conflict could be cataclysmic for both sides. I believe the oracle is aware of this, and so it tolerates our occasional sabotage, and makes allowances for its own occasional small defeat. It continues to make progress, of course, but slowly, yet whilst it *is* still making progress it's happy to maintain the status quo. And so a kind of . . . uneasy stand-off is maintained.' He shrugged. 'This of course is all my own opinion. I cannot speak for the oracle itself. Who really knows how evil thinks?'

He removed his pince-nez, wiped them on a very large, very white handkerchief and carefully replaced them. David watched him, frowning. Trying to order the thoughts in his head, to arrange the myriad jostling questions in there into an orderly queue, was giving him a headache. 'Do you mind if I backtrack a moment?' he said. 'There's still something I'm unclear about – well, quite a lot of somethings actually.'

Max smiled sympathetically and spread his hands in a gesture of compliance. David said, 'How come all this seems to be coming to a head now? I mean, if the Flux as an organisation predates Christ, why is it only in this century that the evil that controls the Flux seems to have been getting the upper hand? After all, there have been tyrants and wars ever since civilisation began. Why hasn't the evil tried to break through before?'

'What we believe,' said Max, 'is that the evil has been growing throughout history, manipulating the Flux to bring about the situation that we have today. The evil, we believe, feeds on misery and suffering and cruelty, all the negative thoughts and feelings of humankind. Now it's true what you say, David, there have been wars and tyrants and atrocities throughout history, but in the last century humankind has excelled itself in terms of techno-logical advancement, allied to which the planet's population has increased dramatically. We see humankind as being like . . . like a car without brakes careering downhill. The more we discover as a species, the more resources we have at our disposal, as a result of which our discoveries become greater and more and more frequent.

'Think about it, David. A hundred years ago, which in the timescale of this planet is a mere click of the fingers, humankind knew only a fraction of what it knows today. We now drive around in cars instead of horse-drawn carriages, we have aeroplanes and tanks, even space rockets. We have weapons of such sophistication and power that we could destroy the world ten times over. There have been advancements in medical science that would have been undreamed of only a lifetime ago. Now, you can argue that many of these advancements have been for the good of humankind, but when you think about it even these apparently beneficial discoveries have brought problems. For example, ever-improving medical techniques mean that more people live longer, which leads to over-population, which in turn leads to deprivation, homelessness, starvation, unemployment, and therefore an inevitable increase in crime. And industrial expansion has led to pollution on a massive scale, and, arguably, an increase in the human emotions of greed, selfishness, ruthlessness.

'Overall, the picture is bleak: wars are more devastating than ever before, crime and unrest are spiralling ever upwards, and the planet is slowly being poisoned to death. And why has this come about? Because the natural evolution of mankind has been manipulated, misguided by the force which controls the Flux. The seed that was planted millennia ago has been tended and nurtured by the Flux. It has grown, blossomed and is now running riot. And the evil just sits there like . . . like a spider in its web, sucking up all the misery and pain, growing bigger and fatter and stronger.'

Max had been growing steadily more impassioned throughout his spiel, and now broke off, his face flushed.

Tentatively David said, 'I take your point, but . . . well, there's still plenty of good in the world surely? More good than bad?'

'You think so, do you?' rumbled Marshall.

David pulled a face, not sure for a moment how to

respond.

Richard Hodge said, 'You're right of course, David. There *is* still a lot of good in the world. But this planet is like a battleground for the continual struggle between good and evil, and unfortunately, thanks largely to the influence of the Flux, the way we see it at the moment, it seems to be evil that's gaining the upper hand.'

'So are you the only group that have ever broken away from the Flux?' David said. 'The only one that has ever opposed it?'

'We think so,' said Ishvak, 'but we can't be certain.'

'The Flux are capable of manipulating history, remember,' said Melanie Hodge, 'including their own. It's possible that earlier opposition groups were wiped out and all trace of them, all *memory* of them, eradicated.'

'Which is probably what'll happen to us,' said Hollis gloomily, 'if we're not careful.'

David sat back, his chair creaking, letting out a long breath that felt as though it was having to fight its way through muscles knotted with tension. 'So where do I fit into all this?' he said. 'And why is everyone after this bottle of mine? Why is it so important?'

'We explained all that in the car,' Marshall grumbled with weary impatience, as though to a tiresome child.

'You told me you didn't know,' David said, more sharply than he intended, 'but in the light of what you've told me since, you must have some idea –'

'We still don't know, Mr Fox,' Marshall said, leaning forward. 'All we know is that the Flux want the bottle and that you were the one who found it.'

David glared at Marshall, felt like asking him what his problem was. Had the old man harboured his bitterness for the past forty years because of what had happened to his wife and child, or was it that he blamed David for reanimating old and painful memories?

Max held up his hands, smiling benignly at Marshall.

'Now, that isn't strictly true, is it, Malcolm?' To David he said, 'We don't know exactly what the purpose of the bottle is, but we do have one or two theories.'

'And what are they?' David said.

'Well, going by what you've told us, it would seem that the bottle is able to be used as a rather effective weapon. You described it as being like a . . . a channel for your thoughts and emotions. Is that correct?'

'Sort of,' said David. 'The bottle seems able to . . . to boost my emotions, to convert them into a sort of . . . radiant light, which, on the three occasions it's been used so far, has . . .' he pulled a face, searching for the right word '. . . *thwarted*, shall we say, the people who've tried to take the bottle away from me.'

'And you say you have to actually be touching the bottle for it to work?'

'That seems to be the case, yes. It wasn't until I actually touched it that it came to life and consumed Worthington.'

'And you say also that it has a limited life? That its power decreases each time you use it?'

'Well . . . I think so. At least when I had my . . . er . . . my vision, that's what the figure that appeared seemed to be saying to me. And the second time I used it, it didn't seem quite as strong as the first time. I found I had to concentrate more. The third time, though, when it killed Worthington, it seemed strong then, but maybe that was because I was so . . . so enraged, so channelled.'

Max was looking at him thoughtfully. David felt a little intimidated by the intensity of his gaze, and was grateful when his attention was diverted by Hollis, who said, 'Or maybe it just realised what a totally evil bastard Worthington was.'

'How do you mean, Pat?' asked Melanie Hodge.

'Well, we've kind of guessed the Flux is after the bottle because it's a threat to them, yeah?' Everyone nodded. 'Right, so maybe it kind of seeks out evil and zaps it. I mean, it makes sense, doesn't it?'

'Hmm,' Max said non-committally, then turned back to David. 'May we see the bottle, David?' he asked.

Even now David felt a little wary of exposing the bottle to view, felt a possessiveness he hadn't known since he'd been ten years old and his parents had bought him a bike for Christmas. However after a moment's hesitation he nodded and reached behind him to his Bogart, which was draped over the back of his chair. He slipped his hand into the pocket and began to draw out the bottle, aware that most of the people round the table were craning forward, eager to see. 'It doesn't really look like much,' he said, as if it was his fault.

He put the bottle on the table in front of him, hesitating a moment before letting go of it. Everyone stared at it silently for a few seconds. David grimaced. 'Told you,' he said.

'Do you think we could see the note, David?' Max asked.

Again David hesitated before nodding. 'Yes, sure.' He unscrewed the cap from the bottle and upended it, and after a bit of jiggling managed to snag the note with his little finger. He unrolled it carefully and handed it to Max, who took it as though it was an ancient and valuable manuscript. The old man read the note, then looked up and asked, 'May I?', indicating that he would like to pass it round.

David nodded and Max handed the note to Violet on his left, who treated it just as reverently as the old man had. She read the note silently and passed it on, as did everyone else except Malcolm Marshall, who grunted and thrust the note disdainfully away from him.

'It's interesting, isn't it?' said Max.

'What is?' said David.

Max tapped his lips thoughtfully with a forefinger, then said, 'What does the note suggest to you, David?'

387

David felt like a pupil being tested by a benign yet respected schoolteacher. It didn't help his powers of concentration that everyone was looking at him expectantly, as if they all knew the answer and he didn't. 'Um . . . well,' he said, 'when we were in the car, Ishvak told me that the note was just a means to an end, that it was calculated to lead me to you, which I suppose must mean that the bottle was intended for you all along. Also you've told me that the note wasn't written by Mr Marshall's son, so therefore it must have been written by . . . someone else.'

'But who do you think could have written it?' said Max.

The note had done the rounds now and was passed back to David, who read it for the umpteenth time. 'I don't know,' he said, shrugging. 'If the bottle's supposed to be used as a weapon against the Flux, then maybe it's a present from God.'

The remark was meant half-jokingly, but no one around the table was even smiling.

'Aw, come on,' said David incredulously, 'you can't be serious? You can't honestly believe that God sent you a magic bottle to fight the Devil with?'

'You don't believe in God, David?' Max said, so reasonably that immediately it put David on the defensive.

'Well . . . yes, I mean . . . I suppose so, yes. But not so . . . well . . . literally.' He laughed without conviction. 'Come on, you can't *really* believe that this is a gift from God?'

No one said anything for a few seconds, not even Hollis, who was usually good for an irreverent quip or two. Then in the same maddeningly reasonable voice, Max said, 'You accept what we've told you so far, David? You believe that the oracle is a force for evil, manipulating the Flux?'

'Well . . . yes, I suppose so.'

'Then is it so hard to accept that there must be a force for good also, to counter-balance the evil, oppose it?'

'Well, no,' said David, 'but I mean . . . God sending you a bottle. It's daft.'

'God is your word, not mine,' Max said.

'You don't believe in God?'

Max chuckled. 'Touché. Very good, David. Yes, I believe in God. But God is just a convenient word that human beings use to describe the indescribable, to imagine the unimaginable. The problem with words, however, is that they are so restrictive. No matter how inspired, they still diminish the true essence of whatever they describe; they impose limits on the limitless. Do you see what I'm telling you?'

'Well, yes, of course, but I still have problems with this. I mean . . . a bottle?' David grimaced and gestured at the scratched and worn object standing in the middle of the table. 'If it is from God, or whatever you want to call it, how come it didn't save the people who were killed in the restaurant? How come it didn't make Burgess shoot himself before he could use his gun?'

'Maybe it couldn't,' suggested Tippi.

'But why not? God's supposed to be able to do anything, isn't he?'

'So's the Devil,' said Hollis.

Max said, 'God gave us free will, freedom of choice.'

'So these people chose to get shot? Is that what you're telling me?'

'Don't be a prat, David,' said Hollis. 'Haven't you ever heard of God working in mysterious ways?'

David snorted an unamused laugh. 'And that's your answer, is it?'

Hollis scowled, his voice betraying a sudden flash of irritation. 'I haven't got an answer. *I'm* not bloody God,' then just as suddenly his humour returned and he added, 'despite what people say about me.'

David reached out and closed his hand around the bottle. It felt solid and rough and cool, not at all like a divine artifact. 'If it is from God or . . . whatever,' he said, 'how come it's only appeared now? I mean, what's so special about now?'

He noticed one or two glances ricocheting around the table. Hollis, who appeared temporarily to have taken on the mantle of spokesman, said, 'We think there's something big about to go down.'

'Something big? How do you mean?'

Hollis looked at Willie, who for the past half-hour or so had said very little. The Scotsman looked tired, as did Ishvak and Marshall, the other two men who had accompanied him here. Ishvak, in particular, looked shattered, and no wonder. Not only had he driven here but he had had to maintain his psychic barrier around the car throughout the journey.

Willie now stirred into life as if Hollis had given him a mental jab in the ribs. Wearily he said, 'For the past year or so, things have been . . . er . . . hotting up in the Flux. Though nothing's actually been said, not ti me anyway, it seems ti me that they've been making . . . what's the word?'

'Preparations?' suggested Tippi.

'Aye, preparations. They're getting ready for something.'

'What sort of something?' said David.

'Don't quote me on this,' said Hollis, 'but we think the big guy from downstairs might be about to attempt another comeback.'

'You mean . . .?'

'Yep. Fire 'n' brimstone 'n' hell on earth. Not something to look forward to.'

'But I thought . . . well, I mean . . . doesn't there need to be a World War? Some great catastrophe or something? Something to give him . . . you know, like a power boost or whatever?'

'Not necessarily,' said Richard Hodge. 'He, or rather it, might be strong enough now without any need for all

390

that.'

'But fifty years ago it wasn't strong enough,' said David.

'Yeah, but think of what's happened in the last fifty years,' said Hollis gloomily. 'The world's gone to hell in a handbasket.'

'So you think the bottle's been sent down to help you?'

'You must admit, it's a nice idea,' said Hollis, 'though what we're supposed to do with it is anybody's guess.'

'And what about me? Am I just the messenger boy? I mean, if this bottle is meant for you lot, why get me to deliver it? Why didn't . . . He just drop it straight into your hands or something?'

'More of those mysterious ways of His?' Hollis suggested.

'No,' said Max. 'I believe, David, that you were chosen for this mission.'

'Chosen? Me? Why?'

'I think you're special. I think that like the rest of us, you have an animis, but one that was . . . how shall I put it? Crafted, *moulded*, to react with the bottle.'

David stared at him. 'Animis? What's that?'

'It's what we call the source of energy inside ourselves that enables us to use our abilities,' said Tippi.

David looked at her and then back at Max again. 'And you think I've got one of these? You think I'm one of you?'

Max nodded. 'Yes, David, I do.'

David barked a staccato laugh and shook his head. 'No,' he said, 'I think you've made a mistake.'

'Do you?' said Max. 'Why?'

'Well, I mean . . . I don't *feel* special. How come I've never been aware of it before?'

'You've never needed it before,' said Max calmly. 'Your animis has been sleeping in you all these years, David, waiting for a time when it will be needed. And now that time has come.'

He spoke as if all this was the most natural thing in the

391

world. David expelled a huge sigh which made his body feel as though it was deflating, and pressed his fingers to his temples. 'This is really hard to take,' he said. 'It's just all so . . . *wacky*. I mean, you're only guessing all this, right, about me being one of you and everything?'

'It's an educated guess,' admitted Max, 'but I feel sure I'm right.'

'I think so too,' said Tippi. She put an arm around David's shoulders. 'Poor David. I remember the first time I found out about all this stuff. I was only fourteen. It's a bit of a shock, isn't it?'

'A bit of a shock,' David repeated and smiled weakly. 'I think you've just made the understatement of the year.'

'Ah, you'll get used to it, mate,' said Hollis airily. 'Welcome to the club.'

David felt mentally dazzled by the evening's revelations, and this combined with his increasing tiredness was making it more and more difficult for him to think straight. 'So what happens now?' he asked wearily.

'We keep our eyes and ears open,' said Max.

'But what about my family and friends? All I really want out of all this is for them to be free.'

Willie yawned extravagantly. 'Aye,' he said, 'talking of which, ah'd better get some sleep. Ah'm off back ti London first thing tomorrow morning wi' Ishvak ti see what ah can find oot.'

He stood up. A thought struck David who asked, 'How come, if the Flux are so powerful, they don't know you're a spy?'

Willie grinned. 'Because ah've been careful. They've no reason ti suspect me. Besides,' he added, tapping his head, 'ah've got so many barriers in here, thanks ti Pat and Ishvak and a few others, that ma brain's like . . . what's the name o' that place where they keep all the gold?'

'Fort Knox,' said Melanie Hodge.

'Aye, Fort Knox.'

As he said his goodnights and trudged off, Ishvak too pushed back his chair and stood up. 'I'd better get some sleep as well,' he said, sounding as though he was half-asleep already. He followed Willie out of the door.

The departure of the two men seemed to act as the cue for a general exodus.

'I think we could all do with some sleep,' Max said, 'I feel that we have some very big times ahead of us.'

As chairs began to scrape back, Tippi took David's arm and said, 'Come along, David, I'll point you in the direction of a spare bed and a toothbrush.' David pocketed the bottle and smiled vaguely at her, though his face must have been betraying the anxiety that his tiredness was causing to resurface in his mind, for she squeezed his arm and added, 'And try not to worry, you're among friends now. I'm sure everything'll work out okay.'

35

This time yesterday, Ellen would not have believed it possible to be as scared as she was now. Even if it hadn't been so cold, her body would have been shaking constantly. Her heart pounded, her stomach churned. On a couple of occasions, despite not eating anything for over twenty-four hours, she had broken into a sweat, certain she was about to be sick. So far she had managed to fight the urge, terrified that if her gorge did rise no one would notice and the tape over her mouth would cause her to choke silently to death on her own vomit. Trussed up as she was, she could no longer feel her arms and legs, and for a while had become obsessed with the thought that lack of circulation might lead to gangrene, which in turn might lead to amputation, or even worse the prospect of literally rotting away down here if she was kept captive long enough.

These thoughts, however, coupled with her constant fears of being tortured and raped and killed, were as nothing compared to her fears for her daughters. The thought of being unable to do anything except watch and listen as they were tortured or molested was almost too much to bear. When the white-haired man had picked Jane up and carried her to the other side of the room, Ellen had almost gone mad with sheer, crushing terror. Indeed, if the man had not been interrupted when he was, Ellen honestly believed that the rage and terror inside her would have stopped her heart.

Although she had not seen the white-haired man for a

long time now, Ellen lived in constant fear of his return. It seemed inevitable that he would come back sooner or later, and so every time she heard footsteps from upstairs, or a floorboard creaking, or a door closing, her body would cramp with tension, her heart would begin to crash in her chest, and the moisture – what little of it there was – would drain from her mouth. Apart from the man and the boy, Bernard, and the fat woman, Ellen had neither seen nor heard any evidence of anyone else in the house. She knew there must be others, though, because their kidnappers had been young men, young and silent and horribly strong. The thought of them made Ellen go cold inside, and not just because they had marched boldly into her house, destroying her privacy, her sense of security, sanctity even, which was what her house had always been to her. No, it was not that, it was that they had seemed so ... merciless, so unstoppable; they had seemed like men to whom human life meant nothing at all. And more than that, and perhaps worse than that, they had seemed so ... familiar to her somehow, and she didn't know why. It was a horrible and elusive feeling, but she was convinced that the men who had invaded her home were people whom she saw every day.

She wondered, if she got out of this, whether she would ever feel safe again. Wasn't it always later that the effects of something like this hit you? She knew, largely through reading articles in newspapers and Sunday supplements, that traumatic memories could often be stored deep in the mind, only to manifest themselves later as nightmares, mental instability, nervous disorders. But again, the bulk of her fears were not really for herself but her daughters. They seemed to be bearing up well, but who could say how all this was really affecting them? Mainly she was worried about Jane, who, since waking up from an apparently deep sleep, had seemed oddly subdued and preoccupied, her eyes gazing vacantly but her face creasing in concentration every so often, almost as if she was listening to an inner voice. Once or twice, Ellen had nudged her daughter and raised her eyebrows in what she hoped was a reassuring manner. Jane had responded fleetingly, but had then slipped back into introspection.

As well as fear, there was another emotion which Ellen felt keenly, and that was anger. Part of it was her outrage at the situation itself, part of it was directed at their captors, but the greater bulk of it was directed at David. Though she really knew very little of what was going on, she still couldn't help feeling betrayed by her husband. She had gleaned enough from listening to the white-haired man's telephone conversation with David to realise that the five of them were being held here as hostages. The group wanted something that David possessed – a bottle, the white-haired man had said. But what could that mean? Drugs? She had been racking her brains to think what else could be kept in a bottle that was important enough to kidnap people for, but could think of nothing that seemed even remotely likely. And so her mind, starved of information, had filled in the gaps: David, in some capacity, had been involved in drugs, and had fled the house because the people who were now holding her and her children and friends, had been getting heavy with him. Which of course, if it were true, meant that his actions were unforgivable. He must have known how ruthless these people were, and yet he hadn't even bothered to warn her.

Ellen looked across the cellar at the young man, Bernard, whose head was nodding on his chest. She had no idea what time it was, though she guessed it was probably the early hours of Monday morning. If this had been a film, she would be working at loosening her bonds now while her captor slept. She would shake off the ropes that bound her, grab his keys before he could realise what was happening, knock him out with one punch, and spring to freedom.

But this was not a film, and her arms and legs felt useless as lumps of wood, her bonds immoveable as concrete. Even if she had been left here alone, she doubted whether she would have been able to free herself. She looked around, the tape that gagged her pulling at her hair as she moved her head. Rachel was sleeping, albeit fitfully, and Ralph was certainly sleeping because Ellen could hear him snoring quietly through his poor battered nose. As for Jane, she had her head bowed forward, and she seemed still enough, but Ellen wasn't sure whether her eyes were closed or not. Diane, she knew, was not sleeping even though she appeared to be. Her eyes were closed and her body seemed relaxed, but Ellen knew, having watched for a while, that she was alert to the slightest danger. All it took for Diane's eyes to spring open and glance around was the sound of someone shifting position or the muted growl of a car passing outside.

Of them all, Diane seemed to be the one who was coping most admirably with their plight. Even after having had her foot bitten, she was still the most aggressive and defiant, still the one who ate food every time it was offered (and used each opportunity to express her displeasure loudly at their predicament through the slit which Bernard cut in the tape in order to feed them before sealing it up again), and the one who made it known when she wanted to go to the toilet.

As for herself, Ellen had not eaten a thing since Rachel had brought her a couple of slices of toast yesterday morning, though she had managed to sip a little water (*and* keep it down, which seemed a feat in itself). She had gone to the toilet as little as possible too, mainly because she found it an awful, degrading experience. It involved being held over a potty by Bernard and the fat woman, and then having to suffer the indignity of being wiped by the fat woman in front of everyone. She was bursting for a pee now, but she was determined to hold on for at least another couple of hours.

Diane, by contrast, seemed to have the knack of turning what should have been her own embarrassment back on to her captors. Indeed, she actually seemed to be making herself pee just to be awkward. Each time Bernard held her over the potty, her jeans pushed down to her knees, the room filling with the sound of her urine hitting the bottom of the metal container, she would twist her head around, defying the tape which wrenched at her hair, and she would stare at Bernard until she had finished, by which time he would be looking anywhere but at her, his face burning red.

Ellen didn't think she had ever admired her friend as much as she did now. The way Diane taunted Bernard, using the only method available to her, made Ellen feel almost sorry for the poor sod. Almost, but not quite, because he was still their captor, and despite his gentleness and his awkwardness she still hated him with a passion. She wasn't frightened of Bernard, she didn't think he would hurt her; indeed, he had even apologised on a number of occasions for having to keep them here like this. And yet if it came down to it, if it meant the difference between escape and continuing imprisonment, Ellen knew she could hurt Bernard and hurt him badly. To save her daughters, she knew she could even kill him if need be.

For the last few hours (or at least what *seemed* like hours; with nothing to use as reference time seemed meaningless here), Ellen was pretty sure that Bernard had been the only one of their captors in the house with them. It was infuriating to think that if just one of them could get free, they might be able to overpower him and escape. What was particularly galling was the fact that Bernard was spending more time dozing than awake just at the moment; he was a sitting duck, and yet one which they were unable to take advantage of. She thought again, wistfully, that if this had been a film there would have been a conveniently jagged object somewhere nearby that they could have shuffled towards and surreptitiously used to saw through their bonds.

She wondered what was going on in the outside world, whether David was all right. She knew the white-haired man and the fat woman had gone off, presumably to meet him and retrieve this mysterious bottle of theirs, and that the agreement seemed to be that if David did hand over the bottle, then she and the girls and the Joyces would be released. Ellen, however, had mixed feelings about this. Part of her wanted to believe that the white-haired man would keep his word. However, she had had a glimpse of how ruthless and cruel and sadistic he could be. Wouldn't it be just as likely that, with the bottle in his possession, he might simply regard them as no longer useful and order them to be killed, especially since none of them had been blindfolded and so could give excellent descriptions of their captors to the police if they were allowed out of here unharmed?

It was a long time since the couple had left, though Ellen didn't know whether the fact was significant or not. The address the white-haired man had given David was a London one, but Ellen had no idea whether she was in London or Leeds or Timbuktu at the moment. Every time she heard a car outside now, she tensed, thinking that the fat woman and the white-haired man were returning. She was dreading their return, and yet in a way was disappointed each time the car she could hear approaching passed by. Part of her wanted to get what was going to happen over with as quickly as possible.

She had her eyes closed, trying to concentrate on quelling another bout of nausea, when the sound of a door slamming upstairs made her jerk her head back with such force that she hit it on the wall behind her. She cried out, the sound muffled by her gag. Sparks leaped from the point of pain and scattered across her vision.

The sound had been unexpected. The white-haired man and the fat woman had left in a car; why hadn't they returned in one? Though the pain in her head was sharp, it was not as strong as her fear, which Ellen felt acutely now, stirring the contents of her stomach, curling in her bowel.

Footsteps thudded overhead, moving quickly. Their echoes made it impossible to tell how many feet were actually making the sounds. Bernard, shocked from his doze, was looking around, alarmed and confused. Diane, fully alert and looking incredibly calm, was watching the cellar steps which tapered into darkness. Rachel and Ralph seemed to be surfacing slowly from sleep, Ralph moaning in pain. Jane, however, was still sitting motionless, head bowed, hair hanging over her face.

The cellar door opened, bringing a breeze which caused the candle flames to flicker, throwing agitated shadows up the walls. Electric light spilled into the cellar, but fizzed out about six steps down as if it had no desire to venture any further. Ellen, her head still throbbing, felt all the muscles bunching in her body, her eyes widening involuntarily, as someone started to descend. She pushed back instinctively with her heels, making herself sit up straighter.

She heard the fat woman panting before she saw her. Her breath seemed to reverberate around the room; perhaps it was this that caused the candle flames to flap like tiny flags. One flame bent double and was snuffed out. The fat woman appeared, looking sweaty and agitated. The curl of grey smoke from the extinguished candle gravitated towards her, sliding around her form and dissipating, as though absorbed into her dark bulk.

Bernard scrambled to his feet, looking guilty, raking a hand through his mop of hair.

'Hi,' he said, and then, registering her appearance, 'Uh . . . what's wrong?'

The fat woman glared at Bernard, glanced at the five captives, and then waddled across the room and turned on the tap above the cracked sink. Water spattered on to the dirty porcelain with a sound that made Ellen's bladder clench in sympathy. The woman thrust a podgy hand beneath the water and splashed her face with it.

'Everything,' she said at last, in answer to Bernard's question.

He took a hesitant step towards her, began to stretch out a hand and then obviously thought better of it. Clenching the hand into a fist and letting it drop to his side, he asked plaintively, 'Why? Didn't you get the bottle?'

The fat woman swung round, her chins wobbling. 'No we didn't!' she snapped. 'It killed Worthington.'

Bernard's eyes widened. His mouth dropped open. The expression was almost comic. 'Killed?' he breathed. 'How?'

Mathilde's doughy face creased in annoyance. 'How should I know? I wasn't there, was I? Worthington insisted on going it alone with just a couple of henchmen for company, playing the big hero. I should never have allowed him to talk me into waiting back at the house, we should have sent a contingent.' She looked up at Bernard, her face grim. 'We think the Schism were involved, judging by the damage done to Worthington's apes, and by what one of them managed to tell us before he died. But what happened to Worthington couldn't have been the Schism's work. When we arrived he was . . .' she creased her face in repugnance '. . . he was little more than a mess on the floor. We only knew it was him because some of his mouths were still screaming.'

'Wow,' breathed Bernard, as though marvelling at the description of some awesome special effect. 'So . . .

where's the bottle now?'

Mathilde sighed, her great bosom heaving. Water was trickling down her face, dripping off her chin. 'Well, presumably, Fox went off with the Schism, so they must have got it,' she said impatiently, then made her way slowly to the steps, where she sat down. She leaned as far forward as her bulk would allow and sank her head into her hands.

There was a short but heavy silence before Bernard asked timidly, 'So . . . what do we do now?'

Mathilde made a muffled sound of exasperation and looked up. 'I don't know,' she snapped. 'What do you suggest?'

Bernard squirmed. He looked at the five captives, his face betraying his anxiety and indecision. 'Couldn't we just let them go?'

'Oh, very intelligent,' said Mathilde heavily. 'That would solve all our problems.' She shook her head as if to clear it, puffed out her cheeks. 'No, we have to . . . get together, have a meeting, decide between us on the right course of action.' She pushed herself, with difficulty, to her feet. 'Oh, I hate this – something going wrong when we're between oracles. The sooner the new oracle makes itself known to us, the better.'

Ellen was bewildered by half of what the fat woman had said, yet her overriding emotion was one of relief that she had returned alone. Indeed, if 'Worthington', whom the fat woman had mentioned in her agitation, was the white-haired man, and Ellen had no reason to assume otherwise, then it seemed he was now dead, 'killed by the bottle', whatever that might mean, which was wonderful news. She was shocked and ashamed to find herself thinking this way, but only a little, and she barely had time to dwell on it before she heard Jane stirring beside her. She glanced to her right, thinking that her youngest daughter must indeed have been sleeping and was now waking up, disturbed by the commotion. Hoping it would be the first thing that Jane would see, Ellen tried to express reassurance through her eyes, but as Jane raised her head her hair fell away from her face, and instead Ellen's eyes widened in shock as she felt something cold lurch inside her.

Her little girl looked ... bestial; there was no other word to describe it. Her face was bathed in sweat, her eyes were rolling, and there was frothy saliva bubbling out from beneath her gag, crusting on her chin. At first Ellen thought that Jane must have contracted a fever, perhaps from the cold damp conditions, but then Jane's entire body began to tremble as though imbued with some kind of energy. Ellen gasped, the sound muffled by the tape, as Jane rose to her feet as if lifted by invisible hands.

Everyone was watching Jane now, their eyes wide. Ellen noticed that the fat woman was smiling as if she knew exactly what was going on. All at once, Jane flexed her arms and legs and the bonds around her wrists and ankles exploded like powder. Astonished as she was, Ellen could not help wincing at the sight of the flesh beneath, which was raw and bleeding, heavily indented with the marks of the rope. By contrast, Jane's hands were very white, as if she was wearing kid gloves.

Now the tape that was wrapped around Jane's head seemed to be shrivelling away of its own accord, as if exposed to enormous heat. It curled and blackened and fell from her face. Beneath, her skin was red, rash-like. All of them watched, not moving, as Jane, now free of her bonds, walked slowly towards the fat woman who was standing by the steps, grinning.

'It is you, isn't it?' the fat woman said eagerly.

In a croak that was utterly unlike her own voice, Jane said, 'Yes, it's me.'

36

Ishvak and Willie arrived back in London just after midday. Ishvak took Willie right into the capital, dropping him off outside King's Cross Station, before heading on down to Portsmouth, which was where his company was based.

Willie yawned and wandered into the station, buying a newspaper from a vendor who was standing outside in the cold, stamping his feet and breathing out steam. The station was busy, as it always was, though it was probably busier than normal just now, with people going home for Christmas and the New Year.

Willie had been hoping to travel up to Glasgow the day before New Year's Eve, to spend Hogmanay with his surviving brother, Fulton, and his wife and children and grandchildren, and with his dead brother Ian's wife, Mary, and her son and his wife and kiddies. It would be a good do as it always was, plenty of the hard stuff flowing freely. However, things being what they were just now, Willie had to face the fact that his chances of actually getting there seemed very remote.

He queued for a burger at the Casey Jones Burger Bar, aware of people trying not to stare at the maroon birthmark that covered the left side of his throat. As a boy, he had been teased unmercifully because of it, had even been beaten up more than once simply for being different to everyone else, and therefore, in the eyes of the other boys, unclean.

It hadn't helped that he'd been the runt of the litter too,

a scrawny little bugger in relation to his two brothers, who were built like his father – barrel chest, spade hands, tree trunk legs. Though his brothers had often acted as minders, they'd only done so because they respected him; if he'd been a pansy, and had come crying to them every time someone called him Blackberry-Face, they'd have washed their hands of him in disgust.

But of the three of them, Willie, despite his diminutive size, or perhaps because of it, had actually been the most volatile. In point of fact, he'd been a vicious little bastard, ready to fly off the handle at the slightest provocation. During his school days, his brothers, older than he was by seven and five years respectively, had been, if anything, a steadying influence rather than a crutch for him to lean on. When they left and started working on the docks, following in their father's footsteps, Willie had become a right little tearaway.

He had been fourteen when, in 1939, war broke out, and his father and brothers went off to fight the Germans. Willie had wanted to go too, but of course had been too young. With only his mother around, preoccupied with her anxiety about her husband and sons at the front, Willie had, for a time, gone completely off the rails. He'd started running with a gang, had got involved in petty crime, and had taken to carrying a knife, which he was not afraid to use in fights with other gangs. Even now, Willie still had the scars to show for those long-ago days, the worst of which were on his stomach where Fudd McStay and Frank Sinclair had once carved out a game of noughts and crosses. He'd got his own back on Sinclair, though; he'd beat him up so bad with a bicycle chain that the older boy had lost an eye. Fate had got McStay before Willie could. If the story was to be believed, the silly bugger had got blind drunk one night and fallen off a cliff.

Despite his opposition to it now, there was one thing about the Flux that Willie still had cause to be thankful for. If his ability had not begun to show itself when it did, which was when he was sixteen, he felt sure he would have ended up lying in a gutter somewhere with his throat cut, very probably dead before his eighteenth birthday. Certainly he could never have foreseen this about himself, fifty years down the line and trying to save the world. Again.

He gobbled his burger in four bites as he ambled across the station forecourt, then licked grease and ketchup from his fingers. A group of foreign schoolkids, wearing purple and yellow ski jackets and scarves like tasselled table-cloths, were pointing up at the vast departure board and arguing vociferously. Willie tried not to think about the fact that he had once been partially responsible for a bomb going off here which had killed fourteen people, including three eleven-year-olds who had been with a school party from Oslo. It was incidents such as this, scenes of unnatural death and suffering and devastation, that provided the evil that manipulated the Flux with the sustenance it needed to burgeon.

This was how Willie always thought of the evil – as some vast tumescent toadstool, growing bloated on all the poison it was sucking from the world, readying itself to erupt from the soil. Because of his need to keep in with the Flux, he himself had been forced at times to participate in some terrible things. However he refused to let his crimes prey on his mind, believing fervently that, in his role as informant, he had helped to undermine a great many of the Flux's plans, thus saving far more lives than he had taken. Like Hollis, Willie played up to the image of washed-out old sot, a vital factor, he believed, in his longevity as a double agent. Within the Flux, he was aware of being held in some contempt, often of being overlooked, disregarded. This was just as he liked it.

The public telephones were just outside the station. Willie hunched his shoulders against the cold and ducked beneath one of the plastic hoods. He lifted the receiver, stuck 10p in the slot and dialled Mathilde's number. Taxis arrived growling, discharged or picked up passengers, and then drove away again. From inside the station a booming, distorted voice announced the imminent departure of the train from platform six. Willie stuck his finger in his left ear and jammed the receiver even harder against his right. The phone was picked up halfway through the fourth ring, and a voice said, 'Yes.'

'Mathilde, is that you?' Willie said, automatically adding a slur to his voice.

'Willie?' Even in that one word Willie could hear the clipped reproof in Mathilde's tone, and he grinned, relishing it.

'Aye,' he said, laying it on thick, even swaying a little in the booth as he got into his role. 'Ah jist thought ah'd ring ti see whit was goin' on.'

'What's going on,' said Mathilde without preamble, 'is that Worthington's dead and the Schism have got the bottle. Where have you been, Willie? We've been trying to get everyone together.'

'Here and there,' Willie said, and then added in a shocked voice, 'Worthington dead, you say?'

'Yes. *Dead*,' replied Mathilde, making the word sound brutal. Then she sighed, as if realising it was pointless trying to get through to him. 'Where are you, Willie? You know the present situation. You know we told everyone to stay close, keep in touch.'

'Aye, well, you know, ah had . . . er, one or two things ti do.'

'You went on a binge, you mean?'

'Well, ah had one or two drinks last night, jist one or two, y'understand.'

Mathilde's sigh was deeper this time. 'And where did you sleep this time?'

'Ah, well, ah'm no sure.'

'Well, where did you wake up?' she asked as though speaking to a simpleton.

'The railway station. King's Cross. That's where ah am noo.'

'Right.' Mathilde seemed to consider. 'Come to my house, and call at Tametia's, bring her with you. She's another one who's gone AWOL.'

'Okay,' said Willie. 'So do we know where the Schism are, where they're holding the bottle?'

Mathilde's expression was so pronounced it made him grin. 'No, Willie, we don't. If we did, we'd try and get it, wouldn't we?'

'Aye, ah suppose so. Oh shit, ma money's run out. Ah'll see you later, Mathilde.'

'Goodbye, Willie. Remember to bring Tam –'

Willie put his finger on the disconnect button. It gave him more than a little satisfaction to cut Mathilde off in mid-flow.

He trooped out of the station and headed towards Bloomsbury, along a Euston Road that was frenetic with Christmas shoppers. With no immediate family, Willie had never paid Christmas much heed. All it meant to him was better telly than usual and a free pint down the local at lunch-time. Yet although he didn't resent Christmas itself, the one thing he *did* resent was people who thought there was something wrong with him or, even worse, regarded him as an object of pity, just because he had had no tree, had sent no cards, and had sat in front of the Queen's speech eating corned beef and baked beans instead of turkey and Christmas pud.

Tametia's flat was located in a building like a small hotel, complete with a uniformed doorman who sat behind a desk. The five-storeyed building was large and white, with railings outside and steps leading up to an imposing front door, painted black. The place always reminded Willie of something from an old musical – *My*

Fair Lady or *Oliver*. He imagined perfectly choreographed flower sellers dancing up the street, singing, 'Who will buy my wonderful morning?' He ascended the steps and pressed a buzzer labelled FLAT 4, one of six by the front door. He waited for Tametia's tinny voice to crackle out of the intercom at him.

Nothing happened. He tried again. Still no reply. He was about to leave, but the thought of Mathilde barracking him for not going inside and making sure that Tametia wasn't asleep or perhaps just pretending not to be there. Or maybe she had a client with her; maybe she was an elephant or an ostrich or a stag beetle or something, in which case she would find it a little difficult to speak right now.

To be honest, Willie thought this last possibility unlikely. He knew how badly the bottle had burned her the other night, and how much pain she was in. Although Tametia was a vain woman, arrogant and selfish and sometimes cruel, Willie felt sorry for her. She had had a very tough life; it was perhaps understandable that she treated people the way she did. There were few in the Flux whom Willie would even have crossed the street to piss on if they'd been on fire, but if it hadn't been so dangerous, he would actually have liked to try to convince Tametia to reject the Flux, to change sides. Maybe he was just kidding himself, but he fervently believed that all she really needed was a bit of genuine affection.

Sighing in readiness for the reception he knew he would get, Willie pressed the bottom buzzer marked LOBBY. There was a bad-tempered crackle, then a voice grated, 'Yes.'

Willie pressed his lips to the intercom. 'Ah'm a friend of Tametia's. Fourth floor. She's no been well lately. Ah thought ah'd pop roond, see how she is.'

'Why didn't you get her to buzz you in then?' the voice replied scathingly.

'Ah tried, but there was no answer. As ah say, she's no been well. Ah'm worried she might be too ill ti get oot o' bed.'

There was a pause, then a prolonged buzz. Willie pushed the door open.

The place smelled and looked gaudily expensive, lots of marble and gold-coloured fittings that gleamed as if they were polished every two minutes. The carpet was a plush burgundy that smelled newly laid every time Willie came here.

The doorman looked like a walrus who had been stuffed into a uniform the same colour as the carpet as a joke. He had gold braid, epaulettes, a peaked cap, the lot. Willie would rather die than be forced to wear such a uniform, but it was obvious that the doorman took great pride both in the uniform and in the position that went with it. He was sitting behind a massive wooden desk with not a lot on it beyond a visitor's book and an old-fashioned gold-plated telephone, and he glowered at Willie as if he was a stray mongrel which had wandered in off the street, his thick moustache actually seeming to bristle like porcupine spines.

'It's all right if ah just go up, is it?' Willie said.

'If you'll just wait a moment, *sir*.' The doorman lifted the receiver of the gold-plated telephone and slowly dialled a number. He listened for perhaps a minute to the trilling of an unanswered phone at the other end of the line, his lips pursed.

Putting the phone down, he said, 'Miss Purdoe doesn't appear to be taking calls at the moment, *sir*. Perhaps it might be best if you came back later.'

'Ah've already told you,' Willie said patiently, 'Tametia's ill. She's not answering her doorbell or her telephone. Noo that gives me cause for concern, and so if you don't mind, I'll just pop up there, see what's what.'

He began to stride towards the lift, leaving the doorman

spluttering behind him. He knew he would not be pursued; for all his bulk and bluster, the doorman was basically a coward. When he pressed the gold-plated lift button, the doors opened at once, accompanied by a musical 'ting'. Willie stepped inside and pressed the button marked 4. As the lift doors started to close he glanced out into the lobby and saw the doorman slumped in his seat, arms folded, glaring at a monitor screen, obviously sulking.

Each flat here took up an entire floor, which meant that the residents hardly ever met each other unless they really wanted to, which Willie guessed they probably didn't. The lift doors opened on to a kind of small enclosed lobby area which always made Willie think of an airlock in a space ship, albeit one that was carpeted and decorated to look like a four-star hotel.

Tametia's door, made of some strong wood which Willie guessed was probably oak, and which had a gold-coloured number 4 above a spyhole in the centre, was directly in front of him. Tametia didn't answer his loud knocking, not even when he called, 'Come on, Tam, wake up. It's me, Willie. Ah've no come ti hassle you.'

He tried the handle and the door opened immediately, which surprised him. Tametia was a woman who normally kept the door locked even when she was in, not because she was afraid of being attacked (being able to turn into a tiger or a crocodile at will had its advantages), but because she was fiercely possessive of her beautiful expensive flat and all the beautiful expensive things in it; she guarded it all jealously, as if she believed that someone was going to come along one day and try to take it away from her.

'Tam?' he called, entering the flat. 'Tam, are you there?'

Silence. A wide hallway stretched before Willie, one door to his left, two to his right, one directly ahead of him at the other end of the hall.

Willie moved forward, opened the closest door, the one to his left which led to the lounge, and looked inside. It was a huge room, winter sunlight streaming through the window. It was furnished in light pastelly colours. The furniture was elegant, feminine. There were two settees, a coffee table with legs like curly vines on which were strewn a variety of magazines – *Vogue, Cosmopolitan, Tatler, Country Living* – and various chairs. There was also a tiled fireplace with an embroidered fire screen in front of it, lots of plants with rubbery green leaves, arrangements of dried flowers in vases, and pictures on the walls, all of which were abstracts in subtle colours and all of which were originals.

Tametia was not here, though the louvred door to the kitchen was half-open. 'Tam?' Willie called, crossing the room. 'Are you in there?'

He looked. She wasn't.

He went back out into the hallway. The door directly opposite was Tametia's bedroom, which was not the room where she entertained her clients. That room lay behind the door at the end of the corridor, which was always kept locked. Willie had never seen into that room, and had no particular desire to. He opened her bedroom door slowly so as not to startle her if she was sleeping. 'Tam,' he called again in as soothing a voice as he could, 'it's me, Willie. Can I come in?'

He knew as soon as he started to push the door open that the room was empty. The place was bathed in daylight, and profoundly still. Nevertheless he pushed the door all the way open, stepped inside and looked around.

The silk sheets on Tametia's four-poster bed were rumpled, her plump lace-edged pillows scattered about the floor. An empty wine glass lay on its side atop a pile of magazines on the bedside table. Other magazines, like the ones in the sitting room, depicting gorgeous people living gorgeous lives, lay about the room as if Tametia had been hurling them around like frisbees.

It could just have been dismissed as general untidiness if it hadn't been for a couple of things. One was that before being thrown aside, many of the magazines had been crumpled, even torn apart, as though in rage. One cover photo of some supermodel or other had had its eyes gouged out with a sharp instrument. The other thing, the thing which really set the alarm bells ringing in Willie's head, was that someone had thrown a half-full bottle of red wine at the wall, which had smashed, leaving a large stain the colour of his own birthmark on the wallpaper. Broken glass and further splatters of wine were spread over the carpet and the dressing table. Willie knew Tametia had a temper, but he also knew that she would never wilfully destroy anything of her own. It was obvious that something was very wrong here.

Apart from the door at the end of the hallway, there was only one other that Willie hadn't tried. He tried it now, the door to the bathroom.

Inside, he found what he was looking for.

Tametia was lying, naked and dead, in a bath of blood.

'Oh, lassie,' Willie sighed, walking in slowly, his feet crunching on yet more broken glass. He had seen enough violent death in his time for it not to affect him physically, but he still felt remorse and a kind of profound weariness. The evil was nothing more than a great mincing machine, chomping up as much life as it could cram between its vast jaws. And now Tametia had succumbed to its insatiable hunger.

With one sweeping glance, Willie was able to guess what had happened here. Tametia had never been a drinker (indeed, Willie had never seen her drink anything but freshly squeezed fruit juice and bottled water) and yet, judging by the debris here and in the bedroom, it seemed that over the course of the last few days, perhaps even in one mammoth session, she had managed to consume two

413

bottles of red wine and a magnum of champagne.

That was a huge amount for a teetotaller, particularly if, as Willie suspected, she had drunk the whole lot in one go. Under normal circumstances she would have been poleaxed on only a fraction of that amount, but what Willie reckoned was that things must have come to a head and she must have been drinking to try to allay the terror that was flowing through her in waves. He knew how scared she was of dying, particularly slowly and badly like her mother, and so whatever had prompted this must have had something to do with that. Perhaps her condition had continued to deteriorate after her encounter with the bottle, perhaps she had looked in one of the many mirrors positioned around her flat and seen her mother staring fearfully back at her. Or maybe she had managed to convince herself, however illogically, that she would recover from whatever the bottle had done to her once it was in the Flux's possession, and had since heard word that it had fallen into the Schism's hands. Whatever the reason, Willie guessed that Tametia had seen her choices gradually whittled down, finally reduced to just two that were really no choice at all: to die badly or to die well. And so she had drunk herself as senseless as she was able, had taken her rage out on all the beautiful healthy women in her magazines, and had then climbed into a bath full of warm perfumed water and opened up her wrists with a razor blade.

She was lying now with her head turned to the side, her face half-submerged in the crimson water. Her eyes were almost closed, her mouth open as if in a pout. Her skin was blue-white and clammy-looking. In death, she seemed waif-like, like a girl twelve or thirteen years old. The razor was lying on the floor by the bath, oily with blood. There was blood on the tiles by the side of the bath, a great smeary zigzag of it, as if Tametia had been trying to leave one last dramatic message to the world.

Willie went into the kitchen and poured himself a glass of water, which he downed in one before pouring himself another. He gulped half of that, poured the rest down the sink and went through into the lounge. He braced himself before calling Mathilde, then viciously stabbed in her number. As her phone was picked up, he forced himself to slip into character.

'Hello?'

'Mathilde? Aye, it's me, Willie.' She would never know that the trembling in his voice was more rage than distress.

'Oh for God's sake, Willie, where are you now?'

'Ah'm at Tametia's. Listen, Mathilde ... it's ... oh God, it's horrible.'

'Why, what's happened?' She sounded concerned, but Willie had never been sure with Mathilde how much of it was put on and how much of it was genuine.

'She's dead, Mathilde. Ah think she killed herself.'

'Ah no,' said Mathilde sadly. 'How did she do it?'

'Slit her wrists,' said Willie, 'in the bath. There's a lot o' blood.'

'Poor Tametia,' said Mathilde. 'I'll send some people over to sort things out.'

She made it sound like a minor business problem. 'Do you want me ti wait here for them?' Willie said.

'No, there's no point. You might as well come here, as originally planned.'

'Okay,' said Willie. 'See you soon.' He put the phone down.

On the tube to Morden, where Mathilde lived, Willie wondered whether 'the people' had arrived at Tametia's house yet. He was glad Mathilde had not wanted him to stay there and wait for them. Some within the Flux referred to them as 'cleaners'. In Willie's day they had been known as 'undertakers', though it hadn't been such a specialised job back then. They were the people who tidied things up when a Flux member died messily, as

Tametia had, or got into serious trouble, as Malcolm Marshall had once. Basically they manipulated things so that the police and press would not get involved. They used their abilities to shape minds and memories, plant false information in files – in fact, to all intents and purposes, they changed history, or at least the history of selected individuals. In Tametia's case, they would probably arrange for her to have died peacefully in a hospice, having been a resident there for the past couple of months. The staff would remember her, the paperwork would be in order, and her possessions would probably be in storage somewhere. Everyone who had had dealings with Tametia in the past few months would be found and approached and their lives altered accordingly.

Willie rubbed a hand across his forehead and pulled the now rather crumpled newspaper he had bought earlier from his pocket. He spent the rest of the journey trying to lose himself in trivialities – football, human interest stories, diet tips, pop stars talking about their sex lives.

It took him an hour to reach Morden from Tametia's flat. When he knocked on Mathilde's front door it was opened by a fat sweaty guy in a blue suit whom Willie recognised as Terry Bull, a solicitor from Crawley who worked in the city.

'All right, son?' said Willie.

'Will,' said Bull, sticking out his hand. 'Good to see you. Come in.'

Willie allowed his hand to be enveloped by Bull's handshake, which was wet and warm and made him think of that vet programme on the telly where they were always sticking their hands up cows' arses. Bull lumbered through Mathilde's hallway, Willie in tow. As usual her house smelled of strange earthy perfumes which evoked memories of the sixties.

'In here,' Bull muttered unnecessarily at the doorway to a room full of people. Willie followed him inside and stood at the back, exchanging nods with a couple of people.

The room was packed. Willie estimated there were fifty or sixty people here. There were perhaps thirty or so London-based Flux members and the rest were from different parts of the country. Whatever was discussed here this afternoon would be relayed far and wide along the grapevine, both verbally and mentally.

In the middle of the room, unseen by Willie through the silent, rapt crowd, a child was talking. She had the strange, flat, rather guttural intonations that Willie had come to recognise over the years as the voice of the oracle. The evil did not always work this way, completely possessing the child it inhabited, using it as a mouthpiece, a body through which to communicate; more often it drew the child into a fugue state which could last for anything from a few minutes to a few hours, and then later, when the child woke up, it would relay the message that had been imparted to it in its own voice, or in some cases would even write down the message during the fugue.

Willie guessed that it was quite a risk for the evil fully to possess a child like this; perhaps it took a lot out of it, or even made it vulnerable to attack. Certainly it was an occurrence that happened quite rarely, usually only when something very important and very major was about to happen, when a lot of talking had to be done, a lot of instructions given, a lot of information conveyed.

Listening to the child, hidden within a ring of motionless adults, Willie began to get a very bad feeling. At the moment she was outlining plans for a major disturbance in Liverpool. Flux members infiltrated every area of society there and in every town and city – the police, political factions, subcultures, the criminal fraternity – and it seemed this time that all of them would be involved in some way in the unrest. Willie tapped Bull's arm. The taller man inclined his head.

'What's going on here?' Willie whispered.

Bull looked excited but nervous. His top lip was beaded with sweat. 'This is it, Will,' he said, 'this is it.'

'What's it?' said Willie. 'What are you talking aboot?'

Vaguely he was aware that the girl had stopped talking about Liverpool now, and was outlining similar plans for Bristol.

'It's the day we've been waiting for, Will. In every country in the world at this very moment the oracles are outlining plans to set it all in motion. It's here, Will, it's here at last. I never thought I'd live to see this. I always hoped but I never *really* thought . . .' His voice choked off. Willie looked up at him.

Tears of joy were glittering in his eyes.

37

Ellen wondered whether she was in shock. She didn't really know what being 'in shock' meant. In films and on TV such people were always portrayed with wide staring eyes and trembling lips, their teeth chattering against mugs of hot tea that they clutched in both hands. To Ellen, being in shock implied being unresponsive to stimuli, oblivious to one's surroundings. She certainly didn't feel like that, but then again she was not entirely sure *what* she felt like. Before it had been easy: she had been terrified and angry. The two emotions, with terror dominant, had filled her so comprehensively that there had been little room for anything else. Now, though, after seeing Jane rise from the floor like a vampire in a film, and break her bonds as if they were made of nothing more substantial than spaghetti, Ellen felt confusion, or rather sheer incomprehension: she had no idea what was happening or how what she had seen *could* have happened. In point of fact, she was actually beginning to wonder whether she *had* seen what she thought she had. Had her stress, her fear, somehow caused her to hallucinate? She couldn't believe that either, but it seemed more acceptable than the evidence of her own eyes.

She had looked to her fellow captives for guidance, but their expressions had not reassured her. For the first time fear had been apparent in Diane's eyes, and the same incomprehension that Ellen was feeling. The same was true of Ralph and Rachel. Was it possible that they had had a group hallucination? Whichever explanation presented itself seemed as unbelievable, unacceptable, as the next.

Jane had gone, apparently willingly, with the fat woman. Indeed, she had seemed to *lead* the fat woman; the fat woman had moved respectfully aside at her approach as if she were a lady-in-waiting and Jane a princess. The two of them had ascended the cellar steps, and then Ellen had heard them leave the house. That had been a long time – ten, fifteen hours? – ago, since which neither of them had returned. Bernard had continued to guard them dutifully, had fed them (Ellen had managed a little cheese and soup this time), given them water, allowed them to use the potty, and had even loosened their bonds and massaged their numbed joints (the pain had been so unbearable at first that it had actually made Ellen cry).

Ellen wondered, as she had wondered constantly since Jane had left with the fat woman, about the strange gruff voice she had heard coming out of her youngest daughter's mouth, and about the words she and the fat woman had spoken to each other. Had Jane's voice sounded like that simply because she had been denied use of it for the past day or so? The words had meant nothing to Ellen, but had she misheard them? If she hadn't, if the fat woman had really asked Jane, 'It is you, isn't it?', and Jane had replied, 'Yes, it's me,' then that seemed to suggest a certain amount of prior collusion, which again was impossible.

One other possibility had occurred to Ellen, but this really *was* unacceptable, far more so than anything that had gone before. Back in the early seventies, Ellen, like everyone else, had seen and been terrified by the film, *The Exorcist*, where a little girl had become possessed by the Devil. During the course of the film, the girl had puked green gunk all over a priest, made her head spin all the way round on her shoulders and masturbated with a crucifix. She had spoken in a deep guttural voice, and had changed in appearance to look like some evil bestial creature. Ellen could not quite get the connection between Jane and the little girl in the film out of her head, no matter how hard she tried. It was ridiculous, of course. *The Exorcist*, for all the impact it had made, had just been a film, after all, with actors and actresses, make-up, special effects, a director and a writer and a camera crew. It wasn't real. It *couldn't* be real . . . Something was wrong with Jane, that was all, some fever or illness. Or if not Jane, then herself.

It had been like this for hours now, the same thoughts playing over and over in her head, like a record on endless repeat. Despite her worry, she had slept a little, exhaustion dragging her into a fitful, nebulous state only just below the surface of her thoughts. When she had surfaced again, the same thoughts had still been there, the needle having worn deep into the grooves in her absence. Her sleep had not relaxed or revived her. Indeed, if anything she felt worse than before, as if she were coming down with a particularly virulent strain of flu. She had felt much the same all day, had even been having little blackouts now and again, strange interludes where it seemed a light was being switched off in her skull, making everything go dark and fuzzy and slow for a few minutes.

Because of this she had no idea what time it was; she was even beginning to lose track of how long they had been here. Was it two days or three? Or had they not even been here two days yet? All she knew was that it was light outside again now, and had been so for a long time. Would it be getting dark again soon? As far as she was aware it could be anywhere between eleven in the morning and five in the afternoon.

Her eyes were closing again, her head rolling around on her shoulders, when she heard the sound of someone upstairs. She jerked awake, not for the first time, the tape yanking her hair at the back. It hurt, but her body was full of pain now; it seemed one big pain, in fact, every joint aching intolerably, every muscle cramping. Even her skin felt tender, as though scoured with a wire brush, and the cold she had been feeling had gone beyond that now, had become an intense chill that had wormed its way into the very heart of her.

Bernard was still slumped against the wall at the other side of the room, reading another of his 'Doctor Who' books. He seemed to have an endless supply of them. Every so often he would finish one and then go upstairs for another, reappearing after a few minutes. At first he had read aloud to them – he had read them the whole of *The Abominable Snowman* and half of a story called *The Daemons*. Then his voice had started getting croaky and he had had to stop. At the moment he was silently reading a book called *The Tenth Planet*.

When the noise came from upstairs, Bernard put his book aside and looked up, as if he could see right through the ceiling. He looked puzzled, nervous, but then didn't he always? Ellen was a little confused. What had she heard exactly? The sound, though she knew it had woken her, had kind of bridged the gap between sleep and wakefulness, and was therefore vague in her memory.

She might almost have believed she had imagined the noise and drifted off to semi-sleep again if it wasn't for Bernard's reaction. He was frowning, licking his lips nervously, as if he was aware of something unpleasant that the rest of them weren't. Awkwardly he clambered to his feet, pushing his fringe away from his eyes. He was shaking slightly, Ellen realised, but then it was bloody cold down here. He kept licking his lips as if he couldn't get any moisture in his mouth.

'Did . . . did you hear that?' he said, turning to them, one hand gesturing vaguely at the ceiling.

They just looked at him, not understanding why he was so nervous.

Suddenly he flinched as if something had touched him

unexpectedly, a cobweb drifting across his face perhaps.

'There!' he said. 'There it was again. You *must* have heard it that time.'

Ellen frowned. She had heard nothing, and it was evident that none of the others had either. Bernard was looking at them with such desperation that she felt compelled to shrug in response.

Bernard's mouth opened and closed, his lips trembling. He looked like a little boy about to burst into floods of tears.

'But you *must* have,' he all but wailed, 'you must have, it was really loud.' His eyes widened. 'There! I heard it again. Don't tell me you didn't hear *that*?'

Ellen was beginning to wonder whether all the time spent cooped up with his captives was starting to affect Bernard's mind too. Was he starting to get paranoid, schizophrenic? The signs were not encouraging. What was it he was hearing? Voices in his head?

As if she had spoken the question out loud, Bernard answered her. 'It was . . . voices. But not human ones. They sounded all sort of . . . buzzy. Mechanical. They sounded like . . .' He gave a short high-pitched laugh that was almost a shriek, and asked, his voice wavering as if on the edge of hysteria, 'Have you seen *The Tomb Of The Cybermen*?'

Ellen assumed he meant another 'Doctor Who' story, not the actual tombs themselves. She shook her head.

'It sounded like them,' Bernard said, 'like the Cybermen from that story. All buzzy and mechanical.' He shuddered. 'Horrible.'

Ellen looked at Diane, who looked back at her, raising her eyebrows. Rachel, who had been sleeping a lot, her head resting against Ellen's aching shoulder, snuggled up closer to her mother as if for protection. Ralph's face, swollen and bruised, was unreadable; Ellen guessed it caused him pain even to raise his eyebrows. Bernard looked at them, and then his head whipped round towards the stairs, his straggly hair lashing his cheeks.

'They're coming,' he hissed, and there was such fear in his voice that Ellen shuddered despite herself. He looked puppet-like, unco-ordinated, as he staggered towards the foot of the stairs and looked up. Ellen was holding her breath; still she had heard nothing. But all at once Bernard let out a wailing cry and threw his hands up in front of his face.

'*No!*' he screamed, staggering backwards. '*No! No! No!*' He began to yell out his denial as he staggered to the other side of the room, and then, to the astonishment of them all, crawled into the cobweb-festooned space beneath the cracked sink.

Ellen saw things scuttling madly over his body, spiders probably. Bernard, however, appeared not to notice. He pushed himself as far back as he could, oblivious to the thick sticky accumulation of cobweb that adhered to his clothes and hair and face. Then he curled into a ball, tucking his head between his knees, enfolding his body in his long ape-like arms. He wasn't screaming any more; he sounded, in fact, as if he was trying to make himself as unobtrusive as possible. Though he was whimpering, sobbing, gulping, it was evident he was trying to bring even these sounds under control.

He's cracked, Ellen thought. His mind has gone, just like that. Though astounded by what had happened, her mind was not so numbed that she wasn't already considering the implications of what this might mean for the rest of them. She had not previously considered Bernard a threat to their safety, but she did now. In the space of a few seconds, everything seemed to have turned upside-down again. If he thought Cybermen were upstairs, wasn't it possible that he might suddenly see the four of them, even trussed up and helpless as they were, as enemies too and turn violent? By doing what he had just done, by being unpredictable, he had opened up the possibility that anything might happen.

She did not have to lie there and think about what might happen for very long, however. Perhaps thirty seconds after Bernard had crawled beneath the sink, the cellar door at the top of the stairs clicked open. It was a small sound, but they were so attuned to it that all four of them immediately looked round. Ellen remembered the Cybermen from years ago, how they had terrified Rachel as a little girl. Bernard's reaction had been such that she half-expected to hear the heavy slow tread such a creature might make, see the silvery flash of its body.

The figure who did appear was far less imposing, but no less bewildering. He was a little scruffy old man wearing a cap and a rumpled suit. He was partly in shadow at first, the light behind him. Then he reached the bottom of the stairs and stepped into the slightly less gloomy cellar. At the sight of him, Ellen's eyes widened; she gave a moan of fear behind her gag.

There was something wrong with the man's face. His eyes were a silvery-purple colour, as if he was wearing weird contact lenses. However, what really frightened Ellen was not so much this as the maroon birthmark on the man's jaw and throat. It was . . . pulsing and squirming – no, not quite squirming. It was . . . changing, coiling within itself, patterns blossoming, opening like petals and then folding themselves back in, like a child's kaleidoscope or the shifting colours in a patch of oil.

As the man approached them, all four of them recoiled as much as they were able, pressing themselves back against the wall.

'Don't be scared,' the man said in a strong Glaswegian accent so incongruous it would have been funny if it wasn't so bizarre. 'The reason ah look like this is for his benefit.' He jerked a thumb at Bernard. 'Ah've come ti rescue you. Ah'm a friend of David's.'

425

Ellen's heart leaped, and then began to hammer. Could this be true? Despite the man's appearance she wanted so much to believe it. Nevertheless as the man approached and then bent towards her, she felt her throat tightening with the urge to scream.

'Ah'm going ti take some scissors out of ma pocket noo,' the man said, 'but it's only ti cut you free. Okay?'

He spoke gently, reassuringly. Ellen tried not to look at his eyes or his pulsing birthmark as she nodded.

'Okay,' the man said, smiling a little. He reached into his pocket and took out a large pair of scissors. Carefully he cut the bonds securing her ankles.

Her feet sprang apart, and were instantly seized by pain. Ellen's teeth clenched. Her eyes brimmed with tears which overflowed, spilling down her face.

'Sorry,' the man said. 'Ah'm going ti cut the ropes round your wrists now, okay?'

She managed to nod and he manoeuvred in behind her, helping her shuffle forward so he could get to the ropes. Within a few seconds she was free.

'Ah'll let you get the feeling back and then you can get the gag off yourself,' the man said. 'Ah don't want ti hurt you.'

Ellen couldn't answer; she just lay there, crying the pain out, unable to do anything for the time being but endure it. The pain was a force inside her, trying to turn her inside-out. When it peaked, she thought she was going to black out, or at the very least throw up. And then, mercifully, it began to fade, little by little but noticeably so.

At last she was able to roll on to her side, though her body still sizzled with the most incredible pins and needles. The man had freed Rachel and was doing the same for Diane. Rachel must have been more hardy than her mother, or perhaps it was simply because she was younger, more supple. Already she was picking at the tape that covered her mouth, though so clumsily she might have been wearing boxing gloves.

A minute or so later Diane and Ralph were both free too. They lay as Ellen had, on their backs, unmoving, their eyes screwed up in agony. The man with the silver-purple eyes and the pulsing birthmark said, 'Ah don't want ti rush you, but as soon as you're able ti walk we should be getting out o' here. If we're found we're dead, me especially.'

Rachel had succeeded in removing her gag. Previously, to feed his captives, Bernard had opened a little nick in the tape with a knife and had then sealed it up again afterwards. He had been very careful but on one occasion had cut Rachel's upper lip and made her squeal.

The bottom half of her face was covered in a rash red as sunburn. There was dried blood crusted on her lips. In a croaky voice, she whispered, 'Who are you?'

'Ah've told you, a friend of your dad's. Name's Willie. Can you stand up yet?'

Rachel tried. Ellen felt absurdly proud of her daughter as she saw her rise shakily to her feet like a newborn colt. There were horrible weals on her wrists and ankles where the rope had cut into her flesh, and her hands were pale, though blotchy with areas of blue and purple and orange, as if she had been out in the freezing cold without gloves for a very long time.

Ellen looked at her own hands. They were the same. At least they responded when she clenched them, albeit in a detached, sluggish kind of way. She tried to rise to her feet too, and almost fell down again; if the wall hadn't been there for her to lean against she would have done so. She felt giddy and sick, not least because the pain in her feet when she put her weight on them was almost intolerable. She felt disgusting, not only ill and in pain, but filthy, almost bestial, like a cave woman. It was horrifying to think that a human being could degenerate so much in just a matter of days. It made her realise how very quickly and easily life could change, how fragile it all was. Diane and Ralph were showing signs of activity. Ellen began to pick at her gag. Beneath the sink, Bernard was still curled into a ball, whimpering.

'What did you do to him?' Rachel asked.

'Ah showed him one of his innermost fears. That's why ah look like this just noo. Ah'm usually quite normal.'

Ellen was unwinding the tape from around her head, unable to suppress small moans as she reached the last layer, which was stuck to her skin and hair. Diane was sitting up now, shuddering as she massaged her ankles, and examining the foot that the white-haired man had bitten so long ago.

Rachel was starting to walk around a little, wincing with each step.

'What are we going to do now?' she asked the man with the birthmark.

'We're goin' ti go and see your dad,' he replied.

38

For a few precious seconds after the sun slanting through the skylight woke him, David felt happy and peaceful. He was warm and comfortable, he could hear birds singing, and the blue sky seemed like the foretaste of a day that was full of promise.

Then he yawned and shifted a little, and it was as though some delicate thread had been broken. His memories came rushing back, seemed to settle inside him like a dark heavy weight. He groaned and sat up, groped for his watch and lifted it to his face. It was twenty-five past ten.

So tired had he been last night that he had not even noticed his accommodation. He looked around now and realised he was in an attic bedroom shaped rather like a tent, the walls sloping up at either side to meet in a point in the middle. The room was effectively divided into two by a supporting beam in the middle of the floor. The far side of the room contained a jumble of boxes and suitcases and bits of worn or broken furniture. The majority of the floor space in David's half of the room was taken up with his bed, though there was also an armchair and an old pot sink with a black-speckled mirror above it.

From somewhere below him, David could hear the murmur of voices and the chink of breakfast pots. After all he had been through yesterday, it all seemed so bizarrely mundane. He pushed back the duvet, got out of bed and padded over to the armchair. He vaguely remembered dragging off his clothes last night and dumping them on the chair before plunging gratefully towards the bed, but now his clothes were neatly folded with a sheet of white paper placed on top of them. He picked up the paper and, bleary-eyed, read the note written in blue biro:

David, thought you might have need of some clean clothes. I reckon we're about the same size. Hope they're to your taste.

Richard.

P.S. Have taken your clothes away to be washed. Hope that's okay. Stuff from pockets is on floor by bed.

David smiled and clumped over to the sink. He tried the taps, which he was surprised to find worked, although they squeaked like tortured hamsters. He washed himself thoroughly, tried to cajole his hair into some semblance of order with his fingers, and put on the clothes Richard Hodge had provided for him. Then he went downstairs.

There was a fire going in the grate, around which sat Malcolm Marshall, nursing a cup of tea, Imogen Butterworth, Violet Turner and Jack Livermore. When David said good morning, the two women responded warmly, Marshall grunted and continued to stare into the flames, and Jack Livermore, wearing a blue blazer and a tie with some kind of crest on it, swivelled round in his chair and barked, 'Morning, young man. Ready for the fray, are we?'

His eyes, whites the colour of dirty ivory, bulged slightly from their sockets, and raw-looking wattles of flesh overlapped the tight collar of his white shirt.

'I won't be ready for anything until I've had some breakfast,' David replied, and was not sure whether he saw a flicker of disapproval on the old man's face before he turned away.

He went through the arch into the kitchen, which smelled welcomingly of bacon and coffee, and not so welcomingly of cigar smoke. The smoker was Hollis, who was sitting at the table talking to Max and Tippi. Before

430

David could say anything, Hollis held up his Panatella and said defensively, 'I'm trying to give 'em up, but if I don't have a couple to kick-start me in the morning I'm a miserable bastard all day.'

'I never said anything,' said David, then realisation dawned. 'You're reading my mind again, aren't you? I wish you wouldn't do that.'

The table was scattered with mugs, bowls, plates and cutlery, the majority of which were used, plus cereal boxes, fruit juices, preserves, a metal rack containing five slices of toast, a half-empty cafetiere and a teapot wearing a tea cosy shaped like a thatched cottage.

David picked up the teapot which felt ominously light and, sighing, wandered over to fill the kettle at the kitchen sink. Tippi told him to help himself to anything he wanted for breakfast, and as he bustled about Max asked him if he had had a peaceful night's sleep. When David sat down, having placed a fresh pot of tea on the table, and reached for the Weetabix, Hollis dropped his half-smoked cigar into his coffee mug, where it sizzled for a second. 'I wasn't enjoying it anyway,' he said wistfully.

'So what are we doing today?' David asked after swallowing a mouthful of Weetabix.

'We're waiting,' said Tippi.

'For what?'

Hollis said, 'Willie went back to London with Ishvak this morning. They should be over halfway there by now. He'll find out what's going on and let us know.'

'And meanwhile we just sit here twiddling our thumbs.'

'I'm sorry, David,' said Max, 'but as I explained yesterday, you must be patient. In our position we have to use stealth. We observe our enemies' movements and counter them.'

David sighed. 'That's all very well, but I wish there was something concrete I could do.'

'There is,' said Max. 'You can arm yourself with

information. You can prepare yourself.'

'I thought I'd done all that last night,' said David glumly.

'Oh, stop feeling so sorry for yourself, you miserable git,' said Hollis. 'Max is right. If you're going to take on the Flux, you have to know as much about them as possible. You've only scratched the surface so far.'

David thought of last night's conversation. 'I don't think my brain can take any more.'

'Course it can,' said Tippi. 'After breakfast, once I've seen to Jean, we'll go for a long leisurely walk by the river. We can talk until the cows come home. How is Jean this morning, by the way?'

This question was directed at Max, who shrugged resignedly and said, 'A little better, though sometimes I think she will never leave that bed, never stand on her own two feet again.'

Tippi leaned forward and placed a hand on his arm. 'She will, Max. It'll just take time, that's all.'

'Ah, time,' he said, nodding slowly. 'Time, I fear, is something that neither Jean nor I have in great abundance any more.'

'Oh, for God's sake,' said Hollis. 'Why is everyone feeling so bloody sorry for themselves this morning? Any more of this and I'll fetch my violin.'

Max chuckled. 'You're right of course, Patrick. I apologise.'

'Shall we go and see Jean now, Max?' said Tippi.

Max nodded and the two of them left. By the time Tippi reappeared, looking pale and a little gaunt, David had eaten his Weetabix, four slices of toast and drunk two cups of tea. He felt a bit guilty holding Tippi to her promise of a walk by the river; she looked as though she needed a lie down. However she insisted she was fine, and the two of them set out into the cold clear morning sunshine just as the Hodges came in, sweaty and bright-eyed from their morning run.

He and Tippi walked and talked for two hours, and then when they got back, Max introduced David, almost shyly, to Jean, who gave him one of the sweetest but tiredest smiles he had ever seen. Though David didn't know what was wrong with Max's wife, he expected her room to be gloomy and to smell of sickness, and so was surprised to see the sunlight streaming across the bed, the old woman's face turned to a breeze which ruffled her grey hair and which smelled of fresh grass and earth and wild flowers. Jean assured him, when he asked, that she was getting a little better each day, and confided that Max, though she loved him dearly, was nothing but an old fusspot.

'Have you come to help us?' she asked him, fixing him with a clear steady gaze which would have been intimidating if it hadn't been so benign.

'So everyone seems to think,' said David a little embarrassedly.

'I think so too,' said Jean. 'I'm not a special person, like Max and dear Tippi and all the rest, but I can sense the goodness in you.'

Then she closed her eyes and seemed to slip almost instantly into sleep. David didn't think he had ever seen anyone look so peaceful.

By the time Hollis and Richard Hodge tried to persuade him to accompany them to the local pub for a lunch-time drink, David was feeling restless, wishing something would happen. His heart was telling him he should have gone back to London with Willie and Ishvak that morning, even though logically he knew that he would have been more of a hindrance than a help. At first, therefore, he refused their invitation, thinking that he should at least stay by the phone, but Tippi assured him she had the phone number of the pub and would ring if anything happened. The pub, called The Half Moon, was actually about four miles up the road in a tiny village whose name David didn't notice and was not particularly interested in finding out. The three men ate chicken and mushroom pie and played pool, and each bought a round of the local brew, which was sweet and dark and had a head so thick you could write your name in it.

The beer, and the smoke from Hollis's Panatellas, made David feel sleepy and headachy for most of the afternoon, and rather than relaxing him seemed instead to exacerbate his agitation. When they arrived back at the house, he went upstairs for a lie down, unable to shake off the notion that by mooching around here, doing nothing, he was betraying his family and friends, turning his back on their plight. Even the thought that Willie, and possibly others too, were out there working for him didn't help. He *knew* he was being unreasonably hard on himself, but that didn't prevent him thinking that he was passing the buck, getting others to deal with his problems. It was only when he took the bottle from the pocket of his Bogart and pressed it to his forehead that he felt anything like calm.

He wondered whether the soothing influence that the bottle had on him in its dormant state was actual or psychological, and was still wondering this when he fell asleep, the bottle still pressed to his forehead like a balm. When he woke up he did so suddenly, feeling momentarily disorientated, aware of the darkness pressing against his face like a smothering hood. He sat up, his first lucid thought the panicked certainty that someone had stolen the bottle. Then he saw it standing upright beside the bed, glinting in the light of the moon that peered at him through the skylight. He must have placed it there carefully in his sleep, or else someone else had.

He held his watch in front of his eyes until its luminous dial made sense to him: it was almost six o' clock. If this had been a normal Monday he would just be getting home from work by now. Jane and Rachel would be watching

434

'Neighbours' while Ellen made some food. He would dump his briefcase, ceremoniously pull off his tie, and wander through to the kitchen to chat to Ellen while she bustled about, chopping vegetables or stirring the contents of pans. Sometimes, if she'd been out in the garden all day and couldn't be bothered to cook, he'd do it, or he'd fetch a takeaway, or even, on occasion, if he was feeling particularly flush and if the girls didn't have too much homework, he'd take the whole family out for a curry or some pasta.

Stop it, he told himself. Thinking like this made him ache inside, actually made his stomach hurt. He doused his face at the sink, then went downstairs, where Violet, Imogen, Malcolm and Jack were clustered around the fire as usual, talking in low voices. David said hello and made some tea, which he dispensed to the fire-worshippers, feeling glumly like an orderly in an old folks' home.

As he sipped his own tea, he reflected on the fact that it didn't seem to be much of a fighting force he had got himself involved with here. What kind of chance did they really have against an organisation as dynamic as the Flux were reputed to be? Of course, there was only a tiny proportion of Schism members here, but even so it seemed to be peopled by ex-Flux members who had realised the folly of what they were doing. Younger members, such as Tippi and the Hodges, seemed the exception rather than the rule, but in the long run did that make any difference? The forthcoming conflict with the Flux which everyone seemed to be expecting would surely be one of minds (or more accurately *abilities*) rather than physical strength. Perhaps a person's ability grew stronger with age. Perhaps the older you got the more powerful you became.

During the next hour or so, most of the house's other occupants drifted downstairs and congregated together in the sitting room and kitchen. The Hodges appeared and asked who was hungry, making it obvious that they were.

For want of anything better to do, David helped them prepare some food, his gaze continually straying to the window as he washed salad, willing headlights to appear in the blackness outside, or at least the phone to ring. By the time the food was ready, it was almost eight o' clock, and everyone sat down to a communal meal of cheese and onion flan, baked potatoes, salad and garlic bread, with the exception of Max, who elected to eat his upstairs with Jean.

By nine o' clock David was standing at the kitchen window with a glass of red wine in his hand, watching pale bluish light crawl across tree trunks and then fade each time clouds stifled the moon. He felt snappy and irritable, resentful of the fact that everyone was just sitting around as if there was nothing to worry about. The old folk were monopolising the area around the fire as usual; the Hodges were playing Trivial Pursuit with Tippi, Richard Hodge saying to his wife, 'Oh, you must know that one, it's *easy*'; Max was still upstairs with Jean; and Hollis was sprawled in front of the TV, sucking on one of the eight cans of Special Brew he'd bought in the pub that lunch-time.

'Come and sit down, David,' Hollis called across to him. 'You know you really should learn to relax.'

David turned so sharply that wine slopped on to his shoe. 'Relax? How can I bloody relax when I don't know what's going on?'

Hollis shrugged. He was lying on the floor, feet either side of the screen, the elbow of his left arm propping him up. 'Worrying about stuff won't change it.'

'Oh right, so you think I should just turn my emotions on and off to suit the situation, do you? You think it's that easy? Just because you've got no one to worry about except yourself.'

'How do you know I've got no one to worry about?' Hollis replied mildly.

David was flustered. He'd assumed that Hollis was a bachelor. 'That's not the point. Your family haven't been kidnapped and held to ransom. I should be out there . . . *doing* something.'

Hollis rolled his eyes. 'Oh God, not again. We've been through this so many times. Look, David, read my lips: There's. Nothing. You. Can. Do. Willie'll have everything under control.'

'Then why hasn't he rung in? Doesn't he realise how bloody awful this is for me, not knowing anything?'

'You want him to ring in every two minutes to tell you what he's doing?'

'Not every two minutes, no, but once in a while would be nice.'

'It's too risky, David,' said Tippi, who had turned from the game. She looked a little wan, having ministered to Jean earlier that evening for the second time that day. 'If it's not essential then it's not done. There's no point taking unnecessary risks.'

Everyone was staring at David now, which somehow seemed to give him an insight into how he must look in their eyes: petulant, frustrated, unreasonable. He turned back to the window, fixing his eyes on the darkness. 'Oh, go back to your bloody TV programme,' he muttered.

He heard movement, but didn't realise anyone was beside him until he felt a hand on his shoulder. He turned to see Tippi frowning at him, albeit concernedly.

'There's no point standing by the window, David. If they're nearby, Patrick will know. Why don't you come and have a game of Triv with us? It'll help pass the time at least.'

David sighed, but nodded and said, 'Okay.' He drained his wine glass, then carried a chair through from the kitchen. He'd always hated waiting. He remembered when Rachel had been born, how long and arduous Ellen's labour had been. At one point Rachel had begun to show signs of distress inside the womb, her heartbeat soaring and plunging erratically, and he had been ushered out into a corridor to allow the doctors room to manoeuvre. It had seemed like an eternity sitting out there on that plastic seat, his stomach churning with helplessness. He remembered thinking at the time that any waiting he had to do in the future couldn't possibly be any worse than this, that as far as waiting was concerned this was the ultimate, the peak, the zenith. Looking back on that now, he realised how wrong he had been. Compared to today, Rachel's birth, for him at least, had been a picnic.

He played the board game mechanically, keeping one eye on the clock. It was just before 'News At Ten', and the Gold Blend couple were enacting a new phase in their coy and irritating love affair, when Hollis suddenly sat bolt upright and said, 'They're here.'

David looked at him, his stomach tightening with apprehension, lizards scurrying up and down his backbone. 'You mean . . . Willie?' He could barely get the words past his dry throat.

Hollis nodded, narrowing his eyes. 'Willie . . . Ishvak . . . and there are others with them.'

David jumped up, his knee catching the edge of the Trivial Pursuit board, causing it to somersault and the plastic pieces to scatter. He ran to the door and pulled it open, tossing an abstracted apology over his shoulder.

Cold air embraced him, teasing his fringe, making him squint. Dry leaves scraped and rustled in the yard, a few blowing into the house, darting around David's feet and taking refuge beneath the kitchen table. He could see nothing as yet through the trees, no approaching lights, could not even hear the distant rumble of a car engine.

'Where are they?' he muttered, feeling sick to his stomach. 'Where are they?'

Hollis, standing beside him, narrowed his eyes and said, 'They're coming . . . They're coming . . . They're here.'

At once the wind brought David the purr of Ishvak's BMW. There was a flash in the trees, the swoop of headlights. David felt giddy with mingled terror and elation. In a few moments he would know; one way or another he would know *something*. He had a sudden vision of Willie getting dejectedly out of the car, meeting his eye and slowly shaking his head.

The car headlights bumped and flashed towards them, occasionally dimmed but never completely obscured by trees.

And then all at once here was the car, bumping into the yard, coming to a halt.

David saw people in the car, dark heads bobbing. He stood transfixed, barely able to breathe.

The car headlights were doused, the engine turned off.

Car doors opened.

People got out.

David saw Ishvak first. He got out of the car, then hurried to the back, where it seemed someone was struggling to push the door open. He held the door open and helped someone out. A woman. Tall. Blonde hair. Limping.

David sucked in a breath that made his head spin. He clapped a hand to his mouth. It was Diane! Oh God, it was Diane!

People were getting out on the other side of the car. David saw Willie offering his hand and helping someone else out. It was a woman – no, a girl. For a moment David didn't dare let himself believe it, and then the girl turned, pushed hair away from her face, and peered bemusedly at the house.

The girl spoke. 'Dad?' she said uncertainly.

'Rachel.' The word emerged as a croak.

'Go to her, David.' It was Max standing by his shoulder who was speaking. He seemed to have appeared from nowhere.

David swallowed, nodded, and began to stumble across the muddy, uneven yard, the wind plucking at his clothes and hair.

Rachel rounded the car, screaming, 'Dad!' and flung herself at him.

David embraced her, and though he was overcome, though he was sobbing, he was still aware of how filthy she was, how bad she smelled.

'I'm sorry,' he kept telling her, 'I'm sorry, I'm so sorry.' He showered kisses on to her filthy hair, her upturned face.

'David,' said a voice.

He looked up, and through the blur of his tears he saw someone else, a woman, looking confused and exhausted and lost, clinging on to the car as he had clung to the farmhouse door a few moments earlier.

Rachel was hugging him so fiercely that he could barely draw breath, but he still managed to whisper the woman's name.

'Ellen,' he said, stretching out a hand to touch her face.

39

By noon the next day the world was in chaos.

It started as a series of isolated incidents, stray sparks which smouldered and flared, began to burn and then, inevitably, to spread. In Britain the first spark was ignited at 6 a.m., when Deepak Kapoor opened his newsagent's shop in the Moss Side area of Manchester, and was bustled inside by four youths who had been waiting outside. The leader of the youths, seventeen-year-old Grant Cundy, demanded money from Kapoor's till. When Kapoor explained, almost apologetically, that it was the start of the day and the till was empty, Cundy pulled a gun from his back pocket and shot Kapoor through the head.

The gunshot exploded through the neighbourhood, waking people up, bringing them to the windows of their houses to peer out. Though the people were not unused to violence here, what Kapoor's neighbours witnessed over the next ten minutes shocked them to the core. First of all, Kapoor's body was dragged outside by two of the youths, its shattered head leaking blood, and dumped in the middle of the road. The two teenagers then ran back inside, reappearing with their friends moments later. The four boys had rounded up Kapoor's wife and three children and now herded them out into the middle of the street dressed only in their nightclothes. At the sight of her husband, Gita Kapoor, already distressed, began to scream, which brought yet more people to their windows to watch. Cundy laughed and pointed the gun at Gita. Panicked, she turned and began to run away, her bare feet slapping the road. Cundy shot her in the back. She fell forwards on to her face, and began to make a high animal-like keening sound. Cundy strolled casually up to her, looked down at her for a moment, then grinned and shot her twice in the head.

The murder of Kapoor's wife seemed to act as a signal to the other boys to slaughter the children. Two of the boys drew knives and stabbed and slashed at the two oldest children, a boy aged four and a girl aged seven, until they were lying still beside their father, their bodies covered in blood. Then the four boys, themselves splashed with their victims' blood, all surrounded the youngest child, a two-year-old girl who was wailing and screeching, and mercilessly kicked her to death, laughing and chanting racist slogans as they did so.

Afterwards, the teenagers heaped the corpses up in the middle of the road, poured petrol on them and set them on fire. They also set fire to the shop, but even now made no move to vacate the scene. Instead they danced round the burning bodies, chanting, 'Niggers out, Pakis out.'

Retaliation was swift and merciless. Less than ten minutes after killing the family, the teenagers themselves were dead, two of them hanging from lamp posts, the other two hacked to death.

When police arrived minutes later, they found a gang of twenty or thirty youths surrounding one of the dead teenagers, trying to remove the boy's head so they could mount it on a javelin.

The police waded in and the youths fought back, hurling bricks and bottles and home-made petrol bombs which seemed to have been manufactured beforehand and in great quantities, as though in readiness for just such an incident. Police reinforcements were called in as the disturbance spilled over into neighbouring streets and then began to spread throughout the entire area like wildfire.

By 7:30 a.m., Moss Side was a full-scale riot zone.

Police were astonished at the speed with which the trouble had flared, particularly considering the time of day. It was almost as though the area had been primed, as though the whole thing had been premeditated, and was now being orchestrated from some central base.

As was common in such situations, the initial reason for the eruption of violence was soon forgotten, or simply used as a feeble excuse for the mayhem which followed. Troublemakers of all colours, creeds and political persuasions converged on the area, drawn by the attraction of creating chaos for its own sake, by the chance to slake their thirst for violence and destruction. But it was not only those with a penchant for splitting heads who were drawn to the scene. The parasites came too – burglars and car thieves, looters and pyromaniacs, all eager to use the turmoil around them as a smokescreen under which to pursue their own nefarious activities.

Although riots had become less uncommon in Britain in recent years, this particular one was odd for a number of reasons. Apart from the astonishing speed with which events had escalated (and the suggestion of premeditation, of organisation on a grand scale) and the fact that no riot had ever begun so early in the day before, and especially not on a cold winter's morning just before Christmas, there was one other factor which made this incident stand out. It was nothing to do with the riot itself, but it was nevertheless the most frightening and significant factor of all. It was simply that the Moss Side riot was no isolated incident. Outbreaks of spontaneous and serious lawlessness were soon being reported not only all over the country, but *all over the world*.

Connections were not made immediately, of course, largely because it seemed outlandish to do so. How could a massacre in Ghana possibly be connected to riots in Manchester, or an explosion at Athens Airport to a sudden upsurge in gang violence in Los Angeles? But as reports continued to flood into every news agency in the world, more and more people in high-ranking positions, risking ridicule, began to suggest that something both terrifying and monumental was taking place. As one newscaster in New York so succinctly put it, 'It seems the world is going mad.'

By mid-morning the apparently impossible phenomenon of a massive and unprecedented crime wave on a global scale was grudgingly becoming accepted as a reality. In every country, without exception, crime figures were soaring through the roof. Civic unrest was rife. In Britain alone, in the space of a few hours, riots had erupted in Manchester, Liverpool, Leeds, Bristol, Norwich, Cardiff, Portsmouth, Newcastle, Derby, Birmingham, Sheffield and London. In some places the riots were not confined to one particular area but spread throughout the city. By 11:30 a.m. *eleven* separate areas of London were reported to be riot zones. Crime of every kind, and not just in areas where riots had broken out, doubled, quadrupled, then doubled again. There were more murders, assaults, muggings, burglaries and incidents of arson and vandalism in just one morning than there had been for the whole of the previous six months.

There was no way, of course, that the British emergency services could cope with the mayhem. Their resources, already stretched to the limit by government cutbacks, were quickly exhausted. In some areas whole streets burned, the fire services simply too busy to deal with them. Murders went uninvestigated, severely injured people lay ignored in the streets. It didn't help that police vehicles and fire engines, even ambulances, were seen as viable targets by the rioters. In one incident in Sunderland, two ambulance men were pulled from their vehicle and beaten to death by a chanting, cheering mob, and the ambulance with its cargo of injured humanity was then set alight.

By noon chaos reigned. It was at this time that the government, after an emergency meeting, decided to impose martial law. However, even within the armed services there was, it seemed, an element of disruption. In many cases orders failed to arrive or were misinterpreted or appeared to contradict previous instructions. Troops were often sent to the wrong place, or their actions anticipated by the enemy. In Streatham seven soldiers were shot dead after being lured into an ambush by armed rioters.

Events then began to take an even more sinister turn. Armed gangs, as many as five hundred strong, turned their attention to the disabling of communications networks. Telephone exchanges and power lines, TV and radio transmitters, and public transport came under attack. Just outside Leeds, an Inner City train was derailed and the passengers attacked by thugs armed with axes and baseball bats. There was an explosion at Gatwick Airport, and nine more in airports and railway stations up and down the country.

Across the globe the story was the same. Little by little people began to lose contact with the outside world. The BBC continued to broadcast for as long as it could, providing the public with continuous news updates. But then abruptly, at 2:15 p.m., the television screens across the country went dark.

The rioters, it seemed, had won.

It was the beginning of the end.

40

'It's crazy,' Diane said, shaking her head in wonderment. 'It's just . . . I can't believe this is happening.'

It was the morning of Tuesday 22nd December. At the safe house in Cumbria, everyone was gathered around the small black and white television, watching the world unravelling before them. They'd been expecting it here, but actually to witness humankind tearing itself apart was more awesome and horrifying than any one of them could have imagined.

David felt hollow, emotionally exhausted. He clutched Ellen's hand as if both their lives depended on it and glanced at Rachel, who was sitting beside Tippi on the floor. He could see her in profile, the light from the television flickering over her face, creating brilliant white pinpoints in her wide eyes. She was transfixed by the horror depicted on the screen, her mouth slightly open, her hands rubbing unconsciously at the rope-marks that braceleted her wrists.

David squeezed Ellen's hand, and was heartened when she turned her head and gave him a definite, albeit distracted, smile. It had taken the whole of last night and most of this morning, with just a few hours of exhaustively restless sleep snatched in between, to achieve even this level of intimacy.

It was only after the car had pulled up and he'd seen his family and friends climbing dazedly out that David realised, despite all the hours of waiting and hoping, that he hadn't really known what to expect from this situation.

At the back of his mind he'd had a kind of idyllic picture of the reunion that would take place: it would involve lots of hugging and kissing and joyful weeping, recriminations swept aside on a tide of love. And at first it appeared that the idyll was becoming a reality; he and Rachel had held each other so tightly, he glorifying in the unbelievable fact that she was *there*, that it must have seemed to onlookers that their mutual joy was such that they were quite prepared to risk crushed ribs and asphyxiation if it meant not having to let go of each other.

Ellen, however, was a different matter. Although she'd spoken his name calmly enough, when he stretched out a hand to touch her face, only half-believing she was not some image conjured by his need, she flinched back, her lips curling and hissed, 'Don't you *dare* touch me!'

David blinked in hurt bewilderment. 'What's the matter?' he said.

Ellen's body was rigid with anger. If she'd been a cat she would have been up on her toes, fur bristling. 'I don't know how you can ask that,' she spat at him, 'after what you've done.'

David realised he should have anticipated her anger after his desertion, after what had happened to her and the rest of them because of him, but somehow, stupidly perhaps, he hadn't, and now he could only gape at her, anguished and confused.

'I'm sorry,' he said, 'I didn't think . . . I never meant for this to happen.'

'You're *sorry*? Is that all you can say? You've torn this family apart and you're *sorry*?'

David raised his hands placatingly. He was distressingly aware of Rachel backing away from him, from both of them, as if she didn't know where to put herself, whom to support, her face full of misery.

'Everything will be all right, Ellen, I promise you,' he told her as earnestly as he could. 'Just give me a chance to

447

explain it all.'

As if she hadn't heard him, she snarled, 'I suppose sorry's going to bring Jane back, is it?'

For a moment the world seemed to tilt on its axis. David's surroundings became a grey blur in which only Ellen's and Rachel's faces seemed to shine with an unnatural light, like twin moons.

Then the moment passed and he looked around as though roused from a dream, peripherally aware of his and Ellen's silent audience, of their emotions laid bare and bleeding for all to see.

'Jane?' he said. 'I don't know what you . . . where *is* Jane?'

He looked towards the car, saw only adult-shaped forms, thought for one ludicrous moment that his youngest daughter was hiding from him, perhaps cowering behind Ralph's bulk.

'She's *gone*!' Ellen hurled the word at him like a blow. 'Those . . . *freaks* did something to her, pulled her strings like a puppet and she went with them. She just . . . she's gone . . .'

She seemed to sag, as if it was only the fury which she had now expelled that had been holding her up. Her head bowed on to her chest and her legs buckled beneath her. She sat down on the muddy cobbles and started to cry.

David moved forward, reaching out his arms, but Diane, despite her limp, got there first. She crouched down, shielding her friend, and snarled up at David, 'Keep away. You've done enough damage.'

David just stood there for a moment, staring at her and swallowing, then he turned to Rachel, who was still standing miserably some distance away, and barked at her, more brusquely than he had intended, 'What did your mother mean? What happened to Jane?'

Rachel looked at him as if she was a foreigner, lost and alone, who didn't understand the language. It was Willie,

448

appearing beside David from his blind side, who murmured in his ear as if imparting a secret, 'It's something we need ti talk aboot, David.'

David swung round on him. 'Talk about? Why? What's happened to her?'

Willie looked uncharacteristically grim. 'Not here and not noo. Later. In private.'

'But I need to know –'

'Ah said later,' Willie snapped, his flare of anger so sudden and unexpected that it shocked David into silence.

For a moment time seemed to stand still, as though everyone was as startled as David by Willie's burst of emotion. Then David broke the moment by nodding and asking in a voice that he hoped was low enough for only Willie to hear, 'At least tell me if she's alive.'

'Oh aye, she's alive,' said Willie, but he sounded uncertain, and his eyes flickered away, unable or unwilling to hold David's gaze.

'How do you know?' David said, Willie's evasiveness making his stomach clench. 'If you haven't seen her, how do you know?'

Willie sighed, fatigued and exasperated. 'We'll talk later,' he repeated again, quietly this time but stubbornly too. 'This isn't the place, son, standing oot here in the dark and the cold and the mud, with all these people aroond us. You need some time with your family, and ah need time ti talk ti Max and a couple o' the others first.' When David opened his mouth to protest again, Willie placed a hand on his arm and said firmly, 'It'll keep for an hour or two. There's people here who need you.'

He indicated Ellen, who was still slumped on the cobbles of the yard, being comforted by Diane. People were coming out of the house now, perhaps prompted by Max. The Hodges helped Diane lift Ellen to her feet, Tippi approached Rachel and introduced herself. There was a general movement back towards the house, Schism

449

members supporting the new arrivals physically if they needed it. David heard Violet Turner say to Ralph, 'Dear me, you have been in the wars, haven't you, young man?', and Ralph rumble something in reply.

The next hour or so was spent gently integrating the Flux's four erstwhile captives into what for them was another new and confusing environment. Introductions were made, wounds bathed, food and drink prepared and devoured, comforting words spoken, hot baths and clean clothes provided. It was a time of calm efficiency, of busyness without bustle, but for David it was a time of longing and frustration.

He wanted to be with Ellen, he wanted to speak to her, to explain his reasons and motives for what he had done; he wanted to make her understand. But she wouldn't come anywhere near him, wouldn't even meet his gaze or acknowledge his presence. David wanted some time alone with her, but she used the people around her like a shield.

At least Rachel was speaking to him, though after witnessing Ellen's reaction to him in the yard, even she was now being a little distant. She sat at the kitchen table with David, nursing a mug of tea which she stared into as though it was a crystal ball, and told him in a quiet emotionless voice everything that had happened since the previous morning. 'Parts of it were like a dream, Dad,' she said. 'I kept thinking I was going mad or something. Some of the things I saw can't have been real, can they?' This was the only time during her account when she glanced up at him and he saw how troubled she was, how much of an effort she was making to keep herself under control. He placed a hand over hers and tried to hide his dismay when she didn't respond to his touch. Her hand simply sat under his, limp and unmoving, a block of flesh. He tried to console himself with the thought that at least she had not snatched her hand away and snarled at him as Ellen would have done.

'You're not going mad,' he told her. 'Maybe you really did see some of the things you described.'

She lowered her eyes again and pulled a face as if disappointed with his response. 'I can't have done, can I?' she said almost petulantly. 'Don't humour me, Dad.'

David was silent for a moment, unsure how to handle the situation. Rachel needed to be reassured, not have her fears that the world was turning upside-down confirmed. But by the same token he couldn't lie to her, couldn't betray her again. And besides, she was going to find out soon enough, wasn't she? There was no way of keeping the truth from his family, even if he had wanted to.

Gently he said, 'If it's any consolation, I've seen plenty of very strange things these last few days as well.'

She was silent for a moment and then she said, 'Like what?'

'Things that I never really thought existed. Wonderful things. Amazing things.' He paused before adding, 'Some scary things.'

He wasn't sure whether her shoulders tensed a little at his words. 'What sort of . . . things?' she persisted.

David sighed. Where to start? If he was going to tell his story from the beginning he'd prefer to tell it to all four of them together with Tippi and Willie and Max and the rest to back him up. But he couldn't fob Rachel off with ambiguities now; he owed it to her to tell as much of the truth as he thought she could handle, whilst at the same time attempting to calm her fears by making what he had seen sound wondrous and exciting rather than terrifying.

'Remember when we used to watch that series on the telly about the supernatural? It was all about mind over matter, reincarnation, telepathy, things like that.' He didn't remind her that it was also about ghosts and modern-day werewolves and demonic possession.

'Yes,' she said warily.

'And remember how we used to say that we thought

human beings only used a fraction of the potential of their minds, and of how exciting it would be if we could train our minds –'

'Get to the point, Dad,' she said, as though insulted by his prevarication.

Her tone made David realise with a jolt of sadness how grown up she had become, how she was no longer a child but hovering on the verge of adulthood. It would hit him like that sometimes. She would say something or do something, or Ellen would tell him something about his daughter, that made him feel as though he had somehow missed a vital chunk of her growing up somewhere along the way.

He sighed and said, 'Okay. Cards on the table, right?'

She pushed out her lips as if considering, then gave a definite nod.

'Are you sure you're ready for this?'

'*Dad*,' she said in exasperation.

'Okay,' he said, 'but brace yourself. This is a very strange story.'

She took it very well considering, or seemed to. She puffed out her cheeks, shook her head in wonder, and breathed out the word, 'Weird,' a few times. She might not have been a child any more, but she still had a child's resilience, a willingness to take on board that which an adult might find more difficult to accept.

'You believe me?' he said when he had finished.

She looked surprised, as if she hadn't considered the prospect that he might have been lying to her. 'Yeah,' she said simply, 'it makes sense.' Then abruptly she stood up and said, 'I'm feeling really kacky. I think I'll have my bath now.' She hovered for a moment, as though unsure how to end the encounter. David thought she might have been about to give him a kiss or a hug, but she seemed too aware of Ellen's presence, of how her mother might feel if she was seen showing affection to her traitorous father,

452

and so in the end she just said rather stiffly, 'See you later, Dad,' before walking away.

'Yes,' he said softly, 'see you later.' He remained seated at the kitchen table, looking through the arch at the activity in the front room. He felt left out, unwelcome. In some ways this was worse than the waiting had been, because he felt more distant from Ellen now than he had when they'd been apart. She was sitting on the settee, talking to Melanie Hodge and Violet Turner who were sitting either side of her. She was the only one of the quartet who was still to have a bath, waiting until last, David suspected, so that she could have a long soak without feeling guilty about it. Her hair was matted, her face grimy-looking despite the fact that she'd washed it at the kitchen sink. Her dishevelment made her look young, vulnerable; David longed to be able to go over there, wrap his arms around her, tell her how sorry he was and that he loved her and that what had happened would never happen again. He looked at her, *stared* at her, for several minutes, but her eyes never once flickered towards him. Was she really as ignorant of his scrutiny as she seemed?

He wished all these people would go away, leave him alone with Ellen. Their presence infuriated him; didn't they understand the situation? Didn't they realise that he and Ellen needed to be alone to sort things out? Didn't they realise how he felt? He felt particularly hateful towards Diane, whose voice, as usual, could be heard above everyone else's. What was she trying to do by keeping Ellen away from him – break up their marriage for good? Didn't she realise that it was thanks to his initiating proceedings that she'd been rescued at all? He realised how unreasonable these thoughts were even as he gave them full rein, but at the same time he felt a sort of seething justification for them.

If the situation didn't improve soon, if Ellen continued to ignore him, he'd have to make a move, but what could he do? He was caught on the horns of a dilemma. If he approached Ellen now, no matter how reasonable he was, she would invariably react as she had done in the yard, as would Diane, thus creating a scene. But if he did nothing, waited instead for her to approach him, then wouldn't that make him look as though he didn't care, wouldn't it emphasise the gulf between them? He supposed the only thing he could do was bide his time, to be as sympathetic and understanding as Ellen allowed him to be. He knew that much of her anger was due to her confusion, to the feeling that she'd been betrayed by someone she loved. He could only hope that somewhere, beneath all that hurt, she still did love him, enough to want to let him try to make amends. Was he only deluding himself in thinking that if she really wanted nothing more to do with him, she'd be more indifferent than angry? Very probably, but he needed something to cling to.

He pushed his chair back from the table and walked through into the sitting room, thinking that if he stayed in the kitchen it would only look as though he was sulking or too timid to risk further confrontation. Max, Willie, Ishvak, Hollis and Imogen Butterworth had gone off together some time earlier, presumably to discuss whatever it was Willie had discovered today. As he entered the room, Tippi gave him a warm smile, for which he was grateful; Ellen studiously ignored him and Diane gave him a glance that seemed both disdainful and dismissive. David wished he could hear what Ellen and the two women were talking about; he hoped that Melanie and Violet were putting in a good word for him. He would have joined Tippi if she hadn't been sitting on the periphery of a conversation between Diane and Richard Hodge, and if Ralph at that moment hadn't beckoned him with a slight movement of the head.

David walked over to him. Ralph was sitting on an armchair by the fire with a blanket wrapped around him, looking vulnerable and bewildered without his glasses and with his face a mass of scars and bruises. He looked old too, as old as Marshall and Livermore, his two silent companions. It hurt David to see him like this, especially since he felt so responsible for his condition. He felt ashamed too that he'd barely acknowledged Ralph's presence since Ishvak's car had pulled up outside earlier that night. The main reason, of course, was that he'd been preoccupied with Ellen and Rachel over the past hour or two, though it was also partly because Ralph seemed like a different man to the one David knew. Since entering the house he'd been quiet, almost unnoticeable, not at all the inquisitive social animal with the commanding presence and booming voice that David was used to. Obviously he was suffering from his facial injuries, but David suspected that the trauma of his beating and subsequent events had resulted in far deeper wounds. He felt slightly awkward now as he sat beside Ralph, and hated himself for it; despite everything, this was still his oldest and best friend, a man he'd known for over thirty years. He was about to speak, to ask Ralph the obvious question, but Ralph got there first.

'How are you bearing up, old feller?' he said as if David was the one in need of care, his voice a low gravelly rumble.

David smiled, instantly feeling more relaxed. '*I'm* okay,' he said. 'More to the point, how are you? You look as though you've had an argument with a brick wall.'

Ralph's face twitched and he groaned. 'Don't make me laugh, it hurts. I wish I had my glasses, I keep wanting to sharpen the focus of the world. I feel as though I'm living in a permanent blur.'

'Just like the sixties, you mean?' said David.

'I was a bit too young for that sort of thing in the sixties.' His voice seemed to drop an octave as he became serious. 'Look, David, what's going on here?'

'It's a long and complicated story, and I'm not being evasive, it just is. I'm surprised you weren't asking questions the minute you stepped out of the car.'

'It seemed too much of an effort talking to strangers. My face hurt too much. I wanted to hear it from you, with no bullshit.'

David sighed, feeling as though he didn't deserve the loyalty and faith his friend still seemed prepared to show him. 'I'm sorry, Ralph. I haven't been a very good friend recently, have I?'

'No,' said Ralph, 'you haven't. You've been a bad friend, a terrible husband and an appalling father.'

'It's okay, Ralph, don't beat around the bush. Give it to me straight, I can take it.'

Ralph squinted at him from the pouches of bruise-darkened flesh around his eyes. 'So are you going to tell me or do I have to guess?'

David sighed. 'Like I say, it's a long and complicated story.'

'That's all right. I don't have any plans for the evening.'

David glanced across at Ellen, who made no indication that she had seen him enter the room.

'She's angry with you, David,' Ralph said, 'but she'll come round.'

'I thought you were half-blind,' said David.

'I am. I just saw the flash of red as your bottom lip drooped, and heard the heavy sigh.'

'Do you think she *will* come round?' David asked.

'She still loves you, despite everything.'

'She blames me for whatever's happened to Jane.'

'She has to blame somebody.'

'Even so,' said David. There was a moment's silence and then he said, 'Anyway, you haven't told me yet who beat you up.'

'Didn't Rachel tell you? I saw you talking to her.'

'She wasn't sure. She says you were attacked at the

house.'

'Yes, by a bunch of young thugs. God knows how they got inside. They were hiding in Jane's wardrobe if you can believe that.' He looked momentarily troubled and then he said tentatively, 'Did Rachel tell you what happened to Jane?'

'She told me what she saw.'

'Yes. Very odd that. What do you make of it?'

'Once I tell you what happened to me, what happened to you will hopefully start to make more sense.'

'In that case,' said Ralph, 'fire away.'

'Okay, but I'd better just warn you before I start that it's a pretty outlandish story. And can I make a deal with you?'

'What kind of deal?'

'I've got to talk to Ellen, but as you know she won't let me anywhere near her at the moment. If an opportunity presents itself, would you mind if I broke off and came back to you later?'

'Of course not,' said Ralph. 'The only thing I want more than to see you and Ellen together again is to have Jane back with us.'

David felt like hugging his friend, but inhibition prevented him. In the end he contented himself with a mumbled, 'Thanks,' and then for the second time that evening he told his story.

It was almost half an hour later, and his throat was sore, by the time he had finished. From upstairs came a glugging sound which evolved into a swirling hiss of water as Rachel finished her bath and pulled out the plug.

'It's an incredible story,' said Ralph, sounding a little shell-shocked.

'It's true,' said David defensively.

'Oh, I don't doubt it.'

David was surprised. Ralph had always been such a pragmatic man. David had used to tease him about his oft-voiced assertion that there was nothing in this world that couldn't be explained logically.

'You really mean that?' he said.

'I don't think I'm in a position to argue against it,' Ralph replied, looking almost glum to have to admit such a thing. 'If you'd told me you'd seen a ghost, I'd say trick of the light, hallucination, wishful thinking, practical joke. But this . . . well . . . unless you're all either lying or mad, which I don't think you are, then it seems I have no choice but to accept what you've told me.'

He still looked very unhappy about having to do so, however. David said, 'It's not so bad once you get used to it.'

'That, I suspect, is a matter of opinion.' He held up a hand as if to prevent David saying anything further. 'I don't wish to be rude, David, but would you give me some time to think about all this? I need to fit some very awkward new pieces into my nice neat jigsaw of how I see the world.'

David smiled. 'Take all the time you need. I'll speak to you later when your mind has stopped reeling.'

'If it ever does,' muttered Ralph.

The door that led to the rest of the house opened and Rachel came in, looking scrubbed and clean, her hair gleaming wet.

'Does everything fit?' Tippi asked, turning round.

Rachel was wearing a pair of jeans and a baggy purple t-shirt that Tippi had lent her.

'It's a bit big,' she admitted, 'but not too bad. It's so nice to be clean again.' She rubbed subconsciously at the weals on her wrists, which looked ugly and red, inflamed by the hot water. 'I've started running your bath, Mum. I put some of those Body Shop bath crystals in it. I hope that's okay.'

Ellen smiled her thanks, and a few minutes later excused herself. A pulse in David's throat began to quicken as he saw his chance to get her on her own. He glanced at Diane, but she was still in conversation with Richard Hodge and Tippi, who was encouraging Rachel to join the group. Rachel glanced uncertainly at David, but he smiled and nodded, and she sat down, half-concealing him from Diane's view.

Even so he waited a minute or two longer before rising as casually as he could and strolling to the door that led upstairs. As he placed his hand on the handle, he expected to hear Diane abrasively demanding, 'And where the hell do you think you're going?' She remained silent, however, as he opened the door just wide enough to slip through before closing it behind him, keeping hold of the handle to prevent it clicking. He breathed a sigh of relief, then sprang up the stairs, taking them two at a time.

From behind the closed bathroom door he could hear the gentle lap and slosh of water. He composed himself, then rapped twice on the stripped pine.

'Hello?' said Ellen, sounding surprised.

'Ellen, it's me,' David said. 'I think we need to talk.'

Absolute silence followed his words; David could no longer even hear the sound of Ellen's body moving in the water. Finally he said, 'Did you hear me, Ellen? I said –'

'I heard,' said Ellen curtly.

Another pause, during which David wondered whether she was going to elaborate. When she didn't he said, 'Well, what do you think?'

'I've got nothing to say to you, David.' Despite her words he felt oddly heartened to hear her use his name.

'Maybe not, but I think I owe you some kind of an explanation. Can I come in?'

'I'm taking a bath,' she said as indignantly as Diane might have done had he asked her the same question.

'Well later then? Will you come up to the attic afterwards so that I can give you my side of things?'

There was another pause. He pictured her lying there,

frowning, trying to decide. At last she said, 'I don't know.'

'Aren't you even going to give me a chance to explain?' When she didn't reply immediately, he persisted, 'Don't you want things back the way they were?'

This time there was an abrupt splash of water as if she had sat up angrily. 'Don't you make this situation between us out to be my fault!'

'I wasn't,' he said, realising he had overstepped the mark. 'I'm sorry, I didn't mean that.'

'It was you who walked out on us.'

'I know, and I admit it was a mistake. I just want the chance to make things up to you.'

'Don't you think it's a bit too late for that, David?'

'No, I don't, and I don't believe you do either. Rachel seems prepared to listen to me.'

'Rachel's a child.'

'She's old enough to know her own mind, and you know that.'

'It's because of you that Jane's been taken away from us.'

'Yes,' said David quietly, 'I don't deny that. But I didn't for one minute think that you and the girls would be in danger, Ellen. I didn't realise what I'd got myself into. You have to believe that.'

'Do I? Why?'

'Because . . . well . . . because it's the truth. And because without you nothing's worth anything. I love you, Ellen.'

'Oh God,' he heard her sigh as if faced with the most appalling dilemma.

'And I'll get Jane back, I promise you that. We'll be a family again soon. Things will be back the way they used to be.'

He could hear her breathing deeply, sigh after sigh, behind the bathroom door.

'Ellen?' he prompted.

'Look, I just don't know, David, all right! I don't know

what to say! I don't know what to think!'

Her outburst seemed to ring off the bathroom walls. David said calmly in the hope it would placate her, 'Well, talking about it might help you decide. We won't get anywhere by not talking, will we?'

There was yet another pause, another sigh, and then finally she conceded, 'All right, we'll talk. But I'm not promising anything.'

'That's all I ask,' said David. 'Will you come up to the attic bedroom when you've had your bath?'

'Yes,' she said, sounding reluctant.

He managed to stop himself from saying, 'Great'; it seemed somewhat inappropriate. 'Okay. Look, I'm going to talk to Willie for a bit. We're going to discuss how we can get Jane back.'

She made a sound that might have been acknowledgement or disbelief.

'Okay, well, see you later,' said David.

He hovered for a moment, waiting for a reply that never came, and then he moved down the landing and tapped on Willie's door, from behind which he could hear the buzz of voices.

'Aye?' Willie called.

'It's me: David. Can I come in?'

There were noises of affirmation and David stuck his head round the door. 'Sorry to disturb you,' he said, 'but I wondered when we could have our chat about Jane, Willie?'

'Come in, son,' said Willie. 'Ah reckon we're aboot finished here.' He looked around at the nods of confirmation. It seemed to have been quite a meeting, judging by the grim thoughtful faces and the cigar smoke which hovered just beneath the ceiling like clumps of thin grey wool.

Max stood up and indicated his seat. 'You can sit here, David, and talk to Willie while we fill the others in. How

461

are your wife and daughter and your friends incidentally?'

'Okay,' said David. 'I've told Ralph and my daughter, Rachel, everything I know. I'm going to speak to Ellen after she's had her bath.'

'Splendid,' said Max, albeit distractedly. 'Well, we'll leave you to it.'

He and the others went out of the room, leaving David alone with Willie.

'Things seem pretty serious,' ventured David. 'Not even Patrick was smiling.'

'Aye, son, they are,' said Willie. He looked troubled, the lines etched deep in his wrinkled face. 'Ah'm afraid ah've got some bad news for you,' he said. 'There's no easy way o' telling it.'

David felt his stomach fall into his shoes. 'Jane's dead, isn't she?' He could barely say the words.

Willie was fidgeting, standing up and sitting down, moving to the window and back again. 'No,' he said, 'she's not dead. Look, son, if you'll just bear with me a wee while I'll explain it from the beginning.'

He told David everything he knew, about the Flux's plans which were to be set in motion the following day, and about Jane becoming the new oracle. David took it reasonably well considering, responding with fury rather than grief. In truth, he realised he'd been expecting the news, though he had been refusing to admit it to himself until now. He jumped up and paced around Willie's room like a caged tiger.

'I'll fucking get them, Willie, I swear it,' he blazed.

'Aye, son, we'll all get them,' said Willie placatingly. He was sitting down now as though he and David were taking it in turns, following David's movements like a tennis spectator. 'Everything's in hand, son. Tomorrow we try and put a stop ti this once and for all. It's all or nothing, son, do or die.'

'You're not going to stop me coming this time?' David's

aggression made the question sound like a statement of fact.

'No, son. In fact, you're our biggest hope. You and that bottle o' yours.'

David paused momentarily and looked at Willie. If he hadn't been full of such self-righteous anger he would have been extremely alarmed to have discovered himself the pivot of the Schisms plans.

As it was, he was only fairly alarmed, which was still enough to sober him somewhat. 'What do you honestly think our chances are, Willie?'

Willie shrugged. 'Ah don't know, son. We still don't really know what yon bottle's capable of, do we? Ah mean, we've only seen what it can do ti people so far. The only certain thing aboot all this is that we cannae afford ti dither aboot any more. We've got ti pin oor hopes on blind faith and go for it.'

Not surprisingly, his words hardly imbued David with confidence. He thought, not for the first time, that the group he had fallen in with here seemed rather a ramshackle bunch. Admittedly they had proved themselves capable of small victories, but their policy of improvisation and counterattack hardly seemed one that would enable them to emerge victorious from the maelstrom of a full-scale war.

He was debating whether to voice his concerns when the little Scotsman said tentatively, 'By the way . . . perhaps ah should have mentioned this before, but . . . well . . . you do know, son, don't you, that . . . well . . . that none o' the oracles have ever survived before?'

David glared at him. Vagueness he could cope with, just about, but this he definitely didn't want to hear. It smacked too much of tempting fate, or admitting defeat before combat had even begun.

His voice a snarl, he said, 'Then Jane'll be the first, won't she?'

Willie puffed out his cheeks and looked away from David. 'Ah hope so,' he muttered.

Later, as David sat on the armchair in the attic bedroom waiting for Ellen to join him, he mulled over what Willie had told him. He'd barely had time to break the ice with Ellen, and yet tomorrow, it seemed, they were going to have to be parted again, only this time he was going to be the one in danger. Willie, to his credit, had not beaten around the bush; he'd told David exactly what to expect, had made it sound, in fact, like a kamikaze mission they were about to embark on. David decided not to tell Ellen what Jane had become and what the implications of that were, and how dangerous their mission to retrieve her and to destroy the evil that controlled her was likely to be. He didn't like the thought of keeping her in the dark – he'd done enough of that in the past two months to last him a lifetime – but at the same time he didn't want her to worry any more than she had to; he felt she had quite enough on her plate to be going on with.

When he heard her coming up the dozen or so winding stairs, he jumped up to meet her so quickly that he bumped his head on the sloping roof. He was rubbing the sore spot and wincing when she came into view, her face set as if it was an expression she'd practised, among others, and had decided to adopt. She looked around and said with more than a hint of bitterness, 'Nice little nest you've got here. Is this where you've been staying since you left home?'

'No,' said David, hating the awkwardness between them. 'I've only been here since last night. Before that I was in London, in a B & B.'

She turned up her nose as if he'd told her he'd been sleeping beneath a mound of rubbish in an alleyway.

'Do you want to sit down?' he said, indicating the bed only because he thought they could sit side by side on it.

'I'll take the chair,' she said as though he'd made an

464

indecent proposal.

'Okay, whatever you like.' He moved to the bed and they both sat down.

'Now that you're here, I hardly know where to start,' he said.

'The beginning's the usual place,' she replied sourly.

'I know that. It's just, I'm not so sure where the beginning is.'

'Why don't you tell me why you stopped being my husband and became someone I didn't like any more?'

He winced and said, 'I've been a real bastard, haven't I? To you, to the girls, to my friends. I've behaved like a real dork.'

'You said it,' she muttered.

'I'm so sorry, Ellen, I really am. If I could take time back, believe me I would. It's taken something like this to make me realise how much I love you and the girls, how you and they are the most important things in my life. I'd do anything to have things back the way they were.'

'So why did you behave like you did? Why did you set out to destroy everything we'd built up together?' Ellen said.

Was it only David's imagination or could he detect the hard edges in her voice softening just a little? He shook his head and said, 'I don't know. I haven't really got an excuse. There was no concrete reason for how I behaved. It just seemed that one morning I woke up and looked around me, and suddenly everything seemed so . . . so pointless. So stifling. I felt that all the . . . the responsibilities in my life – you, the children, the house, my job – were somehow holding me back, preventing me from really achieving something.'

'Oh, thanks,' she said heavily.

'I'm sorry, Ellen, I know it sounds bad, and I didn't want to feel like I did, but I couldn't help it. For a reason I couldn't fathom, which made things even more frustrating, everything just suddenly seemed so ... so black. It probably sounds like a cliché, but I really did feel as though I'd somehow stumbled into a long black tunnel and I couldn't find my way out.'

He grimaced. Articulating his emotions made them sound so insubstantial, so self-indulgent.

'And how do you feel now?' Ellen asked.

'Different,' said David. 'Like I said, I've realised what's important to me. What's happened these past few days has changed me, Ellen. I've seen some terrible things, some really awful things, and I've found out some really scary stuff about ... well, about how things work in the world. But I've seen some amazing things too, and somehow, because of all that, I've managed to find my way out of my own personal tunnel. Some of the things I've seen I don't know if I'll ever get over, but what I do know is that, if you'll have me back, I want you there with me, Ellen. I love you and I want to spend the rest of my life with you.'

He broke off. The air in the room seemed super-charged, pregnant with emotion that neither of them dared yet fully express. David longed to hold Ellen, to kiss her, to have the love he'd offered reciprocated. Ellen had slumped forward in her chair as though weighed down by her own indecision. 'I don't know, David,' she said miserably, 'I don't know what to think. I still feel so confused ...'

Her voice choked off and she bowed her head, running her fingers through her newly washed hair.

'I know,' said David gently, 'I don't blame you, and I don't want to pressure you into anything. I just wanted to let you know how I felt, and I wanted to tell you what's been happening to me these last few days so that you can understand what's happened to you, why things have worked out as they have.'

She raised her head. He half-expected to see tears in her eyes, but all he saw was bewilderment. 'Okay, so tell me,' was all she said.

It was the fourth time he had told his story in twenty-four hours, but this telling he found the hardest of all. Maybe he was wrong, but he couldn't help feeling that his future relationship with Ellen – if indeed there was a future to be had after tomorrow – hinged on his words. It didn't help that his throat felt thick with emotion and scoured with use, and that he was acutely aware of Ellen watching his face the whole time, her unreadable gaze flickering between his eyes and his mouth as if trying to catch him out. It took him longer to tell his story this time because he felt it important to fill in every detail, to leave nothing out, to lay bare emotions which he'd skirted over when he'd told his story to Rachel and to Ralph and to the members of the Schism the previous evening.

Ellen reacted twice to his words – once when he told her about the shooting in the Italian restaurant (she said, 'God, I was lying in bed on Sunday morning with the radio on and I heard about that on the news'), and once when he told her about the death of Worthington (she nodded in grim satisfaction and said quietly, 'Good. It's what he deserved').

When he'd brought things up to date, he spread his hands and said, his voice considerably more croaky than when he'd started, 'And that's it. You know the rest.'

She sat back, shaking her head and blinking as if she'd just woken up from an amazing dream, and expelled a long breath of air.

'Jesus,' she said finally.

'Pretty strange, huh?' said David ruefully.

'Strange? Well, it . . . it's just unbelievable!'

'If I was lying, don't you think I'd come up with a more convincing story?' It was a line he'd rehearsed earlier, anticipating her reaction.

'I didn't say I thought you were lying, did I?'

'You said it was unbelievable.'

'I meant it's . . . difficult to get your head round. Don't you realise what you're asking me to believe here?'

'Of course I do. I know it sounds impossible and crazy and scary, but if you want proof I can arrange it for you.'

She shuddered. 'I don't want proof. I've seen quite enough already, thank you.'

'So you *do* believe me?' David said.

Ellen waved her hands agitatedly as though she was wafting a wasp away. 'Don't hassle me, David, just give me a minute. I need to think about this.'

'That's what Ralph said,' David told her.

'Ralph was right. God, David, I don't know whether I'm coming or going. Perhaps I'm going crazy. Perhaps I'm lying in a hospital bed somewhere, hallucinating all this.'

'You're not,' David said. 'This is all real. It's just something you've never come across before, a secret about the world that you've never been let in on.'

'Or maybe we have,' said Ellen.

'What?'

'Maybe we have come across it before, but were made to forget. You said these people could do that, wipe your memories clean when you found out too much.'

Despite himself, David smiled. 'Maybe,' he said. 'It's a weird idea, isn't it?'

'It's a bloody scary idea,' said Ellen, 'the thought that someone could have messed about with your mind, changed your memories. I mean, anything might have happened to you, and you wouldn't know about it.' She placed her hands on her head as though to test for evidence of tampering, then said in a more subdued voice, 'Mind you, I wouldn't mind forgetting about these past couple of months. When all this is over, maybe you can arrange that.'

That sounded to David like the most hopeful indication yet that she wanted them to remain together. Taking a mental deep breath, he said, 'So now that I've told you everything, what are your thoughts on us?'

She looked for a moment as though she couldn't believe he had asked her that question, and then the instinctive anger that he thought he'd roused seemed to subside slightly. When she replied it was with just a hint of exasperation. 'Oh, I don't know, David,' she said. 'I can't think about that just now. Our little girl is still missing, and I've just been told that everything I always thought was only true in stories really exists.'

'But you think there's a chance? You're not mad at me any more?'

'Don't push your luck, David,' she warned.

'Sorry, it's just that I've been dying to have you back, I've been dreaming about it. The last couple of days have been the longest of my life. There were moments when I never thought I'd see you again.'

'I could say the same,' she said.

'Oh, I know that. I know it's been a lot worse for you than it has for me. I'm not saying it hasn't.'

She sighed deeply again and rested her head on the back of the chair. As though speaking to the ceiling, she said, 'You just have to give me a bit of time, David, and a bit of space.'

He wanted to say, 'But I'm going away tomorrow and I might not come back,' but he wasn't going to stoop to emotional blackmail. In the end he said, 'Okay, I think I can manage that.'

She looked at him, and even managed a faint smile. 'Good,' she said. She looked as though she wanted to say more, but in the end her gaze slithered away from his and she just muttered, 'Good,' again.

'Do you want to go back downstairs and join the others?' he said, hoping she didn't.

'Not just yet. It's . . . nice up here. Quiet. How about showing me that bottle of yours?'

'Best offer I've had all day,' he said, then immediately

regretted it, but the faint smile had reappeared on Ellen's face. 'It's in the left-hand pocket of the coat over the back of the chair you're sitting on. It doesn't look like much when it's dormant. It's just an old bottle.'

She twisted in her seat and pulled at the canvassy material until she found the gash that was the pocket he'd indicated. 'Your Bogart needs a good clean,' she said. 'What have you been doing, sleeping in it?'

It was good to hear her say 'Bogart'. It was one of the little in-phrases that only the two of them shared. In normal circumstances her use of the phrase would have seemed insignificant, but now it seemed to create an intimacy between them, seemed – to David at least – to be another twist of the key in the lock of the door that stood between them.

He grinned at her. 'I might have done once or twice. There, I told you it didn't look like much.'

She held the bottle up to the light and turned it round and round, as though it was a diamond she was examining for flaws. 'It feels sort of . . . warm,' she said, 'like velvet. Or . . . no, more like skin. Like warm smooth skin.' She smiled, perhaps unconsciously, and asked, 'Can I look at the note?'

David nodded. 'Go ahead.'

She unscrewed the cap of the bottle and upended it. When she'd managed to prise out the note she unrolled it carefully, read it and put it back without comment. Then she held the neck of the bottle up to her nose and sniffed.

'What are you doing?' David asked.

'It smells of the sea,' she said. 'It's a restful smell. I've always liked it.'

He took the bottle from her and sniffed it as she had done, and yes, it did smell of the sea, even though the sea couldn't possibly have got inside the bottle while it had been in the water.

Ellen drew her knees up to her chin and wrapped her

arms around her legs. 'Everything's just crazy,' she murmured, then she yawned hugely and said, 'Oh, I'm so tired. I haven't slept properly for days.'

'Why don't you sleep now?' said David. 'We'll change places. You have the bed and I'll sit on the chair and watch over you for a while.'

'I can't sleep while Jane's still missing. I don't think I'd be able to, no matter how tired I am. Besides, it wouldn't feel right.'

'Don't be silly. You're not going to achieve anything by depriving yourself of sleep. Just lie on the bed and close your eyes. Even if you don't sleep, you'll be resting.'

'Okay,' she said, and unfurled herself from the chair. She trudged over to the bed and virtually collapsed on to it as David stood up. He was surprised at how quickly the exhaustion had hit her, and wondered whether the soothing effect of the bottle had had anything to do with it. She was only half-awake when he dragged the duvet from beneath her prone body and draped it over her, and by the time he kissed her forehead and murmured, 'Goodnight, Ellen,' her eyes were closed and she was breathing deeply.

He sat on the armchair and watched her for a while and thought about things, but it wasn't long before his own eyelids were drooping closed and his thoughts were being shunted away and replaced with nonsense. He was thinking of a lake of Weetabix, the dry biscuits turning mushy as gallons of milk gushed on to them from some mysterious source above, when full deep sleep finally claimed him. When he woke some time later it was because of the pain associated with having his upper vertebrae set on fire.

He gritted his teeth in agony, twisted and slapped a hand on to the back of his neck, half-expecting to feel the heat of an oxyacetylene torch crisping the hairs on his hand. But it was only the position in which he'd fallen asleep that had caused his neck to fuse with pain. He scowled and winced his way through gingerly standing up and rotating his joints, hearing things click and pop and crackle, awakening aches that had pooled in various areas of his body like rainwater on an uneven roof. When the discomfort had subsided a little, he glanced over at Ellen and saw her lying on her right side, face half-buried in the pillow, dark hair sticking up like a punk's. He groaned, grabbed the cushion from the chair and dumped it on the floor, then lay down on his back, using the cushion as a pillow, hands interlaced on his stomach.

The second time he woke up it was because too much of his body heat had escaped, and because his back was completely numb. By now he was very bad-tempered. Grumpy and groaning, he clambered to his feet, thinking that whoever said a hard flat surface was good for backache was talking complete bollocks. He wondered whether to go downstairs and sleep on the settee, but thought that with the number of people in the house it was probably already occupied. Besides he didn't want to run the risk of running into someone else who was prowling around, unable to sleep, and getting embroiled in a late-night conversation.

He looked again at the bed. Ellen had moved over to the left side, her arm raised above her head, her mouth slightly open. Would she mind if she woke up in the morning to find that he was lying beside her? It wasn't as though he was taking advantage of the situation, after all. He just wanted a bloody decent night's sleep.

In the end he compromised. He lay on top of the duvet, fully clothed, using his Bogart as a blanket, facing away from Ellen. He fell asleep almost immediately, and woke up in the morning with Ellen snuggled against his back. It was a lovely feeling, a glorious feeling, and for a while he just lay there enjoying the warm, soft proximity of her. Finally, however, she groaned and rolled away from him, starting to wake up, and so he closed his eyes to give her time to get used to the idea of finding him lying beside her, and also to give her time to realise that he hadn't tried anything, hadn't just assumed that it was okay for them to start sleeping together again just because they were in the same room.

He heard her sitting up, sensed her looking at him, even half-expected her to say, 'Okay, I know you're awake. What's been going on?'

But she didn't. For a while she did nothing. And then David almost jumped out of his skin when she began stroking his hair.

He managed to turn his jerk of surprise into a kind of groany sleepy restlessness. Ellen stopped stroking his hair at once, and David cursed himself silently and wished he'd had the presence of mind not to react. He half-turned over on the bed and then settled into apparent slumber again, breathing slowly and deeply, willing Ellen to pick up where she'd left off. Just when he thought she wasn't going to, and had decided to pretend to wake up, she began again, caressing his hair with her fingertips. He lay still, revelling in the sensation, feeling only a little guilty for deceiving her.

Delicious though her attentions were, David was eager to find out how much of her rediscovered affection she was willing to reveal to his conscious self. He made a big show of waking up, groaning and moving around and finally peeping at her through eyes that he hoped looked bleary with sleep. She'd withdrawn her hand immediately he'd shown signs of stirring, of course, but he was delighted to find her smiling uncertainly at him when he looked at her.

'Hi,' he said thickly. 'How are you this morning?'

She shrugged and raised her eyebrows as if she hadn't really thought about it.

'Okay,' she said non-committally.

'I hope you don't mind me being here. I tried the chair and then the floor, but I couldn't sleep a wink.'

'No,' she said, 'that's okay.'

He sat up and said, 'Are you sure you're all right? You look a bit . . . preoccupied.'

'I was thinking about Jane, and about you going to get her, that's all.' She made it sound as though he was just popping out to pick her up from school, but there was a guardedness behind the apparent nonchalance.

'What about it?' he said.

'Well, I was just wondering . . . how dangerous do you think it'll be?'

David wondered what to tell her, and in the end said evasively, 'Pretty dangerous maybe. It depends on a lot of things.'

'But not *very* dangerous? I mean, you will be coming back?'

'I'm planning to,' he said.

She looked at him as if there was so much she wanted to say, but didn't know where to begin, or even whether she ought to. In the end she settled on murmuring, 'Please be careful.'

'I'll be extra careful,' he promised her. 'I'll be thinking of you and Rachel the whole time.'

She looked down at her hands and said in a subdued voice, 'David?'

'What?'

'Give me a hug.'

They held each other for a long time. David buried his face in her hair, kissed her forehead, told her that he loved her. She didn't reply, but she squeezed him tighter when he said it which David convinced himself was just as good.

They might have stayed there for ever if they hadn't heard a noise on the stairs below, and Rachel's voice calling, 'Mum, Dad, can I come up?'

They broke apart, the move instigated by Ellen. 'Course

you can, sweetheart,' David called.

Rachel appeared, looking worried.

'Hi. How long have you been up?' David asked her.

'A while,' she said vaguely. 'Listen, I think you should both come downstairs and see what's on TV.'

Ellen said, 'Why?', but David was already getting a sinking feeling in his stomach and thinking, This is it, it's starting, just like Willie said it would.

'Just come and look,' she said. 'It's really bad.' She looked at David and frowned. 'Dad, Willie says you and him and some of the others are going to go out into that.'

'That's right, sweetheart,' David said gently. 'We have to go back to London to try and get Jane back. But don't worry, we'll be okay.'

'Out into *what*?' Ellen was demanding anxiously, and David wished he'd told her the whole story, wished he'd warned her how bad things were going to become.

'You'll see it for yourself on the TV,' Rachel said, her eyes flickering between her mother and father as if she wanted to commit the sight of them together to memory, 'but Willie described it as the beginning of the end.'

'The end?' Ellen said, looking at David. 'The end of what?'

'Civilisation as we know it,' quipped David blackly. But no one laughed.

5

The Heart of
Darkness

41

The helicopter landed in a field behind the house just before 3 p.m. The wind from its rotors set tree branches twitching, stirred nearby bushes into a frenzy. The occupants of the house collected in a group some thirty or forty yards away to watch it come down. David had one arm around Ellen's shoulders, one around Rachel's. He'd always thought of helicopters as spindly fragile things, but this machine gave the impression of sturdiness, of compacted strength, a factor he found very reassuring. Even from here he could feel the chopping rhythm of the rotors vibrating through his teeth. The grass beneath the helicopter rippled like water as the aircraft hovered, then sank gracefully to the ground.

'Well, I suppose this is it,' David bawled into Ellen's ear.

'Suppose so,' she mouthed back. She tried to smile but it was unconvincing. 'Be careful,' she shouted, then suddenly hugged him so fiercely that pain spasmed through his neck. He threw his arms around her and the next second they were kissing each other on the mouth for the first time in what seemed to David like weeks, years, centuries. It was a sensation so wonderful it made his head spin, but achingly fleeting. When they broke apart her face was flushed, her eyes glittering with tears.

'I love you,' he shouted.

She nodded, but even now seemed unwilling to commit herself as readily. 'I don't want to lose you again,' she told him.

'Don't worry,' he shouted, far more cheerfully than he

felt. 'I've got the secret weapon.' He patted the pocket of his Bogart.

'Bye, Dad, take care,' Rachel shouted when he turned to her. She put her arms around his waist and hugged him hard, the side of her face pressed against his chest.

He wrapped his arms around her, kissed the top of her head. 'See you soon, pumpkin. Look after your mum for me.'

'I will.'

When they broke apart, other people were there waiting, armed with their goodbyes and best wishes. He kissed Tippi, shook hands with Ralph and Max and Marshall. Even Diane gave him a peck on the cheek and said fiercely, 'You come back,' as if he might be considering otherwise.

'The pilot's called Ray,' Hollis yelled. 'He's a good bloke. He'll look after you.'

David nodded and shook Hollis's hand, and then he was moving across the bumpy field towards the helicopter. He turned back to wave and saw Ellen and Rachel clinging to each other, Rachel pulling out a handkerchief which fluttered, wild and white, in the wind. Tears sparked in his eyes. He turned and blinked into the wind, which tore the tears away. As he, and those who had been selected to go with him, came within range of the rotors, they crouched down instinctively. The blades were not actually low enough to take the tops of their heads off, but the noise and the buffeting wind here was incredible. It was like being caught in a hurricane.

The pilot leaned across and opened the door. He raised a hand in greeting as David clambered in. David nodded in response, then turned back to give a hand to Richard Hodge, who was just behind him. Following Richard was his wife, Melanie, then Willie, and bringing up the rear was Imogen Butterworth, whose expression of alacrity was all too transparent, revealing the trepidation beneath.

There was a seat next to the pilot and four behind. Much to David's relief, Richard sat at the front, leaving David to occupy the last available seat, directly behind him, at the end of the row. The pilot, Ray, a burly moustached man wearing a navy blue jumper with padded elbows and shoulders, introduced himself, twisting in his seat to shake hands with each of them in turn. He indicated that they should all put on the earphones that had been provided for them.

Imogen looked unwilling but complied. She lowered the cans on to her coiffeured greying hair as if she half-expected blue jags of electricity to leap out and electrocute her. David put his phones on, taking care not to poke himself in the eye with the microphone which curved round his cheek on its metal rod like a piece of dental apparatus.

'All right, Mrs Butterworth?' he said cheerfully, in an attempt to allay her nervousness.

His question, however, did not quite have the desired effect. She jumped, her eyes opening wide, as his voice buzzed inside her head like a wasp.

She turned to him, brow furrowed in disapproval, and said, a little stiffly, 'Perfectly well, thank you, young man.' He must have looked apologetic for her expression softened almost at once. She confided, albeit to everyone in the aircraft, 'I'm afraid I'm a little nervous. I've never flown before.'

'I gather everyone can hear me clearly now?' Ray said, brisk and businesslike. Everyone nodded. 'Good. In that case, I'd like to welcome you aboard and advise you to hold on to your bellies. We'll be leaving the ground in a moment.'

Almost as soon as he had spoken, the helicopter tipped slightly as it began to rise, then stabilised. David instinctively gripped his seat. Imogen looked almost comically alarmed. David looked out to see the ground falling away, the grass thrashing and then losing definition so that more than ever it resembled a choppy green sea. He put his hand on his belly, which felt as if it was being sucked downwards into his legs. The roar of the engine, though muted by the helmet, filled his head. He closed his eyes, counted to ten, then opened them again and looked out. The helicopter was describing an arc in the air, the ground rotating below. David saw a brown-black weave of trees, the farmhouse like a roughly sculpted rock, tiny ant-people waving antennae-like arms, a green and brown patchwork of fields. He tried to pick out Ellen and Rachel, but couldn't. The farmhouse and the ant-people spun away.

'Everyone all right?' Ray asked. David joined in the chorus of affirmatives.

'This is *fun*!' Imogen said excitedly. David turned to see her grinning now, straining her neck to peer at the swooping land below.

'What sort of helicopter's this?' Richard Hodge asked.

'An Aerospatiale Squirrel. It's the only one we've got at Newcastle.'

'Do the police know you've taken it?' said David. He had seen the emblem on the side.

'Not exactly, no, though I am one of the official pilots. We just . . . . fixed things so that I could borrow it for a while without it being missed. I'd feel guilty if I didn't know this mission was even more important than assisting my colleagues at the present time. Fortunately the army have brought in helicopters of their own, so we're not exactly short of aerial resources.'

David assumed the 'we' who had 'fixed things' referred to other members of the Schism. 'How long will it take us to reach London?'

'The Squirrel's average cruising speed is one-five-oh miles per hour,' Ray said as if giving a lecture, 'so we should be there in two hours or so, depending on conditions.'

'Right,' said David, and settled back in his seat, trying to relax, though in truth he felt as nervous as he could ever remember being. He knew that this was it now, 'do or die' as Willie had said last night. They were about to enter a war zone, to embark on what might very well turn out to be a suicide mission. If they were going to survive, and it was a big if, they would need their wits about them, and a great deal of luck, and they would have to hope that their blind faith in the power of the bottle was not misplaced. Looking around at his companions, as with Willie's vague words last night, did not imbue David with a great deal of confidence. In his opinion, a couple of gym teachers, an old man who drank too much, and a genteel middle-aged woman who would look more at home in an English country garden brandishing a pair of pruning shears did not make a crack combat unit. However, the four of them *had* been chosen to accompany him because of the usefulness of their abilities in the kind of situations they were likely to encounter, so perhaps he was being unfair. Thus far, the only abilities David had actually seen demonstrated among the Schism were Ishvak's and Hollis's mind-reading, Tippi's healing and Malcolm Marshall's talent for pyrokinesis. He couldn't even remember what Imogen and Melanie were able to do, though he did recall that Richard Hodge was able to make people fall asleep. Yesterday, in the pub, Hodge had told David his subjects only remained asleep for fifteen or twenty seconds, however, and that he could only use his ability within a confined area, as the strain it placed on his animis was too great. He had first discovered the ability as an adolescent, and had used it back then to look up female teachers' skirts and write rude words on the blackboard during lessons.

They hadn't been travelling for long before they encountered the first sign of the mayhem that had paralysed the country. Melanie Hodge saw it first and pointed it out to the rest of them.

'That's the M6,' said Ray matter-of-factly. 'You'll see plenty of that sort of thing before we land. In fact, once we get over the Pennines and into West Yorkshire, you'll see whole cities burning, and you'll be able to smell the fires, even from up here. From the air Newcastle looks like hell at the moment. Literally.'

What Melanie had drawn their attention to was a pyre of twisted metal, of cars and lorries and vans, even caravans, which formed a huge roadblock across both lanes of the motorway. It looked surreal and somehow awesome; it made David think of a fat black blood clot plugging an artery. At some stage the heap of mangled vehicles had either burst into flame or been set alight; small fires still danced in the blackened smoking wreckage like sprites. There were no people about, which made the scene even more eerie, though other vehicles, some charred shells, some tipped on to their sides or their roofs, others seemingly untouched, were scattered every which way across the motorway and even up the embankment, like toys carelessly dropped by a toddler.

'It's weird that there are no people about,' David remarked.

'They've done what needs to be done here to create the disruption they were aiming for,' said Ray. 'Doubtless they'll now have made their way to the nearest city or town or village to spread more mayhem.'

'But they can't all have been troublemakers,' said David. 'What about the innocent people who just got here to find the road impassable, the drivers of some of these cars?'

'If there were any they'll either have been killed, or they'll be making their way to wherever they were planning to go on foot, or they'll be hiding out somewhere.'

'How many of these roadblocks are there?' Richard Hodge asked.

'Hundreds. Maybe thousands. It's not just motorways, it's everywhere. It's virtually impossible to drive more than two or three miles anywhere in the country now without coming up against some kind of obstruction.'

'God,' breathed David. Even knowing what he did about the Flux, it still boggled his mind when he considered how much organisation, how much *power*, must have been required to bring civilisation to such a shuddering halt. It was terrifying to think that there were so many people out there more than willing to play their part in tearing the country to pieces. How many of them knew they were being organised on a global scale, he wondered, and how many were just going along with the flow, running riot for the sheer hell of it? Like everyone else, the state of the world had really depressed him at times; Ellen had even gone through spates of refusing to watch the news or read papers because it was all so much doom and gloom. Wars, terrorist atrocities, famine in the Third World, the threat of ecological disaster, crime spiralling ever upwards, endless reports of the most perverse acts of violence and cruelty – it was all here, in lurid colour in every sitting room in the country, served up with the TV dinners and the cups of tea. David had often wondered how and where it would end; well, now he knew. It ended here. Inconceivable as it seemed, the world had lost its mind and created the ultimate nightmare. A society destroyed by its own lawlessness.

They flew on, helicopter rotors hacking the air. Nobody said much, though occasionally someone pointed out another roadblock, or a burning house, or even, on a couple of occasions, people lying in fields or on roads or pavements far below, dead or unconscious, small and indistinct as beetles.

The first really big city they came to, after crossing the

485

Pennines and the A684, was Bradford. They passed over smaller towns first, places like Skipton and Keighley, which provided a foretaste of what was to come. In Skipton gangs were running riot, racing cars up and down the main street, fighting with riot police, looting shops. There were the obligatory fires, including a factory blaze from which the plume of smoke was so thick it resembled a giant black leg with a burning foot descending out of the clouds.

In Keighley it was much the same story. David saw army vehicles blazing, soldiers carrying guns trying to restore order.

Bradford, though, was something else. From a distance it looked as if the whole city was burning.

Somehow, to David, the sight of Bradford burning was doubly shocking. He supposed they must have had plenty of fires there these past seven or eight years, plenty of acts of arson even, but he still remembered the fire at Valley Parade, Bradford City's football ground, back in the mid-eighties, and how horrified he, and indeed the whole nation, had been at the spectacle of people scrambling for their lives, having to climb eight-foot-high spiked fences as the fire raged behind them. To see the city in flames now made David feel that the good that had come out of that terrible tragedy – the compassion and kindness, the rallying together of the community, the enormous fund-raising efforts – had all been for nothing.

He remained silent as they flew over the city, listening to the shocked exclamations of the others, to Ray pointing out this and that in his world-weary, seemingly unshockable policeman's voice. It was like a battleground down there; the devastation was unbelievable. He saw black waves of people flowing this way and that, colliding head-on, indulging in a frightening confusion of violence, then splitting apart again. He saw continuous flashes and sparks among the melee – petrol bombs or gunfire, perhaps. Debris littered the streets; furniture, broken glass, overturned vehicles. Bodies littered the streets too, and were trampled underfoot without compunction. If they had been able to hear anything in the helicopter from the ground below, David was sure they would have heard screams of fear and shouts of rage, alarm bells shrilling untended, the chatter of gunfire, the roar of flame. There was an awful churning coldness inside him. After a few minutes he sat back and closed his eyes, unable to watch any more.

During the next hour or so they passed over other ravaged cities and towns – Sheffield, Nottingham, Bedford. It was growing dark as they approached London, the sky above the capital city lit not with electric light as it usually was but with flame, like some vast pagan festival. Smoke boiled in the air. Even inside the helicopter they could smell it. The aircraft cruised over the outlying districts to the north of London – Welwyn Garden City, Potters Bar, Barnet, Finchley, Muswell Hill.

They had encountered various other aircraft on their journey, mainly army personnel overseeing the devastation, but radio communication had never been anything more than perfunctory. David was a little surprised by the lack of security, by how readily they were accepted as genuine police officers and allowed to proceed. For all the army knew, they could have been terrorists who had hijacked a police helicopter and were now on their way to bomb Buckingham Palace or the Houses of Parliament. However, he guessed that the situation was now so desperate that the various law-keeping forces were too concerned with their own immediate problems to waste time checking one another's credentials. The sensible thing for the authorities to do, he supposed, would have been to get the 'important' people, the politicians and the Royal Family, those who supposedly ran the country, out of the capital and into hiding as quickly as possible, and then to deal with hostile and aggressive activity if and when it happened. Whichever way you looked at it, this policy, if indeed it was the one being implemented, smacked frighteningly of last-ditch measures, of desperation.

David had never *really* realised before how much the stability of the world depended on the goodwill of the ordinary people who lived in it. The army and the police had the majority of the weaponry, of course, and therefore potentially the most physical power, but once the *threat* of using that weaponry had failed to calm the situation, what could you do? Bomb the rioters? Wipe out huge amounts of civilians in the name of peace? It was ironic that the only way they were really going to be able to stop the chaos was by becoming part of it themselves.

He wondered where all the various world-leaders were now, where they had been moved to. Surely nowhere on the planet was safe at the present time? Could contingency plans possibly exist for an emergency of such devastating proportions? He supposed the possibility of a nuclear war had been considered, in which case the privileged would presumably retire to their underground bunkers or their tropical islands, or wherever it was they had decided they should go to wait until the havoc was over.

His train of thought was derailed by a sudden lurching of the helicopter which dumped him unceremoniously into Imogen Butterworth's lap. She in turn clashed heads with Willie, whose outflung arm caught Melanie Hodge in the midriff. Amid the groans and gasps of pain, Richard Hodge, who had been saved from being hurled on to the instrument console by his seatbelt, shouted, 'What's happening?' The helicopter's engine was now making an alarming grinding sound, and the craft itself was continuing to lurch and dip erratically despite Ray's efforts to steady it.

In an admirably even voice, Ray said, 'I think we've been hit.'

Despite his seatbelt David was being hurled this way and that. 'Hit?' he yelled. 'What do you mean?'

'By gunfire from below. We're going down.'

The cabin of the helicopter filled with screams as the machine flapped and squawked and finally began to plummet from the sky like a fatally wounded bird. David's world tipped on its axis; suddenly he couldn't move, couldn't see, couldn't even think. He felt as though he was being crushed back into his seat by an enormous hand. He felt sure that if he opened his mouth, the force of falling would wrench out the contents of his body and turn him inside-out. It hurt to keep his eyes open, so he closed them. Vaguely, through the turmoil, he heard Richard Hodge screaming his wife's name over and over like a war chant.

And then, impossible though it seemed, everything started to slow down. At first, in his confusion, David thought this was merely a prelude to impact and he braced himself. But the sensation of slowing, of settling, persisted. Even his stomach, which had been pressing against the base of his throat, sank back into its proper position in his body.

He opened his eyes and realised that things really were slowing down. It was hard to believe, but the helicopter actually appeared to have stopped falling. Not that David could see much outside, except patches of darkness interspersed with the blocky shapes of buildings given form by the flickering orange light of a thousand fires. The air was hazy and vinegar-coloured; if it hadn't been for the fires it would almost have been like being underwater, drifting through the depths of a sludgy sea.

David's hand slipped into his pocket, searching for the bottle. He was relieved to find it unbroken, though their near-fatal accident only served to remind him that the bottle was no cure-all, no magic shield that would protect him from any amount of danger. The accident had happened so quickly that he hadn't even had time to think about employing the bottle before the pressure in the craft had incapacitated him. Unless the bottle was in his hand and linked to the animis that Max insisted he possessed, he was just as vulnerable as any other human being.

His main concern now, however, was not whether the bottle would have saved them, but what actually had. He looked bemusedly round the helicopter cabin, and then suddenly his ears popped as the pressure changed in them and he realised someone was talking. It was Richard Hodge, his voice low and coaxing. 'That's it,' he was saying. 'That's it, Mel. Go on, you can do it.'

David looked at Melanie Hodge.

She had her mouth wide open and there were cobwebs coming out of it.

No, not cobwebs; more like . . . like mist. But it was a thick, fibrous, almost furry mist, within which shards of matter glittered. Melanie herself was wreathed in the mist; it fizzed on her skin, turned her hair to fog. Her eyes were open but she seemed oblivious to her surroundings. Her body was rigid, fingers outstretched, legs straight and feet at right angles, so that she resembled a mannequin propped against a chair, touching the floor only with her heels.

David realised immediately what was happening. This stuff, this ectoplasm that was gouting from her, was coming from her animis. Whatever her ability was, and David still couldn't remember, she was demonstrating it now.

The mist was drifting around the cabin, though not in an aimless way. Rather it seemed to be searching, exploring, wrapping slow amorphous tendrils around instrumentation, imbuing the entire aircraft with its energy and its presence. Looking out, David saw the rotors whipping by overhead, trailing mist and sparks. Whatever the stuff was that Melanie produced, already it seemed to have made good the damage done to the aircraft, or at least to have compensated for it.

The helicopter seemed now to be hovering in mid-air, held in equilibrium. Though its engine was no longer making the grinding, ratcheting sound it had been making just moments before, neither did it sound how it had for the majority of their journey. It was quieter now, certainly, but there was something else too, something that David found difficult to pin down. He listened hard and realised that there was another noise complementing the whirring of the blades and the steady growl of the engine, a noise so basic and yet so unexpected it was almost subliminal.

It seemed crazy, but the sound most closely resembled the beating of a giant pulse. And it was less a sound, more a sensation; it registered as a subtle but rhythmic pressure change in David's ears. Though the sound seemed to come from outside him, he wondered momentarily whether he was in fact hearing nothing more curious than his own heartbeat, his senses alerted somehow as a result of the helicopter's sudden plunge.

Then, all at once, it came to him. With a flash of memory, he recalled Ishvak telling him what Melanie Hodge's ability was. She was able to breathe life into inanimate objects. And now that he thought about it, the helicopter's engine sounded like . . . like *purring*, didn't it? And the whirring of the rotors sounded more like the beating of vast wings.

Despite everything that he had seen and heard these past few days, the sheer outrageous impossibility of this latest wonder made David laugh out loud in disbelief. Everyone had been concentrating on Melanie, but now they turned to look at him, their faces, which had been stark with panic only a minute or two before, now wide-eyed with surprise, almost disapproval, as if he had laughed in church.

David felt a little embarrassed, and concerned that his sudden outburst might disturb Melanie's concentration.

'Sorry,' he whispered, in what he hoped was an appropriately repentant tone, 'but I've just realised what she's doing.'

Imogen responded with a frown, but Willie grinned at him. Ray, the pilot, was sitting back in his chair, arms folded, staring at the stuff creeping over the helicopter's instrumentation as if wondering whether he would be able to clean it off later, and if not, how he was going to explain the mess to his superiors.

The stuff was still unfurling from Melanie's mouth in a thin stream, and had now formed a kind of shifting film over the interior of the aircraft, so thick that it was getting difficult to see outside. The fires down below were now little more than a golden glow through the opaque skin. The helicopter was looking less like a machine and more like an organic structure with each second that passed; harsh clean lines were being smoothed out, technical equipment disappearing beneath layer upon layer of glittering vapour. There was no smell to the stuff, and though it twined around his ankles and occasionally whispered past his face, it seemed to David that it had no substance.

Just when he was beginning to think that the stuff was going to pour from Melanie's mouth for ever, that they were in danger of being engulfed by it, it stopped coming, tapering wispily to a point like a cloud that resembled a snake. Melanie slumped back with a moan of exhaustion, her eyes closing. Within seconds she was breathing deeply, her chin on her chest, hair falling over her face.

'Well done, love,' Richard Hodge said, and leaned across the seats to kiss the top of her head.

David looked up to see the stuff still moving over the curved ceiling of the cabin, the glittering ever-changing colours producing an almost mesmeric effect. 'Does she do this kind of thing all the time?' he asked.

Everyone laughed. The relief in the aircraft was palpable

now after the panic of just moments before.

'Oh, now and again,' Richard Hodge said airily. And then he added more seriously, 'To be honest, she's never tried it on anything quite so big before, and especially not under such pressure. Normally she needs a minute or two of quiet to compose herself.'

'Aye, she's done us proud this time,' Willie said. 'Ah thought we were all goners for a wee minute there.'

Ray, who had been attempting to peer through the shifting skin of vapour that coated the inside of the aircraft, said suddenly, 'We're moving.'

Everyone turned to look, but of course could see nothing through the coated windows. The sensation of movement was barely perceptible, more akin, thought David, to floating than flying. It was an odd feeling, like sitting inside a giant egg, or, more accurately perhaps, a vast jellyfish, the membrane of which pulsed and shivered with life. The natural phosphorescence which the vapour was imbued with grew subtly brighter with each pulse-beat, reinforcing this notion.

'Where are we going?' said David. He wasn't sure why, but he got the impression they were moving away from their original destination.

'That's the problem,' said Richard.

'What is?'

'We have no control over the aircraft now,' said Ray.

Richard was nodding. 'I'm afraid we'll just have to go wherever the chopper feels like taking us.'

'Doesn't Mel have any say in where the thing takes us?' David asked.

'She might do if she were awake.'

'Well, can't we wake her up then?'

Richard shook his head, and Willie explained, 'The poor lassie's drained of energy. Nothing you could do would wake her up noo. We'll just have ti wait till she's ready.'

'Right,' said David resignedly. 'So I suppose we just have to sit here, floating around inside this giant blob until then?'

'That's about the size of it,' said Richard. 'Still, you've got to admit, it's better than crashing.'

It was fifteen minutes before Mel woke up. She surfaced, groaning and wincing, hands held to her head as though nursing a hangover. At first she was reluctant to open her eyes. When she finally did, David saw that they were bloodshot.

'Are we dead?' was the first question she asked.

Richard laughed. 'Do we look dead?'

She squinted around the cabin, then groaned and bowed her head again. 'I *feel* dead.'

'Well, you're not,' said Richard, 'and neither is anyone else. It bloody worked, love. You saved us all.'

She looked up again, hair tumbling away from her face. 'I did?' she said, surprised. Her bloodshot eyes opened a fraction wider and she looked around. 'I did,' she confirmed to herself in a voice full of wonder.

'We do have a slight problem, though,' said David.

She turned her head to look at him, wincing with discomfort. 'David,' she murmured as though reminding herself. 'A problem?'

'Only a very small one,' said Richard.

'We've got no control over where we're going,' David said. 'We need your help.'

Melanie sat up, blinking her eyes wider. 'Oh, right. I'll see what I can do.'

'Are you sure you're up to this, love?' Richard asked, concerned.

'I've got a bastard of a headache and I'm tired,' she replied, 'but in the light of everything else, I think those are minor problems, don't you?'

'Yes, but I don't want you –'

'Oh, stop fussing, Richard. I know how far to push

494

myself. I'm not going to try to fly the damn thing. I'll just put us down somewhere relatively safe, okay?'

'Okay,' said Richard, cowed. He caught David's eye and pulled a face. David smiled.

'And don't think I can't see you two smirking at each other,' Melanie said.

Willie laughed. 'You tell 'em, lassie.'

Ray, still trying to peer through the opaque film on the window, said, 'I think we're circling something.'

Melanie placed her hands together in her lap, rolled her head back on her neck to relax the muscles there, took a deep breath, and closed her eyes.

Everyone fell silent, watching Melanie's face. After a minute or so, she frowned and pursed her lips. It seemed as if she was peering intently at something, even though her eyes were closed. Behind her eyelids her eyeballs could be seen rolling slowly from side to side. 'There,' she murmured after a few moments.

David felt a subtle shifting in the movement of the helicopter. It seemed to tilt a little to one side. Then he got the impression that it was sinking slowly; the sensation was not unlike being in a lift. The purring of the engine changed timbre. All at once there was a double-bump producing a slight jolt inside the cabin. The engine sound began to wind down, to become slower and quieter.

'What's happened?' he said.

'I think we've landed,' Ray replied.

Melanie opened her eyes, and released a long measured breath. 'Well, we're down,' she said, confirming Ray's diagnosis.

'Where?' asked Richard.

'Well, we're not *too* far from where we're supposed to be, though we have overshot the mark a bit. I've put us down on top of a building in Oxford Street.'

'Oxford Street,' said Richard, pulling a face. 'It's not ideal.'

'It's the best I could do, Richard,' protested Melanie. 'This is bloody exhausting work.'

'Oh, I know that,' said Richard placatingly. 'I wasn't criticising you. It's just the thought of having to make it back on foot.'

She nodded, calmed by his apology. 'I know. It's not going to be easy, is it?'

'Och, we'll be okay as long as we're careful,' said Willie. 'We've got a few tricks up oor sleeves that most of the folk out there won't have bargained for.'

Everyone knew he was making light of what was likely to be a very tough situation, but there were nods all round.

'Right,' said David briskly, 'let's go and kick some bottom.' He unclipped his seatbelt, and then, in a more subdued voice, he said, 'Sorry to be boring, but how do we get out of here?'

Melanie smiled tiredly. There were dark rings around her eyes. 'Don't worry,' she said, 'this won't last for ever. In the meantime, we'll just have to wait. To be honest, I could do with a rest.'

She closed her eyes and immediately seemed to drift into a light doze. Willie sighed and said, 'Och well, if you can't beat 'em . . .' and he closed his eyes too, snuggling down in his seat, hands laced over his belly.

David groaned inwardly, not exactly looking forward to going outside, but nevertheless anxious to expend some of the nervous energy that had been building up inside him throughout the journey. He spent the next ten minutes or so in a state of restlessness, and even when the vapour started to disperse, to shrivel into itself like instantaneous decay, it seemed to do so excruciatingly slowly.

The last minute or two he spent watching the door of the aircraft, the vapour shrinking away from it like a film of mould growth played backwards. The instant the door became accessible, he turned and said, 'That's it. We can get out now.'

The general movement inside the helicopter roused Willie from his snooze, who grumbled, 'Och, it's time ti get up already, is it?'

Richard leaned across and woke Melanie with gentle kisses and soft words. When she reluctantly opened her eyes and peered at him, he said, 'Come on, love. Time to get going.'

They said their goodbyes to Ray, who was hoping to fly back to Newcastle that night if he could get the aircraft fixed, and then Richard opened the door.

Three things struck them at once – the cold air, the stink of smoke, and the noise.

The latter was the most disturbing. Inside the helicopter they had been cushioned from the worst of it, aware only of a general hubbub outside, but now they were able to identify the various different sounds that made up the cacophony below. There were shouts and screams, the crackling of flames, alarm bells shrilling, car horns blaring, and the intermittent sound of gunfire. They could even hear the rapid hacking sound of another helicopter somewhere above and in front of them, but the pall of smoke which hung over the city shrouded the aircraft from view.

Richard climbed down first on to the flat concrete roof, the wind tugging at his hair, attempting to inflate his jacket like a balloon. He squinted and looked around at the panorama of burning buildings and wrecked cars and rampaging mobs of people, as David jumped down beside him. When he turned back, his face was clenched with anxiety, and David knew immediately what he was thinking. His own thoughts turned to Ellen and Rachel, safe in the farmhouse in Cumbria, surrounded by Hollis's psychic barriers. He felt grateful that he only had himself to worry about here, at least until he found Jane. He squeezed Richard's shoulder and said, 'You okay?'

Richard shrugged, grimaced. 'Listen to it down there. It sounds like hell. Looks like hell.'

David nodded, and said more confidently than he felt, 'Don't worry, Richard. As long as we stick together and don't take any chances, we'll be okay. Like Willie says, we've got tricks up our sleeves that make Paul Daniels look like an amateur.'

When all five of them were down on the roof, they waved to Ray, and then made their way to the Exit door that led down through the building. The door, set into a kind of concrete bunker, was made of steel with a lever-bar across it. David expected the door to be locked, but when he depressed the bar and pushed, the door swung open. Beyond he could see a staircase leading downwards into darkness. He led the way.

The staircase was short and led to a landing which had various other doors leading off from it, including a lift and a pair of double doors with reinforced glass panels that presumably opened on to another descending staircase. Though he could see little, David sensed a general air of neglect up here; the smell of accumulated dust and grime scratched at the back of his throat. He coughed, the sound seeming to boom off the walls around them, to reverberate down through the building. Despite the circumstances, he winced, still feeling as though he ought to remain as quiet as possible, that he and the rest were trespassers here.

They moved forward cautiously, David holding out his hands in front of him. Willie, who was at the rear of the group, pushed the steel door closed, but the weight of it took him by surprise and swung it into its frame with a crash that echoed and echoed in the darkness. Instinctively all of them ducked, David clenching his teeth and raising his arms protectively as if he expected chunks of the ceiling to come raining down. With the echoes still ringing in his ears, he turned and glared at Willie, who was now little more than a blurred silhouette against the darkness.

The little Scotsman spread his hands. 'Whoops,' he said.

'Deafened for life,' muttered Imogen.

There was an 'oof' of collision, and then Richard said, 'Sorry, Mel, I thought you'd started moving forward again.'

'Hang on,' said Willie, and next moment his face was hanging in the air like a ghastly yellow skull.

'*Ta da!*' he exclaimed, black shadows seeming to spill from his mouth. His face slid back into the darkness as he flashed the thin beam of the pencil-torch around, the yellowish light showing them a jumble of geometrical shapes – the angles of ceilings and walls, rectangular doors, corners where cobwebs quivered. 'Here,' he said, holding the torch out, 'pass it on.' Imogen took the torch and handed it to Melanie, who in turn handed it to David, by which time Willie had taken another torch from his pocket and was passing that one on too.

He had three in all, the last of which he kept for himself.

'You're a wonder, Willie, you know that,' said Melanie.

'Oh aye,' said Willie, 'a regular boy scout. Ti be honest, though, bringing these along was Max's idea. If it'd been up ti me, ah'd have just brought ma wee hipflask and a packet of peppermints.'

'We're not exactly well prepared, are we?' said David ruefully. 'We should have brought more stuff with us.'

'What kind of stuff?' said Richard. 'Sandwiches? Tents? Hiking boots? Warm clothes?'

'I don't know,' David said. 'Weapons, maybe? No, forget I said that. I suppose nothing can really prepare us for what we're heading for, can it?'

'We have our abilities,' said Melanie, 'don't forget that.'

'So have the Flux,' Willie reminded her, 'and they might be monitoring oor movements this verra minute for all we know. We just have ti hope that this chaos they've created is keeping 'em busy.'

'You think it might have been the Flux that disabled the helicopter?' Melanie said.

Willie shrugged. 'Who knows?'

They moved forward along the corridor. When they got to the lift, David tried both buttons, but nothing happened.

'Looks like we'll have to use the stairs,' he said.

'It wouldn't have been a good idea to use the lift anyway,' said Melanie. 'Too confining. We'd have been terribly vulnerable in there.'

They pushed the reinforced glass doors open, filed out on to the stairs and began to descend, their footsteps trailing ghosts of themselves. David shone his torch down the centre of the stairwell, but all he saw was the black handrail looping down and down like a partly uncoiled spring.

They had descended three floors when he held up his hand and said, 'Shh.'

'Whatever's the matter?' said Imogen.

'I thought I heard something.'

'Aye, me too,' said Willie from the back.

'What sort of something?' asked Melanie.

'I'm not sure. Someone shouting . . . or laughing. I don't know.'

'It probably came from outside,' said Richard.

'No, it was nearer than that, I'm sure of it.'

They stood in silence for fifteen seconds, but all they could hear were the faint distressing sounds of a city ripping itself apart.

'See?' said Richard. 'It must have been outside, like I said.'

'Maybe,' said David, though he didn't sound entirely convinced.

They were another couple of floors down, passing the double doors which provided access to the staircase from the offices of the people who worked here, when they heard a scream. It was high-pitched and full-blooded, a woman screaming in terror and pain. Not only was it inside the building, but it was coming from somewhere very close by, perhaps the floor below, or the one below that. All five of them stopped dead, Melanie so startled that she dropped her torch, the beam of which swooped massively across the wall before rushing towards its source, coming to rest as a bright white pool at the torch's tip.

David had instinctively hunched his shoulders at the sound. For a moment his body seemed to freeze, then his heart began pumping twice as fast as before. Although it had been the scream itself which had shocked all five of them to immobility, it was the sounds that came after it that were actually worse. First of all there was a whiplash-crack, and then a ragged wave of laughter and half-heard jeers.

Willie was the first to speak. 'Torches off,' he hissed, putting his own in his pocket.

Melanie bent, picked up her torch and clicked it off. Before extinguishing his, David said, 'What are we going to do?'

'Torch off,' repeated Willie firmly. David did as he was told.

'Right. Noo we're gonnae keep going doon, okay? Whatever's happening in this building, it isnae oor concern. Ah know that sounds hard, but we cannae afford to stop every time we come across someone in bother. Can everyone handle that?'

There was a sullen and reluctant mumble of agreement. David knew that Willie was right, but if there was a woman being tortured somewhere nearby, then that was going to be an awfully difficult situation to walk away from.

They started down again, moving much more cautiously now, David wondering how often Willie had had to be this ruthless in the past, how many terrible deeds he had had to perform in order to maintain his standing within the Flux.

As they descended, the sound of the revellers grew louder. If it hadn't been for the scream, David could almost have believed that an office party was taking place in the rooms below. Almost, but not quite, because when he listened closely, *really* listened, he was able to detect a hard edge to the proceedings, a kind of viciousness beneath the banter and the laughter.

They had reached the double doors from behind which the sounds were coming when they heard the woman cry out again.

This time it was more of a sobbing, choking sound that she made, though still saturated with just as much pain and despair as the first time. She formed words this time too, a string of pleas splintered by terror, whose repetition, 'Please-no-please-no-don't-please-no-no-please . . .' made David think of a human being reduced to the absolute minimum, to a knot of abject primitive terror.

He stopped on the stairs, sickened and distressed. All five of them clearly heard a male voice spitting out the words, 'Shut up, *bitch*!' and then a dull slap-thud which David knew, instinctively and irrevocably, was the sound of flesh hitting flesh. There was laughter and hooting. Someone shouted, 'Right *on*!' Then, more chillingly, a young male voice, breathlessly excited, urged, 'Give it to her, Stanny, give it to her in the mouth!'

'We've got to stop this,' Melanie said decisively, and she turned and marched towards the double doors.

'Och, ah don't know,' said Willie, though his protests were half-hearted, and already Richard was following his wife. 'Let's just be careful,' he conceded.

David looked at Imogen, but it was too dark to see the expression on her face. He wondered how much she had seen and experienced in her time with the Flux and then the Schism. She gave the impression of having led a sheltered life, and he couldn't help but wonder whether she would prove to be the weak link in their group.

Melanie pushed the double doors open. Despite the darkness, David saw a dull sheen of silvery light, coming from somewhere ahead, slide across the glass. Heads bobbed in silhouette as the group moved into the corridor, David now at the rear. He took the weight of the door which Imogen had been holding open for him, and eased it closed, holding his breath as it met its frame with the minutest bump. Imogen turned back and whispered in his ear, 'Prop the door open. We may have to make a rather hurried exit.'

'Oh,' whispered David hoarsely, 'right, okay.' He felt foolish that he hadn't had the sense to think of this himself. How many times had he been scornful of characters in films blundering into dangerous situations without taking even the most basic of precautions?

Three-quarters of the way down the corridor, on the left, was a door with a frosted glass panel through which light poured. Individual voices could be heard clearly now, a verbal weave of obscenities and exhortations, whoops of delight, vicious laughter.

'Lookit the fucking state of that,' someone cried.

'My fucking turn next,' someone else said.

'Go on, Chad, see how far up it'll go.'

As they neared the door, shapes could be seen moving behind the glass panel. A lot of shapes. David glanced at his companions, whose profiles were outlined in pearly light. Imogen's expression was unreadable, Richard and Melanie looked as nervous and sickened as he felt, and Willie looked calm and determined, *sober*, David thought, his mouth set in a thin line, his eyes watchful.

When they were three feet from the door, Willie, who had moved to the head of the group, raised his hand and flapped his fingers, indicating that they should all seek the shelter of the wall. They did so, then the Scotsman, with another small gesture, drew them into a huddle. Slowly and calmly he outlined what he thought they would find once they opened the door and what he regarded as the best way of dealing with it. Nobody argued with him; they accepted his instructions without question. It was as though he had shrugged off the mantle of the amiable fool, the disguise he normally wore to ensure that his opponents underestimated him.

'Okay then,' he whispered, 'let's go.' He stepped boldly to the door, opened it and went inside.

The others followed without hesitation, immediately stepping aside as Willie had told them to do, so that there was no congestion in the doorway. David had seen some terrible things these past few days – Dean Burgess's gun massacre, Worthington's gruesome demise, entire cities in flames – but the scene he saw in front of him now was by far the worst of all.

The woman who had screamed, actually a girl of perhaps seventeen or eighteen, was on her hands and knees in the middle of the floor. Most of her clothes had been torn from her; her blouse was hanging in shreds, revealing her dangling breasts, her skirt pushed up around her waist. She was surrounded by a group of fifteen or sixteen young men, one of whom – a fat youth with dyed yellow hair – was standing in front of the girl and forcing her to fellate him. Another of the youths, who wore a black leather jacket so new he had probably helped himself to it from the department store below these offices this very evening, was standing behind the girl, trying to force the barrel of a pump-action shotgun up her vagina.

The scene was so terrible, so intrinsically, inhumanely *awful*, that it seemed to David as if it was destroying that part of him that believed blindly in the basic goodness of humanity, attacking it like a virus. His horror seemed to shift his senses into overdrive, so that each detail burned itself into his mind, never to be erased. It seemed in an instant as though he registered the face of every single person in that room and stored it in his memory. The girl's face he would never forget, not just her jaws forced wide by the fat youth's penis, but her eyes squeezed shut, red from weeping, a line of mascara trickling over her bruised cheekbone. He saw a strand of hair that arced down to her chin; a mole on her neck; her earring in the shape of a leaf dangling from her earlobe on a slender gold-coloured chain. He saw too her painted fingernails embedded in the beige carpet, blood on that carpet, blood up the walls, the mutilated bodies of office workers, from which the blood was flowing, sprawled in an obscene, undignified heap by the photocopier.

A number of youths had blood on their clothes and hands; one even had it smeared in stripes on his cheeks, and David thought of the ritual of 'blooding' that takes place after fox hunts, whereby novices are smeared with the blood of the kill. A boy no more than fourteen, with sleepy eyes, a downy moustache, and acne-speckled cheeks, paused in the act of raising a can of beer to his lips, his hands so stained with blood that they seemed gloved with it.

The office itself was a wreck, furniture and equipment smashed beyond repair, Christmas trimmings destroyed and trampled. When the five of them walked in, everything seemed to stop, the voices of the gang members dwindling to silence. Heads turned slowly to regard them. For one absurd moment, David felt like a schoolteacher catching a group of pupils smoking behind the bike sheds. Then the youth with the leather jacket who had been forcing the shotgun up the girl's vagina, jerked it out of her, swung it towards them, and squeezed the trigger.

42

David had time to be shocked that no words were exchanged. In films the bad guys were always curious ('Who the hell are you?'), and almost always gave a warning of the violence to come ('Get 'em, boys!'). But here there was no preamble at all. If Willie hadn't briefed them, they might have been added without ceremony to the heap of bodies by the photocopier in a matter of seconds. However, Richard at least had remembered his role, and even as the leather-jacketed youth was swinging the barrel of the gun towards them, he was doing his stuff.

David didn't see exactly what he did – his eyes were riveted on the second person in a matter of days who was intending to blow his head off. He saw the teenager swing round, his finger tightening on the trigger. And then, before the youth's finger could depress the trigger all the way and fill the room with thunder, everything simply stopped, as though someone had hit the 'pause' button on a video recorder. For an instant the room and everything in it seemed frozen as a photograph, and then, one by one, the eyes of the youths closed and their heads slumped forward. One or two of them even began snoring gently.

Before David had time fully to appreciate the effect, Willie was shouting' 'Go!' into the silence. Instantly the five of them were fanning out, following the instructions that the little Scotsman had given them. David and Imogen began to collect together as many weapons as they could find, to disarm the gang as much as possible. David concentrated on the knives and axes that most of the gang were armed with, and Imogen moved forward to relieve the leather-jacketed youth of his shotgun.

Richard and Willie, meanwhile, moved forward to heave the fat yellow-haired youth away from the girl. They managed the task quickly, the fat youth's penis plopping out of the girl's mouth, and then they pushed him over on to his back. Even as the yellow-haired youth's head was hitting the floor with a sound like a basketball, the two of them were picking the girl up, Richard heaving her on to his shoulder in a fireman's lift.

Unfortunately, in trying to give Richard room to swing round and get the girl out, Willie accidentally backed into the leather-jacketed youth with the shotgun, toppling him over, which is where the plan began to go wrong.

Imogen had been trying to prise Leather Jacket's fingers from the trigger in order to take the shotgun away from him, and had almost managed this when the teenager fell, landing on top of the weapon. 'Ten seconds!' Willie shouted, 'Come on!', and made for the door, waving his arms. David had pulled the front of his sport shirt out of the waistband of his trousers and had raised it to create a sort of scoop of material in which he could carry the weapons. As he staggered towards one of the broken windows, intending to jettison his load, Melanie, who had been collecting stuff to use as a barricade, appeared beside him, carrying the blackened remains of a computer terminal, and shouted, 'Help Imogen get the bloody shotgun!'

David looked back to see Imogen trying to wrestle the gun from beneath the youth's prone body. A vital second or two passed whilst he stood there, uncertain whether to dump the stuff he was carrying out of the window first or drop it and go to her aid.

'Throw out the weapons!' Melanie screamed at him. 'David, come *on*!'

David tossed the weapons out of one of the broken

windows, where they fell like a rain of heavy cutlery that he prayed no one was standing beneath.

He could smell the blood on him. It smeared his hands and shirt and the arms and chest of his Bogart, making him feel soiled and sick. His heart was beating now in time to the mantra in his head, which was the amount of time Richard had told him his animis was effective for: *twenty-seconds-twenty-seconds-twenty-seconds* . . .

They must have had most of that by now and Imogen still didn't seem to be having much luck pulling the shotgun out from under the youth's body. David joined her, tugging ineffectually at the weapon for another vital couple of seconds, before his mind informed him, almost coolly, that he was going about this the wrong way. He grabbed hold of the teenager's shoulder and pulled him over on to his back.

'I should have done that straight away,' said Imogen, distraught. David said nothing. He could see that Leather Jacket still had a tight grip on the shotgun even now, his forefinger crooked around the trigger. He bent down, breathing hard and fast, and tried to prise the teenager's fingers free.

All of a sudden the hand that David had hold of flexed, then made a grab for him. David snatched his own hand back, and looked into the teenager's face. He saw the teenager's eyes open wide and glare at him, saw lips curling back in a snarl that was almost feral. As David jerked back he became aware that the gang was now awakening all around him. Before he could move away, Leather Jacket reached out and grabbed his left ankle.

He was tall and sinewy, and his grip was as strong as an ape's. David only just managed to keep his balance as the youth tugged, trying to bring him down. With his left hand the teenager groped for the shotgun, which was now lying across his body. If Imogen had been more alert, she might have been able to grab the gun – but she wasn't, and the opportunity passed.

The fat yellow-haired youth was sitting up now, blinking and groaning, rubbing the side of his head as if he had the mother of all hangovers. Most of the other gang members were recovering as he was, slowly and confusedly, but there were one or two who were already blinking the sleep away, beginning to take in what was happening.

Leather Jacket had a grip on the shotgun now. Awkwardly, hampered by the fact that he didn't have a hand free with which to lever himself to his feet, he started to swing himself round on to his right side, perhaps intending to roll into David's legs and bowl him over.

David knew he had only seconds before the gang began to recover enough to come to their friend's aid. Frenziedly he began to kick out at the teenager with his right foot, his violence powered by panic and self-preservation. He pistoned his foot into Leather Jacket's body three times, twice into his stomach and once into his groin, before he felt the grip loosen around his ankle.

Yanking his foot free, he almost fell over backwards in his haste to get away. He felt Imogen's arms steadying him as he stumbled. He whirled, and grabbing Imogen's hand, began to run for the door. People were shouting all around him now, but David didn't know who they were or what was being said. It was just a noise to accompany the adrenalin that was surging through him, filling his head with a pulsing roar.

He hadn't run like this in a long, long time. Once it had seemed as natural as breathing, but now he was aware of the stiffness of his muscles, of his perception tapering down to a jolting tunnel vision, the open doorway the prize towards which he was plunging. He was horribly aware of how wide and vulnerable his back was, how tempting a target. Each fragment of a second he expected to hear the bellow of the shotgun, feel himself consumed by searing pain, launched into the corridor by the force of the blast.

And then he was through the doorway, urged on by Willie and Melanie who were waiting in the corridor, and vaulting the heap of debris that Melanie had collected. He was only aware that Imogen was still with him, still holding his hand, when he landed and felt a wrench in his shoulder as his momentum took him forward faster than Imogen could keep up. Their hands snapped apart like the weak point in an elastic band, almost causing David to stumble and fall. Fortunately Willie was there to help him, grabbing him by the scruff of the neck, preventing him from losing his balance. As David made for the darkness beyond the open glass door that led to the stairwell, he risked a quick glance back, half-expecting to see slavering blood-splattered hordes bearing down upon him.

What he did see was Imogen not far behind, holding her shoulder, her face creased in pain. And beyond her, Melanie piling up the stuff she had collected in front of the now-closed office door. There wasn't much – some broken furniture, some cardboard boxes and the burned-out computer she had been carrying when she had shouted at him to get the shotgun – but she was making a good job of things by the look of it, jamming the furniture tightly in the space between the door and wall, using the other stuff to give the barricade weight and solidity. Willie was scampering back towards her, either to help her or to pull her away.

David kept running, his panic and exertion causing tadpoles of light to spark across his vision. He was aware of pain in his shoulder, though only vaguely; he was more aware of the fact that he was breathing too fast, his lungs snatching at air, and that each inhalation was causing pain to stab through his chest.

When he ran out through the door on to the stairwell, he had to skid to a halt, his hands flailing in front of him.

After the brightness of the office, and the shadowy dimness of the corridor, the absence of light out here made it seem as though he had been struck blind. The tadpoles continued to squirm in his vision, though they were blood-red now; he blinked rapidly three or four times, trying to clear them. When he heard Imogen coming up behind him, he began to move forward again, though cautiously, testing the floor with his feet to prevent himself falling headlong down the stairs. Before he reached the stairs he could see them dimly, like a staggered row of giant descending piano keys, as his eyes began to adjust.

He was groping for the first step, his hand on the cold plastic stair-rail, when he remembered the torch. Surely it wouldn't matter now if he used it. There was no longer any need for secrecy. He put his hand in his pocket, and the first thing he felt was the bottle. Perhaps it would be a good idea to keep the bottle in his hand constantly from now on, he thought, or at least to stick his hand into his pocket and grab the bottle at the merest inkling of danger. Of course, he didn't want to drain the bottle's power by using it willy-nilly, but he'd been in two extremely life-threatening situations in the past hour and on neither occasion had he managed to get his shit together in time. He hesitated, and then decided to leave the bottle where it was for the time being. He'd grab it at the first sign of danger in future, but if he carried it in his hand not only would it hamper his movements, but he'd probably only end up dropping it and seeing it smash into a million pieces.

He took out the torch and turned it on. Imogen was just coming through the glass door, Willie and Melanie at her shoulder. All at once David heard the smashing of glass and an incoherent scream of rage, which was swallowed almost immediately by the roar of the shotgun.

It was like an explosion. It echoed and echoed in the square tube of the stairwell. It was a sound so loud that it hurt, like flat-handed blows on David's ears. The four of them raced down the stairs, deafened, as though carried along by the shock waves of the blast, pursuing the shaky circle of light that was David's torch-beam.

For long seconds, as his ears still buzzed from the shotgun blast, David had no idea how close behind them their pursuers were. If they had blasted the barricade apart with one shot, then they could only be the length of a corridor away at most. He plunged down the stairs, only peripherally aware of his companions around him, expecting at any second to miss his footing in the erratic light and fall and break his neck. He desperately wanted to glance back to see if the gang *were* just behind them, but if he did that, then he would stumble on the stairs for sure, unless of course he slowed right down, which at this moment did not seem like a terribly wise idea.

Through the fading buzzing in his ears, he suddenly became aware that people were shouting his name. He felt loath to slow down and turn round, but he had to know what they were shouting for. Twisting, he saw Melanie waving her arms at him, Willie mouthing, 'Git away from the banister! Git away from the banister!' At first David was puzzled, and then, seeing that the others had moved away from the stair-rail, he suddenly understood.

They wanted him to move away from the central banister in case Leather Jacket got the bright idea of pointing the shotgun down the centre of the stairwell and pulling the trigger. Though running down the stairs with nothing to hold on to was going to be treacherous, it was infinitely more desirable than taking the force of a shotgun blast on the top of the head. David veered away from the banister, and almost immediately realised that it was far harder running down the middle of the stairs, unable to rely on the rail for balance, and also slower too. At the bottom of each flight the group had to skid to a virtual halt to take the corner on to the next flight.

David's ears had almost cleared by now. From above he could hear shouted threats, the echoing booms of the gang trying to kick their way out of the barricaded office, the splintering of wood. It was a relief to know that the shotgun blast had not destroyed the barricade, though almost at once there was a mighty crash from upstairs. The whoops of the gang confirmed that the barricade had finally given way. The echoes of their cries as they erupted on to the stairwell seemed to throb down through the darkness like a pulse of air that stirred the hairs on the back of David's neck.

He and the others had already descended six or seven flights, which meant that they probably had a lead of a minute or so. There surely couldn't be many more floors to go before they reached the department store. David imagined the gang members leaping down three or four stairs at a time, using the plastic rail to swing themselves round the sharp corners between flights, gaining on them with each second that passed. Of course, if the worst came to the worst, the group had their abilities to rely on, but it was best to conserve as much energy as possible at this point as their powers were by no means inexhaustible. Yesterday in the pub, Richard had told David that asking someone to use their ability over and over again in a short period of time was like asking an athlete to run one race after another.

Just as he thought this, and of how Richard had told him that using his animis just once in a while exhausted him, David rounded another corner, Willie, Melanie and Imogen just behind him, and his torch-beam picked out Richard and the girl sprawled on the landing of the flight below.

'Who's that?' Richard called, squinting into the light, his voice so tired it blurred the words that he was forcing out between his lips.

'It's us,' panted David, leaping down the stairs towards

513

him. 'What's happened?'

Richard looked exhausted; he could barely keep his eyes open. 'Can't . . . go on,' he wheezed. 'Animis . . . took too much out of me . . .'

The girl was lying across Richard's lap, unconscious, her mind obviously having decided it had had enough trauma for one day.

'Help me get them up,' said Melanie, who had caught up with David and was now crouching down beside him. 'We've got to get them somewhere safe.'

'In here,' Willie said, pushing open one of the glass doors that led into the corridor. 'Come on, quickly.'

David put his torch between his teeth, and then together he and Melanie hauled the girl from Richard's lap and passed her over to Willie, who dragged her through the glass doors into the corridor as Imogen held them open. David and Melanie then heaved Richard to his feet, and half-dragged, half-marched him after Willie and the girl.

The light from the torch clamped between David's teeth showed Willie trying to hold the girl upright with one hand whilst opening an office door with the other. Imogen closed the double doors that led on to the stairwell, then hurried forward to help him. Willie, however, turned his head and hissed, 'No!'

Imogen was taken aback. 'I beg your pardon?'

Instead of answering her, Willie looked at David and Melanie. 'You two prop Richard against that wall there and then the three of you carry on doon. We don't all want to be trapped up here.'

'But –' said Melanie.

'No buts! Just go afore it's too late. We'll try and meet up again later.'

Melanie looked unhappy, but David saw the sense in Willie's argument, and he guessed that she did too. It was pointless all six of them hiding here. Once the gang realised that their quarry had vanished, it would not take them long to deduce why. And then the six of them really would be trapped, with nowhere to head for but the roof, as the gang began working from the bottom up, searching the office complex for them.

He lowered Richard to the floor, spat the torch back into his hand, and said, 'Willie's right. Come on.'

Melanie glanced agonisingly at Richard, but nodded and followed him. Imogen nodded too, though she looked weary, and still pained by her shoulder. David switched off his torch and shoved open the glass doors, and at once the shrieks and roars of their pursuers intensified. Momentarily he froze, thinking that they were too late, that the gang were too close and would spot them emerging from the corridor. It took a push in the back from Melanie to get him moving again. This time they were forced to use the handrail to propel themselves down the winding staircase in order to preserve their slender lead. Three flights further down, the staircase ended abruptly at a pair of large grey double doors. David saw them first, and was dismayed by how sturdy they looked. Praying that they wouldn't be locked, he leaped off the bottom step and hit them with the flats of both hands. He stumbled and almost fell to his knees when they swung smoothly open.

His momentum carried him forward into a clothes-rack which resembled a metal shrub, its branches hung with shirts. Coat hangers, hooks protruding from collars like question marks in place of heads, jangled like wind chimes. David steadied himself and quickly surveyed his surroundings. He was in the menswear section of a large open-plan department store. The dingiest of orange lights, a reflection of the inferno filtering in from somewhere outside, showed him that looters and rioters had had a field day here. The place was a mess, mannequins lying stiffly amid dark mounds of what David hoped were just clothes, display stands and clothes-racks overturned.

Lengths of Christmas tinsel hung like jungle creepers from the ceiling or were strewn about the floor; mirrored columns had been smashed, the carpet sparkling with their shards.

He turned back to see the grey doors, above which was a sign reading OFFICE STAFF ONLY, swinging closed. He caught hold of the handle of the right-hand door and tugged it back open. Melanie was almost at the bottom of the stairs, Imogen half a flight behind her. The gang could be no more than a flight or two above Imogen. 'Come on!' he implored, making a frantic beckoning motion with his hand.

Melanie leaped down the last four steps, David reaching out to break her fall. Imogen arrived at the bottom of the stairs, panting and gasping, seconds later. The three of them stumbled out into the department store, slammed the grey doors behind them, and spent a few frantic seconds pulling overturned clothes-racks and whatever else they could find against the doors. Then they made for the escalator, which was on the far side of the vast room, beneath a sign depicting a large downwards pointing arrow.

As he ran, David felt clothes slithering and glass crunching beneath his feet. Behind him he heard a thud as the first of the gang members reached the bottom of the staircase and threw their weight against the grey doors. The heap of debris clattered and creaked, but held. Whoever had slammed into the door expelled an 'oof' of pain and surprise, which David found gratifying to hear. He even had a fleeting image of a figure juddering back from the door on its heels, like Tom in the *Tom and Jerry* cartoons after being hit by an ironing board.

There was a brief exchange of voices behind the door and then the crash of feet trying to kick it open. The metal barricade squealed and buckled as it fell apart. It took the gang only a matter of seconds to force the doors open and pour through.

'There they are!' he heard someone yell, and the next moment Melanie was barging into him with all her weight, bruising his ribs, slamming the breath from his body, knocking him sprawling into a rack of Fair Isle sweaters.

David's head hit the stem of the rack with a sharp crack. For a second or two he literally saw stars. He knew, somewhere deep in his mind, that he was in terrible danger, that he should be up and running for his life, but he couldn't seem to transfer his urgency into the right sort of energy that would propel his limbs. He was aware, as though in a dream, of his hand flailing, grabbing at material that seemed soft but tough at the same time, like candyfloss that wouldn't tear apart. Then he touched something like ice, and the chill of it seemed to shock him awake. His eyes opened to encounter thick prickly darkness.

A sweater was draped over his face. He clawed it away, trying to work out how long had passed since he had been bundled over. It must have been no more than a few seconds, he realised, for all at once there was a thunderous explosion and a flash of light as the shotgun was discharged for the second time.

The sound tore the last shreds of confusion from his mind, and he understood what must have happened. Melanie had glanced back, seen Leather Jacket taking aim with the shotgun, and had done the only thing possible under the circumstances. Now the shotgun had been fired and David and Melanie were entangled in sweaters, bruised but otherwise unhurt – but where was Imogen? David glanced up, and the first thing he saw was a figure with a missing head.

He felt his throat spasm, but was not sure whether a sound escaped it because the shotgun blast had numbed his ears once more. The headless body was rocking back and forth on its heels, and David was reminded of a scene from the film *Catch 22*, in which the legs of a man chopped clean in half by an aeroplane remain standing for a few seconds before folding gracefully into the sea. For an instant David wondered whether he was looking at Imogen's headless body, still standing upright as though unaware that it was dead.

Almost immediately he realised his mistake. The headless body rocked once more, then came to rest, still standing. Of course, it was a mannequin. It wore a suit, now blackened and partially shredded, and was standing on a podium. How could he ever have believed it was Imogen?

His relief was short-lived. Though his ears still thrummed with the echoes of the shotgun blast, he distinctly heard a voice, buzzing and tinny like an early recording, shout, 'Get the fuckers!'

Fear seemed to reduce his perception once more, to narrow his senses right down. His fall had disorientated him. He had no idea now from which direction the gang was coming, or how close they were. Neither did he know where Melanie was. She might be right beside him, but he didn't feel as though he had the time to look around for her or even to get his bearings. He scrambled to his feet and began to lope away, heading into a shadowy forest of dark bulky shapes, each of which his panic-stricken mind assured him was a crouching figure waiting to pounce.

He rounded a mirrored column, where his own looming reflection startled him, and a lopsided display board hung with ties like dead fish, before he spotted the escalator once more, off to his left. He realised he had been veering towards the right-hand wall and changed direction accordingly. He could hear thudding feet behind him, yells of excitement, of blood-lust. He didn't know whether the sounds were closer now or further away. His chest was hurting again, blood roaring in his ears, his breath rattling in his throat as though sieved through grit.

Behind him he heard someone shout, 'Stop him, Clem, he's heading for the escalators.' He saw movement out of the corner of his eye, and suddenly there was a figure moving into his path, holding something glinting in one of its hands. Desperately David looked round, grabbed something from a rack, and hurled it.

It was a white dressing gown, which billowed briefly like a ghost before dipping towards his would-be assailant. It was only a momentary distraction, but it was enough. As the figure sidestepped, instinctively stabbing out at the garment as though it was a balloon he was aiming to pop, David ran at him with his head down like an American footballer.

His full weight crashed into the teenager's stomach. The teenager folded in half at the waist, his breath rushing out of him. Before he had even landed on his backside, David was plunging towards the escalator. A brief leap of sparks from the topmost step caused David to falter for just an instant, to wonder whether the escalator had somehow become electrified. Then he saw the flash of a knife as it tumbled into the gloom of the floor below, and he hit the metal steps with a shuddering clang and began to leap down them, taking them in threes and fours. About halfway down was a dark huddled shape, a coat or a body which he had to hurdle. He was almost at the bottom when he felt the thumping vibration of pursuit through the metal. He could only hope that Leather Jacket was not at the head of the group.

He looked around in the hope of spotting an exit door or a window, or anything at all that might help him in his plight. Directly in front of him was a mini-optician's, created by the installation of partition walls which were a chain-link of spectacle frames. To his right was the perfume department, or rather what had *once* been the perfume department – now it was little more than a glittering lake of broken glass from which arose the stench of gallons of spilled perfume. It seemed his best bet lay to his left: household appliances, furnishings and kitchenware.

He took the last six steps in one reckless leap, the impact jarring his ankles and shuddering up into his knees. He would dearly have loved a rest but he staggered on, his Bogart flapping behind him. He ran through a corridor of display stands heaped with kettles and crockery, pans and percolators, biscuit barrels, woks and fondue sets. Like the rest of the store, this section too had been prey to vandals and looters – crockery was smashed on the floors, whole shelves cleared of electrical appliances.

David knew that he couldn't run for much longer, knew that if things carried on like this the gang would eventually catch him. Perhaps it would be better to find somewhere to hide while he had the chance, somewhere he could wait out however long it might take for the gang to get bored of searching for him. Certainly, there was an abundance of hiding places in this part of the store. A section of flooring to his right was a maze of washing machines, to his left sideboards of all shapes and sizes vied for attention. Beyond the sideboards was a playground-sized area of beds and bedding. As he moved forward, he noticed a rack of carving knives, each of which was encased in its own plastic sleeve, on a display stand to his left. He grabbed the largest one he could see and dropped it into the pocket of his Bogart.

Then he saw the body.

It was no more than five feet away from him, lying in shadow between two shelving units. It was the body of a plump middle-aged woman lying on her back. Her legs were splayed open, and even in the gloom David could see that her eyes were glaring sightlessly at him, almost bulging from their sockets. She appeared to have been raped and then strangled, though it was just as likely that the two events had happened simultaneously. Her face looked swollen and, in this light, black. Her tongue was protruding from her gaping mouth, and she had a cord tied so tightly around her throat that it made David think of balloon animals, or more particularly of a sausage-shaped balloon that had been twisted in the middle.

He felt sick and saddened and angry, felt the same sense of despair he'd experienced when they had burst into the office upstairs to rescue the girl. Part of him wanted to fall to his knees and give up, to wash his hands of the whole disgusting horror show, whereas the other part wanted to scream out in rage and defiance, to turn on the gang and punish them, hurt them, make them endure the suffering they had inflicted on others.

Of course, he did neither of these things. Instead he ducked into the cover provided by the ample selection of kitchen sideboards. He would have liked to have straightened the woman's legs, pulled her skirt down, given her back what dignity he could, but there simply wasn't time. As he darted along the passageways between the furniture, he couldn't help thinking that somewhere the woman probably had a family – a husband, children – who would be worrying about her now, wondering where she was, hoping she was all right.

He was running along bent almost double, sacrificing a little speed for silence. He could hear the gang somewhere behind him, heard one of them issuing orders to spread out and search. He had reached the bedding section now. He considered diving under a bed, but decided against it. If they came across his hiding place, he'd be trapped. He'd never have time to scramble out, get to his feet and start running again.

Along the far wall, alcoves had been created with partition screens, each of which had been converted into a mock-up of a bedroom, highlighting the different styles of furniture and fabric available. David hurried across to them, weaving between the beds displayed on the shop floor. He winced as his leg brushed against a mattress, causing its plastic wrapping to crackle. He paused momentarily to listen, but the gang gave no indication of having heard the sound. One of the display bedrooms contained a bed that looked big enough to sleep four comfortably and a wardrobe the size of a garden shed, both of which were made of heavy dark-stained wood. The bedding and the curtains framing the pretend window were of a satiny material, edged with elaborate frills and flounces, that shimmered in the gloom. Ellen would have screwed up her face and pronounced the whole effect 'hideous', but the wardrobe was just what David needed. He scurried across to it and pulled it open, gritting his teeth at the horrendously loud click it made. Then he glanced round to ensure he hadn't been spotted, got in and pulled the door shut behind him.

It was so dark that he couldn't even see his hand in front of his face. The darkness smelled of fresh wood-shavings and varnish. He tried to quieten his ragged breathing, to remain as still as possible, because even the slightest sounds he made in here seemed amplified. He imagined the sound of his breathing reverberating through the store, loud as someone sawing wood, leading the gang to his hiding place.

He slipped his hand into the pocket of his Bogart, searching for the reassuring shape of the bottle. At once shock spasmed through his body: the bottle was not there! Frantically he groped through his other pockets, but they were empty of everything but the knife he had picked up, a handkerchief, his wallet and the torch. He checked again in the vain hope that the bottle had somehow eluded him the first time; he even lifted the bottom of his Bogart like a skirt and crumpled it in his hands, just in case the bottle had slipped through a hole into the lining. He checked a third time, then a fourth, unable to believe that the bottle was gone. All at once the air in the wardrobe seemed hot, stifling. The smell of the blood on his coat rose about him, raw and coppery.

He forced himself to calm down, to breathe deeply, and tried to remember when he had last known for sure that the bottle was still in his pocket. It had been at the top of the staircase after rescuing the girl, hadn't it? He thought it most likely that he had lost it when Melanie had slammed into him upstairs knocking him off his feet, though he supposed it could have fallen out of his pocket while he'd been leaping down the stairs or the escalator. The prospect that it might have smashed into a million pieces and lost its power made him go cold inside. He tried to tell himself that if it had done he would have heard it, but he knew that that was not necessarily true; half the time his ears had been throbbing with the echoes of the shotgun blast.

His instinct was to go out and search for the bottle immediately, but of course that would have been suicidal. He reassured himself that even if a gang member came across the bottle he would be unlikely to pick it up. No, the best thing was simply to sit and wait, bide his time, and try not to worry, which of course was easier said than done. At this moment, alone and stuck in a pitch-black wardrobe with nothing but a kitchen knife to defend himself with, David could hardly be blamed for feeling his problems were becoming insurmountable before the task he and the others had set out to achieve had hardly even begun.

Fifteen minutes later, however, he was beginning to think that things just might work out for him here, after all. That was how long he remained in the wardrobe, sweating in the darkness, listening to the gang crashing about outside, getting closer and closer. On more than one occasion he had the almost irresistible urge to fling the doors of the wardrobe open, leap out and flee for his life, but he managed to restrain himself. He was certain he heard other wardrobe doors being opened close by, but miraculously the gang never so much as touched the one he was hiding in. He was holding the knife in his hand by this time, slightly raised so that he could waste no time in slashing down should his hiding place be discovered. He had fumbled the implement from its plastic casing with sweaty trembling hands, and at one point had even dropped the bloody thing, but had somehow managed to catch it between his knees before it hit the wooden floor.

Eventually, after quarter of an hour of almost unbearable tension, he heard someone call out, 'Aw, come on, we're wasting our time here. He's fucked off.' There followed a brief rumbling debate between several gang members, the words of which David couldn't quite catch, and then the sounds of the gang moving away.

When the sounds had faded completely, David breathed a sigh of relief and lowered the knife, which felt fused to his hand. He counted slowly up to one hundred before edging the wardrobe door open. He expected the shop floor to appear lighter after the pitch blackness of the wardrobe, but in fact it was much as he remembered it – gloom and shadows and a jumble of shapes, some recognisable, some indeterminate. He poked his head out and had a good look round before venturing any further, but the place was still and silent. Still holding the knife, he began to retrace his steps, creeping between beds which, bereft of bedding as many of them were, resembled a selection of altars.

He was halfway through the beds when he heard the crackle of plastic somewhere off to his right. It was such a tiny sound that within the split-second it took him to become motionless and attune his hearing to where it seemed the sound had come from, all was silent again. He stood, rigid as though set in cement, heart whacking crazily in his chest, and listened for five, ten, fifteen seconds.

Finally, tentatively, he whispered, 'Melanie? Imogen?'

Just in front of him and off to his right, two figures rose up from where they had been crouching, not quite in silhouette but so dark that they resembled transparent bodies full of thick smoke.

David realised immediately that he had been outwitted. Both figures wore bulky jackets. One had spiky hair and was holding a baseball bat, the other wore a cap whose brim jutted like a beak. The one without the cap whacked the baseball bat into his palm. One of the figures, David wasn't sure which one, said, 'Hello, cunt.'

David turned and ran, and heard the two teenagers bounding after him in pursuit. The chase was nightmarishly slow, because both he and his pursuers had to leap on to and over beds, their feet sinking into mattresses which seemed to absorb their momentum. Even worse was the fact that David's legs now felt like jelly anyway. He wondered whether it would be better to turn and face his pursuers, to fight them, but even as he was considering this, the decision was taken out of his hands.

Something exploded in his right shoulder blade, jerking his arm, sending the knife spinning out of his hand. It felt as if he'd been punched by an enormous fist, with such force that the fist had followed through its blow, embedding itself in his flesh and bone. White-hot pain tore through his right side, then the fist opened, flexing fiery fingers through the rest of his already bruised and battered body. David staggered, the springs in the mattress he had been bounding across conspiring to tip him over. For the third time in the last half-hour he found himself falling, plunging into the space between two beds like a man plunging into a crevasse.

The last thing he saw before the darkness between the beds swallowed him was a giant cigar flipping end over end as it arced through the air. For a split-second he was confused and then all at once the bizarre image made sense: they had thrown the baseball bat at him. It was just luck that they had managed to knock the knife out of his hand. When he hit the floor it felt as though he'd been sealed in a block of pain. Everything hurt, from his teeth to his hips to his ankles. He tried to roll over on to his back, or even under the bed, to make him less vulnerable, but he couldn't seem to persuade his body to obey his instructions. He must have hit his head, for his vision was obscured by a buzzing screen of black static.

Muzzily he was aware of hands on him dragging him upright, dumping him roughly on a bed. He tried to resist, to beat at the hands, but his struggles were ineffectual. He was blinking his eyes constantly, trying to clear them, but it was as though his entire head was stuffed with dust. His hearing was as bad as his vision. Though he could hear the boys' voices, their words were lost amid a mush of distortion.

How long he lay there before his senses started to focus again, flapping at the air, feeling weak and defenceless as a baby, he was not sure, though it couldn't have been more than a few seconds. Yet it seemed like a long time; it seemed as though the black static cleared excruciatingly slowly and only after intense concentration. Likewise his hearing; the first proper words he heard, albeit still fuzzy as bad radio reception, were, 'Here it is.' He had no idea what the 'it' referred to until he heard the other voice say, a bit clearer this time, 'Let's bash his fucking brains out then.'

Like a swarm of cartoon wasps, the static was melding together into recognisable shapes now. David was able to make out two figures looming over him, one of which was raising the baseball bat above its head like an executioner wielding an axe. Still he could not see the two boys' faces, and for that he was oddly grateful. Though he could feel their hatred, their sadistic glee, he didn't want to see it. He tried to shift his strength so he could roll off the bed, but was pinioned easily. He squeezed his eyes shut and prayed that the first blow would kill him instantly to minimise his pain.

Then, only a little distorted this time, he heard someone shout, 'Stop!'

He waited two seconds, still expecting the blow despite the order, then he opened his eyes. The figures, though still in silhouette, were sharper this time. One was still leaning over David, holding his arms above his head, breathing the rank smell of beer and pickle and meat into his face. The other had lowered the baseball bat and was turning towards the new arrival, whom David could only just make out as a dark approaching figure.

The boy holding David released his arms and straightened up, turning towards the new arrival also.

'What's up, Chad?' said the bat-wielder.

Now David could see the figure more clearly. He made out the gleam of his leather jacket.

Before Chad could reply, the kid wearing the baseball cap, the one who had been holding David down, bleated excitedly, 'We got the cunt, Chad. We're gonna splatter his brains up the fucking walls.'

'Shut it,' Chad said. 'If anyone's gonna do any splattering, it's gonna be me.'

'Says who?' said the bat-wielder aggressively, adopting the stance of a fierce dog protecting a bone.

'Says me.' David saw the gleam of the knife which Chad produced and brandished. 'I'm gonna cut the fucker's balls off for what he did to me.'

'Where's the gun?' the bat-wielder said.

'Stanny's got it. We've caught them two birds. Why don't you two go up and get your share while I deal with this wanker?'

'Maybe later,' said the bat-wielder.

'Later'll be too late. You know what Stanny's like.'

'All the same, I'm staying here.'

'I said *I'd* deal with the twat. Are you fucking deaf?'

'We fucking caught him,' said the kid with the baseball cap, who sounded as though he was no more than twelve or thirteen years old.

'I told you to shut it, you little shit,' Chad snapped.

'Why should I?'

'Because if you don't I'll cut your fucking balls off too.'

'Oh yeah, you and whose army?' said the boy, who David noted was taking care to remain shielded behind his bigger, armed companion.

Though still exhausted, bruised and dizzy, David felt a little strength returning to his limbs, his muzzy head clearing bit by bit. His relief at his reprieve had been short-lived when he realised who had ordered it and why, and his spirits had plummeted even lower when Chad had relayed the news of Melanie and Imogen's capture. Nevertheless he had surreptitiously propped himself up on his elbows and was considering whether his legs would be able to respond if he rolled off the bed and made a run for it. They actually felt like tubes of pins and needles held together with bruises, but he had to have a go. Anything was better than lying here listening to his captives decide which of them were going to turn him into dog meat.

'Leave him alone, Chad,' said the bat-wielder, and then he added in a conciliatory tone, 'There's plenty for everyone here.'

Chad shook his head. 'I don't think so.'

'Course there fucking is! I can break the fucker's legs with the bat, we can listen to him scream for a bit, and then you can cut him up while we watch.'

The beak was bobbing in eager excitement, but Chad said, 'I prefer to work alone.'

'Since when?' the bat-wielder exclaimed.

'Since now. So why don't you two just run off upstairs like good little boys and grab yourselves a piece of cunt while it's still fresh.'

The bat-wielder shook his spiky head defiantly. 'No fucking way. We caught the twat, so we're staying.'

'Then you leave me no choice,' said Chad, and moving so swiftly that David barely even saw him do it, he lunged forward and rammed the knife into the bat-wielder's heart.

The bat-wielder's fingers opened, his weapon clattering to the floor. The boy himself remained standing for a good two seconds as though he was unable to believe that his life had been ended so simply and so quickly. Then his legs buckled and he collapsed, his body hitting the floor with the solid abattoir thump of dead meat. Calmly Chad bent and picked up the baseball bat. Both David and the kid wearing the cap gaped at him, shocked into immobility.

As Chad straightened, the kid found his voice and squeaked, 'You've fucking killed him! You've fucking killed –'

He never got the opportunity to finish his sentence. Without ceremony, Chad swung the bat and hit him on the head with it.

The crack of wood on bone was so crisp it reminded David of the sound a cricket bat makes when it impacts perfectly with the ball on a still summer's afternoon. The boy's cap flew off. Poleaxed, he fell without a sound, his upper body crashing on to David's legs, making him yell in pain. Chad tossed the bat on to the bed next to David's, strode forward, grabbed the boy by the scruff of the neck, hauled him off and dumped him unceremoniously on to the floor.

My turn now, David thought, using his hands on the mattress to push himself up against the headboard. His bruised legs were hurting so badly after the boy had fallen on them that he knew he wouldn't even be able to put his weight on them for a few minutes, never mind make a run for it. His only grain of hope came from the fact that Chad didn't now appear to have a weapon. However David fully expected the teenager to produce something large and sharp and gleaming from the creaking folds of his leather jacket.

What Chad did do, however, was very different. He came forward, holding up his hands in what appeared to be a placatory gesture. If this was surprising, what he said then was absolutely astonishing: 'Don't be afraid, David, and whatever you do, don't call out. It's me, Imogen.'

It took a few seconds for the words to register, and then a few seconds more for David to make sense of them. And then all at once it came to him; he remembered that Imogen had the ability to change her appearance, to become anyone that she chose.

'Imogen?' he said wonderingly.

Chad stepped back from the bed, and immediately his form began to alter. His body was virtually in silhouette anyway, but now it seemed a kind of greasy haze was suffusing him, making it difficult for David to focus. It was like watching someone through a not-quite opaque shower curtain. Within the haze, Chad grew taller, thinner. The process took around thirty seconds in all, and then the haze started to clear. David blinked as though the haze had been of his own making, as though it was nothing more than a speck of matter in his eye. All at once, Chad was gone and standing in his place, leaning over him, was Imogen Butterworth.

'Imogen,' David said again, as though feeling the need to confirm the fact to himself.

'How are you?' Imogen said.

'Okay. Well . . . a bit bruised.'

'Can you stand?'

'I think so. Just give me a minute.'

She sat on the edge of the bed, half-turned away from him, looking down at her handiwork, and only now did David notice how much she was trembling. It suddenly struck him what she had done. He didn't know what to do or say, didn't know how to comfort her.

'I know what you're thinking,' she said.

'Do you?' said David, feeling guilty in spite of himself.

'You're wondering how someone like me could be capable of such brutality.'

'No, not at all,' David blustered, hoping she couldn't see him reddening. 'I mean . . . you had to do it, didn't you? You had no choice. You gave them the chance to leave.'

'That's right,' she said in a hollow voice. 'I gave them the chance to leave.' She turned to face him. Though he could barely make out her features, David felt Imogen's eyes on him, scrutinising every nuance of his expression. He got the impression that she was almost hoping to see in his face the disgust and horror she felt sure he must be feeling, that his condemnation was the very least that she deserved.

'Can you stand yet?' she said after a long pause.

David tried. His legs hurt but he managed it. 'Where are we going?'

'We're going to take cover until this nasty little distraction is over. It shouldn't be long now.'

'Why, what's happening? Where's Melanie?'

'She's safe. I left her trying to gather enough strength to use her animis just enough to scare the life out of our little friends.'

'Why? What's she going to do?' asked David. The two of them began weaving their way back through the bedding section towards the kitchenware department, Imogen leading, David hobbling behind.

'Sh,' she said. 'No more questions now. You'll see soon enough.'

They negotiated the forest of kitchen sideboards, passed the dead woman without comment, David averting his eyes from her bloated face, and eventually found themselves back at the bottom of the escalator. From upstairs they could hear the gang moving about, their disgruntled voices. The teenagers were evidently furious that their quarry had got away, and from the sounds of it they were turning the place upside-down, either out of spite or in the hope of discovering a concealed escapee.

Imogen looked around, then said, 'This will do,' and led David over to the optician's stand. A long low L-shaped desk took up one-third of the space. The desk had been studded with computer screens, but now all without exception had been either ripped from their moorings and removed or smashed beyond repair. Imogen and David crouched down behind the desk. From their vantage point they could see almost two-thirds of the way up the escalator. The stink of blended perfume drifted in from their left, making David feel sick.

He commented on the fact that the desk did not provide them with very adequate cover.

'It will do for our needs,' said Imogen. 'Just as long as we can see without being seen.'

'But if they come looking for us, they'll find us easily,' David hissed.

'They won't come looking for us. Not if all goes according to plan.'

David started to ask what would happen if things *didn't* go according to plan, but Imogen shushed him. 'Listen,' she said, 'I think it might be starting.'

David listened. Apart from a few rustles and bumps, it had all gone quiet upstairs. The quiet lasted for perhaps two seconds, and then someone shouted, their voice rising to shrillness at the end of the sentence, 'What the fuck is *going on*?'

A babble of other voices joined in then, panic overlapping panic:

'What are those things?'

'What do they fucking look like?'

'Stand your ground, lads, it's a fucking trick.'

'*Come on, you cunts!*'

'Blast 'em, Chad, blast 'em!'

The shotgun roar swelled, pulsed down the escalator, set David's ears ringing for the third time in less than an hour. On this occasion, because he was further away, the noise cleared comparatively quickly, shuddering out of his head in seconds. From its dying echoes a clamour of voices rose, mostly wordless yells of terror, though David heard someone scream, *'Get out of the fucking way!'*, and another, younger voice, screeching, *'Don't touch me!'* He ducked right down behind the desk as the escalator began to clatter and vibrate with footsteps. Imogen touched his shoulder, and when he looked at her she made a motion with her head to let him know it was safe enough to peek. He did so, and saw a wave of black figures tearing down the metal stairs, shrieking and wailing as if pursued by demons.

The black heap which David hadn't been able to decide was a body or a coat, was trampled underfoot. One of the gang members, barged from behind, slipped and fell. The boy landed at the bottom of the escalator, where he lay, writhing and groaning feebly. The first person who reached him tried to yank him to his feet by his jacket but failed, whereupon the rest just stampeded over him.

Still yelling, the boys, who in their panic seemed to have been reduced to the children that many of them still were, turned right at the bottom of the escalator and ran towards and then through the swamp of broken glass that had once been a perfume department. Glass splintered beneath their feet, the sound providing accompaniment to the shrillness of their screams. David watched them go, listened to their voices fade, and despite all that he had been through, he couldn't help but smile at the thought of the gang trying to act tough out in the streets whilst reeking of Poison and Obsession and Chanel No. 5. He and Imogen rose up from behind the desk. At the foot of the escalator the broken body of the boy who had fallen was sprawled like a rag doll, a black stain expanding beneath his body. Seeing this killed the smile on David's lips.

Staring at the body, David said, 'What frightened them so much?'

If he had had the time to think about it, he would probably have guessed the answer to that question. As if on cue, there was a sound at the top of the escalator, and the hint of a pale misty glow. The sound made David think of someone very old or very infirm descending slowly and tentatively. The glow grew brighter, reflecting off the metal sides of the escalator, turning it to ice. David screwed up his eyes, and saw that the glow was suffusing a figure who was just coming into view. He saw black shiny shoes, rising to a pair of long legs wearing grey pin-striped trousers. The figure took another couple of steps, and now David could see his hands, white and smooth and oddly immobile, poking from the cuffs of a matching grey pin-striped jacket. Still moving stiffly and slowly, as though hampered by arthritis, the figure descended far enough for the rest of him to be revealed.

David took an involuntary step back and gulped out the word, 'Shit.' Above the figure's chest was nothing but a scorched and ragged mess. The figure had no head, just a shifting nub of thick white mist. After the initial shock, David realised that he was looking at the mannequin that had had its head ripped off by the shotgun blast upstairs. Melanie must somehow have managed to find the strength to dredge the sediment of her animis, to bring the thing to life.

The mannequin was about halfway down the stairs now. Behind it, David could see, were at least two others. One was a little boy wearing a raincoat, its bland, vaguely smiling face wreathed in glittering mist; the other was a man wearing brushed cotton pyjamas and a blue and silver Paisley print dressing gown, which moved in an odd

534

crab-like lurch as though its knee-joints were not quite in alignment.

David shuddered and looked at Imogen. 'Creepy, aren't they?' he said.

'But harmless,' she reassured him, and strode to the front of the escalator like a one-woman reception committee for arriving dignitaries. 'It's all right, dear, they've gone now,' she called up.

At once the mist shrouding the mannequins began to dissipate. Imogen stepped aside as the headless figure leading the group tottered for a moment, and then plunged forward. It crashed and bounced down the metal steps, losing a shoe-encased foot and an arm in the process. Its companions quickly followed suit, the little boy sliding down on its face, its head hitting the floor at the bottom with enough force to break its nose off, the pyjama-wearer cartwheeling behind, its dressing gown flapping, its head snapping off and spinning away like a rugby ball ejected from a scrum.

All three mannequins, or at least parts of them, landed on top of the bleeding body of the teenager who had fallen. David winced, and then, when the dust settled, hurried forward. Imogen was already pulling debris away from the boy. When David joined her, she straightened up, rubbing her sore shoulder. David bent down and pulled the teenager gently over on to his back. He felt things shift strangely inside the boy's body, as if there was no support in there, as if his rib cage had been crushed to splinters. He saw immediately that the boy was dead. His eyes were open but lifeless. Most of the blood he was lying in had flowed out of his mouth, and was still doing so. David was no expert on anatomy but he thought that that was probably a sign that the kid's lungs had been torn to shreds.

He stood up, his stomach folding over itself, and stepped back out of the pool of blood he had been crouching in, his shoes making a faint sticky *shluck* noise. Imogen sighed and said, 'Come on,' then began to lead the way back up the escalator. David had blood on his hands. He looked around for somewhere to wipe it, then shrugged and used his Bogart. What the hell, one more stain wouldn't make much difference. Considering what they had been through, his fastidiousness was almost funny.

Halfway up the escalator he confessed to Imogen that he had lost the bottle.

'No you haven't,' she told him. 'Melanie's got it.'

Relief flooded through David. 'Thank God!' he exclaimed. 'Where was it?'

'It fell out of your pocket when Melanie knocked you down. You made such a noise when you jumped up and started running that the gang all converged on you instinctively. That gave Melanie and me a chance to hide and to hurriedly formulate the plan which you have just seen in operation.'

'For a time back there I really thought I was a goner, especially when you showed up as Chad. Thanks for saving my life, Imogen.'

She waved away his gratitude. They had reached the top of the escalator by now. The menswear department looked as though a bomb had hit it. Clothes were strewn everywhere, and seemingly everything that could have been broken or overturned had been.

Melanie was slumped against the wall by the grey doors, head bowed, hair hanging over her face. She looked like a marionette with its strings cut. Even when David spoke her name, she didn't so much as twitch a finger.

'She's exhausted, poor lamb,' said Imogen. David looked at the older woman, who even now exuded an aura of cool gentility. He felt ashamed now of his initial thought that she might turn out to be the weak link in their group. As their ordeal had worn on, she had seemed to grow in stature, to have taken on an air of authority. She had not flinched from being ruthless when she had to be, and though she felt remorse for killing the boys (or boy; David was unsure whether the younger boy had been killed by the blow from the baseball bat or just stunned) she had not allowed it to hamper her. She made David think of an old soldier who had not fought for a long time, but who was now rediscovering the taste for battle. He also noted that using her animis didn't seem to have affected her physically too much.

'You sit here with Melanie, I'll go and fetch the others,' she said, and pushed open the grey doors. David was grateful for the chance to relax for a few minutes. He slumped down beside Melanie with a groan.

He listened to Imogen's footsteps receding, then turned to look at Melanie, who still hadn't moved. He spoke her name, but there was not even the barest flicker of a response. He noticed the neck of the bottle protruding from the triangular space between her bowed back, the wall and the floor. Extracting it almost stealthily, like a pickpocket relieving someone of a wallet, David slid it back into the pocket of his Bogart.

Imogen reappeared a few minutes later with the others and there was a muted reunion. The girl had recovered consciousness now. Willie introduced her as Alison. She was wearing Richard Hodge's jacket, which made her look as small as a child, and she was trembling uncontrollably, evidently traumatised by her ordeal. David sympathised with the girl, but he couldn't help wondering how they were going to be able to cope with her. She said nothing at all, flinched whenever anyone made a move towards her, and stared around with eyes that were both alive with fear and yet so vacant she seemed like a sleepwalker.

Richard Hodge seemed to have recovered a little of his strength at least, though he still appeared tired and sluggish. He crouched down beside his wife, took her head in his hands and tilted her face up towards him. David was shocked by how deathly pale Melanie looked, how tight her flesh seemed, stretched over her skull. She looked ten, even twenty, years older than she was. David couldn't imagine her walking again tonight, let alone using her animis.

'She's out of it,' Richard said. 'There's no way of waking her up in this state. I wouldn't even try.'

Willie nodded gravely, the recipient of unwelcome but not unexpected news.

David looked from Willie to Richard. 'So what does that mean?' he said.

'It means we split up into two groups,' Willie said with a sigh. 'We cannae afford to wait.'

Richard nodded. 'I'll stay here with Melanie. You four go on.'

The girl, Alison, wrapped her arms around herself as if she was cold and shook her head vehemently.

'What is it, love?' Willie said gently.

She looked at him with something like panic in her eyes, her mouth struggling either to find words or allay tears. Finally she whispered, 'I'm not . . . I can't . . .'

'She doesn't want to go outside,' Imogen said. 'That's right, isn't it, dear?'

Alison nodded and whispered, 'Yes.'

'That's all right, she can stay with us,' said Richard. He looked up at Alison and smiled. 'You can help me with Melanie. We'll find somewhere nice and safe to hide until all this is over. Does that sound okay?'

Alison made no immediate comment; she just stared at Richard as if unable to understand the language he was speaking. Then she glanced around, and as though realising she was being spoken to and that some sort of reaction was called for, she gave an abrupt nod.

They spent the next few minutes carrying Melanie up

the stairs and back to the office where Willie, Richard and Alison had been hiding. Once the Hodges and Alison were installed, they said their goodbyes. Richard took David's right hand in both of his and shook it warmly. 'Best of luck, mate,' he said.

'Thanks,' said David. He made a vague gesture around the darkened office. 'Are you sure you'll be okay here?'

'Who can tell?' said Richard. 'Imogen says there's a food department, so we won't starve at any rate. We'll just have to sit tight and see what happens.'

'Yes,' said David, and clapped Richard awkwardly on the shoulder. 'Well . . . see ya. Say goodbye to Mel for me when she wakes up, and tell her it's okay, I've got the bottle.'

'In more ways than one, eh?' said Richard.

'Pardon?'

'Never mind, it's a joke.'

'Oh yeah, I get it. Sorry. Bit slow on the uptake.'

The others said their goodbyes too, Willie crouching down in front of Alison and speaking to her gently and earnestly. David couldn't hear what the little Scotsman was saying, but he assumed Willie was telling her that everything would be okay, that Richard and Melanie would look after her, and that he and his friends were going to get help.

Eventually they were ready to leave. Richard followed them to the landing outside the office like the host of a party seeing guests to the door.

'Hey,' he called as they started down the stairs, 'if I don't see you guys beforehand, have a Merry Christmas, okay?'

43

David, Willie and Imogen had to negotiate the perfume department to find the down escalator that led to the main exit doors. The department store, it turned out, was on four floors, the topmost of which had been the one housing the menswear department. On the way down they found two more bodies, a young man sprawled on his back in a star-shape with a shotgun wound that looked like John Hurt's stomach in *Alien* after the creature had burst out of him, and a woman in a blue suit whose age was impossible to ascertain because of the extent of her facial injuries.

The nearer to street level they got the lighter and noisier it became. The second floor (which was actually labelled 1 on the floor plan they came across, and the one below that labelled G) was bathed in sepia light, the source of which was the down escalator at the far side of the room, beyond the coffee shop and the sports department. From afar the escalator looked like a huge square metal cauldron from whose depths an orange furnace-light pulsed. As they began to descend, David almost expected the metal to be hot to the touch, but it wasn't. If anything, it was colder than it should have been.

The reason for this became obvious when they reached the bottom of the escalator and set foot on the ground floor. The main doors and the huge display windows flanking them had been smashed apart, presumably by ram-raiders, allowing easy access for the cold winter wind that carried the sounds and smells of the night. There was broken glass and debris everywhere, including a ten-foot-tall Christmas tree, which was lying twisted and crushed on the floor like a felled giant, its baubles stomped to powder. The light came from the fires that were raging on Oxford Street, the largest of which engulfed an overturned van on the pavement outside Marks and Spencer's across the road.

Here at street level the noise from outside was horrendous, full of shouts and screams, the crackle of burning, the din of property being destroyed, and an occasional bang that might have been gunshots or distant explosions or the sound of impacting vehicles. People, mainly in groups but occasionally in couples or on their own, were running in all directions like headless chickens. The air was hazy with smoke; the street glittered orange, firelight reflecting off broken glass.

David thought that the scene resembled the aftermath of a city centre IRA bombing he'd seen on TV, only ten times worse. He was about to turn and say something to Willie when the Scotsman grabbed his arm and pulled him back into the shelter of the escalator. David knew better than to question Willie's actions by now. Cautiously he peered around the edge of the escalator.

He saw a group of men stalk past the shattered window, half a dozen in all, rendered nightmarishly pig-like by the gas masks strapped over their faces. Most of the men were carrying guns. Their leader had arms like Arnold Schwarzenegger, and was wearing a sleeveless leather waistcoat unbuttoned over a bare chest. He was completely shaven-headed apart from a ponytail which curled from the back of his skull. One of the men turned his gas-masked head to glance into the store as the group passed, even prodded his gun barrel briefly through the shattered wreckage of the shop's frontage. David drew back into the shadows, heart thumping wildly, hoping he hadn't been spotted. Ten seconds passed, then Willie tapped him on the back.

'Ah think they've gone,' he said.

David expelled the breath he had been holding. 'Why were they wearing gas masks?'

'Mah guess'd be that the military have been using tear gas ti try and clear the streets.'

'Doesn't seem to have worked,' said David.

'Tear gas disperses relatively quickly, and the rioters are far too persistent,' said Imogen.

'So what happens if *we* get bombarded with tear gas?' David asked.

'We run the other way,' replied Willie.

Imogen who had been crouching beside Willie, stood up. 'Ah well,' she said, 'once more into the breach.'

They left the shelter of the escalator and made their way to the mangled main exit doors, their feet crunching on broken glass. On the way David picked up a plastic figure wearing a gown sprinkled with silver-blue glitter. It was the fairy from the top of the Christmas tree, its crushed body tattooed with a smudged boot-print. He tossed the fairy aside and joined Willie, who was looking out into the street.

Few of the people running up and down Oxford Street seemed to be doing anything purposeful. Even the gas-masked gang, still visible some two hundred yards away, seemed to be doing little more than swaggering along, guns cocked, like extras in a post-apocalypse science fiction movie. Maybe most of the people here were just trying to get home or looking for a place of safety, running simply because it made them feel they had more chance of avoiding trouble. There was a disturbance involving maybe twenty people taking place further along the street, but the action was distorted by the smoke and haze of a number of small fires burning between here and there, and David couldn't see whether the apparent violence was being perpetrated against people or property.

There was no sign of the police or military forces, though David realised on closer inspection that the van burning across the street was actually a Black Maria. Just as they had seen on the motorway earlier, wrecked and abandoned vehicles, including at least three buses and numerous black cabs, were scattered around like toys.

'Which way?' David asked, raising his voice above the bedlam.

'Left,' shouted Willie, 'and in case we get separated, which we won't but in case we do, take a right when you get ti Portman Street. Okay, ready?'

David and Imogen nodded, and they plunged into the melee. David almost expected to be set upon instantly, expected people to stop and point them out as somehow different to everyone else. However they were largely ignored, though two teenagers who might or might not have been part of the gang in the department store, shouted something at them which David didn't quite catch but which he gathered from their attitude was some form of threat or goad. They ignored the teenagers, gave them a wide berth, and were not pursued.

They weaved across the street between small fires and mounds of debris. On the central reservation, David noticed with grim amusement that Willie, leading the group, glanced right and left out of habit before stepping off the kerb. They were just coming to the turning on to Portman Street when David heard the hacking of helicopter blades somewhere above them and he looked up. The air was too hazy to see anything, however, and the sound quickly faded. Next moment, from somewhere behind them, came a massive explosion. All three of them flung themselves to the ground and covered their heads.

David felt a hot breeze pass over his back. The echoes of the explosion, accompanied by the thin jagged carillon of breaking glass, seemed to go on and on. Eventually he removed his hands from his head and looked up at his companions. 'Everyone okay?' he asked. Willie and Imogen both nodded. The three of them clambered painfully to their feet, dusting themselves down. David was aching all over.

The explosion, whether caused by bomb or gas leak or electrical fault, had happened close to where the disturbance had been taking place just minutes before. The buildings there had now been consumed by a mountain of flame which clawed at the night sky as if to tear the darkness apart. Even from here, David could feel the heat of the fire on his face. All around people were standing and staring at the conflagration, their own concerns momentarily forgotten. David was not sure, but he thought he could see black stick-like figures capering at the base of the fire as if in celebration. He was screwing up his eyes, trying to make sense of them, when Willie touched his arm and said, 'Come on, son, let's go.'

They left Oxford Street behind, turning right into Portman Street, which was quieter and cooler, though not much. Somewhere along the way, Portman Street became Gloucester Place, a bland thoroughfare of furniture showrooms and big hotels. Most of the people here were running past them, towards Oxford Street, evidently eager to see what had caused the big bang. Most of those that weren't were standing in a semicircle like a street theatre audience, watching two teenagers kicking in the window of a shop selling designer fashions.

They walked on, unchallenged and unmolested, and ten minutes later came across the eerily silent remains of what had evidently been a pitched battle between police and rioters. A barricade, now half-demolished, had been erected using lengths of timber, sheets of corrugated metal, guttering, furniture, trees, cars, suitcases, doors, rolls of carpet, baths, garden statues, parking meters, paving slabs, and a thousand and one other items, which had been pilfered from the buildings round about or stripped like flesh from the bones of the surrounding area. The human debris of the conflict was scattered on the street like items planted on a battlefield by war photographers to achieve poignancy. There were shoes, earrings, handbags, spectacles; knives, broken bottles, tear gas canisters, rocks. There were two policemen's helmets, a discarded riot shield like a car windscreen, and, inevitably, a few guttering fires. All that was missing were the people themselves, the dead and wounded, which in a way made the scene even more eerie. David guessed that they had been removed either by their friends or the authorities, though where they had been taken was anybody's guess.

The three of them walked the length and breadth of the barricade, looking for a place where they might climb over without the whole lot collapsing on them. They eventually decided that their best bet was a section in which most of the space was taken up by a black cab with a crumpled bonnet. Stacked around the cab, in a kind of wigwam arrangement, were wooden beams and lengths of guttering which had been overlaid with mattresses and sheets of tarpaulin. David suggested that rather than climbing over, they could actually go through the barricade via the doors of the cab.

They tried the door nearest to them, which, though unlocked, was jammed into its frame, presumably by whatever accident had befallen the vehicle. Working together, the three of them heaved at the door, David's bruised and battered muscles and bones crying out in protest. At first nothing happened, but then the door came open with a grinding screech, so suddenly that Willie lost his grip and staggered backwards before plumping unceremoniously on to his backside. David and Imogen stepped back hastily as the barricade creaked and shivered above them.

After a moment, to their relief, the barricade settled, although something small and hollow and made of metal (in his mind's eye, David pictured a watering can, of all things) bounced and clattered to the ground somewhere over the other side. 'You all right?' David said, offering his hand to Willie and hauling him to his feet.

The little Scotsman ruefully brushed the seat of his pants. 'Bruised ma pride, that's all,' he muttered.

Imogen was stooping to peer into the taxi cab. 'It seems safe enough now,' she said. 'Shall I go first?'

'Perhaps I'd better,' said David. 'The door might be stuck on the other side too. It might need someone to kick it open.'

'And you think I'm incapable of that do you, young man?' Imogen said sweetly.

David felt himself blushing. 'Well, no, I just thought . . .' He shrugged, his voice tailing off. Imogen patted his arm.

'I appreciate your chivalry, David, but I could always change into . . . oh, what's his name . . . Sylvester Stallone, if I have any problems.'

David smiled defeatedly, and waved a hand at the open cab door. 'Point taken,' he said. 'After you.'

Imogen climbed into the cab, moving as cautiously as she could so as not to disturb the material stacked above it. She slid along the worn leather seat to the far door and tried the handle. The door came open a little way and then jammed. She pushed harder and the door juddered open far enough for her to squeeze through. Above the cab, the barricade creaked once more. David looked up at it, holding his breath. Once again, after a moment or two, it settled and David breathed a sigh of relief. Seconds later, he and Willie had slid themselves through the cab and out the other side.

Ahead of them, still some minutes, walk away, was the end of the road which led to the outer circle of Regent's Park. The park itself was a lightless bulk on the horizon. Here on this side of the barricade all was gloom and shadows, many of the street lights having been smashed, some having even been uprooted to use in the barricade, leaving gaping holes in the concrete. Apart from the devastation, and the sound of a single burglar alarm pealing forlorn and ignored from the depths of a violated antiques shop up ahead, it was hard to believe that the city, indeed the country and beyond that, the world, was in a state of riot-torn crisis. There was no sign of life here, though distantly, underlying the alarm bell, David could still hear the clamour of the crowds on Oxford Street. Elsewhere in the city, he knew, full-scale riots were taking place, but here there was a sense of stillness; if it hadn't been for the alarm bell, he might even have said tranquillity.

A huge hotel to their right was a facade of smashed windows, most of whose rooms beyond were in darkness. The canopy over the main doors hung like a torn flap of skin from a wounded face. Daubed in white across the front of the hotel, in letters the size of a man, were the words, THIS IS GOD'S HOUSE, and beneath that, NO HERETICS OR ATHEISTS BEYOND THIS POINT. Ten yards further along, painted on the road, stretching from one pavement to the other, was another slogan: REVELATION IS NOW.

'As in Book Of, I suppose,' David said.

Willie nodded and gestured at the hotel. 'God's hoose. Mebbe we ought ti call on the old feller and ask him to clear up this bloody mess for us.'

They started forward, but had gone no more than a few steps when a megaphone-amplified voice boomed, 'What do you believe?'

David jumped. The three of them looked around wildly. Imogen pointed up at the hotel. 'There,' she said.

It took David a moment or two to see what she was pointing at. Then he noticed a lozenge of rust-coloured light sliding across the megaphone that a man in a darkened window three floors up was raising once more to his face.

'What do you believe?' the man repeated.

David glanced round at his companions, then yelled back, 'What do you mean?'

The man paused as if David's reply had surprised him. Then he demanded, 'Who sent you to us?'

Once more David looked at his companions, but they seemed determined to remain tight-lipped. Willie raised his eyebrows as if to say, 'Carry on, son, you're doing fine.'

David looked back up at the man and shouted, 'No one sent us. We're just passing through.'

Again the man paused, and David wondered whether he was conferring with someone. Then he said, 'Go back to where you came from with our blessing.'

David pointed towards Regent's Park. 'We're going this way.'

'Turn back now. This is God's country. Only the righteous may follow His path.'

'Hallelujah,' muttered Willie.

'Says who?' David shouted, starting to feel like a schoolboy in a playground squabble.

'It is His word. It cannot be denied,' boomed the man.

'Yes, well, we're going this way,' David repeated dismissively and started to walk forward.

'Only the righteous may follow His path,' the man warned again.

Imogen stepped forward. 'Who exactly *are* the righteous, young man?'

There was another pause, longer this time, before the man replied. Then he said, 'These are they who have come out of the great tribulation. They have washed their robes and made them white in the blood of the Lamb.'

'I think he's quoting from the Book of Revelation,' Imogen muttered to David and Willie. Then, raising her voice again, she shouted, 'We've come to do God's work. You have to let us pass.'

Another pause. Then the man boomed, 'Wait there.'

They saw his silhouette melt into the shadows behind it as he turned from the window. 'What now?' David wondered.

'I'd guess he, or they, are coming down to talk to us,' said Imogen.

'Well, let's just scarper then before they get here.'

Imogen looked around. 'I'm not sure that that's a terribly good idea. They might have set up an ambush ahead. I think it's wise to be cautious. Don't you agree, Willie?'

Willie was peering about him, apparently preoccupied. 'What? Oh, aye,' he agreed.

David put his hand into his pocket and gripped the bottle nervously as people suddenly started pouring out of the hotel and coming towards them.

At their head was a man who resembled a down-at-heel Mormon. He had red-rimmed eyes, a thin stubbled face, and he wore a grubby suit over a white shirt and thin dark tie. His grin was too wide, revealing all his teeth and a greyish-pink expanse of gum. David assumed that he had been the man with the megaphone, but realised his mistake when the man spoke.

'Greetings, friends,' he said in a soft Texan drawl.

'Good evening,' replied Imogen. David and Willie murmured in the background.

'I understand we have a little problem here,' the American said, clasping his hands together and rubbing them as if relishing the prospect of solving it.

'I hope not,' Imogen replied. 'My friends and I just want to pass through this area. We have no intention of disturbing anyone or of causing trouble.'

The Texan's smile widened. 'I'm sure you don't, ma'am. The thing is, these few streets around here have been declared God's country now. It's the divine duty of myself and my brothers and sisters here to protect this area.'

'Divine duty?' David blurted scornfully, which earned him a warning frown from Imogen.

The Texan swept him a dark glittering glance. 'I wouldn't expect *you* to understand,' he said silkily.

Far more politely, Imogen said, 'May I ask who you're protecting this area from?'

The Texan turned his attention back to her. His movements were slow, deliberate, very concise. Perhaps he was simply sluggish from drink or drugs, but David got the impression that beneath his lethargic exterior he was poised and alert, like a snake conserving its energy before striking.

'From the unworthy who bring plague and unjust violence,' he said. 'From sinners who see fit to sully the Lord's kingdom.'

'The Lord's kingdom!' David exclaimed, unable to help himself. 'This is central London.'

'The Lord's kingdom is wherever He wishes it to be,' the Texan said smugly.

Imogen held up her hands placatingly. 'We appreciate what you're telling us, Mr . . .?'

'*Brother* Joseph.'

'Brother Joseph, but let me assure you that we are not sinners. Indeed, quite the contrary. We are here to do the Lord's work too. He told us that if we came this way, you would grant us safe passage.'

The Texan stepped forward until his face was no more than a few inches from Imogen's own. In a voice so quiet that even David, standing beside Imogen, could barely hear it, he murmured, 'Don't bullshit me, little lady. Just get the fuck out of here now or I swear you'll regret it.'

Imogen was momentarily shocked, and then a look of understanding passed over her face. 'I see,' she said, and then raising her voice she declared, 'This man is deceiving you all. Don't listen to him. He's no more a mouthpiece of God than . . . than I am.'

There were murmurs of discontent among the sixty or seventy previously silent acolytes gathered behind Brother Joseph, a restless ripple of movement like a wind ruffling the surface of a calm sea. David focused upon individuals in the silent mass of people for the first time: a thin man with pale, almost translucent skin, bright red lips and a lean, predatory face; a round-faced girl wearing a tasselled skirt and sandals; a young man with bad skin, long straggly hair, spectacles and stooped shoulders; a fat woman with hennaed hair and a black t-shirt bearing the slogan JESUS SAVES.

None of these people looked as if they were prepared to listen to what Imogen had to say. They looked too scared, too desperate for something to believe in, for something that would provide them with a sense of security, comradeship, meaning.

From the middle of the crowd, a woman shouted, 'Why don't you go away and leave us alone?' Her words were met with cries of agreement and support.

'We're happy to do that,' David said. 'Just let us pass through here and I swear you'll never see us again.'

The Texan stepped back, a sneer on his face. Half-turning to his followers but keeping his eyes fixed on David, he called, 'This smells to me, brothers and sisters, of subterfuge, and subterfuge, as we all know, is the Devil's work.'

Another cry of agreement went up from the crowd. Trying to raise his voice above it, David shouted, 'We only want to pass through. What are you afraid of?'

The Texan was getting into his stride now. He adopted a dramatic stance, pointing a rigid finger at David. 'Don't be taken in, brothers and sisters. Stand firm. Take up arms and join me in fighting the fight of the just. For remember, if anyone's name is not found written in the book of life, then he will be thrown into the lake of fire!'

The roar of support this time was akin to that of a

football crowd. David wondered how people could be so gullible, how they could allow themselves to be ensnared by such a transparently obvious shyster as 'Brother Joseph'. There were, of course, examples throughout history of vast crowds of people being manipulated by an unscrupulous few for political, social, religious or monetary gain. The fact that most of the people here seemed frightened and desperate didn't make them any less dangerous. Indeed, on the contrary, their gullibility reduced them to so much putty in Brother Joseph's hands, turned them into puppets whose strings he pulled.

'Let us show these sinners our power!' Brother Joseph roared.

David saw half a dozen long wooden boxes, like rough-hewn children's coffins, being passed over the heads of the crowd and dumped on the ground behind the Texan. As if primed, a number of people peeled away from the main body of the crowd, crouched down and began to slide the lids off the boxes. David saw, packed in shredded newspaper, the black gleam of weaponry. He knew very little about guns, though enough to realise that there was some serious hardware here. A couple of the boxes contained machine-guns, a couple handguns, and there were also a couple that contained what looked like police assault rifles. As these weapons were distributed, Brother Joseph reached into his jacket, pulled out a handgun and pointed it in their general direction. It was a small fat snub-nosed thing; David stared into the blind eye at the end of the barrel, his hand tightening on the bottle in his pocket, fear attuning his senses.

Brother Joseph brandished the gun like a bad guy in a TV movie, but his acolytes, for the most part, looked uncomfortable, as if they had been asked to hold large wriggling fish rather than cold inert tubes of metal.

'Go in peace,' Brother Joseph shouted, which would have been funny if the situation hadn't been so threatening.

David reached out slowly, reluctant to make any sudden moves, and touched Imogen's arm. 'I think it might be wise to do as he says.'

Imogen seemed ready to agree, but just then David became aware of Willie, who had been hanging back and remaining silent throughout the exchange, stepping forward. He turned to speak to the little Scotsman, but instead he recoiled, the words drying in his throat.

Something had happened to Willie's face. His eyes had become flat, silvery, like metal coins, but more nightmarish still was the maroon birthmark at his throat, which was coiling and throbbing as if something was about to burst from it. David realised almost immediately that Willie was drawing on his animis, but that didn't make the sight any less shocking. He stepped aside, anxious not to get too close, as Willie began to walk forward, between David and Imogen, towards the crowd, his steps slow and steady and precise as a tightrope walker.

The effect of Willie's appearance on the crowd was immediate and dramatic. Brother Joseph's eyes and mouth opened in wide O's of horror. All the strength seemed to drain from him and he fell to his knees, the gun swivelling around on his index finger, then dropping off and plumping to the ground. He began to mutter to himself. David couldn't quite hear what he was saying, but thought he might be praying. The Texan slumped forward and prostrated himself on the pavement, arms outstretched like a bank robber caught and surrounded by armed policemen. Face pressed to the tarmac, he began wailing, 'I didn't mean it, I didn't mean it, please don't hurt me, I'm sorry.'

Behind Brother Joseph, others were also dropping to the ground, splaying themselves as he was; some were even crying like children. Guns were clattering to the floor all over the place. For ten long seconds, as this was going on, David gritted his teeth, hoping none of the guns would discharge accidentally. Some of the acolytes took to their heels, seeking the dubious sanctuary of the hotel. One man was lying on his back, arms reaching up, legs pedalling the air, staring at the sky with twitching eyes as if the moon had driven him mad.

Willie, still walking slowly and deliberately, cut a swathe through the throng. David and Imogen followed some half-dozen paces behind. David noticed that a number of the men were tearing their shirts open, revealing upper bodies on which were carved large crucifixes, black-red with crusted blood, the vertical spar stretching from throat to navel. Women were showing him their palms which were scarred in similar fashion. David assumed that the Texan had ordered this self-mutilation as a sign of devotion, of total commitment to his cause. With a flash of intuition, it suddenly occurred to him why the women had carved crucifixes on their hands rather than their chests. Could it be because the Texan didn't want their bodies spoiled? Because he had been anticipating a community in which he, as leader, could make love to a different woman every night?

People were pleading with Willie, or moaning incoherently as he passed through them. David glanced back and saw that Brother Joseph was now whimpering and curled up in a ball like an injured dog. This was a mini-version of what David had always imagined hell to be like – Satan striding majestically through crowds of suffering people who were begging for mercy. The whole scene gave him the creeps. He was glad when they came out on the other side of the crowd and continued walking, towards Regent's Park. He glanced back a number of times to ensure they weren't being followed. Gradually the cries of the faithful died away behind them.

The silver light faded slowly from Willie's eyes. His

birthmark settled, became nothing more than a patch of discoloured skin once again. David looked at him, and tentatively asked, 'You okay?'

Willie nodded slowly. 'Aye. A wee bit tired, but that's all.'

They walked on, and minutes later reached the outer circle of Regent's Park. All seemed quiet here, and relatively untouched by recent events. They made their way into the park itself, coming out on the path beside the boating lake. There was just a hint of smoke on the breeze that ruffled the skin of the lake and cavorted in the park's wide open spaces. Apart from this, and the fact that the park seemed utterly deserted, it might have been any normal day. David didn't know whether the park's walkways were normally lit in the evening, but the whole place was certainly pitch-black now. The only way you could distinguish the water from the land was by the hazy reflection of the moon floating on the lake's surface. David listened hard, but heard only a murmur, a suggestion of sound from somewhere that seemed far, far away.

They started walking around the perimeter of the lake, their intention being to cut through the park and make their way through Camden and Kentish Town and Tufnell Park and Archway, and hence to their destination. They didn't talk much. David felt tired and full of aches and pains. He knew they had a long way to go yet, perhaps a good hour or two of walking ahead of them. It was a daunting prospect, but if they could avoid trouble he wouldn't mind the distance. It would allow his nerves to settle a little before the final onslaught, allow him to get his head together. He'd been through so much this past hour that he felt on the verge of shaking apart, both physically and mentally.

The boating lake was vaguely Y-shaped. There were bridges across each of its three narrowest points. From the air, the bridges might have resembled strips of tape holding the blue water to the earth. David and his companions were approaching the bridge at the top left-hand stem of the Y when David got a sudden and intense urge to pee. It was ages, he realised, since he had last done so.

He looked across at Imogen and Willie. Willie's face was drawn and gaunt. Imogen kept rubbing the shoulder she'd wrenched when she'd been holding hands with David and he'd fallen escaping from the gang in the office block.

'I'm just stopping for a minute,' he told them. 'Call of nature. You go on.'

Willie nodded. 'We'll wait for you on the other side of the bridge.'

David watched Willie and Imogen trudge into the darkness, then he turned and unzipped his fly. His stomach muscles hurt as he pissed a long steady stream into the grass. They'd hurt a hell of a lot more tomorrow, once the ache had really rooted itself – if he managed to live to see tomorrow, that was. He was standing sideways on to the lake, gazing absently into a clump of trees which might have been a mound of coal for all he could tell in this light, when something large and silent slid across the shadowed area at the base of a trunk and was gone.

It was actually only an impression of something, and barely even that, but it was enough of a shock to tighten his stomach muscles so abruptly they hurt and to cut him off in mid-stream. David stood absolutely still for a moment or two, breath suspended, looking and listening hard. Whatever had been there, if anything, did not reappear, however, and after fifteen seconds or so he relaxed enough for his waterworks to sputter back into life.

When he had finished, he zipped himself up and hurried to join Willie and Imogen, whom he could see waiting like standing stones on the far side of the bridge. He looked all around him as he did so, imagining now, of course, that there was constant movement at the periphery of his vision. A breeze sprang up and scampered across the surface of the lake with a sound like the riffling of pages in a book. He hurried across the bridge, trying not to look spooked.

'Better?' Willie asked.

David nodded and tried to make his voice as casual as his smile. 'A great relief.'

'Is something the matter, David?' Imogen said.

His smile was genuine, albeit rueful, this time. 'God, I'll never win an Oscar, will I?'

He told them what he thought he'd seen, chiding himself as he was doing so for his vivid imagination.

'It might have been a person,' Willie said, looking around. 'We'd do well ti keep an eye open.'

David shook his head. 'It wasn't a person. It was too big, it moved too quickly, too smoothly.' He shivered despite himself, then said firmly, 'It was just a shadow.'

'All the same,' said Willie. He looked around, the wind ruffling the hair that jabbed from beneath his cap. 'Come on. We'd best keep moving.'

They started forward again, taking the path that would lead them past the bottom right-hand corner of the zoo and out through Gloucester Gate at the top. The wind was really picking up here, flattening the grass, making foliage shake as if occupied. David felt as if the three of them were walking in the centre of a black bowl, though he knew it was only his imagination that made him think the darkness was sloping up on all sides.

They all saw it this time. They were perhaps five or six hundred yards beyond the lake when something big and black crossed their path, perhaps fifty yards ahead. Again to David it had been little more than an impression of movement; he'd been blinking into the wind and only looked up when Willie gasped, 'Will you look at that!'

557

'What was it?' David whispered. To him the thing had appeared a formless mass, something made of darkness that moved quickly, without sound.

'Something big,' Imogen murmured.

'An animal,' added Willie.

All three of them were stationary now, looking around, drawing together unconsciously into a huddle.

'What sort of animal?' whispered David.

Willie pulled a face to show that he wasn't really sure. 'A big cat, mebbe. Something like that.'

Imogen put a hand on David's arm, making him jump a little. 'Listen,' she hissed. 'I think it's circling us.'

David listened, but after a few seconds confessed that all he could hear was the wind in his ears.

'Me too,' said Willie.

'I can't hear anything now either,' Imogen admitted, 'but just for a moment I'm certain I heard padding footsteps somewhere off to the left.'

They all turned and peered at the place where she thought the footsteps had come from, but saw nothing but blackness. David narrowed his eyes, as if that would somehow enable his vision to slip between gaps in the dark. They stood there for perhaps thirty seconds, watching and listening, before David said, 'Maybe it's gone.'

'Och, we're just being daft,' said Willie, raising his voice above a whisper. 'It was probably just a dog we saw. If it comes back, I'll soon see it off wi' this.'

He walked forward a few paces and stooped to pick up part of a tree branch that was lying in the grass beside the path. As he did so, there was an almighty roar and something erupted out of the darkness on his right.

Whatever it was, it was twice the size of Willie. It cannoned into him, knocking him off his feet. David saw huge claws slashing out at the little Scotsman. There was a sound of tearing cloth and Willie screamed, then came a thud as he kicked out at the creature, his foot connecting with its ribs.

The creature twisted, enraged. It was huge and powerful, but so lithe and quick that its movements were a blur. It flowed over Willie like oil – oil that was a tarnished golden colour. Impossible as it seemed, David realised that the creature attacking Willie was a lion.

'*David!*' Imogen screamed, so close to his ear that he jerked his head away in pain. '*The bottle! Make the bottle work!*'

David put his hand into his pocket and groped at the bottle with fingers that seemed clumsy as chopsticks. Feeling as though he was moving in slow motion and unable to do a thing about it, he dragged the bottle out and held it in front of him. He tried to channel all his energy and emotions into the vessel in his hand, but for long agonising seconds nothing happened. He concentrated hard, concentrated until his head began to pound, but it was as though his emotions were a raging sea hurling themselves ineffectually at a colossally sturdy flood barrier.

'*Come on, David! Come on!*' Imogen screamed.

'I'm trying,' David muttered, 'but nothing's happening.'

Had he used the bottle too much already? Had its power faded, and with it their chance of victory? Perhaps the chaos around them was sapping the bottle's energy, stifling it.

'*Make the bottle protect you!*' Imogen screamed at him.

Was that the answer? Did the bottle only respond when he was in danger? Before he could stop to consider the consequences, he launched himself at the lion. He sprawled over its back, grabbed hold of its mane and tried to pull it away from Willie. Up this close the lion's mane was coarse and hot and smelled musky. The power of the beast was incredible. David's free hand slid over the creature's muscled shoulder, felt the surging piston-beat of its heart. The lion twisted, lightning fast, beneath him, and suddenly he was on his back on the ground, his world filled with the thunder of its roar, its dense meaty breath.

He turned his head away, closing his eyes, and shoved the bottle up towards its maw. Almost at once he felt the familiar surge inside him, felt himself magnified, felt energy squirting through the gaps in the now-crumbling wall. The bottle sputtered with light, then began to glow and finally to blaze; David was aware of it as an umber sunrise behind his eyelids. Cautiously he opened his eyes and the light flooded into them, momentarily painful as bleach. Although not as bright as on previous occasions, the light had engulfed the lion, flowed over it like molten metal. David saw the vaguest hint of the creature squirming within its sac of radiance, like an embryo in a womb.

Shakily, still holding the bottle out like a weapon, he rose to his feet. Beside him, on the ground, Willie was moaning and moving feebly, his left arm a ragged mess. Imogen hurried across to tend to him, pale as a ghost in the bottle's already waning light. The lion had stopped struggling now and seemed to be lying down, perhaps accepting its fate, perhaps deprived of strength, or even of life, by the bottle.

The light faded rapidly. It had burned for perhaps thirty seconds, certainly no longer. David felt drained of energy; his head throbbed like a hangover. The glow faded from around the lion, and David saw that it was lying on its side, its ribs rising and falling as it slept. It was a massive, beautiful, terrifying creature. Its paws, big as tennis rackets, were covered in Willie's blood.

David shoved the bottle into his pocket and crouched down beside Willie. The little Scotsman was still moaning, still struggling, as though in a desperate battle to stave off unconsciousness. Imogen was trying, unsuccessfully, both to calm him and to stem the flow of blood from his wounds with a handkerchief. She might as well have tried blocking up a burst pipe with tissue paper. Willie was leaking like a punctured paddling pool. The handkerchief was already bright red and sopping.

'Hold this here,' she told David, indicating the sodden rag. Her hands, too, were gloved with Willie's blood.

'We need something bigger than a handkerchief,' David said.

'I'm perfectly aware of that. If you hold this here and press down hard, it will give me the chance to take off my slip.'

David did as he was asked. He could smell Willie's blood, like hot oily copper.

'Press hard,' Imogen told him again. 'I think an artery's been severed. If you relieve the pressure he'll spray like a fountain.'

It was tough holding on to Willie, and within seconds David's arms were aching. The handkerchief was slippery as a fish, and what made his task even more difficult was that Willie was still wriggling like one. Bubbles of saliva were fizzing from the Scotsman's mouth; his eyes were half-open but showing only the whites. Bizarrely he was still wearing his tartan cap. His arm looked like a joint of raw meat that had been chewed by a dog.

Imogen reached under her long skirt and pulled down her slip. Though the material looked thin and flimsy, it took a good twenty seconds of gritted teeth and straining muscles before she managed to tear it. Then she was down on her knees again beside David, tying the makeshift tourniquet around Willie's ruined arm. She did it quickly and skilfully. Her hands, though long and graceful, seemed very strong.

'There,' she said, 'that should do it.'

'Is he going to be all right?' David asked.

Imogen expelled a long breath and raised her eyebrows. 'He's lost a lot of blood and is going to keep losing it, despite our efforts. If we could get him to a hospital he'd be right as rain, but of course that's impossible.'

David knew she didn't just mean because their priority was to complete their mission. Hospitals had been high on the rioters' hit list. The health service, like everything else, had been torn apart, as a result of which hundreds, perhaps thousands, of people who wouldn't normally have died – from heart attacks, strokes, illness, injuries like Willie's – were going to because of the lack of medical treatment.

'What shall we do?' David said, feeling completely at a loss. 'We can't just leave him here.'

'We might have to,' said Imogen. When David looked at her, aghast, she added in a softer voice, 'I know. I don't like this any more than you do, David. I'm very fond of Willie. We've been friends for a long time. But he wouldn't expect us to jeopardise everything for his sake, not when we can do so little to help him anyway. If it was me, I'd feel the same. I'd want you – I'd *expect* you – to go on.'

David knew she was right, though the prospect of abandoning a wounded friend sickened him. 'We can give him a bit more time at least, though, can't we?' he said.

'A bit more,' Imogen conceded reluctantly, 'though not much. If the light from the bottle was seen it could bring them to us, if they don't already know we're here.'

'The Flux?'

She nodded.

David shivered and looked around, half-expecting to see their enemies rise up from the ground like the skeleton warriors in *Jason and the Argonauts*.

'Shall we move him?' he said. 'Find some cover?'

'I don't really see the point. If they do come looking for us, I don't suppose hiding behind a bush will fool them for a moment. Do you?'

'Suppose not,' said David. 'We'll just . . . wait here then.' He sat down, cross-legged, on the ground beside

Willie. Already Willie's blood had soaked through the tourniquet. David wiped his hands on the grass, which got rid of most of the blood that was on them, though not its stickiness.

'I guess the lion must have come from the zoo,' he said after a minute or so of silence, looking across at the great cat which was still sleeping peacefully.

'Yes, it must have escaped or been set free – the latter, I suspect. I wonder how many other wild creatures are roaming around here.'

'That's a comforting thought,' said David.

'Isn't it,' said Imogen.

The two of them lapsed into silence once more, too exhausted to speak.

They had been sitting there for ten minutes, during which David became increasingly anxious that Imogen was about to say they couldn't give Willie any more time, when the little Scotsman started to stir. He'd been moaning intermittently since the lion had concussed him, or since the pain and shock of its attack had driven him to seek unconsciousness, but this time he actually seemed to be trying to form words. David tipped himself forward on to his knees and, supporting himself on his arms, leaned over the Scotsman.

'Willie,' he said. 'Willie, can you hear me?'

Willie's eyes opened but appeared unfocused. He blinked sleepily, like an old tortoise coming out of hibernation.

'Willie, it's me, David. Can you hear me?'

Willie's gaze seemed to latch on to his voice and he stared up at David for a moment, face expressionless as a baby's. Then his wrinkled mouth tilted into an attempted grin.

'Did ah win?' he murmured.

'Win?' David glanced at Imogen and raised his eyebrows. 'Win what?'

'The fight, o' course. Ah had him on the ropes, ah know that. Then everything went a wee bit fuzzy.'

David smiled. 'I think it was a draw. You're both out for the count, at any rate.'

Willie gave the smallest of nods. 'Ah well, that's no' so bad. He was a bloody big bugger.'

Imogen leaned forward, making David sit back on his haunches. 'Willie, it's Imogen. Can you understand what I'm saying?'

Willie frowned. 'Aye, course ah can, woman. What d'ye think ah am, daft?'

'Listen to me, Willie. Your arm's very badly injured. You've lost a lot of blood. You've already been unconscious for ten minutes. We need to know whether you can go on.'

Willie took a few seconds to digest this information, then he breathed in and out hard a couple of times, presumably to clear his head.

'Ah'll give it a go,' he murmured finally. He looked from Imogen to David and his eyes were suddenly sharp and clear. 'But understand this, I'll be no burden. If ah cannae cut the mustard, you'll have ti leave me here and go on. Y'understand?'

David nodded. 'Imogen's already explained all that.' He forced a smile and said with a humour he didn't really feel, 'Besides, you don't really think we'd want to drag a useless old codger like you around with us, do you?'

Willie grinned his crumpled leather grin. 'Useless old codger,' he murmured as though mulling over the words. 'Aye, ah reckon that just aboot sums me up.' He closed his eyes and breathed in and out a couple more times, like a weightlifter about to attempt a personal best. Then he opened his eyes again and said, 'Awright, ah'm ready ti give it a go. Help me up.'

Imogen and David got either side of Willie and gently helped him to his feet. Willie gasped in pain as his gored arm was jogged by David's shoulder. David grimaced and apologised; he couldn't help noticing that fresh blood was enlarging the already considerable red stain on the tourniquet. As soon as Willie was upright, Imogen and David let go of him, but his legs started to buckle and they had to rush forward to grab him again.

'Aw Jesus,' Willie moaned. 'Everything's spinning. Ah feel sick.' He began to breathe in and out quickly. His face had gone deathly pale.

'Do you want to lie down again?' David said. The tourniquet was dripping now.

'Naw, I'll be awright. Just give me a minute.' With David and Imogen still supporting him, he bent double so that his face was level with his thighs. Even now his cap didn't fall off.

'It's awright,' he told David in a low weary voice, 'I'm no gonnae puke on your shoes. It's just that all the blood that should be in ma heed is dripping out ma arm.'

The three of them stood like that for a minute or more, David and Imogen listening to Willie's phlegmy rapid breathing. It didn't sound good. Imogen looked at David across Willie's back and pulled a face. It was the kind of expression doctors in films always gave to friends of the fatally wounded just seconds after assuring the patient that everything's going to be fine. David almost expected her to accompany the expression with a tiny shake of the head.

Willie straightened up. 'Ah feel a bit better noo,' he said. 'Ah think ah can –'

Two things happened then, unexpectedly and simultaneously. One was a loud crack, like a dry tree being snapped in half, which made David jump, and the other was the sensation of Willie being plucked from his grasp as though a giant hook had pierced his back and was yanking him into the darkness.

David watched stupidly as Willie flung out his arms and

staggered backwards a few paces before collapsing. The Scotsman hit the ground in such a way, with such a sense of finality, that David knew instinctively that he was dead. He had no time to react to that fact, even in his own mind, before there was another crack and the top of Imogen's head sheared off, blood and bits of stuff flying all over the place like a gory special effect. The elderly woman, always so poised and graceful, spun round in an ungainly, un-Imogen like way and then collapsed without a sound, her body sprawled like a crumpled swastika, skirt riding so high up her splayed thighs that David could see her white underwear.

For a few long seconds he just stood and stared about him, so astounded by what had just occurred that he couldn't conjure up an emotion or a reaction. It was as though the workings of his body had jammed like a machine, as though something cold and hard had fused around his feelings. Somewhere a bland internal voice kept repeating, *They've been shot, they've been shot*, but he couldn't quite seem to grasp the meaning of that. It was the abrupt senselessness of the situation that he couldn't accept, the unfairness of it all. The three of them had come so far together and had endured so much, but had somehow managed to survive. And yet now two of them were suddenly dead – no preamble, no ceremony, no climactic confrontation, no neat tying up of loose ends. Dead. Extinguished. Snuffed out. No chance of a reprieve. It was as though some unseen, unknown opponent had decided to tear up the rule book and had made an illegal, irredeemable move.

Almost disconnectedly David sensed the shell of numbness which had been enclosing him for the past ten seconds or so now beginning to crack like ice, belatedly allowing his emotions to seep through. Horror, grief, despair began to burgeon inside him, kicking in like different drugs injected into his bloodstream. He began to cry. The strength seemed to leak out of him and he dropped to his knees, then lay full-length on the cold damp ground. Suddenly he felt so desolate he wished he could just die here, just close his eyes and forget about everything.

44

It was the sound of a helicopter that made him look up. He saw it hovering fifty feet above the park, silhouetted like a huge black hornet against the vinegar-coloured sky. He screwed up his eyes as its searchlights swept over him. Through the glare, at ground level, he saw armed soldiers dressed in combat gear converging on him, their guns cradled in the crooks of their arms.

He closed his eyes and allowed his head to sink to the ground again. All he could think of, his thoughts bumping across the treacherous terrain of his mangled emotions, was that this was just like one of those films where the main character is haunted by fever-dreams of Vietnam. The chopping rhythm of the helicopter rotors grew louder until it seemed the noise was all around him. He pictured the aircraft landing close by, even felt the breeze of its motion on his face.

The rotors wound down. David imagined the soldiers forming a circle around his huddled body, kept expecting to hear the cinematic clickety-click of guns being primed for firing, of safety catches being released or whatever it was they did. He was vaguely surprised to find that the prospect of his own death didn't much frighten him any more. Though all this business with the bottle had started out with him half-heartedly contemplating suicide, it had been prompted, ironically, by his mid-life crisis, which when you came right down to it, was little more than mortality kicking you up the arse, demanding a progress report, and then belittling what were, in truth, major achievements.

What did frighten him about dying, however, was the thought of the effect his death would have on Ellen and Rachel, and more especially, Jane, wherever she was. Perhaps he was kidding himself in believing that he was her only hope; perhaps all hope for Jane was long-gone. Though the thought of just lying here and letting everything slip away was a comforting, albeit selfish one, David knew that while the possibility remained that Jane was out there somewhere, alive and in torment, then that would be incentive enough for him to carry on searching, and praying for a miracle.

And so he put his hand into his pocket and clutched the bottle, not even knowing whether it would work any longer, then he lifted his head and opened his eyes to see what was going on. There were a dozen, maybe two dozen, soldiers out there. They were surrounding him, though not in a tight circle; the closest was thirty or forty yards away. Their guns were not pointing right at him, but they were not pointing away either. He couldn't see them very clearly, couldn't see their faces at all, because bright headlamps or searchlights or whatever were shining out of the front of the helicopter, right into his eyes, dazzling him.

The helicopter had landed on a flat patch of grass just beyond the circle of soldiers. Because of the lights in his eyes, David could see little more than a massive black shape crouched among the shadows, though the image that came to his mind now was not that of a hornet but of a vast crab. His eyes were hurting with light and he looked away, then wished he hadn't. In the unnatural brightness the details of Imogen's death left little to the imagination. Her mouth and eyes were wide in frozen, awful shock. The top of her head resembled an egg that had been smashed with a spoon, all splinters and dark runny stuff with lumps in it. David turned back to the light, hoping it would scour the image from his memory. He thought he could see someone getting out of the helicopter. Next moment the thought was confirmed.

'David Fox.' The voice was amplified by a megaphone. For an instant, David thought it was Brother Joseph and his band of zealots, come to renew hostilities. He was not sure whether his name had been used as a question or a statement. He brought his arms up and shaded his eyes in lieu of a reply.

'My name is Sir Anthony Woodhead,' the voice went on. 'You don't know me personally, but I think you know the organisation I represent. We've been watching you, Mr Fox, you and your retrograde friends. We picked you up just outside Luton and have been monitoring your progress ever since. You've been very resourceful, though how you could ever have hoped to avoid detection I can't imagine. We've all found it very amusing watching you stumble from one crisis to another, but the time has now come for us to step in and take a hand in these proceedings. I'm here to tell you, if you'll permit me, how the situation's going to be from now on.'

'Fuck you,' muttered David, and climbed shakily to his feet. It wasn't much of a rejoinder, particularly since no one had heard it, but it made him feel a tiny bit better nonetheless. Actually, he was surprised by how much defiance he still had left in him; it had been kicked back into life by the pompous arrogance of the unseen Woodhead, which was moulding his grief, at least temporarily, into a hard poisonous nugget of anger.

'I'm sorry, Mr Fox, did you say something?' Woodhead asked.

David raised his head and his voice. 'Nothing complimentary.'

'Hmm,' said Woodhead. 'In that case, perhaps you'll allow me to furnish you with a few facts? Fact one: your subversive friends have now died and left you all alone in this, um, inhospitable environment. Fact two: you are surrounded by armed troops. And, perhaps most pertinent of all, fact three: your youngest daughter – Jane, I believe her name is – is currently in our custody. Now, I'm sure you want her back more than anything else in the world. More than *anything*. Am I right, Mr Fox?'

David just stood and glowered. His silence was answer enough.

'I thought so,' boomed Woodhead with a smugness which infuriated David. 'Now, Mr Fox, the deal is this. You give us what we want, and I'm sure I don't need to tell you what that is, and we'll give you back your daughter. Fair exchange?'

Still David could only see Woodhead as a dark smear against the shimmering black bulb of the helicopter, beyond the radiance that pinioned him.

Recklessly he called, 'Why don't you just kill me and take the bottle? Wouldn't that be easier for you?'

He envisioned Woodhead's superior smile as he gave his reply. 'After what has happened to various colleagues of ours, I'm sure you'll appreciate, Mr Fox, that we're all rather reluctant to launch a physical attack on your person or to handle the . . . er . . . merchandise. For that reason our . . . um . . . employer has requested that you take the bottle direct to the source of our power and destroy it yourself.'

'And if I refuse, I suppose I'll never see Jane again?'

Woodhead chuckled. 'Quite so, Mr Fox. Got it in one, as they say.'

David was silent for a moment, as though considering Woodhead's proposal, though of course there was really nothing to consider. 'I thought Jane had become the new oracle,' he said.

He half-expected Woodhead to deny it, or at least to be taken aback that he knew. But instead Woodhead said crisply, 'That's correct, Mr Fox.'

'Then there's no hope for her, is there? All the oracles die, don't they?'

'All the oracles up to now have died,' Woodhead confirmed, 'but Jane won't.'

'And how do you know that?'

'We know, Mr Fox, and that's all that *you* need to know.'

David shook his head slowly, surprised at how calm he was managing to appear, and said, 'I'm afraid that's not good enough.'

Woodhead gave a snort of amusement. 'And *I'm* afraid you're hardly in a position to negotiate, Mr Fox.' He paused, and then said in what he evidently considered a persuasively reasonable voice, 'You know, you misunderstand us, Mr Fox. Those retrogrades you've been mixing with have been filling your head with propaganda. We're not an evil organisation. Our methods may occasionally be somewhat, um, ruthless, but believe me we are working towards the ultimate good of mankind.'

David laughed incredulously. 'You have to be joking! You think all this death and destruction is good for mankind, do you?'

'Ultimately, yes. It's part of what we call the pattern – though I wouldn't expect you to understand.'

'Oh, I understand, all right. I understand that you're a group of sadly disillusioned individuals. You follow a god that treats you like . . . like sheep, a god that chews you up and spits you out. Can't you see that you're being used? Can't you see that all you're doing is creating a gateway for evil? I mean, take a look around you. What sort of god tears his people, his world, apart like this?'

During the short silence that followed his outburst, David wondered whether his words had somehow managed to get through. Then, in a wearily patronising tone, Woodhead said, 'Have you *quite* finished?'

David sighed, realising it was hopeless. 'I suppose so.'

'I feel sorry for you, Mr Fox, really I do,' Woodhead said. 'If you only knew how much you'd been used, you'd be thanking us for killing your companions. Your tears would be better employed crying for all the time you've wasted fraternising with the scum you have. We're working towards something glorious here, Mr Fox, and all subversives like this can do is try to destroy it. Not that they ever will, of course, because what they don't realise is that whatever they do is part of the pattern. Nothing can deviate from that.'

'They know it, all right,' David said, 'they just don't believe it.'

'That's what they told you, is it?' said Woodhead, and the tone of his voice had now gone beyond condescension to a kind of pitying arrogance that set David's teeth on edge. He spoke to David as if he were a child who had been misled into doing something illegal by a group of older boys.

'They told me the truth. And nothing you can say will change my mind about that.'

'In that case,' Woodhead said, 'I won't waste my breath any further, except to give you your instructions. What I want you to do is to walk forward slowly to the helicopter and climb aboard. My pilot will take you to your destination. As I'm sure you are aware, a small area in North London known as Crouch End has been, er, psychically cordoned off by our organisation. However, special provision has been provided to allow you through. Once within that area, I want you to locate a small cinema called the Cottage Picture House, which is on the junction between Cottage Road and Edison Avenue. Once there, you will be given further instructions. Any questions, Mr Fox?'

David shook his head.

'Fine. In that case, you may begin walking towards the helicopter.'

David gritted his teeth. He resented being spoken to like a child, but why bother making a fuss? He began to walk into the blazing eyes of the helicopter, armed troops moving back warily before him, keeping their distance, their guns still half-cocked. David wondered whether they were Flux members too. They had certainly been briefed about the bottle's capabilities, judging by their behaviour. The light from the helicopter hurt his eyes, but he tried not to squint too much. For what it was worth, he wanted to present a final image of calm defiance to those gathered here.

The helicopter was a two-seater, considerably smaller than the one he and his companions had come in. When David reached it, he found that apart from the pilot slumped silently in his seat, staring straight ahead, he was alone.

He was not entirely surprised to find that Woodhead had made himself scarce, though he asked brightly, 'Mr Woodhead not coming with us?'

'No,' the pilot said, not looking at him.

'Oh dear, and I was so looking forward to his company.'

David climbed into the helicopter and shut the door. He put his headgear on, though only to lessen the noise of the engine and the rotor blades. He didn't much feel like chatting, and the pilot seemed like the strong silent type anyway. As the rotors started up, he closed his eyes and slumped further down in his seat. He felt exhausted and every muscle in his body ached, but there was no way he could have dozed. Shock and grief and fear and apprehension and anger buzzed in his head like caffeine, forcing his mind to keep working.

The journey was a short and uneventful one. David kept his eyes closed for its duration and his hand clenched tight around the bottle in his pocket. He even kept his eyes closed when he sensed the helicopter circling to land, opening them only when he felt the gentle bump of its impact with the ground.

He saw that they had landed in the middle of a sports field flanked by housing. In fact, they had landed in the centre circle of a football pitch. Nearby, a chain-link enclosure caged four tennis courts. There was not a soul to be seen, though lights burned in the row of fairly standard-looking suburban houses whose rear gardens backed on to the field's fenced perimeter.

It was only when the rotors wound down and eventually stopped that David realised how quiet it was. Not just quiet, but silent, and eerily so. He remarked on the fact to the pilot, who ignored his comment, but pointed at the row of houses and said, 'That's where the barrier starts.'

'What about all the people who live inside the barrier?'

The pilot shrugged. 'Gone.'

'Gone? What do you mean, "gone"?'

The pilot stared ahead, as though he thought David might try to hypnotise him if he established eye-contact. Curtly he said, 'They left. They all decided to go away.'

'You mean the Flux kind of . . . cast a spell on them?'

The pilot raised his eyebrows as if to show that David's comment didn't even merit an answer.

'Are you a member of the Flux?' David asked.

The pilot unzipped his jacket and produced a London A-Z which he thrust at David. Ignoring his question, he said, 'You'll need this. Page 29. It's marked.'

David took the book and turned to the relevant page. In the bottom left-hand corner a vaguely rectangular area of what appeared to be densely-populated land had been outlined in red. In the centre of this area a small red cross marked what was presumably the Cottage Picture House, at the junction between Cottage Road and Edison Avenue.

David found a playing field at the border of the marked area and pointed at it. 'This is where we are now, right?'

The pilot deigned to glance at the book for a moment. 'Right.'

'Okay then, well I'll get going.' David stuck out his hand. 'Thanks for the lift.'

The pilot looked at David's proffered hand as though it was a rotting fish, and said nothing. After a moment David lowered his hand, muttered, 'Please yourself,' and climbed down from the helicopter. He retreated as the pilot restarted the engine and the rotors began to pick up speed, then he watched the helicopter take off, watched it until the night sky swallowed it up. The sound of its engine persisted for a while, then eventually faded, leaving David utterly alone.

He stood for a moment, breathing in the cold winter air, the smell of muddy grass. The stillness and the silence was unnatural rather than peaceful. It was as though his ears had been stuffed with cotton wool, as though the air had been somehow deadened. He turned towards the perimeter fence which marked the boundary of . . . of what?

'The heart of darkness,' he muttered, and failed to suppress a shudder as he walked forward. Three feet from the perimeter fence, a flimsy thigh-high construction of wooden stakes and rusty wire, he stopped, peering at the supposed barrier suspiciously. He could see nothing out of the ordinary, but what did it matter whether or not he could see the barrier? Hadn't Woodhead said that provision had been made to allow him to pass through? But how much could he trust the man's word? For all he knew this might be a trap. Maybe when he put his hand on the fence a billion volts would flow through him, reducing him to a cinder and the bottle to molten glass. It was crude, but who was to say it wouldn't be effective?

He slipped one hand into his pocket and around the bottle, and the other stretched out, holding it an inch from the barrier. He felt nothing; no warmth, no tingle of energy, no pain. He looked around, found a stick and tossed it at the fence. It bounced on the rusty wire and over without any apparent harm, landing on the patio of the house beyond the fence with a strangely muffled sound, as though falling into a pile of towels. He hovered for maybe five seconds more, and then, taking a deep breath, one hand still clutched tight around the bottle, he reached out for the fence, grasped it, and began to swing himself over.

Passing through the barrier was a weird but not unpleasant sensation. It was almost like passing through a sheet of water, but one that was warm and that didn't make you wet. His vision was affected, but only momentarily; the effect reminded him of a TV picture that was threatening to break up, shot through with streaks of light.

And then he was through, lifting and dragging his left leg over the fence, landing in the back garden of the house beyond with a thump that jarred his aching muscles and set his bruises throbbing again. He straightened up and looked back towards the barrier, half-expecting to see something, a shimmer of energy like a heat haze on the horizon perhaps. But there was nothing at all to show that he had crossed any kind of boundary, passed through from one realm into another.

He walked across the back lawn towards a gate that led to a path that ran around the side of the house. Children's toys were scattered on the back lawn and on the patio in front of a pair of French windows – a blue ball, some plastic dinosaurs, a toddler's trike in the shape of a red tractor with yellow wheels. David peered through the French windows, saw a dining room in darkness, no sign of life. His footfalls on the stone of the patio were muffled. The air had a flat, faintly musty smell, like the air in a sealed room.

He opened the gate, walked around to the front of the house and found himself in a tree-lined suburban street, silent and deserted. He stood for a moment and listened, but there was no sound at all – no birdsong, no rustling of leaves stirred by wind, no far-off murmur of activity. Cars were parked on verges, lights burned in windows, but it was as though all the people and animals had simply winked out of existence, leaving only the paraphernalia of lives once lived. It was neither cold nor hot here, but David shivered nonetheless and looked up at the sky. It looked normal. For the first time since arriving in London, he could even see stars.

In order to reassure himself that things were still moving, that time was still marching on, he looked at his watch. It informed him that the time was 7:25, but when he looked closer he realised that the watch had stopped. Ellen had bought it for him as a thirty-sixth birthday present and it had never stopped before. He shook it, held it to his ear, but the watch remained obstinately silent. Had it got damaged somewhere along the way or could whatever lurked in the centre of this web of silence really halt time?

He sighed, pulled the A-Z from his pocket and consulted it. He had to turn left here, then take a right, then another left, then there were a bunch of little roads that he had to negotiate in order to arrive at his destination.

He started walking, his footsteps no louder than if he was walking on sand. The silence and the stillness made him feel vulnerable, made him feel as if he stood out like a black bug on a sheet of white paper. Not that he expected to be able to sneak up on his opponent. Perhaps it was simply his imagination that made him feel it had eyes everywhere, watching him. 'Hello,' he called suddenly, and his voice sounded dead and flat. Not surprisingly, no one replied. He drew his Bogart tighter around him and trudged on.

London was a city of long roads. A destination that looked no more than a couple of streets away on a map could take as long as half an hour to reach on foot. The right turn that David wanted, Berkeley Rise, turned out to be a good ten minutes' walk away. It was just coming into view, for which he was profoundly grateful (he'd been beginning to think that this was all a trick and that he'd been cast into his own personal hell, which took the form of this never-ending stroll through silent suburbia), when a thought occurred to him.

If some of the houses were lit and windows uncurtained, as if the occupants had left in a hurry, then wouldn't someone somewhere have left a television on, or a radio? It was a minor point, maybe, and irrelevant to his mission, but it nevertheless nagged at him enough to make him hesitate in front of the house he was passing, and then turn abruptly and march up the drive of the house to the front door.

He knocked perfunctorily, the sound a series of muffled booms, then tried the door handle. He was not entirely surprised when the door swung open. He walked into a high-ceilinged hallway with a tile-patterned floor and yellow wallpaper. A red mountain bike was propped against the wall to his left; beyond that, an old sewing-machine table with a metal treadle was being used to support a telephone heaped on a pile of directories, beside which was an address book open to the letter C: Crowther, Chinn, Coleborn, Campbell. Beyond the makeshift telephone table a staircase claimed the left half of the hallway and led upwards; doors punctuated the wall on the right, the first of which was ajar and spewing light. David strode forward, picked up the telephone receiver and placed it to his ear; the line was dead. Without hesitation, he crossed the hallway and pushed open the first door, from beyond which more light, soft and orangey, spilled over him.

He went in. The room was large and the decor bright but tasteful. A fireplace was fronted by an embroidered screen that looked Victorian or older; big green plants with fleshy leaves clustered together on an old wooden sideboard. One, taller than a man, with leaves like spades, bowed at him from a corner. Beside a *Good Food* magazine that was open on the plush patterned sofa was a glass ashtray piled with cigarette butts that gave off no smell.

His gaze swept round the room and came to rest on the TV and video recorder. He walked across, checked to make sure the TV was plugged in, then turned it on. Nothing happened. Lamps were burning in the room, but the TV seemed to think that the place was in the middle of a power cut. David sighed, then noticed with a wriggle of fear that on the floor beneath the TV table were two videos. One was a copy of *Pretty Woman* starring Julia Roberts and Richard Gere, and the other was a Maxell E-180, whose sticky label on the spine read, in shaky blue handwriting, DAVID FOX.

David looked quickly round the room, as though half-expecting someone he'd missed when he'd looked the first time to be in there with him, then bent and picked up the video with his name on it. He swallowed a lump of drying spit, licked his lips with a sandpaper-tongue. Then he took the cassette out of the box and shoved it almost savagely into the video recorder.

He scuttled back from the screen as if he expected the machine to explode, and waited. Almost immediately the television fizzed into life, the screen filling with the grey static of empty video tape. There was a blip, then a picture struggled to establish itself. It was grainy and dark and slashed through with white hiccuping lines. At first David couldn't make out what was going on. The image resembled a white grub-like shape moving feebly in green-black surroundings.

Then the picture zoomed in and the whiteness resolved itself into a figure, then a face. The face opened its eyes and mouth wide and began screaming. David recognised Jane immediately, even though her hair was hanging in rat's-tails, her skin was white as death, and her face was covered in weals and cuts as if she'd run through a forest of brambles. '*Daddy!*' she screamed, and David gasped as if punched in the stomach. 'Help me, Daddy,' she sobbed, then abruptly her voice and expression changed and she began to laugh like a dirty old man with bronchial problems. She looked directly into the camera, directly at *him*, and now her eyeballs had changed to a pearly-white, the colour of semen. In a grating voice she snarled, 'This what you expected, Daddy? You've seen all the movies, haven't you? Shall I make my head spin all the way round?' She laughed again, and yellowy stuff, like thin porridge, dribbled out of her mouth. Then she was Jane again, coughing and sobbing. 'Help me, Daddy,' she pleaded, 'help –'

The picture cut out, was replaced by static.

David was shaking so much his teeth chattered. His stomach felt as though it had shrunk to the size of a marble. In a sudden rage, he snatched up the ashtray from the sofa, scattering cigarette butts everywhere, and hurled it at the TV. It smashed right through the screen and became lodged in the machine's inner workings. The TV fizzed and died, a small fire blossoming then being sucked into extinction almost immediately, like a match blowing out. The sound of the TV being destroyed was thick, woolly, slow. It made David realise that Jane's words accompanying the video image were the first undistorted sounds he had heard here.

He couldn't bear to be in this house any longer. He turned and ran out of the room, along the hallway, out the front door, up the drive. His breath rasped in his throat. He didn't stop running until he had turned right into Berkeley Rise, until the house was no longer in sight, and then he stumbled and sank to his knees on the cold pavement.

His breath was coming so quickly it was making his head swim, his heart racing so fast he thought it would burst. Despair washed over him again then, just as it had in the park, as if the makeshift barrier he'd built inside himself to hold it all back was giving way. He thought of Jane, of Willie and Imogen, of the terrible things he'd seen, the violence and destruction, the suffering and death, and he began to sob like a child, the tears flowing freely, darkening the pavement between his knees.

At last the tears stopped and he felt a little better, though not much. He climbed painfully to his feet, feeling old and exhausted, his heart aching as though it was too heavy for his chest. He sighed deeply, wiped his eyes and his nose on his now stained and crumpled Bogart, and then consulted the A-Z. His hands trembled like an alcoholic's, his fingernails still engrained with poor Willie's blood.

He had to take a left at a street called Clarendon Road. He set off, trudging like a fell walker at the end of a thirty-mile hike. He stared at the ground mostly; it seemed too much of an effort to lift his head any higher. Finally he reached the left he was looking for and took it, whereupon he consulted the A-Z again. Ten minutes later, he arrived at his destination.

He was both relieved finally to be here and terrified at the prospect of going inside and facing whatever was waiting for him. The Cottage Picture House was a wedge-shaped building, like a giant slab of cake, and had evidently not been used for many years. Its name had been incorporated into the white stonework above its boarded-up entrance doors and picked out in red paint which had now mostly flaked away like sunburned skin. It must once have been a grand building, but was now little more than an eyesore. On its walls graffiti vied for dominance with overlapping scabs of posters that advertised tour dates for obscure bands.

David approached the building slowly, noting the elaborate spires that sprouted from its roof like horns. As well as being boarded up, the entrance doors had also, for some reason, been painted black. David ascended the semicircle of short steps which led to the main doors and tugged at the nearest handle. The door, though heavy, opened easily. He pulled the door far enough open so that it stayed like that of its own accord, then stepped into the entrance lobby.

Despite the light filtering in from outside it was very dark in here. David remembered the pencil-torch that Willie had given him in the office block. That seemed like hours ago now; he hadn't used the torch since leaving Willie, Richard Hodge and Alison in hiding in one of the offices whilst he, Melanie and Imogen had continued their descent down the stairs.

He produced the torch and switched it on. A thin but bright beam of light lit up the entrance lobby, which was square and cramped with wood-panelled walls. To David's left was the ticket window, then two steps led up to the confectionery counter. On the other side of the lobby were three doors marked 'Ladies', 'Gentlemen' and 'Private'. In the top left-hand corner a flight of steps curved through an arch and thence, presumably, led to the cinema itself. All was grime and cobwebs, the half-rotted carpet beneath David's feet scattered with rubble. A number of film posters sagged from the walls; David was not altogether surprised to see that they replicated posters that he had at home, framed and on his walls: *Casablanca, Brief Encounter, Some Like It Hot, The Birds*.

He took a couple of steps forward, then leaped out of his skin as the entrance door he had propped open crashed shut behind him. He whirled round, glimpsing as he did so a face in his wavering torch-beam which seemed to be shiny and white as candle wax, featureless but for a flapping black mouth containing teeth like splintered almonds.

When he turned back the face had gone. He whipped his torch-beam this way and that, trying to relocate it, but without success. He drew a long shuddering breath and placed a hand on his crashing heart. The worst thing about the face he thought he'd seen was that it had been low to the ground, almost at ankle-level, and he had had the impression it was attached to a sleek feline body, as though a cat had been wearing a Halloween mask far too large for it.

He directed his torch towards the arch through which was the cinema proper. 'Very good trick,' he said loudly, trying to sound both confident and scathing, 'making the door crash shut like that. Very Abbott and Costello.' His taunt received no immediate reply. David realised that his voice sounded normal in here, as did his footsteps on the gritty surface. It was as though someone had made an adjustment to the sound, pulling it back into phase. 'Anybody about?' he shouted, his torch-beam roaming around the room. 'I've brought the bottle.'

Only silence answered him, though it was not absolute silence this time. It was the creaking silence of an old building in a state of gradual but inevitable decay.

Hesitantly he moved towards the steps that led up through the arch, one hand holding the torch, the other closing around the bulge of the bottle in his pocket. He reached the steps and lifted his foot to begin climbing them when he heard something approaching along the corridor beyond the arch, something that moved with a bump-scrape, bump-scrape, as though it had to drag itself along.

David stood, transfixed, shudders rippling through his body, eyes fixed on the point at the end of his torch-beam where whatever was coming would appear. As it got closer, David heard another sound underlying its slow dragging movement, a thin gurgling sound, like someone trying to breathe through a tube full of fluid.

The thing came closer and closer. Now it must be no more than a few feet away, just around the corner, just out of sight. David stepped back instinctively as the thing dragged itself forward, into the light of his torch. His chest felt tight. He couldn't speak.

The body appeared to be that of a teenage girl's. It was dressed in an usherette's uniform, holding a torch in its hand, an ice-cream tray looped around its neck. But there was something terribly wrong with it, for it moved in a lopsided crab-like way, dragging its left foot behind it, the bones of which seemed to have been mashed beyond repair. Grotesquely the shattered and misshapen left foot had been forced into a black patent-leather shoe which bumped uselessly over the rubble-strewn floor in its wake. But more grotesque still was the girl's head, which was encased within a white plastic bag that had been tied tightly at the neck by what looked like fishing twine.

The thin gurgling sound David had heard was the girl's breathing inside the bag. The bag inflated and deflated in time with her respiration. Every time it deflated, it stuck to her face, the flesh of which appeared to be wet and oily.

Slowly, as though it caused her great pain, the girl raised her left arm from the tray, pointed down at David and made a vague beckoning gesture. Then, moving slowly and awkwardly, she turned round and began to drag herself back into the darkness.

The gesture had been obvious; the girl wanted David to follow her. Although she was horrifying to look at, she appeared not to be dangerous. David heard her lurching back along the corridor, dragging her useless foot behind her. His stomach was jumping now with nerves and fear, a pulse pounding in his throat. His legs felt hollow and stiff as he clumped up the stairs after the girl.

The steps stopped just beyond the arch and led into a

narrow curving corridor festooned with cobwebs. David shone his torch ahead of him, and saw lots of little black things – cockroaches, spiders – scuttle away, seeking safety from the light. The girl was just rounding a bend in the corridor, the plastic bag on her head still inflating and deflating like a lung. David stooped after her, clawing cobwebs away from his face.

He moved slowly in order to keep a good distance between himself and the girl. The thought of being close to her made his skin crawl. He suspected that the evil towards which the girl was leading him was playing a game, creating nightmare images in the hope of softening him up, freaking him out. Although wise to its ploy, he still hoped desperately that the girl wouldn't remove the bag, that that wasn't part of the game. He didn't want to think about what might be underneath.

He reached the bend which the girl had rounded some ten seconds previously, and found himself just a few feet away from a pair of wooden doors inset with small panes of glass that were either opaque or so grimy that you couldn't see through them. The girl was nowhere to be seen, but as David approached the doors, moving slowly and hesitantly, ready to turn and run at the slightest provocation, the right-hand door opened with a squeal of rusty hinges, seemingly of its own accord.

It was another horror movie cliché, like the door crashing shut behind him in the lobby, but it was enough to send another ripple of fear down David's back. Beyond the door lay darkness. David shone his torch into it and saw the rounded backs of cinema seats, like rows of teeth or tombstones. He moved forward cautiously, hoping the girl, or something worse, wasn't lurking just out of sight behind the door, waiting to leap out at him.

In the end he sidled right up to the open door and then jumped through it, hunching up his shoulders to protect his head.

Nothing was waiting to leap out at him, though David was half-aware of a rustling sound throughout the cinema, as though his arrival had disturbed a meagre, sleepy audience. He shone his torch around, but it was as though the dust was so thick in here that his torch-beam was stifled with greyness. Nevertheless he was just able to make out vague misshapen forms scattered throughout the auditorium, slumped in some of the seats. They resembled bundles of rags that had been propped up like Guy Fawkes dummies and were held together by dust and cobwebs and what looked like faintly glowing clumps of mould. They looked too insubstantial to be flapping and jerking feebly, as though trying to rise, perhaps to greet him, but David suspected that anything was possible here, that any nightmare, however outlandish, could be given life. He shivered and switched off his failing torch in the hope that the darkness would encourage the lolling things in the seats to slip back into torpor.

Even after extinguishing his torch, however, he realised that a light was still shining up ahead. He pushed his face forward, peering into the gloom. The dimness in here was more like fog than dust; the light was blurred, and seemed to make no impression on its surroundings. David heard a faint sound to his left, like the sliding of silk over skin. He turned and saw a shape slink away into the misty darkness, a shape like a cat with a human head.

Trying to stop his legs from trembling, he walked slowly forward, towards the clot of light. The aisle between the rows of seats was narrow, and sloped downwards like a gentle ski-run. The carpet felt slimy beneath him, and he put out a hand to steady himself, then snatched it back quickly. The seat he had touched was cold and spongy, like flesh bloated with rot. David tried to keep his eyes staring straight ahead, tried not to look at the ragged shapes craning towards him. He didn't even look, merely flinched away, when something so deflated that he hadn't

587

seen it over the back of the seat it was sitting in, hissed at him from a few feet away, then tried to speak with a voice that sounded like something toothless chewing tripe.

As he got closer, he realised that the light was the torch being held by the usherette. He glanced quickly away from her head with a shudder as she breathed in. That time, when the bag had deflated and stuck to her skin he had almost seen the shape of her face. The usherette was probing at an aisle to David's left with her torch-beam. Was this where she wanted him to sit? It was about halfway between the screen and the exit doors. In fact, realised David, the seat which the torch-beam was pinpointing seemed to be in the exact centre of the auditorium. He considered asking the usherette to confirm that she wanted him to sit down, then decided against it. As well as not wishing to see her face, neither did he want to hear her speak.

Checking to ensure that none of the rag-people would be sitting anywhere near him, David approached the row the usherette was indicating and then began to edge his way along it. He had to pass quite close to her in order to do so, no more than four feet of space separating his own face from whatever breathed inside the plastic bag. Apart from the movement above her neck, however, she remained motionless, and when David was installed in his seat, and looking around as though expecting an attack but unsure from which side it would come, she dragged herself back up the aisle and exited through the double doors through which David had entered.

The darkness closed in like fog, making David huddle deep into his seat. Not that the seat afforded him much comfort; it was cold and damp and smelled faintly of rotting vegetables when he moved on it, as though it had been recently retrieved from a compost heap. From all around him he could hear rustling and muttering, even a soft gurgling sound that might have been laughter or old plumbing. He didn't know how long he sat there, but it must have been five, perhaps even ten, minutes. His right hand was stuffed deep into his pocket, clutching the bottle like an alcoholic trying to resist temptation.

He couldn't see more than half a dozen seats to any side of him before the darkness reduced everything to a blurry mass. He wished something would happen, though perhaps something was and he wasn't aware of it; perhaps the things in the seats were inching their way towards him, dragging themselves between the rows, surrounding him on all sides. He considered shouting out as he had done in the lobby, challenging his opponent. But his desire to remain as unobtrusive as possible, coupled with his fear-parched throat, kept him silent.

All at once he heard a sustained swishing noise from somewhere in front of him. He sat up straight and peered hard into the gloom, and immediately got the impression that the pearly opacity of the darkness was receding, parting before him like mist sucked away by powerful extractor fans. Just beyond the front row of seats, David could now make out a great swathe of movement which it took him a moment to realise was a pair of long ragged curtains drawing back from the cinema screen. Not that he could see the screen at all; beyond the curtains was merely a darkness so profound it defied the eye.

He glanced around him uneasily and then back at where the screen should be. The performance, it seemed, was about to begin. He drew the bottle out of his pocket and held it in his lap like a talisman, both hands wrapped around it. There was a sudden sound that made him jump – a sharp click, then a stifled burst of power. Next moment the darkness beyond the curtains erupted into light.

David squinted as white numbers within black circles within white rectangles starting counting down from 10. After the number 1 had flashed up and off, the picture changed abruptly to that of a huge white face, its mouth open, and the sound kicked in, a horrible heart-rending screech so loud and piercing that David thought his eardrums would shatter. The bottle stayed in his lap as his hands rose instinctively to his ears. He had recognised Jane's face immediately, which made the scream ten times worse, made it feel as though it was tearing up through him like an electric saw.

He bowed his head, gritted his teeth, squeezed shut his eyes, but it was no use. He couldn't deny her pain and terror; it was as inescapable as the darkness around him. He raised his head and shouted, 'Stop it, you bastard! Stop it!' at the screen. Or at least, he tried to shout, but dryness made his mouth feel full of sand and all that emerged was a frail croak.

It seemed his plea had been heard, however, for Jane, or whatever possessed her, abruptly stopped screaming and began chuckling instead. David didn't know which was more horrible. At least when Jane screamed she *looked* like Jane, but now she looked like something was wearing her face, twisting it into expressions that David didn't recognise.

The voice too was not Jane's voice. If the thing inside her was using her vocal cords, then it was twisting them, mangling them, using them in ways they were never meant to be used. The voice that emerged from Jane's mouth and boomed around the cinema was deep and somehow muddy, the intonations oddly discordant.

'Just wanted to get your attention,' the thing said, and grinned horribly, curling Jane's lips artificially upwards as if her face was an animatronic mask. Her eyes, big as beachballs, seemed to glare right out of the screen at him, and were filled with a knowledge and a cruelty that David had to assure himself were not his daughter's.

He couldn't think of anything to say that mightn't provoke whatever squirmed inside Jane's mind to hurt her. He wasn't even sure he was able to speak at all now;

horror had not only drained his throat of moisture but seemed to be slowly paralysing it. And so he just sat there and stared dumbly up at the face, filled with a churning sickness, which was a combination of his hatred for the creature and the sour empty ache of his own inability to act.

'You look such a little man down there,' said the Jane-thing mockingly, 'such a little, weak, tired man, a black speck so tiny that you're almost nothing. You feel tired, don't you, David? You just want to go back home, to be with your family, to be safe. You want an end to all this, don't you?'

David said nothing, too full of rage and despair and fear to speak.

'Of course you do,' the Jane-thing whispered, and cocked its head in a ghastly parody of compassion. The eyes rolled and the fat grey tongue, big as a whale, flickered out, drooling a thread of milky saliva.

'Of course you do,' it said again, and its hiss was a lover's hiss. 'You just want it all to end and it can. It's soooo easy.'

The thing rolled its head back on its shoulders, rat-tail hair hanging down, scratches livid on its throat. Then it looked at him again, almost coyly; David thought his disgust would make him sick.

'You know how to end it, don't you?' The thing's voice changed, and suddenly it was Jane who was speaking to him, though a Jane whose voice was sweeter and more wheedling than he had ever heard it before. 'Do it for me. Do it for me, Daddy. Break the bottle.'

David's stomach spasmed involuntarily and he retched, but nothing came up. The feeling passed. He lifted the bottle from his lap, held it up. It glittered in the light from the screen.

The creature's response was immediate. 'Break the bottle,' it rasped, its coyness gone; it twisted his daughter's features into a demonic mask of rage.

The image of Jane on the screen pulled back so that the frame was not filled solely with her face now, but with her head and shoulders and with more of her vague greenish surroundings that David had seen on the video back at the house. She lifted her hand, fingers splayed, palm towards him.

'Break the bottle or I swear I'll tear her apart slowly.'

'No,' David croaked, and he raised the bottle above his head, intending to smash it over the back of the chair in front of him. His muscles bunched in readiness for the downward motion . . .

And there he hesitated.

Was it really going to end like this? Had he come all this way for such an ignominious conclusion? Was he going to simply smash the bottle over a chair and allow all the evil, all the darkness, to come flooding through into the world? He couldn't do it, but he *had* to do it, for Jane's sake. But he couldn't, and even if he did would the creature let him have Jane back, safe and well? And if so, would there be a world and a life worth returning to? He looked up at the screen, his face creased in an agony of indecision.

All at once, with the gristly crackle of a chicken leg being torn from a carcass, David saw the smallest finger of Jane's outstretched right hand get ripped away from the rest of her as though by an invisible force. The finger spun away into the darkness like a tossed pencil as blood gouted from the wound. For an instant the shock and pain brought Jane to the fore, or perhaps the creature was merely allowing David to glimpse the effect his indecision was having on his daughter. The little girl began to scream and scream, tears erupting from eyes that were suddenly crazed with pain. Her body shuddered and sagged, and seemed to be plucked upright by invisible wires, like a marionette. Then mercifully her eyes rolled back in her head and she seemed to faint on her feet, the pain evidently too much for her.

'*No!*' David screeched, but the word came out as a thin reedy whistle. He started crying and retching and he couldn't breathe. Black blobs danced in front of his eyes. He felt hot and cold in rapid succession. He was so shocked by what he had seen that every nerve in his body seemed to jam up. The bottle slipped from his numb fingers and hit the seat in front of him without breaking, and from there bounced into the gulley between the rows of seats.

Up on the screen, the creature was making Jane hold up her now-mutilated hand. Blood was pumping steadily from the terrible gap where her little finger had been, and running down her palm in thin red rivulets. The creature spoke through Jane's mouth. 'Break the bottle.'

This time David did find his voice, and screamed the loudest, even louder than Jane, when the third finger on her right hand was ripped away in a tiny explosion of flesh and bone and blood.

'Stop,' he sobbed, 'stop, stop.' Still fighting back the urge either to faint or throw up, he threw himself over the seat in front of him in his desperation to retrieve the bottle.

For a few terrible seconds he couldn't find it, and then his desperately roving right hand bumped against it and he snatched it up. He shoved himself back to his feet and raised the bottle, his right hand encircling its neck, his arm shaking as if palsied.

On the screen, blood spurted from the ragged stump where Jane's third finger had been like ink ejected from a fountain pen. The creature was still holding the little girl upright, still using her mouth, her vocal cords. In its mushy voice it said, 'Break –'

David didn't want to witness for the third time what would come at the end of the phrase. With no thought this time for the consequences of his actions, he brought the bottle down hard on the seat in front of him.

It smashed at once, though even as the shrill, splintered cry of breaking glass filled his ears, the moment seemed to stretch, to fold around itself, to slow down. David was aware of a number of things. Physically, he was aware of thousands of shards of glass glittering and spinning and falling and erupting around him, and of the feel of the glass on his face, not sharp and stinging, but cool and almost refreshing, like a fine spray of clear spring water. And mentally, like an echo of his own act, he had the sudden and strange impression that he was looking out of hundred of eyes simultaneously, occupying many different bodies in many different places. It was like a telepathic impulse, a surge of thought, the catalyst to which was this simple act, the breaking of the bottle. Suddenly David got the feeling – no, more than that, David *knew* – that he was not alone. All around the world, at precisely the same moment, dozens, perhaps hundreds, of unremarkable people just like him were also being forced to break bottles that they had found on beaches and rubbish tips, in gutters and abandoned buildings, tangled in under-growth and embedded in the silt of lakes and ponds, in steaming swamps and arid deserts, in attics and cellars and outhouses and a hundred other secret and silent places.

For a moment, just a moment, he saw faces of people he had never met before but whom he felt he knew intimately. The faces were of all colours, all nationalities, and they were calling out to him, just as he was calling out to them, using names he had never heard, but which he instinctively knew were right. It was a glorious moment. Never before had he experienced such a sense of community, of camaraderie. But then, as the moment ended and the raining glass pattered and tinkled to the ground and became still, the faces and his knowledge of them dwindled and died, and suddenly he found he was alone again, in the darkness and the silence.

That was when the truth hit him, the realisation that he had lost, that the evil had won. He realised too that the heart of darkness had not been confined to this insignificant place, that evil, darkness, the Devil, call it what you will, was a beast of many hearts, all of which were beating at this moment with increasing strength, a crashing tattoo of triumph and power. With the Flux's misguided help, the evil had engineered a situation and a moment in which the darkness had massacred the light, shattered it beyond repair.

David stood in a daze, unable to believe that it had all ended in such abject failure, and gaped up at the screen, which now depicted Jane, his little girl, lying on the floor of the greenish-black room, curled up like a question mark, whimpering and shivering, her mutilated hand cradled against her body. The picture flickered, broke up and then shakily re-established itself. And then all at once the screen cracked like a building in an earthquake, and stuff began to pour out of the crack, stuff that looked like tar and smelled of decay.

This is the start of it, David thought, almost calm now that it was over. He wondered what he should do. Run away and try to outpace it? Or just let it flow over him and hope that his death would be painless and quick?

He decided, without really thinking about it, on the latter. He just didn't have the strength or the inclination to run any more. Still standing and facing the screen, he closed his eyes. The stench of decay rose as the darkness poured forth and made his head spin, filled him so completely that it was almost as though he were decaying himself, rotting quickly from the inside. His stomach cramped then lurched, and he finally did what he'd been threatening to do since he'd entered the cinema. The vomit burned like acid as it tore up through his stomach and throat and out through his mouth.

He doubled over, retching and retching, until all that he could produce was green frothy bile that he spat out in strings. Finally he looked up, sweating and red and empty and wretched. The screen had burst now like an over-ripe melon, and the darkness was still bubbling through, nullifying everything it touched. Already it had engulfed four rows of cinema seats, sucked them into itself, reduced them to nothing.

It was then, creeping forward, that it must have made contact with the first shard of glass from the bottle.

The result was instantaneous, like a spectacular chemical reaction. David didn't realise what had happened immediately; he was simply aware that all at once he was standing in what appeared to be a forest of light. Vertical bars of radiance, some as thin as wire, sprang into being all around him. There were hundreds of them, thousands of them, stretching from floor to ceiling. It was as though myriad holes had been punched in the floor of the auditorium and the most brilliant radiance imaginable shone through. The greatest conglomeration of light was just in front of David, where he had smashed the bottle. Here the separate bars were so close that they seemed to meld together like strips of sinew, forming a vast tree of light that became a blaze of white fire at its apex.

Each chunk and splinter and sliver of glass from the shattered bottle must be pouring forth light, David realised. So by breaking the bottle he had not destroyed the light at all; he had merely distributed it. Indeed, the light, though dispersed, actually seemed more plentiful now than ever. Perhaps by breaking the bottle he had released it, like a genie. Perhaps he had even been *supposed* to break the bottle; perhaps this moment had been engineered not by the darkness, as he'd thought, but by the light.

He stood entranced within the light, held out his hands and raised his head and laughed delightedly, like a farmer welcoming rain after a long drought. He felt a warmth and a serenity that was almost somnolent flowing through him. The light seemed to be revolving around him now, like a pattern on a spinning top, coming together into a definite shape.

Beyond the light, the darkness seemed to be mirroring the light's movement, lashing and snapping like thick oily tentacles, coiling too into a solid definable form. Was it really David's imagination or were the light and the dark metamorphosing into humanoid figures, giants that were even now lumbering towards each other like colossal warriors about to engage in combat?

There was so much confusion that David was not sure exactly what he did see. He felt disorientated now, even disembodied, as though he were trapped within a circle of stroboscopes, his mind whirling as though with drugs or fatigue, mangling his perceptions.

Suddenly the building seemed to shake and he staggered, only preventing himself from falling by grabbing hold of a seat-back. There was a roaring sound, as of a huge fire. In front of him, through a haze of light and darkness, David thought he saw the giants locked together, but perhaps that was merely his mind trying to create some sort of sense out of the chaos.

Something tickled his neck and he put his hand there instinctively. It came away smeared with a white chalky deposit. He looked up, and was shocked to see the ceiling moving and interlaced with cracks, plaster sifting down. Even as he watched he saw a lump of masonry the size of a door detach itself from the angle of wall and ceiling and crash to the ground below, scattering rubble and completely destroying half a dozen seats. He looked around, and realised through the flickering of radiance and shadow that the whole building was swaying and buckling around him. Using the seats for leverage, he began to propel himself towards the aisle that sloped up to the exit doors.

He had almost reached the top of the aisle when he saw, through the ever-increasing clouds of plaster dust, a small roly-poly figure dart across the narrow landing behind the back row of seats. Instinctively David felt certain that the figure was not one of the nightmare creations he had previously encountered – these now seemed to have all vanished like ghosts – but a human being, flesh and blood, just like him. He put on a spurt of speed, and reached the doors just a couple of paces behind the figure. He lunged and grabbed the figure by the arm. It turned, shock and surprise on its face, and he saw that it was a woman of perhaps sixty with long hair greyed by plaster dust.

'Who are you?' he yelled above the din of the collapsing building.

'Let go of me!' the woman snarled, and kicked out at him.

David evaded her foot and increased his grip on her arm, his fingers sinking into her doughy flesh.

'Are you with the Flux?' he shouted.

'Fuck off!' she screamed. 'We'll all be killed!'

'Not until you answer my question.'

'All right, yes, I'm with the Flux. Now let me go or I'll use my animis to break every bone in your body.'

'Where's my daughter?' David shouted at her, ignoring the threat. 'Where's Jane?'

With vicious satisfaction, she replied, 'She's dead! She's fucking dead! Now let me go!'

David grabbed her other arm and slammed her back against the closed exit door. She struggled but was no match for his strength.

'Where is she?' he snarled into her face.

'I told you, she's dead, just as you deserve to be. You spoiled everything, you bastard. You stupid fucking bastard. You don't know what you've done.'

She sounded more upset than angry now, looked as

though she was about to burst into tears. The doorframe behind them creaked and splintered. Rubble pattered on to their shoulders and heads like heavy rain.

'Dead or not, I'm not letting you go until you tell me where she is.'

The fat woman nodded to her left. 'She's in the projector room. Through the door in the corner there and up the stairs. Now let me go!'

As David's attention was diverted to the door the woman had indicated, she twisted in his grasp, then turned her head and bit down hard on his left hand. David shouted in pain and instinctively snatched both hands away. With a swiftness that belied her size and age, the woman ducked away from him, slipped through the exit doors and was gone, waddling as fast as she could along the corridor.

David let her go, ran instead towards the door in the corner. He was relieved to see a faded plaque reading PROJECTOR ROOM – PRIVATE clinging to it with rusty screws, but it occurred to him that if she'd been telling the truth about this, then she might well have been telling the truth about Jane's death as well. The door opened easily and as he vaulted up the stairs beyond it, he wondered whether it was she who'd been filming Jane, wondered what sort of person could simply stand there and watch a little girl get her fingers ripped off. The stairs stank of damp and mould, and seemed to vibrate beneath his feet. At the top of them was another door whose plaque was too dark to read. David twisted the handle and pushed.

The door didn't open immediately, so he put his shoulder to it, wondering whether someone was holding it closed from the other side. He realised, however, when he almost fell into the room, that the door had been sticking because the frame had buckled. The projection booth was small and stuffy, bereft of equipment, full of dirt and cobwebs. There was just enough light to tell that the walls had been painted olive-green. A shape that could have been a figure or a coat lay curled on the floor.

David dropped on to his knees beside it. It was Jane. Her white face, composed now, was turned upwards; her knees had been raised almost to her chest. He reached out a hand and touched her face. It was cold as marble. A bubble of emotion was swelling inside him, readying itself to burst, when she murmured and frowned.

He almost collapsed with relief. 'Jane,' he said, then decided against waking her. Conscious, she would be in terrible pain. He slipped an arm behind her neck, another behind her knees and scooped her up. His own battered body cried out as he rose slowly to his feet, cradling his daughter. His arms and back ached intolerably; if this had been anything or anyone but Jane, he would have proclaimed himself incapable of walking another step.

He staggered to the door and down the stairs, the building shaking so fiercely now that he felt like a drunk in an earthquake. Somehow, bouncing off walls and shoulder-charging doorframes, he made it to the bottom of the stairs and back out into the cinema.

As he stumbled towards the exit doors, head bowed to avoid falling masonry, he glanced once towards where the screen had been. He saw no figures this time, but what he thought he saw was a kind of tornado composed of darkness and light, whipping this way and that, tearing itself and its surroundings apart. It was only a momentary glance and then he stumbled on, through the exit doors and down the winding corridor towards the foyer. Walls and ceiling were cracking and falling all around him now; he could barely see ahead through the dust. And then he was at the top of the steps leading down to the foyer and the black-painted entrance doors.

He staggered down them, picking up speed towards the bottom, his knees feeling as though someone were trying to saw through the tendons in there. His legs were all over the place as he made for the door that the fat woman must have left open, Jane weighing him down like a sack of rocks. Somehow he managed to keep hold of her, managed to stay on his feet. He plunged through the doors into a night that suddenly seemed vast and cool and fresh. As he lurched down the semicircle of stone steps in front of the cinema, he realised that he could feel wind on his face. The barrier sealing this area off from the rest of London must have broken down.

He managed to lurch another thirty or forty yards and then he could go no further. He hoped it would be far enough away from the cinema, which now seemed certain to collapse. He sank to his knees, lowering Jane gently to the pavement, cushioning her head with his hand. He moaned at the sight of her mutilated right hand. Blood was still seeping sluggishly from her wounds.

He turned his head wearily and looked back at the cinema. It was shaking as though in the midst of an earthquake, though all the other buildings around it were still and silent. One of the horn-like constructions on its roof had already collapsed, and the roof itself was punctured in a number of places. Strange intertwining columns of incredibly intense light and absolute darkness blazed from these gashes and became lost in the smoky night-clouds overhead. There was a screeching roaring sound, like a vast machine gone haywire, and all at once the building collapsed, imploding into a mountain of its own dust and rubble.

Something happened then that David was never quite able to describe. Something vast rose from the debris of the wrecked building, something which defied the eye to such an extent that it was impossible to tell whether it was composed of darkness or light. At first the something seemed to resemble a vast lizard, like a dragon or a dinosaur, then it became a horned colossus that stood upright and bellowed at the sky. Then it was a man, then simply a vast face, beatific and serene. And then it unravelled and a moment later it was gone, leaving behind a silence that seemed to hum.

David stared at the place where the shape had been, but now there was only the blue of a night sky, smoky with settling dust. He heard a groan, felt Jane squirm against his knees. He turned to look at her just as her eyes opened and she stared up at him with an expression of wide-eyed puzzlement. He smiled, feeling plaster dust prickle on his face like a thin mask crumbling.

'Hello, Jane,' he said, his voice brittle with dust and emotion.

Jane's lips moved slowly. And after a moment, as if he was the most unexpected sight in the world, she murmured, 'Daddy?'

Epilogue

The car pulled up over the rise, then indicated and turned
cautiously right, through a narrow entrance in a high
chain-link fence. A hand-written sign looped through the
fence links read XMAS TREES FOR SALE. The car
park beyond was merely a ledge overlooking the
Yorkshire Dales, pitted with ruts that had iced over and
which cracked, oozing mud, when the car's tyres passed
over them. There was one other car in the car park, a
silver-blue Citroën, the owners of which, a young couple,
were perusing the two dozen or so fir trees lounging
against the fence.

David brought the car to a halt and reached for the
gardening gloves on the dashboard. As he pulled them on,
he said, 'There's plenty of choice anyway.' He glanced into
the rear-view mirror and saw Jane bouncing up and down
on the seat and pointing with her three-fingered hand,
Rachel trying to be cool, to hide her excitement.

'Can we have that one, Daddy?' Jane cried. 'That big
one there? Can we, *please*?'

David turned and smiled at her. 'We'll see,' he said.
'Remember the freshness test. We don't want something
that's going to have shed all its needles by Boxing Day.'

The car doors opened and the family tumbled out, Jane
racing across the muddy car park to the tree she had
already fallen in love with, eager to claim it before the
young couple could. David and Ellen looked at each other
and grinned, rejoicing in her excitement. This last year
had been very tough for all of them, but for Jane in
particular, even though she had adapted to her deformity
surprisingly quickly. She was drawing and writing now as

well as she ever could, and did not seem anywhere near as self-conscious as she had been a few months ago.

It was the mental scars that lingered longest, however, that resulted in her, a year after the event, waking up screaming and crying in the night. Tippi had been a great help, of course, not only to Jane but to all of them, but still it would take a long time, perhaps years, before Jane was able to put the trauma of her ordeal firmly behind her.

David slipped his arm around Ellen's shoulders as they strolled towards the identity parade of trees, and Ellen reciprocated by slipping an arm around his waist. Rachel walked beside them, quiet as always. She had really grown up this past year, had become very reflective and level-headed, more adult than child. At times, especially when she had been comforting Jane after a nightmare or during one of her bad days, David had been astonished to see how closely she resembled Ellen. It was almost as though she had grown up secretly, when he wasn't looking, and it gave him a pang of wistful regret, made him feel he was somehow responsible for stealing away a little of her childhood before she should have been ready to relinquish it. Certainly she seemed a little more serious than she should have been; nowadays it was a relief rather than a joy to see her laugh. On the whole, though, she had coped well. She had become firm friends with Tippi, despite the four-year gap in their ages.

Jane was standing in front of the tree she had chosen, rubbing the needles between the thumb and index finger of her mutilated hand and sniffing them. As David, Ellen and Rachel approached, she turned, eyes shining, cheeks red with the cold, and held the hand out.

'It's fresh, Daddy. Smell,' she ordered.

'That's not very nice,' said David, 'calling me a smell.'

She rolled her eyes and punched him playfully on the arm. 'No, *smell*,' she explained as if to an imbecile.

David sniffed her fingers dutifully. They smelled of pine,

a scent that reminded him more than any other of Christmas.

'Ahh, Bisto,' he said, and she punched him again. 'What do you two think?' he said, turning to Ellen and Rachel.

Ellen looked doubtful. 'It's a bit big, isn't it?'

'You always say that, Mum,' Rachel said, 'but it never is. It's always just right.'

'But how will we get it home?'

'You always say that too,' Rachel said, smiling wryly.

'We'll slap it on the roof rack like we always do,' said David, 'and I'll drive along at ten miles an hour. Either that or Jane can sit up there and hold it. What do you reckon, Janey?'

Jane looked alarmed. 'No way,' she said, making them all laugh.

'Well ... okay,' Ellen conceded after a few more seconds of deliberation.

'Yay!' shouted Jane, loud enough to cause the young couple to look round and smile. To the tree she said, 'You're coming home with us, Mr Tree, and we're going to make you look really nice.'

'I'll go and pay Mr Murray,' David said, and clomped through the muddy puddles in his Wellingtons to a ramshackle shed on the far side of the car park. The door of the shed was open, so he leaned in. A fat red-faced man with white hair tufting from beneath a checked cap was drinking tea from a plastic cup.

The man looked up, and the flesh of his cheeks folded into ridges as he smiled. 'Hello, Mr Fox,' he said. 'It's good to see you again. Brought the family with you, have you?'

'Yes,' said David.

'Oh, that's good. How are they all?'

David hesitated, wondering whether he should mention Jane's hand. In the end, though, he just said, 'Fine.'

'Oh, that's smashing. It's done me good to see some of

my old customers coming back this year. After last Christmas, you wonder what's happened to some folk, and if they don't turn up, well you fear the worst, don't you?'

'Yes,' said David. 'How have you been, Mr Murray?'

'Oh, can't complain, lad, can't complain. It's nice to see things getting back to normal.'

David paid him for the tree and waived the offer of help with getting it on the roof rack, saying that the four of them would manage. He went outside and looked across the car park at his family, who hadn't seen him emerge. Ellen was standing with her hands stuffed into the pockets of her quilted jacket, chatting to the young couple; Jane appeared to be showing Rachel some kind of complex dance movement which involved spinning on the spot. Instead of walking straight back over to them, David wandered to the edge of the ledge and looked out over the valley, breathing in cold air that smelled of pine and rain and fresh earth.

A haze hung over the land, blurring the horizon, but it was still beautiful: the undulating hills, fields like tiles whose colours didn't quite match, woodland like clumps of broccoli spears, farmhouses like sculptured boulders linked to the sky with umbilical cords of smoke.

'Back to normal' Mr Murray had said, and out here it was easy to believe that things were or soon would be. Of course, things were much better than they had been, and were improving all the time, but it would be a long while yet before the world would be able to outpace the echoes of last year's events.

The Christmas Riots. That was what the chaos had become commonly known as. David suspected the phrase had been chosen to make what had happened seem more innocuous than it really had been, to make it manageable, understandable. Of course, very few really understood what had happened, or more accurately *why* it had. Apart from the Flux and the Schism, only he and a handful of others, including those whose faces he had glimpsed an instant after smashing the bottle, really knew the truth.

The world had suffered in many ways – psychologically, economically, politically. Priests and philanthropists were trying to mend its spirit, aided by the people themselves, by the kind of generosity and sense of community that seems only to show itself in times of great crisis. Psychologists and historians were trying to understand what had happened, to reduce the disorder into neat theoretical patterns and cold statistics. The mechanics of the world, however, the nuts and bolts, was a different matter. Channels of communication had been repaired and restored relatively quickly, but such was the devastation that the economic systems of many countries had all but collapsed. Big businesses had gone under, dragging numerous small businesses with them. Insurance companies had been unable to cope with the demands placed upon them, as a result of which thousands of people were now destitute, living on government hand-outs and charity. The health service, too, in a bad enough state before, was only now getting back on to its knees. A rough estimate put the number of deaths in Britain alone on that fateful night at three hundred thousand, but thousands more had died as a consequence of the night's events, simply because the resources needed to treat them were no longer there.

Three hundred thousand dead. The worldwide figure ran into millions. Everyone, it seemed, knew someone who had died. Everyone had a story to tell, a nightmare nestling in their mind.

David thought of Ralph and Diane, who would be coming over tomorrow with the boys and their dog, Boss, to help the Foxes celebrate David's forty-first birthday on Christmas Eve and then Christmas itself. They had arrived back home to find their house razed to the ground, all their belongings reduced to ash, and with no hope of compensation. Since then they had been living a nomadic existence, staying with friends here, relatives there, and even occasionally with members of the Schism, such as the Hodges or the Fleischers, all of whom had been very kind. Twice they had stayed with the Foxes, and on the second occasion David had been shocked to see how defeated, how ground-down by life, their friends had seemed. With no call for private gynaecologists and no vacancies in the health service, both Ralph and Diane had had to try and find work in other areas. Ralph had found the odd temporary job, working mostly as a builder's labourer, but his earnings had been meagre, nowhere near enough to support a family of four.

The boom professions this past year had been building and undertaking, though even these had had to be reliant for the most part on government funding. Many families could no longer afford to pay for the funerals of their relatives. It was hard enough keeping the living alive, never mind spending money on the dead.

David felt arms slide around his waist from behind, a chin press softly into his shoulder. 'What're you thinking?' said Ellen.

'I was just thinking about Ralph and Diane, and about how lucky we were to still have a house, and for me to have a job.'

'Do you still feel unworthy?' she asked.

He turned to face her. 'Wouldn't you? Thousands are starving, and we're living the life of Riley.'

'Hardly that.'

'Okay, but at least we can afford a Christmas tree. Some people can't even afford food. In some areas of London they've taken to eating dogs and cats, for God's sake.'

'That's just a rumour and you know it.'

'Okay, whatever. But you know what I mean.'

'You deserved to get that job, David. You're a good

608

journalist, and an honest one. People need to be kept informed.'

'Maybe so, but there were lots of people ahead of me in the queue, people with more experience of proper journalism, not bloody film and video reviewers for a pissant little magazine. You know I only got the job because Max and his cronies pulled a few strings for me, used their influence . . .' He pulled a face. 'Whichever way you look at it, it stinks, Ellen.'

'Resign then if you feel so strongly about it.'

'You know I can't do that.'

'Well shut up then and give me a kiss and try to give your conscience a rest for once. You *deserve* that job, David. It's the very least you deserve. You saved the world.'

He laughed, a little bitterly. 'Did I? I don't know what happened that night.'

'Well, you must have done something because all the . . . all the badness stopped, didn't it?'

'That wasn't my doing. I was just the messenger. I even broke the bottle before I realised that that was what I was meant to do just so that that . . . thing would stop hurting Jane.'

Ellen tilted her head towards him and kissed him on the mouth. Her lips were cold and her tongue warm. It was a delicious combination.

'What was that for?' he said when they broke apart.

'That was to shut you up, and to let you know that you're a wonderful man and that I love you.'

His frown remained for a moment longer and then suddenly he smiled. 'I love you too,' he said, 'more than words can say.' He slipped an arm around her shoulders and hugged her to him, kissing the dark honey-warmth of her hair. 'Shall we go?'

'Where to?' she asked.

'Home. Let's go home. Let's go and make things nice for

Ralph and Diane.'

She smiled up at him, the wind pushing her hair, which had grown long this last year, away from her face.

'Good idea,' she said.

Only Forward
Michael Marshall Smith

A truly stunning debut from a young author. Extremely original, satyrical and poignant, a marriage of numerous genres brilliantly executed to produce something entirely new.

Stark is a troubleshooter. He lives in The City - a massive conglomeration of self-governing Neighbourhoods, each with their own peculiarity. Stark lives in Colour, where computers co-ordinate the tone of the street lights to match the clothes that people wear. Close by is Sound where noise is strictly forbidden, and Ffnaph where people spend their whole lives leaping on trampolines and trying to touch the sky. Then there is Red, where anything goes, and all too often does.

At the heart of them all is the Centre - a back-stabbing community of 'Actioneers' intent only on achieving - divided into areas like 'The Results are what Counts sub-section' which boasts 43 grades of monorail attendant. Fell Alkland, Actioneer extraordinaire has been kidapped. It is up to Stark to find him. But in doing so he is forced to confront the terrible secrets of his past. A life he has blocked out for too long.

'Michael Marshall Smith's *Only Forward* is a dark labyrinth of a book: shocking, moving and surreal. Violent, outrageous and witty - sometimes simultaneously - it offers us a journey from which we return both shaken and exhilarated. An extraordinary debut.'
Clive Barker

ISBN 0 586 21774 6

Night Sisters
John Pritchard

The first novel from a talented new horror writer

YOU'LL NEVER FEEL SAFE IN HOSPITAL AGAIN

CLINICIANS

A word that will come to haunt Casualty Sister Rachel Young through the dark nights ahead. A word she hears from a terrified patient, brought dying into her department after driving a stolen car straight into a brick wall. Still trying to escape from someone who has surgically mutilated his brain.

He isn't the first; he won't be the last. People are disappearing into the darkness; the lost ones, with no shelter from the night. Those that are found again have hideous post-operative injuries.

For centuries they have pursued their cold and merciless quest for knowledge, leaving death and mutilation in their wake. And tonight they have come for Rachel Young. For here they have a special role . . .

'A good old fashioned tale of battling evil, which turns into a roller-coaster ride to heights of gut-churning suspense and real terror'   Ramsay Campbell

'A taut and fast-moving tale with bags of authentic detail and a slam-bang finale'   Stephen Gallagher

'*Night Sisters* is one of the creepiest and most shocking novels I've read in a long, long time. The writing is superb. The story brilliantly eerie, marked by stunning shocks of violence'   Richard Laymon

ISBN 0 586 21769 X

Brian Lumley

The Necroscope Series

Dead Girls

Richard Calder

'Dark, edgy, and inflicted with just the right degree of lyricism'   WILLIAM GIBSON

Is Primavera a self-replicating cyborg bloodsucker or a poor little dead girl? Ask Ignatz Zwakh, when he stops bleeding.

Nanoengineers have unleashed machine consciousness. Only Primavera and her wild teenage lover Ignatz, who tells this story, know what power is really behind the microbiotic army dedicated to overthrowing the human gamete. They will try to reach Dr Toxicophilous before the CIA or the pornocrat Kito or their combined assassins and nanomachines reach them. But, meanwhile, quantum magical allure fuels the doll plague in the West and old fashioned software viruses work another sort of genocide in the East: two parts of an infinitely sinister equation.

This dazzling first novel by Richard Calder depicts a future that bites.

ISBN 0 586 21455 0

Everville
Clive Barker

Five years ago, in his bestseller *The Great and Secret Show*, Clive Barker mesmerised millions of readers worldwide with an extraordinary vision of human passions and possibilities. Welcome to a new volume in that epic adventure. Welcome to *Everville*.

On a mountain peak, high above the city of Everville, a door stands open: a door that opens onto the shores of the dream-sea Quiddity. And there's not a soul below who'll not be changed by that fact . . .

Phoebe Cobb is about to forget her old life and go looking for her lost lover Joe Flicker in the world on the other side of that door; a strange, sensual wonderland the likes of which only Barker could make real.

Tesla Bombeck who knows what horrors lurk on the far side of Quiddity, must solve the mysteries of the city's past if she is to keep those horrors from crossing the threshold.

Harry D'Amour, who has tracked the ultimate evil across America, will find it conjuring atrocities in the sunlit streets of Everville.

Step into Everville's streets, and enter a world like no other . . .

'Clive Barker is so good I am almost tongue-tied. What Barker does makes the rest of us look like we've been asleep for the last ten years . . . His stories are compulsorily readable and original. He is an important, exciting and enormously saleable writer.'
Stephen King

ISBN 0 00 647225 7